KRISTEN BRITAIN

WINTERLIGHT

First published in Great Britain in 2021 by Gollancz
an imprint of the Orion Publishing Group Ltd
Carmelite House, 50 Victoria Embankment
London EC4Y 0DZ

An Hachette UK Company

1 3 5 7 9 10 8 6 4 2

Copyright © Kristen Britain 2021

Map by Kristen Britain

A CIP catalogue record for this book is
available from the British Library.

ISBN (Trade Paperback) 978 1 473 22649 4
ISBN (eBook) 978 1 473 22652 4
ISBN (Audio Download) 978 1 473 23343 0

Printed in Great Britain by Clays Ltd, Elcograf S.p.A.

www.kristenbritain.com
www.orionbooks.co.uk
www.gollancz.co.uk

For Melinda Rice-Schoon

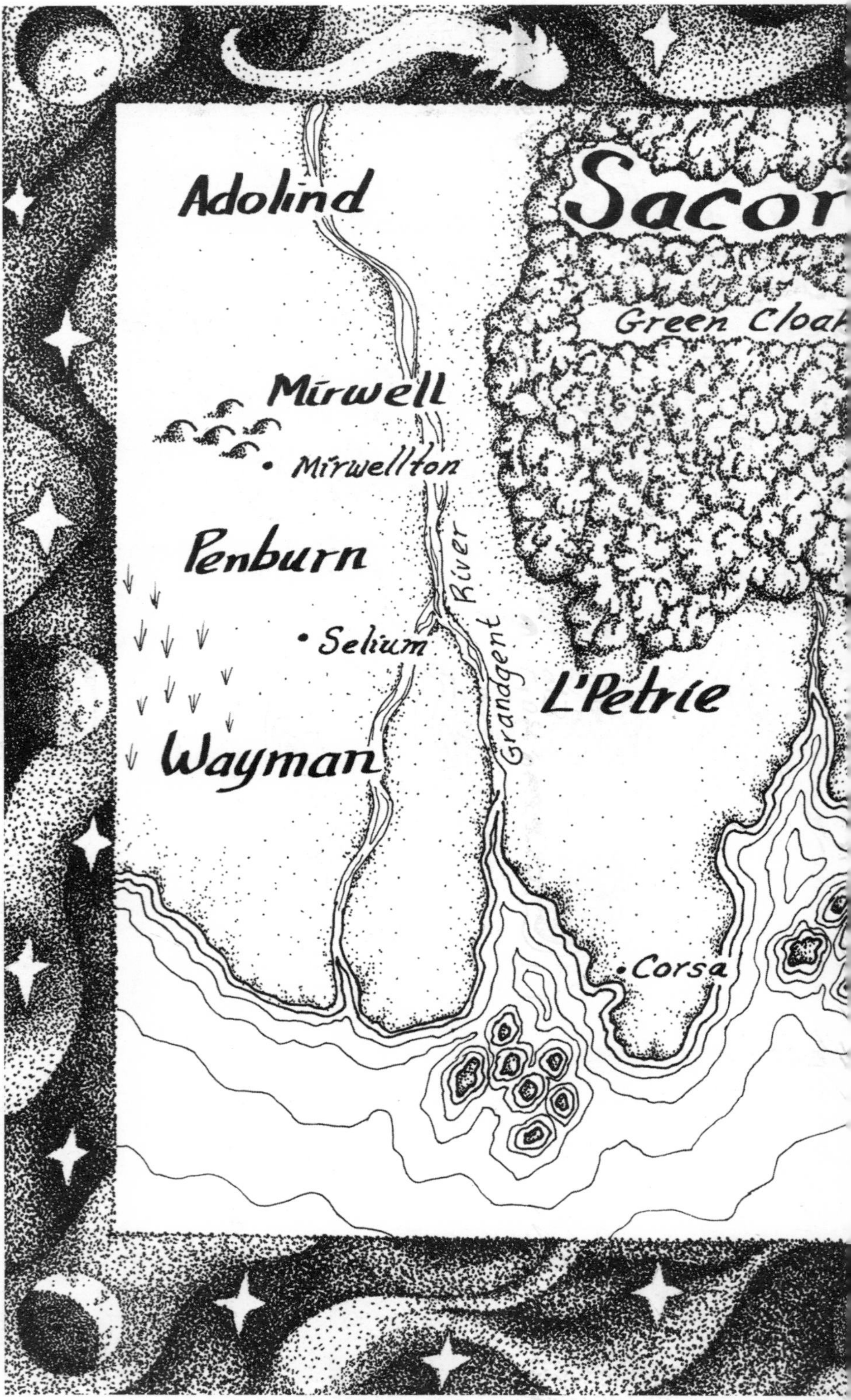
Adolind
Sacor
Green Cloak
Mirwell
Mirwellton
Penburn
River
Grandgent
Selium
L'Petrie
Wayman
Corsa

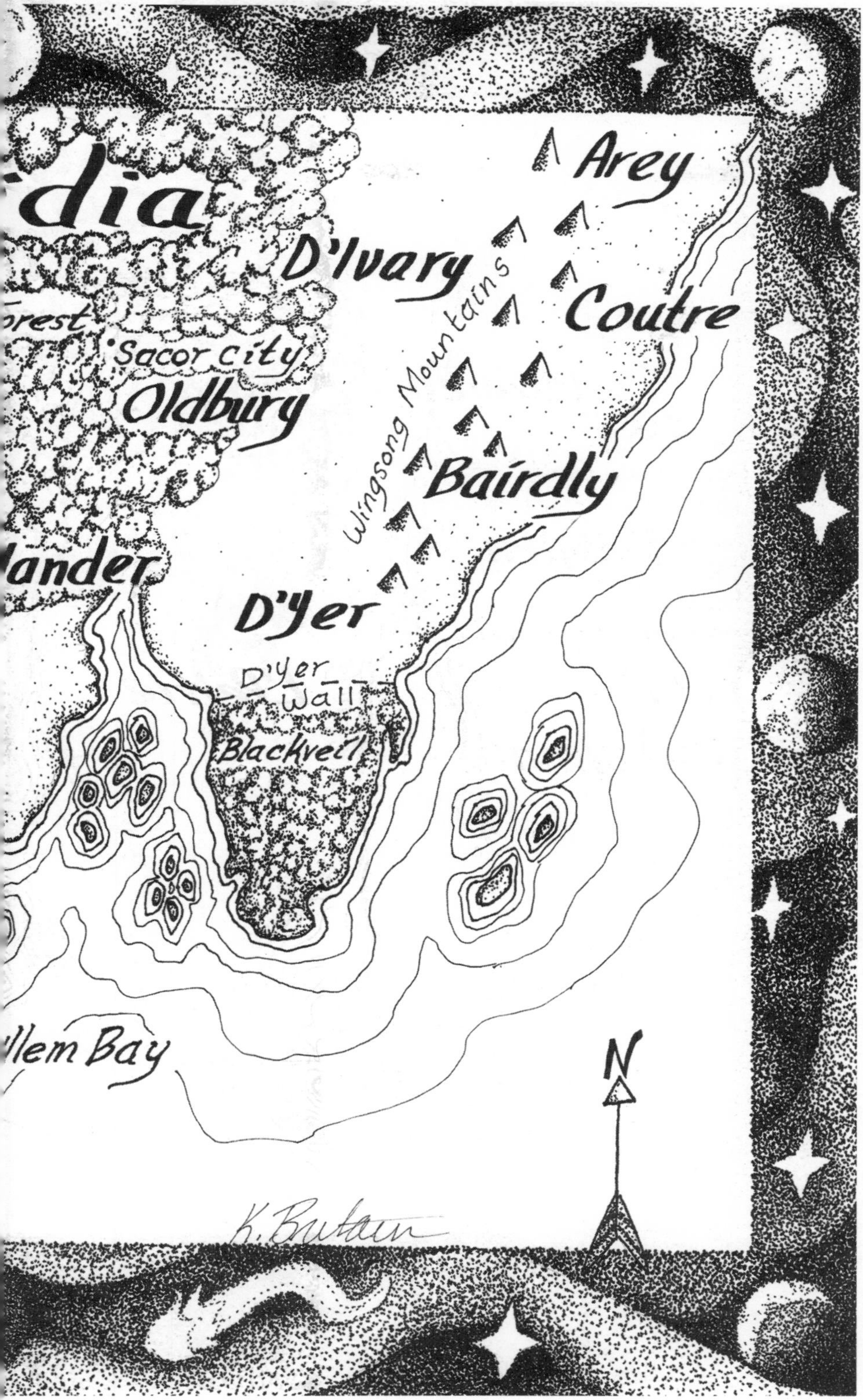
dia
Arey
D'lvary
Wingsong Mountains
Coutre
orest
Sacor city
Oldbury
Bairdly
lander
D'yer
D'yer
Wall
Blackveil
llem Bay
N
K. Britain

⋙ SHORTCUTS ⋘

Waldron Gates cradled his broken arm to his chest and huddled in the lee of his overturned cart to shelter against the drizzle. He lay upon shards of broken pottery, all that remained of his winter's work. Unfortunately, it wasn't just the pottery he'd lost in his encounter with the brigands, but the goods he'd traded for, as well—foodstuffs, tools, seeds— all the necessities that would see him through the coming year. They'd even robbed him of his poor old mule. He supposed he ought to be grateful he still had his life.

Shivers racked his body. He needed to get dry and warm, but every time he tried to stand, his vision dimmed and his knees buckled. When the cart tipped over during his attempt to escape the brigands, he'd hit his head. A little rest was what he needed. Yes, a little rest to regain his strength so he could make his way back to Boggs where the townsfolk could help him. He tried not to dwell on how long a walk that would be.

Dusk would soon fall, and Waldron resigned himself to spending a cold, miserable night beside the road. He'd faint hope of passersby helping him as the "road" was little more than a backwoods trail that was scarcely fit for a laden cart, but it was a shortcut to a settlement northward where he had planned to sell more of his wares.

Some shortcut, he thought.

The chances of a friendly traveler passing by and offering aid were pretty slim.

"Should make a fire," he murmured, but he hadn't the strength, and how could he manage with just one arm?

He dozed off, waking now and then out of some nightmare

1

of skull-faced men tormenting him, materializing out of the woods once more to chase him down the road.

A snap of a twig, the plod of a hoof.

He jerked to full wakefulness, sweat mingling with raindrops on his face, to find his nightmare come to life. A horseman wreathed in mist loomed above him. The horse pawed the road. Harness jingled when it shook its head. Fear flooded through Waldron's veins. Maybe he was already dead and this was some kind of spirit come to carry his soul to the heavens, like it was said the death god did. Or was this the leader of the brigands come back to finish him off? Did the rider have a skull face? He could not tell in the deepening dusk.

"Have you come back to kill me? P-please—please have mercy. You got all I had." Tears streamed down his cheeks.

"Are you badly hurt?" The question was spoken in a perfectly natural woman's voice. Not the skull-faced man, not a death spirit.

Waldron sobbed in relief. "Think my arm is broke."

She dismounted and knelt before him. In the gloom he could not make out her features, but from her silhouette she seemed to be wearing some kind of uniform.

"We need to get you warm and dry," she said. "How long have you been here like this?"

"Don't rightly know. Maybe since midday." His teeth chattered.

"That is a long time. What's your name?"

It was so kindly asked that he fought the urge to sob again. "Waldron—Waldron Gates."

"Well, Waldron, I'm going to see if I can find a dry patch in the woods and set up some shelter." There was the glint of brass buttons as she removed her coat—and to his astonishment—blanketed him with it.

"Will you be all right while I look after things?" she asked.

Waldron nodded, already feeling warmer beneath the coat. It was not wet all the way through like his was. He lost track of time and drifted off while she went about her business. This time the nightmares stayed away as though the coat were a shield.

A while later, he didn't know how long, she gently shook

his shoulder to wake him and helped him to a spot amid a group of pines where a small fire crackled.

"Some of the crates that held your pots were still dry," she explained. "Nice seasoned wood. The straw and sawdust helped, too."

Yes, he'd used straw and sawdust to protect the pots during transport.

She'd placed tarps over branches to help keep the drizzle off. The ground beneath the protective boughs of the pines was relatively dry. She guided him to blankets next to the fire, then tended to his injuries. When she splinted his arm, he nearly fainted from the pain. He watched her as she worked now that he could see her a little better in the glow of the fire— short, shaggy hair, one eye covered by a patch. A winged horse was emblazoned on the left sleeve of her shirt in gold thread.

"Green Rider?" he said in surprise. It was a rare sighting here in the backwoods. "What's a king's messenger doing out here in the middle of nowhere?"

"Rescuing potters, it would seem." A brief smile flickered across her lips; then she made a final knot with a cloth to hold his splint in place and sat back on her heels. "Actually, I think I got a little lost. I decided to take a shortcut, but it ended up not being so short."

Waldron barked a laugh. "My shortcut didn't work out so well, either."

She smiled again, and again it was brief. "I am boiling a pot of water for some willowbark tea," she said. "It may help your pain. If you feel up to it, I have some food I can share, as well. Maybe while we wait for the water to boil you can tell me what happened here."

She listened gravely as the story spilled out of him—of the band of cutthroats emerging from the woods as if out of the air; of his short mad dash in an attempt to escape them until the cart wheel broke off and he went flying.

"They took everything I'd acquired in trade," he said. "They weren't much interested in my pots, though."

"Where were you coming from?"

"Boggs," he replied. "I stop there every spring. The Antlers Inn always takes some of my pottery."

"So this *is* the Boggs Road," she murmured.

"Guess you *really* were lost if you didn't know."

"I came out of the woods," she replied. "Was bushwhacking for days before I found the road. I thought it probably led to Boggs but wasn't sure since there were no wayposts." She handed him a mug of tea. "What can you tell me about these men who robbed you?"

He pressed the mug against his chest. The heat penetrated through his clothes and he sighed in contentment. "I was in and out of consciousness after the cart went over. Maybe I looked dead enough that they didn't kill me."

"Or maybe they wanted you alive to spread word of them, which would cause fear among the populace," she said. "But please, continue."

"I think there were half a dozen of them. I didn't see much, but they seemed . . . not just brigands, but trained warriors the way they moved. They had some discipline about them. And their leader . . ."

"Yes?"

He closed his eyes summoning the horrible image to his mind. "Skull face."

"Skull face?"

"His face was tattooed so it looked like a skull. He'd no hair but for a topknot. Have never seen the like, and never want to again." The nightmares were going to come back, he just knew it. "The others called him Torq."

"Torq," she echoed. She did not reveal to him if she'd seen or heard of this Torq before, but asked, "Anything else you can tell me? So I can take news of it to the king?"

"No. They took my things like I said and disappeared."

"Disappeared?"

He paused to consider. "I must have blacked out because when they left, it was almost like they disappeared."

The Green Rider didn't reply, just tossed more wood onto the fire. Sparks flurried upward and glinted in her one eye like stars. He shuddered once more and turned his attention to the hardtack she'd given him, though his stomach wasn't much interested in food. When he finished his tea, she took the cup from him.

"I think you should sleep," she said. "It'll be a long day tomorrow to get you back to Boggs. Someone there with mending skills should be able to fix you up right."

She helped him lie down.

"Those brigands won't come back, will they?" The anxiety had been building in his chest. "What if they see the fire and come back?"

"They already got what they wanted," she replied. "They won't bother to return."

"Are you sure?"

She hesitated. "I don't think they will, but I'll be keeping watch in any case. Rest best as you can. I'll be right here if you need anything."

He felt almost like a child as she pulled a blanket over him. He tried to get comfortable, but his splinted arm made it difficult. It hurt so much, and the willowbark tea had done little to ease the pain. He watched as she returned to her place on the other side of the fire. Drops of water plopped onto the tarp overhead. Her horse shifted nearby.

He thought of his mother when he was a lad and how she'd take care of him when he was hurt or ill. How she'd sing him to sleep. "Could—could you sing something?" he asked. "It'd help me sleep."

She chuckled. "No. No it wouldn't. I can't carry a tune to save my life. Sorry."

Maybe he'd been silly to ask this of one of the king's own messengers, but with her taking care of him, she'd put him in mind of his dear mother, long buried and resting in peace. Sleep began to descend even without a song. "You got a name?" he asked her as he drifted off.

"Karigan."

"Goodnight, Rider Karigan," he said, his voice beginning to slur.

"Goodnight, Waldron."

His last vision before sleep took him was of the Green Rider sitting alert by the fire with a staff resting across her lap. He was not plagued by nightmares, after all, and he slept soundly, feeling quite safe with Rider Karigan to watch over him through the night.

 ⋘ THE BOGGS ROAD ⋙

"**Y**ou're going to have to help me," Karigan told Waldron. She was trying to get him mounted on Condor, and she couldn't do it by herself. "Lean against Condor with your good arm and I'll guide your foot into the stirrup."

Waldron wavered on the rock that served as a mounting block. It was flat on top and a good height, and Condor stood patiently and still, but Waldron's broken arm and head injury had taken their toll so that even simple tasks were difficult for him.

He did as she asked but could not seem to propel himself into the saddle. He gripped the cantle so hard his knuckles turned white, and he shook with the effort.

She tried to hoist him by the belt and push him from below, straining her own not-quite-healed back injuries. Finally, after several attempts, he was able to haul himself the rest of the way into the saddle. Afterward, she stood trying to catch her breath and stretching her back. Once she was sure Waldron was secure, she picked up the reins to lead Condor down the Boggs Road.

The morning was chill as mornings often were in early spring. Crystalline drops clung to the tips of pine needles and mist crept low over the ground. The weather had left Karigan perpetually damp and cold and aching ever since her departure from the Lone Forest up north. Getting lost had not helped. She could only blame herself for trying to follow the Eletian "ways" to get home. She and her companions had followed them to shorten their travel north, but when she tried to use them on her own to go home, the ability to see the magical paths had eluded her, and she wondered if it was because there'd been no Eletian with her this time. She could have had Enver guide her home, but she'd been adamant she would undertake this journey alone.

And alone she'd certainly been, especially during the long days of bushwhacking through the woods. If only she'd had her friend Garth's special ability of wayfinding, she'd have never gotten lost.

She could only guess at what her fellow Green Riders back at the castle thought of her delay. Maybe they imagined she'd fallen prey to some toothy predator, or maybe that she was lying in the woods somewhere with a broken limb just as she'd found Waldron. They seemed to believe she had a knack for getting into trouble, and they weren't wrong.

Condor plodded alongside her, steam blowing from his nostrils. They'd been through a lot together, she and he. She slapped his neck companionably and walked on trying not to think about who else awaited her back at the castle.

"How are you doing?" she asked Waldron after a couple miles. He'd been very quiet, and she who had traveled so long by herself had become accustomed to silence, but she also knew that it sometimes meant trouble in a sick or injured person.

"I guess I'm fine," he replied. "I've not sat a saddle in quite a while so I reckon there will be parts of me that hurt more than my arm."

She smiled.

"Tell me, Rider," he continued, "the news of the realm. I hear rumors now and again of this Second Empire fighting our Sacoridian soldiers. What do you know?"

Messengers were often called upon to provide the latest news as they passed through towns and villages, or settled in at a generous farmer's house for the night, so it was no surprise that Waldron asked.

"I can't say as I know much of anything current," she said, "as I've been busy traveling and getting lost." He laughed. "However, I can tell you the king dealt Second Empire a blow at the end of winter."

She had Waldron's full attention as she described the Battle of the Lone Forest. He whooped when he heard of the demise of the group's leader, Grandmother, who had been a dangerous necromancer. Karigan left out her own part in those events, as well as the supernatural aspects. The miles slipped by as she spoke.

"Those imperialists are traitors," Waldron declared. "If they want to rule so badly, they can go back where they came from."

If only it were so easy. The ancestors of those who called themselves Second Empire had arrived on Sacoridia's shores one thousand years ago from the far-off empire of Arcosia. They'd sought resources lacking in their own land and attempted to take what was not theirs. When the Sacor Clans defied them, war erupted. In the end, the Sacoridians defeated the imperial forces, and with no way to return home, the Arcosians melded into Sacoridian and Rhovan populations. Though Second Empire sought to preserve the purity of its bloodlines, that purity was so diluted as to make them more Sacoridian than Arcosian. Karigan herself was descended from one of those original Arcosian invaders, but she had never felt anything other than Sacoridian.

"From the sound of it," Waldron said, "you were in the thick of the action."

He gazed at her as though he expected her to tell him all that she'd done during the battle, but she simply replied, "I was there. I am on my way home now."

"To Sacor City?"

"Yes."

By midday the mist had burned off into a sunny haze leaving the air stifling with humidity. They took a break so Waldron could rest and she could check his splint. They drank water and ate hardtack. Karigan was relieved to be heading toward a town where she could freshen her supplies. She had given Waldron the last of her willowbark tea the previous night, and now her last piece of hardtack. She had skill enough to forage in the woods if she had to—all Green Riders learned how—but she didn't want to if she didn't have to. Despite the heat, he professed to feeling chilled, so she took off her great-coat and placed it around his shoulders.

"Will you really tell King Zachary?" Waldron asked from the mossy log he sat on.

"Hmm?" she asked, startled from her reverie.

"About me," he said. "Will you really tell him what happened to me?"

She nodded. His was not the first encounter with brigands she'd heard about, though it was the first evidence she'd seen. Rumors spread among travelers of robbery here, a house ransacked there, and of hapless merchants on the road stripped of their goods. She heard stories of murder and abuses cruel enough to give anyone nightmares. The incidents appeared random in nature, and too widespread to be the work of one group. She imagined much of it was exaggerated hearsay, but some kernel of truth must lie at the center.

Yes, she would certainly take Waldron's story to Zachary, the one story she could verify. She would tell him about the others she'd heard, as well, and let her superiors decide how much to believe and what was to be done about it.

When they were once more under way, Waldron said, "I am sorry to make you walk after you stayed up all night keeping watch."

She was tired, yes, from a night without sleep, but at least she'd been spared the nightmares of amorphous shadows and torture that had plagued much of her journey.

"I could take a turn," Waldron said. "Let you ride."

"I'm fine," she assured him. Truth was, he'd only slow them down and she'd grown accustomed to walking, anyway. The condition of her back had necessitated she take long breaks from the saddle. In a way, it had been good for her, forcing her to improve her conditioning and to restrengthen injured muscles. Unfortunately, the walking had just about ruined yet another pair of boots. How many pairs had she gone through since joining the Riders? The quartermaster, as usual, was not going to be happy with her.

The afternoon continued in companionable silence, and the shadows of trees lengthened across the road. There were more signs of habitation—cart wheel tracks and hoofprints, and narrow trails wending off the road into the woods to unknown destinations. In the distance, farms came into view, with their cleared fields.

"Not far now," Waldron said.

Karigan noticed the strain on his face and how he sagged in the saddle. It would be a good thing for his sake if he was right that Boggs wasn't far. To her relief, they soon came upon a sign nailed to a tree with "Boggs" and an arrow painted on it.

She started to pick up her pace, when a voice cried, "Halt!" from the woods and an arrow planted itself at her feet.

⊰ THE ANTLERS ⊱

"**W**ho are you and what is your business in Boggs?" the voice demanded.

Karigan fought an urge to flee, but stood her ground and gazed into the trees. Whoever it was that threatened her was well concealed. A rustling to her left indicated the speaker was not alone. Carefully she shifted her gaze and thought she caught a bit of color amid the undergrowth. She took a step forward.

"I said," came the voice, "don't move. Answer my questions."

Karigan raised her hands to show they were empty of weapons, but they shook, and so she lowered them. What if these were the brigands she'd been hearing about? But from all accounts, they were not ones to ask questions.

"I intend no harm in Boggs," she said. "My companion here was robbed by brigands on the road, all his goods stolen. He requires the attention of a mender. I, in turn, am a Green Rider in need of supplies."

There was a pause, then, "Prove your identity."

Waldron stirred atop Condor. "Redmon Terr, is that you?"

"Waldron?"

"She speaks the truth. Has been aiding me."

Branches cracked as three men stepped out of the woods onto the road from various positions around her. Each was armed with hunting bows and arrows. One possessed a short-sword.

"It is against king's law to impede the passage of travelers on the realm's roads," she told them.

The one she thought to be Redmon Terr gave her a

thorough look up and down. "Tell that to the family of farmers raiders massacred not far from here." He then dismissively turned toward Waldron to hear what happened to him.

Waldron gave them a brief explanation of his encounter with the bandits and how Karigan had found and helped him. They did not press him for it was clear he was not well.

Redmon Terr yanked his arrow out of the road. "You are free to pass," he told Karigan. "Go to the Antlers. Waldron can be seen to there, and you can get your supplies." He turned and, with his fellows, disappeared back into the woods. Clearly they were skilled hunters able to hide themselves so efficiently.

She would have to wait until she reached the village to find out more about Terr's reference to the massacre at the farm. That was something Zachary and his advisors would want to hear about. She took up Condor's reins once more and led him forward passing the spot where Terr had vanished into the undergrowth. She couldn't blame them for setting up a watch to safeguard their village, but it was her duty to remind them of the king's law. She would not report them.

The village of Boggs wasn't much. It was composed of only a few houses, a smithy, a mercantile with a "closed" sign in its window, and the inn. The village mainly served farms and woodsmen that were off long winding roads and trails. She turned Condor toward the inn, the huge rack of moose antlers over the entrance making it obvious this was, in fact, "the Antlers."

At first it appeared no one was about, but as soon as she began to help Waldron dismount, a man and woman emerged from the inn, and a girl trotted out of the stables, to help. Karigan found herself pushed aside as the others took over. She was just as glad, too weary to see to the potter herself. As the trio got him off Condor, the man peppered him with questions.

"Leave him be," the woman said. "Let's take care of him and then ask questions."

"He was robbed on the Boggs Road," Karigan said, answering the most pressing question. The trio paused and glanced at her as if just noticing her existence.

"Lori," the woman told the girl, "see that the horse is

settled in, then go fetch Omey. She'll want to know." The girl nodded and took the reins to lead Condor into the stables.

The woman gave Karigan a once-over. "You'll be wanting something hot to eat. Come in and find yourself a place to sit while we care for Waldron."

And that was all.

Before entering the inn, Karigan took a moment to stretch her sore back. Once inside, she found a few trestle tables and a large hearth with another rack of antlers over the mantel. The only patron was an old, gray-faced hound dog sprawled before the fire. It made sense the place was empty, as most folk would be at their labors during the day.

She dropped into a chair before the hearth, stretching out her legs, but not so far as to disturb the hound, and closed her eyes. Warm and dry for the first time in ages, she dozed off into a sleep blessedly free of nightmares. She must have been out for quite a while for when she woke up, voices buzzed around her and she sensed people moving about. She stood with a yawn and tried to shake off the grogginess. When she turned, she found patrons at each table. The hound now sat alertly at the feet of an older woman as she supped, waiting for some tidbit to fall to the floor.

Redmon Terr and his men stood up from a table and clomped out of the inn. Terr gave her a look in passing, but no other acknowledgment.

The woman who had invited her in to the inn saw her and came over, wiping her hands on her apron.

"You're awake. I didn't want to bother you—it seemed like you needed some rest. Why don't you come over to a table and I'll bring you a hot meal."

At the thought of food, Karigan's stomach grumbled and she sat at the table Terr and his men had just vacated. In moments the woman was back with a bowl of venison stew, a loaf of bread, and a cup of ale, which she set before Karigan.

"How is Waldron?" she asked.

"Resting. He'll be just fine. You did a good job splinting his arm and taking care of him. I set the bone, and it doesn't look like it will fester." At Karigan's look, she explained, "My name is Elda. I help here at the Antlers, but I also do some mending when it's called for. Now eat your stew before it gets cold." And then she was off to tend other patrons.

The stew was very good, and Karigan took her time savoring every spoonful and letting it warm her belly. After a while, however, she felt the gaze of another on her. She looked up and found the older woman, with the hound now lying beside her, watching her.

"I don't mean to be rude," the woman said, "but the king's messengers never travel through Boggs. At least, not that I've ever heard. But it was a good thing for Waldron."

As Karigan could not disagree, she nodded, then turned her attention back to her stew. The woman's chair scuffed the floor as she stood and moved to hover over Karigan's table.

"Rider Karigan, isn't it? I am Omey. Do you mind if I sit with you? I intended to wait till you finished your meal to speak to you, but I was never good at waiting."

Karigan schooled her annoyance. She had become too accustomed to silence and was not particularly interested in conversing with a stranger, but she gestured to the chair across from her. No doubt the woman wanted the news of the land as Waldron had.

"I sit at the head of the village council," Omey said, taking the proffered chair.

Karigan's spoon scraped the bottom of the bowl. The village had enough people to sit a council?

"Can you tell me what the king's plan is for dealing with the cutthroats terrorizing the countryside?" Omey asked.

Karigan set her spoon aside and straightened. This was a more formal kind of inquiry, and she had to do her part as a representative of the king.

"I have been away from Sacor City for some time, and when last I was in the king's presence, this issue of banditry had not arisen."

Omey nodded. "Waldron told us as much, but I wanted to confirm."

Karigan did not relax for the older woman's gray eyes remained keen, and still she did not ask for the usual "news of the land," not even about the Battle of the Lone Forest, which Waldron must have mentioned if he were repeating the conversations she and he had had along the road. The danger of Second Empire must seem far off to most common folk, but that of the bandits far more present.

"You heard about the farm nearby that was massacred?" Omey asked. "The Ferris place?"

Karigan nodded.

"Good people. Worked hard to carve fields out of the forest and grow crops on rocky land. But the raiders destroyed it. Took what they wanted and murdered six members of our community."

"I'm sorry," Karigan replied. "I will certainly tell the king."

"I appreciate that, Rider, as we are all grieving, but I want more. In the morning, after you've rested some, I want to take you out to the farm so you can see what was done, as a witness. I want you to be able to tell the king what you've seen with your own eyes."

Karigan shifted in her seat, a certain dread tugging at her. "My plan was to start very early to Sacor City in the morning. The sooner I—"

"This won't take long, Rider. You can start back as soon as we're done and have the whole day ahead of you." The steely resolve in Omey's eyes brooked no argument. And, she was right, of course. As a king's messenger, it was Karigan's duty to bear witness to that which affected the realm and its people. She gave Omey a curt nod and rose.

Elda, who must have been watching and waiting for the right moment, came over and said, "Rider, we've put you in room three, just up the stairs and to the right. Your coat that Waldron borrowed, and all your gear, are there."

"Thank you," Karigan murmured.

"We'll see you in the morning," Omey said.

Without another word, Karigan headed for the stairs, uneasy for what the morning would bring.

Lady Omelia Vinecarter watched after the Green Rider as she walked across the room toward the stairs. She could tell the Rider had been through hard times—not just from the eyepatch she wore, or the fading scar on her cheek, or even the state of her uniform. She could see it in the Rider's face and how she moved as though wounded. Omey's husband, Nickold, had been an officer in King Amadon's army during the hostilities with the Under Kingdoms. Bad things happened to him and his comrades down there. She was not sure exactly what. He had visible scars, but he refused to speak of his experiences even at the end of his life. Her Nick, the love of all her years and her true heart mate, was never the same after his return. He'd passed away fifteen years ago, her only solace that he no longer suffered. She saw something of Nick in that Rider.

As the Rider passed beneath brighter light, Omey saw that the back of her shirt was crisscrossed by faded brown stains that were unmistakably old blood. There were a few fresher stains, as well, long and narrow stripes that layered over the old. If a wound was deep enough, it could ooze for months, especially if the injured person were too active and did not get the wounds tended regularly.

"Rider," Omey called as the young woman started to climb the stairs, "don't you think Elda should take a look at your back?"

The Rider paused and shook her head. "No, it's fine."

As she disappeared up the stairs, Omey thought there was little about that Rider that was "fine."

STORMS AND NIGHTMARES

Thunder shattered the night and Karigan sat up, eyes wide open and heart pounding. Sudden pain lanced through her right eye as it often did when left uncovered. She clapped her hand over it with a small cry of agony until she could pull on her eyepatch. Covering it helped, but it remained a source of irritation even then due to the nature of the injury.

Lightning flashed the plain lines of her room into bright relief, then faded. She threw off her blankets and rose, shivering as the air cooled the perspiration on her skin. She padded over to the window. Rain pattered against the clouded glass.

She did not know whether it was the storm or the nightmares that had roused her. The storm was certainly bad enough on its own to unsettle her. Thunder and lightning never used to bother her, but she'd grown sensitive to it and other loud, sudden noises. This one was bad enough to make her hands tremble.

More lightning crackled across the sky, and in the corner of the room, it revealed the shadowed figure of her torturer as dream merged into waking nightmare. Nyssa Starling gazed at her, whip in hand.

"No," Karigan murmured, stepping back.

Nyssa smiled at her with sadistic pleasure before darkness absorbed her.

An ear-splitting peal of thunder rattled the window, thunder like the crack of a whip. Karigan cried out and sank to the floor, and drew her knees to her chest. She shook all over.

These visions, or visitations, were becoming more frequent. She closed her eyes and there was Nyssa again, with her sick grin, the thongs of her whip writhing like snakes and trailing blood, the same as in her dreams.

"Go away, go away, go away," she whispered.

I am always with you, Greenie, Nyssa told her. *You are mine.*

Nyssa was dead, and logically Karigan should have nothing to fear from her, but logic seemed not to matter, for the torturer's reach extended from beyond the veil of death. Enver had taught her how to use a sort of meditation to seek the peace of a starry meadow where Nyssa could not reach her, but she'd been unable to do so since their parting, as if a barrier blocked her way. As the avatar of Westrion, god of death, she should have been able to banish Nyssa to the hells, but that power, too, appeared to be lost to her.

The wailing of an infant leaked through the wall, the poor thing also awakened by the storm. The family—four children, their parents, and a granny—had arrived late, and now she could hear voices and the creak of floorboards as they attempted to soothe the baby.

The thunder rumbled in the distance, the storm's intensity spent. Karigan sighed and returned to bed. She closed her eyes before once more removing the eyepatch, not only to avoid the pain, but to prevent unsettling visions, for no ordinary injury had stolen the sight of her right eye. The shard of an arcane device, a looking mask, had lodged into it and turned the whole of it into a mirror. Anyone who gazed into her mirror eye saw visions reflected back to them as if it were a miniature looking mask, and caused her to see, on occasion, a blur of images, of fates past, and those yet to come, all intersecting and diverging across the loom of the heavens as brilliant threads, weft and warp.

Visions, she thought in derision. Between the nightmares and being haunted by the ghost of her torturer, the last thing she needed was the shard inflicting more visions on her.

There were still a few hours before dawn and she needed to try to sleep no matter how bad the dreams. It was not until the storm diminished completely that the baby quieted, and that she drifted into a gray, uneasy sleep.

The family left at dawn. Karigan had heard them chattering and yelling to one another and banging around as they packed, and so she'd been deprived of yet more sleep. At breakfast down in the common room, she lingered over her tea and gazed out the window. The rain had stopped, but tree limbs hung heavy with their burden of rainwater.

"Waldron is doing fine," Elda was telling Karigan. "He's still abed sawing wood. Of an entire forest, or so it would seem." She grinned. "Now how about more eggs?"

"No, thank you." Karigan was glad to hear she was leaving Waldron in such good hands.

"If you don't mind my saying, you look like you could use some meat on your bones. What would your mother say?"

Karigan had no idea. Her mother had been gone since she was a small child. She knew Elda was right, though. Her clothes were loose, and even her hands looked boney. Message errands usually took the weight off her, but this was worse than usual.

"No eggs," she said, "but I'd have more tea and another cinnamon muffin."

Elda looked delighted and bustled to the kitchen. At that moment, Omey stepped into the common room from outside, bundled in an oilskin coat and wearing mud-caked boots.

"We're ready," she said.

"Ready . . . ?" It took Karigan a moment to remember she was to accompany Omey to the farm that had been hit by the raiders. Actually, she had not forgotten, but had hoped Omey would, and had pushed it to the back of her mind.

"We're going out to the Ferris place so you can see what was done."

Karigan nodded and stood.

Elda hurried over with muffin in hand. "Omey, she hasn't finished breakfast."

"She can bring it with her." Omey turned on her heel and headed for the door.

Elda made a disparaging noise and handed Karigan the muffin. "There will be more when you return." Then she returned to the kitchen.

Karigan shrugged and took a bite of the muffin. It was still warm from the oven. She did not hurry, and by the time she reached the horse yard, she found Omey there, mounted up on a fat pony, an old sword that looked too long for her girded at her side. A man in a battered helm and leather jerkin, and armed with an ax, sat on a mule.

"Are we expecting trouble?" Karigan was not ready for a fight if it came to that. She had not healed enough.

"It is a precaution. I do not think there is anything of value left at the Ferris place to draw the raiders back, but I'm bringing Clem along just in case. He fought in the Under Kingdoms with my husband."

Clem did not look any more ready for a fight than she or Omey, especially against these dangerous raiders.

Lori led a freshly groomed and tacked Condor from the stables. There wasn't anything for it, so Karigan mounted up. The sooner they got this over with, the sooner she could be back on the road to Sacor City.

Once they left the village center, they urged their steeds into a steady trot and turned onto a dirt track bordered by a tangle of scrub alder and pines barely wide enough for a cart. Lori had done a fine job of grooming Condor, but mud already splattered his gleaming hide. The track was flooded where it dipped into a fold in the land, but they splashed through with no trouble. The farm, Karigan learned, was about four miles from the village. The ordinariness of chipmunks scurrying into the brush ahead of them, and the courtship songs of birds, relaxed her. Nothing felt off. It was just a normal spring morning.

She judged they were three miles in when Omey called a halt and said, "Around the next bend the path opens to farmland. If anyone is up at the farmhouse and looking, they'll be able to see us coming."

"What do you propose?" Clem asked.

"No one has been up there since we laid the Ferris' to rest," Omey replied. "I believe it would be wise if our Rider scouts the scene to ensure it is safe."

Cold settled in Karigan's belly, and when she did not respond, Omey asked, "Isn't this the sort of thing you Riders do? Scouting and whatnot?"

"Yes," Karigan replied in a flat voice. Then she shook herself. "Of course. I will check it out." She reined Condor about to continue on alone.

"White as a sheet," she heard Clem tell Omey. "The Greenies I knew back in the day were like steel."

Karigan squeezed Condor into a trot so she would not have to hear more, but when she reached the bend in the path, she halted him before they lost the screening of vegetation.

What is wrong with me?

You are broken, Nyssa whispered.

Karigan tightened her hands on the reins in an effort to quell the voice of the torturer. She believed Omey was right, that the raiders would be long gone, never to return to the farm, that there was no danger ahead. And yet, she hesitated. She had chosen to journey by herself from the Lone Forest back home to Sacor City to regain her confidence after having been at the mercy of Nyssa Starling, but she'd only discovered that being alone with her thoughts for so long allowed inner voices to tell her how incapable she was, how vulnerable to harm, how weak.

The Karigan of old would not hesitate. The Karigan of now feared it would happen all over again, that she'd be held helpless as she was beaten nearly to death. A jolt of pain coursed up her back at nightmarish memories. The old Karigan could save herself from danger. Until Nyssa. With Nyssa, she hadn't been able to save herself.

When she'd come upon the wreck of Waldron's wagon yesterday, she'd almost turned Condor around and run away. It was like wanting to protect a wound, but *all* of her was the wound.

She closed her eyes for a moment, trying to clear her mind of doubts, of the internal voices that told her how unfit she was, how broken. Condor turned his head to look back at her and gave a gentle whicker. He was picking up on her distress. She patted his neck, and with a trembling exhalation, nudged him forward at a walk. When they passed from the concealment of the woods for the open expanse of farm fields, she fought an inclination to wheel Condor around and retreat. But she could not let Omey and Clem see her fear, so she continued on.

She scanned the landscape. Some fields were freshly furrowed and smelled of having been fertilized with dung. Stone walls rambled around the edges of the fields. The farmstead, or what was left of it, was located on a hillock, a haze of smoke hovering around the remains of the house and barn.

If anyone observed her from the hillock, there was not much she could do to conceal her approach in such openness during daylight hours. Whether she rode fast or slow, she would be spied by anyone watching. She had to go one way or the other, so she settled on moving Condor out at a crisp trot.

Other than smoke, nothing moved as she approached the farmstead. When Condor trotted into arrow range, she knew she made a fine target. Though no projectiles came tearing through the air at her, she found the stillness as she entered the farmyard disquieting. There should have been at least the song of birds. Only a few insects buzzed around her head. All else was silent.

She pulled Condor to a walk and drew her bonewood staff from its sheath across her back. The bonewood was light compared to her saber. Even if she wasn't up to her full strength, its leather-wrapped iron handle could still do damage to an opponent. With a shake, she extended it to full length.

Her disquiet built as she halted Condor in the farmyard. No dog raced toward her barking a challenge. No chickens pecked the ground near their coop. Untended laundry rustled on a line.

The barn was a heap of ash and scorched timbers atop its foundation, smoke still lazily wafting above it. It would likely smolder for days despite the rain, before it finally burned out. When some of that smoke hit the back of her throat, she coughed until tears ran down her cheeks. She drew a handkerchief from her pocket and covered her nose and mouth to protect lungs made too sensitive from inhaling the smoke of a different fire. She reined Condor around toward the house. The chimney still stood, as did a portion of a wall with a window, its glass blasted outward from the intense heat. Beneath it was a planter of wilted flowers.

A cloying floral scent penetrated her handkerchief and drew her to the far corner of the house, where a fine specimen of a lilac bush that had been lovingly cared for bloomed in full spring glory. The blossoms closest to the house, however, were browned and wilted.

Nearby, a rope swing hung from an oak, swaying back and forth as if nudged by the small hands of children. Beyond were six freshly mounded graves. Two were very small.

⋘ SKULL AND SWORD ⋙

The graves, particularly those of the little ones, were proof that evil truly existed in the world. She gazed up at the gray sky, the clouds laden with more rains to come, and wondered where the gods were in all this. They were selfish and self-serving, too far above Earthly concerns as they walked among the stars. They only cared about *how* they were venerated by lowly mortals, not for the mortals themselves. They offered nothing in return that Karigan could perceive. Though she'd once been skeptical about the existence of the gods, she now believed in them full-heartedly after having been forced to serve as Westrion's avatar. She was only worthy of his notice for how useful she could be.

Abruptly she reined Condor away from the graves and directed him around the house. She continued to explore the farmyard. A shed door wavered on sighing hinges, and she caught a glint of steel just inside. She dismounted to get a closer look. The shed was full of small tools hung or shelved in neat rows, the sort used to dig a post hole or sharpen and mend larger farm implements such as plow blades. It was completely intact, unlike the rest of the buildings on the property.

She knelt to examine the metal that had caught her eye, a wicked-looking dagger coated in blood. Not fresh blood, but crusted. A couple days old at least. As her gaze adjusted to the dark of the shed, she found a blackened patch where more blood had soaked into the earthen floor. Was this where the farmer met his demise?

The dagger was finely made with a bone hilt. She stepped outside to see it better in the light. The blade was heavy and sharp, and beneath the blood, a skull with a sword thrust through it was etched into it.

Not very likely the farmer's, she thought.

She wrapped the dagger in her handkerchief and tucked it into her message satchel knowing that Zachary and his advisors would want to see it. She positioned it so it would not touch the tiny pouch also inside her satchel that contained a horsehair bracelet. She longed to wear the bracelet, as it was a warm memory of he who had given it to her, but her hard journey had caused it to start unraveling, so she kept it in her satchel for safekeeping before it could fall apart completely.

As she settled the shoulder strap of the satchel over the pommel of Condor's saddle, she was overcome by the sensation of being watched. She whirled around, but saw no one. The feeling dissipated quickly, and she chided herself for being so jumpy. Considering the circumstances, she supposed it wasn't surprising to feel on edge.

She continued to search around the shed for clues as to the owner of the dagger, but found only a pitchfork lying nearby in the grass. Blood that the rain had not washed away appeared to stain the tines. Or maybe it was rust. No, she determined, not rust. If the orderliness of the shed was any indication, the farmer had not been careless with any of his tools. She picked up the pitchfork for a closer look.

"Farmer Ferris died protecting his family with that pitchfork, and not without taking one of the murderers with him."

Karigan whipped around to find Omey standing there, and Clem sitting his mule some distance off, holding the reins to Omey's pony.

Karigan's heart hammered in her chest. "Please don't sneak up on me like that again."

"I thought we were making enough noise as we entered the farmyard," Omey replied. "It appears, however, you were quite absorbed."

Karigan realized she'd been holding the pitchfork in a position ready to skewer Omey and, thinking of how it had been last used, lowered it. Then, in deference to the farmer, she leaned it against the shed instead of just tossing it back onto the ground.

"Where is the raider's body?"

"Clem and some of the men rode some distance from here and tossed it into a ravine. We did not dignify it with burial or a fire. It will be fodder for wild animals to rip apart."

It was so calmly said that Karigan thought that Omey was a woman she dare not cross. The body might have been useful to look at if the villagers had held onto it, but she had to admit she was relieved they hadn't. Still, there were some questions she could ask.

"Did you search the body before it was disposed of? Any distinguishing details you can think of?"

Omey's keen eyes seemed to reappraise her. "Clem," she called, "come forward and tell Rider Karigan about the body."

Clem nudged his mule forward and halted before Karigan. "Not much to say. Ordinary fella in most ways. Had some old fighting scars, it looked like, and a purse with a few coins—"

"Which we put into the village treasury," Omey interjected.

"He was missing a dagger from its sheath."

"I found it," Karigan said, "and am taking it to the king. Anything unusual about his dress? Any tattoos?"

"Don't remember any tattoos, but we didn't look under his clothes. He wore rough travel garb in good repair, nothing special. Oh, and a necklace of human teeth."

"Those went into the ravine with him," Omey said.

Karigan shuddered. What kind of savages were they dealing with? Clem's description, and the dagger with its sword and skull, however, might prove useful to Zachary and his advisors.

"Are you done here?" Omey asked.

Karigan nodded and mounted Condor, and gazed once more around the ravaged farmyard. "What will happen to this place?" she asked Omey.

"Hard to say. Maybe when memory of what occurred here has faded, someone else will come and rebuild and make a go of farming the land. I fear, however, with so many young people being called to war, it will lie fallow for years to come, go back to forest."

Perhaps it was best that nature cleanse the ugliness of

what had happened at the Ferris place. Until then, however, it would be a haunted ruin.

"Let us return to the village," Omey said, "so we can provision you for the rest of your journey to Sacor City."

Karigan, more than eager to leave the dead behind, rode right past Omey and Clem at a trot.

Upon Karigan's return to the Antlers, Elda ensured her saddlebags were filled with provisions. Waldron was up and about and ambled outside to see her off.

"Mind you watch for those brigands," he said. "They will take everything you have and more."

"I'll be careful," she promised him.

He clasped her shoulder and squeezed. "You saved my life, young lady. I am indebted."

Karigan's cheeks warmed. "It's just luck I came along when I did."

"Luck? Well, not everyone would stop to help out a poor old potter."

Karigan smiled, and hauled herself back into the saddle.

"One more thing," Waldron said.

She looked up from the reins. "Yes?"

"No shortcuts."

She actually laughed, and the sensation surprised her for it had been a long time since she'd had reason.

As Waldron made his way back into the inn, Karigan turned Condor to leave, but just then, Lori hurried up to her.

"Rider?"

Karigan paused. "What is it?"

"Omey asks that you carry this letter to the king for her."

The letter was handed up and she turned it over, a little surprised to find the wax seal stamped with a coat of arms, a catamount rampant and a sheaf of arrows. She looked up to ask Lori about it, for clearly Omey was more than just the head of the village council, but the girl had already run off to the stables. Karigan shrugged and placed the letter in her message satchel. Omey would remain a mystery for now as Karigan desired no further delays. It was time to leave Boggs far behind and go home.

⋖⋗ TRAILING HER ⋖⋗

Over the next few days, the sky remained gray and heavy with foreboding, but the most it produced was a light drizzle, which was miserable enough. Karigan was still two days out from Sacor City, but she consoled herself with the fact that riding along the Kingway was much easier than bushwhacking through the woods, and that she'd be staying at the Hawk's Tail in Deering the next night where she'd be able to dry out again, get a good meal, and best of all, take a steaming hot bath. It was the blissful thought of that bath that propelled her through the gloom.

All that lay beyond Deering and the Hawk's Tail would prove more complex. She looked forward to seeing her friends and sleeping in the comfort of her own bed, but she did *not* look forward to the inevitable looks and questions she'd receive, for surely they'd heard what had befallen her in the Lone Forest.

Even more complicated was knowing Zachary, her sovereign, the man she loved, awaited her there. A man who was married, and whose wife was expecting twins. She both thrilled at the prospect of seeing him again, and dreaded it. She longed to be near him, to be held in his arms—imagining it made her feel feathery inside, but she knew she must keep her distance.

"Why must it be so complicated?" she asked Condor.

He twitched an ear at her. She patted his neck and drew him to a halt so she could dismount and stretch her back, maybe walk alongside him for a while. When she was down, he nudged her shoulder.

"You just want another of Elda's muffins."

He bobbed his head.

"Greedy beast. You had one this morning and the last one is mine." He gave her such a look of dejection that she laughed. "All right, maybe I'll share." She pulled it out of her saddlebag and gave him half.

They continued on at length, but then she paused.

Paused, and watched from the corner of her eye. Listened hard. Condor, as if sensing the need for silence, stood stock still. There was the persistent drip of water from tree limbs to the forest floor on either side of the road, *thunk, thunk, thunk, plink, thunk* . . . Nearby a stream overflowed its banks from the rains and rushed and gurgled. A woodpecker tapped on a tree somewhere in the distance and leaves rustled. A biter buzzed by her ear.

What was she searching for? An indefinable something, some sound buried beneath the ordinary sounds of the forest, some vague shape absorbed into shadow and leaf. But she never observed anything for certain, whether it was a predator stalking her, man or beast, or even a ghost.

Or, maybe she was just tired. She didn't get the best sleep with the nightmares, and memories of the devastation of the Ferris farm with its tiny graves were not helping. Keeping alert for raiders also kept her wakeful.

It was all probably just her imagination. Plus, Condor did not seem concerned. Still, she removed the bonewood from the sheath across her back just in case. She used it like a walking cane as if she were simply out for a stroll in the country, and led Condor on, one part of her listening for that latent *something*, and watching with her peripheral vision.

As she went on, her perception of being watched evaporated and the tension eased out of her neck and shoulders. She fell into a rhythmic stride that carried her at a good pace down the road, and proved meditative.

As they started around a bend in the road, Condor balked beside her.

"Wha—?"

She looked up and saw ahead of her three men sitting on their horses looking as surprised to see her as she them. A feeling of alarm rang through her. Even as she thought to mount Condor so she could run, the men spurred their horses forward. She hadn't even gotten her toe in the stirrup when they bore down on her. She let go the reins and stirrup and shook the bonewood to staff length, but before she could raise it to defend herself, it was booted out of her hands. She stumbled back as the horsemen crowded and grabbed her. Condor whinnied and kicked. One of the horsemen reached for his reins.

"Run, Condor!" she cried.

He hesitated, his ears pricked.

"Run!"

He bolted. Karigan watched for a fleeting, frozen moment until one of the horsemen grabbed her and hauled her onto his horse in front of him. She kicked and hit to no effect. The man held her securely, and the horse stood stolid, unaffected by her struggles. It was happening again, she was helpless. She could almost hear Nyssa laughing at her.

"Let's go," the man told his companions.

She expected them to ride off. Instead, one of the men withdrew a spherical object from his belt pouch and twisted it. The woods, the road, and the sky melded together into a nauseating whorl. It made her light-headed, and reality turned unreal, birdsong turning to a painful high-pitched squeal that hurt her ears, her mind. The visual and aural torment became indistinct until consciousness left her.

It all unspooled, the blue, the green, the brown, until it once more became the sky, the woods, and the ground. The ground upon which her captor had dropped her. She lay sprawled on her stomach, and a wave of dizziness caused the world to whirl around her again, which in turn aroused nausea. She brought up Elda's last muffin and a good portion of her breakfast. She closed her eyes, willing the motion to stop. It did not.

A man laughed. "The Greenie don't like traveling. Don't worry, happens to us all until you get used to it."

The vertigo was too hard upon her to consider his words. She dug her fingers into soil as if to root herself and thus stop the spinning. It helped. As the world gradually slowed down, she caught some of the conversation of the men.

"—don't want to tell him," one was saying. "He'd just have them killed."

"Hard to keep a secret like this in a busy camp, and if the general finds out, he'll—"

She didn't hear what their general would do, for her rebellious stomach brought up the rest of her breakfast. She groaned and rested her head on her arm.

"—do as I say," a third man said. His voice was low, resonant. "Put her in with the other."

They hauled Karigan to her feet and roughly dragged her forward. It occurred to her the air was sharper, drier. That couldn't be right, but when she looked, the world now stilled, she realized they had in fact traveled, that she was no longer even in the Green Cloak, for the jagged peaks of the Wing Song Mountains, still cloaked in snow, reared up before her.

Enver of Eletia fell back and bided his time in the woods when it became clear the Galadheon sensed she was being followed. She'd be incensed, he knew, if she discovered that he was trailing her. She'd almost detected him at that ravaged farm the other day. His skills as a *tiendan* were failing because of his desire to see her.

It had not been easy to track her, as he'd sent his mount, Moonmist, back to her people, the *terrial'ada,* after he and Karigan had parted in the north. He'd taken his time wandering alone away from people, whether Eletian or human, to master the wild emotions and needs of *accendu'melos,* which every maturing Eletian endured. It had come upon him in the Galadheon's presence without other Eletians to intervene, endangering her with his lack of control. He'd sent her away, and just in time.

The mad fever of it overrode all reason, gave in to instinct only. He passed his hand across his brow at the memory, and continued his passage through the woods just out of sight of the road. He'd hung back just enough to calm her suspicions about being followed, but close enough to ensure her safety. His hearing, as acute as any Eletian despite his being a half-breed, picked up the sounds of hoof falls and her voice as she talked to her horse. He smiled.

His mind was clear now, and he was horrified and humiliated by what he'd almost committed upon her in the midst of accendu'melos. The scent of her still called out to him, but it was calm, not a storm. A gentle tug. He refused to open himself to it for she did not love him.

After wandering in the north for a time, he had come upon her trail as she journeyed south. It was cold, but having filled himself with the scent of her during their travels, it was not hard to find. He sensed her continued suffering from pain, both mental and physical, imprinted in the traces of her presence. Concerned, he had followed.

Her trail had cut through wild lands and dense forest, which made no sense. Why did she not keep to established trails and roads? At her camping spots, though her fire was cold by weeks or days, he perceived the residue of nightmares and the taint of wounds still seeping blood.

She did not travel fast. She walked much of the time hindered by having to bushwhack through the woods. He finally caught up with her two days out of Boggs, watched over her as she writhed in bad dreams during the night. He yearned to comfort her, to help her find peace, but he knew she'd only withdraw further from him, and so he did not interfere and kept watch to ensure her safety from a distance.

Once she entered the gates of Sacor City, he would at last turn toward Eletia, leaving her none the wiser he'd been following her.

When he deemed enough time had passed for her suspicion of being followed to have waned, he resumed walking, keeping as silent as any Eletian in the woods. But when he heard more horses than just Condor, sensed men on the road near the Galadheon—*dangerous* men—he leaped into motion.

"Run, Condor!"

Her cry froze his heart. He tore through the woods, ran hard, but when he reached the road, the world screwed in an agonizing miasma that left him writhing on the ground. When it passed, he rose unsteadily to his feet and discovered that she and the men were gone. Gone beyond his ken. He could not sense her anywhere nearby.

He frantically searched the ground for clues and found Condor's hoofprints where he had dug in and bolted. She'd cried for him to run, and Enver imagined he would not stop until he reached Sacor City. There were the confused hoofprints of other horses. An imprint that may have been from the Galadheon's boots, but they just ended as if she'd been carried away. And carried away she'd been. His miasma had been caused by powerful magic. Ancient and powerful, but not Eletian.

He caught the after-scent of her fear and desperation, but all else was *gone*. He tilted his head back and howled his despair to the sky. What now? What now? He had failed her.

Then he saw her staff. She had dropped it, and it had rolled to the side of the road or been kicked there. He approached it with care. The black lacquered wood was almost like a blank space in his vision. It contained some minimal power to negate magic. He had borne it before, had carried it to her in Sacor City after it had returned from the future time with Lhean. Still, it required careful handling. Clearly it did not disturb the Galadheon's special ability, but she was not a creature of magic as was he.

With some trepidation he grasped the staff—bonewood, she had called it—and almost dropped it for it nettled his hand. He'd expected it, but expecting it didn't make the sensation any more pleasant. After a moment, it settled and just numbed his hand.

Now he must decide what to do. He certainly was not going to return to Eletia now. He could go to King Zachary and tell him what had befallen the Galadheon, but that would only slow him, and he had no wish to see the man she loved. No, he was on his own, and he would find the Galadheon. He would bring her to safety, but where could she be? The road offered no clue, nor could he sense her. He would have to rely on instinct. He would search all the lands if he must to find just a trace of her. He would find her, but he hoped it would not be too late.

⊰ RIDER ASH ⊱

 Rider Anna Ash stood a polite distance away by the door while Colonel Mapstone finished up with Captain Connly. The two were sitting at the colonel's desk hashing out lists and assignments.

"Is that all?" the captain asked.

"You want more?" Dusty daylight poured in through a window and flashed on Colonel Mapstone's red hair, briefly outshining the gold braid of her uniform. "How would you like to stand in for me at the next high officers' weekly grumble? Meeting, I mean."

"That is above my pay level."

The colonel sighed. "Then you may be excused."

Captain Connly smiled, his chair scraping on the floor as he stood.

"You will let me know the moment our wayward Rider returns," the colonel said as he walked toward the door.

He paused. "Which one?"

"Either of them."

"Yes, Colonel." The humor had gone from his face. "You'll be notified immediately." He nodded to Anna on his way out.

The colonel seemed to slump at her desk, lines of care etched in shadow around her eyes.

Before Anna had become a Rider, she'd been a servant, mostly caring for the hearths around the castle. An ash girl. Servants were trained to mind their place and their business, which was not too hard when most people who visited or lived in the castle disregarded their existence. They were fixtures so commonly seen that they were unseen. The best-trained servant enhanced this effect by learning how to fade into the background. In the course of their duties, it was impossible to not overhear unguarded conversations.

She had picked up enough to know that the increasing dangers from brigands, in addition to Second Empire, were prompting the colonel to requisition some sort of armor for her Riders. From bits and pieces of the colonel's conversation with Captain Connly, though never directly stated, Anna discerned that striving with the higher officers of the military was wearing on her a great deal, and that she was worried about two of her Riders who were overdue. One was Sir Karigan who should have arrived from the north weeks ago, and the other, Fergal Duff, who was a few days overdue from a run to the capital of D'Ivary Province. With the roads more dangerous of late, being overdue did not bode well.

The colonel looked up as if surprised to find she was not alone. "Oh, Anna, I'm sorry. I'd forgotten you'd come in. What is it you need?"

Anna stepped up to the desk. The clutter atop it was more unruly than ever with open ledgers, scattered papers, dog-eared books, ink pots and pens, and no less than three dirty teacups. She had to fight her natural inclination to tidy it up. At least Elgin saw to keeping the rest of the office and colonel's quarters neat.

"It's not rightly what *I'm* wanting, Colonel," Anna said.

"Oh?"

"It's Arms Master Gresia."

A look of suspicion deepened on the colonel's face. "And what does the arms master want?"

"She asked me to stop by after my training session to remind you of yours next bell. She thought you would—"

"Conveniently forget?"

Anna nodded.

Colonel Mapstone gazed at the piles on her desk in dismay. "I don't have the time."

"Arms Master Gresia said you'd say that, and that I was to tell you that you are wrong." Now she tried to use Gresia's exact wording. "She said, 'If she dies in combat for lack of training and conditioning, then her work won't get done, anyway. At least not by her.'"

"She said that, did she?"

"She also wanted me to remind you that your sessions are by order of the king."

The colonel groaned.

"Arms Master Gresia wished me to further remind you—"

"There's *more*?"

Anna nodded. "Yes. She said that if you wish to achieve full use of your shoulder again, that you'd best not find an excuse to miss the session."

The colonel raised her eyebrows. "Is that all?"

"Yes'm."

"Very well." She sat back in her chair with an air of defeat. "This means I'll have to reschedule my visit with the queen. Actually, I'll just send you instead."

"You want *me* to attend the queen?"

"Is there a problem? She's never tried to bite you before, has she?"

"*Bite me?* No'm!"

The colonel chuckled. "Good. I really just want you to deliver these reports to her." She dug through piles of paper and pulled out a sheaf. "Nothing more complicated than that. Besides, she might enjoy seeing a fresh face and find out for herself how you are doing."

Anna accepted the papers. She had served on Queen Estora's household staff before becoming a Rider and had found her to be warm and kind, but was sure the queen would have forgotten about her by now. "Oh, I can't imagine the queen would remember the likes of me."

"On the contrary, she asks after you often," the colonel said. "Now you best get on, and do clean up before you go to see her."

"Yes'm." Anna hugged the papers to her chest and headed out. The queen asked after her? While it was true Anna had helped protect the queen a time or two during attacks made by the aureas slee, an ice elemental, she was surrounded by

much more important people. Anna had been just a simple
servant, after all. But now she was a Rider, and with the
queen's blessing.

She rushed across the wet grounds to the castle, and in her
chamber changed from her sweaty work tunic and trousers
she'd worn for arms training into a fresh uniform. She wiped
the mud off her boots and splashed her face with water. She
gave herself a quick look in a hand mirror and deemed herself
acceptable to appear before the queen. She was proud to wear
the uniform of forest green, but it lacked the one thing a *real*
Green Rider possessed, and that was a gold winged horse
brooch. Sometimes she felt like an imposter because she did
not have that brooch, that she had not been called to serve in
His Majesty's Messenger Service by a magical compulsion as
the other Riders had been. Those other Riders had an underlying special ability the brooches augmented. Anna did not,
and she'd become a Green Rider simply because Colonel
Mapstone had taken a shine to her and was willing to try an
unmagical, mundane ash girl in the service.

Though she was hard on herself, the other Riders, once
they had gotten over their surprise at the colonel's decision,
treated her as if she really were just one of them, for which she
was grateful. That's just the way the Riders were, a family, but
better than a family because they were accepting, and she
knew they would always stand behind her. The truth, however, was that without a special ability and no brooch, she'd
never be a full Rider.

But now she had to set that feeling aside and take the papers to the queen. She left her chamber in the ancient corridor the Riders were now inhabiting. In her old life, when she'd
been cleaning the Rider hearths, she'd found these corridors
creepy if she happened to be working when no one else was
around. Some believed them haunted, and she did, too. But
when the corridors were filled with Riders, it was lively and
friendly, and thoughts of spirits far off. Come to think of it,
she hadn't felt ghostly presences there in a long time. Just the
heavy and shadowy quality of ancient stone walls and flickering lamps.

She passed by Sir Karigan's door, which was always kept cracked open when she was away, just wide enough so her cat, Ghost Kitty, who was not a ghost, could come and go.

She turned the corner into the main corridor of the Rider wing and waved to a pair of Riders in the common room playing a game of cards. It was home. The first time she had ever felt at home. And now she was off to see the queen. Who would have guessed that this would be her life, she who had been abandoned at the castle by her family, she whose future had held only servile drudgery?

From the Rider wing she entered the flow in the castle's central corridor. It was so much busier these days with uniformed soldiers going to and fro, ambassadors and courtiers and officials on war business. The crowd was in fact so suffocating that Anna stepped into an alcove to catch a breath.

"Oh, look. If it isn't the high and mighty Anna *Ash*," came a voice from behind her. "What a silly name to give yourself."

"Nell Lotts," Anna replied. "What are you on about?"

The girl, just slightly older than Anna, sat on a bench carved into the alcove wall, with her feet tucked beneath her and a feather duster at her side. She wore the livery and apron of a general castle servant, the same as Anna had once worn.

"I guess you are so high and mighty," Nell said, "we can't call you Mousie anymore. How about Rider Mousie?"

"Shirking your duty, Nell?" Anna shot back.

The girl shrugged. "No one notices if I don't dust and polish every day, so why bother? I find other things to do."

Anna shook her head and looked back out at the bustle in the main corridor.

"You look to be shirking your duty, too," Nell remarked.

"I'm not. It's just crowded out there and I'm catching my breath."

"Poor Rider Mousie. Not welcomed anywhere. I'm sure the other Greenies barely tolerate having an ash girl among them."

"That's not true," Anna retorted a little too hotly. She'd never had friends down in the servants quarters and Nell was playing on one of her fears—of actually being hated by the

Riders who had to put up with her existence among them. She knew it was not true, but the dark fear of it still nagged at her.

"I doubt the Riders will keep you around for long," Nell said. "After all, you're a nobody, no one special."

That was hitting too close to her sensitivity about having no magical ability. She took a deep breath and prepared to enter the busy corridor to get away from Nell and her mocking, but then paused.

"I may be nothing special," she said, "but I have a job to do, which I actually *do*." She gave Nell a disparaging look. "And today, that job is visiting with the queen. Not bad for someone who is nothing special, eh?"

She didn't wait for Nell's response, but plunged into the crowd to make her way to the west wing and the royal quarters.

 A VISIT WITH THE QUEEN

Anna was fuming so much about her exchange with Nell Lotts that she arrived at the queen's door before she knew it, and found herself standing beneath the stern gazes of two Weapons. They were always so tall and intimidating, especially in their black uniforms, which, she guessed, were good traits for the king's and queen's personal guards.

"Do you have an appointment?" the Weapon, Ellen, asked.

"Colonel Mapstone does, but she couldn't come, so she sent me with some papers."

"Yes, we were expecting the colonel," Ellen replied, and she shared a quick glance with her comrade, Willis. "Are you carrying any sickness?"

Anna shook her head.

"Very well. I will check with the queen to ensure she wishes to see you."

Ellen entered the queen's quarters, closing the door behind her. Anna spent a few painful, silent minutes under the scrutiny of Willis. When finally Ellen returned, she exhaled in relief.

"The queen is pleased you have come," Ellen said. "She is finishing with another visitor, so take care when you approach."

Willis stepped aside so she could enter and actually cracked a smile. "I assume you remember the way?"

Anna did indeed, and as she passed through the public areas of the queen's quarters and into the private section, she found not much had changed since her days as a member of the queen's household staff, even if her own fortunes had changed dramatically since then.

She encountered Jayd, the queen's personal maid, who was heading in the opposite direction with a tea service. Porcelain cups clinked against one another on the silver tray. There were the remains of tiny cakes on plates.

"Oh, Anna," Jayd said, "how nice to see you. The queen is so pleased to have you visit. Go right in. She is saying farewell to the luin prime."

Jayd continued on, but Anna hesitated. The luin prime? The chief of all the priests in Sacoridia? Well, if she could be among the likes of the queen, the luin prime shouldn't be so great a stretch. She took a breath and walked into Queen Estora's bed chamber. She stepped discreetly against the wall endeavoring to be as quiet and inconspicuous as she'd ever been as a servant.

The luin prime was standing beside the queen's bed, his pristine white robes aglow even in the dismal daylight flowing through the windows. The other servants had always whispered about the prime's handsome features and how the gods must have blessed him with such favor. He was good looking, Anna thought, but maybe a little too good looking, especially for a priest. At the moment, with the light upon him, he certainly looked virtuous, and rather ethereal. Her own preferences leaned toward those who did not look so—so perfect. Like King Zachary, or Weapon Fastion. She felt her cheeks heat up. She shouldn't think about the king in that way, especially not in his wife's bed chamber!

"I do not think you should worry," the luin prime said. His voice was deep, and Anna could well imagine it filling any chapel of the moon and inspiring his congregants. "Your husband will understand that you were deceived."

"Perhaps you are correct," Queen Estora said. It had been a while since Anna had seen her, confined as the queen was in her gravid condition, but she looked well, her belly enormous. "But Zachary prefers to keep his private life, well, private. People will read these romantic poems that make even me blush, and what will they think of their king?"

"That he is madly in love with his queen. I see it only as an advantage for the populace to see Your Majesties in so strong a union. Besides, perhaps he will not hear of it."

The queen lifted a small book from her lap. "This is by Lady Amalia Whitewren, Sacoridia's most celebrated living poet. Everyone is talking about it."

"Perhaps among your ladies," the luin prime replied. "After all, you have not been out and about for quite some time."

"I know it all too well."

"I suspect your husband is, at any rate, too preoccupied by war plans to notice."

"That may be, but I will have to discuss it with him, and he will not be happy."

"Would you like me to be present when you do?"

The queen reached out and took his hand. "My dear Brynston, you are a solace to me, but this I must do on my own. There *is* one thing you can do for me, however."

"Yes?"

"Pray."

They both laughed and then the luin prime bowed and, his voice now grave, said, "I always do. But now I must leave you to your rest, and I've novices to chivvy."

"You will return soon?"

"Yes, my queen." He bowed again.

Anna waited for him to leave, but as he swept by her, he turned, his beautiful face ruined by anger.

"You, girl, were you eavesdropping on our conversation?"

Anna went cold all over. "N-no, Your Eminence. I was, I mean, I was told . . ." She couldn't seem to make her tongue work right, which was not a good omen for her life as a Green Rider.

"Brynston, I invited her here," the queen said. "This is Anna, Rider Ash. Before she was a Green Rider, she was a trusted member of my household."

The anger left the luin prime's face, but his gaze remained cold. He turned back to Queen Estora. "As you say, my queen. However, I wish you would not put so much trust in these *messengers.*"

He said "messengers" with such distaste that Anna wondered if he thought the Riders ogres. They were often looked down upon by the other branches of the military, though maybe less now than they used to be, but she never expected such antipathy from someone like the luin prime.

"They are the king's own messengers, and *mine*," Queen Estora said. "They do dangerous work for little recognition, and are honorable. Both Zachary and I entrust our lives to them."

"My mistake," the luin prime said. "I will take your words to heart."

He glanced once more at Anna before he strode from the room, but he looked no friendlier.

"Anna," the queen said, "come sit beside me and tell me all that is new with you."

First, Anna handed over Colonel Mapstone's papers, then haltingly spoke of her studies and training, still amazed the queen was at all interested. She paused to take a breath, and her gaze wandered to a vase on the queen's bedside table filled with wispy branches abloom with yellow flowers.

The queen followed her gaze and smiled. "Beautiful, are they not? Forsythia. The chief gardener cut them for me yesterday from the castle gardens. They were not more than buds when they were brought to me, but look at them now. They have come along nicely."

They were, Anna thought, bright and cheery.

"I do miss my strolls in the gardens," the queen said with a wistful look in her eye.

"You must be sad they're being dug up."

"Yes, and no. It's being done for a good reason. I had heard about the refugees with no prospect for work, and so I thought this might help at least a few of them."

Refugees, fleeing the insecurity of the countryside, crowded the lower city and camped outside the city gates. They were being given work to transform some of the castle's ornamental gardens into vegetable gardens. The idea was that the refugees would earn a small amount of coin as well as a portion of the harvest for their efforts, and the castle would also be provisioned against shortages. No few refugees were farmers and their fields were going unworked. Soon the shortages would become very real. Anna had not known it had been all Queen Estora's idea.

"I miss the flowers and trees and birds," the queen continued. She reached to touch one of the flowers and it seemed to perk up, but Anna guessed it was just her imagination. "Once the children come, I can go outside again. The gardens won't be the same, but one day, when the war is over, they will once more flower as they used to. I made the chief gardener promise to save all the seeds he could."

The queen smiled, but it was a little melancholy, and Anna thought she must imagine rambling the pathways of the gardens with flowers in full bloom, the tinkle of King Jonaeus' spring in the background, all currently so out of her reach. But then suddenly she came back to the present and brightened.

"Now, Anna, tell me how you are faring with your riding lessons."

Anna straightened in her chair. "Much better. I haven't fallen off in weeks." She loved the riding and was usually paired with a retired cavalry horse named Lion. Perhaps in battle he had been a fierce lion, but in lessons he was as sleepy as an old house cat and hard to get moving. The queen laughed at her descriptions of her lessons, but underneath Anna held her own sadness, knowing that since she did not have a special ability with magic, she'd never be matched with one of the very special horses the real Green Riders rode.

Not a real Rider, came the thought from a bleak place within even as she smiled at the queen.

✵ RIDERLESS ✵

The queen kept Anna for over half an hour in conversation. They talked about the Riders, the queen's preparations for the children, and the murky weather. Though they spoke of mostly light topics, all was underlain with the foreboding of war and the perils of childbirth. Their visit only came to an end when Jayd returned proclaiming it was time for the queen to rest.

"What have I been doing if not resting all the time?" the queen demanded. "I need a rest from all this rest." But she gave Anna a good-humored smile. "I have enjoyed our visit, Anna. Please do come again."

Anna bowed and left the queen's bed chamber. She'd been invited back for another visit! What would Nell Lotts think of *that?* She held her chin a little higher as she walked.

When she reached for the door to exit the queen's apartments, she heard voices out in the corridor. When she stepped through the door, Weapon Ellen stayed her with a hand on her shoulder. Anna quickly saw why—the king and a knot of his advisors were choking the corridor.

The king was addressing General Washburn: "It is true the Eagle's Pass Keep has never fallen to the enemy, but I do not intend that there be a first time during *my* reign."

"With due respect, Majesty," the general said, "the keep is impenetrable. Our additional forces could be used elsewhere."

The king was very still. There was an intensity to him that made Anna not want to be the object of his regard. And yet, he did not lash out, and his movements were quiet, controlled.

"With due respect, General," the king said, his words

rimed with frost, "the D'Yer Wall was deemed impenetrable, as well. The Eagle's Pass is vital for our landward troops to move east and west. We must ensure its safety."

The general opened his mouth to speak, but a man in black, Les Tallman, who was the chief of all Weapons and one of the king's close advisors, interjected, "I think we should take to heart the recess that was called and reconvene later as agreed, when all have cooled off and rested."

The king nodded. "Very well. We will meet again in an hour's time."

At first the general looked like he would argue, but then nodded as well, and with that the group dissipated. Ellen released Anna's shoulder so she could continue on her way. She had to cross paths with the king, so as he approached, she stepped aside and bowed her head.

"Rider Ash, right?" he said.

"Yes, Your Majesty."

"Do you bring news? Perhaps of our missing Riders?"

He asked after Riders, but she suspected she knew which one he really wanted to hear about. "No, Your Majesty. I brought some papers to the queen from Colonel Mapstone."

The king did not allow disappointment to show on his face, but she could sense it anyway.

"Very well. Captain Connly knows I wish to be notified immediately when we've word." With that, he turned on his heel and headed for his apartments.

Anna took a deep breath and continued on, her boots silent on the plush carpeting. She suspected that she most certainly wasn't the only Rider who knew that there were feelings between Sir Karigan and the king. She'd picked up on veiled comments between Captain Connly, Colonel Mapstone, and Lieutenant Mara. It had to be hard for two people who were in love not to be together, but the one she really felt bad for was the queen.

Love, it was a sketchy business at best.

"What do you want with that old map book anyway?" Gil asked.

They were walking across castle grounds from their geography lesson to stable duty. Anna carried the large and heavy atlas, wrapped in oilskin against the weather, hugging it to her chest like a baby.

"I wanted to look up a few things," she said. Like the Eagle's Pass. Thanks to her lessons, she had a much better grasp of what her country, and others, looked like. She was also learning how to read maps, but they had not covered specific geographic details, and after overhearing the king's conversation a couple days ago, she wanted to know more about the Eagle's Pass. After some cajoling, Master Foley had allowed her to borrow his beautiful atlas for the night.

Gil shrugged. She knew he'd rather use his free time to play games in the Rider common room with friends than have anything to do with books. She tried not to hold it against him.

Her foot squelched in mud in the pathway. "I wish this rain would quit. I just shined my boots."

"You'll wear 'em out with all that polishing," Gil replied. He was just as indifferent to his boots as books, but Anna was proud of her real, black riding boots. They were finer than anything she'd ever owned.

A Green Foot runner trotted past them on her way to deliver someone a message. Troops marched in formation here and there around the castle, their cadence songs ringing out sharp and strong. Wagons moved supplies around to various outbuildings, and the sword practice rings near the field house were in near constant use by warriors who needed to hone their fighting skills. Cavalry soldiers likewise practiced on the castle's west side, and sometimes, if Anna had free time, she went to watch the riders in blue charge across the field.

"Well," Gil said, "at least you aren't cooing over that book of poetry like everyone else."

All the *girls*, he meant. And she didn't have to ask him which book of poetry he meant. She, too, had seen girls and ladies tittering and blushing over it. She had known the queen was not happy about the book, and if the queen were aware of the silliness around it, it could not be making her any happier.

They were just abreast of officers quarters when the pounding of hooves from behind made them jump off the path just in time as a horse galloped by. Both were pelted by mud kicked up by the horse's hooves, much to Anna's dismay. With castle grounds so busy, they kept aware of horses coming and going, but it was generally accepted one did not gallop except in designated areas. That rider should have hollered a warning.

"It's one of ours," Gil said.

Anna looked up from her mud-spattered greatcoat to see the horse circling in front of officers quarters. He was Riderless, but despite his coating of mud, it took Anna only a second to realize which horse it was.

"Condor!"

He was thin, and a lather of sweat mixed with the mud. He was fully tacked. His sides heaved as he fought to catch his breath. How far had he run? Where was Sir Karigan?

"Get the colonel!" she ordered Gil.

He opened his mouth as though to protest, then shut it and jogged off to bang on the colonel's door. Captain Connly stepped outside and froze when he saw Condor. Color drained from his face. When he collected himself, he stepped up to the gelding to remove the message satchel that dangled precariously from the saddle's pommel.

"Anna, please walk Condor out, take him to Hep to look over."

Anna shifted the burden of the atlas in her arms in order to do as he asked.

"I'll take that," Gil said when he returned.

Gratefully she handed over the book and went to Condor to loosen his girth, then took up his reins. Colonel Mapstone arrived a moment later, and spying Connly with the message satchel, said, "Let's have a look at the saddlebags, as well."

Anna halted Condor so they could remove the saddlebags. The colonel patted the gelding's neck. "Poor Condor, you've been running hard, haven't you, but you don't seem lame, and I can't see any obvious injuries. Hep will get a better look on that count. But where's Karigan?"

If the colonel expected an answer, Condor wasn't giving

one. Then she and the captain disappeared into the captain's quarters with Sir Karigan's gear.

Gil fell in step beside Anna as she led Condor toward Rider stables. "This can't be good," he said.

Anna just kept stroking Condor's neck knowing that Gil was right. Where was Sir Karigan?

SACORIDIA'S WORST ENEMY

Zachary was maintaining his composure well, Laren thought. He'd much practice over the years of reining in his emotions, of wearing a mask. He and his advisor, Les Tallman, were going through the contents of Karigan's message satchel as Castellan Javien watched. They'd cleared out a meeting of Zachary's war chiefs to do this, and a map of Sacoridia with markers placed in various positions remained on the long conference room table.

"Some old reports from Captain Treman," Les Tallman said holding up a sheaf of papers.

"I saw those when we were in the north." Zachary betrayed nothing with his words, but his expression was taut.

Laren glanced at Connly standing beside her, practically at attention, his face a little pale. He had yet to lose a Rider under his command. Not that they'd *lost* Karigan. They didn't know what had happened to her, but the potential was there. Messenger horses were not easily parted from their Riders. She and Connly had found nothing among Karigan's effects to explain why Condor had run to the castle without her.

"My goodness," Les said as he pulled out another sheaf. He flipped through it while Zachary and Javien gazed over his shoulder. "She did it. She actually did it." He looked up in wonder. "She found the p'ehdrose and drafted an alliance with them."

Laren and Connly had already known this after having dug through her message satchel themselves, but her pride in her Rider expanded as others saw her success. Zachary's mask faltered, emotion rippling across his face.

"You were right to send her after all, sire," Javien said. He had not had much faith in the venture, but now he gazed at the document with barely suppressed excitement. "She deserves a commendation. If we see her again."

Zachary's jawline went taut at Javien's words. Laren wanted to shake the castellan for his callousness, but instead said, "She will return, I've no doubt."

Neither Javien nor Les seemed to hear her for their attention was fixed on the document.

"We will have to send a delegation, make plans with our new allies," Les said. "I honestly believed the p'ehdrose were long passed into myth, but she found them."

"Rider G'ladheon has always been an exceptional Green Rider," Laren said.

"Yes," Les replied absently as he pulled a knife wrapped in a handkerchief out of the satchel.

Laren knew the symbol on the blade well. Javien blanched when the handkerchief fell away, revealing he did, too.

"Is this mark what I think it is?" Les asked.

"The sword and skull ever belonged to one group," Zachary murmured.

"Yes," Laren said. "The Darrow Raiders are back." They'd suspected it from the descriptions of attacks they'd heard about happening across the realm. Oh, yes, Laren was quite familiar with their ways.

"How did Rider G'ladheon come upon it?" Les asked. "It's stained with old blood."

Les and Javien spoke among themselves making guesses. Zachary gazed at her, and she gazed back. Had Karigan come upon the scene of an attack? Had she been involved in one? Was the knife a message she intended for them, the only way to send them word? Surely the blood was not hers.

Eventually, much to Laren's relief, Les set the hideous thing aside, the blade once more draped. "Rider G'ladheon has given us quite a mystery," he said. He turned his attention back to the satchel. "One more item." He withdrew a sealed letter. "It is addressed to you, Your Majesty, with the Vine-carter seal on it."

Laren and Connly had seen the letter, but had not read it

since it was clearly intended for Zachary, but she knew the
Vinecarter name well as it belonged to Zachary's Aunt Omelia. Even before they saw the contents of the letter, it was a
clue that indicated Karigan had gotten at least as far as Boggs
before she'd been separated from Condor.

When Zachary finished reading the letter, he said, "All but
Colonel Mapstone leave me."

He and Laren stood in silence while the others exited the
room. When the door was shut once more, Zachary dissem-
bled little, even though it was just the two of them. They continued their silence for some moments before Zachary chose
to speak.

"My aunt tells me a farm was hit in Boggs by raiders, an
entire family wiped out, including children. That's where
Karigan picked up the knife. Apparently the farmer killed a
raider before he in turn lost his life."

Laren closed her eyes and let out a breath of relief. It was
not Karigan's own blood on the knife, then. But it did not
explain her whereabouts.

"My aunt further recounts that Karigan aided a pottery
merchant who was also attacked and injured by brigands on
the Boggs Road, most likely raiders, as well. Unfortunately,
she gives little information on that account, expecting Karigan
to fill us in. She just wanted to ensure I was aware of what was
going on in the countryside."

They knew all too well, with more and more reports coming in every day, along with refugees seeking safety in the city.

"My aunt then speaks of Karigan herself." Zachary turned
away, gazed into the distance. "She praises Karigan, but suggests our menders take a good look at her. She reminded my
aunt of her late husband Nickold after the war in the Under
Kingdoms. I remember my grandmother explaining how his
spirit had been deeply wounded in the conflict."

Laren knew that story well. Nickold had returned home so
shattered by his experiences that he gave up his lands and
duties to lead a quiet life in the country.

Zachary turned abruptly to face her once more. "Laren,
where is she?" Finally he revealed his pain. It was in his eyes
and voice. "It is Blackveil all over again."

"I don't know where Karigan is," Laren replied softly. "Neither her gear, nor Condor, offered any clues, but no, it is not Blackveil all over again. We can investigate. Once I saw Lady Vinecarter's seal, I immediately sent out Tegan and Brandall to search for her between here and Boggs."

"Good thinking. She could be hurt along the road."

"Yes," Laren said, but did not add that in that case it was unlikely Condor would have run off without her, though if she were conscious at the time, she might have commanded him to leave in hopes they found enough clues on Condor to come looking for her.

Zachary swept back and forth pacing in agitation, barely able to contain himself. "I'd go myself."

"But you can't."

He paused. "No, I can't." He looked up at the ceiling. "And I have to act like she means no more to me than anyone else."

"I am afraid it is true," she said, "but you know you can always come to me if you need to talk."

"Will you tell her father?"

Oh, gods. She hadn't even given Stevic a thought. Thank the gods he was in Selium for the funeral of Lord Fiori. "No," she said. "Not till we know more."

"Omelia seemed to think Karigan was suffering." Zachary shook his head. "I feel so helpless."

"Anyone would suffer after what she went through, but we both know she is strong, and if she is in some kind of trouble, she can handle it. You know how she is."

"It's killing me," he said, "that I can do nothing."

"I know, Moonling, I know." Karigan was not the only one suffering. Zachary, too, had been tortured at the hands of Second Empire, though most of his wounds were on the inside.

Their story was a tragic one of two people inexorably drawn to one another, but kept apart because of class and politics. The attraction had begun very early on, but circumstances kept them apart, permitting only a distant yearning between the two. Until the north.

Until the north where they'd been far away from court and gossips, and helped one another through the depredations of Second Empire. Zachary told Laren little, but Connly, who'd been there for some of the time, spoke of how protective Zachary had been of Karigan, and how she had cared for him through wound sickness. The intense situations they faced would have deepened their feelings even more for one another, she was sure. If only Lady Fiori, Karigan's best friend who'd been there with them, could have returned to Sacor City. She would know everything, but of course she'd had to return to Selium to bury her father.

"If only I'd commanded her to come home with the rest of us," Zachary said.

"Then she would not have gotten the alliance with the p'ehdrose."

"Even so. And I would like to know, where is the Eletian in all this?"

It was a good question. He was supposed to have traveled home with Karigan, but there was no sign of him, and Lady Omelia had apparently made no mention of an Eletian in her letter.

Zachary gazed at her, his mask firmly in place, and said, "You will inform me the moment you hear from the Riders you sent out."

"Yes, of course. I will also ask Hep to keep an eye on Condor." Messenger horses often sensed something of their Riders even when far apart. If Condor stopped eating, became very depressed and listless, it was a good indication that things were not going well for Karigan. "She will be fine," Laren reassured him. "She can take care of herself."

"But she has not fully healed."

Laren knew that, and she knew Karigan might not be fine, but she had to keep Zachary's hope up. There was too much on the line with battle and troop movements and a war stance in the offing.

"I almost forgot," she said. She pulled the pouch from an inner pocket. "This was also in Karigan's satchel. I didn't leave it there for Javien and Les to gawk at. I figured you might know what it was."

He took it, loosened the string to look inside. A muscle spasmed in his cheek. "I do."

Just as she'd thought. Such tokens were gifts between lovers.

He removed the bracelet made from Condor's chestnut tail hairs. It was frayed and might have grown too loose on Karigan's wrist.

"Clearly she wanted to keep it safe," Laren said in case he thought Karigan was hiding it, or in some way rejecting it and thus him. "If you like, I can leave it in her room. For when she returns."

He replaced the bracelet in its pouch. "No need. I'll repair it."

Laren saw that as a good sign, that he did have some hope Karigan would return none the worse from whatever had delayed her. Laren knew she shouldn't do anything to encourage Zachary's and Karigan's feelings for one another, but trying to keep them separate certainly had not worked. It reminded her of those old stories about true heart mates.

In the distance, the bell down in the city rang out the hour.

"I've a meeting with the lord-mayor," Zachary said.

Laren took it as a dismissal. She stepped outside, glanced over her shoulder to see Zachary with head bowed, the pouch clenched in his hand. She quietly shut the door.

Les Tallman, who waited for her in the corridor, asked, "Everything all right?"

"Fine," she replied. "He says he has a meeting with the lord-mayor."

"That's not for another half hour."

Then Zachary was, she decided, taking time to compose himself. "I would not disturb him, in any case."

"How does he seem to you?" Les asked quietly.

Laren sighed. It was not the first time they'd had this discussion since Zachary's return. "Hard to say. You know how he hides what is on his mind."

If Les were aware of Zachary's feelings toward Karigan, he did not speak of it. "I fear his experiences in the north will just fester. It is difficult to know what will happen when it breaks him down as it eventually must."

Les referred not to the situation with Karigan, but to his

torture at the hands of Second Empire, and he was right to be concerned.

"I sense him second-guessing himself, his strategy," Les continued. "He doesn't know what information he gave the enemy when he was held captive, and he is questioning his every move, wondering if he is playing into their hands."

"I agree," Laren replied. What Les did not mention was the possibility of a spell placed on Zachary by Grandmother, the former leader of Second Empire and a necromancer. Zachary was highly aware one or more may have been placed on him, and must wonder if a spell was influencing his decisions. She hoped any spells had died with Grandmother, but thought it unlikely. If only their other missing Rider, Fergal, were here with his ability to see magic in others. Then they would know for certain if a spell had been placed on Zachary.

In the meantime, the wondering, the waiting, must eat at Zachary. Sacoridia's own king could turn out to be the kingdom's worst enemy.

⋙ NEWS FROM SELIUM ⋘

"These came in while you were out," Elgin said as Laren entered her quarters. He handed her a letter and a parcel, and then continued clearing old teacups off her desk and onto a tray, careful not to disturb the disarray of papers in the process. If only she could work in a more organized way, she thought. Connly's desk was always so neat and tidy.

With a sigh, she sat heavily in her chair.

"I heard about Condor coming back without his Rider," Elgin said. "That's never a good sign." He should know for he had been Chief Rider when she had come into the messenger service, when she was just a youngster, really. After years of retirement, he'd returned to the castle at her request to help train new Riders. He assisted with other tasks as well, such as combing through old documents for references to the Green Riders during wartime, and he'd taken it upon himself to serve as her orderly.

"No, not a good sign," Laren echoed.

"How did the king take it?"

There were few secrets between her and Elgin, which meant he was aware of the romantic bond between Zachary and Karigan, but they did not engage in idle gossip, and anything they discussed certainly did not leave her quarters. The lack of secrets between them ensured that someone she trusted knew what she knew should the worst ever happen to her. Mara and Connly were aware, as well, but perhaps not with as much detail as she shared with Elgin.

"He is often hard to read, even for me," Laren replied,

"but for all that, he did not take it well. What folly for him to fall in love with a Green Rider."

"A folly for any," Elgin said. "Happens, though."

For all her words, Laren was distressed for Zachary. He was a deep thinker, and he felt deeply as well. Perhaps a little too much for a king who must make all kinds of difficult decisions that affected tens of thousands of his people. It would eat a lesser man alive. It wasn't that Zachary allowed his feelings to interfere with his duty, but Karigan was a different matter, and if she had fallen into the hands of the Darrow Raiders? Laren tried not to entertain that possibility and what it would mean for both of them.

She turned in her chair to find Elgin setting aside the tray of dirty cups and preparing to polish her dress boots. "Elgin, there is something you should know."

"Eh?" he asked as he sat on a stool and inspected one of her boots.

There was no easy way to say it, so she decided to be direct. "The Darrow Raiders are back."

He looked straight at her, froze, then slowly nodded. "I've heard about all the attacks. Does sound like the Darrow Raiders, but we finished them off."

Like Laren, Elgin was a veteran of those terrible days, when the Riders were deeply involved in trying to stem the anarchy the Darrow Raiders sowed across the countryside.

"I am afraid we didn't."

"How can that be?" His voice was full of denial.

"Karigan had evidence in her message satchel." She explained about the knife.

"Maybe this current crop are pretenders," Elgin said. "Just using the name."

"I wish it were so." She understood his need for the return of the Darrow Raiders to be untrue. They'd seen their fellow Riders butchered and tortured in gruesome ways. "It's my fault," she said. "I let Torq get away."

"But he was killed."

"We never knew that for sure. It was hearsay."

"But—" Elgin began.

She knew he wanted to say how after that one last battle,

after they'd killed or rounded up most of the Raiders, cleared them from the countryside, they'd had peace all these years.

"All I can figure," she said, "is that the survivors went to ground and bided their time. My guess is that our upheaval with Second Empire has brought them out of hiding, that they have decided they can attack while we are otherwise occupied."

"What are we gonna do, Red?"

"I don't know. The fact it is the *Darrow* Raiders is new, so there has not been time to strategize." They would have to strategize, and carefully. The Raiders would remember and have learned from what was done in the past. She'd also have to sit with her Riders and explain exactly what they were up against. She could only guess that after all these years, the Raiders held a great deal of animus for the Green Riders who had defeated them. "I do think Zachary is keen to reinforce the Eagle's Pass Keep and then make some major move on Second Empire." Unfortunately, after the fall of Grandmother, another stepped into the breach as leader—General Birch, formerly of Mirwell Province's militia. Whether it was Second Empire or the Darrow Raiders, you cleared out one nest of snakes and another erupted. Her own priorities were about to shift, she knew, especially if Zachary decided to use his Riders to eradicate the Darrow Raiders as Queen Isen once had.

Both she and Elgin fell into silence to ponder the gravity of it all, or relive nightmarish memories. Laren tried to shake off the spell, and remembering that Elgin had brought her a letter, she picked it up from her desk. It was from her daughter, Melry. Soon Melry would come home as her studies at Selium concluded at spring's end. They'd have to find her some position in the castle. Despite Melry's greatest wish and expectations, she had not heard the Rider call.

Laren broke the seal, unfolded the letter, and started reading. After a few minutes, Elgin paused the brushing of her boot and asked, "How is Mel?"

"Doing well, it would seem." Laren was pleased. Melry had blossomed at Selium, making many new friends, seeing new sights, and being exposed to a wide range of experiences she would not have been had she remained at the castle. An education at Selium ensured plenty of challenges in all its lines of study. "Says her masters are happy with her work." Melry wasn't being disingenuous, Laren knew. Her marks had been above average all along. It gave Laren hope that Melry would find some occupation after school that would interest her that had nothing to do with the messenger service.

Melry then described the somber atmosphere in Selium, with black bunting draped everywhere, and mourners arriving from across the realm and beyond to pay tribute to the Golden Guardian. Zachary had sent a special delegation consisting of officials, nobles, and admirers of Lord Fiori.

Estral, or should I say the Lady Fiori, hasn't arrived home yet, Melry wrote, *but a soldier with the honor guard rode ahead to inform the dean she was getting close.* Considering how long it would have taken Melry's letter to reach Sacor City, she assumed Lady Fiori had reached Selium some time ago and that funeral ceremonies were well under way.

Yesterday, I ran into Karigan's father and he treated me to supper, Melry continued. It pleased Laren that Stevic would take Melry to supper. It was very good. At some point, she and Stevic would have to tell their daughters about their relationship. That was, of course, if Karigan returned home safely. The last thought darkened the lightness she felt at reading Melry's mostly cheerful letter.

She turned to the next page, but grew increasingly dismayed as she read Melry's plans for after school. By the time she finished, she was brimming with displeasure.

"You look like you swallowed a hornet," Elgin said from where he sat on his stool.

Laren turned to him. "She says if I won't let her be a Green Rider like that 'Anna girl' she's heard about, she wants . . ." Words failed her.

"Wants what?" Elgin said, working oil into one of her boots with a soft cloth.

"She says," Laren tried again, "that she wants to be a *Weapon.*"

Elgin made a low whistle.

"This is not exactly what I was hoping for when I sent her

to Selium. Who would put such an idea in her head?" For all that Selium should have opened up the world to her, this was what she wanted? It was almost as bad as becoming a Rider. Laren loved her Riders, but she wouldn't wish the call upon anyone, especially not her own daughter. A Weapon was the shield of royalty and must put the life of her monarch before her own. Hells, their motto was, *Death is honor*. It was also an ascetic life. Weapons did not marry or have families. Laren wanted Melry to have the widest range of options possible available to her.

"Maybe the lass will change her mind," Elgin said. "Maybe it's a—what is the word?—a *phase* that she's going through."

"I certainly hope so. I bet that Rendle, who is arms master at the school, has put notions in her head. Can you imagine Melry as a tomb Weapon, working down in those cold and dark catacombs every day?" Laren sure couldn't. Her daughter was too lively, too sociable for such work.

"Can't say as I know Mel terribly well." Elgin set the boot down beside him and dipped his cloth in oil to begin working on the other. "Last time I saw her she was just a bitty mite."

Laren stood and paced. She had the urge to throttle someone. If only she knew who to hold responsible.

"Before you go about strangling someone," Elgin said, guessing at her thoughts, "maybe you should look at that parcel I brought you."

So occupied by Melry's letter had she been that she had forgotten about it. She took it off her desk and saw her name and address written in Stevic's broad strokes. Hastily she tugged loose the strings that bound it. Whatever it was, it was wrapped in an outer layer of oilskin to keep it dry. She then tore apart a few layers of protective paper, and then a length of muslin, to find silk, deep indigo silk. She caught her breath as she lifted it from its wrappings. It was a scarf of high quality silk shot through with filament-fine silver threads like tiny stars.

Elgin cleared his throat. She'd forgotten he was there. "Something you wanna tell me, Red?"

Her relationship with Stevic, still very new, was one secret she had not shared with Elgin. Not with anyone. She feared

others would think she showed Stevic's daughter favoritism
because of it. And certain personal things she liked to keep
to herself.

She turned toward Elgin, the gossamer scarf flowing across
her hands. It was lighter than a cloud. "Uh . . ."

"At a loss for words, are you?"

Laren found that, indeed, she was.

"Then I will tell you," he said. "That merchant is keen on
you, isn't he? Karigan's father? And you are keen on him, too."

Laren looked down at the silk, then back at Elgin. "Yes?"

"That's a question?" He laughed. "Thought so, with all the
time you two spent together while he was here, supposedly
working out supplies and shipments, and you with a light in
your eyes like I haven't seen since you were a new Rider with
the wonder of it all filling you."

"Is it that obvious?"

Elgin nodded. "I figured it out some while ago, I did. Now
you're blushing."

Laren put her hand to her cheek. It was hot. "Elgin—"

"No need to explain, Red. I get you don't want your Riders to think you're treating Karigan special because you are
being courted by her father, though I think you are underes-
timating them."

"Well—"

"I'm just happy you're happy. I worry that you've been too
alone all these years."

"You're one to talk."

"Not me, I've got my girls."

His "girls" were chickens and a milk cow.

"Elgin . . ."

He set aside the newly oiled and buffed boot and stood. "I
am an old bachelor and won't be changing my ways anytime
soon. I like things the way they are. I got the Riders and you,
and that's all I need. Speaking of which, I'm due to meet Merla
down in the records room."

"Merla?"

Elgin nodded. "The latest translations of those old Rider
documents are done and some are about warding. Could be

helpful to Merla so she doesn't get hives every time she tries to cast one."

"That would be good," Laren agreed, trying to regain her composure. Poor Merla had been setting wards around the royal apartments and elsewhere, and it was painstaking work that left her swollen and itching with hives. She watched Elgin leave, then pressed the silk against her face. So . . . soft. The indigo was so deep. What would she wear with it? Did she own anything that wasn't green and part of a uniform?

Hidden among the wrappings she found a note: *To my dearest Laren, till we see one another again.* He was as brief as his daughter when it came to notes, but the scarf itself said volumes.

Then she remembered his daughter was missing. She'd already had to tell him once that Karigan had gone missing and was presumed dead when they thought she'd been lost in Blackveil. Would she have to do so again?

⇨ WITCH'S BAIT ⇦

"**K**arigan, why are your hands shaking?"
She clasped them together hoping
that would make them stop and ignored Fergal's question. She was sitting on the dirt floor
beside him, he leaning against the stone wall of the old crofter's hut in which they were being held. Pin beams of daylight
stabbed through the roof and broken shutters, and played
against Fergal's wan face. His shoulder was saturated with
crusted blood.

"Has no one come to check your wound?" she asked.

"Not since they threw me in here and yanked the arrow
out. They bandaged it and that was that. What do they want
with us? Who are these people?"

"I'm not sure," she replied. "Bandits—raiders have been
hitting around the countryside." Her hands shook with renewed ferocity. She sat on them. "The ones I ran into on the
road were as surprised to see me as I them, so I don't think
they were specifically looking for me."

They'd compared notes and found Fergal had lost track of
time, but reckoned he'd been there two days before they
brought her in. He'd been riding back from an errand in
D'Ivary when he was ambushed. In an attempt to escape, he'd
been brought down by an arrow. He remembered the earth
reeling, a great deal of sickness—which could have been a
reaction from his special ability, or the effects of the traveling
device, or probably both—and darkness, only to awaken in
the hut. He winced as he adjusted his position.

She rose to her feet. "I'm going to try to get someone's
attention out there, get you a mender."

Their captors likely would not help. When food had been brought to them earlier, their guard had offered nothing when asked.

"You didn't answer my question," Fergal said, "about why your hands are shaking."

"What shaking?" And she pounded on the door before he could reply. In truth, all of her was shaking and she couldn't seem to stop. She swore she could feel Nyssa the torturer's pleasure at her plight. To be held captive again, helpless. She'd been broken once before, and now she just wanted to scream her distress. Instead, she channeled it into yelling and pounding on the door.

When she paused to catch her breath and rub her throbbing, still-shaking hands, she glanced at Fergal and saw his wide eyes.

"Never knew you had lungs like that on you," he said, "though you did shout at me a time or two on my training run."

Despite it all, she smiled. Then she kicked the door again, kicked it to shuddering on its hinges. She was poised to kick it again when she heard the rattling of chains and snick of a lock outside. The door opened, and she averted her face from the blinding light. Next thing she knew, she was slammed to the ground.

"Pipe down!" a man bellowed. "What the hells you making a racket about?"

Karigan blinked up at the hulking figure in the doorway. This was a different guard than had come in before. She pointed at Fergal, but when her hand shook too much, she pulled it back to herself. "He needs the attention of a mender. And we could do with more blankets. A fire would help, too."

"Anything else?" the man asked. "Maybe the queen's jewels?"

Karigan knew better than to respond. She tried to rise to her knees, but the man booted her back down.

"If you start screaming and kicking the door again, I will gag you and truss you up like a pig."

He then stomped over to Fergal, and a second guard, armed with a crossbow, filled the doorway. Karigan levered herself into a half-sitting position trying to conceal how much

the rough treatment hurt, and watched as the first guard
loomed over Fergal.

"You need a mender, boy?"

Fergal spat on the man's boot.

No, Karigan thought, fisting her hands. Sure enough, the
man kicked Fergal in the side. Fergal grunted and fell over.

"Mind your manners," the man said. He then turned to
Karigan. "And remember what I said about the noise. You
don't want to rouse the attention of certain people out there,
trust me."

"Why are you holding us?" she demanded.

He paused in the doorway. "You're bait for the witch."
Then he was gone, the door slamming behind him.

At Fergal's groan, she scuttled to his side. "Anything
broken?"

"Don't think so. Gonna bruise, though."

"You shouldn't have provoked him."

Fergal snorted. "It's the same as you'd have done."

Not anymore, Karigan thought. In the past, she might have
even tried to attack the guard, but maybe she had grown a
little more sensible with experience. And after Nyssa, she just
wasn't the same.

What's happened to the brave Greenie? Nyssa whispered.

Karigan tried to shake that voice out of her head.

"What was that about a witch?" Fergal asked.

"I have no idea. Maybe he meant Grandmother and doesn't
know she's dead." But why would they think Grandmother
would want a pair of Green Riders? Grandmother *had* wanted
Karigan, not because she was a Green Rider, but because she
served as the death god's avatar. Grandmother had wanted
the avatar to release the demons of the hells to defeat Sacoridia, and she'd almost succeeded.

"What now, Chief?"

"Chief?"

"That's right," he murmured. "How would you know?"

"Know what?"

"The colonel promoted you to Chief Rider."

"She *what*? What about Mara?"

"She's lieutenant."

She must love that, Karigan thought. "So Connly is captain?"

Fergal nodded. "Beryl Spencer is major. Not that we'll ever see her."

That was for certain. Beryl was a Green Rider, but with her special ability to assume a role, the king used her for more secretive missions. In any case, Karigan had not expected a promotion, and under the circumstances it seemed a distant thing, but it still kindled a flush of pleasure. As Chief Rider, she wouldn't be sent on so many runs, which both pleased and dismayed her. Pleased because she could get to know her fellow Riders better, and frankly wouldn't be in as much danger, and dismayed because she wouldn't experience the freedom of the ride very often, to be out in the countryside with the wind in her hair and a fast horse beneath her, though thoughts of rain, snow, mud, and sleeping on the ground did diminish the romance of it to a degree. As Chief Rider, there would be the difficulty of sharing the same roof as Zachary and his wife for longer periods of time. She supposed it was all a displaced concern as there was no telling what would become of her and Fergal in the hands of these brigands.

She wondered if Condor had reached the castle and what Zachary would make of it. She could not imagine he and Colonel Mapstone could even guess where she and Fergal were, and finding two lost messengers certainly would not be a priority, even for Zachary, no matter what he felt for her.

She and Fergal spoke for some time, he filling her in on the latest at the castle until he grew weary.

"How are you feeling?" she asked.

"Could be better."

She knelt beside him and placed her hand on his forehead. "Your fever has spiked," she said. This was not good, especially if their captors would not bring him a mender.

She fetched him a ladle of water from the bucketful the guards had left them, and made him drink. Then they both rested in silence, though she could sense Fergal's discomfort.

Hours later, when the guards brought them supper, she stood steady though she fought the urge to retreat to a corner. "We need a mender," she said. "His fever is up."

The guard glared at her, and left two plates of some kind of gruel and burned pan bread on the floor before clomping out of the hut and slamming the door. Karigan took one of the plates to Fergal.

"Not really hungry," he said.

"You've got to try and eat. You need to fight the fever."

She considered once more peeling off his crusty bandages and trying to clean the wound, but she feared doing more harm than good. She also possessed no clean bandages with which to replace the old. She settled beside him deciding to take her own advice and eat her supper so she'd have the strength to fight whatever was to come.

⋘ A MENDER ⋙

Karigan splashed icy water on her face where a spring formed a pool, and gasped. It jolted her from her groggy state and felt so good to clean up. Being out of that dark hut beneath the sun and sky also helped, but there was no time to revel in it for the guard kicked her leg.

"Get the buckets and get moving," he ordered.

Karigan stood. She'd filled two buckets and now she must carry them, she with her bad back, but she did not hesitate, preferring not to provoke the guard. What was it Arms Master Drent pounded into the heads of his trainees? *Lift with the strength of your legs, not your back.* She did this, and fortunately two buckets meant balance. She followed the path back toward the hut, concentrating on not spilling water, and trying not to scream when it felt like all the wounds on her back were ripping apart. Tears of pain filled her eyes.

Even so, she looked around as best she could as she went, and took in the jagged profile of mountain summits above the treeline. She sensed a lot more people, like an encampment, through the woods—the distant sounds of voices and banging and horses, the scent of wood smoke.

And then they were at the door of the hut and she was ushered inside. With a cry of relief and tears streaming down her cheeks, she lowered the buckets to the floor. On her journey from the north, she'd done a certain amount of lifting and carrying of her gear, Condor's tack, firewood. Fortunately, when it came to picking out Condor's hooves, he lifted them for her. She had not tried to carry more than she could handle. The buckets had been heavier than anything she'd lifted

69

since the wounding of her back, and as her scored muscles shifted into place, it was all she could do not to scream. She walked in a small circle with her knuckles pressed against her lower back, the tears tracking down her cheeks.

Finally, when the pain settled, she became conscious of Fergal and another man watching her. At first she thought the newcomer was a guard, but then she saw he was not garbed in fighting gear, and in the dim light his features took on a familiar cast. She wiped the tears out of her eyes with her sleeve to make sure. Her heart beat rapidly. She stepped toward him.

"Cade?" she whispered. She was ready to fling herself into his arms believing that somehow he had survived the cataclysm of the future time and had traveled to her present.

But then he moved into a shaft of light and she saw the gray in his hair, features that were similar to, but not, Cade's. A man of middling years with a haggard expression gazed at her with specs propped on the end of his nose. They flashed in the light.

"Beg pardon?" he said.

"They brought me a mender," Fergal said from where he sat against the wall. "His name's Renn."

Renn nodded. "Rider."

Still too shocked, she said nothing.

"He's fixed me up with a poultice and new bandages," Fergal explained. "And some awful herbal concoction."

"Yes," Renn said, "you must see that he drinks the rest of it tonight."

Karigan nodded numbly, noticed her hands shaking again and hid them behind her back. Renn set about packing a basket with the medicaments he'd brought.

"I'll be back to check on you tomorrow," he told Fergal, "if they allow it."

"I thank you either way."

Renn started to leave, but paused before Karigan. "Looked like your back is hurting you. Would you like me to check it?"

Karigan shook her head.

The man who-was-not-Cade, but strongly resembled him, gave her a long appraising look through his specs.

"As you wish, but backs are tricky and should be cared for. Think it over, and I'll check it tomorrow if you like."

"C'mon, mender," a guard grumbled. "It's not a social."

"Tomorrow," Renn said softly, and he left. Even as the door shut behind him, Karigan stood mutely, gazing at nothing. Could he be an ancestor of Cade's? The resemblance was definitely there.

"Karigan?" Fergal said.

She shook her head, realizing she'd been staring into space for a while. "Yes?"

"You look like you've seen a ghost."

In a sense, she had.

"I kept talking," Fergal continued, "but you didn't hear me, like you weren't even here."

She exhaled a long breath. "I brought some fresh water. Want some?"

"No, not until you tell me what the hells is wrong with you."

"Besides being held captive in this bloody hut?" Then she moved to sit beside him, grimacing at her twinging back, and said in a lowered voice, "There's a large encampment out there, not too far away."

"Two, actually."

"What?"

"Renn couldn't say much with the guard hanging around, but he's a captive, too, taken from his village to serve as mender for our captors, and he said there's an armed encampment of Second Empire nearby."

"We've got to get out of here."

"Tell me something new. You're the one with the useful ability."

Her ability would be useful only if she could find a way out, and she wasn't going to leave Fergal behind. He still looked feverish, and he couldn't use his one arm.

"Renn brought us blankets, at least." Fergal rested his hand on two beside him that were neatly folded.

Karigan picked one up. It was woven of rough undyed wool and smelled of cedar as if just removed from storage, and appeared to be in good condition—not moth-eaten or infested with insects. She guessed it had been plundered from someone's home. She thought of the farm in Boggs and set the blanket down.

"So what is wrong with you?" Fergal asked. "The way you looked at Renn and called him 'Cade.'"

"He reminded me of someone."

"Cade was the fellow in the future time who helped you."

"You've heard about him?"

"I hear things."

"Yes, he reminded me of Cade."

"There's more to that story, I reckon," Fergal said.

There was much more to that story, but Karigan did not elaborate. She'd spoken candidly of it only to her best friend, Estral. When she'd been forced to travel to the future time, Cade Harlowe had indeed helped her, but even more, they'd fallen in love. She'd tried to bring him back with her even as his world shattered, but by whatever forces were in play, they were torn apart and he remained in his own time, and she returned to hers. The memory of it cut through her chest with pain worse than that of her back, and she turned away from Fergal. He made a grunting sound as if she'd confirmed something he'd suspected.

"Must've really looked a lot like your Cade fellow the way you reacted," he said softly.

She nodded, still not looking at him.

Through much of the rest of the day, Fergal dozed fitfully and asked no more questions. When he awoke for brief periods, she offered him water or helped him to the slops bucket to take care of business. Otherwise, she lay on her stomach on her new blanket, or paced in circles to pass the time, and wondered what their captors intended for them and why they were situated away from the other encampment. One of the guards had said there were those she wouldn't want to know about her presence. The question was why.

She then thought about escape. With her special ability to fade from sight, she might be able to sneak out of the hut, slip through the night. She gazed at Fergal. Sweat glistened on his brow and he murmured unintelligibly. She couldn't leave him behind, and she certainly could not carry him. And what about Renn? If he was indeed Cade's ancestor, she could not leave him behind. If their captors killed him, Cade might never come to exist in the future.

When the guards brought supper, she paid attention this time. The twilight would be dark enough for her to fade out completely, but the guard who carried their supper in left a lantern in the doorway. There were more lanterns outside for other guards to see by. Guards with crossbows, like the one watching her with a discomfiting intensity.

She looked away until the one guard withdrew and the door was closed and locked. So much lantern light would prevent her from fading out completely. There would have to be a major distraction.

She took a bowl of what appeared to be stew over to Fergal and gently woke him. "They've brought us supper."

He took the bowl and sniffed. "Actually doesn't smell too bad."

It didn't taste too bad, either, she thought. It was full of meat chunks—venison, potatoes, and some wild herbs. It was decent fare for a pair of lowly captive messengers. Their captors wanted to keep them well enough to lure their witch. After that, she didn't care to think about it.

⋘ RIDER NOTMAN ⋙

 In the morning, Karigan awoke with a start, heart pounding. She looked about, but all was calm, soft light leaking through the cracks and holes of the hut. Fergal lay wrapped in his blankets gazing at her.

"Bad dreams?" he asked.

She passed her hand over her eyes. "Nothing new. How are you this morning?"

"Still tired of this hut."

"That makes two of us." She forced her aching body to get up, and she stepped over to Fergal to check his fever. "Still warm, but maybe not as bad."

At that moment, the guards burst in and ordered her to empty the slops bucket outside. Then they brought her back in to fetch the water buckets and head down to the spring for refilling. She was able to splash her face again before the guard prodded her along. Tears of pain rolled down her cheeks at the strain of carrying the full buckets with a back already sore from the previous day's effort.

You are weak, Nyssa said in her mind.

Leave me alone.

No, Nyssa replied. *I will always be here.*

Karigan perceived in her peripheral vision the approach of another. It was not a guard, but Renn who fell in step beside her. "Let me take those," he said.

"No," she replied through gritted teeth, and she continued on as swiftly as she could without spilling water. If having the strength to carry buckets of water was a way to defy Nyssa, she would do it. Once she made it into the hut, she set the

74

buckets down with a splash, and fell to her knees, breathing hard. Renn crouched beside her. She dared not look at him.

"I may be able to help you, if you'd let me." When she did not answer, he added, "I'll check on Fergal first, then you can decide."

He left her side, and she closed her eyes. She heard him conversing with Fergal and checking his wound. It was not just Renn's appearance that reminded her of Cade, but his manner, a certain gentleness about him.

"—torture," she heard Fergal say, though he'd spoken in a low voice.

Silence.

"Isn't that right, Chief?" he said more loudly. "I heard something of what they did to you up north."

"It is not your place to speak of it," she said in a tight voice.

"Renn's a mender. He can help." To Renn, he said, "She won't even talk to me about it."

She closed her eyes and exhaled, trying to ease the tension that had caused her to snap at Fergal. She glanced over her shoulder at their guards. They were not paying attention, but rather were engaged in an animated conversation outside the door. One leaned against the doorframe sucking on a pipe.

"Let him take a look," Fergal said. "He can help."

"I'm not sure anyone can," she murmured, and she didn't mean just her back. She staggered to her feet and loosed an involuntary cry as pain rippled down it.

Suddenly Renn was beside her again. He touched her wrist. "May I have a look?"

He can't help you, Greenie, Nyssa said. *No one can.*

Nyssa aroused Karigan's rebellious streak once more, and she decided to acquiesce to Renn's request. She removed her greatcoat and allowed him to lift the back of her shirt. He had to peel it free where it stuck to some of her still-oozing wounds. To his credit he did not exclaim at the horror she presumed her back to be. Fergal did.

"I wish the light was better," was all Renn said.

He used a wet cloth to wash the wounds that were still weeping, and she shivered with the cold. He then spread a pleasant herby-smelling salve on the wounds.

When he was done, she tugged her shirt down and pulled her greatcoat back on. She turned to face him. "Thank you."

"The pain, I suspect, has more to do with your muscles trying to adjust to the deep scar tissue. I will mix up a liniment that will ease them. The lacerations are healing. Considering the damage, someone did remarkable work to mend them early on."

"Yes, he did." She flashed to Enver tending her over all those days back in the north, but it always made her feel guilty to think of him and how badly they had parted.

"I actually think carrying the water buckets, if done properly, is not a bad thing for you. It will help loosen up the scar tissue and strengthen the muscles." He showed her some stretching exercises she could do. Then he hesitated before speaking again. "You are a very strong person." He adjusted his specs on his nose, picked up his basket of medicaments, and left. The guards shut the door.

"I knew what they did to you was bad," Fergal said. "I didn't know it was *that* bad."

She turned to him and thought he looked a little pale in the dim light.

"It was bad," she agreed, but she felt encouraged by Renn's words. She would do the stretches he'd advised.

"I hope you got that torturer," Fergal said.

"King Zachary killed her." It was a hazy memory at best. She'd been trying to free him from Second Empire, and Nyssa had leaped out of the shadows and attacked her. Zachary somehow released himself from his bonds and used Karigan's knife to stab Nyssa.

"Good," Fergal said.

"Did Renn leave another concoction for you?"

"Aye." He nodded at the stoneware jar at his side. "I am to take it tonight."

"In the meantime, we've got to get you back on your feet. It's not just me who's got to stretch and move."

When she extended her hand to him, he groaned. "Right now?"

"Get up, Rider. And that's an order."

*   *   *

Later, as they were finishing their midday meal of gruel, the
door slammed open. Karigan looked away from the shock of
light, but discerned a figure stumbling in. Then the door was
shut once more. Whoever it was turned and banged on the
door. Karigan blinked until her sight resolved. It was a Green
Rider.

"Let me out!" the young woman yelled.

"We've already tried that," Fergal said.

The Rider whirled around and her eyes widened when
they alighted on Fergal. "Fergal?"

She was not a Rider Karigan knew, which wasn't surprising considering how much she'd been absent from Sacor City.
Might this Rider have a useful ability to help them escape?

"Aye, it's me," Fergal said.

The Rider barely spared Karigan a glance before rushing
to his side. It did not appear she'd been injured in any way
when she'd been captured.

"You're hurt!" she cried.

"Just an arrow wound."

"*Just* an arrow wound? Here, let me see."

Might she be a true healer? But no, when Fergal pulled the
poultice back for her to see, she paled and backed away.

"Oh, Fergal!" she cried. "You poor thing."

"It's fine, really."

She placed her hand on his forehead. "You've a fever."

"We know," Karigan said.

The woman turned on Karigan with a toss of her curly
hair. It was all shiny and nicely coiffed. She placed her hands
on her wide hips. It didn't appear she'd been on a hard ride by
any means when she was taken. It was difficult to tell in the
dim light, but her uniform appeared to be in perfect order,
and even her fingernails looked well-shaped and clean. That
was an accomplishment when dealing with horses. Oh, how
Karigan yearned for cleanliness.

"Why aren't *you* caring for him?" the Rider demanded of
Karigan.

"What do you expect me to do?"

"Make him more comfortable. Place a damp cloth on his forehead."

Karigan looked around the empty hut. "Trust me, I'd give him a feather bed if I could."

"She's been helping me as much as she can," Fergal told the Rider. "Not to mention she's coping with her own wounds. A mender checked me out, too."

"What's your wound?" the Rider demanded of Karigan.

"Bad back."

The Rider did not look impressed, and dismissing Karigan as of little concern, gazed around the hut's interior with disgust.

"This is totally unacceptable," she said. "Where am I supposed to sit?"

"Help yourself to a bit of dirt," Karigan said.

The Rider glared at her, looked her up and down, and from the sour expression on her face, she found Karigan wanting.

"I don't know you," she said. "Who are you?"

"Rider Megan Notman," Fergal said, "meet our Chief Rider, Sir Karigan G'ladheon."

"*You're* her? The one they all talk about and worry over?"

"I don't know anything about the talking and worrying, but yes, I am Karigan, and according to Fergal, I am the Chief Rider."

"I was expecting someone a little more—"

Karigan just waited with a raised eyebrow.

"A little more . . . *more.*"

"Sorry to disappoint."

"Really, Megan?" Fergal said.

"Well, you know, the Sir Karigan I hear about has done all these things, and in real life she looks . . ."

"Small?" Karigan suggested. "Haggard? Threadbare?"

Megan nodded. She suddenly looked abashed. "Sorry. My mouth tends to run on. I shouldn't even be a Green Rider. I was a milliner and I miss it, the shop and wearing nice dresses, and the fancy customers. But now I am stuck in this green *uniform* and in this hut with only dirt to sit on. What do I know about swords and things? What do those rough men want?" She burst into tears.

Karigan and Fergal exchanged glances as if expecting the other to comfort Megan.

"You're the Chief," Fergal mouthed.

Karigan scowled at him, but figured he was right. And she knew from experience that being in a situation like this was frightening, especially for someone like Megan whose previous life sounded genteel and sheltered. She slowly rose to her feet. Megan was now dabbing her tears with a lacy handkerchief.

"Look," Karigan said, "you aren't alone here, and it's all right to be afraid."

"I want to go home. I don't want to be a messenger."

"I understand."

"No, you don't."

"You might be surprised." Karigan smiled grimly, recalling how she'd tried to resist the Rider call. "You aren't the first to be pulled away from the life you were living by the call, and you won't be the last. It's a big adjustment, I know. But look at me, I've adjusted pretty well."

Megan looked, and wailed. When Karigan went to place a comforting hand on her shoulder, Megan backed away as if she carried the pox.

Hells, Karigan thought, at a loss. She wondered what the colonel would do in this instance, and realized she had no idea.

"I don't," Megan said in a sniveling voice, "I don't wanna be like you!" She wailed again and dropped beside Fergal and started to sob on his good shoulder.

He patted Megan's back and looked up accusingly at Karigan and mouthed, *"Good job, Chief."*

⋙ TORQ ⋘

Karigan decided the best course of action was to let Megan have it out, to bawl on Fergal's shoulder, no matter the ugly looks he cast her. Once Megan cried herself dry, they could talk. Karigan was curious to know where and how Megan had been captured, and about the nature of her special ability. Might the latter be useful in an escape attempt? She glanced down at the dirt floor beneath her feet. She'd considered tunneling and had even tried to claw out a test hole, but determined the dirt was but a thin layer over solid rock ledge.

It took some time for Megan to wind down, and she stayed at Fergal's side resting her head on his shoulder. He more or less took it in stride. She told them how she had been taken right off the street in Woodhaven, the seat of Clan D'Yer. She had just delivered a message to Lord-Governor D'Yer and had paused in town to gaze into the window of a dressmaker's shop.

"I didn't even get to go inside before they grabbed me," she complained. "And oh, I hope someone takes care of Bug."

"Bug?" Karigan asked.

"My horse. Her name's Deer Fly, but what kind of name is that for such a pretty girl? So I call her Bug. I left her hitched there in front of the dressmaker's shop on the main street."

Before she could lapse into tears again, they reassured her that someone kind had probably taken care of Bug. She told them that her captors' use of the travel device had made her mildly queasy, but she suffered no further ill effects the way Karigan had.

Karigan then lowered her voice. "Megan, what is your special ability?"

"I haven't the faintest. I've certainly not asked for one."

Karigan was surprised. At the very least, her ability should have manifested when she was captured. Extreme danger seemed to trigger most Riders' abilities, but it was not the same for everyone. It could be that Megan's ability would not have been useful in that particular situation so it did not emerge. She glanced at Fergal.

"I can't tell," he said. "My ability shows magic, but doesn't always tell me what it is." He looked hard at Megan, then shook his head. "Can't see magic in her, but I'd say that's normal for Greenies whose abilities haven't awakened."

Talking helped pass the day, and seemed to keep Megan calm. No, she hadn't seen much of their outer environs when she arrived, and no, she hadn't been assigned to go to the wall while in D'Yer Province. They *did* get a rundown of the fashions worn by the ladies in Woodhaven, and an outpouring of distaste for her captors.

"They were foul-mouthed and vulgar, and grabbed at me inappropriately. They did not smell very good either."

As the light dimmed and they ate their suppers, more of the stew, Megan demanded, "Where do we sleep?"

Fergal swept his hand out to indicate the extent of the hut.

"I *hate* sleeping on the ground."

Karigan handed her an extra blanket and she of course inspected it for vermin. Karigan didn't hold it against her since she'd done the very same thing.

The door to their prison opened allowing much-welcomed fresh air to rush in, and they rose to their feet. A guard bearing a lantern entered, followed by a taller, broad-shouldered figure who remained shadowed until the guard turned around and illuminated the man. Karigan could not suppress a gasp for his face was a grinning skull. She recalled Waldron's terror at the skull-faced brigand who had attacked him on the Boggs Road. Megan screamed and buried her face into Fergal's shoulder. At that moment, a strange look came into his eyes.

It took a moment for Karigan to realize the man's face was actually flesh and blood, that it was tattooed in such a way that the lines and shading were inked to define the jaw and teeth, the contours of the skullcap and eye sockets, that it created the illusion of a skull-faced man. He wore a topknot of steel gray hair, the rest of his scalp shaved. His eyes, lost in the shadow cast by the lantern, glinted, but otherwise really were like the gaping eye sockets of a skull. Dressed in hard leather armor, he was clearly a warrior.

"I am Torq." His accent indicated he was from the Under Kingdoms. "I am the leader of *Deija*, or as you know us, the Darrow Raiders."

The *Darrow Raiders!* But they'd been vanquished years ago. Yet, Karigan did not doubt his words. She hid her trembling hands behind her back. If these were truly the Darrow Raiders holding them captive, she, Fergal, and Megan were in very bad trouble.

He launched forward and grabbed her arm. She tried to pull away, but his grip was like iron. He twisted her arm just enough to see the Black Shield patch on her sleeve and then let her go. He laughed. "It is true. Dunner said you were a Black Shield Greenie and I did not believe him. I now owe him five silvers. But if you are a real Black Shield, you would have fought your way out by now, eh? Or maybe there is a reason you have not, for I find you pathetic, more likely to hurt yourself than anything."

Torq's words were all the more cutting for being true.

"You have nothing to say?" he demanded.

Karigan did not speak, just stared straight ahead.

"I see." He gave the others a quick glance before settling his gaze on Karigan once more. "Which of you is the ranking Greenie?"

"She is," Megan said hastily, pointing at Karigan.

"Is this true?"

Karigan nodded. There was no use in denying it.

"You," he said pointing at her, "are responsible for the behavior of the others. Understand? You will keep them quiet—no banging or shouting will be tolerated. Should our friends of Second Empire learn of your presence here, it would hasten your demise. Do not doubt it. General Birch hates Greenies almost as much as me since one killed Second Empire's leader."

Karigan kept her peace not wishing to implicate herself. She had not killed Grandmother. An ice elemental had. But she'd been there, and that was, at the very least, guilt by association. In her peripheral vision, Fergal swayed on his feet. She shifted her gaze just enough to see he was holding onto Megan hard and that his complexion had taken on a green tinge. Megan herself was wide-eyed.

When Torq's gaze started to stray in their direction, Karigan said, "Your guards told us we were witch bait. What does that mean, and why are you keeping us from Second Empire?"

"Ah, you *do* speak." The grotesqueness of his tattooed face increased with his smile. "Birch would kill you outright, whereas I intend to make use of you. We work with Birch while it's to our advantage in our quest to reclaim what is ours."

"And what would that be?"

"A land for ourselves to live as we wish. No king or queen will rule. No emperor, either."

That was interesting since Second Empire was all about the *empire*, which strongly suggested an emperor. Would the Raiders turn on Second Empire if an alliance no longer suited them?

"And what about witch bait?" Karigan asked.

"You don't know? Don't they teach you Greenies about your own history?" He shook his head. "It is all about vengeance." He turned on his heel and swept out of the hut. When the door was firmly shut behind him, Fergal fell away retching into the corner and Megan . . . floated?

"Ah . . . ah . . . ah . . ." the Rider said as she bobbed up to the rafters. She grabbed one and held on to it with all she had. "Cobweeeebs," she wailed. "Someone get me down. I do not like this."

Torq's appearance must have set off Megan's special ability. But *floating?* She could only gaze at the Rider in wonderment before springing to action.

"Megan, breathe deep."

"*You* breathe deep."

"Listen to me." Karigan's patience with her was being sorely tried. "Breathe deeply, exhale slowly." The only way to even begin to bring her down was to calm her.

"I tried to hold her down while Skull Face was here," Fergal said. He slid to the ground looking exhausted. "But I couldn't hold back the sick for long when her magic came."

Fergal's was one ability Karigan was glad she didn't have, especially when its use caused him to get sick. It took her a while, but she finally got Megan to calm herself, and now she had to coax her back to the ground.

"Close your eyes and imagine you are slowly descending." Karigan had no idea if this would work, but it was worth a try.

"I'm afraid to let go."

"I thought you didn't like cobwebs. They are probably full of spiders."

Megan screeched and let go of the rafter, and fell.

"Well, *that* worked," Fergal said.

Karigan knelt beside the clump of green on the floor that was Megan. "You all right? Anything broken?"

Megan looked up at her with an odd glint in her eyes. Cobwebs trailed from her curls. "I. Did. NOT. Want. This."

The door opened again and a guard stormed in. "Torq told you to be quiet. Who screamed?" He gazed down at Megan.

Something of the old Karigan stirred and she stood. "I did. It was me."

He cuffed her and she stumbled back.

"If I hear anymore from you lot, I'll do worse. Got it? If I had it my way, we'd skin you alive like the old days."

"Got it," Karigan mumbled. She touched her hand to her stinging cheek.

When he left, she shook her head and extended her hand to help Megan up, then helped dust her off. This time Megan did not recoil. "Thank you," she said in a small voice, then she grabbed her blanket and curled up against the wall, her back to them.

Karigan stood there, her cheek throbbing. If this was what it meant to be Chief Rider, she'd happily give the position back to Mara. If ever she got the chance, that was. Just because Torq didn't want them to be killed by Birch didn't mean they wouldn't be killed in the end, and what she had heard about the Raiders of old was that they were not merciful. From Torq's terse explanation, it would appear they held a grudge against the Green Riders for their earlier demise. Vengeance, she knew, could be messy.

SELIUM

The Smiling Sow was one of Selium's finer dining establishments, and Melry had been very impressed when Stevic brought her there.

"It's awfully nice of you to bring me to The Sow," she said. "My friends were quite jealous when they heard where we were going."

He watched her dig into each course with enthusiasm. For dessert, she enjoyed a mug of warm drinking chocolate, while he sipped a nicely aged cognac. He'd treated her to dinner the night he arrived in the city, but that had been at an ordinary pub. Here the servers bowed to their guests, cleaned their hands with steaming towels, and made the food look like works of art on their platters.

"It would please Karigan that I took her friend out for a meal," he replied, "and it seemed a good place for a farewell dinner." Taking Melry to dinner reminded him very much of bringing Karigan to The Sow while she was still in school. "This was Karigan's favorite place to eat out."

In truth, he probably would not have treated Melry out a second time had he not been in a relationship with her mother. It seemed a good opportunity to get to know the girl better other than just as Karigan's chatty friend. He noted Melry had matured a good deal since last he'd seen her, and the chattiness had more or less abated. She was still, however, a lively young lady who was easy to talk with, and who, unsurprisingly, surrounded herself with a wide range of friends.

During the main course, she had revealed her plans for after school to train as a Weapon. He could not imagine her as one of those solemn statue-like sentinels silently guarding the king, or worse, the royal tombs, nor could he imagine Laren being happy about it when she found out.

"So, what inspired you to want to become a Weapon?" he asked, returning to the topic of her future.

"I've done well with arms training here with Master Rendle."

"But you've done well with your other subjects, as well. Surely there are many directions you might choose."

Melry held her mug in both hands as if to warm them as he'd so often seen Laren do. They were not mother and daughter by blood, but they still shared certain mannerisms.

"I always planned to serve the king," she replied. "I mean, as a Green Rider. But I've never heard the call, and the colonel won't let me join like she let that Anna girl. So, I am going to be a Weapon instead." A cloud settled over her usually sunny features. "I am of age to make my own decision, but the colonel has final say when it comes to the Green Riders."

Stevic had known from Laren that there was some conflict in that regard. Melry used "the colonel" interchangeably with "mother," but he picked up a hardness to it now. He wondered how much of her desire to be a Weapon was retaliation against her mother for not letting her be a Green Rider. As the father of a Green Rider, he understood Laren's stance on the issue better than most. He knew too well it was not a safe occupation, and never more so than when he heard his daughter had been tortured. How was a parent supposed to live with that? He'd been ready to storm north to avenge her, but Laren calmed him, told him King Zachary had killed the torturer and led troops in victory against Second Empire. Karigan would heal, she reassured him. Afterward, he'd gone to the chapel of the moon, something he hadn't done in a long time, to light a candle of prayer for his daughter's healing, and a second one in thanks that Sacoridia had such an exemplary king.

It still ate at him, though, the torture of his daughter, and it always would. But how to explain the anxiety of a parent to Melry so that she would understand and not cause her to become more entrenched in her decision? He was not certain he could find the words.

"At least Master Rendle and General Whitestall support me," Melry said.

"Who is General Whitestall?"

"The commandant of the academy on Breaker Island."

The Forge, Stevic thought, where Weapons were made.

"He came here in the fall," Melry said, "looking for talent. He watched us advanced arms students train. He says he'd very much like me to attend the academy."

Stevic hid his misgiving by taking a sip of his cognac. He let the liquid tingle on his tongue for a few seconds before swallowing. There was nothing wrong with becoming a Weapon. It was, in fact, a very honorable profession, but he always sensed something of a fanatical nature about them, a cultish aspect brimming with secrets that stretched all the way back to their founding during the Long War.

"It seems," he began carefully, "an austere choice with your whole life ahead of you. Weapons do not have families, for instance."

Melry waved it off as inconsequential. "The Weapons have one another. General Whitestall explained it to me."

Not the same thing, Stevic thought. As much as he wished to voice it, he did not. This was a matter for parent and child, and Melry was not his daughter, at least not yet. Or, maybe he was just being a coward, not wishing to turn her against him even before his relationship with Laren had been announced to her. He had to admit he'd left most of the difficult parental discussions with Karigan to his sisters.

He took a deeper sip of the cognac this time and dabbed his lips. "I hope that life as a Weapon is all that you wish."

She smiled. "That's if I pass all the tests and am good enough. General Whitestall thinks I am. But if not, I can be an arms master somewhere."

They discussed his leave taking with Lady Fiori set for the morning, and how composed Estral had been during all the various ceremonies of mourning for her father. The people who served Selium, the dean and all the school's staff, rallied around her and seemed to have all in hand. It would make her transition to being the Golden Guardian easier to bear. He thought Karigan would be pleased to hear how well Estral was being cared for.

Finally he took his last sip of the cognac and rose. "Let us find you a cab to take you back up to campus."

When they stepped out of The Smiling Sow, the evening was misty, but it did not deter crowds milling about the streets in search of entertainment. There were more people filling the city than ever with both the funeral ceremonies attracting mourners from all over the realm and refugees fleeing the attacks in the countryside. To Stevic's displeasure, the theater across from The Sow had just let out and there was no cab to be had.

"I will walk you to campus," he told Melry.

"Oh, there's no need. I—"

He forestalled her with a raised hand. "Humor me, please. I would do the same for Karigan were she here. Besides, my legs could use a good stretch after all that food."

Melry did not argue further. As they walked on among the throngs, the theater-goers chattered and laughed all around them, and he thought Lord Fiori would be pleased to see so many continuing to enjoy the arts in his city even in his absence. The night deepened as they continued on. Lamplight rippled across puddles on the cobble street.

Stevic kept an eye out for trouble. This was a prime hunting ground for thieves—so many people in good spirits and paying little attention to their surroundings or purses. Though he spied nothing suspicious, he had an itch, which was a sort of intuition he had for pickpockets and the like. Not surprising, he supposed, there'd be a few working this crowd.

Soon they arrived at a brightly lit square where minstrel students were playing lively music. A crowd had gathered to listen. Some clapped to the beat and others twirled and danced. It would be difficult for him and Melry to work their way through the press. They were already hemmed in and getting bumped into by onlookers.

Melry paused to watch the dancing and he followed her

gaze. Three men engaged in a step dance battle. Onlookers hooted and hollered and clapped their encouragement. Two looked to be students, but one was older.

Melry laughed. "That's Master Franks and a couple friends of mine." She had to shout to be heard above the music and boisterous crowd.

The young men were hard pressed to keep up with the tempo of the music and it was only speeding up, but Master Franks seemed to have no trouble. A frenetic quality enveloped the square with the musicians playing hard and the crowd laughing and shouting. The dancing, the excited atmosphere. The mist spread lamplight like an otherworldly vapor over the scene. Stevic felt unmoored as if the world slipped out of kilter.

Then he realized that he'd gotten separated from Melry by a surge of onlookers. The "itch" intensified. He tried to reach Melry, pushing through the revelers, but could seem to make no headway. A group of drunken young men knocked him back even farther. He shoved and jostled his way through with a renewed sense of urgency. He looked up and glimpsed Melry some distance away. A hooded figure seemed to loom up from nowhere behind her.

"Melry!" he cried, but his voice was lost in the clamor. He pushed and shoved some more, but it was taking too long. He cried out again just as the hooded figure grabbed her. She screamed. The crowd shifted around Stevic like a riptide carrying him away.

The world reeled, all the light and shadows streaming around him, and he was stricken by a momentary miasma. People nearby were also affected and cried out. When Stevic's equilibrium returned, he saw only an empty space where Melry had been standing.

"Melry!" But his shout was met only by the blank looks of strangers who chattered anxiously near him. In the square, the music played on unabated as if nothing unusual had happened.

He rushed forward in search of Melry, and asked the people around him if they'd seen her. They'd been momentarily overcome by a sick feeling, they said, and they hadn't noticed her. Then a student rubbing his temple nodded.

"I saw her, aye. We have a languages class together. I saw a man grab her and then—and then—" The young man looked like he could not believe his own words. "And then the magic or whatever hit, and he and Mel vanished just like that. I was just gonna go look for a constable."

"Aeryc and Aeryon," Stevic murmured. He was not going to look for a constable. He was going to go straight to the city's power, and he knew she would see him without question.

He pushed himself clear of the crowd and headed up the street toward campus. How would he explain to Laren that her daughter had been snatched right in front of him?

☙ ESTRAL'S CONFESSION ☙

*I**fear it is Me, this time, who must tell you Dif-*
ficult news of your Daughter . . .
Stevic dipped his pen in ink before hastily
explaining to Laren in his letter what he had
witnessed happen to Melry in his presence. He wrote in haste
and was regrettably brief, but a messenger waited on him, and
he wanted that messenger on the road as soon as possible.

When he finished, he folded the letter and sealed it with
wax that Estral, the Lady Fiori, had provided him from her
own supplies, then turned to face the others in the Golden
Guardian's drawing room. Estral looked pensive as she handed
a letter of her own to the messenger, a city guardsman who,
Stevic was told, often carried messages on behalf of the lord-
mayor, and occasionally the Golden Guardian, when there
was need for swift delivery. Still, they could have wished for a
Green Rider to do the duty, but the two who had attended the
funeral for Lord Fiori on Laren's behalf had already departed
the city.

He handed the guardsman the message, quavering with
the guilt of having failed to ensure Melry's safety. Now he
knew how Laren must feel when she had to tell him that
something had happened to Karigan.

"Is there anything else, my lady?" the guardsman asked.

"Be professional and precise in your approach," Estral advised him. Her voice was hoarse, the result of a spell enemies
had used to steal her voice. Stevic was told it came and went
and she often resorted to chalk and slate to express herself.
"Colonel Mapstone is not only the chief of the king's own
messengers, but has his and the queen's favor, and my esteem,

as well, so comport yourself as befits her status. Also, keep in mind she is the mother of the student who was abducted tonight. A gentle touch will be most helpful."

The guardsman bowed and was dismissed by Captain Croyden of the city guard. "He'll do very well for you, my lady," the captain said. "He is a fine guardsman and our best rider."

"You will keep me apprised of your investigation?"

"Yes, my lady, and speaking of which, I must return to see how it is proceeding." He clicked his heels and bowed his head, and turned, his boots making a sharp report on the floor as he left.

The other man in the room, Dean Crosley, stepped forward. "We will keep close touch with the guard to ensure we hear the latest details of the investigation with expedience."

The dean's demeanor was calm and efficient, the same as he'd displayed throughout the mourning period for Lord Fiori, which must be a great help to Estral. Stevic thought him a far better administrator than his predecessor, who had treated Karigan so poorly when she was a student. At one of the banquets after the funeral, Dean Crosley had pulled him aside to tell him how proud he was that one of their students served the king and realm so well, and though she may have had troubles in her early years at the school, that she'd been a gem in the rough.

"I appreciate your assistance, Dean Crosley," Estral said. "Would you stay for a nightcap?"

"Thank you, my lady, but my wife expects me home and morning arrives all too quickly."

He bade them farewell leaving Estral and Stevic to gaze across the room at one another. Estral looked weary, even more so with the dean's departure. He could only guess how the weeks of funeral rites and ceremonies had taken their toll on her.

"Perhaps I should say goodnight, as well," Stevic said.

"Please stay for a little while," Estral said. "We have not had time to speak but in passing, and I think you would like to hear about the north before you leave the city."

Stevic sat straight in his chair. He *did* want to hear about the north, and yet, he did not. Laren had told him the little she knew before he'd left for Selium. Learning of his daughter's torture had been painful, but at least he'd known she would recover.

The butler entered with two cups on a tray, their nightcap. Stevic took his and sniffed the contents, inhaling steam and cinnamon. It was warm, spiced wine, and he was glad of it.

Estral set hers aside and stared into space with a sober expression. Her big shipcat, a bushy gray-brown tabby, lumbered into the room and launched himself onto her lap. At first she looked startled, but then absently petted him as he kneaded her thighs before finally settling into a round lump of fur and emitting rumbling purrs.

"I am not sure how much you know," she said.

"Very little," he replied. "Colonel Mapstone informed me of the torture."

She sat silent for a time before speaking. "With all that has happened, with having to say good-bye to my father, it has been overwhelming. When I lie in bed at night and cannot sleep, my thoughts grow heavy and I cannot stop reliving the awful memories of what happened in the north. I can't help but think of my own responsibility for what was done to Karigan. As you may guess, I have been rather short of sleep."

"I do not understand why you consider what happened to Karigan your responsibility," Stevic said.

"My actions caused both of us to be captured, which led to the torture. I—I thought I could just walk into the Lone Forest by myself and rescue my father. Karigan told me to wait, that when she was feeling better, she'd scout ahead, and then we'd get the River Unit to help."

"Feeling better? Was she sick?" Indeed, there was much Laren had been unable to tell him.

"Before we reached the plains between the Green Cloak and the Lone Forest, Karigan inhaled the hot smoke of a pyre. We burned the remains of men murdered by Second Empire in a lumber camp. Spirits of smoke wanted to show Karigan how they were killed. They forced her to inhale them."

Stevic frowned. He knew Karigan had some "facility" with the dead. Laren said it had to do with her Rider ability, but his sisters also claimed there were ancestors on Karigan's mother's side who could converse with spirits. It was unsettling.

"I feared for my father, that he was a captive of Second Empire, and did not want to wait for Karigan to feel better. I decided to set out on my own. Some hours later when she saw I had left our camp, she came after me. I should have known she would. Maybe I *did* know, and went anyway." She could not meet his eyes. "That's when we were captured."

Her words carried the tone of a confession, Stevic thought. Her feelings of guilt must drive her to speak thus. "What of your Eletian guide? Where was he in all this?"

"Enver had gone scouting, looking for the p'ehdrose, but he did rescue us when he found that we were missing from camp. Karigan suffered for my foolishness."

"It is my understanding," Stevic said, and it was difficult to offer her consolation at that moment for he agreed she *had* been foolish, "that Karigan's capture led to the rescue of the king." Laren had been quite assertive on this point. "Who knows what would have been done to him had he remained in the hands of Second Empire any longer. I am certain they would have used his captivity against the realm to, at the very least, demoralize us all, and who knows what other despicable things would have been done to him."

"Yes," Estral said. "Karigan saw him, and so she and Enver were able to rescue him and my father. But might she have done the same if she had scouted ahead on her own time and not been captured?"

Stevic did not know, but it was likely. He repressed a surge of anger and tried to remind himself that Estral was not responsible for what had been done to Karigan, that it had been Second Empire's doing. He drank deeply of the mulled wine and it eased him with its warmth. They sat in desolate silence for a while, but for the purring of the cat.

Stevic finally asked, "How was it between you and Karigan when you parted?"

"She . . . There was no blame."

He nodded. Undoubtedly, it had made Estral feel worse rather than better. "Then you should not dwell in your guilt.

I grieve for what was done to my daughter, but she is, in the end, the arbiter of forgiveness, not me."

"As her father, I thought you would—"

"Lay blame? I will admit this is difficult for me, but Karigan also made choices that day, and perhaps not the best ones. My lady, you did not invent Second Empire and their bloody ways. If any mistakes were made, you have more than paid the price."

With that, the air seemed to clear between them, and whatever oppression weighed on Estral lifted.

"I have carried much guilt," she said. "Others helped me confront it, which was of great help and a relief, but my experience is that one must live with it for a time to come to some accord. I think speaking with you, Karigan's father, has helped me absolve the worst remnants in a way the others could not. And yet, I must ask, is there nothing I can do to answer for my foolish decision that day in the north?"

"Perhaps you could tell me more of the details. Laren— Colonel Mapstone—was able to give me only fragments before I left Sacor City, which was, unfortunately, before the king and Karigan returned."

"Of course." She took a deep breath and told him the story in depth, using her slate when her voice failed her. She left out the grisly details of the torture, much to Stevic's relief, but his imagination was enough when it came to picturing what had been done to Karigan.

She spoke of Enver's rescue with the help of gryphons, and how he tended Karigan's wounds over the ensuing days. Stevic had never been enamored of Eletians for their interference in the lives of his late wife and daughter, or for their magical ways, but now he found himself profoundly grateful for this Eletian and how he'd cared for Karigan.

"Karigan wanted to go back and rescue the king right away," Estral continued, "despite the fact she was weak and couldn't even stand." She described how Karigan went on to lead the rescue of the king and Lord Fiori. Stevic had never felt greater pride for his daughter.

"She grew dark afterward," Estral said. "The ghost of

Nyssa, the torturer, haunted her, but Enver helped her again. The king also proved . . . supportive."

The last was a curious statement, Stevic thought, but before he could question her about it, she continued her tale all the way to the Battle of the Lone Forest.

"I can't tell you much about the actual battle," she said, "as I stayed in camp."

"With Karigan."

An odd look came over her face, and she hesitated before replying. "She was too injured to join the fight."

He narrowed his eyes at her and set aside his long-forgotten wine. "What is it you aren't telling me?"

"I believe," she replied, her voice growing faint again, "it is Karigan's story to tell if she wishes. Beyond that, there is not much I know, for once I heard of my father's death, I was not thinking about anything else."

Stevic forced back his need to press her. Estral was exhausted and grieving. He would question Karigan when he returned to Sacor City. "I thank you for your willingness to tell me of your terrible experiences."

She caressed her cat who was still contentedly curled on her lap. "Thank you for hearing me out." Her voice was now a bare wisp.

"I must bid you farewell tonight instead of taking part in the official leave-taking tomorrow. In light of Melry's abduction, I will depart ahead of the delegation so I can reach Colonel Mapstone as soon as possible to speak to her, as witness."

"I am sure your presence will be a comfort to the colonel."

Stevic looked at her sharply. "A comfort?"

"I understand the two of you have become a couple."

"You know?" he asked incredulously.

"Karigan told me."

"Karigan *knows*?"

"Apparently she espied the two of you in Rider stables during an intimate moment."

He felt his cheeks warm. That explained a curious conversation he'd had with Karigan in a carriage not long after. At least it solved the problem of having to tell her.

He stood, and Estral set the cat on the floor to walk him to the door.

"I wish we could have visited under more auspicious conditions," Estral said. "I pray your journey is a safe one, and please tell the colonel that we'll do all we can to recover Melry. And please give Karigan my love when you see her."

Stevic promised to do all, but as he stepped out into the rainy night, he had grave doubts that the city guard of Selium would have much luck in finding Melry, not with the magic that had been used to take her. He could only guess she was miles away, but to what purpose she had been abducted, he could not guess.

 ⇜ NO WAY OUT ⇝

Karigan sat up when the hut's door burst open, fluttering the flame of the lard candle the Raiders had deigned to give them as a result of Megan's incessant pestering. The guards threw a girl inside and slammed the door shut again. The girl fell to her knees retching, her sickness no doubt caused by the traveling device. Oddly, she was not a Green Rider, or at least she was not wearing a Green Rider uniform, but a dress and jacket fine enough for one to wear out on the town. When she climbed unsteadily to her feet and wiped her mouth with the back of her hand, Karigan saw no brooch.

Megan, of course, was right there with her hands on her hips and demanded, "Who are you?"

The girl, wobbling slightly, peered into the gloom. "Green Riders? *Fergal?* Is that you?"

"Mel?" he said, rising to his feet.

"Mel?" Karigan echoed in disbelief. Her friend had matured into a tall young woman, no longer the coltish girl she remembered.

Mel gazed back at her, eyes squinted. "Karigan?"

It seemed time had wrought enough change in both of them that they did not recognize one another right off. Karigan rose and crossed the space between them and they started talking at the same time.

"What are you doing here?" Karigan asked, realizing belatedly it was a stupid question.

"Is that really you?" Mel asked. "I didn't—you look—you are . . ."

"I know," Karigan said. "I look like a one-eyed scarecrow

who has seen a few too many seasons." She plucked at her shaggy hair.

Mel did not argue, which only confirmed how awful she looked, but then Mel threw herself into Karigan's arms.

"What is this place?" she asked when they parted. "Why are we here?"

"Who is this person?" Megan demanded again.

"Megan, this is Melry Exiter, our colonel's daughter."

Megan took a step back, looked Mel up and down. "I didn't know she had a daughter."

"Never talked about me, eh?" Mel asked. "Typical."

"We hardly see the colonel." Megan shrugged.

"Well, *I* know Mel," Fergal said. Now she hugged him, too.

"You're hurt," she said.

"It's nothing. Mender says I'll be fine."

There was another round of hugs, and Karigan assured herself that Mel was unharmed. Afterward they settled into a circle on straw the Raiders had supplied them, also at Megan's insistence.

"We should tell you what we know," Karigan said, "though it's not much."

When she finished, Mel said, "But I'm not a Green Rider. And what does a witch have to do with Green Riders, anyway? Are there even witches for real?"

"You are closely affiliated with the Green Riders," Karigan said, "and there is always the chance it's coincidence and they aren't targeting Green Riders at all." But as she said it, she knew it to be false. "Are witches real? I guess it depends on how you define 'witch.' Grandmother was a necromancer, but some might call her a witch, and some call the entities of lore in the Eastern Sea witches, but others may have worshipped them as goddesses at one time."

"Traditional witches did simple magic," Megan said. "They were versed in herb lore and healing, and would cast curses or create potions to make someone fall in love, for instance." When Karigan looked at her in surprise, she said, "What? I used to hear all kinds of things in the milliner's shop." With a toss of her curls, she added, "And it's said the witches died out during the Scourge."

The Scourge had ravaged the lands of magic and magic-users after the Long War. It had been no plague, though, or at least not just a plague, but the organized extermination of magic and users of magic by people who feared, and thus hated, it after battling the sorcerous Mornhavon the Black for so long.

"Oh, the witches aren't all gone," Fergal said. "At least not along the coast of the eastern provinces. They call themselves witches, at any rate. Don't know if they have real magic, though."

They then asked Mel how she'd been taken.

"I was on my way to campus from dinner. With your father actually," she said, gazing at Karigan.

Karigan was gratified to hear her father had both attended the funeral ceremonies for Lord Fiori, and spent time with Mel. She could only guess he'd made a special effort because of his relationship with Mel's mother.

Mel explained the circumstances of her abduction. "It was very sudden," she said. "The streets were busy and I got separated from your father, and then someone grabbed me from behind. Next thing I knew, I wasn't in Selium anymore and then was thrown in here."

They continued to discuss their predicament in low voices so they wouldn't be overheard by their captors.

"I say that the next time a guard comes in we grab him and run for it," Mel said with a surprising amount of enthusiasm, but when the Riders just stared at her, she said, "There *are* enough of us to overpower him."

"And what about the guard who stands in the doorway with the crossbow?" Fergal asked.

"Or the others just outside?" Megan added.

"Besides," Fergal said, "I'm not much good for fighting or running just yet."

"So," Mel said, "we sit here and do nothing?"

"No," Karigan replied, "we develop a plan." When they all gazed expectantly at her, she said, "We can't just make a run for it. I'm not particularly fit, myself."

"I could take both those guards with my fists," Mel said.

Karigan knew Mel had been training with Arms Master

Rendle, but that wouldn't be enough. "As Megan pointed out, there are more Raiders we'd have to get through. We are also next to an encampment of Second Empire."

"I didn't know that."

"Also," Karigan continued, "we don't know exactly where we are, other than near the Wing Song Mountains."

"Your abilities—"

"Lower your voice," Karigan said sharply.

Mel looked stung by her rebuke.

"Show me magic," Fergal said, "and I'll puke on a guard or two."

A smile flickered across Mel's lips, just as Fergal must have intended.

"So what is the plan?" Megan asked. She twisted a length of hair around her finger as if to fix her tousled curls. They were not holding up well in captivity.

"Can you float your way out of here?" Karigan asked.

"Float?" Mel asked.

"I have no idea," Megan said.

Karigan looked up at the hut's roof. Might it be in enough disrepair that Megan could break through?

"*Float?*" Mel asked again.

"Want to give it a try?" Karigan asked Megan. "At least see if you can get through the roof?"

"I guess so. Could someone hold the candle high so I can have at least some light up there? It's so dark." She shivered.

Karigan climbed to her feet and held the candle aloft. The roof ridge was high up, as the roof had a steep pitch to cope with what must be heavy snowfalls. Megan didn't bother to stand. She simply floated upward in a sitting position.

"Aeryc and Aeryon," Mel whispered. "I haven't seen anything like that before." Having been raised around Riders, she knew all about their magical abilities and may have witnessed some in use, but the ability to float was one Karigan had never heard of before, either.

Up Megan rose, vanishing into the shadows beyond the rafters, beyond the light of their meager candle.

"Ow!" she exclaimed.

"Are you all right?" Karigan asked tersely.

"Bumped my head."

They followed her best as they could as she scrabbled across the underside of the roof. At one point she sneezed forcefully. "Dusty," she muttered. She paused at one of the holes, tugging at the sheathing.

Then to Karigan's horror, the door opened. She lowered the candle. A guard stepped inside, and as always, a second one with a crossbow stood outside with the lantern at his feet.

"What is the noise?" the guard demanded. "What are you doing burning a good candle when you should be abed."

"Get me a real bed and I'd be abed," Fergal said.

Karigan was afraid Fergal was going to get himself beaten again for his insolence. She blew out the candle hoping that it would help conceal Megan, but the lantern still let in an awful lot of light. "We are going to bed."

"Where's the other one?" the guard asked. "The bossy girl—Curly?"

"Taking a piss," Fergal replied. He pointed at a dark corner where they had hung a blanket to afford themselves a modicum of privacy when using the slops bucket.

The guard fetched the lantern and brought it inside as though he planned to go check that corner. Karigan caught her breath, but then Megan stepped into the light.

"All done," she said brightly. "And it would be so much better if we could dump the slops bucket more than once a day. Especially with the new girl here."

"Bossy." The guard grunted and left, taking the light with him. Karigan silently thanked the gods that he hadn't seemed to notice Megan had been almost ashen with dust and cobwebs.

Thunk!

"What was that?" Mel asked.

"I think it was Megan," Fergal replied.

Karigan lowered herself to her hands and knees and felt around. As her night vision improved with the help of a little moonlight leaking through holes and cracks, she found Megan. Her face was clammy and she seemed to be unconscious.

"Is she all right?" Mel asked.

"Hard to say."

Moments later Megan groaned. "I'm not waking up from a nightmare, am I. I'm still in this wretched hut."

"You are," Karigan said.

"It made me so weary, the floating," she replied.

"You did well. Could you get through the roof?"

"The holes are too small and I couldn't break through. Am I really bossy?"

"Rest up," Karigan said. "We'll find another way out. We should all rest."

They retreated to their respective sleeping places. Mel curled up beside Karigan so they could share a blanket.

"I still have so many questions," Mel whispered. "What happened up north? I know something did, but no one knows anything, and if they did, they weren't telling me."

Karigan fluffed the straw that served as her bedding. "Try to sleep. Tomorrow will be soon enough to talk."

"Even Estral wouldn't tell me."

"Go to sleep."

She lay on her stomach as Mel moved restlessly beside her. Soon Mel stilled, and her breathing became slow and even. Karigan tried to emulate her, but she felt Nyssa nearby, just beyond her vision, whip in hand.

You cannot escape, Greenie, the torturer whispered into her mind. *You are doomed.*

Karigan whimpered, tried to bury her head in her arms. *Go away. You are not real.*

I am more than you imagine, and I am not done with you.

⋯ SPIDERS ⋯

A scream shattered Karigan's sleep. To her surprise, it was not her own.

"Bloody hells!" cried Mel, who sat up beside her.

"What's going on?" Fergal asked, his voice thick with sleep.

It was too dark to see anything.

"Megan?" Karigan asked. "You all right?"

"Sp-sp-spiders. All over me! I swear!" Sounds of rustling and swatting came from her direction.

"Wouldn't be surprised if there were mice in this place, too," Mel said.

"*Mice?*" Megan squawked.

"Not helping," Karigan informed Mel.

Mel yawned and slumped back into her straw, taking most of their shared blanket with her.

When Megan continued to fuss and sounded like she was weeping again, Karigan said, "Megan, what makes you think you are covered in spiders?"

"I was up there in the rafters, in their webs."

"I know. Do you feel like you are being bitten?"

"*Bitten?*"

Karigan could well picture the horror on her face. "Are you?"

"I—I don't know. Now I feel itchy all over, and ticklish like they're crawling all over me with their *legs*." The last came out with immense loathing.

Karigan took a moment to consider how spiders would be crawling on Megan if not with their legs. "Tell me, before you

105

started feeling . . . tickled, were you dreaming or thinking about spiders?"

"Of course I was. I was up in the rafters with them. I was covered in their webs."

"Could you have been having a vivid dream?" Megan might well be covered in spiders, but Karigan doubted it, and there wasn't much they could do about it even if she were, except to blindly swat at her in the dark. The thought did hold some appeal.

"I—" Megan said. "Maybe."

"Dreams can do that to you." Karigan knew it to be true. "Are the spiders tickling you now?"

"Uh, no. I don't think so."

"Then try to relax and think of something pleasant."

"Mmm," Megan said. "Yards and yards of ribbon in every color . . ."

Karigan sank into her straw once more, tried to tug some blanket from Mel's iron grip, and had a feeling she was about to dream about spiders. Dreams of spiders, however, were overshadowed by the familiar fear and darkness of torture and helplessness repeatedly playing through her mind. Nyssa was a huge shadow that loomed over her, her whip hissing through the air. The flaying of flesh, the splatter of blood. Karigan was locked in place, unable to move, unable to cry out.

She woke panting with sweat streaming down her face, and found the world still enclosed in night. Her fellow captives remained asleep, their breaths peaceful. She must not have screamed and was thankful for it. Then she started shivering, not sure if it was the sweat cooling on her skin or the fear evoked by the dream. She tried to clamp her mouth shut to quiet the chattering of her teeth, and reclaimed some of the blanket from Mel.

Then she worked on slowing her breathing, and though she was loathe to close her eyes, she did so. She called on the visualization she'd used to reach the starry meadow. Enver's voice seemed to whisper to her and guide her along the tranquil path, but she hadn't gotten far when a wall slammed down blocking the way.

"What?" she murmured. It had happened before, but never so soon, never so forcefully.

Your Greenies blocked me out before, Nyssa said, *but you didn't think I could do the same to you?*

"You are dead," Karigan whispered.

And you speak with ghosts.

There had been a time when she could command ghosts, but it had never worked with Nyssa. She was not even sure if Nyssa was, in fact, a ghost or her own mind punishing her.

Either way, I am here.

"Go to the hells," Karigan said.

Nyssa laughed as she faded away. Karigan sat in the dark shivering.

"You look terrible," Fergal told Karigan in the morning.

Megan's expression indicated she didn't think this was anything new.

Everything hurt. She'd dozed on and off, sitting against the stone wall. The cold had seeped into her back.

"Are you sick?" Mel asked, raising herself onto her elbow.

"No. Didn't sleep well." She had been waiting all night for Nyssa to return and taunt her. She almost dreaded the wait more than the actual experience.

The usual morning guard came in and pointed at Karigan. "You. Get the slops."

With some difficulty, Karigan wearily climbed to her feet and tried to hide the pain as she straightened up. The others watched as she fetched the slops bucket. When she stepped outside, the fresh air did little to revive her. After she dumped the slops, she was sent back for the water buckets.

"One of us can do that today," Fergal told the guard.

"No. *She* will do it," the guard replied.

Karigan gathered the water buckets. It had been good of Fergal to speak up, but he would not have been able to carry both with his wounded shoulder, and she didn't want to expose the others to the additional danger outside the hut, especially the young women with all the "rough men" around, as Megan had called them.

When she reached the spring, she didn't splash her face this time, but dunked her whole head in, and it helped wake her some. Carrying the buckets back was even harder this time, however, and it was all she could do to keep from screaming. As it was, she had to set them down and rest for a moment. The guard smirked the whole time.

When she stepped back into the hut, she set the buckets down immediately and stretched her back. She restrained the tears this time, not wanting the others to see. She did try to walk the pain out, using some of the stretches Renn had shown her.

"I don't get it," Fergal said, "why do they choose only you to go for the water?"

"They know," Karigan said, "that it is difficult for me and it amuses them."

"Difficult?" Mel asked. "How?"

"She—" Fergal began, but Karigan's glare stopped him.

"Bad back," Karigan said. Fergal might know the truth, but she felt she had to show some strength for Mel and Megan.

After their morning meal, Renn arrived leaning on a stick and walking with a pronounced limp. A bandage was tied around his thigh.

"What happened?" Fergal asked.

"Torq's lieutenant didn't like the taste of the medicine I gave him for his indigestion, so he stabbed me in the leg."

Megan's hand went to her mouth.

"Fortunately I am a mender," Renn said, "and could treat the wound. I see we have another person here . . ." When Mel was introduced, he said, "I thought they were only collecting Green Riders. Where are you from, young lady?"

"Selium," Mel replied. "Well, Sacor City, actually. I go to school in Selium."

"She's not a Green Rider," Karigan said quietly, "but our colonel's daughter."

Renn gave Mel another look. "So you are guilty by association."

That made Mel smile. "Very."

He then turned to Fergal. "Let's take a look at that shoulder." As he passed through a beam of light, it revealed a welt and bruise beneath his eye.

When he finished with Fergal, he asked Karigan, "Have you been doing your stretches?"

"Yes, but carrying water buckets is still hard."

"I brought more liniment. I can apply some now, and later one of your friends here can put some on for you."

"No," Karigan replied. "What you put on will be fine."

He looked at her for a moment, then nodded. "Very well." He removed a jar from his basket. Mel and Megan watched expectantly.

"Would you two mind giving us some space?" she asked.

They exchanged glances, shrugged, and moved to sit beside Fergal.

Karigan made sure her back was away from them before removing her greatcoat so Renn could get to work. He lifted the back of her shirt and began to apply the liniment. It was aromatic and he worked it in with gentle expertise. She sighed as he loosened stiff and sore muscles and the liniment soothed the pain. It was not as efficacious as the evaleoren of the Eletians, but it was very good.

"How is Fergal's wound?" she asked in a quiet voice.

"He is mending well despite the circumstances."

"Thank goodness." She winced when he placed pressure on a tender spot. "We need to get out of here—you, too."

"I would like nothing better, Rider, but I am not leaving without my family."

"They have your family here, too?"

"Yes. To ensure my cooperation."

"I'm sorry." That complicated an already complicated situation. "How many in your family?"

"My wife, Cora, and two children, a girl and boy, nine and twelve, respectively."

How would she get all those people out? A wrong move and the Raiders would not hesitate to kill Renn's family. Not only would that be a tragedy for all concerned, but she believed it might very well prevent the existence of Cade in the future.

⫷ YOLANDHE'S ISLAND ⫸

**B**eryl Spencer hugged her arms to herself. Even when the sun shone over the island, the air was damp and cold. Raw. She missed the hills of Mirwell Province where it wasn't so damp that it made your bones hurt. Clouds flowed in streamers overhead and cold landward breezes combed through her hair. She watched as Yap sliced through the belly of another fish. She was heartily sick of fish—roasted fish, dried fish, stewed fish, raw fish, fried fish. Even the occasional seabirds Yap trapped tasted like fish because that's what seabirds ate. Seabird eggs weren't too bad, but they were usually fried in fish oil, so they, too, tasted like fish.

Yap pulled out the guts of the fish and tossed them aside. Before they could slap the rocky beach, Scorch snapped them up and hastily swallowed them, then crooned in anticipation for more.

"Yer a glutton, and that's for sure," Yap told the little dragon.

Little, Beryl reflected, as in the size of a pony. *Dragon*. She was still having a hard time accepting the concept of dragons present and living in her world. They had always ever been ancient myth, the province of bedtime stories and the poems of long-dead bards.

Scorch hopped in place and flicked his tail in anticipation as Yap held another treat aloft. When he tossed it, Scorch caught the fish head neatly in his maw very much like a well-trained dog. A dog, that was, with gray-brown scales, lizard-like feet with long talons, and membranous wings. Scorch couldn't fly for his wings were too small, stunted. He was a

runt or otherwise inferior to, and rejected by, the other dragons, or so Yap claimed. She had to admit that Scorch was
easier to take than the big ones. There wasn't much in the
world that made Beryl Spencer shudder, but the big ones did.

"Come here, my lad," Yap told Scorch. He patted his leg
to get the dragon to follow him. They went to where there was
a pile of driftwood. "C'mon, do yer thing."

Scorch drew his head back, then hacked and belched until
fire flared from his jaw and sparked the wood. The dry fuel
exploded into flame. Yap patted Scorch's head and scratched
between the ridge plates of his neck. The dragon crooned. It
was convenient to have a fire lit so easily.

"We'll have a good stew tonight," Yap cheerfully told the
dragon.

Beryl pulled up the hood of her coat against the incessant
wind. *Great. Fish stew.* "You said Lord Amberhill has gone
to the east side of the island this morning?" she asked Yap.

"Aye. Him and the lady."

The lady, the sea witch, Yolandhe. The east end of the island reared out of the water in high vertical cliffs and was
exposed to the full brunt of the open ocean. It was there that
Amberhill went to commune with his dragons, the big ones.
Beryl didn't know exactly what this entailed as she was forbidden to leave their cove. Scorch was not only Yap's pet, but
her guard dog. As appealing as his size and snub-beaked nose
was, he would not think twice about biting off her leg.

Amberhill had recognized her when she floated half-dead
to shore after her sailing dory pitched over in the raging currents near the island. They'd pulled her to land and tended her.
She thought Yolandhe might have used some sort of magic to
help heal her worst hurts, though she still had headaches and
blurred vision from having cracked her head on a reef.

They also knew she wasn't there by chance. They had no
reason to suspect King Zachary wanted Amberhill returned
to Sacor City because Karigan G'ladheon had seen what he
would become in the future, what he'd do to their world. They
had no reason to suspect that if she could not drag him back
to Sacor City, she was to assassinate him. All she'd done thus
far was recite the king's wish that he return. No reason given,

no ultimatums made. And yet, she sensed they suspected. Yolandhe was a witch, after all, and who knew what she could divine.

It would seem Amberhill was not there by chance, either. As Yap explained it, Amberhill had been drawn across the sea. He knew not by what means, and at the same time to where, but the pull to the island had proved relentless. Like Beryl when her dory had gotten caught in the hazardous currents around the islands of the Northern Sea archipelago, so had theirs, and they had likewise crashed upon the shore.

Scorch suddenly whimpered and leaped behind Yap's legs. Yap looked out to sea and she followed his gaze. Glowing orange eyes and a row of dorsal ridges appeared above the crests of waves. No wonder Scorch was scared. She backed up the beach, herself, and a good thing for the dragon reared up with prey in its great jaws, and with a toss of its head, launched a corpse ashore. The heavy body of a seal crashed onto the stone beach just inches from where she'd been standing.

The dragon regarded them for a moment with its blazing eyes, its huge head perched on a neck that was as tall and straight as a ship's mast. Wet scales of aquamarine glistened in the sun. And then it sank into the water and disappeared. Scorch sighed, exhaling a puff of smoke.

"Why do I get the feeling that dragon was deciding whether or not to eat us," Beryl said.

"Naw," Yap replied. "My master says they have enough prey in the ocean that they won't bother with us scrawny, boney people."

He had told her that the dragons, large as they were, could kill a small whale individually, and the largest of whales if they hunted in schools. Herds? What did one call a group of dragons?

"We'll have seal and fish stew tonight," Yap said in satisfaction. He drew his knife out again and made his way over to the dead seal.

It would still taste just like fish, she thought.

Beryl stood off some distance from where Yap slaughtered the seal in order to escape the stench of raw, bloody meat and exposed offal. Some time passed before Amberhill and Yolandhe returned. They strolled out of the woods and onto the beach. Yolandhe wore a simple kilt of seagrass green and a necklace of pearls and sea glass. She never seemed to feel the cold. As for Amberhill, Beryl had hardly recognized him. When last she had seen him, he'd a lean-muscled build, but now he was thin and wiry. His clothes hung off him in rags, but he carried, in contrast, a jewel-encrusted knife at his side, and she wondered where he'd acquired it. His hair and beard had grown long and wild. But it wasn't just his outward appearance that had changed. When he gazed at her, sometimes she sensed someone else wise and ancient surveying her, but then he would seem to return to himself, an ordinary man befuddled as if he didn't know what was going on around him.

Before Beryl had been sent on her mission to find Amberhill, she had been briefed by the king's spymasters on what was known of Karigan G'ladheon's excursion to the future time. Karigan herself had forgotten much of it, a strange quirk of traveling from the future to the past, it seemed. But before her memories had completely disappeared, she told King Zachary and Captain Mapstone what she could remember, and the captain transcribed her words. Beryl had read and reread the transcription trying to piece it all together. Karigan's memories had been sporadic and confused, but it was clear Amberhill was a danger to the realm, that with the use of some great weapon, he had deposed the king . . . *would* depose the king in the near future. This thing about time was confusing. In any case, he would depose the king and crush any opposition, and would somehow continue to exist almost two hundred years into the future as a tyrannical emperor inhabited by Mornhavon the Black. Karigan had described the harsh existence of ordinary people in that time, and how slavery was condoned. The Sacoridia of the future had been devastated.

With this knowledge brought back by Karigan, King Zachary hoped that preemptive action would prevent Amberhill from using his great weapon, and that Sacoridia and its people would be spared. Karigan had not learned what this "great weapon" was, but Beryl thought she now knew.

"Is the seal satisfactory?" Amberhill asked Yap. Despite his feral appearance, he retained the refined speech of one who was raised in the aristocracy.

Yap popped up from his work on the belly of the seal corpse, his hands covered in gore. "Oh, aye, sir! It will make a fine stew and supply us with lard. The hide will also make a good blanket."

Amberhill did not really seem to care, nor did he give Beryl a second look. Yolandhe certainly did not. The two were probably going to return to their cave to do what they always did. They never tired of it.

On impulse, she asked Amberhill, "What are you training those dragons to do?"

Amberhill paused, and Yolandhe beside him. "Training?" he asked. "I suppose in a sense it is that, but is it they who are being trained, or me?" Then his tone grew sharp with that odd, swift personality change. "How do you know this? Have you been spying on us?"

It was the switch of tone that always took Beryl aback. He'd be his congenial self, then change and become hard, like a completely different man. Karigan had alluded to this, that Amberhill as emperor had been volatile due to the conflicting personalities that inhabited him.

Yap popped up again, some stringy gore clinging to his cracked specs. "Sir, sorry, sir, but I may have told her." Before Amberhill could lash out, he hastily continued, "Seeing as we're all stuck on this island for eternity, sir, I didn't think it would hurt anything."

The anger melted from Amberhill's face and he was once more himself. "No harm," he murmured. He and Yolandhe started to walk on.

"You didn't answer my question," Beryl said. "What are you training the dragons for?"

"Does it have to be for something?" Yolandhe asked.

Yolandhe was always protective of Amberhill, and Beryl was acutely aware she did not like the presence of another woman on the island at all, that Yolandhe considered her a rival for Amberhill's affection.

"Perhaps," Amberhill said with a slight smile, "I do not wish for them to eat us."

So much for Yap's explanation that the dragons wouldn't eat boney humans. Beryl did not press Amberhill, and he and Yolandhe continued on. She was not in the position of power she required to get all the answers she wanted. She was not precisely a captive, but it was close enough. Yolandhe was an unknown. If she were indeed some kind of sea witch, she might have powers that would easily overcome Beryl. Could Amberhill turn the dragons against her? She watched Scorch slurping up seal entrails. Sending their "watch dog" against her would be bad enough, runt though he may be. She did not care to die from immolation or to be shredded by his toothy maw.

She would bide her time, let them get used to her presence. Let them think she was resigned to being stranded on the island. They'd get careless after a while. Not watch her as closely. She could use the time, she decided, to sort through the various obstacles before her and figure out how to overcome them. If she killed Amberhill, how would she get off the island and past the dragons? And what would that mean for people should the dragons decide to maraud the mainland? Even if she managed to take Amberhill alive, she faced the same problems, only he might be able to command the dragons to stop her escape. Flames and munching. That's where all her plans led, to flames and munching. There wasn't even a way *off* the island. And maybe that was the answer to everything, to just surrender to life there and make sure Amberhill and his dragons never left.

It was not, of course, what she wanted. In any case, if a way off the island came to light, she'd best stick to the plan of letting them get used to her. In time, her injured head might clear, too.

The toe of her boot nudged something and she bent to pick it up. A fish head.

"Hey, Scorch," she said. When the little dragon looked her way, she tossed it to him. "Catch, boy!"

He deftly caught it in midair and gulped it down. It was her first step in getting them to accept her.

❧ FORMS, AND A RED HOT POKER ❧

Megan sat with her eyes closed tight, lines of concentration forming across her forehead. "Anything?" she asked.

"No," Karigan replied. "Relax."

They had decided to test the parameters of Megan's new ability to levitate. They'd wanted to find out if she could use her mind to lift objects other than herself. The jar of Renn's liniment remained frustratingly unmoved in the center of their circle.

"So, it's different than the sort of ability Ereal had," Mel said.

The late Ereal M'Farthon, gone three years now, had been able to lift and move many different kinds of objects with her mind. Her final act had been to use her special ability to re-unite Karigan with her saber during battle.

"It was worth a try," Karigan said. They had also wanted to see if Megan could lift the weight of another person when she floated, but when she tried to do so with Mel, Mel just proved to be an anchor. All of this, of course, was to see what might be helpful in an escape attempt. Plus, it kept everyone busy when they had nothing else to do all day. If they just sat around, dark thoughts would haunt them, maybe even hopelessness would set in. Karigan knew rescue was unlikely, so she kept them busy to keep them from dwelling on their uncertain future.

"Let's take a break," she said. She didn't like to push Megan, whose ability tended to render her unconscious if she used it for any length of time.

She stood and dusted off her breeches, and paced around

a bit before working on the stretches Renn had showed her. She thought they were helping, and the liniment he slathered on her back was like a gift from the gods for the relief it gave her. As she worked, she slipped without thinking into sword-fighting forms. Even without a sword the practice helped muscle memory and strength. She was pleased by how it all came back to her so easily. Perhaps her execution of the forms was not as precise or as smooth as it had once been, but she had not forgotten, and the movements did not leave her in excruciating pain.

Mel clapped. "Crayman's Circle!"

Karigan paused in surprise. "You know Crayman's Circle?"

"Master Rendle taught me, and others besides."

"That's an advanced form."

"Yeah, what of it?"

Karigan noted Mel's defensive tone and chose not to respond to it. Instead she said, "Show me."

Mel looked surprised, but then lightly rose to her feet and demonstrated Crayman's Circle. "Feels weird without the sword."

"That was good," Karigan said, "but you need to widen your stance a little more."

Mel adjusted her feet and tried again.

"Better. Master Rendle has really worked with you, hasn't he."

"Yes. When school is done, he is going to recommend me for swordmaster initiate training."

"I'm impressed." And Karigan was. Arms Master Rendle did not support just anyone in that manner. "And then what?"

In a defiant voice, Mel said, "I'm going to train to be a Weapon."

Karigan knew surprise must show on her face, but she restrained her initial impulse to respond negatively to Mel's announcement. Instead, she asked, "What made you decide that?"

"I'm good at weapons." Mel spoke not as one bragging, but as one stating fact. "And obviously, Mother will not let me be a Green Rider since I haven't been called."

Karigan nodded. There was so much she could say against

this course. She could enumerate the dangers, but also the tediousness of the work. She could tell her there were so many other things a bright young woman could do. She just didn't want to see her friend give up all of life's possibilities to be a somber guard in black. However, she kept her misgivings to herself. It was Mel's choice. Mel had grown up at the castle so she actually knew what it was the Weapons did, and had an idea of what their lives were like. She could tell Mel was judging her silence.

"Well, then," she said before Mel could accuse her of one thing or another, "let us work on a series of forms. Yes, it will be different without a sword, but the practice will do us good. I'll lead the first set and you follow along, and then you can lead the next."

There was such gratitude in Mel's eyes that Karigan guessed that all Mel ever heard in reaction to her aspiration was negative. Whether the negative reactions came from her mother, her teachers other than Rendle, or both, Karigan didn't know. Karigan was neither. She was Mel's friend. Mel had been the first friend she'd ever made at the castle, and so she would support her in whatever course in life she chose.

They went through several sequences, one mirroring the other. There were some that Mel did not know, so Karigan showed her. It felt good to go through exercises, even when the movement aggravated scar tissue.

"Now if only you two *swordmasters* had *swords*," Megan said in a scornful voice, "we could get out of this miserable hut."

"Karigan *is* a swordmaster," Fergal said, "and a Black Shield."

"Honorary," Karigan said. "Honorary Black Shield."

Megan gave Fergal a roll of her eyes. "I *know*. It's all they talk about back in the Rider wing. Karigan this, Karigan that. But look at her now—she's a swordlessmaster."

Megan's words dug unexpectedly deep. Yes, she was swordless, but even if she had one, she hadn't the strength, still, to properly wield it.

Even these others see how feeble you are, Nyssa told her. *How feeble I made you.*

The torturer's words weighed on her. A sense of hopelessness crept into her mind and she felt Nyssa's pleasure at it.

Mel strode over to where Megan sat and fisted her hand. "Green Rider or no, I ought to punch you in the face."

"Mel," Karigan said, feeling suddenly very tired, "there will be no punching. The last thing we need is to fight among ourselves. We have enough problems. Those are the *Darrow Raiders* holding us. They are treating us well for now, but you've heard some of the stories."

"My mother won't talk about it at all," Mel said, "but I know she fought them."

Megan just reclined on her blanket. "Let me know when you finally come up with a useful plan for getting out of here."

You will only fail them, Nyssa whispered.

Karigan had to agree. She could hardly take care of herself much less anyone else. How was she to help them survive the Raiders and escape? As Chief Rider, they were her responsibility. Her hands began to shake again and she clenched them into fists.

"Get up," she told Megan and Fergal.

They exchanged glances.

"What for?" Fergal asked.

"We're going to work on sword forms."

"Bit of a complication," he said with a nod at his shoulder.

"Doesn't matter. You'll use your other arm."

"But—"

"No buts. I had to train with my left side back when my sword arm was injured. Now get *up.*"

He pushed himself to his feet, but Megan stayed where she was.

"Megan?"

"I hate the sword stuff," the Rider said. "And it's silly without the swords."

"I am not asking," Karigan replied.

"Are you going to make me, *Chief* Rider?"

Karigan quelled her anger best as she could. Whoever had trained Megan had fallen short in some areas. "No, I am not going to *make* you. If a time does come when we have to fight our way out of here, we should be limber and in shape enough

to do so." Then she turned her back on Megan. "Fergal, Mel
and I are going to teach you some advanced swordfighting
techniques."

They were only on the second form when Megan decided
to join them.

"You think you can lead them?"

Nyssa infiltrated Karigan's dreams. Instead of wielding her
usual whip, she held a red hot poker. In the dream, Karigan
sat up and found she was not in the hut by the mountains, but
back in Nyssa's workshop in the Lone Forest. The brazier
glowed a garish orange against the wall. It was hot and she felt
sweat pouring down her face.

"You think you can lead them to safety?" Nyssa demanded.
"You are being held by the Darrow Raiders."

"You are dead," Karigan said.

"Am I? Then why are you here?"

Karigan wanted to wake up. She tried, but she felt stuck in
the dream, unable to move. "This is just a dream."

"Is it?" The glow of orange flame flickered against Nyssa's
face.

This is a dream, this is a dream, Karigan thought, but it
did not go away.

"Where are your precious ghost Riders, eh? They won't
protect you, nor will your god of death. Even your king won't
come for you. It is just you and me, Greenie, and you are
mine."

"No—"

"Look at yourself. All alone and terrified."

Karigan was no longer sitting, but hanging by her wrists
which were chained to a beam overhead. "No," she whispered.
Blood stained her side where Nyssa had plunged the knife.

"Remember this?" Nyssa waved the hot poker before
Karigan's face.

"Please . . ."

Nyssa brightened. "You said *please*!" She laughed and
plunged the poker into the wound.

Amid the scent and sizzle of Karigan's own flesh burning,
she screamed.

⋘ HOSTAGES ⋙

"**K**arigan, wake up!"

It took Mel shaking her to release her from the pain and terror. She blinked in the gray light of predawn and peered up at the three worried faces gazing down at her. Her side still throbbed with pain so she was not convinced she was actually awake. As the others watched, she threw off her blanket and pulled up her shirt just enough to see the wound.

There was no blood, it was not burning. There *was* a nasty scar of cauterized flesh over the old stab wound. Megan put her hand over her mouth. Karigan hastily pulled her shirt back over it.

"Um, nightmare, I guess," she said.

"You *guess?*" Fergal asked.

She nodded.

"You are restless on the best of nights," he said. He passed his hand over his eyes. "But your screaming just now nearly gave me a heart attack."

"Sorry." She couldn't help but notice that his hair was standing up on one side of his head.

"Truth of the matter," he continued, "is that none of us are getting good sleep between Megan and her spiders and you and your nightmares."

"You go up to the rafters next time," Megan said indignantly.

"I don't ask for these nightmares," Karigan said.

"I know," Fergal replied in a quiet, earnest voice, "but maybe if you talked about things and let us help you, they'd go away."

Maybe if Mara or Estral were here, she'd talk to either one of them, but she did not want to pass her nightmares on to these relative youngsters. "I'm sorry. I didn't mean to wake you up." She lay down on her side and curled into a fetal position, and pulled the blanket over her shoulder.

She heard the others moving to their sleeping spots. Mel lay back down beside her.

"What happened to her?" Megan whispered to Fergal just loud enough for everyone to hear.

"Go to sleep, Megan," he replied.

"You know you can talk to me," Mel told Karigan, "if you want. I'll listen."

When Karigan did not reply, she stretched out beneath her portion of the blanket. Karigan listened as the others quieted and their breaths became long and even. She did not sleep, but waited out the rest of the dawn awake against Nyssa's return.

Groggy and still shaken later in the morning, Karigan attended to the chores her captors demanded of her. She stumbled taking the water buckets to the stream and cursed under her breath.

"Clumsy for a Black Shield, aren't you," her guard observed. "That's what the insignia on your sleeve means, right? You are a Black Shield and Greenie."

Karigan said nothing, but knelt by the pool to fill the buckets.

"You're in pretty sad shape to be a Black Shield."

She tried to ignore his goading, but he was not wrong. After she filled the second bucket, she splashed her face with cold water. It gave her some clarity, and she remained kneeling as the rings from her disturbance drifted away. The pool reflected the surrounding trees and a patch of sky in which birds flew. She frowned thinking one looked disproportionately large.

She looked up and saw that her guard was watching the sky. She followed his gaze to where crows cried as they harassed a huge raptor circling on air currents high above. The crows were tiny insects compared to the raptor, and it occurred to her that it was a great gray eagle. It was too far up for her to see it in any detail, but its size told the story. It flew off, the crows a disorganized gaggle behind it, darting in pursuit. Rare as gray eagles were, she supposed it was not so surprising to see one out this way, as the mountains were their domain.

"C'mon, hurry up," the guard barked at her.

She picked up the two buckets and noticed that it didn't hurt as much as it once had to carry them. Renn's stretches were helping. She glanced up, but the eagle had not reappeared. If only it had been Softfeather who had helped her about five years ago in a battle against a monster out of Blackveil Forest, and that he was coming to her aid once again.

"Why hasn't Renn come today?" Fergal muttered.

"Maybe because your wound has improved," Karigan replied. It had, but she, too, wondered, and frankly worried about Renn when he did not make his usual appearance to check on Fergal. Maybe he was needed elsewhere. Or, maybe there was a much worse reason. She tried not to think the worst and what it could mean for Cade, or for the man himself with his calm and reassuring manner for whom she'd taken a genuine liking. She wouldn't let anyone else apply the liniment to her back.

Meanwhile, Megan had taken to whining and sulking about their situation, the curls of her formerly lustrous hair hanging long and limp. The tension in the hut escalated as a restless Melry paced about, scuffing her heels on the dirt floor, and humming to herself as if to block out Megan's incessant complaints, which in turn only served to increase Megan's ire.

"Why don't you sit down," Megan told her.

"I don't feel like it. Why don't you stop bellyaching about everything?"

"Just because you're the colonel's daughter doesn't mean you get to tell me what to do."

"Just because you're a Green Rider doesn't mean you get to tell me what to do," Mel mimicked. "In fact, you're a disgrace as a Green Rider. Do you know how special it is to be called? It's all I ever wanted, and yet you're the one who gets chosen, and all you ever do is whine, whine, whine. Look at Karigan and Fergal. Are they whining?"

Megan burst into tears.

"Enough," Karigan told them. It was the boredom and uncertainty of their situation that was getting to them. The boredom she could diminish by teaching them swordfighting forms, but only for so long. There was not much she could do about their situation, for she was as uncertain as they. As Chief Rider and senior among them, she tried to put forward a calm and confident demeanor, but it was all a facade undermined by night terrors and self-doubt.

Megan sniffed and blotted her tears with a lacey, and rather soiled, handkerchief. "Well, *you* haven't come up with any plans to get us out of here."

"If you have any ideas, you are welcome to share them," Karigan reminded her.

"Why did *I* have to get stuck here?" Megan said, launching into another refrain of a familiar lament. "I miss the shop and all the fine things, the ribbons and feathers, all my notions."

A quizzical look crossed Fergal's face. "What notions might those be?"

"The ones in the shop."

"Your shop has . . . notions?"

Karigan chuckled, and Mel smiled.

"What?" he said.

"It's a *millinery* shop," Megan replied.

Karigan and Mel laughed at Fergal's blank expression. Megan's perturbed look only made it funnier.

"Why are you laughing?" he demanded. "What notions is she talking about?"

It was more than likely Fergal had never stepped into a millinery shop or bought sewing goods. And from what she knew of his past, there had probably been no one in his life who did those things, either. She sobered, and became aware of a commotion somewhere outside. She rose to her feet and moved to the boarded up window. She could not see much through the cracks, but there were people headed their way.

"Guards coming," she warned the others.

Fergal and Megan stood, and they and Melry moved close

to her. If something was about to happen, they would face it together despite any irritation among them. They waited while the door was unlocked and then thrown open, and blinked to accustom their eyes to the inrush of daylight. Someone was shoved inside. He stumbled, barely keeping to his feet. A Green Rider.

"*Ty?*" Karigan said.

He looked up, his face swollen and bruised and bloody. He had been beaten badly and he pressed his hand against his ribs. He seemed barely able to stand, but alert enough to know who he was seeing.

"Karigan?"

A guard clenched his hand around the back of Ty's neck. "You taking this in, Greenie?" He forced him to look at each of the prisoners. "You know who they are?"

"Yes," Ty said.

"Ty, what—?" Karigan began.

"No questions," the guard snapped.

"They got me as I came down from the Eagle's Pass," Ty said hastily.

The guard cuffed him and he went down on his knee. A second guard menaced them with his crossbow so they would not try to help him. The first guard hauled him to his feet.

"You sure you got a good look at those faces?" the guard asked.

Ty nodded.

"Good, because we'll start taking these prisoners apart one piece at a time if there is no response. Understand?"

"Yes."

Megan whimpered, hid behind Fergal.

The guard jerked Ty around to push him out of the hut. The door was slammed shut and locked.

"Poor Ty," Mel murmured.

"What was all that about?" Megan asked.

"Can't you see?" Fergal said. "We're hostages. They want something from the king, and they're sending Ty with their demands. And if their demands are not met . . ."

"They'll cut us up!" Megan buried her face in Fergal's shoulder.

"Crying's not going to help us any," Fergal said, but he tolerated her hanging onto him.

"We at least have a clue as to where we are," Karigan said, "thanks to Ty."

"Below the Eagle's Pass," Mel said.

"Makes sense, doesn't it," Karigan mused. "Eagle's Pass is the major east-west crossing through the mountains, and would of course be of interest to Second Empire. I wonder if they intend to take it? Or, maybe they already have."

Fergal gave a low whistle. "That would be a big victory for them, blocking the eastern provinces from the west. But isn't the keep supposed to be impossible to take?"

"I don't think they'd be here if they didn't have some plan to take it."

"Then why would they send Ty on with intelligence about Second Empire's position? Doesn't make sense."

"They must figure the king already knows. He must certainly have his scouts keeping an eye on them. And keep in mind the Raiders do not seem to be entirely in step with Second Empire and may not care." She needed to think of some way to use that to their advantage.

"Will the king negotiate for our release?" Megan asked.

Karigan slowly shook her head. "It's unlikely. The crown's policy is not to negotiate with criminals who take hostages and demand some sort of ransom. At least, *we're* not important enough for negotiations, unless one of you has high noble blood I don't know about, or has been promoted to general."

"They won't try to rescue us either, will they?"

The others watched her expectantly. She shrugged. "If the opportunity arises, they might try. At least they'll know where we are now." Before they could grow more downcast, she said, "I think maybe it's time to take a chance and get outside for a look around."

⇜ ANGRY-MAD ⇜

Anna gazed at the homely, one-eyed horse, and then back at Master Riggs. "Is there a reason she's called Angry-Mad?"

Master Riggs leaned against the door of an empty stall. "I'll be truthful with you, Anna. She's got attitude and you've got to be careful around her. I don't know the exact circumstances of her life, but she wasn't treated well by her previous owners. So, it's going to take time to build trust. I think with patience and care she will turn out to be as fine a horse as any."

Angry-Mad watched them with her one eye, and it was not a friendly regard. The mare was thin, hips and ribs protruding. There were scars on her bay hide from ill-fitted saddles, ropes, whips, and who knew what else. Horse Master Riggs had rescued her from the knacker.

Anna had looked forward to the day she got her own messenger horse, but of course, because she possessed no special ability, she wasn't a full Green Rider, and as such, she was not paired with a true messenger horse. There was some sort of magic that drew a particular Rider and horse together. Without a special ability, Anna would never know what that bond was like. She couldn't even ride a retired cavalry horse like the ones they'd been using for lessons, including dear old Lion, because every sound horse was being called back into service for the military. Some hauled supplies, others were noncombat remounts for officers. Master Riggs had to go to the very dregs just to find her a sound horse.

The mare's missing eye reminded Anna of Sir Karigan,

127

who remained unaccounted for. She glanced down the aisle where Condor poked his head out. He'd been slightly off his feed since returning, and sometimes he worried around his stall, but he did not act overly distressed. If he did, Anna had been told, they'd know something was terribly amiss with Sir Karigan. That's how closely they were bonded. Fergal's palomino, still too young for long errands, behaved similarly. Fergal also remained overdue.

"We'll try to get to know Angry-Mad slowly," Master Riggs said. "We need to gain her trust."

"What about her missing eye?" Anna asked. "Won't that be a problem?"

"As she begins to trust you, you will become her other eye."

"Oh."

Anna must have sounded underwhelmed enough that Master Riggs said, "I'm sorry she's not like the other messenger horses, Anna, but despite her challenges, or maybe because of them, I think she'll do much better than we expect. As for her appearance? Besides being thin and missing one eye, she is in decent health. She'll fill out with the good feed she's getting now, and her coat will improve, too. With you taking care of her, I've no doubt she'll shine."

The mare did have a nice star beneath her forelock, and some good grooming would make her less rangey. Still, it was something of a disappointment as much as she'd come to accept that she'd never be like the other Riders with their special abilities and special horses.

"Where do we start?" she asked.

"The same as when you met Mallard for your very first lesson."

Anna frowned at the mention of friendly Mallard, who had been her first lesson horse, but had since been claimed by Hoff, a new Rider.

"Go ahead and introduce yourself to her," the horse master continued. "Do so confidently, but not aggressively. No quick moves, and stay on her sighted side. Be wary, she might try to bite."

The last did not instill in Anna the confidence that the

horse master said she should project. Nevertheless she approached the stall staying in the mare's line of sight.

"Hello, I'm Anna."

At first the mare just watched, then blew through her nose. It did not sound like the friendly chuff Anna was accustomed to from the other horses. The closer she got, the more the mare's ears lowered.

"Keep it slow," Master Riggs reminded her. "No sudden movements."

Anna tried talking nonsense in a low voice. When she got within reach, the mare seemed to retract her head.

"Watch out, she's gonna—" Master Riggs started.

Angry-Mad lunged and Anna leaped back, the mare's teeth snapping just inches from her arm. The mare then whirled and kicked the stall door for good measure. Anna's heart pounded wildly.

Master Riggs placed her hand on Anna's shoulder. "That was close, but you've good reflexes. It will take a while, it appears, before you can do a whole lot with her. Visit her as much as you can. Let her get used to you, your scent, the sight of you, the sound of your voice."

"I don't know," Anna replied, "but I am thinking I might be better off going back to cleaning hearths. I don't think I am ready for this."

"No? Maybe that's so, but you've faced worse. Give it time. I think you both deserve a chance."

Anna wondered what would happen if the king needed all his Riders ready to ride, even the new ones like her. She and Angry-Mad would have to come to some understanding quickly.

"Remember, all she knows is that people are cruel," Master Riggs continued. "We'll show her otherwise. In the meantime, I'd better put a warning sign on her stall. You Riders are so used to good-natured horses that no one will be expecting her behavior."

They were heading for the exit when Master Riggs paused and peered out the door into daylight. "What's this?" she murmured.

Anna looked out and saw a Rider slumped over the neck of a tall horse she did not recognize.

"That's Crane," Master Riggs said, and she trotted outside with Anna on her heels.

The horse was huffing as he circled in the stable yard. The Rider appeared to be unconscious. His face was swollen and bloody.

"HEP!" Master Riggs yelled.

The stablemaster emerged from behind the manure pile and charged toward them.

"Anna," Master Riggs said, "run to the mending wing and tell them to prepare for an injured Rider. Then locate your captain and colonel and tell them Rider Newland is back and injured."

Anna obeyed. Even as she sprinted off, Hep and Master Riggs were pulling the Rider off his horse.

Rider Newland, Anna thought as she raced toward the castle. That would be Ty, who had been off to the east coast over much of the winter, probably in Coutre Province or some such. They had not met since he'd been gone before she became a Rider, though chances were she and he had crossed paths in the Rider wing when she was on hearth duty.

What could have happened to him? The colonel had spoken to them about the Darrow Raiders and how terrible they'd been in the past, and now they were back. Had Rider Newland encountered them?

She hurried her steps thinking that this, along with Angry-Mad, were good reasons to resume her status as a servant and forego the green uniform. She was not fit, hadn't the courage, but she'd entered into this aware of the dangers. She just had not expected them to present themselves with such immediacy.

She leaped a puddle and dodged between two porters and hurried to the castle entrance to herald the news of Rider Newland's arrival.

⋙ THE RED WITCH ⋙

In the mending wing, Anna stood outside the room in which they'd placed Rider Newland in case the colonel had some need of her. The door was cracked open just enough that Anna could hear what was being said within.

"Broken ribs," Rider-Mender Ben Simeon said. "Broken arm and smashed knee. Fractured cheekbone and broken nose. All the fingers of his left hand have been smashed."

Anna winced as Ben worked his way down the list. Colonel Mapstone and Captain Connly remained silent.

"Master Vanlynn has given me permission to heal the breaks that would otherwise result in crippling his ability to use his limbs properly. His knees, for instance. I won't be doing a full healing, but enough to get the process under way."

Ben's Rider ability was as a true healer. He could magically heal a wound or illness, but it took a great toll on him. Anna knew Master Vanlynn, the chief of all the menders, forbade him to use his abilities except in dire emergencies, for he was to remain ready in case something went awry with the queen's pregnancy.

"Is his head injured?" the colonel asked. "I mean, in addition to his facial injuries?"

"A concussion," Ben replied. "I've already given him a touch of healing and that should be all right. In fact, he seems to be waking up."

Anna gazed both ways down the quiet corridor, and when she saw no one was about, crept to the door and peered through the crack. She could see the foot of the bed, but nothing really

131

of Rider Newland, just the lumps of his body beneath his blankets. Ben leaned over him on one side, and the colonel and captain on the other.

"Ty?" the colonel said. "Are you with us?"

"Captain. Must speak to captain." Rider Newland's words were dull and slightly slurred.

"I'm here," Captain Connly said.

"I think he means me," the colonel said. "He's been gone long enough that he can't have heard of our promotions. Ty, I am right here. You are safe now. Can you tell us what happened to you?"

"Darrow Raiders . . . caught me when I went through the pass."

"Eagle's?" the colonel asked.

Anna had looked up the Eagle's Pass in Master Foley's atlas after hearing the king speak of it. It was the easiest passage, she had learned, from one side of the Wing Song Mountains to the other. There was also an ancient keep there embedded into the side of Stormcroft Mountain to guard the pass—the one General Washburn had claimed was impenetrable. She'd sought to do further research in the castle library, but most texts on that area, and about the keep, were signed out. The one or two books that remained had very little to say about the Eagle's Pass, but she'd found an intriguing reference to a great plaza that had been constructed across the pass from the keep atop a cliff on Snowborne Mountain, called Eagle's Landing. In the old days, the book claimed, the great gray eagles would alight there to parley with the Sacor Clans. When she asked Master Foley about it, he scoffed at the idea of birds parleying, and that the landing must have had a defensive purpose for the sentinels at the keep. Anna didn't brush it off so easily, as she'd heard that Sir Karigan had once conversed with a great gray eagle.

Rider Newland must have indicated that he'd indeed been caught at the Eagle's Pass because the colonel then asked, "About where?"

"Forest to the west. Large encampment, I think. Somehow shielded. Didn't see it until I was upon it and rode right into a trap. Then . . ." He struggled for a breath. "Then they brought me to just outside of Sacor City. With magic. I—I have message from the one called Torq."

The three leaning over the bed went so silent and still that it was like Anna looked upon a tableau of wax figures at the Sacor City War Museum. The colonel paled, which made her look particularly like a wax figure.

"Go on," the colonel said.

"Torq has three of our Riders."

"Which ones?"

"Fergal, Megan, Karigan."

"Megan, too?" Captain Connly said in dismay. "She was not due back for a while so we wouldn't have known. But I guess the mystery of our other missing Riders is solved."

"He also has . . ." Rider Newland paused to swallow.

"Yes?" the colonel urged.

"He has Melry."

That was the colonel's daughter, Anna thought. The colonel did not move, did not make a sound.

"Are they all right?" Captain Connly asked.

"Yes. When I saw them, but Torq, he says he will take them apart one piece at a time if the Red Witch does not give herself over to him on the next full moon."

"Red Witch?" Ben asked. "Who or what is that?"

The colonel straightened. Her expression was flat. In a soft voice, she replied, "I am the Red Witch. It is what the Darrow Raiders called me. Now they wish to repay me for all I did to them so many years ago."

Rider Newland had grown quiet. "He's asleep," Ben said. "He needs his rest."

"Send a runner for us when he awakens again," the colonel said. "He may have more information for us."

"Yes, Colonel," Ben replied.

When the colonel and captain moved to leave, Anna scrambled from the door to her proper waiting place. When the two emerged, Captain Connly looked more worried than the colonel. Aside from her pallor and a certain stiffness, the colonel hid her concern for her daughter and Riders.

"What now?" Captain Connly asked the colonel.

"I go to the king. He will want to know that Ty can back

up the scouts' reports about an encampment this side of the Eagle's Pass."

"Do you want me to go with you?"

"No. I want you to be available when Ty wakes up again."

"What are we going to do about our people?"

Colonel Mapstone gazed down the corridor and took a deep breath. "The Riders know the dangers of their calling. We all do. We all have uncertain futures as king's messengers." She turned back to Ty, her expression set. "It is not the realm's policy to be extorted by criminals. But I will tell you one thing, Connly, I *will* see the Darrow Raiders destroyed."

Connly watched after her as she strode down the corridor, his gaze thoughtful. "Her own daughter," he murmured. Then he shook his head.

"Sir?" Anna said.

He looked at her in surprise. "I'd forgotten you were still here."

"Is the colonel really just going to leave her daughter and our Riders in the hands of the Raiders?"

He sighed. "You heard her. It's the realm's policy not to give in to ransom demands. It would only encourage our enemies to take hostages. I imagine she will bring it up with the king and he will decide. He won't want to sacrifice the colonel, and that's for certain. Hells, none of us want to sacrifice anyone."

Anna wondered what the king would decide when he heard that Sir Karigan was one of the captives.

"Sir?"

"Yes, Anna?"

"Why do you think the Raiders call the colonel the Red Witch?"

"I'm not sure, to be honest," he replied. "I imagine the 'red' part has to do with her hair, and the 'witch' may refer to her using her ability against the Raiders, but she never talks about those years, and I can't be certain. Now, don't you have duties to take care of?"

"No, sir, except that the colonel asked that I stand by while you both went in to see Rider Newland in case she needed a runner."

"Well, then, dismissed. I will be off to my quarters."

The captain left her, and she paused to glance into Rider Newland's chamber where Ben leaned over his patient, his hands emitting a soft blue glow.

Anna made her way back to the Rider wing, feeling downcast after all she had just heard. It was hard to think of her Rider friends, especially Sir Karigan whom she admired, in the hands of the Darrow Raiders, and no rescue likely. She couldn't imagine how the colonel felt, as much as she tried to hide it, with not only her Riders being held, but her daughter, too.

She tried to remind herself that Riders were resourceful and they might rescue themselves, and that Sir Karigan had gotten herself out of many a difficult situation before and might again. Plus, Rider Newland had said they looked well when he saw them.

"Anna, have you seen Hoff?"

Anna was startled back to the present by Lieutenant Mara standing before her with her hands on her hips.

"Hoff?"

"Yes. He's supposed to be at arms training, but you know how he loves *that.*"

Anna looked around herself, then pointed at the old cabinet at the end of the corridor.

"You think he's hiding in there?" the lieutenant asked.

"Not exactly in," Anna replied. "Do you remember a cabinet in that spot?"

The lieutenant scratched her head. "Now that you mention it . . . Ah, I think I get your meaning."

She strode up to the cabinet and stuck her arm *through* it. "Rider Jay Bishoff, come out immediately." Then a look of triumph crossed her face and she pulled. Hoff popped out of the cabinet, the lieutenant hauling him by his collar. The cabinet dissolved as if it had never existed, and in fact, it was never more than an illusion. Hoff, whose special ability was to create illusions, was very good at it, an artist really.

"You are going to arms training whether you want to or not," Lieutenant Mara told him.

Hoff liked his desserts and made frequent trips to Master

Gruntler's Sugary on payday, but otherwise disliked exerting himself.

Lieutenant Mara continued to drag him down the corridor. "You continue to do this," she warned him, "and you'll be on laundry duty for a month."

Anna smiled as she watched after them, but it was fleeting when she recalled the dire things she had heard that afternoon. She continued down the corridor and turned the corner. As she passed the door to Sir Karigan's room, she wondered what King Zachary would decide.

❧ ESTORA'S GARDEN ❧

Estora smiled as her husband stood in the doorway of her bed chamber taking in all the greenery. He'd brought her a bouquet of spring flowers, but they were overwhelmed by all the pots and vases of plants that already filled her room.

He glanced down at the bouquet. "These would seem rather inadequate."

She reached out. "Please bring them to me. I love them."

He came to her bedside and handed her the flowers. "I know you tire of being cooped up, so I thought to bring a little spring to you."

"Irises," she said. "How lovely. Jayd, might you locate another vase?"

The maid, who had been folding linens, smiled. "I will try," she said, and left.

"What is all this?" Zachary asked, gesturing broadly at all the plantings as he sat.

"Master Fairhouse is preserving some of the plants from the courtyard garden as it is being converted to vegetables. Most are going to the greenhouse, of course, but he thought I'd enjoy some in here." And she did, very much so. She loved the scents of soil and blooms. She loved the textures of the leaves beneath her fingers—some smooth and waxy, some rough or fuzzy, some nubby. Master Fairhouse had even potted a balsam fir sapling for her so she could enjoy its woodsy fragrance. She'd some fear that the plants might not do well inside, and that maybe they would not get enough sunshine, but to her surprise, they thrived.

During the times she was allowed to rise from bed, she

took on the job of watering the plants herself, though Jayd did all the fetching of water. She loved living in a garden, and she thought that maybe after the children were born, she might keep the plants indefinitely.

She was especially pleased that Zachary had brought her flowers because she suspected they were a peace offering after some heated words they'd exchanged over the book of poems by Lady Whitewren citing their love as inspiration. Her suspicion was confirmed when he next spoke.

"I am still displeased by this book of poems," he said, "but I understand my imposter had undue influence in the matter." His imposter had been the aureas slee, an ice elemental that had abducted him and taken his form and place. "I apologize for being so cross about it."

"I should have known it was the sort of thing you would not find appropriate," she replied, "when the imposter agreed to it. I should have guessed it was not you." There had been so many clues, but she'd been so pleased, so full of joy that the one who she thought was her husband had started to pay her so much attention, that it had overcome her good common sense and suspicion.

"I realize I am not an ideal husband," he said.

"You are a king, and that comes with a responsibility first to the realm."

"That is why I have come to see you now."

She'd been expecting this moment, dreading it. She'd known he would not be satisfied watching his soldiers march off to war without him.

"I leave in two days' time," he said, "to join our troops on their progress east toward the mountains."

"The children will likely come while you are away."

"I know, and I am sorry, but it cannot be helped."

She could see it in his face, etched in the lines around his eyes. She looked down at the flowers in her hands. "I am sorry, too." Would he come home? Would their children know their father?

"I wish to be here for the birth, but I also wish to give my children a stable kingdom. A safe kingdom."

They sat in silence, each lost in their own thoughts. What

else was there to say? Zachary was leaving again, leaving her alone to face the fruition of their marriage on her own, an event that was as frightening to her as it would be joyous.

Jayd reappeared in the doorway and cleared her throat. "Your Majesties, Colonel Mapstone is here to see you."

"Send her in," Estora said. Maybe Laren could talk sense to Zachary. Remind him that his place was to govern, not to die in battle. The colonel could talk to him in ways that no one else could.

Laren stepped into the bed chamber and bowed.

"Welcome, Laren," Estora said. "Will you sit with us?"

"I am afraid I am here on business, my lady. Rider Newland arrived not an hour past."

"Ty?" Estora asked eagerly. "Has he brought news of Coutre?"

"He may have," Laren replied. She hesitated, then said, "He is in the mending wing recuperating from a confrontation with the Darrow Raiders. He was not conscious long enough to speak of his errand to Coutre, but he did speak of other things."

Estora felt Zachary stiffen beside her. "Explain."

Laren did, relating how Ty had been taken on the west side of Eagle's Pass. "He corroborates what your scouts have told you about the enemy encamped near the pass, though he says they are now shielded by some magic."

"Magic, despite Grandmother being dead," he murmured. "They must mean to make an attempt against the keep. Continue."

She described how terribly Ty had been beaten, then said, "And they used him to bring a message from Torq to the Red Witch."

"The Red Witch?" Estora asked. "Who is that?"

"Laren," Zachary said. "It's what the Raiders called her back in the day. She was required to use her ability extensively to sift the truth out of Raiders who had been taken prisoner. And what was Torq's message for the Red Witch?"

"That I must meet him at a certain location by the next full moon or they will torture and kill certain captives they have taken."

"Our missing Riders?"

"Yes, Rider Duff, Rider G'ladheon, and Rider Notman. And also . . . my daughter."

"Your daughter!" Estora exclaimed.

"Yes."

It struck Estora how clearly Laren had shuttered away emotion. How she could do so when it concerned her own daughter, Estora did not know. And Karigan. The Raiders had Karigan. She gazed at her husband, who had risen to his feet. His expression was grim, but he did not expose any deeper emotion though she knew it must roil inside him.

"What do they want?" Zachary asked.

Laren smiled a smile that was anything but. "Me. They will exchange the captives for the Red Witch."

"That is an impossible choice," Estora said.

"There is no choice," Zachary said.

"What do you mean?"

"The realm does not treat with the enemy in regard to hostages in this fashion."

"You are just going to let them kill the captives?" Estora asked incredulously.

"We cannot make exceptions," Laren said.

Estora could not believe this. "Have you both gone mad?"

"I wish I had," Laren murmured. To Zachary, she said, "I will be riding out with a cohort of Riders as soon as all are ready. It appears I failed Queen Isen in her prosecution of the Darrow Raiders. I aim to correct that. Unless you say otherwise, of course."

"I, of course, expect the Green Riders to assist the realm in eliminating this menace."

"Then if you will excuse me, I've preparations to make." When Zachary gave his assent, she bowed and departed.

"This is maddening," Estora said. "How can you both be so calm?"

"I assure you, we are not the least bit calm."

"And what is Laren doing? Is she going to sacrifice herself to those Raiders? Surely they'll just kill the captives anyway."

"That is likely." Zachary gazed at the doorway Laren had just passed through. "But it would be against the realm's policy for her to give herself to them as they demand." He turned once more to Estora. "You must excuse me, my lady. I have some matters to attend to."

"Of course," she murmured, but he was already out the door.

And so they would all leave her alone while they went to fight. But hadn't she been alone all along?

⫷ A LONG, BAD JOURNEY ⫸

"**W**e are going to war," Laren told an astonished Connly and Mara. Connly had already briefed Mara on the plight of their captive Riders and, of course, Melry.

"Against the Darrow Raiders or Second Empire?" Mara asked.

"Most likely both, but our focus will be the Raiders."

Silence fell over Connly's quarters as they took in her words. The Riders had not gone to war since the first appearance of the Darrow Raiders.

"This is not a rescue operation?" Mara asked quietly.

"If we are able to rescue our people in our attempt to quell the Raiders, so be it, but our primary mission will be to destroy the Raiders." Laren was determined she would see both done. She could tell Mara was itching to say something about Melry, or maybe she was wondering how a mother could be so heartless as not to put her daughter first. But it wasn't like that. There was the official mission, and then there was the *other* mission.

They spent a long two hours hammering out what needed to be accomplished to get the Riders ready. Mara looked both relieved and frustrated that she would have to remain at the castle to oversee the Riders who would not be riding to the mountains, namely the green Greenies.

"I need experienced people," Laren said. "These are the Darrow Raiders, and our new Riders wouldn't have a chance." But there *was* one she planned to take along. "When Ty is back on his feet, he can assist you here, and if the opportunity presents itself, you may join us at the front."

Mara nodded. "Yes, Colonel. What of message errands?"

"The king will, of course, have all of us at the front to fulfill his needs, but here in the city, our green Greenies will be up to doing only local runs. The other services will have to pick up the slack, even for the queen's correspondence. I expect, however, it won't be much of an issue with the king away."

When they'd gone over everything, she decided to go sit with Ty for a time. The quiet would do her good, let her think things through, and maybe he would awaken again. She relieved Tegan who had been sitting with him.

"Has he awakened?" Laren asked.

"Not while I've been here," Tegan replied.

She dismissed Tegan and sat beside the bed. It was something she liked to do when possible, sit with an injured or ill Rider. She didn't know if her presence ever helped, but it was the same as her captain had always done when she was a young Rider, and it had always helped her, made her feel less alone, and valued and cared for.

Sitting with her Riders made her feel as if doing this one small thing made some difference in their well-being. Alas, she could not be with those out on the road who were hurt or ailing. Many died alone. She couldn't do anything about that, but *this* she could do if even for a short while.

The mending wing always had a serene atmosphere, as well, and she could sit and think while her injured Rider slept or remained in an unconscious state. This time, however, she did not want to think, for that would lead her to worrying about her daughter in the hands of the Darrow Raiders, and whatever horrible things they'd do to her. No, she must not get trapped in what-ifs. Ty had said the captives looked well when he saw them. She must hold on to that. And Karigan was there. She would protect Melry to the best of her ability.

As Ty slept oblivious to her presence, she kept her mind active with lists. Lists of the Riders she was choosing to take with her. Lists of the gear she needed for herself. Lists that would be useful in supplying the complement of Riders and horses that would be going. She'd ride Loon, but take Bluebird as a relief horse for the ride out. Bluebird no longer had the endurance for combat and he was technically retired, but he'd be fine for simple riding. Besides, the two geldings had become inseparable companions and each would be lonely without the other.

Ty murmured and she looked up. His eyelids fluttered. His face was so swollen and bruised that he was almost unrecognizable. He looked about as if trying to discern where he was.

"You are in the mending wing," she said. "Do you remember?"

"Captain?"

She smiled. "It's colonel now. Would you like some water?"

"Yes, please."

She stood and poured him a cup and helped hold it to his bruised and split lips.

"Thank you," he said after a few sips, and he sank back into his pillow and seemed to fall asleep again, but then he asked, "How long have I been out?"

"A few hours or so. Do you remember your last awakening?"

He was silent for a moment, then said, "It is dim, but I think I told you about Torq's message."

"Yes, you did. We still have questions, but you needed to rest first."

"I was snared like a green Greenie," he said. "There was no warning from the guards at the keep, but probably they couldn't see past the magic shield around Second Empire's encampment."

"You don't think Second Empire has taken the keep yet?"

"No."

"How long ago was it that you passed by the keep?"

"Yesterday. They had some sort of travel device, more magic, that got me outside the city in seconds. Very disorienting."

Laren nodded. "When last we fought the Raiders, we always suspected they used some form of magic to move around. One minute they'd be there, and the next gone. It made them very difficult to track down and fight. It was a tremendous advantage to them." She wondered why they hadn't used it to enter the city or the castle itself, but thought maybe there was some ancient magic in the stone walls that deterred the travel device.

"I—I am sorry I couldn't do anything for the captives."

"You did the best thing you could under the circumstances," she replied. "You brought me the Raiders' message. You complied with their wishes and did not get yourself killed."

She was fond of Ty. He was an excellent Rider and would have been promoted to Chief Rider but for the fact he lacked the right leadership skills. He'd get bogged down in the picky details when what the Chief Rider needed to do was get new Riders trained, and messengers heading out on errands supplied. It required organizing several people at once and making sure they adhered to strict schedules and duties. It required the ability to make people move at a moment's notice. Most importantly, it required a certain charisma to lead others in a way Ty lacked. He was much better one-on-one as a mentor, and now that he was back, he could resume that role once he recovered.

Unless they were in full-on war . . . All hands would be needed.

She asked if he had spoken with the captives.

"No, I was not allowed. The Raiders just wanted to make sure I saw who they had, and that I knew who they were. They looked in good condition. Mostly, anyway."

Laren's chair creaked as she sat forward. "Explain."

"Fergal looked like he had been wounded, but he was standing fine on his own, so he must not have been too badly off. Karigan looked . . . unkempt."

"Unkempt?"

"Like she'd been on a long, bad journey. Her hair was short, too."

"Ah. Yes, she'd been on her way back from a very difficult mission when she was taken."

"Captain—I mean, Colonel—as for my other errands in Coutre, I brought back greetings from the queen's mother and sisters, but I was also able to meet with Beryl."

"Is this something for the king's spymasters?"

He shrugged and winced. "Not much that is secretive. It took her most of winter to find clues to Lord Amberhill's whereabouts. When we met in Midhaven Harbor, she said she'd tracked down the master of a sealing ship who'd transported Lord Amberhill and a servant to an archipelago off Bairdly Province."

"Did she say what he wanted there?"

"She didn't know, as the archipelago was uninhabited. Had a bad reputation among mariners. Lost ships, sea monsters, the usual superstitious rubbish passed on by sailors. At any rate, she planned to go to the archipelago to find him and bring him back as the king wished."

Laren sat back. This thing with Lord Amberhill seemed a distant worry with the Darrow Raiders back in action and Second Empire encamped before the Eagle's Pass. And, of course, her daughter and Riders being held captive. She was about to ask him for more explicit details about the Raiders and anything else he may have seen, but his eyes drooped, and closed, and he was asleep just like that.

She stood, needing to get on with her day. She'd ask someone else to sit with him, maybe Anna or Elgin. Anna had a maturity for this sort of thing that most of the new Riders did not.

When she stepped outside, she was surprised to find Zachary standing in the corridor, a pair of Weapons keeping watch nearby.

"He's just fallen back asleep," she told Zachary, indicating Ty.

"I heard most of it," he replied. "I am pleased Rider Spencer was able to find some clue to the whereabouts of my cousin. Frankly, I would feel much more confident about the future were he brought in."

Laren would, too, considering what they'd learned about Sacoridia's dire future from Karigan's travel through time, and Lord Amberhill's part in it.

"Beryl is good at what she does," Laren replied by way of reassurance.

"I know. But I can't help thinking that there are more forces at work than even she may be capable of handling. As for Ty's information about Second Empire and the Raiders at the pass, it appears we'll have to wait for him to awaken again to acquire more specific logistical information."

They walked slowly along the corridor. Menders going about their duties stepped aside and bowed their heads to the king before continuing on.

"You and your Riders will be ready to ride soon?" he asked.

"Sooner, I've no doubt. You will have to hurry to catch up with us."

"You wouldn't be planning anything rash, would you?"

"Rash? Of course not."

He halted. "Laren, I know you well. They have your daughter."

She faced him, looked him squarely in the eyes. "During the original uprising of the Darrow Raiders, your grandmother charged the Green Riders with squashing the Raiders into nonexistence. We failed, and citizens across the realm are paying for that failure. We failed the queen, and we failed our people. I am in command of the Green Riders now, and I do not intend to repeat that mistake."

"Your daughter, Colonel."

"I will draw up my plans for you, Your Majesty. I would be interested in seeing yours. Will you be concerned mainly with Second Empire, or will you strike the Darrow Raiders at the same time? They do not fight in a conventional manner, nor do they possess honor."

"You need not give me a history lesson, Colonel. And I think you know my answer."

Laren looked up and down the corridor. They were alone except for the Weapons, and *they* didn't count. Still, she lowered her voice. "You are, I am guessing, quite concerned about one captive in particular. *You* aren't planning on any special objectives when you reach the mountains, are you?"

"I am concerned about all the captives."

He spoke truth, but she also knew the other truth, about the one captive who had his heart.

"There is much that concerns me about the realm and its people," he said softly, "and I know that I cannot endanger any of it for just one person, or even a handful of people. I know my duty. But should the opportunity arise to rescue those captives without imperiling the rest of the operation? Most certainly I will be there. But I expect the Riders will make my involvement unnecessary."

A half-smile formed on her lips. It sounded like tacit approval for her plans. The Raiders, she thought, would answer for their crimes.

≫ DEIJA ≪

The Darrow Raiders had gotten their name from a prosperous town in Wayman—not because that was where they were from, but because it was one of the first in Sacoridia to be utterly destroyed by them. The populace was massacred to the tiniest soul, anything of value looted, and all the buildings burned to the ground. They, however, did not call themselves "Darrow Raiders," but *Deija,* which in the tongue of the Under Kingdoms meant "death." It was, Laren thought, a pretentious name, but fitting.

Corpse flies. All the corpse flies.

She sat in the darkness and silence of her quarters, eyes closed, finally allowing herself to let her guard down out of the view of all, even her Riders. An ache throbbed in her temple. Corpse flies, always the corpse flies swarming the dead the Raiders left in their wake. Even now she could hear the incessant buzz of wings, see flies clouding above the bodies, crawling over an eye, or into the gaping mouth of a victim who had been cut down in the middle of a scream. Corpses alive with larvae eating them from the inside out.

She could hear it now, the buzzing, smell the peculiar stench of rent bowels and sweet rot. How it would cling to her for days afterward. Hastily, she sipped a cup of whiskey. She hardly ever touched the stuff, but this night she needed to feel its burn because the Darrow Raiders—*Death*—had her daughter, and because their return caused so many memories to resurface that she had worked so hard to bury.

The town of Darrow and its inhabitants were long dead. What happened there had been horrible enough that no one

148

ever tried to repopulate it. Only the forest reclaimed the streets and the remains of foundations, and it no longer appeared on maps. Darrow was gone, but the Raiders were back.

She thought about how innocent she'd been before hearing the Rider call and becoming a Green Rider. She'd led a carefree life on the river in Penburn, with her brothers always around to protect her. The only deaths she knew of were the peaceful passings of elders, and the occasional river-running accident. When she'd become one of Queen Isen's own messengers during the age of the Darrow Raiders, all that changed.

She took another swallow of her whiskey. She'd been able to fend off the memories earlier while she spoke with Ty, while she sat and planned with Connly and Mara, while she met with Zachary, but no more. The images came at a furious rate, images of the mutilated remains of her fellow Riders, of innocent children, of people caught in the most mundane of acts—hanging laundry on the clothesline, sitting down for dinner, working the fields. Then there was the last time she'd seen her Sam. He'd been a post rider, a job almost as dangerous as a Green Rider's for the amount of time spent on the road, the parcels the post rider carried a target of robbers in the best of times. He had been taken on one of his rounds and tortured, parts of him sent back to his post master's headquarters in the very bags that held the mail, strapped to his pack mule. Her Sam. Her first love.

A keening swelled in her chest, but she clenched her fists, and trembling, throttled it back. At the time, she had wanted to end her own life, for without Sam, it had seemed the end of everything worth living for, but her captain had redirected her grief by brutally stoking her need for vengeance so that she'd once again be useful to the Green Riders and Queen Isen. Isen had charged her Riders with eliminating the Darrow Raiders, and so they in turn became a favorite target of the Darrow Raiders. Laren rose quickly in the ranks, not solely because she was so good at her job, but because so many of her comrades were killed and someone had to take their place.

The Raiders called her the Red Witch because she was able to tell when those they managed to take prisoner were lying or speaking truth. She'd been made to endure the interrogations of several of them as they boasted about their slaughter. It had hardened her still more.

She splashed more whiskey into her cup, then pulled out the wooden box that contained her medals and opened it. Elgin kept them at high polish. Medals of courage, bravery, mostly for her actions to end the scourge of the Darrow Raiders. She turned up the lamplight and tilted the box this way and that to see how they glistened. She wore them only on formal occasions, and only because Elgin insisted on it.

Medals for the slaughter she herself had committed. The Darrow Raiders held no dominion on brutality. The nadir of the queen's plan to destroy the Raiders had been Laren's own strategy. They'd discovered the Raiders' base camp and poisoned the water, but it had only made them sick and had not killed them. So she and her comrades entered the camp and killed the ill men where they lay on the ground groaning and rolling in their own waste. She'd gone mad with blood lust, using her sword with unnecessary savagery. She'd saved Urz, their leader, for last and hacked him to pieces until she wore his blood from head to foot. Red Witch, indeed.

For the slaying of sick men unable to defend themselves, she was given Sacoridia's highest military honor, the Crescent Moon. She threw the medals on the floor and covered her eyes with her hand. There were no tears, not even for Sam. The time for tears was long past.

"Red," said a quiet voice.

She looked up with a start, hadn't heard Elgin come in. He looked at the medals scattered on the floor, but did not move to pick them up. He reached for the bottle of whiskey and squinted to read the label.

"That's good stuff," he said.

"Is it? Zachary gave it to me years ago. A Night of Aeryc gift, I think."

"How much have you had?"

That was a good question. She was a bit fuzzy-headed. "One or two. Or three. Four?"

Elgin raised an eyebrow, but he didn't remark on it. Instead, he asked, "Mind if I join you?"

"Help yourself."

He rummaged around her quarters for a clean cup, found a mug, and poured. Then he settled down in a chair across from her and sipped.

"This is the kind of stuff you take your time drinking," he said. "Savor."

"Not why I'm drinking it," she mumbled.

"I figured. I heard about Ty's news."

"And?"

"I heard you are going to the mountains where the Raiders are. I'm going with you."

"Elgin—"

"Now don't you deny me, Red. It's my history, too, and I also lost friends. I still have ghosts whispering in my ear in deepest night begging me to save them."

"I know."

"I won't let you sacrifice yourself."

"Tell me, Elgin, what would you do if it were your own daughter being held by the Raiders?"

"I'd make 'em pay."

"You wouldn't try to rescue her?"

Elgin shifted in his chair, took a sip of whiskey. "I don't rightly know what I'd do. I don't have children. Likely I'd do anything I could to get her back."

"And if official policy forbids treating with hostage takers?"

"Policy be damned."

Laws, rules, policies were usually set for good reasons. The policy of not negotiating with criminals was a good one, but this time it was personal and Elgin's words mirrored how she felt.

"I'd sacrifice anything for my daughter."

"That's what I'm afraid of, Red," Elgin replied.

"I will not let them harm her."

"I know that."

"Then if you are coming with us, you'd best sharpen your sword."

"It has never been dull."

She believed it. "Then, to begin with, you can help Mara and Connly get the Riders ready to go."

"Who you leaving behind?"

"I'm leaving Mara in command here with most of the new Riders. Maybe Merla so she can keep working on the wards around the castle."

"Most of the new ones? You are taking some green Greenies with us? Won't they be underfoot?"

"Just one, actually, and you know very well green Greenies are never underfoot."

"Red, just what are we up against?"

"We're not up against Urz, and that's a good thing." She passed her hand over her eyes to clear them of the vision of the Raider's expression as her saber hacked into him. "Torq isn't as clever as Urz. Urz was the brains. Torq was always more the enforcer. However, he was never stupid, and who knows what scheming he's been up to over all these years. Besides figuring out how to bait me for his revenge, that is."

"Where do you think he's been hiding all this time?"

She shrugged. "Sulking somewhere in the Under Kingdoms, no doubt." Urz and Torq, brothers, were from the Under Kingdoms, of course, and it was where they formed their group of raiders after the Under Kingdoms had been subdued by Sacoridia in war. Sacoridia had not been a gentle victor, and resentment against the victors had been the foundation of the Darrow Raiders. "Thing is, he has a point."

She hadn't realized she had spoken aloud until Elgin asked, "What point? And who?"

"Torq. About vengeance."

"Now I know you've had too much to drink."

"Elgin, you weren't there in the end when we finally took out the Raiders, Urz."

"They had it coming."

"But from Torq's viewpoint, we killed his brother and fellow Raiders in a dishonorable way, and he's right about that."

"Torq knows nothing of honor," Elgin said. "The Raiders never showed honor toward Riders or any of their victims."

"And Sacoridian troops committed atrocities in the Under Kingdoms, which in turn produced the Darrow Raiders. Where does it end, Elgin, this vengeance? It just goes round in circles. His eye for mine."

"It ends when we take down the last of the Raiders."

"And what will that spawn? In some places, and not just in the Under Kingdoms, they are folk heroes."

"You don't seem to want my answers, Red, and I can't help you with that. I can only help you with the here and now, and the answer to that is stopping Torq and his band of criminals from ravaging the countryside again."

She considered his words, but the whiskey had dulled her thoughts. He had no answers, nor did she.

His mug clinked on a side table as he set it down. "Well, then, I suppose I ought to start getting my gear ready." He stood.

Laren looked him over critically. "You need to wear some green."

"Eh? I'm not a Green Rider, not anymore."

"Retired or not, you are. Elgin, we are going to battle. You may not be at the front line, but others need to identify you as one of our own. I will speak with the quartermaster."

"I guess I don't know what to say to that, except to wish you good night. Never expected to be facing Raiders again."

"Raiders and, very likely, Second Empire."

He nodded. "Now don't you drink much more, Red, you'll regret it in the morning."

"Goodnight, old friend."

She watched him limp his way out into the night. He and his ancient mare, Killdeer, were not up to active combat. She'd ensure they remained well out of the fray.

She stood and the room heaved. She caught the back of her chair. *Oh, dear.* She was indeed going to regret having imbibed of the whiskey come morning. There was so much to do, too. First thing on her list was to sharpen her saber.

~❧ ENVER ❧~

There was much fear in the land. Enver could feel it. He stood atop a granite ledge beneath the stars. The ground fell steeply away beneath him into a valley where a small village slept uneasily. The wind carried tales of ambush and murder from other settlements much like this one. Whole populations massacred. Fear permeated the very dreams of the folk who slept uneasily in their cottages and farmsteads below.

He did not sense immediate danger, but decided to keep watch, and maybe sing of peace so the folk would be less troubled for this one night. And why not? They were kin to the human half of his blood. He folded his legs beneath him and sat down on the ledge, and placed the bonewood staff beside him. He'd grown used to its touch, its negation of magic. It was but a minor sensation now.

He sang the healing. Fear *was* a sort of wound, after all. His was a song without words, quiet and attuned to the natural world around him, the stars like bright notes. The wind, the sound of crickets chirruping, the rustle of leaves, were all drawn into the song and poured out across the valley.

When he finished, the feel of the village was more peaceful, and he nodded to himself in satisfaction. He would keep watch this night, with his bow across his knees, to ensure their safety. Thus settled, his senses ranged farther out into the world to take in its greater mood.

The lands of the Sacor Clans were in turmoil. Raiders terrorized the countryside and armies moved. There were skirmishes in the north, not far from the Lone Forest. A large force continued to move in the direction of the mountains eastward. It was there, he had determined, the Galadheon had been taken, for he could feel the darkness of that large force, its intention to conquer and subjugate. It was overpowering enough, however, that he could not sense *her* specifically, but he knew he must use intellect as much as intuition to locate her. Both told him she was there. Earlier he had entered the *aithen'a* in search of wisdom from his *aithen,* but the spirit that came to him in the form of a turtle did not appear.

As he sat in quiet communion with the life force of the world, even as he maintained vigil over the village, he began to sense something else from the north and west, from his own homeland of Eletia. As a halfblood he was unable to feel the essence of Eletia or that of his fellow Eletians the way others of the tree kindred could, but now he did. Something was happening, or was soon to happen there. Something momentous, but he could not tell if it was good or disastrous. He felt it like a call to return home, to return home as he should have when first he parted from the Galadheon.

But the song of the Galadheon rose up in him once again. The urgency of it almost made him leap to his feet and continue his journey immediately, but he mastered himself and remained seated. He'd been searching without pause for many days, and even Eletians needed rest now and then. He closed his eyes, feeling the tug of both Eletia and the Galadheon pulling him in opposing directions. He resolved that he would rescue the Galadheon, then return to Eletia for whatever was about to transpire. What could be happening in his homeland for him to hear its call, he dared not guess.

⋙ TEMPTED BY FREEDOM ⋙

Megan sat with an expression of fierce concentration on her face.

"Megan," Karigan said.

"Shh! This is important."

So was their timing. "I just need—"

"Blue!" Megan exclaimed. She lifted the ribbon from her lap and waved it in victory. The myriad others she had pulled from the inner pocket of her greatcoat remained draped over her leg. "It matches your eye."

Karigan had a mind to argue that the gold matched her uniform, but she didn't want to waste more time. She accepted the ribbon gratefully and pulled her hair back to tie it into a pony tail. It was finally long enough to do so except for a few tendrils that she tucked behind her ears.

Megan, meanwhile, carefully stashed her precious collection back into her inner pocket. When Karigan finished, Megan nodded to herself in approval. "Yes, blue is good on you."

That settled, Karigan rose to her feet and patted straw off her breeches. Her own greatcoat covered a form on the floor shaped from straw to look like she was sleeping. The blanket was pulled part way over it. In the dark, it might convince the guards it was actually her. That was what they hoped, anyway.

"Are you sure you want to do this?" Fergal asked.

No, she wanted to say. She would fail, the Raiders would catch her and hurt her. They'd torture her as bad as or worse than Nyssa had. They'd kill her.

You will fail, Nyssa agreed.

Karigan knew in her heart that Nyssa was right. She knew it with every breath.

"What choice do we have?" she asked Fergal.

"There are always other choices."

"None good."

He grunted in agreement.

Mel gave her a quick hug, then sat beside the straw form of sleeping Karigan, and huddled her knees to her chest. Fergal retreated to his usual place, and Megan stood. She had actually agreed to create a distraction since it would be in keeping with her character. Karigan took her place by the door.

The passage of time was interminable even if it were mere minutes, but finally she heard the voices of the guards bringing their supper, and the sound of chains as a key was fitted to their lock. Karigan nodded to Fergal and he blew out their little candle. She then passed her hand over her winged horse brooch and faded out. She briefly closed her eyes as the door opened.

"Well, it's about time!" Megan declared as the first guard stepped in with a pot of steaming stew. "We're starving in here."

"Is that so?" the guard said.

The other stood outside as usual with his crossbow at the ready, his lantern at his feet.

"Give me the pot," Megan said, and she grabbed the handle.

"Hey!" the guard cried.

A tug-of-war ensued, but did not last long, for when the guard yanked hard on the pot, Megan simply let go. The guard bowled backward through the door, tripped on the lantern and overturned it, and then crashed into his companion with the crossbow. The two fell into a heap howling as the stew scalded them.

"There goes our dinner," Fergal commented.

It had gone better than Karigan had hoped. She glanced back at Megan who looked immensely pleased with herself. She prayed none of her friends would get hurt over this, and darted through the doorway past the struggling guards, and into the night.

She paused when she was far enough away from any light source. She was free of the hut! A sudden overwhelming

desire to run away came over her, to just run from the camp
toward freedom, to make her way to the closest populated
place and try to get word back to Sacor City. No one would
blame her if she did so, even if it meant leaving her companions behind, would they? Wouldn't they do the same? After
all, she'd be bringing intelligence back to the king about the
Darrow Raiders. All would forgive her. She put the mountains to her back and started walking. Walking turned to a
jog, and before she knew it, she was running. Damp meadow
grass whipped at her legs as she ran. She stopped only when
she reached a copse of aspen trees. She breathed hard, her
heart pounding. Could freedom be within reach? She dropped
her fading to conserve her energy, for the copse was concealment enough.

From her vantage point, she could observe the activity
down by the hut quite well. One of the guards yelled for a
mender. A crowd had gathered in the entryway. A man was
dragged to the hut and she could only guess it was Renn to
attend the guards who moaned with their burns. Would they
blame Megan, and if so, how would they punish her?

Her hands started to shake and once more she turned her
back to the camp.

Run, Greenie, Nyssa persisted. *Run to freedom.*

Karigan took a hesitant step. This was not the plan. The
plan was for her to look around the encampment, to see if
there was a way for all of them to break free, and take Renn
and his family with them. She must ensure that Cade's ancestors endured so he would exist. And still the magnetic pull
westward to freedom forced her to take another step away. If
she headed west, she could rouse a group of fighters to come
back for her companions, but who and where? It would take
nothing short of an army to defeat Second Empire and the
Darrow Raiders, and they might decide to slay all their prisoners out of hand should they come under attack. It was not
the answer. To run was to condemn her fellow captives.

Look out for yourself, Greenie, Nyssa told her. *Run to
freedom. Why should you be the one to suffer all the time?
Would not your king rejoice to see you? Go to him, go to him.*

The thought of returning to Zachary, of falling into his

arms, was alluring. He would not blame her; he would be overjoyed to see her. She knew this. She would go to him, feel his strong arms around her and—

Yes, Nyssa purred. *Yesss.*

Karigan shook her head. No. No, that was not how it would go at all. Yes, he would be happy to see her. No, she would not fall into his arms, for back in Sacor City was also his wife. Certain things could not be. Such a reunion with Zachary was no more than a fantasy no matter how much she and he might desire it. She turned back around. Fading out once more, she strode into the encampment, away from freedom.

Reconnaissance. That's all she was supposed to do this night, reconnaissance. Then she'd return to the hut and finalize an escape plan *with* her companions.

You are very stupid, Nyssa said.

She worked her way around the Raiders' encampment, taking especial care to stay away from any direct light that would betray her presence. The tents of the Raiders were not pitched with the precision of a military camp. They seemed to have been put up wherever the Raiders felt like it. A restless breeze rippled canvas walls and bent the flames of campfires. She saw mostly men in the camp, but there were some women drinking, dicing, and eating right alongside their male counterparts. A shout went up as a victor claimed a pot of coins.

She found a supply tent and slipped inside. It burgeoned with goods, probably stolen by the looks of it—sacks of grain with labels from several different mills, an assortment of blankets and furs dumped in a pile, hand tools and tack. The items did not have the uniform look one would expect if they'd been acquired from a military supplier, or a mercantile. The labels on some of the goods indicated they had come from all over the realm.

Nearby was Torq's tent, brightly lit with the flaps wide open as he played a card game and drank with his lieutenants. Taking a deep breath, she edged close and peered inside. The men were intent on their game, so spoke of no useful intelligence, but among the weapons, furs, chests, and equipment that filled Torq's tent, one object set in a place of honor in the middle of his table stood out—a coffer of gold embedded with gems and etched with strange lettering. It looked ancient, the gold rubbed away in places and some gems missing from their settings. It must contain something old and very special, and her thoughts went immediately to the traveling device. She would bet on it. If only she could get inside to see, and snatch it if it were so. She would prevent the Raiders from engaging in their bloody raids and give the king an advantage in defeating them, and Second Empire, too.

Footsteps approaching from behind startled her and she fled deeper into the shadows. A man in a tabard strode toward the tent accompanied by a Raider. Torq and his companions looked up from their game. Karigan squinted, but it was hard to make out the colors on the tabard in the dark and with the fading obscuring her vision, but the crude design sewn into it was clearly visible: the dead tree of Second Empire.

"The general requests your presence," the man in the tabard said.

"For what?" Torq demanded. "To dress me down again for the lack of discipline of my troops?"

"No, sir," the man said. "They are ready to proceed with the keep."

Torq sat back in his chair. "Are they now. And they need me for what?"

The man in the tabard did not seem rattled by Torq's manner. "The general simply thought you'd enjoy viewing it, as we are, after all, allies."

"Oh, so now he's being polite."

Torq's lieutenants chuckled.

"As you say, sir," the man in the tabard said.

"I guess I cannot refuse such a polite invitation then." Torq rose. "Gerts, you keep watch here, and don't drink all my good ale."

One of his men, Gerts, grunted and nodded. Torq and the others left to go with the man in the tabard.

Karigan made to follow, but she paused and gazed back into the tent. If she could get in there and take a look in the coffer . . . But it was too well lit, and Gerts did not look like he was going anywhere. In fact, a couple fellows appeared to be joining him. He called a greeting and started shuffling the cards for another round of play.

Karigan gave up on the coffer for the time being and went after Torq's group, keeping to the fringes. Across the camp she saw a fenced area with makeshift shelters filled with civilians. Prisoners. It was likely where Renn and his family were being held. She couldn't investigate though if she wanted to see what Second Empire was up to in regard to the keep— Eagle's Pass Keep. She kept her distance, but needed to remember to be careful when she almost stumbled into a sentry on the outskirts of the Raider camp. He seemed to sense something, but she kept stock still, and he moved on. Once the way was clear, she hurried along.

She was a little surprised by how small the Raider camp was. There were maybe a couple hundred when she had expected hundreds more. She recalled that the Raiders of old numbered over five hundred. Best guesses from that time were near a thousand, but their stealth and surprise tactics of warfare made them hard to count. There could be more Raiders now, but they just weren't encamped here.

She came across more sentries between the two camps, so continued to tread carefully. However, it was only when she mounted a wooded hillock and peered out that she saw the extent of the Second Empire encampment. Whereas there may have been a couple hundred of the Raiders, judging by the campfires and rows of tents here, she judged there to be at least a few thousand of Second Empire, probably more.

To her right she could see the silhouette of the mountains rearing against the starry sky, divided by a huge cleft that was the pass. On one side of the pass, tiny lights twinkled in the windows of what must be the keep. The fifty or so soldiers who served at the keep should be able to hold it, but for how long she did not know. She hoped Ty was able to get through to King Zachary with news of Second Empire's presence here, but even if he did so, it would take some while to move the realm's army in an attempt to defend the keep and pass.

Torq and his escort had gone deep into the Second Empire

encampment. With all the fires, lanterns, and torches alight among the tents, she hadn't a chance of passing though unseen. She sank to her knees overwhelmed by the enormity of it all and dropped her fading once more to save her strength and ward off a debilitating headache. What lay before her was too big for her to face alone. What could she possibly do on her own?

✎ A LITTLE MAD ✎

Nyssa took advantage of the opening Karigan had created. *You are right to be afraid. They will kill you, all the Greenies, and your king, too.*

Karigan shuddered. *I am NOT afraid.*

Then go down there. Go down there and not be afraid, or run away free.

Karigan could do neither. She could not move. It wasn't just her hands shaking now, but all of her. Self-loathing flowed through her. The old Karigan would have found a way down there. The old Karigan would not have hesitated. But everything was different now. What if they caught her? How would they hurt her?

Go or flee, Nyssa said. *Either way, you lose.*

The fears and self-doubts were always there, the fear of being helpless as someone methodically and intentionally hurt her. Nyssa's ongoing presence in her mind had only served to augment those feelings and spur her into darkness and inaction.

A few years ago, Jametari, the crown prince of Eletia, had invited her to gaze into the Mirror of the Moon, a bowl of reflective water that was a remnant of Indura Luin, a lake revered by the Sacor Clans and Eletians alike for its visionary qualities, and destroyed by Mornhavon the Black for that reason. In it she had seen all her fears stripped bare, fears such as losing her father, or what would happen to Sacoridia should Mornhavon rise again. From those visions she had realized it was fear more than anything that propelled her into action,

163

not duty, and certainly not courage. She had feared outcomes more than facing the danger head-on.

Nyssa and her whip, however, had changed all that. Fear now produced hesitation. Inaction.

At about the same time as she had gazed into the Mirror of the Moon, the spirit of Lil Ambrioth, the First Rider, had come into her life. Lil had been a hero of the Long War who recklessly rode into battle and miraculously survived. Karigan had helped in one of those instances after having been pushed back in time. She remembered Lil's mad charge down Kendroa Mor, now known as Watch Hill, single-handedly taking on the legions of Mornhavon the Black while her Riders escaped down another route. Linked by their brooches—Karigan's had been made for Lil—Karigan experienced Lil's determination firsthand. Yes, she'd been a little mad, but who wouldn't have been under the conditions of the Long War?

Karigan needed to be more like Lil, a little mad. And if emulating Lil and facing her fears head-on made Nyssa shut up? She rose to her feet and shrouded herself in the fading, and after taking a deep breath, walked down the hillock, shaking all the way, her steps uncertain, but at least she moved forward.

She, of course, could not walk into the camp near light and with so many people crowded together, and she must be watchful on the fringes for sentries. She could roll up her shirtsleeves and hide her Green Rider and Black Shield insignia, but she didn't think it would fool anyone. If she couldn't get close to what was happening within the encampment, it would make it difficult to ascertain what Second Empire was up to. So, when she came upon a line of laundry strung between a couple trees, she filched a plain woven cloak with a hood. She put it on in the shadows. It was still slightly damp and smelled of wet wool, but it would allow her to move more freely among the enemy.

The encampment was laid out like most she'd known, the latrines and pickets, and supplies on the outskirts. Tents, unlike the Raider camp, were pitched in neat rows with large cook fires evenly spaced. Families and camp followers were confined to one section on the far side of the encampment.

The tents of lowly foot soldiers surrounded those of officers. At the very center she would find command.

Walking into the enemy's camp was one of the hardest things she'd ever made herself do. She was surrounded by people who would not hesitate, if they found her out, to harm or kill her. She tamped down such thoughts as best she could so Nyssa would not amplify them. If she did, Karigan was not sure she'd be able to continue. She licked her lips and pushed on.

Soldiers played games before their tents, sipped tea, or ate late suppers. Some cleaned and honed weapons, or oiled leather gear. Others laughed at a joke. One played a pipe for his fellows. It could have been any encampment, a Sacoridian encampment, and it struck her that the two sides were more alike than they were different. The only thing that set them apart was the dead tree emblem they sported on their garb.

A soldier stepped in her way. "Well, hello," he said. "Mind keeping me warm tonight, darlin'?"

"My husband would certainly mind," she replied. She stepped around him and hastened on.

"Maybe he wouldn't mind sharing?" the man called after her.

No, the differences between encampments were few. When she found an unattended handbasket, she snatched it and hung it over her wrist so she, in fact, appeared a wife intent on an errand for her husband.

Sooner than she thought possible, she came upon the command section of the encampment. The tents were larger, the personnel wearing more official-looking uniforms with more insignia. Many of the officers were attended by aides. In this area Karigan would look out of place, so she moved around it and found a group of people heading out in the direction of the mountains. She followed, as there seemed to be an assortment of people making way, many cloaked like she was. Others fell in behind her as they went.

When they reached the edge of the encampment, they formed a half-circle around a small group and a huge pile of firewood. Torq was there with his lieutenants, and a uniformed man with short white hair and a general's insignia on his coat pointed toward the pass. Karigan recognized him—General Birch. She'd met him when he was but a colonel in the Mirwell provincial militia. He'd risen in the ranks in Mirwell, yes, but it turned out he'd always been an agent of Second Empire.

Birch and Torq were in deep discussion, and Karigan worked her way through the assembled as unobtrusively as possible to find a better vantage from which to see and hear what was going on.

"So, they can't see us because of a magical shield," Torq said. "I know this. And you keep telling me you are going to take the keep, but never when or how."

"I have appreciated your patience in the matter," Birch replied. His back was ramrod straight, each movement calculated. The sailors of Corsa Harbor, from whom Karigan had learned a good deal of colorful language, would have described Birch as having an oar up his aft. "This night, the time has finally come."

"And how will you do this?" Torq demanded. He gestured toward the camp. "Your soldiers sit idle."

Birch smiled the smile of one who is superior dealing with an imbecile. He held out his hand toward his audience. "Come, Lala."

Karigan caught her breath. The onlookers murmured. A girl stepped away from the audience and walked over to Birch. She looked up at him with an impassive expression, and then at his hand. After some consideration, she grasped it.

Torq, for his part, laughed. "You expect this little girl to infiltrate the keep?"

"Show him what you can do, Lala."

The girl dropped Birch's hand. She pulled a wad of yarn out of her pocket. A pin-prickling sensation spread across the back of Karigan's neck, for Grandmother had cast spells using knotted yarn. Lala blew on the yarn and a glow rose from her hands, and then a bright dove formed of light sat cradled on her palms.

"Very pretty," Torq said. "A child who can do pretty tricks."

"This is not just any child," Birch said. "She belonged to Grandmother, was trained by her. In fact, Grandmother once told me she thought Lala would far exceed her in ability."

Lala tossed the bird of light into the air. It fluttered its wings and hovered so very lifelike, then dove at one of Torq's men and hit his chest. The man cried out, then fell over dead or unconscious.

"What did you do?" Torq roared.

"A demonstration only," Birch replied. "Not to worry, your man but sleeps."

Torq nudged the man with his boot, but he did not rise. "How long will he be out?"

"Hours, as it will be for the defenders of the keep. Long enough for our forces to break in. Lala?"

Light played across Lala's face as she formed another dove, and another, and another, until a flock cast a brilliant glow above the assembled. Lala shooed them away and they flew off like a comet, sparkling in an arc through the night until they shrank smaller and smaller as they closed in on their destination.

Now Karigan knew how Second Empire intended to take the keep, and there wasn't a thing she could do about it.

"It's the sign!" someone cried out.

Even Birch looked surprised when a dozen men stepped forward and threw off cloaks that were much like Karigan's own, revealing scarlet robes and swords girded at their sides.

"It is the sign," the man cried again, "that Mornhavon the Great is rising again!"

❧ THE LIONS REBORN ❧

All around Karigan swords were drawn at the unexpected uncloaking of the robed men, who did not draw their own swords in return.

"Who are you?" Birch demanded.

The man who had shouted the declaration about Mornhavon stepped forth. His scalp, like those of his fellows, was shaven.

"Greetings, General Birch," he said. "My brethren and I have been observing the work of Second Empire from afar, but only now have decided it was time to make our existence known. I am Brother Pascal, and my brethren and I are the Lions Reborn."

Quiet descended as Birch stared incredulously at them.

"We honor the one god," Brother Pascal continued. He turned to address the crowd. "And, of course, the empire. When Mornhavon has risen, we will serve him as the Lion Regiment of ancient days once did."

Even as a frisson of excitement passed through the assembled, Karigan was too fascinated by the swordsmen with their curved blades girded at their sides to be appalled. A gold buckle gleamed on Brother Pascal's belt, a lion's head. She knew a little about the ancient Lion Regiment from reading the memoir of her ancestor, Hadriax el Fex. The Lions had been the best of warriors who served Mornhavon and the Arcosian Empire. Hadriax recounted how Mornhavon, after years of war, actually sacrificed his Lions in gruesome fashion to infuse their life essence into a powerful magical device called the Black Star. Hadriax broke with the clearly insane

168

Mornhavon after that and turned himself over to Lil Ambri-oth and the Green Riders, and provided them with valuable intelligence. But knowing all that, why would anyone declare themselves a Lion and want to serve Mornhavon? Then again, logic was not a trait one associated with fanatics.

"We have studied and trained generations of our breth-ren," Brother Pascal continued, "for a millennium, awaiting this moment. This moment when the prophesied necroman-cer in the guise of a young girl demonstrates her power as she has so gloriously done this night." He bowed to Lala. "And so we offer our swords to you, General Birch, to reclaim what was lost and be ready for Mornhavon's return. You will find no better swordsmen in all the lands. Even the enemy's Black Shields are no match."

Karigan couldn't blame Birch for his incredulous ex-pression.

"Where have you been hiding all these years?" he asked.

"Deep in the desert lands," Brother Pascal replied. "We established a monastery there to honor God and study the teachings of Mornhavon the Great. We only left to supple-ment our ranks with more of the faithful, walking the lands in disguise to find those of true blood. We have kept our pres-ence secret, but now the Lions are ready to roar again."

"All twelve of you, eh?" Torq said with a belly laugh.

"This Unbeliever may mock us, and it is true our numbers are not what they once were, but there are nearly a hundred of us in total."

"Where are the rest of you, then?" Birch asked.

"Nearby, waiting to be welcomed into the fold."

"I don't have time for this right now," Birch told one of his officers.

Was that a glint of suspicion in the general's eye? Karigan would be suspicious if it were her.

"Carver," Birch said, "take these, er, brothers and see to their comfort."

"Yes, sir," the officer replied. He and some soldiers ush-ered Brother Pascal and his companions back into the en-campment, onlookers murmuring after them. Birch laughed at something one of his men said.

"We will need to test their intentions," Birch said, "but if they pass and can carry a sword, all well and good. If they are as skilled as the Pascal fellow claims, then we've got something."

"They will be good," Lala said softly.

Karigan stilled at hearing the voice of her friend Estral coming from the girl. Lala had stolen it from her with a spell. It was a perversion of Estral's beautiful voice to be used by this strange child of Second Empire.

"You know so, do you?" Birch said.

"Grandmother told me the Brotherhood of the Lions would return to help restore the empire to its full glory."

"Of course she did," Birch said in a dismissive tone.

It was interesting he sounded disdainful of Grandmother, who had led Second Empire before him. Perhaps he was that way to all women, but maybe especially those who held power. What if Lala was right about those brothers? If they were anywhere near as good as the Black Shields, one hundred of them made a significant fighting force.

"And what of your spell, girl?" Birch asked. "Is it done?"

"They sleep."

Birch smiled. His eyes held a sickening gleam as he turned to a soldier holding a torch aloft. "Light the beacon to let our people know. The Sacoridians sleep, and they will never know what happened."

"Over the side, eh, sir?"

"Yes."

Karigan's stomach churned. He would throw defenseless, sleeping people over the side? The keep walls were hundreds of feet high. She looked about herself wondering what she could do, but the officer had already touched his torch to the beacon.

"No," Karigan whispered.

The fuel caught and whooshed into flame. They must have soaked the wood in fat to make it burn so readily. She wanted to act. Could she find some means to douse the fire? But when she looked about, she found Lala staring at her with flames reflecting in her coal eyes.

Lala pointed at her and said, "You were supposed to die."

Some people standing nearby followed Lala's gaze, including Birch and Torq.

Run, fool! a distant voice cried in her mind, and it wasn't her own, or Nyssa's. Karigan did not wait to find out who it belonged to—she simply obeyed and ran, pushing aside anyone who got in her way, leaving startled and indignant exclamations in her wake. She had to get away from the light, and the beacon was bright.

"Stop her!" Birch shouted.

She leaped over a cook fire, stumbled over a tent stake, and fought to keep to her feet. Hands reached for her, but her desperation was great, and having walked so many miles from the north had strengthened her legs and endurance so that she could run fast.

She veered away from a soldier with sword drawn, and kicked a lantern into a tent causing it to blaze. Destruction was good, but causing fires did not help her find the degree of darkness she needed to fade out completely.

Fortunately, most people she encountered had no idea what was going on or what Birch was yelling about.

"The general needs you," she told a knot of confused soldiers. "Go to him at once." Having been given a direction, they obeyed.

And then she was off, and turning again to make a beeline for the immense darkness of the meadow that stood between the encampment and the mountains. Overhead she sensed something large sweeping across the stars. Behind her there were screams and shouts of consternation. She did not pause to look behind to see what it was all about, but leaned into her run and called upon her ability to fade and become one with the night.

Eamon Birch, general and leader of Second Empire, watched in dismay the confusion of his troops as they ineffectually ran about and shouted as the great eagle dove and swooped above their heads. It flew low over the pickets, driving their horses mad, then shredded a tent with its huge talons, scattering its contents across the ground. Before anyone could regain enough sense to impale an arrow in its oversized breast, it winged aloft into the deeps of night. Even though the eagle was gone, the idiots still ran in circles as if the world was ending. With an aggravated sigh, he turned to one of his officers.

"Lieutenant, get this under control. Afterward, put together some teams to hunt the spy down. She can't have gotten far."

"Yes, sir!" The lieutenant gave him a smart salute and set off to do as ordered.

Birch observed that the Raider, Torq, stood quietly by, his skull-tattooed face pensive, an odd gleam in his eye.

"I think we will send out hunters of our own," he said.

Birch nodded. "I appreciate it. If you find the spy, bring her here."

"I will return to my camp to organize the hunt."

Birch watched as the Raider lumbered away, leaving one of his men to shoulder and carry the other whom Lala had put to sleep. The main event of the night, the magicking of the guards of the keep, had been overshadowed by the arrival of these brethren who claimed to be the "Lions Reborn," and the discovery of a spy in their midst. However, he could only assume activities at the keep were going as planned and it would be theirs by dawn. As for the spy? He turned to Lala.

"Who was it?" he demanded. "You said you knew her."

Lala looked up at him with that unsettling impassive gaze of hers. "She killed my grandmum."

"You mean that Greenie?"

Lala nodded. "Nyssa striped her good and she should've died. But she came back and killed my grandmum."

That Green Rider, Birch thought, had more lives than a cat. They'd actually crossed paths before, back when he was Colonel Birch of the Mirwellian provincial militia. She'd come to Lord Mirwell with some invitation or other from the king, something innocuous, to give her an excuse to spy. She'd foiled Grandmother's grand schemes more than once. Even worse, she was descended from the empire, from Hadriax el Fex, who had been Mornhavon's right hand and most contemptible betrayer. She carried on the betrayal by serving as one of the empire's great enemies, a Green Rider.

And now she was spying on them out here in the shadow of the mountains? How had she gotten into their encampment? Greenies had some small gift of magic, or so Grandmother had believed, or perhaps this one was inordinately skilled or blessed. Not for long, though. They'd find her and discover what she knew, and they'd do so in a far more thorough way than Nyssa Starling had. While he'd not been an admirer of Grandmother's—her methods had been too dependent on faith and magic, and were thus faulty—her murder also required an answer.

No matter. They'd find the Greenie and punish her accordingly, and one day ensure the extermination of that bloodline entirely.

 A VOICE FROM THE SKY ❦

K arigan awoke to a chill, damp dawn glad she'd held on to the cloak she'd stolen from the encampment. After running heedless through the night to escape Second Empire, she'd taken cover down a stream bank and, as morning light broke in the sky, found herself in the midst of a beaver meadow that lay in the shadow of Snowborne Mountain, with ponded water dotted with islands of stick and mud lodges. A dragonfly hovered before her face, its iridescent blue-purple brilliant in the rising sun. Birds chirped and sang, and darted to and fro among the shrubbery and grasses that skirted the pond.

She peered above the bank to take in her greater surroundings. To her north-northeast, sunlight blazed through the gap between Snowborne and Stormcroft Mountains that created the Eagle's Pass. She was close enough that she could make out the battlements of the keep carved into the side of Stormcroft. A large banner was too distant to make out its exact design, but it was not black and silver, but rather, crimson.

She looked in the direction of the encampments across the valley to the west. Her view was partially obscured by the terrain and patches of trees amid the meadowy expanse, but she could see the encampments as dark masses with the plumes of campfires drifting in the air. Had they sent searchers after her? Torq would not be pleased he'd lost some of his "witch bait," and to Birch it would appear his ranks had been infiltrated by a spy. She did not think either man would forget about her, and so now, in daytime, when her fading ability would not work well, she'd have to be very careful about her movements.

The question was, what to do next? Torq knew she was free, so there was no use trying to sneak back into the hut as if nothing had happened as originally planned. *Sneaking* of any sort was out of the question as both Second Empire and the Raiders would have most certainly increased their guard. She worried about her friends, and hoped the Raiders didn't take out their anger at her escape on them. She worried the most about Melry, the youngest, who wasn't even a Green Rider, but a schoolgirl. Then Karigan remembered she'd been Melry's age, and a schoolgirl, when she'd gotten caught up in her first Green Rider adventure. If anything, this revelation just worried her more.

When it came down to it, there was nothing she could do for her friends at the moment, and trying to work her way around the encampment so she could head west would be foolhardy in daylight. She'd have to lie low for the time being.

Her stomach growled, and she decided that before she did anything more, she needed to find something to eat to maintain her energy. She stood and stretched her back, then started trekking upstream, plucking wild raspberries as she went and popping them into her mouth. She collected watercress and dug out cattail tubers, and continued on as the terrain grew rockier and started to ascend near the base of the mountains.

Water flowed down a jagged course among boulders and talus, forming small, clear pools. Here, of course, there were no beaver ponds, but it was the source of water that the beavers dammed in the meadow below. Karigan flung herself down beside one of the pools to drink deep. She had not quenched her thirst near the beaver ponds, knowing that those stagnant waters could make her sick. She was less worried where the stream moved rapidly, and found it cold and refreshing. She then removed her cloak to wash up in the bracing water. Afterward, with a delighted chill, she drew her cloak back on and proceeded to munch on all that she'd foraged. Leafy vegetation and berries were not particularly satisfying, but they would do.

As she ate, she continued to assess her situation. Had all

gone as planned, she and her fellow captives would have discussed next steps based on what she had found out on her scouting mission around the encampment. It had not been much of a plan, but it was all they'd had. Now that she was outside, was there a way out for all of them, and any other captives the Raiders held, such as Renn and his family? It was hard to think what she could do on her own.

Logic dictated that when dusk fell she make her way back toward Sacor City and safety, and report everything she'd seen, and yet, she couldn't just leave her companions behind.

She sat long considering her options as the rising sun reeled back the shadows cast by the mountains. She caught a flash of metal out in the meadow. She rose, hiding her movement behind a boulder, to take a better look. Two figures on horseback swept back and forth in a search pattern. That they searched for her, she had no doubt. A glance toward the encampments revealed movement. The tents were going down, and the mass that was all the people, livestock, and supplies of Second Empire was moving toward the mountains via the road that led to the pass. Now she looked toward the keep. Its details had shifted with the morning sun. Among the rocky outcrops beneath its walls, she could now discern lumps that must be the corpses of those Sacoridians who had manned it. She looked away, sickened.

Duck, fool!

The voice came into her mind like a kick in the head, and she dropped immediately into the shadow of the boulder. She called on her fading ability and hoped that it and the shadow would be enough to hide her.

Good, the voice said. *I can almost see you, but they won't.*

Again, Karigan didn't know who spoke to her. It could be she was going mad, or already had. After all, she'd been hearing Nyssa in her mind for months. And yet, there was a familiar guttural quality to the voice she recognized, and she sensed its higher tones as being female.

As for the "they" the voice had spoken of, Karigan heard the clack of rocks and footsteps, and conversation as searchers neared her hiding place. She'd been keeping watch toward the meadow, not the stream.

"She's probably gone west to meet up with her king," a woman said.

"I don't know," a man replied. "Were it me, I might hide out here where the water is good. Might take a drink myself."

The footsteps approached closer. The man's knees crackled as he knelt to drink at her pool. She hoped she had left no evidence of her presence there.

"Greenies are tricky," the woman said. "Torq claims they have magic—not just the witch. How else did this one get away?"

The witch was a Green Rider? Karigan wondered.

"She's also a Black Shield," the man said. "They are very skilled. She slipped out while those idiots were crying about being scalded."

"Maybe." The woman's boots crunched nearby. In fact, she moved next to the boulder and just about stood over Karigan. Karigan held her breath.

There was the screech of a raptor overhead and a winged shadow flowed across the ground. The woman, a silhouette above, raised her crossbow.

"Don't waste the bolt," the man said.

"It'd be a great prize, a bird like that," the woman replied.

"It's too high."

Footsteps retreated as the pair started downstream. Karigan let go her breath and sighed. She waited until long after she could no longer hear them to rise and take a look. When she did, they were well downstream, hopping across rocks, their attention headed away. She dropped the fading with relief and sank once more to the ground, her back against the boulder to wait out the headache that came with every use of her ability.

She gazed up into the sky, hoping to glimpse the eagle that had screeched at just the right moment, but saw only clear skies. The voice she had heard in her head—it must have been one of the gray eagles, and if so, she had a very real ally.

She tried to reach out with her mind's voice as the eagle, Softfeather, had once taught her. *Hello? Can you hear me?* But she received no answer.

She settled in for the day. There were few moves she could make while the sun was high. When dusk came, then she might be able to accomplish something. She rested, and occasionally peered out to see what progress Second Empire was making as it marched toward the pass, and to ensure there were no searchers nearing her hiding place.

The westering sun painted the mountains in soft magenta hues. Karigan had no more close calls with searchers. They were still out there, yes, but none had come close. Throughout the day, she observed Second Empire close in on the Eagle's Pass. It had been a lengthy affair to move all those troops and corresponding support personnel and equipment across the valley and into the gap between the mountains. Not only had they claimed the keep and pass, but they had the high ground, as well, should the king's forces mount an attack.

She wondered if the Raiders had moved their camp, too, and where her friends were. She decided this night she'd find out. It would be a hike to reach the pass, and she would not be able to use her fading ability the entire time, so she'd have to be careful.

As the sun went down, it took most of her concentration to watch her footing on the treacherous rocky ground. She also had to climb quite a bit to reach the level of the pass. She paused for a rest and wiped sweat off her brow. Even in the chill mountain air she'd worked hard enough to become overheated.

As she sat on a rock still warm from the day's sun, she realized the one thing she had not thought about since she'd slipped out of the hut the night before was her back. It still hurt, but it was no longer at the front of her mind. She found she could exert herself, work hard in a physical manner, and it made the pain no worse. Her flesh did not peel open and bleed. In fact, she was moving easier than she had just a couple weeks ago. Perhaps trying to deal with bigger problems distracted her from worrying about it all the time, which meant she wasn't always guarding it against additional hurt.

With a final deep breath, she stood to take on the rest of the distance to the pass. She would search for her companions and free them if she could.

⇜ RIPAERIA ⇝

 If the occupants of Second Empire's new en-
campment in the pass saw a movement from
the corner of their eye, they shrugged it off as a
glimmer of moonlight or a flicker of a torch.
If they thought they heard footsteps or some other sound, but
no one was there, they put it down to their imagination or the
flutter of a tent wall. After all, the Eagle's Pass funneled the
wind in odd ways.

Karigan moved through the encampment as a ghost, keeping away from the bright light, but sometimes when she did
step too close, she appeared as a moment of blurred translucence. She collected useful items as she went—a knife that she
belted to her waist, a waterskin she slung over her shoulder. If
anyone missed the items, they blamed their neighbor or for-
getfulness.

As she looked about, she observed that some number of
Second Empire's folk had moved into the keep and that the
main gates were left open for people to pass freely. Guards
kept watch on the battlements and above the murder holes
that were a primary defense of the keep. The encampment
itself, unable to spread out as it had down in the valley, was
densely packed. The road through the pass was barricaded,
and to its side she located Renn and his family, and other
prisoners, penned up. Nearby stood Torq's tent, but her companions were nowhere to be found. Were they still being held
down in the hut? Made sense if Torq was still intent upon
keeping their presence a secret from Birch. It would be impossible to do so here at the pass.

As she scouted, she was also greeted by the curious vision

179

of the Brotherhood of the Lions as they prostrated themselves eastward in an attitude of prayer, their long, curved swords beside them.

She made her way to the kitchen tent. The cooks were a short distance away scrubbing pots and pans in a trough. No one tended the entrance, so she slipped in. She found an empty flour sack and filled it with a hard sausage hanging from a central tent pole, half a wheel of cheese, a jar of preserves, a couple loaves of pan bread, and a tin of hardtack. Hunger gnawed at her belly the whole time. She dared not take more for fear of being overburdened as she worked her way back to her hiding place.

As she left the encampment and retraced her footsteps along the steep slope of Snowborne, she wondered if there was a way to use her ability to better effect. She couldn't take on the whole army of Second Empire, or even just the Raiders, by herself, but she could do some damage. Stealing Torq's travel device would be quite a coup, and a great prize to present to Zachary. However, by the time she deemed herself a safe distance from the encampment and dropped her fading, her head hurt so fiercely she never wanted to use her ability again. It even made her stomach so upset she was given to dry heaves and subsequently lost any interest in the food she had pilfered. When she came upon her hiding place, a grouping of boulders that had tumbled together in such a way as to make a sort of cave, she curled up inside, leaning her head against the cold rock in an attempt to find relief.

She dozed fitfully, dreaming over and over of terrible slaughter, of her friends and Renn's family being cut apart by the curved blades of the Lions, or by the Raiders, or by some faceless enemy. Even worse, Nyssa appeared covered in sprayed droplets of blood.

Yes, Nyssa said, *this is how it will go.*

Stupid human, another voice chimed in. *Stop screaming. They will hear.*

Karigan shuddered to wakefulness only to find herself being intently regarded by a large pair of raptor eyes, the tip of a razor-sharp beak just inches from her face. Startled, she backed farther into the cave. The eagle cocked its head quizzically.

Perhaps, it mused through mind speech, *they will think it coyotes.*

"Coyotes? What coyotes?"

Your screams. Or maybe it will have sounded to them like raccoons in heat.

The eagle's body blocked the exit. Karigan took in the talons that gripped the surfaces of rocks and swallowed hard. They could rend a human in no time.

The eagle pushed its—her?—head in farther, bringing the sharp tip of that beak even closer. Karigan had pressed as far back as she could. There was nowhere to go.

You should not scream, the eagle said.

Karigan nodded emphatically, wanting to do nothing more at the moment than just that even though the eagle showed no inclination to tear her apart, and had, in fact, been helpful during her escape from Second Empire's camp the previous night and warned her yesterday of the searchers. Softfeather, the only other gray eagle she had ever met, had been friendly, if taciturn, but out of caution she didn't assume all eagles were of the same disposition, and she had yet to learn the nature of this eagle's agenda. Above all, it was one thing to see a giant gray eagle soaring high and distant among the clouds, and quite another to awaken abruptly from nightmares to find oneself nose to beak with one of them.

You are afraid? Of me? the eagle asked. She sounded genuinely surprised.

"You are large and well armed. Taloned, I mean. You don't plan to eat me, do you?"

The eagle made a chortling noise that Karigan took to be a laugh, then gave her an assessing look. *You look too scrawny, too stringy and bony. Not particularly palatable, though if there were nothing else?* She paused to ruffle her feathers, her eyes bright. *You need not be afraid.*

Somehow that wasn't as reassuring as it could have been.

I am called Ripaeria, the eagle said.

"I'm Karigan. A Green Rider for His Majesty King Zachary. I met one of your folk some years back. His name was Softfeather."

Ripaeria chortled again. *Softfeather is my mother's nest*

*brother. He and his mate are busy with a new clutch of eggs.
That is why I am here.*

"To find me?" Karigan asked incredulously.

*No, foolish wingless one. To watch the pass. We became
aware of an army building in our territory, so I was sent to
scout it out.*

"Oh, well, thank you for your help yesterday. It *was* you
who gave me that warning, wasn't it?"

*Yes. And I scared the humans to distract them, too. It was
fun.* She bobbled her head as though reliving the excitement.
*We favor Green Riders over the aggressors who break an-
cient law.*

"Ancient law?"

*As stipulated by your first king and our people in a treaty.
The law of your land is not to kill gray eagles, yes?*

Karigan nodded, though she did not know how many were
actually aware of it.

*It is a law of good will, and represents the alliance of our
peoples during the Long War. The realm of the Sacor Clans
has been permitted, by treaty, to maintain the keep at the pass
since that ancient time so long as we remain undisturbed and
unhunted. In turn we do not concern ourselves with human
activities. Your kings and queens used to parley with our folk
on the Eagle's Landing high above where we now perch, but
this has not happened in centuries. These aggressors shoot
their arrows at us. This does not please us.*

The history was interesting, but Karigan was more interested in the present. "Have you seen, in your scouting, the
whereabouts of some companions of mine? We were held
captive in a hut down below. From what I can tell, they weren't
moved to the pass with everyone else." She wondered if they
were being held inside the keep and that was why she hadn't
seen them.

I believe they are where I first observed you, Ripaeria replied, *in that hut. Some of the aggressors remain there on
guard. I have seen them force a whining hen to carry water
and the bucket of foulness.*

Karigan smiled. The "whining hen" could only be Megan.

May-gun, Ripaeria pronounced.

"You could hear my thought?"

A little.

"I tried to reach out to you with my mind yesterday after you helped distract the searchers."

I heard you. It seemed best to keep my silence at the time.

"But now you are willing to talk to me?"

I was curious about the screaming, and I knew you should stop lest the aggressors hear you.

"Bad dreams," Karigan replied.

I dream of fish. Big, delicious fish.

They would have to be big, Karigan thought, to satisfy a great gray eagle. Ripaeria chortled and Karigan guessed her thought had been heard.

I like talking to you, Ripaeria said. *You are the first human female I have met. You are much more interesting than our male.*

"You have a human male?"

His name is Duncan. He stays with us at the eyrie.

"Um, oh. Perhaps we can meet sometime." Karigan wanted to hear more about this human male who lived among the eagles, but she had more pressing needs at the moment. "Ripaeria, there are some things I need to do. There are people I need to free from the, uh, aggressors. They are innocents taken against their will. Would you help me?"

The eagle cocked her head again, and listened while Karigan outlined her plan. When she finished, the eagle said she would think it over. She wasn't, she said, supposed to interfere in the affairs of humans, just observe and report, but interfering sounded much more fun. Karigan began to think the eagle was quite young, though her plumage was that of an adult.

Ripaeria soon announced it was time to leave, and launched from the cave, her wingbeats gusting into Karigan. When all settled, Karigan sighed, too tired to eat any of her food, but she forced herself to nibble a few bites of pan bread anyway, and wash it down with water.

I will give you credit for the audacity of your plan, Nyssa told her, *but—*

"But it will fail," Karigan provided. "That's what you were going to say, right? Frankly, you are beginning to bore me."

Her words were met with stunned silence, and she wrapped her stolen cloak tightly about her and tried to get as comfortable as she could in her rocky space, and drifted to sleep uninterrupted.

She dozed throughout the day, eating small amounts of food to keep up her strength. She had gotten so thin from the ardors and deprivations of the last several months that she really needed to punch another hole in her belt so she could tighten it up, but that would have to wait.

Around noon, she shielded her eyes to watch a gray eagle circling very high above, but it was too far away to know if it was Ripaeria. She spied some movement in the valley below, some figures who must be Second Empire scouts patrolling the area, and perhaps still searching for her. She also saw a thin line of smoke that must be from near the hut. Though Nyssa did not speak, Karigan still sensed her in her mind, waiting and watching. It made her sleep uneasy, but she recalled no full-blown nightmares.

Finally, as the sun westered, she took a long, deep drink from the waterskin, retied her ponytail with the precious ribbon Megan had given her, and stepped out of her rock cave. With any luck, she'd at least be able to move Renn and his family out of harm's way, and more of the prisoners if she could manage it. Cade's life, his future existence and all he had meant to her, depended on it, she believed. Without him she would not survive the future time.

✍ *WHERE?* ✍

*A*re you with me? Karigan mind-asked Ripaeria.

I fly far above, yes, came the eagle's response.

Cloaked by her fading ability and the cover of night, Karigan worked her way toward the pickets, where she loosened the tethers that secured horses and mules in place. From there she moved to one of the large supply tents, cutting through the side wall so she didn't have to confront the guard at the front. It was filled with crates and barrels of goods, and to her pleasure, bushels of arrows. When she detected a pungent fishy scent, she followed it to a cask set on its side on a pair of support braces, with a spigot pounded into it. Beneath the spigot there was a small puddle of whale oil where it had dripped. The gods were surely smiling on her. She opened the spigot and let the whale oil pour freely onto the ground.

She slipped outside and grabbed the nearest torch. If no one cried out, it was because they were too surprised to see an apparition carrying away a torch. She threw it inside the tent toward the cask of whale oil. She smiled at the thought of all those arrows burning. As she hurried on to her next task without a backward glance, shouts went up behind her and people ran in panic as fire consumed canvas.

She was headed toward the pen that held the captives when she glanced toward Torq's tent. He was standing in the opening watching the commotion. She thought about his travel device. Would it be within?

She moved to the back and slit the canvas as she had with the supply tent. She had to move more carefully than ever for

185

the front flaps were tied open and Torq was standing right there, though looking outward with his back to her.

She entered through the slit, stepped around his cot, and looked for the gold coffer she'd seen before. It sat on his table beside a stack of playing cards and dice. She crept to the table, her luck holding. The lid was open and within sat the travel device, a silver orb nested in velvet. She had not seen it close up when the Raiders had captured her, and now she took in the decorative etching on its surface, the fine script that was like nothing she had seen before. It shone untarnished and unscathed even after what must have been extensive use by the Raiders over the years.

"*You!*" Torq's bellow was like a crack of thunder.

She looked up to see him charging her. She snatched the device and, as she turned and ran, wished she knew how to use it. She remembered when she had been taken how the Raider had twisted the two halves of the orb. She leaped through the slit she'd made in the tent wall and felt Torq's hand swipe her shoulder in his attempt to catch her.

She twisted the sphere. *Where?* came a gentle query in her mind.

She pictured the pen where the prisoners were kept and the world spiraled around her and she was carried away by the traveling. When it ended, the ground spun beneath her feet and she staggered.

"Karigan?" asked a shocked voice.

She promptly vomited and fought for her balance. When her vision settled, she found Renn standing before her. He placed steadying hands on her shoulders. As the miasma subsided, she became aware of the turmoil around her, of the scent of smoke mixed with that of her vomit, and the shouts of panic from the encampment's inhabitants.

"I've come to get you out," she told him. "You and your family."

"How? How have you—?"

"No time. Where are they? Your wife and children?"

A guard who had been watching the excitement across the encampment suddenly took notice of her. "Intruder!" he shouted. "Intruder!"

"Hurry," she urged Renn. Then she saw Torq and a handful of other soldiers storming their way toward the prisoner pen. *Ripaeria!*

I come! the eagle cried with unrestrained enthusiasm, and a winged maelstrom started tearing tents from the ground and flinging them around. She overturned carts and screeched at the humans who ran in terror before her.

In the pen, prisoners screamed and scattered in confusion as guards poured in. One swung at Karigan with a cudgel, and she ducked just in time. Then Renn was there and he bashed the guard over the head with a bucket. Even as the guard hit the ground, Renn thrust a woman and two children at her.

"I love you," he told his family. To Karigan, he yelled, "Go!"

Before she could grab him, he turned to fend off another foe. There was a flash of steel and the tip of a curved sword emerged through his back. His wife wailed.

"Renn!" Karigan cried, still reaching as he sank to the ground and slid off the blood-slicked blade. He would not rise again. His wife tried to go to his side, but Karigan grabbed her wrist. "Hold on to me," she instructed the children. The boy clung to her arm, and the little girl to her leg, crying out for her papa.

Karigan twisted the sphere. *Where?* it asked, its voice calm in contrast to the surrounding chaos.

Ripaeria swooped low over the pen raking a guard aside with her talons. *You go,* the eagle told Karigan. *I go scare horses now.*

Karigan told the orb the first place that came to mind, and as the travel began, a sword blade sliced across her side, leaving a burning trail of pain across her ribs.

This time the world's whirling lasted much longer, but eventually she slammed into the ground spinning, and then she thought she blacked out for a few moments.

When she came to, she shook her head, which only worsened the dizziness. She disgorged whatever remained in her stomach. "Dear gods."

When everything finally stopped turning and her stomach settled down, she found Renn's wife hugging her children nearby. The little girl was sobbing inconsolably. Karigan had no idea if the travel had made them sick, but at least they appeared to be in one piece. Some distance away stood the main gates to Sacor City and she was never so glad to see them. Many small campfires flickered in the night among tents, shanties, and wagons huddled up alongside the city wall. Refugees, she thought, seeking safety from Raiders and war.

She rose unsteadily, another wave of vertigo making her stagger. She quelled it with a deep breath, then winced with the pain in her side. "Cora, isn't it?" she said to Renn's wife. "I am going to take us up to the castle." She wished she'd been more specific with the instruction she had given the travel device.

"I am not putting my children through that again," Cora told her. "It's bad enough they had to see their father slain before their eyes."

Guilt surged within Karigan. If only she'd called upon Ripaeria sooner, or had managed to grab Renn before the swordsman stabbed him.

"I'm so sorry," she said.

Cora gazed at her in accusation. "And what of all the poor people you left behind? It would've been better if you'd just left us alone. I thought you Riders were better than this."

Karigan wanted to argue she had done her best, that she had been on her own for the rescue, that it was most important to save Renn and his family to ensure Cade's future. Instead, she said in a tired voice, "If you'd like to rest here, I'll send help back to you."

Cora did not reply, but hugged her children hard.

Told you, Nyssa said, sounding well pleased. *You failed.*

Before her torturer could say more, Karigan moved away from Cora and her children so they would not be affected by the use of the travel device. This time when she twisted the halves and it asked, *Where?* she pictured her bed chamber in the Rider wing.

Everything spun 'round again, but abruptly she hit what felt like a wall and bounced back onto the ground.

"Ow," she whispered. The stars above rotated in her vision. There was the Hunter chasing mischievous Ru'uth, the river otter, in a glistening stream of heavenly light. Fortunately, the universe soon stopped moving and she discovered she hadn't gotten far.

What had stopped her? She tried again with the same result. Did something about the city walls or the castle prevent her from using the device to enter? Were they warded against its magic?

Guess I'll have to walk.

She approached the gates under the curious gazes of refugees and guards. The guards blocked her passage with crossed pikes.

"What is your business?" they demanded. "Who are you?"

"I am Rider G'ladheon. I'm on business for the king."

They did not look convinced, and she had to admit she probably didn't much resemble a Green Rider in her current condition, especially with the plain cloak. She pulled it off her shoulder to reveal the embroidered insignia of the gold winged horse on her sleeve. They still looked skeptical.

"Oh, for the sake of the gods," she said. "I have important news for the king."

The guards exchanged glances. A third sauntered up and said, "It's all right, lads. She is who she says she is."

Finally. "Thank you, Sergeant Keen. Might I have a horse? I need to speak with the king and his advisors immediately. There is also a woman and her two children who came with me, and they need some assistance." She roughly explained how they had escaped from Second Empire.

"We can certainly assist the lady and her children, Rider. Private Seften, please go see to them."

"Yes, Sarge." The private trotted off.

"As for the king," the sergeant continued, "he's long gone with his troops to fight Second Empire in the east."

"To the Eagle's Pass?"

"That is the rumor I hear. Castellan Javien remains at the castle if you need to speak to someone. The queen, too."

"Colonel Mapstone?"

"She and a fair host of Riders left about the same time as the king."

She sighed, very tired by it all. And now Zachary wasn't even here. "How long ago did they leave?"

"It's been a couple weeks, Rider."

She calculated travel time and distance, and thought that they should have reached Oxbridge by now. "Can I have that horse?"

"You're going to ride after them?" the sergeant asked. "Excuse me for saying so, Rider, but you look like you could use a rest, and the services of a mender, too." He pointed at her side.

She glanced down at her shirt where it had been rent by the swordsman's blade, and in the light of lanterns, she saw it was stained by a good deal of blood.

"It's not deep. There is no time to lose."

A horse was found for her along with a freshly filled waterskin and some provisions from their personal stock. She appreciated the gesture, but hoped she'd not need them. While she waited for the horse, she wrote a message to be taken to Mara who, she was to understand, commanded what remained of the Riders in the absence of Colonel Mapstone and Captain Connly.

She mounted the horse with some pain to her side. Nothing, however, hurt as much as seeing Private Seften returning to the gate with Cora and her children, but no Renn. Guilt washed over her once more and deepened her own grief. Renn had reminded her so much of Cade. He'd put the lives of his family before his own, as she'd imagine Cade doing in a similar situation. He had, in fact, sacrificed himself for her. At least, for Renn, she had brought his wife and children to safety. She prayed that if he were indeed a progenitor of Cade, that it was through his children that Cade would one day live.

"Thank you for your assistance," she told Sergeant Keen.

She reined the horse around and clucked her into a canter. She would have loved to have gotten her Condor from Rider stables, but it would have taken too long and she'd be subjected to too many questions from Mara, Javien, and perhaps even Estora.

When she was some distance from the city gates and

people in general, she pulled the mare to a halt. She grasped
the sphere in both hands and twisted.

Where?

"Oxbridge." She pictured the village square and the world
whirled away.

⇜ OXBRIDGE ⇝

Karigan slumped over the mare's neck and twined her fingers into the mane so she wouldn't fall out of the saddle while the world unraveled around her. The mare did not seem perturbed by the travel. Karigan groaned and dry heaved.

"Dismount immediately and identify yourself," a man shouted at her.

When everything stopped spinning, she discerned the tip of a swordblade in her face.

"Is this Oxbridge Square?" she asked.

In response to her query, several ungentle hands grabbed and hauled her off the mare's back.

"Hey!" she cried.

They then relieved her of her knife and the traveling device. She reached after the orb. "Be careful with—unh!"

A blow to the back of her head sent her into blackness. The next she knew she was lying face down on a stone-paved surface, her hands tightly bound behind her back. The rough hands dragged her to her feet but she couldn't quite get them under her, the world still unsteady around her.

"I'm Rider G'ladheon," Karigan said. "Seeking King Zachary."

"You can tell the countess all the lies you want," the first man said. "Now move."

They prodded her along what she perceived to be a street—it was all fuzzy. There were hazy globes of light she thought must be street lamps. Fluttery things dipped and dove around them. Either they were bats, or the traveling device combined with the knock to her head had loosened something in her

192

skull. There were others on the street with her and her captors—they were like shadow demons changing shape and size. She blinked trying to clear her vision.

Eventually, a building loomed above her, very brightly lit and glaring into her eye. She was propelled up steps and inside. The scent of cooked food made her gag. They pushed and pulled her into a large room. Someone stood before her and she was forced to her knees.

"Lady Clary," one of the captors said, "this intruder used Raider magic to suddenly appear in the village square. She must be a Raider."

"Not a Raider," Karigan murmured. "Rider. I am a Green Rider."

"If she is a Raider," Lady Clary said, "then she will know justice."

"What do you suppose is going on out there?" Laren asked. She held her wine glass poised to sip. Lady Clary had laid out a sumptuous table fit for a king, no doubt because it was for a king. There'd been courses of soup, fresh lake trout, wild turkey, beef, garden vegetables, and endless side dishes. The countess was not suffering the food shortages other parts of the realm were.

Zachary's expression was inscrutable. "Fastion?"

The Weapon, who had been watching through the doorway to see what was happening across the hall, turned to address his king. "It appears the countess's people have caught an intruder. A Raider, perhaps, who arrived with the use of magic."

Laren sat her wine glass down with a thump and stood abruptly.

"Laren," Zachary cautioned, "don't go charging in there."

She did not charge, but strode with purpose from the dining room, across the corridor, and into the parlor, with Zachary right there beside her. Fastion, and a second Weapon, Ellen, followed. If it was a Raider, she'd see him put to her blade. After an interrogation, of course.

What she saw within the parlor were two burly constables standing over as wretched a creature as she had ever seen, wearing a dirty, colorless cloak, lank hair spilling from a ponytail into her face. A torn and stained shirt—there appeared to be a bit of blood—draped from a starved-looking figure whose hands and wrists were all bone. She swayed as if drunk or ill. She was a contrast to the elegantly gowned and bejeweled lady who stood in judgment over her.

"If she's a Raider," Lady Clary said, "then she will know justice."

Zachary suddenly rushed forward. "Release her immediately!"

Laren gazed at him in shock.

"Your Majesty?" Lady Clary said, equally surprised.

"Release her!" he roared.

To everyone's astonishment, he knelt before the captive and gripped her shoulders. He looked up at the constables. "Cut her bonds, damn you, and fetch a mender."

They practically tripped over themselves to obey. When the bonds were cut, the captive's arms flopped lifelessly to her sides and she slumped against Zachary's chest. He held her steady.

"Who is it, Your Majesty?" Lady Clary asked.

"Rider G'ladheon," the captive murmured into Zachary's shoulder. "Must see the king."

"*Karigan?*" Laren exclaimed.

Zachary gazed up at her, and all at once she saw his desperate concern. How had she not recognized Karigan, her own Green Rider?

"She was carrying this." One of the constables displayed a metallic orb on his palm. Could it be the traveling device of the Darrow Raiders? Had Karigan somehow managed to capture it from them? Laren had only been able to dream of obtaining it. She reached for it, and the constable handed it gingerly to her as if he feared it might discharge malevolent magic of its own accord.

Zachary gathered a limp Karigan into his arms and, under Lady Clary's guidance, carried her to a guest chamber.

"Who is she?" the countess whispered to Laren as they followed Zachary into the room.

"One of my Riders."

"Is he always so *ardent* about his common messengers?"

Laren pursed her lips deciding the best answer was to pretend she hadn't heard the question.

Zachary laid his burden on the bed so gently it was as if he was afraid he'd break her. Laren had seen Karigan in bad shape before, but this was exceptional. Her difficult time in the north combined with captivity with the Raiders had taken their toll on her. Her cheekbones jutted sharply, and indeed, a section of her shirt was slashed and bloody. Her breeches were torn and no longer looked Rider green.

Karigan raised her hand to her temple. If she was aware of her surroundings, she made no indication.

"Karigan," Laren said, "our Riders, and Melry, are they all right?"

"I—I need to go back for them."

"Not right now you aren't," Zachary said. He then gave Laren a look of admonishment. Laren raised an eyebrow. Then he turned back to Karigan. "Karigan, it's all right. A mender will be here in a moment."

"Zachary? Your Majesty?" Karigan said in surprise. She tried to sit up and grimaced.

Zachary gently pressed her back into her pillow. "Easy now, until the mender can take a look at you." He sat on the bed beside her, gazing down at her. He brushed a stray lock of hair out of her face.

Laren shook her head. The countess's query about Zachary being ardent about one of his common messengers was by now well answered by this display.

"Colonel," Karigan began.

"Karigan," Zachary warned.

"The colonel should know," Karigan said. "Colonel, Melry was fine when I last saw her. And the others, too."

Laren exhaled with relief at this news and immediately wanted details, but then Mender Howell bustled in with one of his assistants and asked those crowded in the room to please step out. They obeyed, and the mender closed the door. Laren glanced at Zachary and saw that he was trying to mask his concern. It was, she thought wryly, a little late for that.

"Shall we resume dinner while we wait, then?" Lady Clary asked.

They returned to the dining room, but dinner had grown cold, and Laren did not feel like eating for she was anxious to learn all that Karigan had to tell them. She patted the magical device she had carefully stowed in her pocket. It was truly a coup that Karigan had obtained it, and she looked forward to hearing that part of the story, but she was even more anxious to hear about her daughter.

Lady Clary attempted to carry on a conversation all by herself. Zachary, it appeared, had lost his appetite, as well, and it was clear that his thoughts were elsewhere. Laren felt bad for the countess for she'd been quite hospitable, not only to her and Zachary, but to the troops encamped just outside the village. Many of the local populace housed them in their homes or invited them to camp in their fields. The king could have ordered the populace to do this, but that he did not have to spoke well of the countess and the village of Oxbridge.

Soon a servant entered and whispered in Lady Clary's ear.

"Excuse me," she said, and followed the servant out into the corridor.

Zachary watched after her, then turned to Laren. "Once I know Karigan is well and hear what she has to say, it would be best if I leave. Lady Clary's hospitality is very fine, but it's preferable that I remain among my troops."

"Of course," Laren replied. She knew what he said was true, but she also knew what he was not saying. He loved Karigan, but it was best that he put distance between them to forestall gossip, and . . . well, to keep apart.

Lady Clary returned just then. "Mender Howell awaits in the parlor if you wish to speak to him about your Rider's condition."

Laren and Zachary immediately rose and followed her into the parlor. Mender Howell, with his satchel slung over his shoulder, bowed to the king.

"How does my Rider fare?" Zachary asked. "Can we speak to her?"

"She is in fair health generally, sire," the mender replied, "but exhausted. There is disorientation due to the use of the arcane device. Says it makes her dizzy. She's also a bump to the head which does not help. The effects of the arcane device appeared to ease even as I examined her. I've cleaned and bandaged the cut across her ribs. It is not deep and so does not require suturing, but she did lose some blood. Previous . . . grievous injuries . . ." Howell looked deeply disturbed. "Lashings she says she received in early spring are healing well, thanks to someone with excellent mending skills. Whatever she has been through more recently has not undone that healing."

"That is very good news," Laren said, observing Zachary relax his stance beside her.

"I think with rest and some good meals she'll be her old self soon enough. Especially if she stays away from the magic." He visibly shuddered. "Let her sleep the night through, and then perhaps she'll be ready to report and answer any questions you have for her. If there is need, do not hesitate to call upon me again." He then bade them goodnight.

Lady Clary said, "Your Rider is, of course, welcome to stay here until she recovers. We'll see to her needs. I've also had rooms made up for both of you."

"I thank you," Zachary said, "on behalf of my Rider, and for the generous accommodation you've offered, but I deem it best to return to my troops."

"I, for one," Laren said, "intend to accept your offer of a room whole-heartedly." She'd discovered, to her dismay, that she was getting too old for tents and sleeping on the ground. A feather mattress in Lady Clary's house would be a welcome change from her days on the road.

Lady Clary was about to speak when an unsteady form staggered into the parlor.

"Karigan?" Laren said.

Karigan grabbed the back of a heavy chair before she could fall over. "I have much to tell you."

❧ *HOME.* ❧

The Weapon, Ellen, who was closest, moved to help Karigan into the chair.

"Mender Howell said you should rest until morning," Laren told her.

"I'm fine."

She didn't look fine. She was still dressed in her ragged clothing that looked even worse than Laren remembered, including her cracked and worn boots, but there was more color in her cheeks, gaunt though they were. Not that Laren was going to argue too much if Karigan wanted to talk. She needed answers.

"Perhaps we might all have a sit down," Lady Clary said. "I will see to some refreshment."

Laren and Zachary did sit as Lady Clary swept from the room presumably to arrange for refreshments.

"You have information for us, Rider?" Zachary asked, Laren noting that he did not address her in a familiar way.

"The Eagle's Pass Keep has been taken by Second Empire."

It was not good news, and Zachary questioned her intensively about the situation at the pass, and they listened in dismay as she described the manner in which the pass had been taken. Then she told them how she and the others had been abducted.

"The Raiders are using us as bait," she said. "Bait to draw in some witch."

"The Red Witch," Laren replied without emotion.

"You know? Oh . . ." Realization dawned on Karigan's face. "Of course it is you. Why I didn't figure it out sooner . . ."

"You have had a lot to contend with," Laren replied.

Lady Clary returned, followed by servants who carried in a platter of pastries and supplied each of them with a hot toddy. She made to leave, but Zachary invited her to stay.

"You know the approach to the mountains well," he said.

"Yes, born and raised in their shadow," she said with a smile.

"Rider," Zachary said, "please describe the scene for Lady Clary, the locations of Second Empire and the Raiders, and the terrain."

Karigan obliged. When she finished, Lady Clary said, "I know that hut. It was used seasonally by a sheep herder, but from Rider G'ladheon's description, it sounds as if he's moved on and no one else has taken his place. It's too bad as that is good grazing. As for the pass, there is not much to say about the area that you don't already know, Your Majesty. My husband occasionally went there on business, as it was an extension of his holdings.

"I do not recall much cover in the approach to the keep," Lady Clary continued, "though there are the pockets of woods as Rider G'ladheon stated, and perhaps it has grown up with no sheep there to graze the land."

"It corresponds with what our scouts have been able to tell us," Zachary said. "Is there anything further you can add, Rider?"

Karigan was gazing into her mug. "Prisoners," she said. "Civilians taken by Raiders or Second Empire, besides Melry and our Riders. They are being held in the pass. I—I got a few out."

"How?" Zachary asked.

She hesitated, and Laren suspected it had to do with her special ability and not wanting to speak of it in front of Lady Clary.

"It's all right," Laren said. "Lady Clary is discreet."

Karigan nodded and explained how she had escaped the hut using her special ability.

"I wondered how that had been managed," Lady Clary said.

Karigan continued to describe how she infiltrated the

encampment in the pass and stole the travel device. Laren felt a great deal of pride for her Rider for her quick thinking and persistence, and immense satisfaction for the sabotage she had committed. Everyone was astonished by her description of Ripaeria the eagle.

"I have never!" Lady Clary exclaimed. "I've heard the old stories, of course, and I used to see those great birds at times soaring high above when I was growing up. I used to make up stories about them and wish they would speak to me."

"It is not the first time a great eagle has spoken to Rider G'ladheon," Zachary said. His own pride in her shone in his eyes and could be heard in his voice. "But that is a story for another time."

Karigan then spoke of how she used the travel device to rescue the one family. She hid her face in her hands. "I lost him, I lost him . . ."

"Lost who?" Zachary asked. "And why did you choose to rescue this family over the others?"

"Cade," she said, her voice muffled. "*His* family."

Laren exchanged a look with Zachary. To Karigan she said, "Surely this wasn't your Cade."

"Who is Cade?" Lady Clary asked.

"Another long story, I'm afraid," Laren replied with an apologetic look to the countess.

"His—his ancestor," Karigan said. "I am sure of it. His name was Renn Harlowe. And now he is dead because I failed him."

"You saved his family," Zachary said quietly, "and that is no small thing."

"Yes," she whispered. "But I failed *him*, and I failed all the others, the rest of the prisoners. I need the orb so I can go back."

"Karigan G'ladheon, it is not up to any single person to do all the rescuing, to solve the world's problems. You could not even stand after the use of that device. You are going nowhere, but to bed to get some rest and recover as the mender ordered."

"But—"

"The responsibility is not yours."

"We *do* have the device," Laren told Zachary, "thanks to Karigan's cunning, and we should use it. It will be of great advantage to us."

"But it does not have to be Karigan—Rider G'ladheon—who has to make use of it."

Laren understood what was in his heart all too well. He didn't want to put Karigan in further danger. She didn't want to either, and one of the hardest parts of her command was ordering her people into difficult and dangerous situations. To increase the odds of a mission's success, and the safety of her Riders, she made it her business to assign the best person suited to a given job.

Quietly she said, "But Rider G'ladheon has been there. She knows how everything is laid out, and she is the one who made contact with the eagle."

"We will discuss this later, once I've had a chance to meet with General Washburn and his officers."

He did not look happy, which meant he'd heard the logic of her words. She sipped the last of her hot toddy, which had become lukewarm.

"I am curious," she told Karigan, "about your time among the p'ehdrose and your return journey from the north. We know you made it as far as Boggs before the Raiders captured you."

Karigan, who looked so exhausted, brightened. "Condor made it home, then?"

"Yes. We found your messages and papers in your satchel, so we received the letter from Lady Vinecarter."

"Now there is a name I have not heard in years," Lady Clary said.

"*Lady* Vinecarter?" Karigan asked.

"Why, yes, sister to King Amigast."

"My father disowned her when she married against his wishes," Zachary explained to Karigan, "a situation I intend to rectify. Lord Vinecarter was an honorable man, but beneath her station, so it was not an advantageous marriage for the realm, in my father's opinion."

"It happened before you would have been born," Lady Clary told Karigan, "so it is not surprising you had not heard of it."

As requested, Karigan began to recount her quest to sign an alliance with the p'ehdrose. There was hedging when she discussed how she finally convinced them that they should renew the old alliance, though it did not register as a lie. Laren assumed it was something she didn't wish to say in front of Lady Clary despite the countess's discretion.

"I *explained* what the future could look like," Karigan said, adjusting her eyepatch in a way that was not lost on Laren. She'd shown the p'ehdrose her mirror eye? Visions of the future then, were what must have convinced them.

Zachary interrupted when she discussed parting with Enver. "He was supposed to accompany you to Sacor City."

Laren did not miss the angry undertone in his words.

"I decided I needed to travel on my own," Karigan replied.

There had to be, Laren thought, far more to the story than that. She would get to the bottom of it another time. She had a feeling it was something that would displease Zachary.

Karigan described bushwhacking through the woods until she came upon the Boggs Road, her time in Boggs, including the scene at a farm that had been massacred by Raiders. Then she went into more detail about her abduction on the Kingway and her conditions as a prisoner of the Raiders.

"Curious the Raiders were keeping you a secret from Birch," Zachary mused. "I wonder how that can be exploited to best effect. But unless you have more that you must tell us now, perhaps you should get some rest. You look done in."

"There is one more thing, and it may be of special interest to Fastion and Ellen, and the rest of the Weapons." If they were surprised to be addressed, Fastion and Ellen did not show it. "While I was scouting around the encampment of Second Empire, a group of swordsmen appeared." She poured out the story of the Lions Reborn.

"A hundred of them?" Fastion asked.

"Yes."

"I shall look forward to meeting them on the battlefield."

Laren shook her head at Weapons and their desire to live up to their motto of *Death is honor.*

"That is the last of what I've to report," Karigan said. "I can think of nothing more."

Lady Clary rose. "Here then, with your king's and colonel's permission, let me return you to your guest room."

Laren and Zachary gave their assent, and Karigan stood unsteadily. "Oh, I can make my own way, but is there a chance of a bath?"

"Of course. I will order that one be prepared for you."

When the two left the parlor, Zachary slumped in his chair and shook his head.

"I know how you feel," Laren said. "Karigan has been giving me gray hair for years now."

"I don't wish for her to use that device again, and return to the danger she only just narrowly escaped."

"I understand, but if she can return and bring out our people, *my daughter,* then it is worth considering. Plus, you heard of the sabotage she committed. Imagine what more could be done with the orb, and she doesn't have to do all of it."

"I suppose not, and using the Raiders' own device against them has appeal."

"I know you hate to send her back in, and why, but Zachary, she is a Green Rider and it is her job. If I might speak plainly?"

"Why not? I've never stopped you before."

"You cannot play favorites, no matter your true feelings."

"You don't think I know that? I admit, I did not do well tonight before Lady Clary and her people."

"No, you did not, but fortunately, as I told Karigan earlier, Lady Clary is discreet."

They sat in silence for some moments before he said, "Don't you think Karigan has done her share?"

"I admit she does seem to end up with the weightiest assignments." Laren decided she'd best step carefully to quell his anger. "The combination of her ability and experience, and, frankly, her skill at handling herself in difficult situations, explains why, don't you think?"

"Difficult situations? Like nearly being flogged to death? Gods, Laren, you did not see what . . . what was done to her." He shook his head. "Yes, she handled all that very well."

He still had, Laren thought, unexpressed rage burning inside him from all that had happened up north. She was not going to get through to him with this mood upon him. Fortunately, Lady Clary returned at that moment.

"Your Rider will soon get her bath," she said. "She is quite remarkable, meeting with p'ehdrose, traveling with Eletians, and speaking to eagles. I am so pleased to have met her."

"Yes, she is remarkable," Zachary said, and he stood. "More than you can know. I do thank you for your kindness toward her, and for your hospitality to all of us, but I must return to my troops now. I've much to discuss with my officers."

"Do you wish me to attend?" Laren asked.

"I will simply be reiterating what we've learned from Rider G'ladheon, so there is no need. However, you *will* notify me if she remembers anything else she wishes to convey." He then bade them goodnight, Lady Clary accompanying him to the entryway.

Laren removed the orb from her pocket and gazed speculatively at it. Her reflection was distorted in its silvery surface. Perhaps they didn't necessarily need it to be Karigan who went back to rescue the prisoners.

When Laren returned to her guest room, she found Elgin snoring in her chair, a polishing rag in his hand. She should have made him stay behind in Sacor City. He was not a young man and the journey had been harder on him than her. She gently shook his wrist.

"Chief?" she said. "Chief, wake up."

"Wha-a-a?"

"You were dozing."

He looked groggily about. "Asleep? Nah, I was just resting my eyes."

"Of course. If your eyes are rested, I wonder if you might go find Tegan and help her gather some uniform parts for Karigan. Everything needs to be replaced, and Tegan ought to be able to judge Karigan's size."

"Karigan? What in bloody hells did I miss?"

Laren told him, and displayed the travel device on the palm of her hand.

"So that little thing is what gave the Raiders the advantage over us," he said.

"It would seem so." If only she knew how to work it.

"I see that look in your eye," Elgin said. "You aren't thinking about doing anything stupid, are ya?"

"Of course not." She placed the orb on the table beside his chair. "Please do as I ask and go find Tegan."

"I'll do that, Red." He dropped the rag into a bucket with other polishing tools and pushed himself out of the chair. She watched him leave.

Once he was through the door, she closed it softly behind him and turned about, taking in her luxurious room filled with furniture upholstered in velvet and silk, and a huge postered bed that had steps one must ascend to reach the high mattress. It would be so easy just to go to bed and leave everything for the next day, but the shiny orb drew her eye like a crow to a silver coin.

She strode to the table and took the orb in hand again. It appeared to be divided into two halves with a hairline groove around its circumference. Karigan had not explained how she made the device work, except that she told it where she wanted to go.

I could bring my daughter to safety now. I could rescue her and my Riders just like that.

It sat glistening on her palm in the lamplight as she considered for a long moment. Then she shook her head.

"No," she murmured.

She was too disciplined, knew how badly so rash a decision could end. She'd too many years of command not to see how much more successfully a rescue could go with proper planning. They had the travel device, and they would use it to best effect against Second Empire and the Darrow Raiders. It would not be just one person against all of them, but the full backing of Zachary's army and her Riders.

She set the orb back down on the table and sat in Elgin's chair. She picked up a book she'd borrowed from Lady Clary's extensive collection with the hope of relaxing before she went to bed. It was a tome of a novel by a Second Age author who had practically invented the form, but she did not know how much time passed before she realized she'd been turning pages without taking anything in. Her mind was too much on the plight of Melry and her Riders. She glanced at the orb and was surprised to see it emitting a red glow from the fine script on its surface.

Curious. She picked it up only for it to start quivering on her palm.

"What the—?"

The quivering intensified and the two halves of the orb rotated in opposing directions. *Home,* a calm voice said in her mind.

The world reeled and Laren was swept away, swept away in a whirlwind to someplace new. She sprawled headlong onto the ground. Her surroundings spun around her, and the orb rolled off her open hand and away. She closed her eyes against the sickening disorientation.

"Well, well," said a man.

She dared to squint to see who spoke, and gritted her teeth against the vertigo. The face of a leering skull looked down on her. Tent walls rippled in the background.

"What a gift the gods have brought me," said Torq, leader of the Darrow Raiders. "The Red Witch in the flesh."

She frantically reached after the orb, but he stepped on her wrist and placed his weight on it. She felt her bones straining and she grunted with the pain.

"Did you not know that after a certain amount of time and use," he said, "the orb must come home to restore its power?"

Even as she watched, the orb floated into the air and then flew across a table and deposited itself into a gold, jeweled coffer. The coffer's lid immediately snapped shut of its own accord.

The pressure on her wrist ended when Torq knelt beside her. He grabbed her braid and yanked her head back to bare her throat. He placed the edge of a knife there. "I think it was time we caught up, yes?"

⊰ THE SKIN OF
A MONSTER ⊱

Brown hair clippings wafted at Karigan's feet. "Thank you," she told Tegan as she studied her reflection in the full-length mirror. Not only had Tegan brought her fresh uniform parts to wear, but she offered to trim her hair, something she had a knack for, and for which many Green Riders sought her out. The unruly mop had been evened out, and now it would grow in more uniformly.

"Glad I could help, even in such a small way," Tegan said. While she worked, she'd hesitantly asked what had happened to Karigan's hair. When Karigan explained that Nyssa had cut off her braid with a knife to keep it out of the way of flogging, Tegan blanched.

"Your help is no small thing," Karigan said. "I appreciate it more than you know." Her hair had once fallen below her shoulders and she'd taken some pride in it, which Nyssa most certainly recognized, and knew that cutting it off was another way to hurt her. But now, the trim lessened the hurt, allowed Karigan to reclaim some small control over her life when so often she'd been at the mercy of others.

"Anytime you want another trim, just ask." Tegan's smile of pleasure told Karigan it had given her friend a measure of relief that she could do something to help.

It had almost felt like old times as they gossiped together about all the doings in the Rider wing and Sacor City. After Tegan cleaned up and headed downstairs, Karigan gazed back into the mirror. It was the first time she'd a good look at herself since leaving Sacor City in late winter. In her reflection she saw hardship, how her grungy clothes hung off her, a scar on her cheek visible when she angled her face into the light just right, dark circles beneath her eyes. But the haircut had made a difference, and the overdue bath would do wonders. She would definitely smell better! She glanced at the steaming tub and thought she should get to it before it cooled off.

But first . . . First, now that she was alone, there was something else she had to see. She bolted the door to make sure no one would walk in unexpectedly. Then she slipped off her clothes and unwound the bandage that dressed the wound given her by the swordsman. From the dressing table she took the hand mirror and used it to look over her shoulder and survey her back as reflected in the full-length mirror.

She tried to examine the damage as a mender might, dispassionately, as if it were not her own. Oddly, it was the boniness of her spine that caught her attention first, the protruding nobs that looked like they belonged to some strange creature rather than a human being. She then took in the scars, the wounds left by the torturer's whip. These, too, seemed the markings of a deformed beast. How could it be her? How could anyone not see her as anything but grotesque? A monster.

It is art, Nyssa said with obvious pride. *You were one of my best canvases.*

Karigan did not reply or fight or protest. She simply gazed at where leather and wire barbs had torn away strips of her skin, ripped her open, leaving furrows gouged into her back. Some of the scars had healed raised. Some of the lines were spidery, others deep and sure and straight. Some were more healed than others. She would not have healed at all if not for the mending skill of Enver. He had surely saved her life, and without him, the mass of scarring wounds would look even worse.

Suddenly depleted, she sank to the floor and hugged her knees to her chest. She did not weep. She was beyond tears, but there was grief for the person she had once been, the girl, the young woman, who had known life without torture. Nyssa had changed everything and Karigan would never be that person again.

Eventually she rose and, without once gazing into the

mirror again, stepped into the blissful heat of the tub. As she settled into the water, she grimaced at how it stung her wound, but then her muscles relaxed; she dozed off and dreamed. Not nightmares, not of Nyssa and her whip, but amorous dreams of Zachary sharing her bed, their arms and legs entwined, his skin hot against hers. She was unscarred in this dream, wore no patch over her eye. She was not a monster, but the Karigan who had not known hardship or injury. His hands caressed the length of her smooth, unblemished back and buttocks, and moved to more delicious, private places. So potent was the dreaming that she awoke overheated even in the cooling bath water. She stepped out of the tub and padded dripping to the wash basin to throw cold water on her face. A need was on her to go to him that instant, not just to dream.

Steady, girl, she told herself, and she practically poured the whole pitcher of water over her head and the back of her neck.

She wrapped herself in a towel and dropped into a chair. The cool evening air raised goosebumps on her arms. Had seeing him earlier triggered the dream? That longing to have his hands and lips on her and—

She got up and poured the rest of the pitcher over her head. Her need for him pulled on her like a wild horse she could not control. A wild, *lustful* horse.

"Dear gods," she muttered as she dripped over the basin. How was it going to be when she saw him for real again, probably in the morning? Then she remembered she was no longer the young, unscarred woman in the dream, but that she now wore the skin of a monster. What man would want her? Her heightened ardor diminished even as a small inner voice told her, *Zachary would.* She could not allow herself to believe it. He was beyond her reach, anyway.

Her morose thoughts were interrupted by a sickening, familiar sensation that washed over her. She staggered out into the hall wrapped in her towel, holding herself up with her hand against the wall, her stomach churning. Tegan pounded up the stairs followed by Lady Clary and some servants.

"What the hells was that?" Tegan demanded.

"The travel device," Karigan replied. "It's been used."

"Who had it last?" Lady Clary asked.

"The colonel."

The vertigo eased and they made their way to the colonel's room. Karigan pounded on the door, and when no one answered, she flung it open and they all filed in. The room was, as she expected, empty. A book sat open on the table, the pages fluttering in the air current.

"Did she—?" Tegan began.

Drops of water, now turned icy cold, slipped down Karigan's neck and shoulders. "She must have. You didn't see her leave?" she asked Lady Clary.

"Rider Oldbrine and I have been having tea down in the parlor discussing the Oldbrine dye works. No one has come or gone."

Karigan faced Tegan. "She must have used the device to go after Melry and the others."

They made a hasty search of the room for the orb but could not find it.

"We need to inform the king immediately," Karigan said. "If she is caught—"

"—the Raiders will have their Red Witch," Tegan finished, and she sprinted for the stairs.

Without a second thought, Karigan pelted after her leaving behind a trail of droplets. She did not slow down until she was out of the house, across the street, and at the village square. Tegan had already turned around and walked toward her.

"I ran into Donal," Tegan said. "He will inform the king, but he'll likely have questions for us. Not that we have answers. Uh, you might want to get dressed for that."

"What?"

"Remember Darden?"

Karigan looked down at herself. What the hells was she thinking running outside in only a towel? Well, she was thinking her colonel was—

Karigan?

She looked up into the sky at the familiar voice, though she could only see the darkness of night beyond the street lamps. "Ripaeria?"

"Ry-peer-what?" Tegan said.

You are there! the eagle cried in a plaintive voice. *You vanished away and I've been searching.*

"Um, Karigan, you all right?" Tegan asked.

"I'm fine," Karigan reassured both the eagle and Tegan, "but our colonel has gone missing."

"I know," Tegan said. "I was—"

Tree branches tossed and rattled with the backdraft of enormous wings as Ripaeria landed in the square. Horses nearby neighed in fright, and a pair of constables on duty fell back in surprise, then drew their weapons.

"No!" Karigan cried. "She's a friend." She ran into the square to where Ripaeria had landed.

"This is who you've been talking to?" Tegan said.

"Tegan, this is Ripaeria of the Wing Song Mountains. She helped me escape at the pass. She is very brave."

"And very beautiful," Tegan said in awe.

Ripaeria preened at the praise.

"And Ripaeria, this is my friend, Tegan Oldbrine. She's a Green Rider, like me."

Very honored, the eagle said.

Tegan jumped. "I heard that! In my head!"

At that moment, several booted feet pounded up to them, and Ripaeria shied, stretching her wings as though to take off.

"Wait," Karigan said. "This is Sacoridia's king and some of his advisors."

The ones with hands on their swords?

"His protectors. Stand down," she told the Weapons. "This is Ripaeria and she is a friend."

More introductions were made and Zachary bowed in a courtly manner to Ripaeria, who seemed very pleased by the gesture.

"It would appear we have an emergency," he told the eagle. "The leader of our Green Riders, and my trusted advisor and friend, has vanished with the arcane device Rider G'ladheon liberated from the enemy." He glanced at Karigan, then took a second look, eyes widening. He cleared his throat. "We fear she will encounter trouble, get caught trying to rescue those of our people who remain captive." Without pausing, he removed his longcoat and placed it over Karigan's shoulders. She felt the heat creep up from her neck into her cheeks, and something of her bath time dream flashed in her mind, which only intensified the feeling, especially embraced by the pleasant scent of him rising from his coat.

"Is there some way the eagle can help?" General Washburn asked gruffly. "Maybe go take a look and see what's happening in the enemy camp?"

Ripaeria said, *I am not an owl. I can see in the night better than an ordinary tiny eagle, but not that well.*

The general grimaced at hearing the eagle's voice in his mind.

"If all has gone well, Colonel Mapstone should return any moment with our people," Karigan said. "The travel is instantaneous."

They all looked anxiously about as if the colonel would suddenly appear before them, bringing the captive Riders and her daughter along with her. She did not, and the ominous feeling that had been growing on Karigan only intensified.

"We need to go after her," she said.

A look from Zachary indicated his concern, as well, and suddenly she realized there was no more likely chance of a rescue mission than there had been before.

"I am afraid we'd never make it in time," Les Tallman said, "even without the army behind us."

They knew what it meant: that if Colonel Laren Mapstone of His Majesty's Messenger Service was not dead already, she would be soon.

❧ PLUMAGE ❧

There had to be something they could do. If the colonel had fallen into Raider hands and was slain, there would be nothing holding the Raiders back from killing the others, as well. Karigan couldn't let this happen, she just couldn't.

"I'll take the Riders," Connly said. "We can ride swiftly."

"Not likely swiftly enough, I'm afraid," General Washburn said, pity in his eyes.

Karigan looked at the faces around her, and all held that look of resignation. "You're all just going to give up?"

"Karigan," Zachary began, his eyes full of sorrow.

Failed again, have you, Greenie? Nyssa's voice and laugh wormed into her mind. She suddenly felt so tired, so useless. What hope was there?

Ripaeria looked up then and cocked her head. She made some inarticulate vocalization Karigan interpreted as eagle for, *uh oh.*

A wind rushed down on them that shredded leaves and pinecones from tree limbs. Ripaeria sidestepped to make room for another larger, gray eagle to land. A pouch hung slung around its neck, and incredibly, a man sat upon its back.

"Two in one night," someone said. "Unbelievable."

Ripaeria and the newcomer engaged in what appeared to be an argument consisting of screeches and other vocalizations, and silences that must have been mind-to-mind communication. After a short time of this, Ripaeria shrank into herself as if chastened.

This is my esteemed uncle, she told the assembled in a meek voice. *Softfeather of Snowcloud Eyrie.*

213

"Softfeather!" Karigan cried, and she stepped forward.

He gazed down his long beak at her with his intense raptor eyes. He blinked slowly. *I remember you. The Green Rider who helped me destroy the creature of Kanmorhan Vane some years ago. Well met. It is good to see you well and surprisingly alive.*

Karigan let the last pass unremarked. His "voice" was much deeper than Ripaeria's, and with his arrival, it became clear that Ripaeria was very young as Karigan had suspected.

I apologize for this intrusion and any disruption my wayward niece has caused you, Softfeather said. *She was told not to meddle in human affairs, only to keep watch, but she is young and headstrong.*

If it were possible, Ripaeria seemed to shrink even more into a large feathery ball.

"May I make proper introductions?" Karigan asked.

"Please do," Zachary said, gazing at the two eagles in wonder.

When this was done, the man on Softfeather's back said, "What about me?"

Softfeather closed his nictating eyelids, and it seemed the equivalent of a human eye roll. *Of course,* the eagle said. *This is Duncan.*

Karigan suddenly remembered Ripaeria mentioning a human male who lived with them at the eyrie. That must be quite a story.

The man slid off Softfeather's back and stood with his hands on his hips. "Yes, I am Duncan, and I cannot tell you how pleased I am to be off the ledge and among humans again. When I heard where Softfeather was going, I made him bring me along."

He was a virile specimen of a man with a chiseled, square chin, his hair swept back just so, and a muscular build accentuated by his choice of trousers and shirt, the latter of the overly tight variety leaving little to imagination. His shirt was open to the middle of his chest, and she wondered if it was cold flying thus attired.

He in turn was gazing at her, and not at her face either. She tightened her hold on her towel and shrugged deeper into Zachary's longcoat.

"Interesting nightwear," Duncan commented. His smile was perfect and beautiful. A little too perfect. "The coat kind of ruins the effect, however."

"Who are you?" Zachary demanded. He stepped forward as if to make Duncan back off from Karigan.

Duncan did not, but made a graceful, sweeping bow, his gaze trailing down Karigan's body as he did so. "I am a humble mage, Your Gracious Majesty." Then he gave the Weapons present a keen look. "Your dark wardens of ages past failed to slay me, or imprison me in one of the towers of the D'Yer Wall."

The assembled erupted with questions and generally chattered all at once. Duncan looked quite pleased by the effect he was having on his audience.

"A mage, as in a great mage?" Karigan asked. "You knew Merdigen, Itharos, and the others?"

"Oh, I knew them all. They were my teachers, but they were hidebound, had no imagination, and so I struck out on my own."

My ancestors gave him sanctuary during the Scourge, Softfeather said. *And so we are stuck with him.*

"And I remained stuck at the eyrie of the Snowclouds for centuries. I've known Softfeather since he was an egg."

"If that is the case, then—" Karigan poked him, but her finger traveled through nothing but air. "You are like the others, an illusion."

He placed his hand over his heart. "No, dear lady, I am a *projection* of the great mage, Duncan."

Karigan gazed at the pouch hanging around Softfeather's neck. She'd heard a bit about Alton's experiences with the tower mages and had met Merdigen. "And Softfeather is carrying your tempes stone so you can be, er, present."

"That is *very* personal information," he said.

Oh, there is more than a tempes stone in this pouch, Softfeather said, *to allow him to exist among us.*

"Softfeather," Duncan said in a warning voice.

The eagle clacked his beak shut and said no more.

"This is all very interesting," Zachary said, "but we have something of a crisis on our hands."

Then I shall take my niece away immediately, Softfeather said.

"Please stay, if you would. I understand Ripaeria has been of some assistance to Rider G'ladheon."

Against the wishes of her elders and our Lord Drannonair.

"Ripaeria saved my life," Karigan told Softfeather, "as you once did."

Someone needed to slay the creature of Kanmorhan Vane, he replied, *and there you were, and able to use a sword, too.*

"The fact of the matter is," Zachary said, "that there has been some mutual aid between your folk and mine. We were allies during the Long War." He outlined for Softfeather the situation with the colonel and the other captives.

I like him, your king, Ripaeria told Karigan, and Karigan was pretty sure she directed her comment to her only. *He is well-spoken and strong. His plumage is admirable. Or would be, to a human, and his displays subtle but unmistakable.*

His plumage? His displays? Karigan glanced at Zachary anew.

He watches you a lot when he thinks you do not notice, Ripaeria observed. *His blood runs hot because of your plumage.*

Karigan coughed and reddened.

I feel sure he desires you as a mate. Did you not see how he challenged Duncan? Yes, I think he is worthy. You should mate and nest.

Heat flushed through Karigan's body. Ripaeria the eagle was telling her to—to *nest* with Zachary.

*You are surprised by this? You respond to his plumage and displays as an interested eagless would. I also sense between the two of you, the—*and here was a vocalization no human could interpret.

Karigan was so mortified she didn't know how to respond except to ask, *What is—is that thing you just said?*

I do not have the human expression for it. "Bond" for a mated pair is not strong enough. But when a pair has this thing, ah, it is the stuff of romantic ballads. Eagles are great poets, you know.

I, uh, didn't know, Karigan told her. Might she be referring to something like "true heart mates"? It was also the stuff of romantic ballads in the human world.

I like that, Ripaeria said. *It expresses what I mean. I see that your hearts are bonded.*

Karigan could not believe she was having this conversation with a bird, albeit a magnificent one. Ripaeria's eyes glittered in the lamplight, and she made a chuckling noise.

It cannot be done, Softfeather was saying.

"What cannot be done?" Karigan asked, wondering what she had missed while discussing "plumage" with Ripaeria.

"Your general wishes to ride eagleback into battle," Duncan answered, "like I can. But he weighs far too much." When General Washburn began to sputter, he added, "You all do. I am weightless, and so Softfeather can manage me."

The eagles of the mountains were much larger and stronger in the past, Softfeather said, *and though they found such conveyance distasteful, as I personally still do, it is said to have happened during times of dire need. But alas, we are a diminished people from what we once were.*

"The alliance between our people," Zachary said, "has never been terminated, not since its creation over a thousand years ago. Is there no way you can aid us? Our need is urgent to reach the mountains."

Softfeather stood there, wings tightly folded to his sides, beak lowered.

"He does not want to get in trouble with Drannonair, do you, old boy?" Duncan said.

Softfeather gave the great mage a fierce look. *Remember who it is that carries your entire existence in a pouch.*

Duncan put his hands up as if warding against a blow. "I am only speaking the truth of the matter. But it *is* possible that *I* may be able to help."

"You?" the general scoffed.

"Yes, me. I may be a mere projection of the great mage I once was, but I still have, shall we say, access to a few abilities."

"Then please," Zachary said, "if there is a way for you to help us—"

"Tut, tut," said Duncan. "I do have a condition."

"And that is?"

Duncan smiled.

Karigan lugged the pouch containing Duncan's tempes stone, and whatever else was in there, over her shoulder and into Lady Clary's house. It was not light, but Duncan refused to help with a rescue unless it was *she* who carried it. She glanced out the door where Zachary continued to speak with Softfeather about the old alliance. Meanwhile, many of the others had scattered to make preparations for the rescue. Karigan was not best pleased by Duncan's plan, but she could think of no other alternative. She closed the door behind her.

"Very nice," Duncan said as he strode beside her and looked around. "Look at all the art, the soaring ceiling. No dingy keep is this. Humanity has progressed."

"Haven't you been in a house recently?" Karigan asked. She shivered as she stepped onto the marble floor with her bare feet.

"No. You would think living with eagles would allow you to go many places, but they just fly about from eyrie to eyrie, or go hunting. It's quite boring, actually. And yes, they may be poets, but you hear one eagle ballad, you've heard them all." He leaned in toward Karigan. "You should probably clothe yourself, my dear, before you catch a chill."

That was her intention. She started up the stairs holding Zachary's coat tight around her. Softfeather had looked so relieved, nay, *joyous,* to hand the pouch over to her. She made him promise to take it—thus, Duncan—back when all was said and done.

The mage followed her up the stairs, admiring everything from the millwork to the rugs to the sculptures. "Very civilized. Much better than the cliff."

Karigan supposed it would be. She entered her guestroom and let the pouch slide off her shoulder onto a chair.

Duncan jumped onto the bed. His action did not disturb the covers or mattress, but he stretched out like he could really feel it beneath him. "Oh, very nice." He patted the space beside him. "Join me?"

She scowled at him and picked up the uniforms Tegan had brought her.

"Now don't be like that, dear lady. It has been many a year since I've had the privilege of female company. Er, human female company, at any rate. You know, women did always find me irresistible." He tossed his hair back just so.

Dear gods, Karigan thought. What had she gotten herself into?

She stepped behind a screen to change. She removed Zachary's coat, taking in the scent of him as she did so.

"Nice shoulders," Duncan said, suddenly there beside her.

She squawked and dropped the coat. "Get out!"

"But—"

She pointed to the other side of the screen. "Get *out!* Or I will drop your tempes stone to the bottom of a lake."

"Easy now, dear lady." He backed away *through* the screen as though she were a wild mare about to trample him. "But do not forget who is getting you to the mountains within a few minutes instead of a few days, eh?"

She was beginning to regret their agreement that she be the steward of his pouch in exchange for his getting them to the mountains quickly. If he tried anything like that again, she *would* throw it in a lake, or at least out the window.

Once she had rebandaged her wound and dressed, she felt much better and not at all chilled. The uniform pieces were indeed a bit baggy on her, but they'd serve. The boots, however, were perfect, and it was even better that they were already broken in.

"Well, well," Duncan said when she emerged from behind the screen.

She ignored him and took up the pouch again, and with Zachary's coat draped over her arm, she left the comfortable room with some regret. She could really use several days of sleep, but the colonel and her fellow Riders came first.

She trotted down the stairs and found Lady Clary awaiting her.

"I wanted to wish you the best of luck," the countess said.

"Thank you," Karigan replied. "You've been most gracious, and I only wish I could have stayed longer."

"Perhaps another time. You would be quite welcome. I was wondering if I might have a private word with you before you depart." She looked significantly at Duncan.

When Duncan did not move, Karigan strode down the corridor and set the pouch on a chair. "Stay," she told him.

He crossed his arms and, with a petulant look, said, "I am not a dog." But he obeyed as Karigan returned to the countess.

"These are very strange days," Lady Clary said, "with all the magic returning to the world." She shook her head. "But what I wanted to talk to you about has nothing to do with magic. Rather, I wish to warn you."

"About what?"

Lady Clary hesitated, then said, "The danger of kings."

THE DANGER
OF KINGS

"The danger of—?" Karigan faltered.

"I saw how King Zachary looked at you," Lady Clary said. "It is obvious to at least me that there is rapport between the two of you. Perhaps more. I admire all that I've heard of you just this night. Not just a messenger, but knighted, and a hero of some repute. Both King Zachary and Colonel Mapstone were glowing in their comments about you. I also see that you are a grown woman, but still young, and perhaps not as sophisticated in regards to the world in which kings and queens inhabit."

"I'm sorry, Countess, but I don't really have time for—"

Lady Clary placed her hand on Karigan's wrist. "Please hear me out. I do not mean to criticize, but to help. You see, I have been around influential people my whole life. Not just influential, mind, but the ruling class. Our King Zachary is a good and just ruler, but you should know that people who wield such power can change on a whim. One moment you are their favored servant, and then the next? One should never forget kings are above us all and it is they who make the rules over which we, their servants, must abide. Kings can turn on one without provocation no matter how much we are presumed a friend or are favored."

Zachary, Karigan thought, was not like that. "If that is all—"

"No," Lady Clary said. "There is more. You should also know that those held close by a king are also targets. They are in danger from others jealous of his attention, or wanting something from him, or those suspicious of the undue

influence a favored servant may bring. It is even more dangerous if it is feared one may supplant the queen's position."

Karigan was horrified. What had brought Lady Clary to
say such things? Had anything she said, or had been said by
Zachary, caused the countess to draw certain conclusions?
No, she thought, not what had been said, precisely, but what
had been done. She'd been out of it when she was brought to
Lady Clary's house. Using the travel device so many times
had depleted her, and then one of the constables had hit her
over the head. A very dim memory came back to her of being
carried up to her room, of being held in arms that made her
feel safe, protected. The next she remembered was Zachary
sitting beside her as she lay on the bed, concern and, yes, love,
in his eyes. And Lady Clary had seen it all.

She glanced down at Zachary's coat draped over her arm.
It wasn't just anyone who had offered their coat to keep her
warm while she stood wrapped in only a towel out in the
square. No, it had been Zachary, king of Sacoridia.

Oh, dear. Aloud, she said, "You don't think—"

"It does not matter what *I* think. It is what others may
perceive. Cemeteries are filled with the remains of those who
were not cautious in their dealings with kings. You head off
to battle this night, but also, every moment others suspect the
king's favor of you, you are in danger. In their minds, they
presume favoritism and access equate with undue power. The
royal court is a different kind of battlefield. I hope you accept
my words out of friendship as no malice is intended. I just do
not wish to see you hurt, and appearances have been the undoing of many a good soul."

Karigan did not know what to say, so she stammered her
thanks and a farewell to Lady Clary, collected the pouch and
Duncan, and headed out into the night, attempting to absorb
Lady Clary's words.

"Got a real lecture, didn't you," Duncan said. "So, are you
the king's favored mistress?"

She turned on him. "You heard our conversation? And
NO, I am not."

"My hearing as a projection is actually more acute than if
I were corporeal."

She would have to remember that. Lady Clary's words filled her mind. No, she could never believe Zachary would turn on her. He wasn't like that. Power had not corrupted him. The rest, however, she could believe, the petty jealousies of others wanting the access and favor for themselves. Her own life had already been in danger because of this. Before the Blackveil expedition, Estora's cousin, a courtier, had believed she would interfere with the impending marriage between Zachary and Estora. He'd gone so far as to send an assassin with the expedition to kill her. Clan Coutre had had much to lose if the marriage failed to go through.

She tried to shake off Lady Clary's warning, and put her mind to the task at hand. To her wonder, she found the square full of Green Riders tightening girths, mounting up, and digging into saddlebags. There were several cheery, "Hello, Karigan!" greetings. Lanterns and street lamps gleamed on the cuirasses and helms each Rider wore. Softfeather and Ripaeria were nowhere to be seen, and so must have already departed for the mountains. She espied Zachary speaking to some of his officers. With Lady Clary's words fresh in her mind, she hesitated, but then took a deep breath and strode up to him.

"That will be all," Zachary told his officers. They bowed and left him, the gazes of a few of them lingering on Karigan. What did they suspect? Her heart hammered in her chest when he turned to her. "Yes, Rider?" he asked. His gaze fluttered over her shoulder, and suddenly she remembered Duncan.

She bowed her head. "I wish to return your coat, Your Majesty. I thank you for its use."

"I am pleased it helped." He accepted the coat with a small bow of his own.

Karigan was aware of Duncan watching the exchange with rather too much interest. "I, uh, guess I'd better find a horse."

"Before you go," he replied, "might I have a quiet word with you? Alone?"

"Yes. Of course. One moment." She walked over to Brandall.

"What are you doing?" Duncan asked.

"Could you hold on to this for a moment?" she asked Brandall.

"Sure."

"Thanks." She slipped the pouch off her shoulder and handed it to him. To Duncan she whispered, "No eavesdropping."

"But—"

She shook her head curtly and returned to where she'd left Zachary. He stood there straight and tall with his hands clasped behind his back. His beard had grown nicely since she'd seen him in the north. She smiled.

They strolled over to a quiet corner of the square where it was unlikely anyone would overhear their conversation. Lady Clary's words about the danger of kings remained fresh in her thoughts, and she was conscious of how others might perceive Zachary having a private word with her. She made sure not to stand too close to him.

"I won't detain you long," he said, "but we haven't had a chance to speak. I . . ." He seemed strangely at a loss for words. "I was very concerned when you did not return to Sacor City; then I heard you'd been captured by the Raiders. I also missed you. A great deal."

She glanced back into the square where the Riders continued to make adjustments to their gear in preparation for leaving. They were not paying any attention whatsoever. However, there were a few villagers awakened by the late night activity observing the goings on, and some, indeed, were gazing in the direction of their king. It was, for many of them, a once-in-a-lifetime opportunity to see the man who ruled over them, and so it was not surprising they watched him.

She opened her mouth to speak, but he shook his head. "I know it is complicated between us, but I wanted you to know you have been greatly in my thoughts and I want you to come home safely."

She nodded. It seemed they were always taking leave of one another. "I have often thought of you, too." It seemed a safe enough thing to say, but her dreams played unbidden through her mind. Once again their sensuous nature overheated her and she resisted the urge to fan her face.

Zachary smiled down at her. "There is one more thing. Fastion?" The Weapon stepped forward from the shadows

and handed him a small oblong box. "With the recent promotions, it came to our attention that the Chief Rider position
claims no special insignia. Your colonel thought that wrong,
and I agreed. I know she would have liked to give you this
herself, and she had brought it along in hopes of recovering
you alive and well from the Raiders."

He opened the box and inside lay a brooch in the form of
a gold feather. It was about the length of her hand.

"It's gorgeous," she said, and it was, for it had been made
with an eye for detail, and it shone brightly in the lamplight.

He removed the feather from the box. "From now on, the
Chief Rider will always be known by a gold feather. This one
was made by the royal jeweler."

Such a fine thing, she thought, for a lowly common
messenger.

He stepped close to pin it to her coat, and the heat intensified. She forced herself to stand steady and breathe naturally. It was a relief when he stepped back. He seemed to
admire the feather on her, and then nodded in approval.

"Congratulations, Chief Rider Sir Karigan G'ladheon," he
said.

"Thank you," she murmured.

He gazed into the square. "I suggest you get ready or
they'll leave without you." When she hesitated, he said, "That
is all, Rider. For now."

She bowed again, wondering about the "for now," and hastened back among her fellow Riders. She collected the pouch
from Brandall.

"Nice bauble," Duncan remarked, pointing at the feather.

"New insignia," she said.

She looked about for the little mare she'd borrowed from
the guards in Sacor City, but instead, she spotted Tegan and
Elgin jogging toward her with a spotted horse in tow.

"Loon?" she said.

Elgin grinned even as he huffed and puffed, and Karigan
was further astonished to note he was attired in Rider green
though he wore no brooch.

"Good to see ya, lass," he said. "Your Condor isn't here,
so it makes sense for you to ride your colonel's horse. He's

fast! She can have him back when we find her. I'll be ponying Bluebird in the rearguard."

"That all right with you?" she asked Loon.

The gelding tossed his head high and whinnied. It was answered by several of the other horses packed into the square.

"I take it that's a yes," Karigan said with a smile.

"It'll have to be, I guess," Elgin said. "He and Bluebird are riled up with their mistress gone, and Loon still being so young might be a handful."

"I understand." As Karigan recalled, it was Loon who had caused the colonel to dislocate her shoulder in early spring. He practically danced in place, eager to be off to rescue his Rider. They'd get a sense from him and Bluebird as to the colonel's situation through their bond with her. So far, Loon appeared upset, but not so much that it made her think the Raiders had killed the colonel.

"I also took the liberty of borrowing a couple of the colonel's things for you to use," Tegan said. She helped Karigan buckle on the colonel's cuirass, which fit well, but was definitely an unfamiliar addition to her usual gear.

Tegan tapped her own cuirass. "These are discards from the light cavalry."

"Discards? Really?" The cuirass was polished and ornamented with a delicate filigreed pattern. There was nary a sign of wear on it that she could see.

"You know how the light cav is," Tegan replied. Then, "This is the colonel's saber."

"Tegan, I can't."

"You can't go unarmed."

"I can't use it. My back. It's not strong enough yet."

Elgin whispered in Tegan's ear and she nodded. "The colonel will need her saber when we find her, just like she'll need Loon, so you might as well carry it even if you don't use it."

Karigan protested no further at their logic and belted on the sword, along with its matching longknife.

"Your saddlebags are provisioned so you are all set." Tegan then hurried off to get herself ready.

Elgin tightened Loon's girth and held the reins while Karigan mounted. The wound on her side stung as she stretched it pulling herself into the saddle. The colonel was a smaller person, so Karigan had to lengthen the stirrup leathers.

"Loon's a good-hearted horse," Elgin told Karigan, "but untried in battle. He'll do his best for you though." He handed up Duncan's pouch and left her so he, too, could prepare.

Duncan vanished one moment only to reappear sitting behind her on Loon. She could not feel him there, and Loon seemed unperturbed by his additional, weightless, passenger.

Connly nudged his gray mare, Will, short for Whip-poor-will, over to her. "Trace will stay with the king's host so we can keep each other apprised of our progress and what we encounter." Their complementary special abilities allowed them to communicate with one another through their minds. "We are twenty-two strong going. The rest, some forty Riders, will also remain with the king's host. I would like you to speak to the group about what lies ahead."

At Connly's direction, she followed him so they could position themselves before the assembled messengers. As she looked upon so many Riders in green, some she knew, such as Tegan, Brandall, and Harry, and others she had yet to meet, she could not help but be proud to be one among them.

Connly stood up in his stirrups. "Riders," he said, "the night wanes and we are losing time. We are going to the mountains to rescue our own, but we will be traveling strange paths that will help us reach our destination in very little time. Only your Chief Rider has walked these paths, so she and the mage, Duncan, will speak on it to prepare you."

"We will be entering a transitional place," Karigan told them. "It will be unlike anywhere you've gone before." She'd been unhappy to hear Duncan's suggestion of using the "white world," which he called the "Blanding," to travel to the mountains. He could open a way for them, he said, with Karigan's help. She went on to describe the white plains, how disorienting they could be. "It is a place not of our world or corporeal existence. It may present images and symbols that look real, but are not. Do not panic, do not be deceived by anything you may see there. Anything you want to add?" she asked Duncan.

"I wish to stress that you do not stray, and do not cross any bridges we encounter under any circumstances, unless I lead you there."

Zachary then appeared at Karigan's stirrup. "If I could have a word or two?"

Connly bowed in his saddle. "Of course, sire."

Zachary turned to the assembled Riders. "You are a small group heading into enemy territory. Small, but swift and able. Do not forget, however, you will be dealing with Darrow Raiders. Their desire for vengeance is great, but your goal is not to engage with them, but to get our people out, then return to the main body of the host. Is that clear?"

The Riders responded with, "Yes, Your Majesty."

"Good," he said. "I expect you will do me and your colonel proud. May the gods hold you close."

With that, Connly ordered the Riders to move out. Zachary watched them go, his hands once more clasped behind his back. He watched them all, yes, but Karigan knew he especially watched her. She thought of the softness in his brown eyes when he looked at her. The true danger of her king, she thought, was what he did to her heart.

⤳ THE BLANDING ⤳

**"Y**ou need to use your ability now," Duncan said from behind Karigan. In his "diminished" state, he explained, he did not have as much access to etherea as he'd once had as a corporeal being. Karigan's ability to cross thresholds, he said, was all he needed to open the way into the Blanding.

While Connly and the rest of the Riders waited behind her, she touched her brooch and called on her fading ability.

"Very good," Duncan said. "Hold it until I say otherwise." He then spoke in a singsong language she did not know. Perhaps his words were incantations, for a mist grew before her eyes and Loon sidestepped beneath her. He paused, then spoke in the common tongue: "Enter. Walk into the mist."

She clucked Loon on, and sure enough, when they passed through the mist, Oxbridge Square, and the known world, disappeared behind them with only the white world stretching in all directions, a featureless white plain with a milky sky. All was silent, unless emptiness was a sound. The other Riders followed behind with gasps and exclamations of astonishment though they'd been told what to expect. The telling, of course, simply could not do it justice. The intensity of the white world was enough to wash out the green of their uniforms.

When Elgin, the last in line, rode through on his mare, Killdeer, and leading Bluebird behind him, Duncan told Karigan, "You may release your ability."

She did so, and in her vision, the white world became whiter, if such were possible. She rubbed her temple to ease its throbbing from the use of her ability. "Which way do we go?"

"It does not matter," Duncan replied.

"It doesn't?"

"We will arrive where we intend."

Karigan squeezed Loon on in the direction they faced.

"Remember," Connly told his Riders, "we stick together."

The air was still as they moved out, horse hooves thudding dully on the white ground. Loon was uneasy, sidestepping and tossing his head.

"Easy, boy," Karigan told him. She patted his neck when he quieted, and kept reassuring him with soft words of encouragement. He swiveled his ears to hear her voice. "That's a good boy."

It seemed odd to be riding a messenger horse other than her Condor. Condor was older and more experienced, and while maybe he wouldn't take the white world in stride, he would have been steady and solid. Loon had that flightier feel of a green horse. It helped that Will walked beside them. As mature as Condor, she had a calming influence on Loon. Perhaps, Karigan thought, they should bring Bluebird up front. Maybe he—

"What's that?" Connly asked.

A pile of rubble appeared before them. The stones were scorched black. White glared around the rubble as if affronted by the existence of any other color.

"A bridge," Duncan said. "Or, what's left of one."

Karigan had seen such on previous journeys through the white world, half-destroyed bridges with scorch marks on them.

"What happened to it?" Connly asked.

"Not all battles in our history occurred on the plane of reality," Duncan explained. "Magic users who were able to transcend the layers of the world entered the Blanding and built bridges that allowed them to move quickly from place to place. As you can imagine, the Blanding and its bridges were useful during times of war, but when the opposing side discovered what was happening, how war mages were sneaking up on them, they began to use the Blanding, too, and built bridges, as well. Inevitably, conflict among multiple factions erupted here."

"This was during the Long War?" Karigan asked.

"The Long War and those that came before. Back into the Black Ages. Maybe even before then. The Blanding has always been."

Chatter died among the Riders as the ruined bridge fell behind them. They rode on in the heavy silence. Even the horses seemed to keep as quiet as possible. The sameness of the terrain and sky made it seem as though they simply moved in place, making no forward progress. It was impossible to tell how much time passed. Weariness settled over Karigan like an oppressive weight. Was it really the same night she'd rescued Renn's family with the Raiders' travel device? The same night she'd then "traveled" to Oxbridge and the colonel vanished? Was it still night in the real world? Was there a real world where night existed?

Do you exist, Greenie? Nyssa asked in a hushed voice.

Karigan sat upright, realized she'd been slumping over Loon's neck. Mist rolled away before her like gauze pulled across her eyes. She recalled that it usually presaged something unpleasant was about to appear.

"What is it?" Duncan asked. "Do you see something?"

A figure materialized as the mist peeled away in layers. She was as Karigan remembered, her cruel smile, her clothes splattered with blood, a whip clenched in her fist. She stood there more real and alive than in any nightmare. Blood dripped from the whip and stained the white ground. The stain spread.

Loon, sensing Karigan's distress, snorted and tossed his head. A choked cry left her throat and her hands shook, rattling the reins.

"What's wrong?" Connly asked.

"The Blanding is showing her something," Duncan answered.

"Don't you see her? Doesn't anyone see her?" Karigan asked.

"Who?" Connly said.

I am here only for you, my pet, Nyssa told her, and she

grinned, her eyes dark pits as she watched Karigan pass by. *I will never leave you.*

Karigan kicked Loon into a gallop to get away.

"Dear lady!" a startled Duncan cried out. "Remember, it's not real!"

She heard Connly call after her, but then she hauled on the reins when Nyssa reappeared right in front of her.

I will always be here with you, Nyssa said.

The blood stain continued to expand beneath Loon's hooves, across the empty land, and even the sky, until the white world turned crimson. The skin of her hands was cast the color of old blood.

"No," she murmured. "No . . ."

"What is it?" Connly asked, once again beside her.

"Clearly, she's seeing a disturbing vision, a vision just for her," Duncan said.

"Karigan," Connly said, "there's nothing here, just us."

"Snap out of it, dear lady," Duncan said. "You know the nature of this place better than most."

Most had not been hearing Nyssa in their mind for months and dreaming of her.

"Karigan," Connly said quietly, "you are making the others nervous."

She raised her head, looked and saw no Nyssa, no whip, no blood, but plenty of Riders shifting in their saddles and looking uncertain. She loosed a rattling sigh, but her hands shook.

"What did you see?" Duncan asked.

"My torturer," she whispered. "Blood. Lots of blood."

"Oh. That would explain it."

"Explain what?" Connly asked.

"Why only she saw the vision. It was, I take it, highly personal."

"You could say that," Karigan replied bitterly.

"Everything all right up there?" Elgin called from the end of the line.

"Fine," Connly answered. "Karigan, do your best. We have to keep moving."

She nodded numbly, tried to compose herself. Here she was, the one who had warned everyone not to believe anything they saw in the white world, and yet who was the first to fall for its lies? She clenched her still-shaking hands, not able to look any of her fellow Riders in the eye.

"How much farther?" Connly asked Duncan.

"Hard to say. There is no exact measurement of time or distance in the Blanding."

They continued on, the horses trudging along for what felt like years. It was easy to let one's vision blur, for the landscape was all the same, without definition or character, taking on a mesmerizing quality reinforced by the staccato rhythm of plodding hoofbeats. On and on it went without relief, sensory or otherwise. The impression of a great deal of time passing when they needed to reach the mountains quickly made her anxious, and she tried to keep in mind Duncan's words about time moving differently in the white world.

To forget about Nyssa, she thought about Zachary instead, his kind eyes and reassuring presence, but soon started to drowse again, so bereft of sleep was she. The quiet conversation of the Riders became part of a half-dream where she was being draped in funeral shrouds, layer upon layer upon layer.

"What is that?" Connly said.

She dreamed they came to a burbling stream, and their surroundings were not white, but green and mossy. The shrouds fluttered away in a breeze.

"Oh, very good!" Duncan exclaimed. "I never expected to see it again."

Karigan shook herself awake. There was no stream, no moss, but an object that appeared before them. As they approached closer, she realized it was a large three-tiered fountain. Water spouted from the top and tinkled and chimed into the basins of the lower tiers. It seemed odd to hear so musical a sound after the dull silence of the white world. The presence of water, real or imagined, suddenly made her very thirsty.

Duncan disappeared from behind her and reappeared beside the fountain. Closer up, she could see on the surfaces of the basins depictions of gryphons and p'ehdrose and eagles, and even humans.

"Come!" Duncan exhorted the Riders. "Come, let your poor steeds drink from the Fountain of Winthorpe."

"It's real?" Karigan asked.

"I understand your skepticism," Duncan said. "There are few real things in the Blanding, but this is one, created by an elemental mage of a more altruistic nature named Winthorpe, who specialized in working with water. He knew the Blanding could be dry and featureless for the wanderer, so he established the fountain to slake the thirst and bring joy back to the heart."

"Don't anyone drink," Connly said, "until I make sure it's clean, that it won't sicken us or the horses."

"Heavens," Duncan said, "it will do anything but. Winthorpe used powerful magic to create it. He may have pulled the water from some other layer of the world, but it is wholesome."

"I'm still going to check first." Connly dismounted Will and strode up to the fountain. He let the water spill into his cupped hand, then sipped of it. "Tastes excellent," he reported. "I think it's safe."

It was too bad, Karigan thought, that Dale Littlepage was not with them. Her ability was to find good, drinkable water, and she could verify its safety, but Tegan had told Karigan that Dale had been ordered to return to duty at the D'Yer Wall.

"Well, you're not dead yet," said Brandall. "Can we let the horses drink?"

Connly grinned. "Yes, everyone take a break."

All the Riders seemed to sigh in relief as they dismounted and led their horses to the fountain. Loon drank enthusiastically from the basin that made up the bottom tier of the fountain, and Karigan, like Connly, cupped her hand under the water spilling from the middle tier to sample it. When she did, she found it clear and cold and heartening. Perhaps it was just that it slaked her thirst, but as she drank more, it seemed to dilute the darkness of Nyssa and the heaviness of the white world. She and the other Riders refilled their waterskins from the Fountain of Winthorpe.

She was about to lead Loon away to make space for another horse when the figures carved on the basin of each tier came to life.

WHISPER WRAITHS

She jumped back and spooked Loon, who tried to drag her away.

"Whoa." She held the reins firmly and calmed him down with soft words and by stroking his neck. Then she looked again at the figures. The other Riders were commenting on and pointing at them.

"You can all see it, too?" she asked.

"Yeah, this time," said Constance. "Really strange."

P'ehdrose loped along, eagles swooped and dove, gryphon tails thumped. Then those figures blurred and new ones formed—horses and riders. Karigan looked closer. Not just any horses and riders, but messenger horses and Green Riders.

"Hey," Daro said, pointing, "that one looks like the captain."

The Riders started picking out images that resembled one another. Karigan caught a glimpse of herself riding a spotted horse, her eyepatch unmistakable. Round and round the rims of the basins the images galloped.

She turned to Duncan. "Why is it doing that?"

He shrugged. "In addition to being altruistic, Winthorpe had a whimsical streak."

Soon the images stopped moving and became graven into the stone of the fountain as though they'd always been part of it. It made her uneasy that their images were left there for anyone to see, or at least anyone or any*thing* that might venture into the white world. If there were other travelers, she had no idea, but she had certainly found herself there enough times, so the idea that there were others was not too far-fetched.

After everyone had had enough to drink and refilled their

waterskins, Connly announced it was time to mount up and they rode off into the white monotony, leaving the Fountain of Winthorpe and its cheerful plash and murmur to fade into the distance.

After some time, Karigan began to wonder if they were going to make it through the white world without encountering further disturbing visions, but an uneasy feeling grew on her as a cloud bank formed before them, a thick billowing cloud with beckoning tendrils of mist that settled on the ground as if waiting to consume them.

Loon tossed his head and backed away. Will, who was much more experienced, stood her ground and snorted. Horses behind them whinnied with anxiety.

It did not help when Duncan said, "This can't be right. Could it be?"

"What?" Karigan asked, glancing over her shoulder at him. Loon pawed the ground, raising puffs of white dust. "What could it be?"

He squinted into the mist. "They shouldn't exist anymore but—"

"*What?*"

"Whisper wraiths—RUN!"

Connly didn't wait. He turned Will on her haunches. "Riders, retreat!"

The Riders reined their mounts around without question and galloped in a full charge, horse hooves kicking up chalky clods of earth. Loon was more than eager to sprint after them. Karigan looked back and saw the cloud tumbling in their wake. She did not know what whisper wraiths were, but if Duncan feared them, she wasn't going to wait around to find out.

Loon, with his long strides, wanted to race ahead, but she held him in check to maintain her pace alongside Connly as rearguard. The mist quickly gained on them, spreading along the ground beneath Loon's and Will's hooves like the leading edge of a wave rolling ashore. Only, it did not retreat as a normal wave would, but kept surging ahead.

"You must go faster," Duncan shouted.

She ignored him and held Loon steady. As rearguard, she

would not race ahead of the other Riders who were already moving at a full-out gallop. She observed with dismay that elderly Killdeer, bearing Elgin who also led Bluebird, was tiring and falling back. They would be unable to keep up the mad pace. None of them would if it went on much longer. She and Connly checked their speed so Elgin would not fall behind.

Meanwhile, the mist continued to swell around them. Tendrils reached past her, between her and Connly, separating them.

"No, no, no," Duncan moaned. "You must *outrun* it."

Unfortunately, Elgin, Killdeer, and Bluebird had fallen so far back that she had to rein in Loon even more. Loon continued to fight her, yanking on the bit and tossing his head so he might be free to charge ahead, but a whinny from Bluebird steadied him. Duncan cursed as the pace slowed.

She could barely see Connly beside her, and the mist rushed ahead graying those who rode before her. It was like a great, opaque fist closing around her. Then the whispers came. At first they were innocuous and barely perceptible beneath the sound of galloping hooves, but gradually they insinuated themselves into her hearing and mind. She shook her head in an attempt to dislodge them, as if they were biters whining in her ears, but to no effect.

"Don't listen," Duncan told her, "don't believe a thing they say."

As she rode on through the mist, now sundered from her companions and isolated, the whispers grew more distinct, but less bothersome, almost gentle. They calmed her panic at losing sight of the other Riders, and encouraged her to slow down, that it would be all right. They cajoled her to take her ease. At first she tried to resist, but the whispers made so much sense, and she was *so* tired. It *would* be nice, she thought as her heartbeat gentled and a languor slowly flooded through her body, to halt Loon, close her eyes, and nap for a while. It would be good to take a break. Everything had become so hard, this rescue mission, the riding, simply holding the reins. Why couldn't she just rest? Hadn't she done enough for one night? For one lifetime?

Yes, Karigan, the whisperers told her, *you have done enough. You should rest now.*

In some corner of her mind, she thought she should be alarmed that they knew her name, but the hypnotic whispers quelled any suspicions, only offered her restful peace.

Any energizing benefit she had received from drinking from the Fountain of Winthorpe had vanished, leaving her head feeling so heavy she could barely hold it up. Her eyelids drooped. She just wanted to sleep. She shook her head again, this time to stay awake, but the whisperers chipped at her resistance, urged her to stop and rest, promised her painless slumber and sweet dreams.

The cloud had grown thick around her, enveloped her so completely that the world faded away. Fading, fading . . .

Loon's stride faltered as she slumped over his neck and dropped the reins.

Peaceful dreams, find rest, Karigan, and painless slumber . . .

"No!" Duncan cried. "Don't give in! Don't listen!" But his voice was distant, almost imperceptible.

Loon stumbled to an uncertain walk.

Fading, fading . . .

She rubbed her temple, feeling as clouded in her mind as the mist that engulfed her, even as Duncan railed at her. Loon went to his knees, and she spilled out of the saddle onto the white earth. It was a relief. She could stretch out and rest.

The cloud undulated and rustled around her, its ebb and flow trailing coils of vapor in mesmerizing waves. The whispering voices were pleasant, warm, reassuring. She could rest now, they told her. Others would carry on whatever task she'd been undertaking. It felt so good to just let go.

Yes, Karigan, there is no need to fight anymore. Leave it to others. Let go.

Fading . . .

White shrouded figures drifted out of the mist and surrounded her. The ragged edges of their shrouds billowed like wings. They whispered with papery breaths that she should not be alarmed, that they would care for her so she could rest undisturbed.

Peaceful dreams, painless slumber . . .

They took the heavy pouch from her shoulder. She could not remember what it contained, but it was a relief to be unburdened of its weight. Soon she would have tranquility. She did not have to fight anymore. They would take care of everything. Then they removed her swordbelt and the cuirass, and then the helm and her coat. A gold feather gleamed as the coat crumpled to the ground. Someone had given it to her, a man who she had . . . loved? Her memory of him melted away into the mist.

She was lifted by many pale hands, lifted up, up, up, her arms outspread as if to embrace the sky. She was weightless, insubstantial, floating on clouds, a euphoric dream of herself ascending to the heavens and greeted by white starblaze.

Peace, Karigan, painless rest . . .

It was true, there was no more pain—the many hurts she'd accrued since becoming a Green Rider, the injuries and torture, the loves and losses fell away as leaves on the wind. She cared not, for it was all part of some other life, some other dimension.

Somewhere in her consciousness, the torturer yelled in her mind, *Wake up!* But it was so far away, she was so submerged in mist, that it held no power, and it did not occur to her to wonder why the torturer would care. Even farther away, she heard the grief-stricken cry of an Eletian who loved her. It no longer mattered. Nothing mattered as she sank deeper. She sought only painless slumber where no one could hurt her. Peaceful dreams. The whispers supplanted all else, embraced her in serenity.

I am fading, she thought. Letting go.

They lowered her onto a raised bed of stone, but she felt only comfort. She smiled up at her benefactors.

The yelling man leaned over her. She knew not what he said. She saw his mouth moving and fear in his eyes, but heard nothing. She tried to tell him it was all right, that all was well and her pain was gone, but she could not seem to muster the energy to speak.

Rest, Karigan, be not bothered. Tranquil slumber . . .

The whisperers moved around her like clouds forming and

reforming. If she glimpsed a face, it was beyond beauty, though sometimes she thought she saw something grotesque beneath a facade, but then it was gone and there was only beauty. They whispered her back to peace, and she drifted.

Drifting, fading, sinking . . .

They rolled up her sleeve and exposed her wrist with its pulsing vein. *Just a little prick,* they reassured her. She thought that would be fine.

A whisperer caressed her wrist. A stinger with a venom sack emerged from its fingertip and was pressed into the vein. Even the pain was far off, and the whisperers stroked her and sang to her to keep her calm. She was so happy to please them. When the stinger retracted, a yellow drop of venom hung from the tip. Crimson bloomed on her skin. She was not distressed.

They caressed her face and whispered praise and reassurance as waves of cold flowed through her body and extremities. They whispered of peace. *Peaceful dreams, Karigan,* they told her. Everything dimmed even as a whisperer licked the blood off her wrist with a prehensile tongue that rasped her skin.

Darkness.

Peace.

Nothing.

Karigan ran through a field holding aloft a dandelion gone to seed. She was so small that the emerald grasses of the field were above her waist. She giggled as she ran, and, one by one, a bit of fluff bearing a seed detached from the dandelion head and drifted into hazy golden sunlight.

Across the field, her parents awaited her with open arms. Seed fluffs floated in her wake, drifting . . .

Drifting . . .

When she reached her parents, her father lifted her into the air, laughing. Her mother smiled, the golden light upon her face. Their love infused Karigan like the sunlight that washed over the scene.

Time to go in, Kari, her mother said. *Time to sleep.*

Karigan didn't want to go in, but her mother sang to her of sweet dreams and moonbeams.

Drifting . . .

Days spun by, days of love and happiness. One day her mother sat in the garden. *Guess what, Kari,* she said, *I am not going to that trading fair, after all.*

Why not, momma?

People have been getting very sick, and with your little brother or sister on the way, I thought I'd better not take the risk.

A distant memory of sorrow lifted from Karigan's heart.

Drifting . . .

As the years spun by, she grew up with a little sister and lived a life with her mother present to care for her and guide her into young adulthood. She thrived as she worked with her father in the clan merchanting business, and at a trading fair she met and fell in love with another merchant's son, Telamir. Their fathers approved of the match and they married. She bore Telamir two sons and a daughter. Though strange things were happening in the realm—the king murdered by his brother, magic returning to the land, rumors of darkness to come, none of it touched her as she and Telamir flourished unto old age.

Peace, Karigan, rest in peace . . .

It had been a good satisfying life. A whole lifetime so quietly lived. No torture, no fear, no pain.

Sleep in painless peace . . .

In the end, cold darkness enveloped her.

⊰⊱ ANETHNA ⊰⊱

Enver looked out from the cover of the woods toward the mountains. The jagged peaks loomed above the land against a backdrop of stars and moon-limned clouds. She had been here. The Galadheon had been here, but suddenly she was not. He did not panic, but stretched his senses to search for her and caught a hint of her farther west. All the way to Sacor City? He pondered how she could travel so far so fast. Did it mean she'd escaped her captors? Then she moved again. and he received a much stronger feeling that she was closer. How was it possible? It was . . . disorienting. What magic was at work that allowed her to move across the country with such speed? Despite it all, he sensed no overt distress from her.

Reassured she was well, he folded his legs beneath him to meditate on it, to observe what would happen next. Time passed with little change until he picked up a surge of urgency. It was frustrating not to know exactly what was happening, but he was only able to sense so much, and whatever was happening in Eletia was interfering. He blocked out Eletia's calling and focused on what he remembered of the Galadheon, her bright eye, the brown hair, the scent of her that filled him. He lost all awareness of time as he immersed himself in her so that it was a shock when he felt a different magic swallow her and she entered *anethna*, nothingness.

"No, Galadheon, you must not," he murmured in consternation.

It was a fold of reality, another layer of the world, the anethna, a transitional place that, for all that it was empty, could cause madness with its visions and endless white plains if one lingered too long. And it was not without physical dangers, for it was not uninhabited. He knew she had crossed through it before, but she'd been fortunate to survive as well as she had. Eletians avoided it, knowing its calm was an illusion, for many battles of magic had been fought there, and the ghosts and residue of the magic did not just settle and decay.

"Be careful," he whispered. He could not help her there. He could only hope she had good guidance and would not tarry.

His connection to her ebbed the deeper she traveled into the anethna, but he managed to maintain her thread. He felt her exhaustion, the nagging desire to sleep. Whispers scraped against his mind.

NO! He jumped to his feet, heart pounding. Wraiths! Wraiths as old as the anethna itself, parasites born of it that the Eletians had defeated long ago. *Do not listen,* he thought to her. *Do not hear them.* But they overcame her, and he screamed in grief and despair and swayed on his feet, engulfed in his own darkness.

"Enver, you must disengage," came a quiet voice.

"Father?"

"Yes. We have been searching for you." Somial placed his hand on his son's forehead. "You must let the Galadheon go."

"I cannot." His anguish was poured into those simple words.

"You must. I will not lose you this way."

There were two others with his father, and they sang to him, sang of strength and love.

"Come, my son," Somial said, "back into the world of the night forest. Leave the nothingness. You cannot help her this way."

As his connection with the Galadheon stretched too thin and receded, he could no longer feel her. The song of her was replaced by that of those who accompanied his father and drew him back on a tether. When he returned to the world, he wept. "She is lost, she is lost to me."

Somial knelt beside him. "My son, that is the only conclusion you can draw? You are so sure?"

"The wraiths of the anethna have claimed her."

Somial seemed to consider. "That is not good, but be not so fast to underestimate the Galadheon. You most of all should know not to."

"They've taken her . . ."

"If it is so, we will sing and grieve for her, but now you must be here. You must come with us."

"Come with you?"

Lhean and Idris moved closer, starlight shining in their eyes.

"Have you not heard the call to return to the Great Wood?"

"Yes, but I needed to rescue the Galadheon. She'd been taken . . ."

"My son, I fear your bond is consuming you, and it is not reciprocated."

"I am not bonded."

Somial raised his eyebrows as if in surprise. "The Galadheon's path winds a different course than yours. You only do yourself harm in pursuit of it."

"*You* loved a mortal woman."

"Yes," Somial said. "Very much so, and grief almost killed me when her life ran out in old age."

Enver closed his eyes. "I remember."

"Your mother returned my love. The Galadheon will only bring you sorrow."

"But her spirit sings to me."

"I know, my son, but there are other forces that influence her path—powers greater than you or me, and others whom she serves. All that she is, all that she has done, lends her *kheireithin*. It is, in part, what draws you to her, it's what fills your senses."

Enver clenched his hands. "I know."

"And the pain is terrible. I can see it in your eyes. I am sorry, my son, but she is not for you. But be at peace knowing that your love is not wasted. She feels it, is strengthened by it, and it is part of what makes her who she is. You will always be a part of her, as she is of you."

"What of the wraiths?"

"We will stand vigil with you," Lhean said, stepping forward, "for the Galadheon and I shared much in the past, and the future, as well."

"Yes," Somial agreed, "we will stand vigil, but then it will be time to leave, to return to Eletia."

They listened to the voice of the world, the currents of nature, the darkness of battle, the call emanating from Eletia. Enver, eyes closed, could not help but return his senses to the nothingness, to reunite with the Galadheon. For all his father's wisdom, he could not just forget, he could not just abandon her. Through the hazy layers of mist he went, deep, deep, and deeper, and he thought her completely lost to him until he found a faint spark that was her steeped in darkness. A cold dark enveloped him until she, and thus he, were seized by all-encompassing pain.

⭜ THREADS ⭝

She was seized by an all-encompassing pain. Darkness peeled back to reveal the heavens full of stars that seared her mind's eye, and the weaving of threads. Great threads of sizzling light beamed through the well of darkness surging infinitely onward, and fine spun threads cut intricate patterns against a backdrop of deep midnight blue that was spangled by the pulsations of distant suns. She knew these to be the strands of lives and worlds, of time and place, as she had once seen through the faceplate of a looking mask, the shard of which remained in her right eye.

A thread of light impaled her chest, shredding the illusion of a life where her mother had lived. It showed her the reality, her mother on her deathbed, her father and aunts collected around her as she breathed her last.

Karigan screamed, but the sound was lost to the vastness of the universe. The whisperers tried to rein her in, to sing to her, to bring her peace, their voices taking on a note of urgency, but cold fire burned through her veins.

More threads intersected or ended, or snagged and tore loose. Others continued their weavings, warp and weft, all in good order: *The colonel slain, blood drips from a Raider's blade. The Riders save the colonel. The colonel is held captive aboard a ship. Estora in labor, beads of perspiration on her brow.*

A peaceful stream burbles in a mossy glade.

A terrible battle, a great dark host on the horizon advances.

Zachary sits proud and brave on his warhorse, his army thronged behind him.

Karigan lifts the hem of her white linen gown to step into the stream. Icy water sends a chill through her body.

Screams of the wounded, the clash of blades, the song of arrows soaring through the air.

It is cold, *Karigan says as she places her foot into the stream. Enver holds her hand to steady her.* It will bring you peace, *he says,* painless slumber and healing.

Swords slash and lancers try to hold back the terrible horde, the monsters of Blackveil. Fire in the sky. Zachary raises a great shield emblazoned with a flying dragon toward the inferno that rains down on him.

It will not feel so cold once you grow accustomed to it, *Enver says.*

Hooves pound and pennants snap in the wind. The stench of gore.

She settles into a pool formed by the stream. It is clear, perfect, with mossy boulders to either side of her. I will always keep watch, *Enver says.* I will keep you safe. You will never be alone.

Corpses of horses and defenders are strewn about the battlefield. The foul avians of Blackveil feast on the dead.

She submerges all the way into the pool. Currents flow along her body in whorls. She need not breathe, just sleep. She is at peace and without pain, and Enver will keep watch.

Zachary reigns victorious. Zachary is cut down by arrows. Sacor City shines in the setting sun as the realm enters a golden era of peace and prosperity led by the descendants of Zachary and Estora. The dark host swarms across the battlefield and invades the city. Its citizens are slain or enslaved. All is decay and walls crumble. The stain of darkness and defeat spreads across Sacoridia and all the free lands.

The flight of arrows. Always the arrows.

The beat of a god's wings surrounded her, and she was cast back into her body.

She burned. Cold fire scalded her veins, her scream echoed by those of the whisperers. Duncan shouted at her, and Nyssa, too. Far away in a copse of trees near the mountains, Enver cried out. Their voices, all the rage, the fear, the pain, punched through her to the pith of her existence.

She snapped into a sitting position and threw off a gauzy shroud that had been spread over her. The whisperers stepped away in consternation, and her winged horse brooch slipped from the fingers of one who had been examining it. It thumped to the white ground, raising a fine puff of dust. Their faces were not beautiful at all, but bloodless and misshapen with oozing pustules and deep seams that contorted their features in an inhuman lack of symmetry. The nearest hissed and flicked its tongue at her.

"Get up! Get up!" Duncan yelled.

Stupid, Greenie, Nyssa said, *don't just sit there!*

She half fell off a stone slab that looked like an altar or a coffin rest, and staggered a few steps before falling to her knees. Her legs and feet were numb, her mind so terribly muddled.

"Get up!" Duncan cried. "They are stealing me!"

A whisperer held a large, polished stone of green tourmaline in its hands, Duncan's tempes stone, and what looked like a human thigh bone tucked under its arm.

Get the sword! Nyssa shouted in her mind.

Karigan crawled toward where the colonel's sword had been discarded, dragging her left arm which was completely useless and trailed blood. When she reached the sword, she drew it from its scabbard and used it to help her stand. She lurched after the whisperer that was carrying away the tempes stone and bone, and putting all the fire of burning pain into pursuing it, she caught up and ran it through with the saber. The creature fell, the stone and bone thudding to the ground. The other whisperers closed in around her and walled her in with a thick mist. To her horror, tentacles snaked out from beneath their shrouds, reached for her.

"Come closer at your peril," she warned them. She did not wait, but jumped at them and cut off the closest tentacle, then pivoted and struck down another whisperer. That was all it took. The rest screamed away into the mist and the cloud that had surrounded her evaporated until there was no trace of it.

"Thank the gods," Duncan said, hovering nearby.

She used the tip of her sword to prod the shroud of the whisperer crumpled at her feet, but the creature itself was gone. No blood, no corpse, it had vanished like the mist. She raised the saber, noting with some surprise, that she had actually used a sword and it had not hurt. Then she saw herself reflected in the blade. No eyepatch there, just her mirror eye reflecting infinitely into the blade and back. She shook her head and turned to find all the Riders and their horses scattered about the white landscape as if dead. She dropped to her knees.

"They are not dead," Duncan said hastily. "Just asleep. The whisper wraiths weren't as interested in them as they were in you and me, though they would have gotten to them eventually. You saved all of us. Though, I might add, it took you long enough." He chuckled. "I do not think they've ever had a victim fight back before."

She wiped cold perspiration from her brow and then collapsed into the darkness of oblivion, this time without the whispers in her mind.

"Drink this, Karigan."

Cold water moistened her lips. A damp cloth was applied to her face.

"Drink in little sips," Connly advised her, supporting her and holding the waterskin to her lips.

Karigan obeyed and slowly began to feel her senses return. The numbness had vanished from her body except for her left arm, and her mirror eye throbbed with pain. When she looked up, twenty Green Riders looked down at her, and a number of horses, too.

"Put this on." He helped her place her eyepatch over her

mirror eye. Any Riders who had not known about it, that it was more than just a simple injury, did now. "I explained it to them," he said, guessing her thoughts.

It was kept secret, as much as possible, by Zachary and the colonel, to protect her from those who would covet its power, and those who despised all magic and magic users. Fortunately, the Riders knew how to keep secrets, but she couldn't help but think that it was one more thing that made her strange, and a stranger, to them.

"What . . . what happened?"

"Duncan said you saved us," Connly replied, "for which we are grateful." His statement was followed by murmurs of agreement from the others. "What do you remember?"

Her memory was vague about what had happened. "Trying to escape the mist, then peacefulness." Several Riders nodded as if their experiences had been the same. Much of the rest was like a jumbled, half-remembered dream. "Visions of my childhood and my life, but it wasn't really my life. An alternate life." Suddenly she was overcome by sobs realizing anew that her mother was gone and had been for many years, and that the husband and children she had loved hadn't been real. When she calmed down and made use of a handkerchief Connly provided, she said, "I lived a whole other lifetime." After a pause, she added, "They must have looked into my mirror eye because I had all sorts of visions."

"They did," Duncan said. "They very much wanted what is in your eye, and it threw them when the magic worked on *them*. Who can say what sorts of things they might have seen, but it was ultimately their undoing and they lost control of you."

"It woke me," she said. "They were after the mirror shard in my eye?"

"The wraiths wanted the magic. They are parasites that prey on magic and siphon it, sometimes keeping their victims alive for long years to do so."

Karigan was appalled to think that might have been her fate.

"They were intrigued not only by your eye," Duncan continued, "but by your particular ability. I fear you will never be safe in the Blanding again. They will hunt you down."

A good reason for her to never return. She tried to lift the waterskin for another sip, but her left hand and arm remained lifeless. She glanced down and found her wrist bandaged and stained with a spot of blood. Purplish-black striations ran up the inside of her arm from the wound.

"They poisoned you," Tegan said.

"Not enough to kill," Duncan said, "but enough to keep you under their power. Captain Connly eliminated much of the poison."

Karigan looked up at him, wondering if he'd acquired a new special ability. He smiled. "I got it out the same way as I would snake venom. Sucked it out. My uncle taught me how. There were timber rattlers in the woods by his farm, so it was a necessary skill."

"Oh!" She inquired after the others, and to a one they were unharmed, though some remained drowsy. Their dreams had been pleasant and peaceful, too, but they'd not been subjected to the same horror as Karigan.

"You rest while we get ready to ride again," Connly said. "Drink some water. Best we don't stick around in case those wraiths get brave and come after us again."

He and the rest of the Riders returned to their horses to prepare to leave.

Karigan turned to Duncan. "I remember something about a bone. A human bone."

Duncan actually blushed, which seemed an odd thing for a "projection" to do. "That is, er, my leg bone, and having others see it is a little like being naked. When a great mage dies, their bones are supposed to be burned to ashes because they contain power that can be misused, but the eagles don't use fire, so mine were never destroyed. As a result, I am not just confined to being a projection. With the power of my bones intact, I can travel the outside world and do some small magic. The bone has to be with my tempes stone, of course. The wraiths almost had a great prize in both of us." He shuddered. "I would like to hear about how you are *Mirare* sometime."

Karigan touched her eyepatch. She didn't feel prepared to go into that just now. "Do you have, er, the rest of your bones?"

"They are at Snowcloud Eyrie. Yes, all of them. They are too heavy for Softfeather to carry all at once along with the tempes stone, too, and it is safer this way. I hate to think of the wraiths or anyone else in possession of them all. I'd appreciate you not telling anyone about them."

The water they'd filled skins with from the Fountain of Winthorpe helped Karigan feel much better. There was even some tingling in her arm and hand after a short while. Tegan came over to help her with her coat—winged horse brooch once more pinned to it. Karigan touched the feather, and it grounded her more than anything else as she remembered who had given it to her. Tegan then helped buckle her cuirass back on and girded the swordbelt around her waist.

"I'm glad my ability just helps me predict the weather," Tegan said with a smile. "It keeps me out of trouble, unlike you and yours." She then gave Karigan a leg up onto Loon's saddle, and handed her Duncan's pouch.

"If you ever want to trade," Karigan said.

Tegan laughed and returned to her horse.

As the Riders continued on their journey, Karigan tried to shake off the residue of the spell the whisper wraiths had put her under. Briefly her mind strayed, drifted, ranged across the white world on ragged wings, seeking peace and painless sleep . . .

Yes, come to us, the wraiths whispered in her mind. *We will take care of you, bring you peace.*

She started to rein Loon away from the others.

"Snap out of it," Duncan said in her ear.

Idiot Greenie, Nyssa chimed in, *inviting it in.*

"Problem?" Connly asked, urging Will closer to Loon's side.

Karigan shook herself to wake up fully.

"What's left of the venom is still holding sway over her," Duncan said. "We'll have to keep an eye on her."

"Smack me if I seem to drift away," she told Connly. "Really. Smack me hard. What they offer is tempting."

"Oblivion, humph," Duncan said. "You are better than that, stronger than them. You must not give in to temptation."

Karigan was not sure she would be strong enough if the wraiths came for her again. There was only so much pain, so many trials, one person could endure. What the wraiths offered was an escape from that. Not that she wanted to be the body they fed off for long years, but the allure remained.

Do not be seduced by the easy way out, Nyssa told her.

Why do you care? Karigan had a dim recollection of Nyssa trying to wake her up from the grip of the wraiths' spell. *Why did you help?*

Because you are mine, and mine alone. Your giving in would have been a disappointing end to our dance.

And, Karigan surmised, it would have ended Nyssa's own existence, whatever kind of existence it was. She sighed, wishing that everyone would just stay out of her head.

❧ CONNECTION ❧

When Enver could breathe again, he sat up from where he'd fallen on the ground, elation filling him.

"She is well," he told his father, Lhean, and Idris. "She overcame the wraiths, though she still wanders the anethna."

"I am pleased for the Galadheon," Somial said. "However, I am less pleased that you did not sever your connection with her. I fear for the harm you do yourself, my son. You listened to my words, but you did not *hear* them."

"I heard them, father. I just did not *heed* them."

"He reveals his human blood in his insolent nature," Idris said.

"You have not bonded yet," Lhean reproved her in a soft voice, "to know what that connection is like, and so you cannot judge."

Enver was pleased by Lhean's support, though Idris looked unmoved. Many Eletians had biased views of mortals as inferior, and thus him. Idris clearly was not immune. Lhean had once been of that nature. However, traveling into Kanmorhan Vane and the future with the Galadheon had helped reshape his opinion.

His father checked the sky for the moon's progress, seemed to listen to the hoot of an owl. "It is time we took to the ways and resume our journey to Eletia."

Enver stood, the Galadheon's black staff gripped in his hand. "I wish to seek out the Galadheon once she has left the anethna. I wish to ensure she is well."

"No," Somial said.

"No?"

"My son, what will your next excuse be? The Great Wood calls. We must answer."

Enver stood fast. "I will not go. I am not a child."

"In that you are wrong. Forgive me."

Before Enver knew what his father was about, moon-gold motes of dust sparkled in his face. A sudden weariness came over him. The staff slipped from his fingers, and he would have fallen but for Idris and Lhean catching hold of him and lowering him to the ground.

No, he thought. He had to seek the Galadheon. It was his last thought before he slept.

"**W**e must ask the terrial ada to carry us," Somial said to Lhean and Idris. "We cannot bear him all the way to Eletia."

"He will not be pleased when he awakens," Lhean said, "and it will only make him more determined to reach the Galadheon."

"I know," Somial replied, "but we must answer the calling, and perhaps being beneath the eaves of the *Vane-ealdar* will ease his ardor."

"Either that, or the Galadheon must break him of it," Idris murmured.

"It may be so," Somial said.

Idris nudged the staff with her toe. "What of this weapon of the Black Shields?"

Somial gazed down at his peacefully slumbering son. "Perhaps we leave it. It only fuels his obsession, and such wood as that has no place in Eletia."

"I will carry it," Lhean replied. "I have done so before, and no harm came of it. It may be the Galadheon will have need of it again one day."

⇜ BRIDGES ⇝

Karigan stumbled back across the bridge, spitting sand and brushing it off her sleeves. "That definitely was not the mountains."

"It's an easy mistake," Duncan said. "A lot of these bridges look similar."

She rubbed more sand out of her eye and saw they were once more in the white world, and all the Riders were watching them curiously. Loon made a plaintive whicker.

"What's on the other side?" Tegan asked.

Karigan glanced back at the bridge. It was not a large span, but more like a picturesque stone bridge one would find crossing a stream on a country estate. This one crossed nothing, or at least nothing perceptible. Only when one walked over the arch and suddenly arrived elsewhere did one learn that what the bridges transversed were layers of the world.

"A desert," Karigan said, "with two suns and a dust storm."

"Two suns?" Tegan said. "How is that possible?"

"The bridges do not always align with our own world," Duncan replied.

Which begged the question: what other world or worlds were there? One that was obviously hot and dusty. She went to Loon's side and sipped from her waterskin, only to spit out the water to expel more sand. It was going to take a while to get rid of all the grit crunching in her teeth.

"We'd best move on," Connly said. "Time is running out for the colonel."

"Remember," Duncan said, "it may feel like hours have passed here, but time moves more slowly in our world. Perhaps only minutes have passed."

They were, Karigan thought as she dragged herself back into the saddle, very *long* minutes, and stepping into that dust storm had made being under the influence of the whisper wraiths an almost enticing alternative.

Do not dare to even think that way, Nyssa told her.

"I was being sarcastic," Karigan muttered.

Tegan gave her a strange look.

"Talking to myself again," Karigan said.

You were not being sarcastic enough.

Perhaps not. Nyssa wasn't the one with sand in her hair and clothes, and in her eyes and mouth. Which Karigan would probably have for days. She was so damn weary, and the only rest she had gotten recently was with the wraiths.

"Perhaps," Duncan said, once more popping behind her on Loon's back, "the next bridge will be the one we are looking for."

They rode on, everyone sunk into his or her own thoughts. The white world seemed to extract animation from a person with its ponderous white expanse the way the desert would deplete a person of moisture.

For her own part, she thought back to the alternate life she had experienced under the influence of the wraiths, one in which she had not been called to the Green Riders. Had the visions shown her what her life might have been like had her mother lived? It had been so perfectly normal—no sword fights, no magic, no political intrigue, just joining her family in the clan business and marrying a merchant's son. She wondered if Telamir was someone who actually existed, or if it were all a fiction. He lingered in her mind with memories that felt as though she had lived them: birthdays, holidays, family picnics, working together at trading fairs, birthing her first child . . .

Grief caught in her throat, the loss of Telamir and her children all too real. She grieved quietly as she rode beside Connly at the head of the Riders. To think all her suffering and hardship as a Green Rider might not have occurred had her mother lived.

This, however, was her reality, this green uniform, the white plains before her, the horse she rode, the torture, and the loss of friends. She did not regret her life as it was, for she knew she had real purpose, especially when it came to defending the realm. If she hadn't become a Rider, she would have missed out on making friends with Tegan and Mara and Yates, and all the others, and she would never have met Colonel Mapstone, Alton, or Cade. She would never have gotten so close to her king. Maybe it would be better if the last had not come to pass, but in that alternate reality given her by the wraiths, he had died at his brother's hands. She could not bear the thought of that.

Mercifully, she could not linger in such speculation as they soon came upon another bridge. This one had a long sweeping curve to it. They paused while Duncan considered whether or not it was the one they wanted.

"I thought you were an expert about these bridges," Connly said. They were all, by now, feeling a little irritable.

"It has been a long time since I last traveled through the Blanding," Duncan replied. "*You* try remembering what you once knew a thousand years ago."

After some hemming and hawing, he decided, ultimately, it was not the one they wanted, and they moved on. Karigan was just as glad he hadn't asked her to carry his pouch across so they could have a look.

The next bridge appeared more promising to him. "We will cross it," he said.

The bridge was made of rough stone like the others, but it had three arches. Karigan dismounted with a sigh. She and Connly had decided to risk only one Rider to accompany Duncan across the bridges, and since she was the custodian of his pouch as per their agreement back in Oxbridge, she was the one Rider. Duncan, of course, approved, adding that, indeed, depending on what might lie at the end of some of the bridges, just one Rider would be less of a target. This did little to improve her disposition toward the whole endeavor.

"Do you want someone else to go this time?" Connly asked her.

"A deal is a deal," Duncan said.

"Surely you can give her a break."

"It's all right," Karigan said, handing Connly Loon's reins.

She was pretty sure a certain amount of annoyance colored her words. She adjusted the strap of the pouch on her shoulder.

Duncan stood by the end of the bridge and gestured to it. "After you, dear lady."

Karigan grumbled to herself. He could be as charming as a prince and fashion his image to look as stunningly handsome as he wanted, but at this point his efforts left her unmoved. She scratched at her wrist where the wraiths had punctured it. As feeling returned to her arm, it grew more itchy and painful like a bad sting.

"Don't scratch it," Duncan chastised her. "You'll just make it worse."

She grumbled again and stepped onto the bridge. There was no telling what they might encounter on the other end so she kept her hand to the hilt of her sword as she approached the center arch. They came to a thin wall of mist that marked that they were about to leave the white world and cross into another place. She held her breath against the possibility of another sandstorm and pushed through.

And found herself in a pleasant wood-paneled room with towering shelves of books and an open bay window that looked out over the ocean far below. Seashells were lined up on the sill and a pleasant breeze flowed in that smelled of briny air. She breathed deep of it for it was a balm after so much time spent in the deadening environs of the white world.

"Huh," Duncan said. "I have been here before, but long, long ago."

"Where are we?" The room was circular and appeared to be part of a tower. A desk sat in the middle of it, set with paper and some sort of writing implement, as if waiting for someone to sit down and write. She gazed at the books on the shelves but was not able to read the titles on the spines for they were all in a language she did not know.

"It is not of our world," Duncan replied.

"It isn't?" Aside from the different language on the spines of the books, she could be standing in a tower room looking upon the shoreline of almost anywhere along the Sacoridian coast.

"Some layers of the world are just slightly offset from our own," he replied.

She picked up a book from the desk and found in its pages beautiful lifelike renderings of birds—all very familiar. Exacting type on shiny paper like she'd never seen before must describe each bird.

Just then, a terrier with folded ears and a red coat scampered into the room. Actually, he was . . . transparent, and when he started barking at them, he sounded muted, far away.

"Is he—?" she began.

"A ghost?" Duncan nodded emphatically. "He is, and we best leave lest he rouse someone."

Another ghost? she wondered.

"Fergus!" a woman shouted from below, followed by the sound of footsteps ascending a creaking spiral staircase.

Karigan went to set the bird book back on the desk, but spied another ancient-looking tome there with a cracked leather binding and very faint lettering, which was, to her surprise, in the common tongue. She picked it up but could not quite make out the words they were so blurred with age. The dog growled as he tried to gnaw on her ankle, but being a ghost, he could not grab on and she felt only his cold presence, not a jaw full of teeth.

"Come on!" Duncan said.

"Fergus?" the woman called again, her footsteps nearing the top. "Who's up there?"

Karigan went to replace the book on the desk but missed. Pages fluttered as it fell, and she glimpsed wording on the title page:—*and the Green Riders: A History, by Lady Estral*—

It hit the floor with a boom, which was followed by an exclamation by the woman climbing the stairs. Karigan dashed after Duncan toward the bridge even as the ghost dog barked at them. The bridge faintly glowed and seemed to superimpose itself on a wall of books. Karigan and Duncan hastened onto it and into the mist. She assumed it would disappear from the tower room and whoever lived there would not be able to open the way to the white world and cross it unless she possessed the right magic.

As she reentered the white world, she idly wondered if the

woman who yelled for the ghost dog could communicate with ghosts like she could.

"That wasn't so bad," she said as she stepped off the bridge. The ocean breeze had been a refreshing change from the white world. She would have liked to have lingered and looked at the book. She'd known Estral had been working on a history of the Green Riders, and apparently would manage to finish it at some point, but it also made her wonder how it had migrated into that other world. Others, perhaps, had found their way across the bridge? She would probably never know.

The Riders who awaited her and Duncan were not even looking her way to hear about what the two of them had seen. Instead, they faced in the opposite direction, silently staring. She stepped up onto the bridge's parapet wall to see what they saw, and immediately wished she had not.

A cadaverous army of dull blacks and grays marched mutely across the plain, bearing tattered banners. At the head, beneath the shredded silver and black banner of Sacoridia, rode a skeletal king in helm and armor on the rotting corpse of a warhorse. He was not close enough to discern fine details, features, but it was *him,* his armor, the way he carried himself even as one dead. A scream built inside her. He was followed by cavalry and foot soldiers. The other banners featured the provinces, and pennants for regiments and units— the River Unit, the Mountain Unit, and so on. Then came the Green Riders, all rotting, some with arrows stuck in them, or missing limbs, even heads, all riding silently on.

Karigan thought the white world was sparing them the stench of dead, but it was not to be so. A wafting breeze carried an overwhelming odor of decay, and Karigan was not the only one who turned and gagged.

"It's not real," Duncan reminded them. *He* wasn't gagging. Apparently "projections" lacked a sense of smell. When she looked again, the dead army vanished behind a tumbling cloud.

"What does it mean?" Constance asked, voice trembling.

"Sometimes," Duncan replied, "it's a warning, and sometimes the Blanding just taunts you. But on the whole, the why and what-for of it all is beyond even me."

Karigan gazed at her fellow Riders and saw some in tears. Others had a pallid cast to their faces.

"We should get them moving," Karigan told Connly. "This wasn't the bridge we were looking for."

Connly shook himself. "Right."

She took the reins to Loon and mounted. "Everyone form up," she told the Riders.

As she clucked Loon to the head of the line, she observed one of the Riders wiping tears off his face. He was a green Greenie, quite young, and not exactly fit for the life of a messenger. She was surprised he'd been brought along on the journey to the front, much less chosen by Connly for the rescue mission. It must have something to do with his special ability, whatever it was.

"Hoff, isn't it?" she asked. They'd been briefly introduced.

The boy nodded, but gazed straight ahead, not willing to look her in the eye.

"Don't let the white world—the Blanding—get to you too much. It likes to show the worst visions."

"All right," he said, still not meeting her gaze.

"We'll be out of here soon." When he did not reply, she continued on to the head of the line.

"His specialty is illusion," Duncan said, making her jump. She'd forgotten about him and his tendency to just appear behind her.

"You can tell that's his ability?"

"I can, just as I can tell what yours is. His is not an easy form of the art to master."

"I'm sure it will be useful." And now she understood why the colonel had chosen to bring him to the front, and why Connly had chosen him as well for this mission. Still, it was a harsh introduction to the reality of his calling.

When Connly joined her at the head of the line, she asked, "About Hoff—did the colonel have some plan in mind for him?"

Connly smiled. "She did."

When he told her what it was, she said, "Very crafty." She expected no less of their colonel and only hoped they found her in time.

 THE BRIDGE TO THE DAY BEFORE ⥱

The journey continued. There were no more visions, no more wraiths, though Karigan could feel them waiting for an opening, waiting for *her*. It was disturbing enough that she did not allow herself to doze even a little bit despite her exhaustion and the endless monotony of the terrain.

"Ah ha!"

Duncan so startled her she jumped. "What the hells?"

"Bridges ahead."

Karigan squinted. They were mere dots on the horizon, but even at a walk, the bridges grew larger and closer in disproportionate leaps. She'd be very glad to leave the white world and its abstract unreality.

There were three identical stone bridges, simple single spans with no ornamental flourishes but for the abutment walls scrolling out to rounded end posts. Karigan hoped they would not have to explore what lay across each of them.

Duncan vanished from behind her and reappeared to stand on the ground before them. "I remember."

"So, which one is it?" Connly asked.

"Patience, Captain, give me a moment. I remember this configuration of bridges, but not which one."

Karigan could tell Connly struggled with himself, that his patience and that of the others had just about expired. There was an edginess to their demeanors that indicated they were barely holding themselves together. She could relate.

"My lady, Karigan," Duncan said, "let us start with the middle."

Once more Karigan dismounted and handed Connly

Loon's reins. She joined Duncan at the middle bridge, and without prompting, headed across with her hand to the hilt of her sword, only hesitating for that passage through the mist at the center of the arch.

On the other side she was greeted by daylight and the roar of water that rushed down a steep slope and pounded into cottage-sized boulders. The mist it raised moistened her face, and she traced the course of the torrent with her gaze to where it fanned out far below, parting and twining through swaths of rocky debris until it eventually emptied into a lake bordered by a meadow and forest. The trees of the forest, even from her distant vantage, appeared to be giants with expansive crowns that concealed all beneath their eaves.

She pulled her attention back to what lay immediately in front of her, for she and Duncan were not alone. Arrayed before them were numerous Eletian warriors in their pearlescent armor, who stood upon flat boulders, their bows bent and all their arrows aimed at her. The water frothed and gyred around them creating a scene of perilous beauty as the play of sun and spray cast the arc of a rainbow behind them.

A single swift arrow carved through the air. Its white feather brushed her cheek as it sang by her. She forced herself to calm, stood her ground even as every fiber of her being urged her to run, for she knew the warning for what it was. These archers were too good to miss.

She released the hilt of her sword and raised her hands so that they could see she intended no harm. They did not waver. Beside her, Duncan placed his hands on his hips. It occurred to her that even *his* beauty was diminished by that of Eletians. No mortal could rival them in this regard, except possibly Queen Estora.

"Well, how about that," he said, "the Alluvium of the Elt Wood." Another arrow, its tip flaring in the sun, ripped right through his chest, with no damage, of course, and clattered onto the deck of the bridge behind him. "That was not very hospitable," he said with a sniff.

The Alluvium was the seat of power of the Eletians, and indeed, a familiar figure stood beyond the archers in long emerald and blue flowing robes. He swept past them, leaping gracefully from one rock to another, until he reached the foot of the bridge. He approached no closer, however.

"Greetings, Galadheon," the crown prince of Eletia said, clearly heard over the tumult of the current, though he did not raise his voice. Sunlight glanced off droplets caught in his long gold hair as though it were adorned with diamonds. No other crown did he need.

She bowed. "Prince Jametari."

"You do know such trespass upon the Alluvium merits death, do you not?"

"I did not, though I know non-Eletians are not welcome in the Elt Wood."

"And yet, here you are."

"It is my doing," Duncan said. "We have been trying to find the right bridge to the Wing Song range. I have not traveled the Blanding in a very long time, and so I forget which bridge is which."

"I would ask how a great mage came to guide a Green Rider in the anethna," Prince Jametari said, "but that sounds a long story and there is much else that concerns me at present." He gazed hard at Karigan. "The law says you must be executed for your trespass."

She thought all she needed to do was back one step into the white world and its dubious safety, but the Eletian archers were too keen. She hadn't a chance.

"It was an accident," Duncan insisted.

Prince Jametari raised a hand to silence him, his gaze never leaving Karigan. "It is not your first trespass into Eletia, is it," he said.

"No." She had saved the Sleepers of Argenthyne, had brought them through time to Eletia by a different bridge, to deliver them from the encroachment of Blackveil Forest. When she'd crossed, she encountered the prince's father, King Santanara.

There was the hint of a smile on the prince's lips. With a minute gesture, the archers released the tension on their bows and lowered them as one.

"It would be inappropriate," he said, "to slay she who saved so many of our kin from Argenthyne, she who was favored by Laurelyn, she who *is* favored by our ally, the king of Sacoridia."

Karigan's cheeks warmed a little at the last, but she found that now she could breathe much easier.

"It is well," he said, "that I was here at your arrival and not some other. They would not have hesitated."

She did not doubt his words. "Your folk are fortunate that Eletians do not encounter the same harsh laws in Sacoridia."

"Sacoridia is not Eletia."

The heat of anger crept up her neck. Eletians carried themselves as superior beings. It was true they were eternally lived and outshone any mortal being, but that didn't make them better in the ways that counted. She pursed her lips so as not to say anything imprudent that would cause the archers to reconsider skewering her with arrows. From the corner of her eye, she observed Duncan watching her with apprehension. He was probably more concerned about the contents of the pouch she bore than her should the Eletians decide to kill her.

Then she released a breath. "You are correct. Sacoridia is not Eletia. My king would not have sent an individual on a mission who was a danger to his fellow travelers. You had to have known Enver was near his unfolding and that he—" She waved her arm, unable to go on. The unfolding, as she understood it, was when an Eletian came into sexual maturity and needed to mate. He should not have been sent out into the world unaccompanied by other Eletians so close to his time. His feelings for her had only increased the danger to her, for as she'd seen, the unfolding consumed him, and if not for his own inner strength to resist his need, his nature, she likely would have ended up his unwilling partner.

Prince Jametari simply gazed at her with a subtle smile as though she were talking about a garden party.

"Why would you put us—Enver and me—in that position?" she demanded. "Of what benefit would it have been to Eletia?"

He cocked his head as he gazed at her, the cascades roaring behind him filling in for his silence. Finally he said, "I have no knowledge of it."

She almost laughed at the absurdity of his answer. He'd had no knowledge of *what?* Enver's unfolding? That he'd been on a mission with her without the support of other Eletians?

"If any of my folk have behaved in an untoward manner or served you poorly," he said, "I apologize."

He was not, she thought, at all apologetic, but it was hard to tell for certain, for Eletians were fey and could not be read in the same way another Sacoridian could be. What she did know was that Eletians played a long game, they with their eternal lives.

"During the mission, Enver saved my life, and during the unfolding, he—he controlled himself to give me time to escape."

He nodded as if she told him things he already knew. The desire to push him off his boulder into the swift current came over her, but death by dozens of white arrows did not seem worth it.

"I am pleased," he said, "that our tiendan served you well. Actually, you are a source of intrigue to my folk, Karigan Galadheon, as well as frustration. We do not know what you will do next, which is hard for a far-seeing race to accept. What is the term your folk would use? A 'wild card'? And so we take an interest. After all, your actions may be a great asset in the dark times that now threaten, or not. There is one thing I have foreseen, and that was your arrival here on this day."

Of course he had. And if he had such pressing business, why not begin with this rather than playing games and making her fear for her life by threatening execution? *Eletians.*

"This is the day before your present," Prince Jametari said, "so you are slightly off-time here. You should cross the bridge that is to your right hand as you leave this one. It will deliver you to the mountains and the correct time. I have a feeling, depending on which paths you take, we will see you here again. It seems we cannot do without you."

"Thank you," she murmured with a slight bow. She hastily backed into the mist before he could say more. It was not the first time she'd heard those words from an Eletian: *We cannot do without you.* Since she'd become a Green Rider, the Eletians had regarded her with curiosity, and some with animosity. One had tried to kill her. And yet, they'd called upon her to seek out the p'ehdrose with Enver. She would never understand, and the politics within Eletia would remain a mystery.

Duncan made a low whistle as they reentered the white world. "There is a lot more to you," he told her, "than I guessed. Not everyone would have held their own against Jametari."

"Thanks, I think."

Back in the white world, she and Duncan told Connly and the others where they'd been.

"I would give my firstborn to see Eletia," Brandall said.

"I would not recommend it," Duncan said. "They'd put an arrow through you on sight. They did me, but fortunately they can't hurt me that way."

"Why didn't they put an arrow through Karigan?" Harry asked.

"They're used to me." It was the best response she could think of.

She and Duncan then crossed the bridge Prince Jametari indicated would lead to the mountains. Sure enough, when they reached the far side, they found the mountains draped in night and that the stars appeared in the same position as when they'd left Oxbridge Square.

"We made good time despite being delayed by the whisper wraiths," Duncan said. "I'd say only a few minutes have passed."

It could still be, Karigan thought, too late.

Rubble clattered underfoot when she shifted her weight, and she realized she was walking on the remains of a human-made structure, maybe a foundation to some building, and not a natural pile of stone rubble. Duncan watched as she turned over a small block with the toe of her boot.

"Used to be an order of great mages who kept a hall here," he said, "no doubt to retain easy access to the bridge and the Blanding. Must have been razed during the Scourge. Nothing left of them but this."

It was the first she'd seen him sad. He'd existed, in one form or another, for so long without his own people. She could not imagine it.

"Best get the others across," she told him. "They will be happy to be out of the white world, and we need to find the colonel."

*   *   *

From the white world side of the bridge, Karigan watched as Connly led the Riders across the bridge and vanished on the other side. Some moved faster than others, and she couldn't blame them. She tried to maintain her own patience until it was her turn at the end of the line. Loon practically danced beneath her, knowing that a green world lay on the other side. Mallard swished his tail as he carried Hoff through the mist at the arch.

When only a few remained, she began to feel an itch on the back of her neck. She turned Loon around. There on the plane stood a lone figure in white that almost blended entirely into the background—not Nyssa, not a cadaver, but an almost mirror likeness of herself, brown hair, familiar features. The lengths of her gown flowed in an unearthly breeze.

"Mother?" she whispered. Was this a cruel vision of the white world, or . . . ?

"Karigan?" Tegan said.

Kari, the figure said, *my daughter.*

Karigan nudged Loon forward. He balked, but she pressed him. "Mother? Is it really you?"

The figure emanated love and peace. *I left you too soon and for that I am so sorry. I am so proud of you, of the woman you have become.*

Loon tossed his head when she urged him forward. She needed to get closer, to see if it was truly her mother.

"What's she doing?" she heard Elgin ask.

I love you, the figure of her mother said. *Know that I always will.*

"Karigan?" Tegan repeated.

"The wraiths appear to be after her again," Duncan said. "Don't listen to anything they tell you, dear lady. It's a trap."

Her mother retreated. When Loon wouldn't follow, Karigan jammed her heels into his sides. He half-reared.

"Mother!" she cried as the figure grew more distant.

I love you, my daughter.

Karigan fought with Loon to chase after the figure, but still he resisted.

"Karigan." Tegan grabbed Loon's reins. "Look at me."

"My mother—"

"*Look* at me."

She looked. Saw Tegan's set, but worried, expression, the green of her uniform, her living flesh, the reality of her existence. When she glanced away, she saw that the figure of her mother was gone.

"I don't know what you think you saw," Duncan said, "but the wraiths were no doubt trying to lure you back."

She allowed Tegan to lead Loon back to the bridge. Tegan made her go ahead of her right behind Elgin.

"That's better," Duncan said from behind her. "Remember what the Blanding does, the deceptions it sends you."

Wraiths, deceptions, she wasn't so sure. The warmth, the love the figure emanated, had felt so genuine, and had demanded nothing in return. Tears flowed down her cheeks as Loon passed through the mist at the center of the arch and into the real world.

Though unsure of what she had really seen in the Blanding, whether it had been some vestige of her mother or not, her tears soon dried in the verdant valley beneath the mountains for it was all real. She could smell the fresh green growing things, hear the rustle of leaves and small mammals, feel a fragrant breeze upon her face.

The horses rested and grazed while the Riders plotted. Constance had been sent forward to do some scouting near the hut where Karigan and the others had been held. When she returned, she reported it was still guarded by a handful of Raiders.

"It's good news," Connly told the others. "It means our people are still alive. We'll enclose the Raiders in a snare. There are only half a dozen of them, but remember, these are the *Darrow* Raiders. Take no chances. To begin, we'll need a distraction."

"I have an idea," Karigan said. She gazed at Duncan, who was inspecting his fingernails and not seeming to pay attention.

"What now?" he asked.

Karigan smiled.

GIBLETS

"You there, hellooo," Duncan called.

Two guards had just forced Fergal to his knees beside Megan at the campfire. Their hands were tied behind their backs. The guards, and their brethren located in various places about the small camp, stopped what they were doing to gaze at Duncan in surprise.

"You wouldn't happen to know the way to the steaming baths of Mount Avernil, would you?" he inquired. "I seem to have lost my way and I am deeply in need of the steam. It's the ague, you know."

The guards drew their weapons. "Who are you?" one demanded.

"Name's Duncan of Snowcloud Eyrie. Who are *you?*"

"Grab him!"

"Oh, that doesn't sound very polite." He turned and ran off into the nearby copse of trees.

The apparent leader of the six guards pointed at two of his men. "Go and bring him back."

The two pursued Duncan. Karigan smiled from where she stood invisible away from the glow of the fire. His appearance was followed by that of a muscular Rider with Hoff's doughy face riding a stunning white charger who galloped into the midst of the camp. The charger reared and the Rider drew his saber.

"Release my people," came Hoff's voice.

A Raider loosed a crossbow bolt at the Rider who reined the horse aside just in time, though no weapon could harm him, but the Raiders didn't know that. The illusory Rider galloped around the camp and then out into the dark to lure away more Raiders.

"We're under attack," the leader declared. He then called out for the first two who'd gone after Duncan, but they did not respond, nor did they reappear.

The Rider and charger circled back and cantered around the outskirts of the camp. Duncan walked back into the firelight.

"Hello, me again."

"Get him!"

All was going according to plan, with the rest of the Riders waiting in the dark to pick off Raiders pursuing either Duncan or Hoff's illusion. With the remaining guards distracted, Karigan crept up behind Fergal and Megan unseen beneath the cloak of her ability.

"It's me," she whispered to them. Megan jumped, but did not give her away. Karigan sliced through their bonds and said, "I am going to fade you out. Don't lose contact with me, and keep quiet."

She extended her fading to them and pulled them away from the fire. Megan, rather unexpectedly, obeyed and kept quiet. She led them away from the camp. They almost collided with a panicked guard at one point, but she pulled Megan out of the way just in time. She smiled when she heard the uproar from behind when it was discovered the captives had disappeared. She retained their invisibility, painstakingly moving over uneven ground and through the woods. Only when they were truly out of sight did she drop the fading and release them.

"You are visible," she told them, "and we're far enough away that we can talk now."

As though unable to contain herself any longer, Megan wailed, "They were going to cut off our heads! What took you so long?"

"Shh! Talk, don't yell," Karigan told her.

"We're very glad to see you," Fergal said in a more solemn voice. "Thought it was the end. They were going to cut off our heads like Megan said. They were sharpening the ax."

"I am going to leave you in a moment. Elgin is just over the next rise, and I want you to go to him. But first, what of Melry and the colonel? Are they all right?"

"The colonel—is she here, too?" Fergal asked. "I haven't seen her since I left Sacor City. They did take Melry away about an hour ago. Felt them use that travel device."

"Oh no." It couldn't mean anything good. Karigan directed them to go on to Elgin's position, and ran back toward the Raider camp. Horses whinnied and hooves pounded. There were shouts. By the time she got there, though, it was all over. Five dead Raiders, their leader now a prisoner bound and on his knees. All the Green Riders appeared alive and uninjured, for which she sent a silent prayer of thanks to the heavens.

Connly kicked open the door to the hut and entered with Harry on his heels. Others stood over the prisoner. Connly stormed back out of the hut in short order and over to the prisoner. "Where are Melry Exiter and Colonel Mapstone?" he demanded.

The prisoner did not answer. He was the guard who usually made Karigan dump slops and fetch water. He looked up as she approached.

"Remember me?" she asked.

He gave her a sideways look. "So, you came back."

"I did."

"You are a witch, too, are you? One who can just disappear from an armed camp?"

"I am a Green Rider, royal messenger of the king, as are my companions."

Duncan popped into existence out of nowhere. "Not me. I'm a great mage."

The prisoner's eyes widened at his sudden appearance.

"Tell us where Melry Exiter and Colonel Mapstone are," Connly snapped.

"You think you're going to make me talk?" the man asked. "I don't care what magic you got. Those two are long gone anyway."

Karigan tried not to let the dismay she felt at his words reach her face. It meant they had either been taken away, or were dead.

"*Where?*" Connly demanded.

The prisoner did not respond, nor did he look likely to offer up information anytime soon.

I would torture him were I you, Nyssa said. *A good, sound flogging.*

Nyssa was now giving her advice?

I don't need your help, Karigan thought.

No? I don't think your Greenie honor will get anything out of him.

Karigan wasn't sure if flogging would get anything out of him, either. She was sure Beryl Spencer could, but Beryl's brain worked much differently than her own, and, of course, Beryl was nowhere nearby to offer her services. Connly's anger certainly wasn't helping, either. It just seemed to amuse the prisoner.

"You going to spank me, Greenie?" the Raider asked.

Connly fisted his hands; his face turned red. Karigan stepped over to him and touched his wrist. He turned his hard gaze on her.

"I think I know how to make him talk," she said.

His anger melted to curiosity. He backed away and gestured for her to take over.

The Raider laughed. "Not man enough, eh? Gotta let a girl do it for you?"

She peered down at him and said nothing while he carried on. Her silence only seemed to bolster his courage. "What are you going to do to me, witch? Eh?"

"It has been suggested to me that I give you a sound flogging," she replied, ignoring Connly's odd look. "But I have something better in mind." His laughter became less certain.

Ripaeria! she called with her mind.

It was mere moments before the backdraft of giant wings announced the arrival of the eagle. The prisoner averted his face as he was showered with sparks and ashes from the campfire.

I have arrived, the eagle declared.

You certainly have, Karigan replied, then told her what she had in mind. A glance at the prisoner, who gawked at the eagle, made her think her plan might work. Aloud, she asked

Ripaeria, "Does this man look like the one who shot arrows at you?"

Ripaeria extended her neck so that her hooked beak was but an inch from his nose. He sat wide-eyed and trembled.

Yes, Ripaeria said. She must have said it so all could hear for the man gibbered incoherently. *Shall I rend him with my beak and talons?*

"We'd actually like to get some information from him," Karigan said. "Could you rend him slowly to see if we can get him to tell us the whereabouts of our colonel and her daughter?"

I would rather gobble him quickly and messily, Ripaeria said. *But I could just start with his liver.* Her penetrating regard was intimidating enough from a distance. Up close it was terrifying. *I like liver.* She made an anticipatory throaty sound and flexed her talons for good measure.

The man soiled his pants.

Ripaeria nudged his shoulder with the tip of her beak and knocked him over, and he curled into a fetal position. "Don't let her eat me!" he cried. "Please!"

You must let me eat him. You can't just wave this giblet before me and then say no.

Karigan knelt down beside the man. Tears ran down his cheeks. "I can protect you from the eagle," she said, "if you tell me what you know. Otherwise, I'll let her feed."

He nodded emphatically. "I'll tell you everything—I swear."

"Then talk." In the recesses of her mind, she could sense Nyssa's approval.

⋘ VAROSIANS ⋙

L aren was not sure if it was the effect of the travel device that Torq had used to transport her and Melry from his tent up in the pass to some distant valley, or his all-too-obvious enjoyment of beating her that was making her see double and her ears ring. She'd fallen to her knees in meadow grass near a pond that gleamed in the moonlight. The sonorous croaking of bullfrogs and the other chirps and squeaks of pond creatures were backdrop to her disorientation.

Torq casually kicked her in the ribs and she toppled over, unable to use her bound hands to stop herself. The pain darkened the world around her. Somewhere, seemingly far off, Melry shouted angrily at their captors. Her Melry, her girl, so full of fire. She'd fought hard when they brought her to Torq's tent and scored some impressive hits and blackened an eye or two before they managed to restrain her. She'd been trained well by the arms master in Selium, but it had not been enough. So far they hadn't hurt her badly. They seemed mindful of her appearance. They had not taken the same care with Laren, though she was surprised they hadn't done worse.

It was tempting to just rest in the grass and breathe deeply of the earthy scent of the meadow, to listen to the chorusing of frogs, but she could not show weakness. She could not for Melry's sake, or for that of her Riders. By sheer will, she forced herself back onto her knees, repressing a scream at the pain to her ribs. Back in Oxbridge, she'd thought herself too old for sleeping on the ground, and now this. She laughed. It was a harsh, raspy sound.

"What's so funny, Witch?" Torq demanded.

Two of him stood over her, and she squinted at him through blood dripping into her eyes. When she didn't answer, he cuffed her.

"Leave her alone!" Melry shouted.

"I'm tired of the girl's voice," Torq said. "Gag her."

Melry's protests were cut short.

"Let her go," Laren whispered. "You've got me, let her go." It took a great deal of concentration to speak.

"Oh, it's not that easy," he replied.

Of course it wasn't. They were using Melry to keep her compliant.

"Why not just kill me?"

Torq knelt beside her. "Because, Red Witch, I have something much more satisfying in mind. Have you not wondered what happened to the remnants of Deija after you murdered defenseless men writhing in sickness?"

She had in fact wondered. She'd never been satisfied that they'd been fully defeated, and it gnawed at her as the years passed, but less so as the danger of Blackveil arose. It turned out he required no prompting to tell her.

"We journeyed," he said. "We journeyed across the lands and across the Western Sea. Travel is good. You meet new people, make new friends, engage in trade."

As he boasted about all the places he'd been to and the people he'd met, she picked at the thread that held a button to the cuff of her coat. She pried and plucked despite fingers benumbed by bonds that were too tight.

"It is a big world," he was saying. "So much more to be explored."

"Then maybe you should go," she mumbled.

Torq laughed. "Maybe I should. Oh, look. My friends have arrived."

To Laren's surprise, her sight had cleared enough that she no longer saw two of everything, though her vision remained blurred around the edges. A caravan of riders and pack animals was moving toward them and included two highly ornamented carriages. Only as the carriages drew closer could she discern the complex symbols among the decorations.

"Varosians?" she said in incredulity. Varos lay across the

Western Sea and was a kingdom that did not welcome outsiders, nor did its sovereign seem to allow its citizens to venture outside. Zachary had sent embassies in an attempt to develop relations between the two countries, but they were turned back.

The caravan came to a halt. Someone was helped out of the carriage and guided to Torq by a servant bearing a lantern. The newcomer halted before Torq. He was a small, middle-aged man attired in long silk robes so finely embroidered it clouded her mind. He wore an odd, tall cap. He and Torq bowed to one another in greeting as was the custom among Varosians. Then he turned to Laren.

"This is it?" he asked with a heavy accent.

"As promised," Torq replied. "The Red Witch."

The man walked around her once, twice, as if assessing livestock. As it turned out, that was precisely what he was doing. "It does not look like much," he said. "It is old."

Old? He was probably older than she.

"You said His Excellency was interested in function," Torq said, "not youth or beauty."

Laren shook her head to make sure she had heard him correctly.

"One naturally desires all the best attributes," the Varosian said. "Still, its unusual hair color may be amusing to His Excellency."

Torq was selling her to be a slave? A concubine?

The little man peered down at her. "Does it speak?"

"Yes, *she* does," Laren said.

"It was not asked directly. It will be trained in appropriate conduct in the court of His Excellency."

"Like the—"

Torq struck her across the face, and once more she was lying in the grass, her cheek stinging.

"Its tongue is offensive," the Varosian said. "His Excellency may wish to cut it out."

Torq grabbed her by the collar and hauled her back onto her knees. "You hear that? Speak only when you've been told."

"I am Tol Asmerand," the Varosian told her. "I serve His

Excellency, King Farrad Vir of Varos as finder of rare objects for his collections." He then turned to Torq. "I require a demonstration."

"As you wish," Torq said.

Tol Asmerand gazed speculatively at her. "I will speak truth or a falsehood. It will tell me if I lie."

"I certainly will not," she replied, but things were beginning to make more sense. Tol Asmerand didn't want her for her body, but for her special ability.

Torq did not hit her this time, but he grasped her chin. "If you do not cooperate, we will hurt your daughter bad."

Melry was dragged into the lantern light. Even trussed and gagged as she was, she struggled. One of Torq's men put a knife to her throat. Laren's spirits sank.

"If I were to say," Tol Asmerand said, "that the production of grain was up three *kersats* in Varos this summer, would I be lying or telling the truth."

False, Laren's ability told her. "True," she said with as little inflection as she could.

Torq and Tol Asmerand gazed at one another.

"I suspect it is attempting to deceive us," the Varosian said.

"Cut the girl," Torq ordered his men.

"No!" Laren cried.

Tol Asmerand held up a hand. "There is a more definitive way to judge." He withdrew a small vial from his belt pouch, as well as a pair of fine tweezers. "Hold its head steady."

Torq grabbed her head. When she struggled, he booted her in the ribs again. It left her in so much pain she could not breathe or move. He seized her head once more and held it steady in an iron grip. Tol Asmerand stepped closer and dipped his tweezers into the vial. He pulled out a long and wriggling insect with many undulating legs and dangled it before her eyes. Sharp claw parts near the thing's head snapped at her.

"An Ekedian centipede," he said. "Very rare, and very useful." He directed Torq to tilt her head so that one of her ears was facing upward.

She struggled as he bent over her with the dangling centipede. The tiny legs feathered against her neck. She fought with all she had, but Torq was too strong. She felt the thing crawl into her ear and she squeezed her eyes shut against the sudden agony.

"Now, again," Tol Asmerand said. "If I were to say that the production of grain was up three kersats in Varos this summer, would I be lying or telling the truth?"

Laren looked dazedly at him, her mind fogged, and revolted by the thing that was deep in her ear distorting sound and piercing her head with needle-sharp pain. Warm blood dribbled from her ear down her neck and soaked into her collar.

"Answer," Torq said, "or we cut your daughter."

Laren gazed at Melry as if through a tunnel. Tears trailed down her daughter's cheeks.

"Truth," Laren whispered. Her vision went white with pain and she screamed.

"Ah," Tol Asmerand said.

"What happened?" Torq asked.

"The Ekedian centipede is sensitive to etheric impulses. If the gift is subverted by the gifted, the centipede becomes distressed and injects venom into the subject. It is very painful as you can see. The prisoner purposely gave me a wrong answer and the centipede reacted accordingly."

"Like a fail-safe," Torq murmured.

"Observe." Tol Asmerand turned back to Laren. "If I were to say the border of Gaska Province is defined by the Rind River to the east, would I be speaking true or false."

False, Laren's ability told her.

"Tru—" Her answer turned into another scream, the pain so potent she wanted to bash her head against the nearest rock. Torq restrained her from doing just that. This time the pain did not abate. "False!" she shouted. "False!" Now it settled and quickly faded away. She slumped in exhaustion.

Tol Asmerand then tested her with a series of questions. This time she answered as her ability indicated and avoided the centipede's wrath.

"It has learned to use its gift more wisely," Tol Asmerand

was telling Torq, "and will please King Farrad Vir. Now, as for your fee, we are being more than generous."

False, her ability told her. Might she use the Varosian's lie to turn the two against one another? "He is lying to you," she told Torq. "He is underpaying the true value of your finding me."

Torq laughed. "Perhaps. But don't you understand? It is not about the fee. It is about selling *you* into slavery. You see, on my travels I heard how all the kings of Varos used to have truth-tellers in their courts as a way of keeping the upper hand over their subjects, knowing when they were lying— using them the same way King Zachary uses you. And naturally, because no others in the Western Sea possessed such, the kings of Varos could brag about having something special the others did not."

"Zachary does not *use* me."

"No? How about Queen Isen?"

She did not dare answer. It cut too close to the truth.

"In any case," Torq continued, "I wondered what it would be worth to King Farrad Vir to have a truth-teller of his own. The kingdom has been without one for nearly three hundred years. He was very interested to learn I could provide him with one.

"And you know what? It is so much more satisfying to sell you than to just kill you. You lose your freedom and position— no more colonel. You have that thing in your head for the rest of your life now, and you will find that Varos is a very different place than here. Women are not people. They must rely on protectors—fathers, husbands, sons, masters—to exist at all. Who will protect *you?* I can only imagine how unpleasant it will be for a foreign female slave."

Tol Asmerand removed a small disk from his pouch. It was about the size of a coin, and in fact it looked like new copper. He leaned down and pressed it against her neck.

"What the—?" It burned and she could smell her own flesh cooking beneath the disk. The agony was short-lived, but she could still feel the sting of it.

"The disk is now melted into your skin," Torq said. "It is a

Varosian brand. You are now the property of King Far-rad Vir."

Tol Asmerand handed Torq a purse that jingled with coins. Two husky men in livery of an exotic sort that marked them as Varosian came and lifted Laren to her feet.

"One more thing," Torq said. "Or maybe two. We will tear apart any of your Greenies who come into our possession—you can count on it. Even better, I am taking your daughter back to camp. I am sure my men will find a way to make use of her."

"*No!*" Laren lunged and fought and kicked, but the Varo-sians held on to her and started to drag her toward one of the carriages.

"Momma!" came Melry's muffled cry through her gag as Torq's men pulled her away.

"*Melry!*" Laren lunged again, but her neck burned. She cried out, and only the grip of the Varosian guards prevented her from collapsing to the ground. "Melry," she sobbed.

"Silence," Tol Asmerand said.

"No, you—" Again, the burning on her neck, this time long and intense.

"I will teach, and it will obey," Tol Asmerand said. "It will serve King Farrad Vir well. All else is pain. As for the daughter, it will be forgotten in due time."

"No—"

She did not know how he caused the brand to burn, but he did, until she screamed and lay limp and near unconscious in the arms of the guards. Tol Asmerand stepped away to speak to someone in one of the carriages. She felt the button dangling from her cuff. She snapped it off and dropped it into the grass.

One of the guards jabbed her where Torq had kicked her in the ribs, and finally she blacked out, even as Melry could still be heard calling for her mother.

❧ THE BIG POND ❧

"**M**omma . . ." Melry's whisper, muffled through her gag, was imbued with all the pain of seeing her mother beaten and taken away. She sobbed as the caravan disappeared from sight.

Torq laughed. "It all came together pretty well. The only thing I would have liked better was for your mother to witness my men doing what they wish with you, but the Varosians wanted her as soon as possible and we ran out of time."

Melry's fingers twitched. She wanted to gouge his eyes out with her thumbs so that the appearance of empty eye sockets created by his tattooed face wasn't just an illusion.

He laughed again. "You are a fierce one. You'd kill me with a look if you could."

I will *kill you and get my mother back*, she thought at him, twisting her hands in their bonds before her, but his attention was turned elsewhere as he dug into his belt pouch and removed the orb, the travel device. He rolled it around on the palm of his hand in an attitude of contemplation.

It all seemed so hopeless, her mother sold into slavery in a far-off land, Torq planning to destroy the Green Riders, and she to be—no, she couldn't even think of it, the horror they would subject her to. The worst part was knowing how her mother would feel, how she would grieve. Melry was terrified for her mother and herself. She didn't know what to do. As much as she wanted to roll into a ball and sob, she knew it would do little to help.

Torq tossed the orb into the air. It glinted in the moonlight. He caught it neatly. No, she thought, she must not give in to despair. Her mother needed her. But what could she do? Up went the orb, and down it came. Torq was enjoying his game, no doubt gloating over his victory. Karigan, she thought, wouldn't give up, though the Karigan she'd seen during their imprisonment was much changed, and not just in appearance. There was a darkness about her, and a hesitation. Melry didn't know all that had gone on with her in the north, but Fergal had told her the little he knew, and some of it had been pretty bad. Her nightmares that had awakened them all were another clue. Still, the Karigan Melry knew wouldn't give up.

The orb arced into the air, but before it could descend, she lowered her head and charged. She rammed into Torq's gut. It knocked the air out of him and he doubled over. The orb bounced to the ground and rolled away. Torq's men were so surprised, they were slow to react when she ran. They attempted to intercept her, but she dodged around them and dashed across wet ground in a beeline for the pond. They yelled and pounded after her.

Her feet sank into mud, but she drove ahead and threw herself through a stand of cattails. When Torq shouted orders at his men, she did not glance behind her, but splashed through water that soaked her skirt and weighed her down. She pushed on up to her thighs. When she was in up to her waist, she held her breath and dove into the inky water among the pickerel weed and lily pads. She frog kicked to propel herself along trying to use her bound hands best as she could.

She was blind in the night dark of the pond, but swam ahead with certainty that whatever lay behind meant only torment and death. Soon the water grew deeper and cooler. When her lungs felt like they must burst, she surfaced for a breath and saw before her the silhouette of a beaver lodge. A crossbow bolt skimmed along the pond's surface beside her. A quick glance behind revealed two figures wading knee-deep looking this way and that.

"But I can't swim," one of the men said.

She sank into the water again and swam for the lodge, kicking furiously, but a shocking pain stabbed her leg and she screamed bubbles. She thrashed and swallowed water and rose once again for another desperate breath.

"You're just wasting bolts," one of the men complained.

"Thought I saw something."

She glanced ahead and the lodge was close now, and she submerged. Each kick sent agony through her leg. The resistance of the water pulled on the shaft of the bolt causing the head to dig into muscle. Then she almost gouged her eye on a sharp stick. Instead it dug into her cheek, but it was nothing for she had reached the beaver lodge. Despite hungering for air, she sank deeper. In natural history class, Master Fisk taught, among other things, about beavers and how their mud and stick homes had underwater entrances. This helped them evade predators and allowed them to enter their lodges when the ponds were iced over in winter. Master Fisk had actually crawled into lodges himself to see what they were like.

The need for air crushed her chest, but she probed beneath the lodge for the opening with her bound hands. When she found it, she pulled herself through it, hoping there wouldn't be angry beavers awaiting her inside. When her head broke the surface, she gasped the air, then worked on squeezing through the entrance into the cramped space that was a beaver's home. No beavers greeted her, and only the faint scent of animal musk and castor, mixed with that of decayed wood and mud, remained. Perhaps this lodge was abandoned.

Immediately she pulled the gag from her mouth, then probed her wounded calf. She had to bite her lip to keep from crying out. At some point, the shaft of the bolt had broken off leaving the head embedded in her leg. There was not much she could do about it but maybe staunch the blood. But even that was not easy to do in the cramped space. She wrapped her leg with the gag. Then she heard voices.

"Not her," said one of the men, not too far off. "It's a log."

"Where'd she go?"

"Maybe you hit her after all. Or she's drowned."

She hoped they hadn't taken a natural history class with someone like Master Fisk.

The voices faded as the men moved on, searching along the shore. She curled up on her side with her knees tucked to her chest in the close space. And she waited.

And waited.

Then she heard the men again. They were closer.

"Gone," one said. "Maybe we did get her."

"Doesn't matter." This time she recognized Torq's voice. "What's important is what the Witch *thinks* we've done to her daughter. She'll never know the difference."

One of the men grumbled.

"I know, I know," Torq said. "You wanted some fun. When we get back up to the pass, choose one of the captives there, maybe that little girl you've had an eye on, and use her as you wish."

Melry swallowed a sob as their voices once again faded and she heard only the croaking of frogs. She started to shiver for her clothes were wet and the intensity of her flight had worn off. The lodge, however, kept her warmer than if she were out in the open air. Finally she gave in to racking sobs for whatever fate her mother would meet in the hands of the Varosians, for the unnamed girl who would suffer in her place in the camp of the Raiders, and for her own sorry circumstances.

She wondered if Weapons cried, and doubted it. They were hard, like granite. To an outsider they might not even appear wholly human. She tried to emulate them, but found she could not. In the mud and jabbing sticks of the beaver lodge, lonely and bereft, she wept until exhaustion took her.

They were down to sixteen Riders in total. Connly had directed Fern and Oliver to accompany Fergal and Megan, and the captive Raider, west to meet up with the king's army. There'd been a happy reunion between Fergal and his old cavalry horse, Sunny, whom the Raiders had been using for their own needs. Karigan smiled at the memory of Fergal throwing his arms around his horse's neck.

But now she and her companions were hunting for Torq and Colonel Mapstone. Ripaeria, who was currently off somewhere making a hunt of her own for sustenance, had scared the Raider into revealing the location of where Torq was meeting with some foreigners—for what, he could not say, no matter how frightening Ripaeria made herself. With the mountains to their left shoulders, the Riders rode as the night sky turned to the gray of morning dusk. They were exhausted, but determined.

Connly, in the lead, called a halt and stood in his stirrups to peer into the distance. "Sandy," he shouted, "up front!"

The Rider trotted his horse up beside Connly and Karigan.

"Do you see a pond ahead?" Connly asked.

Sandy, whose ability was exceptional vision, also stood in his stirrups. "Yes, Captain, a large one with beaver lodges as the Raider described."

"See anyone?"

"No people. Just a couple deer browsing near the water's edge."

Both men eased back into their saddles.

"Let's hope it's the right pond," Connly said. There had been a lot of wet areas they'd passed by, smaller ponds dotted with beaver lodges, but this one was supposed to be particularly large. It had no name and did not merit note on any of their maps as beaver ponds were ephemeral things, turning back into meadows when the beavers moved on. The Raiders had just called it the Big Pond.

Connly gave the word, and they trotted out in two columns, Karigan and Connly leading. By the time they reached the pond, though the valley remained shaded by the mountains, the meadow grass and leaves of aspen and birch took on an emerald-golden cast. Fish surfaced in the pond creating ever-widening rings, birds swept over the water after insects, and beavers swam along bearing branches in their mouths.

There was clear sign of human disturbance in the wet ground near the pond—hoofprints and carriage tracks pressed into the earth. Sandy once again used his special ability to examine the ground while the rest of the Riders stood back so as not to confuse the scene. He squatted and pried something out of the grass which he brought to Connly.

"Brass button," he said. "And blood staining the ground. Not a whole lot, but some."

Connly took the button and held it in the growing light. "From a Green Rider officer's coat, do you suppose?"

Karigan, in turn, examined it. A piece of gold thread hung off it. She nodded, her spirits plummeting. "Looks right."

Connly then called Peri forward. Though she wasn't a green Greenie, she was relatively new and the extent of her ability was not known.

"Can you verify that this button was the colonel's?" he asked her. "I can't honestly think of who else it would belong to, and I am sure she left it for us to find."

Peri took it from Karigan and closed her eyes in concentration. "It was the colonel's, and she was alive when it fell to the ground," she said without hesitation. Then she yelped and jumped backward, dropping it as if it stung her. "Pain," she whispered.

Karigan exchanged an uneasy glance with Connly. The colonel had been alive when she was brought to this location for the meeting with the foreigners. However, when she and Connly asked Peri for more information, all she could tell them was that there had been fear and pain.

⋙ MELRY'S STORY ⋘

"**T**hey need a rest," Karigan told Connly. "You and I need a rest. Not much time slipped by out here while we were in the white world, but in the white world we went on for hours."

Connly brushed his hair out of his face. "If we stand around, it just gives the colonel's captors a bigger lead."

"Look at them." Karigan pointed at the weary Riders and their horses.

"Good thing I don't get tired," Duncan said.

Karigan and Connly glared at him and he slunk away. Karigan was ready to drop the pouch containing his tempes stone and leg bone into the pond. Her back was killing her, her wrist where the wraith had stung it itched like mad, and she thought maybe she'd just fall off Loon in her exhaustion.

As for Loon, the poor horse was worrying himself to pieces over the colonel, circling and pawing at the ground, and tossing his head. He wouldn't be much good for anything if they kept on. Fortunately, Bluebird, who was also clearly upset, but more mature, calmed him with gentle whickers and by keeping close.

"Look, I'm as eager to catch up with the colonel and her captors as anyone," she said, "but it won't do the colonel any good if we're too tired to fight."

"All right," Connly said. "Half an hour."

Karigan raised an eyebrow.

"Three quarters of an hour?"

She nodded. It wasn't a lot of time, but would allow the Riders a chance to relax, maybe eat some travel rations. The horses, likewise, could rest and graze. They'd all be better for it. She gave the Riders the word and they fell out with many sighs of relief.

Before Connly could wander away, she touched his arm. "What does Trace say?"

"They've begun the march from Oxbridge," he replied. "The king is aware we made it to the other side of the Blanding and are in pursuit of the colonel, and he approves that we continue on and confront the foreigners who have seized her."

Karigan nodded in satisfaction and went to loosen Loon's girth and halter him so he could graze. Afterward, she lowered herself into the meadow grass with a wince.

"I believe I will take a rest myself," Duncan said, appearing by her side. "Don't let anything untoward happen to the items in my pouch." He vanished, and Karigan thought once more about the pond with a certain amount of wistfulness.

"How are you holding up?" Tegan asked, sitting beside her.

"About as well as can be expected." She started scratching her wrist.

"I've got some Priddle cream with me that should help," Tegan said. She dug into her pack and produced a jar.

"A thousand thanks," Karigan said. She opened the jar and slathered it on her wrist.

"Looks nasty," Tegan said of the welt.

"Better than it was." The Priddle cream smelled rank, but soothed the irritation almost immediately. She corked the jar and, when Tegan told her to keep it, stowed it in her saddlebag. She then lay down on her side and dropped off to sleep even as she closed her eyes.

A scream woke her from a sound sleep. She sat up blinking rapidly. The dusk of dawn had changed to morning brightness.

"What's going on?" she asked Tegan, who looked more asleep than awake.

"Not sure. Something down by the pond."

Karigan stood unsteadily and drew her sword. Sophina was running toward them, away from the pond. Most of the other Riders were awakening from a nap just like Karigan after having been startled out of sleep. Then she saw why as a creature of mud and pond weed rose out of the water and staggered toward shore. It slipped and fell to its knees. She shook her head. This was no creature. Ignoring her own weariness, she raced toward the pond, followed closely by Tegan and Brandall.

As she neared the pond, she realized who it was. "Mel?" She hurried to her friend's side. Melry smelled of mud and decaying vegetation, and rather strongly of an animal musk. "Are you all right?"

"No," Mel said, with an edge of hysteria to her voice. "I spent the night in a damn beaver den and have a bolt stuck in my leg, *and they took my mother.*" Tears streaked through mud on her cheeks.

Karigan wrapped her arms around her as her body spasmed with sobs. "She's freezing cold," she told Tegan. "She needs a blanket." She thought it was shock as much as being wet that left Melry chilled.

"Right." Tegan trotted back to where the Riders had taken their rest.

Melry eventually calmed down, and by the time Tegan returned with the blanket, her story had begun to spill out. She told Karigan and the others how the Raiders had used the travel device to take her to Torq's tent in the pass where they already held her mother, then brought both of them to this place where they met the foreigners.

"They took her away." She lapsed once more into tears, but after a time said, "They're from Varos, the foreigners."

"They came from some distance," Karigan said. She knew a little about Varosians through her father, who'd done some limited trading with the otherwise reclusive folk. They must have really wanted the colonel to have left their borders and travel so far. "What did they want with her?"

"They wanted her for her ability," Melry said. "It's rare in Varos or something. Torq sold her to them."

Such an ability, Karigan thought, was considered rare among the Green Riders, as well. There hadn't been anyone with the ability to detect honesty since the time of Gwyer Warhein until the colonel. It was an ability that had made

Gwyer Warhein a thorn in the side of King Agates Sealender leading up to the Clan Wars.

"And then they put a centipede in her ear," Melry continued.

"A *what*?"

When Melry explained, Karigan's stomach churned in revulsion and dismay for her colonel, for whom she held the utmost regard. How dare those Varosians steal her away from them and harm her? Melry concluded with how she escaped Torq's men and what they had intended for her, and how she came to spend an uncomfortable night hiding in a beaver lodge.

Karigan was impressed by her quick thinking. "You did well," she told her.

"We have to get my mother back."

"That is the plan," Connly said, crouching beside her. "But first, we've got to do something about that bolt head in your leg."

He and Brandall supported her all the way up to their rest area. They gently set her down to examine her wound while Karigan fetched her waterskin.

"Sips," she told Melry, and handed her the waterskin.

"Oh, look, a leech," Brandall said, pointing at Melry's leg.

Karigan shot him a pointed glance.

Sophina, who'd been hovering nearby, squeaked and reeled away.

"The bolt needs to be cut out," Connly told Brandall.

"Agreed," Brandall replied.

"What do you need to do it?"

"What do *I* need?"

"That's what I said."

"Me?" Brandall's expression was stricken. "Just because my mum's a mender doesn't mean I know how to do this stuff."

"Would somebody do *something*?" Melry demanded. That edge of hysteria crept back into her voice.

Connly and Brandall soon came to an accord about how to deal with the wound. Brandall conceded he'd assisted his mender mother on occasion and theoretically knew what to do. Karigan held Melry's hand and told her about the rescue of Fergal and Megan as they cleansed the wound and cut the bolt head out. Melry's screams echoed through the valley and mercifully she passed out during the process. Brandall sutured the wound while she slept.

"We need to go after the colonel," Connly said, "but we can't take Mel with us. She's in no condition for hard riding."

"You know how angry that will make her," Karigan replied.

Connly shrugged. "If she wants her mother back, she'll understand."

And thus their numbers were reduced by another two Riders. Brandall and Elgin stayed with Melry by the pond while the rest pursued the caravan of the Varosians. Connly was confident they'd have no problem catching up with the caravan that included slow-moving carriages.

Duncan chose that moment to reappear. "It was a very fine rest." Then he glanced down at the unconscious Melry and bloody bandages, and asked, "What did I miss?"

"I can see far," Sandy said, "but in this understory and brush, I can't see much."

It wasn't that they couldn't find the tracks of the colonel's captors—they had left behind numerous hoofprints and wheel ruts. It was just hard to tell how far off they were. The horses were already exhausted by their full night of travel, and it was not desirable to send scouts ahead on mounts that had already been pushed hard.

"Karigan?" Connly said.

"Right." *Ripaeria?* she called with her mind. *Did you feed well?*

Oh, yes, came a somnolent reply. *A nice buck fat on spring grasses.*

Could you help us again?

My belly is very full and I am napping in the morning light.

Karigan wished she was, as well. *We could really use your help.*

I might get in more trouble with my elders. Ripaeria did not sound entirely displeased by the notion.

Picking up on that note of impudence, Karigan replied, *I am sure they'd be very displeased. However, I am also sure that in time, the rest of the eagles will recognize how very brave you are.*

Oh, yes, I am very brave. But I'm so comfortable in my roost.

Are there heroic eagle ballads about those who stay in their roosts? Karigan asked.

Well . . .

No? Well then, I guess there will be none about Ripaeria of Snowcloud Eyrie.

This was met with silence. *I want to, but the sun feels so good.*

Very well, Karigan replied. *We'll go on without you.*

Wait—are you sure about the ballads?

Yes, I am fairly sure they will not sing of Ripaeria who roosted.

There was a pause, then: *I come—don't leave without me! But where are you?*

Karigan smiled and gave her their general location.

"Is she coming?" Connly asked.

"Yes." Karigan listened for a moment and laughed. "She demands to be made a Green Rider. Or, perhaps, a Green Flyer."

"If she can help us," Connly said, "she can be a green whatever-she-wants."

Karigan relayed his words to Ripaeria, who responded, *I come even faster!*

THE BENEFITS OF COMPLIANCE

Laren awoke to a constant drubbing in her head. No, not *in,* but against. Her head was bumping against the side wall of the carriage. She shook it, but vertigo caused bile to rise in her throat. She gagged and tried not to think about the centipede in her head.

"It will soon settle," said a man across from her who was not Tol Asmerand.

She did not remember seeing him before. He had a kindly face fringed by snowy whiskers. He wore long, dark robes. His command of the common tongue was excellent, but his accent was not Sacoridian or Rhovan, nor even Varosian.

"Who are you?" she whispered in a hoarse voice. "Where is Tol Asmerand?"

"Perhaps you would like a drink of water." He held a waterskin for her.

She raised her hands to take it and realized her wrists were manacled. A heavy chain clinked on the floor of the carriage where it was bolted. Her ankles, too, were cuffed and chained to the floor. She gazed at the man.

"Please forgive the precaution," he said. "You are not the first, nor will you be the last, to be so transported."

"Into slavery," she said. She accepted the waterskin and drank slowly, fearing nausea would just bring it back up.

"Many find it a great honor to serve King Farrad Vir. Good service is well rewarded."

"Even that of slaves?"

"Even so."

She thrust the waterskin back at the man. "I already serve

a king, and he is not going to be well-pleased that you abducted his loyal advisor and friend away from him."

The man took the waterskin and dribbled water onto a clean cloth. "I am rather under the impression he is going to be too busy to do anything about it. Still, we have taken precautions."

She glanced at her manacles wondering just what he meant. He then leaned forward to dab her face with the cloth. She jerked back.

"Now, now," he said. "I only mean to help, and the Deija were not kind to you."

"They are murderers," she said. "Did you not know who you were dealing with?"

He did not reply, but she gave in to his gentle ministrations as he cleaned blood from her face and beneath the ear through which the centipede had entered. Then he applied an herb-scented salve to her cuts.

"When we reach our ship," he said at last, "the ship's physician will see to your injuries in a more thorough manner."

"Mending for a mere slave?"

"Ah, but you are not a mere slave, but King Farrad Vir's truth-teller. You will be held with great esteem."

"Then why these?" she rattled her chains.

"Would you have come otherwise?" He chuckled. "You are a Green Rider, and we are aware of the resourcefulness of King Zachary's messengers."

She closed her eyes as the carriage juddered over some obstacle, but her head still swam. When the episode passed, she glanced at the curtain covering the carriage's window, wishing she could open it to see where they were, but her chains did not extend that far.

She wondered about Melry and abruptly shut down that line of thought, for imagining her daughter in the hands of Torq and his men was more than she could bear. Her knuckles turned white as she fisted her hands. She would escape, and when she found Torq, she would disembowel him slowly and painfully.

"Hmm, I sense your intense anger, the seeds of vengeance," the man said. "There is pain and fear, and grief, too."

She gazed at him. "You *sense* it? It seems to me such feelings for someone in my position would be rather obvious."

He gave her a small smile. "Perhaps, but I can *feel* what others feel. When I say I sense your emotions, I mean it literally."

"You're an empath?"

He nodded.

None of her current Riders were empaths, but she'd known one in her past, and it was an ability she would not wish on anyone. It was related to her own, only hers was devoid of emotion, and an empath did not get a direct true or false reading from people, but emotions that would suggest lying or the telling of truth.

"If you are an empath," she said, "why doesn't King Farrad Vir make you his truth-teller?"

"Though I can feel the emotions around falsehoods, my readings are not as pure or direct as yours. Empaths receive not only indication of a falsehood, but all the shades of gray around them. It is not reliable enough to be used in that manner."

"You are not from Varos," she said.

"No. I was born in Bince."

"How did you end up in Varos?"

"Oh, I was young and a seeker of adventure. Became a sailor on a merchant vessel. Once in port, the captain, having learned of my ability, sold me for a great sum to the king's man."

"So, you are a—?"

"A slave?" He nodded, and with great dignity, turned his head and lowered his collar so she could see the disk melded into his flesh. It was inscribed with the image of a two-headed eagle, the sigil of Varos.

Her own was still extremely painful. "Yours is gold." She recalled her own was copper.

"Yes. I oversee the king's personal slaves. The gold denotes my status. If you serve the king well, your status may improve, which would allow you more freedom and other privileges. I've a fine house, my own servants, freedom to move about the city, and a dozen wives."

But not real freedom, she thought. "Did they put a centipede in your ear?"

"Yes, but as I am a good servant and use my gift as the king wishes, it is almost as if it is not there. It lies quiescent."

"They haven't removed it? It hasn't crawled out on its own?"

"To remove it would cause the death of the host, or at least cause him to go insane."

To Laren's dismay, her ability confirmed the truth of his words.

"My name is Navid," he said, "and I will help you navigate the new world you are entering. It is quite different from the one you know. You must forget your king, your daughter, and that you once held a position of authority. You must forget your personhood. In Varos, the status of females is on par with livestock, but in some cases, not even. You will have more value than some females, even more than some men, because of your gift, but do not expect the accord with which you are treated in the court of King Zachary. If you displease your handlers or King Farrad Vir, you will be punished by those like Tol Asmerand who like to train slaves." He tapped the disk on his neck, and she remembered how Tol Asmerand had somehow inflicted pain through hers. "You will be trained so that you understand the benefits of compliance and how to please the king."

With those words, she determined she would do everything in her power to resist. She was sure Zachary would not simply forget her despite the war. At the very least, he'd send an embassy to the court of King Farrad Vir to protest. But in the meantime, she would not capitulate.

The carriage suddenly ground to a halt. Navid looked surprised. He opened the door and leaned out to query the driver in the Varosian tongue. Quite a discussion erupted, and then she heard the sound of hooves and shouting.

A hundred Green Riders stood on a ridge barring the caravan's path of travel. Meanwhile, a great eagle circled overhead. The caravan was, Karigan thought, smaller than she expected. It consisted of one carriage, half a dozen mounted guards, and a supply cart. With Duncan riding behind her, she and Connly advanced. The hundred remained on the ridge, ready to charge in when ordered. Just as well they kept their distance as the illusion that they were would not hold up well to close scrutiny. This was how the colonel had intended to reclaim her captive Riders from Torq, Connly had told her. It was ironic that they were now using it to release the colonel from *her* captors.

The rest of the real Riders had concealed themselves in the forest, ready with bows and arrows and swords should the encounter with the Varosians get ugly. The representative for the Varosians rode forward, a captain from the looks of his insignia, accompanied by his lieutenant. They met halfway.

"I am Captain Connly of His Majesty's Messenger Service," Connly announced. "More of my people are keeping close watch on you and your caravan from concealment. I would not make any ill-considered moves were I you."

"There will be no ill-considered moves," the Varosian captain replied in heavily-accented common. He then bowed at the waist. "I am Captain Erl Avanon of Varos. There is no reason for hostility."

"No?" Connly said. "You have abducted Colonel Laren Mapstone of His Majesty's Messenger Service, who is also King Zachary's esteemed counselor and friend. You abducted her on Sacoridian soil, and for that the king will pass judgment on you."

"I am afraid there is a misunderstanding," Captain Erl Avanon replied. "We have done no such thing."

"He is lying," Karigan murmured.

"I quite agree," Duncan said.

The Varosian gave her a peculiar look, then said to Connly, "It is gifted to tell truth from false?"

"*She* is," Karigan said. He did not seem to want to look directly at her. "But perhaps not in the manner in which you are thinking."

"I will not speak to females," he told Connly.

Duncan laughed. "Your loss, friend."

"You are in Sacoridia," Connly replied. "You'd best get

used to it. Rider G'ladheon is our Chief Rider and a knight of the realm."

"I am also the sub-chief of my clan," she said. "A merchant clan as it happens, so I am pretty good at spotting a liar, though not as good as our colonel."

"Release Colonel Mapstone immediately," Connly said, "or you will face the consequences." He nodded back at Hoff's illusion.

"There is a mistake here," Captain Erl Avanon said. "I but escort a gentleman, a servant of King Farrad Vir."

A man suddenly stuck his head out of the carriage's window and shouted in Varosian. The captain struggled not to show his aggravation. He did manage to respond to the man in a respectful tone.

"Apologies," the captain then told Connly. "The gentleman wished to know why we have stopped."

Karigan glanced over her shoulder at the illusory Riders. She wasn't sure how long Hoff could hold it. Some of the figures appeared to waver.

"I may be able to help," Duncan whispered, picking up on her concern, and he disappeared. The Varosians gasped, and the captain exclaimed in his own tongue.

"We will search your carriage," Connly told the captain before the Varosians could dwell on Duncan's magical disappearance.

"That is not acceptable," the captain replied. "The gentleman is a favorite of King Farrad Vir. Under whose authority—"

"The king of Sacoridia on whose lands you trespass," Connly said.

He and Karigan urged their horses past the sputtering captain and his lieutenant and made for the carriage. Karigan yanked the door open and Connly demanded the occupant exit in the name of King Zachary. The man complied, but to Karigan's disappointment, there was no sign of Colonel Mapstone or anyone else within.

"I am but a finder for my king," the man was explaining to Connly. He said his name was Tol Asmerand. "I seek collectible treasures, unique curios—art and antiquities and the like. I have been given an additional mission of determining if this realm is worthy of formally collaborating in trade, but thus far—" and here he glowered, "—I find it wanting."

Most of it rang true to Karigan. The man was who he said he was. But something was off. "Your king does not like outsiders. Why would he like the objects and art of outsiders?"

The Varosian pointedly ignored her. "It offends me," he told Connly with a sniff. "I will not speak to it."

Karigan had heard a little about this facet of Varosian culture from her father. She sighed, and while Connly barked questions at the man, she looked to the sky.

Ripaeria, do you see anyone hiding nearby? Not our Riders, but other people who belong to this caravan?

I can see no one.

This just wasn't right. Melry had witnessed Torq selling her mother to the Varosians. When she turned her attention to the scene before her, Tol Asmerand thrust a paper in Connly's face.

"You will see I have the proper seals for passage through your country, and additionally, a letter of introduction from Prince Theron of Rhovanny. An ally of your king, no?"

Connly examined the paper, then tilted his head in a thoughtful manner that Karigan associated with his using his ability to communicate with Trace, who must be relaying information to King Zachary in turn. Good. Not that Karigan didn't trust Connly's judgment, but Zachary's would be the final word.

"Well?" Tol Asmerand demanded.

Connly blinked rapidly as he ended his communication, but he did not immediately respond to the Varosian.

"Chief Rider, instruct our, er, Riders to stand down."

"What? Why—?"

"Do not question me. Do as you are ordered."

Karigan was about to retort, but restrained herself. Although it was hard to get used to, Connly was now her captain and commander. She must obey.

She reined Loon around and cantered into the woods where Hoff concealed himself, with Duncan sitting beside him. She passed on Connly's order and the young Rider looked relieved, while Duncan gave her a questioning look.

"Later," she muttered, and she watched as the illusions rode off into the woods where they promptly dissolved into nothing. The Varosians then continued on their way, unhampered.

She rode back to where Connly sat watching the caravan disappear over the ridge.

"Why?" Karigan demanded. "Why are we just letting them go?"

"Their papers were in order," he replied, "and the king told me to let them go."

"What of the colonel?"

"I don't know, Karigan."

Loon snorted and danced beneath her, echoing her displeasure. She reined him around as if to pursue the Varosians.

"You know that man was lying," she said.

"Most likely, but we have no proof."

"I could go after them, see what I—"

"*No,*" Connly snapped.

Karigan stilled in her saddle, by turns startled, angry, and—much to her shame—relieved that she would not be allowed to face the possible danger that could come with trailing the Varosians.

"The king wants us to meet him at the pass," Connly continued in a more measured tone. "*All* of us."

"Why won't he let us go after the colonel?"

"He need not explain himself to us," Connly replied. "You will follow orders." It was not a question. "I don't want you haring off."

Haring off?

"You are not on an independent mission," he continued, "where you decide what to do next. You obey the king like the rest of us, or you will be charged with disobeying an order at best, and desertion at worst."

Karigan's mouth dropped open. Did he really think her so intractable that he had to threaten her? Yes, she'd briefly entertained the idea of looking for the colonel on her own, but it wasn't like she routinely disobeyed orders, though it was true that she—*all* of them—were accustomed to working on their own as the job required without orders of any kind to guide them in the interim. Considering her penchant for finding trouble, she supposed it was not surprising Connly singled her out.

But maybe it wasn't about her. She peered at Connly as he sat in the saddle, staring at the ridge. Maybe, just maybe, he was insecure in his new position as captain, and now with the colonel missing, he was in charge.

"Look," Connly told her quietly, "I don't like it anymore than you, but orders are orders. Especially those that come from our king."

"I understand," she said. Relief once more flowed through her, with the accompanying shame. This day she would not have to confront fears of danger, of possible capture and torture, but the guilt of her relief would cling to her until they could get the colonel back.

Loon proved balky when the Riders formed up to leave as if he knew they were giving up the search for his mistress. He half-reared, and when she brought him down, she patted his neck. "Sorry, boy. We'll get her back, I promise, but the king needs us now and she'd want us to go to him."

The question was, *when* would they get the colonel back, followed by what means? And who would do the getting? She tried to remind herself that Zachary was not given to making arbitrary decisions, especially when it concerned someone as dear to him as the colonel, and perhaps he had some other plan in mind. She could not imagine what, however, when he had pulled them off the trail.

"What's going on?" Laren asked Navid when he ducked back into the carriage. She hoped against hope that it was, by some miracle of time and distance, her Riders out there to reclaim her.

"It would appear we are being rejoined by Tol Asmerand," he replied. "He served as a decoy, and was intercepted by a large force of your messengers, but they let him go, as we hoped would happen in such a situation, when they found no evidence of you." He smiled briefly. "No one was hurt, and the wards concealing us from your people proved effective."

Laren's hopes plummeted to despair. She closed her eyes and tried to contain her emotions. Her Riders had come after her, had come so close, but the Varosians succeeded in deceiving them.

Someone knocked on the carriage door. Navid opened it, and after a brief conversation in Varosian, he told Laren, "Excuse me again. I am afraid they require me for a consultation."

She watched, devastated, as he stepped out of the carriage once again. If the Varosians could hide her so effectively from her own Riders on home soil, what chance had she of rescue once they left Sacoridia's shore? She must find her own way to escape, but as her chains clinked and rattled with her every movement, her prospects seemed ever more bleak.

Without warning, a sharp pain, accompanied by vertigo, stabbed through her head and left her gasping. The centipede was moving around. Blood trickled afresh from her ear. Intense white pain exploded in her skull and she passed out.

She blinked rapidly when she came to, sweat gliding down her face. Her head and ear throbbed, but the intense pain had subsided. As she regained equilibrium, movement on her arm caught her attention. The centipede. Its multitudinous legs trailed her own blood down her sleeve. She shook it off in disgust, and it coiled up when it hit the carriage floor. She squashed it with her heel.

Why had it crawled out? Navid had said they could not be removed. Not that she had *removed* it; it had crawled out on its own, and perhaps that was the difference. She nudged its remains beneath her seat. She had no wish for her captors to realize their etherea-sensing centipede was no longer in her head and give them cause to put a new one in. Without it, she would be able to lie about her readings of truth and falsehood, and they would be none the wiser, and best of all, its absence meant she would not be put in excruciating pain when she did so. It was an unexpected bit of good fortune she'd been lacking until now.

Even as this positive development sank in, she became aware of another change. Something . . . Something was missing, as though a part of her had gone dormant. She was oddly put in mind of what it must be like for the Lady Fiori to have lost her beautiful voice. Or maybe what it was like to lose one's sight or hearing.

"I have black hair," she said, and waited.

Nothing.

"I look forward to being the slave of King Farrad Vir."

Again, nothing. No response from her ability.

She glanced down at her coat for the reassuring golden glimmer of her winged horse brooch, but it was gone. She looked wildly about trying to see if it had fallen off in the carriage, but she could not find it.

Then she stopped. She did not know whether to laugh or weep. Her brooch had abandoned her. It had once belonged to Gwyer Warhein, and she had worn it for most of her life. It was gone, and that meant she was no longer a Green Rider.

The tears and laughter came at the same time. The brooch that had tied her to the messenger service, the lifetime occupation into which she had poured her identity, had abandoned her, and all her sacrifice was for nothing.

The Varosians' truth-teller had lost her magic.

Losing the centipede had not been lucky after all, but an effect of her brooch abandoning her. She sobered, realizing her peril had increased significantly. If the Varosians learned she no longer had her magical ability, they'd kill her on the spot.

The carriage leaned as Navid climbed back inside. He took his seat opposite her, and a smile froze on his face when he gazed at her. "Oh, my," he said. "It would appear the centipede has been giving you some trouble." He started dabbing his cloth at the blood around her ear and neck. "Sometimes it takes a while for them to settle in."

The blood and her tears must suggest to him that this was indeed the case. She certainly was not going to enlighten him.

She would have to bluff her way with the Varosians while she attempted to devise a plan of escape.

"The ship's physician should have something for the pain. We are now to make our way to Storm Harbor where our ship awaits at anchor. If you can bear it for a little longer, we'll be there before you know it."

The carriage lurched into motion. Laren did not respond to Navid. Let him believe she was nearly incapacitated by pain from the centipede. It would be her first performance of many.

⇜ FAILURE ⇝

 *T*he caravan of the little man has turned southwest, Ripaeria told Karigan. *It has not met up with any other. If your colonel is out there, she is beyond my range.*

"Thank you, my friend," Karigan told her.

I must go now. I tire and am far from home, and my elders will be beyond displeased with me.

Karigan bade the eagle farewell and relayed what she had been told to Connly, who in turn relayed it to the king through Trace. The Riders then rode on at a desultory trot. Loon bowed his head in an attitude of dejection and heaved a bone-rattling sigh.

They backtracked, bearing east toward the mountains, the sun warm on their backs, and did not push their weary mounts. The Riders spoke little and their expressions were downcast. Karigan knew they all felt as keenly disappointed at the failure of their mission as she did. No, not the failure of the mission, but failing Colonel Mapstone. She prayed that Zachary had some plan to bring her back.

Duncan, in contrast, whistled a jaunty tune behind her as if they were out for a pleasant day's hack in the countryside. She ground her teeth as her irritation rose.

"Would you *please* stop whistling?" she told him.

"Oh, sorry. The eagles like it. They find it entertaining."

"*I* am not an eagle."

"All right, all right. Gloomy bunch you all are."

More than one Rider gave him a dark look.

When they finally reached the big pond, Elgin and

Brandall hurried to meet them, but the hope on their faces quickly faded. It was Melry's cry of *"Where is she?"* from where she sat on a blanket with her injured leg propped up that speared Karigan's heart.

"I'm sorry," Connly said. He dismounted and led Will to the edge of her blanket. "We couldn't find her."

"Why aren't you still out there?" she demanded. "Why aren't you still searching?"

"The king ordered us back."

"What the hells!" She tried to stand, but fell back with a cry of pain.

"Easy there," Brandall warned her, helping her settle back down. "You don't want to start the bleeding again."

"Give me a horse—give me Bluebird, and *I'll* go find her."

When she attempted to rise again, Karigan dismounted Loon and hurried to her. "Mel, you're going to reopen your wound."

"Why aren't you out looking for my mother? *You* of all people?"

Momentarily taken aback, Karigan wondered if Melry now expected miracles of her. She knelt beside her friend. "I'm sorry, Mel, but the king ordered us *all* to return."

"Since when do you follow orders?"

"What? I—"

"I hate you. I hate you all!" Tears ran down Mel's flushed face.

Karigan drew her into her arms. "I'm sorry, Mel, but we have to follow the king's orders."

Mel sobbed against her shoulder. "Why? Why would he call you back? I thought he loved her."

Karigan had thought so, too. She rubbed Mel's back. "He does. He absolutely does. We don't know why he decided we must give up the search, but it may be he has some plan in mind."

"I want my momma."

"I know, Mel, I know." Melry's grief almost brought Karigan to tears, but she knew she must not give in. She couldn't let Melry or the other Riders see her lose hope that they'd get their colonel back.

While she comforted Melry, the Riders watered and rested their horses, and prepared to resume their journey.

When Connly indicated they were ready to go, Karigan said to Melry, "When King Zachary arrives, why don't we find out how he plans to get the colonel back."

"Better be good." Melry wiped the last of her tears away and consented to be helped into Bluebird's saddle by Brandall.

Karigan wearily mounted Loon and rode beside Melry and Bluebird, both horses carrying on with heads hung low. They knew their Rider was in danger and worried about her.

The sun continued to descend behind them as they approached the mountains.

"Now look at that," Duncan said. "Look at the color on the peaks."

The sun washed the mountains in magenta with its setting.

"I never got to see it from this perspective in the eyrie. Would Softfeather ever take me out to see the sunset? No, he wouldn't. He never took me anywhere, really, unless I bothered him enough about it. It was terribly boring, and when you consider the only entertainment was those terrible ballads of theirs? Gah.

"Softfeather had a cousin, though, named Airghost. What a preener! He was actually kind of interesting, always bragging about all the eaglesses he mated and how many eggs he attributed to his virility. He refused the mate-for-life thing and claimed the females positively swooned over him, like they do me. Since we had something in common, we became friends."

He continued on in this vein, filling in for the weary silence of the Riders, long after the colors faded from the mountain and dusk set in, until finally it became too much.

"Shut up," Karigan and Connly told him in unison.

"Well!" he huffed. "I know you've had a bad day, but it's no reason to be rude." He vanished, probably to sulk. Karigan sighed in relief at the peace and quiet.

They were ordered to regroup and camp just outside the valley Second Empire had occupied before they moved up to the keep, and await the king's army. They found a spot well out of sight and took turns keeping a distant watch on the pass so they could report anything of interest. All they could tell, however, was that Second Empire was making itself at home there.

Within a day and a half, the vanguard of the army arrived to root out any of the enemy that might be lingering in the valley, and any traps they had left behind. Among the vanguard's complement were those who planned the arrangement of the encampment.

Karigan and the Riders watched as that night and throughout the next day troops marched in, pennants held high, and a tent city arose in the valley with astonishing speed.

The Riders picketed their horses and helped set up their section of the camp. Elgin, meanwhile, escorted a protesting Melry to the menders.

"But I want to talk to the king," she said.

"I know, lass," Elgin said, "and he will want to talk to you, too, but first things first."

Connly found Karigan as she tapped tent stakes into the ground, and said, "The king wants to see us."

They ran into Fergal, who had returned with the army.

"How are you?" Karigan asked.

"Fine." He leaned toward her and said in a quiet voice, "We need to talk."

Before he could explain, Connly called for her to come along, but she paused. "We have to go see the king now, but could you do me a favor?" She slid Duncan's pouch off her shoulder and passed it to him. "Could you hold onto this for a little bit?"

"This is, er, Duncan's?"

"It *is* Duncan. He seems to be keeping dormant at the moment." She didn't want him to suddenly materialize while she and Connly were reporting to Zachary. At Fergal's uncomprehending look, she explained, "He's like the great mages down at the wall."

"Oh, I see. Huh." He glanced about, and once again quietly said, "Don't forget. We need to talk."

She nodded, wondering what was on his mind.

"Karigan!" Connly cried.

"Coming!"

They made their way to the king's tent with the royal standard, emblazoned with the firebrand and crescent moon, planted before it. A pair of black-clad Weapons stood between flickering torches, guarding the entrance. They parted the flaps so Karigan and Connly could enter.

The tent was large and divided into "rooms." The first room held a couple tables. The king and his officers hovered over one that was covered in maps and lit by the golden glow of a lamp. The other held mugs and pitchers, the remnants of a meal, and an Intrigue board. The curtained-off spaces were Zachary's private quarters.

Counselor Tallman leaned toward Zachary to speak into his ear, then pointed at Karigan and Connly. Zachary nodded, said something to his officers, then turned to take in his Riders. Karigan and Connly approached and bowed.

When Karigan looked up, his expression was carefully neutral. Even though he already knew the particulars of the Riders' attempt to rescue the colonel, he listened intently as Connly described in detail all they had seen and done, beginning with the journey through the white world. When Connly came to the part about the whisper wraiths, concern glimmered in Zachary's eyes.

"From here on," Zachary said, "the white world, or the Blanding as Duncan calls it, will be off limits as a means of passage. There is too much we don't know about it, and apparently a good deal of danger."

It was a decision Karigan applauded, though in her experience, entering the white world was not necessarily a matter of choice.

When Connly described Karigan using Ripaeria to get their captive Raider to talk regarding the colonel's whereabouts, Zachary said, "That Raider was still gabbling about the eagle and giblets when he was brought to us," he said. "She made quite an impression."

Ripaeria, Karigan thought, would be pleased to hear it.

When Connly finally concluded his narrative with watching Tol Asmerand's small caravan leave them, Zachary told them, "You did as well as you could. Thank you, Riders."

It was a dismissal, but Karigan couldn't help herself. "What about Colonel Mapstone?" she asked.

He turned his unreadable gaze on her. "It will be dealt with."

"But we should have kept on her trail, or at least pressed the Varosians more."

"Karigan," Connly said in a warning voice.

"They were lying," she said, ignoring him.

"It will be dealt with," Zachary said. "You are excused."

His response, toneless and almost cold, left her speechless. Connly grabbed her arm and dragged her out of the tent, and then he pulled her aside.

"I don't know, or at least I don't want to know, the extent of what is between you and the king," he whispered, "but this is the *king* and you are his messenger, his *servant*. You obey his orders. You leave when excused. You do not question him. I don't know how much of this insolence the colonel tolerated from you, but *I* won't allow it."

Karigan was flabbergasted. Before she could respond, he added, "Whatever the two of you do in private is one thing, but when you are on duty as a Green Rider, he is your king and nothing more. You especially won't question him when others, such as his counselors and officers, are present. You will also obey me when I give you an order. Do you understand, Rider?"

"I—"

"Do you understand?"

Not knowing what to say, she nodded.

Connly sighed. "Now that you are Chief Rider, you have an example to set for those we lead, and I expect nothing but professionalism from you."

"Yes, *sir*," she said, and she refrained, if barely, from bringing up his relationship with Trace, a subordinate, and how they would be keeping one another warm in his bed this night. It was understood among the Riders that their shared abilities forged the bond and intimacy between them, a bond that was broken only in death, but what sort of example was *he* setting?

"Get some rest," he told her. He strode off leaving her standing by herself overwhelmed by feelings of guilt in addition to her sense of failure at not having rescued Colonel Mapstone.

He was right to put her in her place as far as the king was concerned. She was not off on a message errand making her own decisions in her own way. This was a different situation, where she must fall in line and obey orders from her superiors, and she must especially not question those from Zachary, her king. It was for the better. Their regard for one another had caused her to forget he wasn't just any man, and that she was nothing more than his servant.

She shook her head. They were all on edge after failing to rescue the colonel, and Connly, especially, must be feeling the pressure now that he was fully in charge.

She was about to go in search of her tent assignment when a hand gripped her shoulder. She whirled to find Willis, one of the king's Weapons, gazing down at her.

"Sir Karigan," he said, "the king wishes you to return in two hours."

"What? Why?"

"He likely has further questions for you."

"Oh. Of—of course." Or, was it an excuse to see her? It was so confusing. He'd been distant, almost cold, and now he wanted her to return?

"Also, on the morrow, we will begin training. First crack of dawn."

"We will?"

He nodded. "We need to get you back into fighting form."

Fighting form, she thought as she stumbled in a daze to the row of tents occupied by the Green Riders, the banner of the winged horse rippling above. She was on the one hand pleased to be getting back to ordinary activity and regaining strength and honing her skill, but on the other hand, nervous that that strength and skill would not come back, that the torture had so injured her that she could not attain the same level of sword mastery she'd once possessed. She paused and closed her eyes. Even worse than all that was the worry that even if she got fit and was able to wield a sword at the same level as before, would she lose her nerve in a fight? She trembled.

"Karigan?"

She opened her eyes to find a concerned Tegan standing before her.

"Are you all right?" the Rider asked. "You're looking a little pale."

"Just tired," she replied. It was true. She had not quite recovered from the night she stole Torq's travel device, their adventures in the white world, and pursuing Colonel Mapstone's captors.

"Well, then, I have our tent assignment and we're together. Why don't you get some sleep?"

She followed Tegan to the tent and, once inside, dropped into one of the bedrolls and remembered no more.

⋙ AT THE D'YER WALL ⋘

Alton swung a sword at the creature with his right hand, and a torch with his left, the flame flaring in a long arc.

"Keep those fires burning!" he shouted at his soldiers, and barely missed being disemboweled by one of the creatures.

They had come at dusk, scrambling over the repairwork of the wall's breach, agile as squirrels, as large as shepherd dogs, and bearing quills like a porcupine. Unlike porcupines, they were not content to amble along on their own business. These fought with rabid tenacity, using sharp fangs and claws. They did not like the light, so the soldiers of the breach had built bonfires and bore torches and lanterns to push them back. The creatures cast hideous, bristled shadows against the wall, the fever dreams of Mornhavon the Black brought to life.

The torch hissed as Alton pushed it into the face of the creature. It reared and hesitated, and he thrust his sword into its belly and slashed. Steaming entrails spilled out. In the defenders' favor, the creatures appeared to be rather dull-witted.

He glanced around camp. Soldiers fought and shouted. Some lay on the ground injured and moaning. No few had quills stuck in them. Captain Wallace fought with his legs bristling after wading into a cluster of the creatures to help one of his overwhelmed warriors. It had to hurt.

Mister Whiskers, one of the wall encampment's resident gryphons, screeched as he leaped onto a creature, his tawny flank golden in the firelight. Part catamount and part raptor—except when he chose to present himself as a house cat—he had the best ensemble of predatory tools to shred the creature to bits—talons, claws, beak.

Alton braced himself as another of the monsters hurtled out of the dark straight at him. For all their ferocity, they made no roars or growls, but grunted and chuffed with the occasional squeal. This one's beady green eyes flickered in the light of his torch. He tried to jump aside to avoid its charge, but it deftly turned with him. Once again he employed the torch, but the creature kept coming on. He hacked with his saber, but the quilled hide might as well have been armor. The blade bounced right off. The difficulty was getting at the underbelly where there were no quills, which meant provoking the beasts into rising onto their haunches and facing fangs and claws.

It snapped at his leg and he jumped back. Instead of wearing himself out by uselessly hammering on it, he waited. Waited for it to spring forward, jaw agape, and when it did, he rammed his sword right down its gullet. The creature pushed itself up the blade to reach Alton, but stopped at the guard, before finally slumping and sliding back off onto the ground, dead. Alton withdrew his sword, and backed away, then wiped the mucusy slobber and blood off the blade onto the ground.

When he looked up to see where he could help, he discovered the fighting had quieted significantly. He directed the menders to aid the wounded, and knelt by the side of a young soldier clearly beyond help. He bled from a torn throat.

"Easy," Alton said softly, not sure if the soldier heard him. "You're not alone. Easy, now."

He continued to comfort the soldier and stayed by his side until the light was gone from his eyes. It was the hardest part of this business, losing people like this, and he knew it was only going to get worse. Afterward, he rose to find Captain Wallace standing beside him, his legs still full of quills.

"You need to see the menders, Captain," he said.

"I will. Just letting the severely wounded get seen to first." He gazed at the dead soldier and shook his head. "If not for that gryphon, we'd be a lot worse off."

Alton glanced at Whiskers who tore into the gut of one of the creatures and tugged out entrails, purring happily as he fed. It was Whiskers who had given the encampment the warning it was about to be attacked. The human guards at the breach had been overrun before they could sound the alarm. It was indeed lucky Whiskers had come with him to the encampment for his usual inspection of the wall. He wondered if there was a way to convince him to stay and keep watch, but with a brood of gryphlings to help care for, Alton was doubtful. When the gryphlings were old enough, however?

The captain, he noticed, was shivering. "You need to get to the menders," he said. *"Now."*

Wallace nodded and limped away.

Alton caught sight of Corporal Manning and called to her.

"Sir?" she asked.

"I think we should make another bonfire right in front of the breach. Maybe burn the corpses of these creatures. Think you could organize a crew to do that?"

"I'll see to it at once."

The light would be, he thought, a deterrent against more creatures crossing over, and with so many of the wall's people wounded, help with keeping the breach guarded.

"Take extra care in the handling of the corpses," he told her. "Their quills, and even their blood, could be poisonous."

As the corporal set off to attend to the dead creatures, Whiskers took flight with a hunk of meat clenched in his talons, undoubtedly destined for his mate, Midnight, and the gryphlings in Tower of the Heavens. Since the feeding of the young had begun, the tower smelled of rot, and he was constantly cleaning out bits of bone and hide of the various prey animals that were brought in. In one case, he'd found an entire rack of deer antlers. He hung *that* over the tower's hearth.

He glanced around at the carnage. There'd been a couple dozen of the beasts, and all were slain. He was unsure of the human casualties, but saw the bodies of at least two others nearby.

When he was satisfied the encampment's dead were being cared for and a more than adequate pyre prepared for the corpses of the creatures, he set off for the dining hall, which had been turned into a makeshift house of mending. Smells of herbal concoctions competed with that of blood and the stew they'd had for supper. Leese and her assistants were tending bites and clawings, and pulling quills out of the defenders. No one else appeared to have died in the attack. He found Captain Wallace laid out on a table, a blanket drawn to his chest, seemingly deeply asleep with a pile of quills beside him.

Leese left what she had been doing to join him. "We put the captain out," she said. "He was just too full of quills and it was easier on everyone when it came to removing them."

Alton could imagine. He was more relieved than ever that he'd made it through the attack unscathed. "Poison in the bites or quills?" He knew Blackveil Forest and its predilection for poisonous flora and fauna well.

"Not that we can yet tell," she replied, "though we are taking precautions to treat the wounds as if they have been poisoned."

"Good." Leese had been, Alton thought, stationed at the wall long enough to know the ways of the forest.

"Is it my imagination," she said, "or are these incursions growing in frequency?"

"You are not mistaken," he replied quietly. The forest had become more restless of late, more awake, or at least that was the consensus of those who guarded the breach, and Alton's own observations.

"And we're not going to get more help, are we?" Leese asked, just as quietly.

Alton shook his head. D'Yerian forces had been mustered northward to join the king's army, and additional Sacoridian regulars certainly would not be sent down. They were needed for whatever moves the king was planning to make against Second Empire.

"What are we going to do?" Leese asked.

He looked down at her as she absently wound a bandage into a roll. "What we have been doing, and hope those gryphlings mature quickly and cooperate." He'd also be sending more reports to the king, imploring him to provide more troops. If there was a concerted invasion, the encampment would offer no impediment. He picked up one of the quills that had been stuck in Captain Wallace. It was as long as his forearm with little barbs that made it stick in the flesh of victims. "Do you need these for any reason?"

She shook her head and raised a questioning eyebrow. He smiled in return. He'd write a report about the incursion for the king. Perhaps including a bundle of quills with it would help bring the seriousness of the situation to the forefront of his mind.

If not? Well, then he and the others would continue to face whatever the forest sent their way on their own. It was all they could do.

⭆ BOBCAT ⭅

Alton took his morning kauv outside and sat on a bench. The birds fluted and warbled in the woods sounding perfectly normal despite the previous night's violence. The embers of a fire upon which they had thrown the corpses of Blackveil's unnatural creatures still crackled and spit by the repairwork of the breach. Smoke plumed above the pyre, staining the fresh blue sky. To either side of the repairwork, the D'Yer Wall rose infinitely. The actual stonework was about ten feet high, but magic made it soar to the clouds. That magic had been lost to them over the centuries, and even if they'd the knowledge of it, it would require blood magic, the sacrifices of thousands.

Had all those lives been worth it to build the wall? Alton only knew that it had kept Sacoridia and the free lands safe from Blackveil for nearly a thousand years, and it would have continued to do so for another thousand had an Eletian with dark intent not broken it. Now, that weakness, the breach in the wall, could prove disastrous should Mornhavon the Black awaken again and call upon the dread denizens of the forest to cross the breach and invade Sacoridia.

He waved away a biter that hovered near his ear and took a sip of his kauv. Hot and bitter, just what he needed after a night of too little sleep. Then from the corner of his eye, he observed movement near the woods. His hand found the hilt of his saber, and he waited.

A bobcat limped out of the underbrush and watched him. Alton was relieved it was not one of last night's creatures, but was this an ordinary bobcat, or a Blackveil bobcat? Most wild cats would usually hide rather than reveal themselves to humans. It took a few more steps forward and it was then that Alton saw it was full of quills.

Someone walked up behind him. "Lord Alton—"

He raised his hand for silence, then pointed at the bobcat.

"Huh," Corporal Manning said in a hushed voice. "I was about to report that we found two more creatures while on patrol. They'd been shredded like what Whiskers did last night. I assumed it was his work, and maybe it was. This fellow looks too small to have done much damage to those things."

Alton agreed. "See if there is some of that sausage or ham left over from breakfast. Tell the cooks that I am ordering it brought out."

Manning obeyed, and when she returned, she brought a pan of sausages and ham oozing with drippings. She was followed by Leese.

"There is more if we need it," Manning said.

"Poor thing," Leese said, observing the bobcat. "It needs help."

Alton took the pan and carried it toward the bobcat, moving slowly so as not to spook it. He set the pan down and retreated to the bench. They sat in silence for some time waiting to see what the bobcat would do, but he just crouched there and watched them with wary eyes. Leese eventually left to check on her patients, and Manning headed off to attend to her duties, leaving Alton to wait on his own.

"C'mon," he coaxed. "That's good meat."

The bobcat crept forward, but paused when a great winged shadow passed over him. Suddenly Whiskers dropped out of the sky and landed beside the pan. He screeched and spread his wings in an unmistakable display. The bobcat did not slink away, but enlarged, sprouted wings, and roared. Another gryphon! He was compact, as dappled and bobtailed as his bobcat form, and reminded Alton of a falcon. The two gryphons growled at one another.

Would the new one stick around? Not if Whiskers proved too territorial. Their growling was intense enough Alton could feel it vibrate through his body. Whiskers leaped aggressively toward the bobcat gryphon. The bobcat gryphon leaped toward Whiskers. The two hissed and snarled and swiped. They tussled and parted before pacing one another with yowls and deep growling.

Afraid there was going to be a full-scale gryphon fight, Alton grabbed a nearby bucket of water and ran toward Whiskers. "Leave off!" he shouted, as if a gryphon would listen to him. Whiskers growled and gnashed his beak at him.

"Bad gryphon!" Alton prepared to toss the water on him.

But to his surprise, Whiskers sat. "Meep?" he said. It was such a small sound for such a large creature.

Water sloshed over the rim of the bucket as Alton stumbled to a halt. "Don't hog all the meat. That's for our new friend there."

"Meep?"

"Yes, meep," Alton replied, though he had no idea what Whiskers had said.

"Mhirr?" the bobcat gryphon said.

Whiskers swiveled his head to gaze at him. "Meep."

"Mhirr."

Whiskers then backed from the pan and mantled his wings. Alton, too, backed off and set down his bucket.

At first the bobcat gryphon circled the meat aggressively with wings outstretched, but then folded them and settled before the pan. He sniffed cautiously at the food, then snapped up a sausage and gulped it down.

Leese returned and said. "He's a gryphon! I can't believe it. I hope he stays. Isn't he a beauty?"

"Yeah, but I don't know how we're going to get those quills out."

"We've been talking it over inside and have a plan. Of course that's before I knew he was a gryphon, but leave it to me."

Leese acquired more meat and dosed it. The gryphon gorged himself and, after, lay full length in the sun and nodded off. Leese and her assistants approached him with care. They trussed his legs and pulled a sack over his head in case he awoke while they worked on him. Alton left them to it, as he was overdue to inspect the breach.

Aside from the remains of the bonfire, there was little evidence of the previous night's battle. The repairwork remained fine and sturdy, and the wall to either side as immutable as ever. Closer inspection revealed, of course, the D'Yer Wall was not so permanent, and the edges that bordered the repairwork were riddled with fine cracks. They, in fact, extended in either direction for quite a distance. He'd been monitoring their advance, and though they'd not changed much recently, even a little was a blow to his clan. His ancestors had created the wall to last for all time, but over the generations, their vigilance in maintaining the wall had lapsed, causing it to become vulnerable to the dark magic of one Eletian who opened the breach. It was a grave dishonor to the clan. Should Mornhavon the Black throw the might of Blackveil against the wall, all of Sacoridia would pay the price for Clan D'Yer's failures.

He pressed his palms against the cool nubbly surface of the wall next to the breach. Silver runes flickered briefly between his hands. They were an old warning of damage to the wall. Merdigen had taught him enough of the ancient Sacoridian and Kmaernian to decipher the runes.

If he focused hard enough, he could sense the song and rhythm of the wall guardians within stone and mortar. When he returned to Tower of the Heavens, he would commune more deeply and sing with them, strengthen their rhythm, which in turn would help maintain the strength of the wall. The guardians were not enthusiastic about him, and he suspected some were still suspicious of him after Mornhavon had tricked him into nearly destroying the wall. The one they really wanted was Estral, and he was sure she'd be here helping if only her voice had not been stolen.

He looked up at the approach of a horse and rider. It was Dale Littlepage on Plover. She halted before Alton and dismounted.

"Mad Leaf told me there was an incursion," she said before any greeting could be exchanged. Mad Leaf was the mage at Tower of the Trees, where Dale was stationed with a small encampment. She was the only Green Rider King Zachary spared him. She must have traveled all night and pushed hard to arrive here so early in the day. She'd be particularly concerned about Captain Wallace, he knew.

He told her about the battle with the creatures. "We lost three of our people," he said. "Wallace was hurt, but is recovering fine."

She leaned against Plover's neck in relief. The mare nickered and turned her head to look at her Rider. Dale and Wallace had been a couple for a while now.

"You look exhausted," he said. "After you check on Wallace, rest up for a bit. I have an assignment for you."

She looked up at him. "You do?"

He nodded. "I need you to go to King Zachary with a message. He's leaving us too vulnerable down here."

"Are you expecting something . . . imminent?"

"Imminent or not, we need reinforcements."

He watched after her as she led Plover away, hopeful the king would heed his plea for help, but, in truth, expecting that they'd have to face whatever came next on their own.

A JOYOUS AND FRAUGHT TIME

"Look," Anna said, pointing across the pasture.

Condor sidled a few more steps toward Angry-Mad even as he grazed. The mare flicked her ears back but continued grazing. She did not squeal and move away in a huff as she had when any of the other horses neared her.

"She's more accepting of him than the others," Mason said. He was a new Rider who had arrived shortly after Colonel Mapstone and King Zachary left for the mountains. He had just begun an apprenticeship with an animal mender in Hillander when he heard the call. Horse Master Riggs was so pleased to have an animal mender among them, even with only nascent skills, that she intended to ask Colonel Mapstone to allow him to continue his apprenticeship with a local animal mender as his Green Rider duties allowed. "And do you notice that he stays on her sighted side?"

Anna had not, but she nodded.

The two leaned against the pasture fence, enjoying the peaceful scene of horses grazing, insects droning over the top of the grasses, and small birds darting after them. Tails swished at flies, and the horses made contented sighs as they tore and munched on grass and the sun warmed their backs. To Anna, thoughts of war were far off, except for the fact that there were too few horses in the pasture.

"You say she was found at the knacker's?" Mason asked.

Anna nodded. "She was so skinny you could see her ribs."

"Looks like she still has a ways to go," he replied, "but she's probably much improved from where she was."

325

Angry-Mad had not made quite the progress they had been hoping for, despite the good, regular feedings she received at Rider stables, but yes, she'd come along miles from the sorry, abused creature she had been. Her coat now gleamed and her mane and tail lacked snarls due to Anna's diligence. Anna might risk life and limb grooming the tempestuous mare, but she got the job done. Angry-Mad put on a good show of fighting the rigorous grooming, but Anna thought she actually liked it. Riding was another matter, however, and Anna had the bruises to prove it.

"I was thinking," Mason said, "maybe you ought to start calling her something else other than Angry-Mad."

"Like what?" Anna called her a lot of things when she was acting up, most of them not very nice.

He shrugged. "I don't know, but it's like when you call a thing a thing, it becomes that thing."

"You mean that by calling her Angry-Mad, it makes her angry? And mad?"

"There are certainly other reasons for the way she is, but what I'm saying is that by calling her Angry-Mad, you are predisposing yourself to expect that behavior, and horses are sensitive. She can pick up on how you feel, and she is only too willing to accommodate you. It's like a—a self-fulfilling prophecy."

"Huh." Anna had never thought about it that way. Angry-Mad had come with the name, and she hadn't changed it because she thought it was appropriate.

"Names have power," Mason said.

She thought he might be right. She'd changed her surname to Ash when she signed on to the messenger service. Her family had abandoned her at the castle when she was little, so she abandoned her family name. The Riders were her new family, the one she had chosen for herself, and "Ash" represented who she had been and her pride in that person, as humble as being an ash girl had been. It also represented that she was rising out of the ashes, so to speak, as she entered her new life as a Green Rider.

"You are very wise," she told Mason.

He laughed. "Oh, I don't know about that. My grandsire

was always saying stuff like that, and I guess I picked up on it."

However he had gotten it, he'd sure given her something to chew over.

"I'd better go," he said. "I'm due to clean stalls and I don't want Hep to think I'm shirking my duties."

Anna watched him saunter off toward the stables. She was done for the day with her classes and chores, but when she returned to the castle, she got a pot of tea and a couple scones from the kitchen and carried them on a tray all the way to the Rider wing where she knew Lieutenant Mara would be hard at work on accounts, or scheduling, or whatever needed doing since she was in charge of the Riders still at the castle and all the administrative details that went along with managing them.

As expected, she found the lieutenant in her room at her desk poring over a ledger, old burn scars on her face puckered as she frowned at the figures on the page before her. The room was a dreary contrast to the sunshine in the pasture and Anna knew she'd made the right decision.

The lieutenant looked up when she noticed Anna. "What's this?"

"I used to look after the colonel like you always asked me to," Anna replied, "but since she's away, I can look after you."

"It's very kind of you, but not necessary." The grateful expression on Lieutenant Mara's face said otherwise.

Anna poured her a cup of the tea. "No honey or sugar, I'm afraid. Nor cream. The cooks are hoarding what they've got."

Lieutenant Mara accepted the teacup and sighed. "Shortages. I hear there are ships in port from the Cloud Islands filled with sugar and fruit, but they're just sitting there because no one is willing to transport goods overland with the Raiders at large. They're dumping the rotting fruit into the harbor."

"Maybe we can have honey soon," Anna replied. "They're setting up hives in the gardens." The central courtyard gardens, once flourishing with decorative plantings, had been transformed into orderly rows of sprouting vegetables.

"I actually prefer honey." Mara sighed. "But I guess it will be a while before the likes of us get any." She sipped her tea.

"Anything I can help you with?" Anna inquired, eyeing the piles on Mara's desk.

"How is your arithmetic?"

Now Anna frowned. "It is not my best class."

"It was never mine, either." Mara thumped the ledger in front of her. "Daro and Karigan are the ones who are good at this. I just mess it up."

Daro Cooper was off with Colonel Mapstone and the other Riders, and Karigan was . . . Well, it was hard to say where Karigan was. She'd been a captive of the Raiders, but just the other night, Lieutenant Mara had received a message from her that she'd arrived outside the city and that she was going to set out for Oxbridge and try to catch up with the king and colonel. The note was terse, but she'd said the Eagle's Pass Keep was now occupied by Second Empire, and that the Raiders still held Fergal, Megan, and Melry. There'd been no details about how she escaped the Raiders, how she had ended up at Sacor City with such suddenness, nor how she expected to catch up with the king and colonel. Lieutenant Mara and Castellan Javien, Anna had heard, had not been best pleased that she had not come up to the castle to report in person.

"Anything else?" Anna asked.

"It's good of you to ask," Mara replied, "but if I'm not mistaken, you are off duty for the rest of the day."

"Yes'm, but I thought—"

"None of that, Rider. Take it from me, when you've got free time, enjoy it because there will be too many times when it won't be possible."

"Yes'm."

"You are dismissed now. I thank you for the tea."

Anna started to leave, but paused in the doorway. "Lieutenant?"

"Yes, Anna?"

"Do you think Fergal and the others are going to be all right?"

Mara turned in her chair to gaze at her. "Well, if Karigan managed to escape—and that's a story I'd very much like to hear, by the way—it gives me hope for the others. But I don't know, and it will be a while before we get any other news."

Anna nodded and headed down the corridor. It was quiet with so many Riders away, and those who remained were mostly at class or training. When she reached the common room, she peered inside. One Rider sat sprawled in the armchair in front of the hearth. The weather was warm enough that no fire had been lit.

"Merla?" she asked.

The Rider made a noise and Anna strode across the room to where she sat. Merla's face was so swollen with hives that she could barely open her eyes.

Anna placed her hands on her hips. "You've been working too hard again by the looks of it."

"Finally finished placing wards in the royal apartments and corridor." She waved her hand in the air, and it, too, was swollen, her fingers stubby sausages.

One benefit of not having a magical ability, Anna reflected, was not having to "pay" for its use in some unpleasant way, like Merla and her hives. "Don't you think you should go to the menders?"

"It'll go 'way in a few minutes. Now the job is done like they wanted. No magical attacks or trespass on the queen or babies."

That was why she'd been pushing so hard, Anna thought, to be sure she completed the warding before the babies came. She sat in a rocking chair next to Merla. It creaked as she slowly rocked. She'd stick around to make sure Merla's swelling went down as she claimed it would.

"What next?" she asked.

Merla sighed. "The castle, from top to bottom. The Eletians said there are already some wards around, old ones that need refreshing. I haven't come across them yet, but the Eletians said I'd sense them as I worked."

In the winter, visiting Eletians had shown Merla how to go about setting wards to protect the queen after an attack by the aureas slee. The slee had slipped in anyway after disguising itself as King Zachary. Merla had then worked on strengthening the wards to prevent something like that from happening again.

"How long will it take?" Anna asked.

Merla laughed. "Years. But at least the babies will be protected for now, and probably just in time. Queen looks ready to burst."

"Burst?"

"Any day now."

It was both a joyous and fraught time, the birthing of heirs that would ensure the continuity and stability of the throne. The happiness of new life was tempered by the threat of all that could go wrong. Anna's mother had suffered no hardship in pregnancy and birthed many healthy children—it was why Anna had been abandoned—too many mouths to feed. But it was different for everyone, and this being the queen of Sacoridia and a time of war, any loss of queen or heirs would be a loss for the entire realm, and a victory for the enemy.

⊰⊱ THE UNCALLED RIDER ⊰⊱

That the west castle grounds were empty was a testament to the realm at war, so many soldiers pulled north and now to the east to face Second Empire. Usually there were cavalry soldiers exercising their horses, or units drilling in formation. Today, there were only Anna on Angry-Mad and Horse Master Riggs riding Condor. The west castle grounds was a large open sward with the castle rising to one side, and the castle's curtain wall to the other. Anna, who had only ridden the mare in the close confines of the paddock with a fence around her, felt insecure in the openness. No doubt Angry-Mad, or "Maddie," as Anna had decided to call her after her talk with Mason, could sense her apprehension.

Master Riggs sat Condor like it was more natural than standing on her own two feet. The gelding, she said, needed exercise, and she was certain Karigan would approve of her riding him. He certainly didn't look as if *he* minded. She also said that since he and Maddie seemed to be getting on, or that Maddie at least tolerated him, that his presence might prove reassuring to her.

Anna had groomed her without injury. Most of Maddie's attacks had become half-hearted as she grew accustomed to the attention, but half-hearted could still hurt. Anna also got used to Maddie's ways. The mare gave off signals when she was about to explode, and Anna's reflexes had grown swift. Of course, avoiding the mare's sensitivities was the best way to prevent problems, but it wasn't always possible, and some of her outbursts were due to ill-humor and sheer orneriness.

"Posting trot," Master Riggs ordered.

Anna squeezed Maddie's sides and they circled Master Riggs and Condor at a trot. Maddie had been well-trained at some point in her past and knew the signals. In fact, her gait was lovely and smooth.

"Very good," Riggs said as Anna made her circuits. "The more I think about it, the more I believe she was someone's fine riding horse. She really does have elegant movement."

Anna was pleased her one-eyed, angry-tempered mount had some positive attributes. She was actually enjoying the ride until she realized Maddie had laid her ears back and was dropping her head.

Oh, no! Anna tugged on the reins to pull the mare's head back up, but was too late. Maddie bucked and Anna was flung forward in the saddle. She grasped a handful of mane for the second buck and held on.

"Good save," Master Riggs said. "Now see how keeping your heels down aids in maintaining a good seat so you don't get thrown?"

"Yes'm," Anna replied, feeling slightly rattled.

"No telling what set her off, though," Riggs continued. "Your hands were quiet, so it wasn't that."

For Maddie's part, she behaved as an obedient horse as if nothing had happened. The lesson proceeded more calmly until Riggs asked Anna to ride at a canter down the length of the field. Maddie started tossing her head, bucking, and twisting until she succeeded in dislodging her desperate Rider. Anna hit the ground and the air *whooshed* out of her lungs. For a moment she was not sure what happened, but then she saw her horse calmly grazing just a short distance away.

"Ow," Anna said.

Maddie flicked her ear and swished her tail, and generally looked pleased with herself.

Master Riggs trotted up on Condor. "You all right?" she asked.

Anna wanted to say that no, she was not all right, but replied with the expected, "Yes'm."

"Good," Riggs replied. "You know what to do."

Anna did. It was certainly not the first time she had ended up on the ground thanks to Maddie. Still, it was with no small amount of trepidation that she took up the reins, put her toe in the stirrup, and swung up. The mare tossed her head and stamped, but otherwise tolerated being mounted.

The rest of the lesson went more or less without incident. A small buck here, vigorous head tossing there, and resistance to Anna's commands, but no spills. The one was going to be enough to make her very sore by the next day.

Following the lesson, after the horses were untacked and brushed down, she and Master Riggs gazed at Maddie in her stall. Maddie gazed back at them with her one eye.

"It's not just orneriness from abuse," Master Riggs said, "though that's a lot of it. She's trying to tell us something, but for the life of me I can't figure it out."

The mare blinked, then went to her hay rack, leaving the pair to gaze at her rump.

"We've given her the gentlest bit," Master Riggs continued, "had her thoroughly examined by a mender and farrier, and treated her well, but something is still not right."

Mason appeared beside them with his pitchfork. "How'd it go today?" he asked.

"The usual," Anna replied. "Only got thrown once this time, though."

Mason's eyes were keen as he gazed at Maddie. "She's a fine-looking horse up close as she was at a distance yesterday. She looks healthy, but . . ."

"But?" Master Riggs said.

An odd look entered Mason's eyes. "Could be better."

"She was in rough shape when we got her," Master Riggs said, "and she's been on a long road to recovery."

"Hmm," Mason said. "Anyone look at her teeth?"

"Of course. They were floated just—"

Not seeming to hear the horse master, Mason handed his pitchfork to Anna and went to the stall door. Maddie whirled and lunged, but he dodged her teeth just in time.

"What are you trying to do?" Anna asked.

He did not answer. In fact, there was a faraway look to his eyes as if he was unaware of anyone but the horse. He slowly advanced on the stall door again. "Easy," he murmured.

Maddie laid her ears back again.

"Easy." He continued to speak softly, and Maddie held herself ready to lunge but did not act. In fact, she seemed to relax as he continued to murmur to her. Then something curious happened. A blue glow formed around his hand, just like Anna had seen when Ben worked on healing Ty.

Maddie appeared mesmerized by Mason, and he by her, as if they were in rapport. Her ears slowly went to point, then flickered to pick out his words. She did not react when he placed his hand on her cheek. The glow pulsed and it seemed to flow into her cheek; then after several seconds, it vanished. His hand dropped to his side and he stumbled backward. Master Riggs caught his arm to steady him.

"You all right?" she asked.

"I—. Yes. What just happened?"

"You healed Maddie," Anna said. "Or something."

"Oh." He wiped the back of his hand across his forehead. "Guess I did. It—it just flowed out of me, the energy, and somehow I knew what to do."

"What did you heal?" Master Riggs asked. She'd been around Green Riders enough that she was aware of their special abilities.

"Tooth infection," he said. "Back tooth, just starting to form an abscess. That's why she was tossing her head so much and being picky about her food. Whoever looked at her in the beginning missed it. Easy to do, I suppose, especially when she's so hard to handle. Also, her eye socket, the empty one, was bothering her. It gets itchy from dust and whatnot and should be cleaned with a damp cloth now and then."

"You got rid of the infection?" Anna asked.

He nodded. "I repaired the tooth and gum. She'll eat with no trouble now, and I expect she'll get to her full weight in no time."

"Aeryc and Aeryon," Master Riggs said. "I'm afraid I wasn't seeing past her personality to know she was hurting." Despite her own misperception, the horse master looked extremely pleased. "Not only are you an apprentice animal mender, lad, but a true healer. This is wonderful. Your services will be in high demand."

He gazed at his hand, opened and closed it. "I can't believe it. It was so clear what to do." He looked at Maddie again and grinned. "She's feeding easily."

Maddie indeed tugged at her hay and ate with enthusiasm.

"Thank you," Anna said, and returned the pitchfork. "I think Maddie thanks you, too."

"You found another name for her. I like it."

Anna nodded. "Doesn't sound, well, so angry."

"I think I need to go sit down," Mason said. "Feeling kind of weak all of the sudden."

They watched after him as he made his way down the aisle and sank down onto a hay bale, his back against the wall.

"No doubt that's his ability exhausting him," Master Riggs said. "Keep an eye on him until he feels better, and then tell him to report to Mara. She'll want to know. And I'm sure he and Ben will have a lot in common to talk about when they've a chance." She turned back to the stall. "As for you, Lady Maddie, I am sorry I missed the signs you were hurting."

Maddie flicked an ear in acknowledgment.

The horse master chuckled. "Good lesson today, Anna. Now that Maddie's painful issue has been worked out, I expect more improvement in the coming days."

After Master Riggs departed, Anna approached the stall. Maddie whirled again with ears pressed back.

"All right, I know," Anna said. "You are still you, but I'm glad you feel better."

Maddie snorted and returned to her hay. Anna started down the aisle to check on Mason, but paused to pat Condor on the neck. He nuzzled her shoulder and blew softly through his nostrils. She was under no illusions that she'd ever be able to have these kinds of moments with her own horse, which, of course, hurt in a lonesome way; nor would she be able to wield such incredible and important magic like Mason. Imagine! The ability to heal! Sometimes, actually, a lot of times, it depressed her that she couldn't have a real Rider horse or do magic, but at least she was a Rider. She could never be unique in the way they were, but maybe among them, she was the unique one. The uncalled Rider who lacked a special ability and rode a one-eyed horse. She laughed and decided she'd just keep telling herself how unique she was.

 ⊰ AN ATTACK ⊱

The next day, Anna was, as predicted, quite sore from her fall. However, it did not excuse her from arms training or any of the other tasks required of her. She was heading to her chamber in the Rider wing when Lieutenant Mara poked her head out of her doorway and called to her.

"Yes'm?" Anna said.

"Do you have time to run some reports up to the queen?"

"I do."

"Good. I was going to send them with a Green Foot runner, but there's been some sickness among the servants and the runners have been pulled to cover other duties. Besides," Lieutenant Mara added with a smile, "the queen likes you."

Anna accepted the reports still bewildered by the idea the queen thought anything about her whatsoever. She hurried to change and wash up before heading to the west wing of the castle. On the way, she wondered what sort of sickness had hit the servants this time. It wasn't unusual, given how close they lived and worked together.

She strode through the main castle corridor. It was much quieter than usual, like castle grounds, with so many off to fight Second Empire. The corridor seemed all the more cavernous and echo-y.

She paused in a seating alcove to fix the buttons on her shortcoat—in her hurry she'd done it up unevenly and it just wouldn't do in the presence of the queen. Unfortunately, the alcove was occupied by her old foe, Nell Lotts. She groaned and turned to move on.

"Well, if it isn't Anna *Ash*," came Nell's mocking voice.

Anna took a deep breath and turned back around. "Hiding from your work again, Nell Lotts? And with so many other servants sick?"

"So? No one ever notices. And I suppose you are *so* important you are on your way to see the queen again."

"As a matter of fact, I am."

"You're just a runner. The queen probably doesn't even notice you."

Anna smoldered, wanting to tell Nell how the queen liked her and had actual conversations with her, but the best answer was to walk away. Nell, however, decided to make another jab.

"Not trying to ride that ugly horse of yours today? And I mean *trying*. I hear you end up in the dirt more often than not."

So, someone was keeping an eye on her to see how she failed. "At least I have a horse," Anna retorted. "How many do you have, Nell Lotts?"

She did not await an answer, but charged out into the corridor and fixed her buttons as she walked. She should report Nell for neglecting her work, but the last thing she wanted was to get entangled in the affairs of servants again, especially if it meant confronting Master Scrum, who oversaw them. He'd made her life miserable before she had left to join the royal household to serve the queen. When she became a Rider, she'd thought herself well free of it all. She then felt guilt at her parting jibe at Nell. Servants, of course, were not wealthy enough to own horses, and few could even hope to aspire to a level where they could. She knew all too well what the life of a servant was like, and how futile hopes and dreams could be, and pointing it out to even Nell Lotts was insensitive in the extreme.

She tried to put it out of her mind as she entered the west wing and climbed the stairs to where the royal apartments were located. When she reached Queen Estora's door, she found it guarded by a pair of Weapons she did not know. They must have been brought up from the tombs to replace those who'd gone east with King Zachary.

"I'm Rider Ash," she said. "I've some reports for the queen."

"Are you healthy?" one of the Weapons asked.

"Yessir." Of course they would not want anyone with the sickness that was going around to enter the queen's presence.

"Wait here a moment," he said. He passed inside, leaving Anna to wait uncomfortably beneath the deceptively impassive gaze of the other. Little, she knew, escaped the notice of Weapons.

When the first Weapon returned, he said, "You may enter. The queen awaits you."

Before she proceeded, she worked up her courage and asked, "What are your names?"

The two exchanged surprised glances. She assumed they were rarely asked down in the tombs.

"I am Lennir," said the one who had gotten the queen's permission for Anna to enter.

"And I am Scotty," said the second with a slight bow. He was clearly the younger of the two.

"Please call me Anna. I am pleased to meet you."

This brought tentative smiles to their otherwise stern faces, and it pleased her. She couldn't imagine working in those tombs all the time, which she thought must be so gloomy.

When she reached the queen's chamber, it was bright with the drapes drawn back. There were even more plants than before, filling up floor space, and any other flat surface. It was a garden gone wild. Many of them leaned not toward the light, but toward the queen on her bed.

"Anna," the queen said, "I am so delighted to see you."

A servant was handing her a glass. "Your concoction from the menders, my lady. You must drink up."

"Thank you, Felice. Rider Ash will see that I do. You may be excused."

The maid, whom Anna had never met, hesitated before bowing her head and leaving.

"Come sit beside me," the queen said.

Anna obeyed and sat in the chair at the queen's bedside. The queen herself looked, if anything, even more enormous than the last time, and fairly uncomfortable.

"Master Mender Vanlynn says my time is very soon. It will be such a relief. If I remain in this prison much longer, I will go mad."

Anna did not know what to say to that, so she said, "Lieutenant Brennyn asked that I bring you these reports."

Queen Estora smiled. "Keeping me informed as I had asked your colonel to do. You may set them on my bedside table and I will look them over in a while."

Anna found a spot for them beside a bushy fern.

The queen took a sip of her drink and grimaced. "My concoction from the menders. It's a little more bitter than usual. It's supposed to relax me and be healthful for the little ones. Now, tell me all that you've been up to since last you visited."

The queen was eager for even the most trifling news, and so Anna told her of her continuing trials with Maddie, including the healing Mason had performed.

"Another true healer," the queen said. "That is wonderful news. I wonder if his gift works only with animals, or if he can use it with people, too?"

Anna certainly did not know, but the queen's curiosity aroused her own. Surely the two abilities couldn't be all that different, but she'd never heard of Ben true healing an animal. She'd have to ask.

As they talked, the queen sipped her drink, her expression growing ever more pinched.

"I don't think Felice prepared this correctly," she said. She poured the remaining contents, more than half the glass, into the fern plant. "Don't tell her I did this."

"I won't," Anna said.

"Felice is kind and helpful, but she isn't my Jayd, or even one of my other maids." She sighed. "They all came down ill, even Mistress Evans, and that woman never gets sick."

The conversation moved on, the queen asking how the courtyard gardens looked, and she showed Anna a baby blanket she was embroidering. It featured frolicking Hillander terriers, and each square featured a border of flowering heather. Anna, who had not learned the finer stitching techniques noblewomen were expected to perfect, was duly impressed. But then, while describing how the stitching was done, the queen trailed off and an expression of discomfort flickered across her features.

"Is something wrong, Your Majesty?" Anna asked.

"Just feeling . . . I'm all right." She smiled and started to explain how the blanket would be pieced together.

Felice entered the chamber to collect the empty glass. "Is there anything else you wish of me, my lady?" she asked.

"No, thank you, Felice."

The maid bowed her head, but paused and gave the queen an odd look before turning to leave.

"Now, where was I?" the queen asked.

Anna's gaze drifted to the fern plant the queen had poured her drink into. It had wilted.

"Oh, yes," the queen said. "The stitching of the border. It was—" The color suddenly drained from her face and she doubled over.

Anna jumped to her feet. "What is it, Your Majesty?"

"Terrible cramps." She moaned.

"I'll get Ben right away," Anna said, but when she got to the door, Felice blocked the way.

"No, you won't," the maid said.

"What? The queen needs—"

A knife flashed in Felice's hand, and with reflexes honed by working with Angry-Mad, Anna jumped back. Felice pushed forward and swiped the blade, and Anna again evaded it with a sidestep.

The queen cried out in pain. A quick glance revealed she was curled on her side.

Felice cut at Anna again, but Anna managed to evade the knife once more. *"LENNIR! SCOTTY!"* she cried at the top of her lungs.

A look of alarm, then determination, came over Felice's face, and she charged toward the queen. Anna ran after her. Without thinking, she grabbed a flowerpot with a lily in full bloom, and as Felice raised her knife to strike the queen, Anna bashed the pot over her head. Felice sank to the floor unconscious.

When the Weapons arrived, Anna said, "Something is wrong with the queen and the maid tried to kill her. I'm gonna get the menders."

She did not wait for Lennir's reply, but set off at a run and did not stop until she reached the mending wing. She babbled at the menders until they understood what was wrong. Ben was found, and he and two others charged from the mending wing. Master Mender Vanlynn hobbled behind with her cane at a much more sedate pace.

"Come, Rider," Vanlynn said in a calm voice. "Carry my kit for me and tell me exactly what happened." When Anna did so, the mender said, "And the maid attacked you, and then tried to attack the queen?"

"Yes'm."

"Are you hurt?"

"No'm. My horse trained me to move quick." Anna just felt shaky from the excitement of it all, both full of energy and just ready to collapse, but she kept by Vanlynn's side at her slow, slow pace.

"Good. That means just one patient." Was that a smile playing on Vanlynn's lips? How could she be so calm with the queen in distress?

"Will Queen Estora be all right?"

"There is no telling until we have a look at her, see what we're dealing with. Help me up these stairs, child, then you must tell Lieutenant Brennyn to come to the queen's apartment to wait with the others."

"The others?"

"The higher-ups who will be witness to whatever outcome there is for the queen. When a monarch is ill, it's very important business as to how the realm proceeds, and if the worst should happen, well, decisions must be made."

Anna helped Vanlynn up the stairs in the royal wing. Already, important looking-people were congregating outside the queen's door. Weapon Scotty guarded it, looking fierce.

"Go now," Master Vanlynn told Anna.

Anna hurried down the stairs and to the Rider wing, praying all the way that the queen and her babies would be all right.

THE CLAMOR OF THE BELLS

"**Y**ou're not doing anyone any good pacing like that," Gil said. "You'll wear out your boots." He sat at the long table in the common room playing a card game with Merla. There had been no news about the queen, and there was no getting near the royal wing at all to try to find out what was going on. The way was blocked by a wall of Weapons, and there was no openness to their demeanors. They were steel, and they did not look at all like they would budge. Not that anyone would try to force their way through, anyway.

"How can you just sit there and play cards?" Anna demanded.

"I got no use for pacing," Gil replied, "so might as well play cards."

He hadn't had a knife drawn on him and he hadn't seen the queen doubled over in pain, so maybe it was no wonder he was calm.

"Hah!" Merla exclaimed. "I've got three cats." She laid her cards down.

Gil groaned. "Good thing we're betting only coppers or I'd be in big trouble."

Anna wanted to take their deck of cards and throw it at the wall. As she was contemplating doing just that, another Rider entered the common room. Ty Newland made his slow, limping way to the table and sat heavily in one of the chairs. He'd only recently been released from the mending wing, and remained off duty while he continued to recover from the injuries delivered by the Darrow Raiders.

"Evening," he said.

"Good to see you, Ty," Merla said. "Can we deal you in for a round of Cats and Mice?"

"Afraid I don't know that one," he replied. "I've actually come to let you know that Mara sent me a runner with the news that the queen is in labor."

"Is she all right?" Anna asked.

"Mara said nothing more than that."

Was it coincidence, she wondered, that the queen went into labor after the servant, Felice, pulled a knife, or had that somehow set it off? She loosed a trembling sigh and finally sat down next to Merla. Merla patted her on the shoulder.

"I'm sure Queen Estora is receiving the very best care from Master Vanlynn and Ben, and she'll be fine. You had a hard day, too, what with that woman pulling a knife on you."

"You had good sense smashing that pot over her head," Gil chimed in.

"I hope no one else tries anything," Anna said.

"Too bad my wards only help with magical attacks," Merla said.

"No doubt the Weapons are scouring the castle and grounds to make sure there aren't more people with ill-intent skulking about," Ty said.

A shadow filled the common room's doorway. "That we are," said the Weapon who stood there. They had not heard her approach. "I am Sergeant Brienne Quinn, and I am looking for Anna Ash."

Anna stood. "I'm her. Anna Ash."

"I would like to have some private words with you, Rider Ash."

Chairs scraped the floor as the other Riders stood and departed.

"Please sit," the Weapon told Anna.

"Am I in trouble?"

"I just want to hear your version of events from this afternoon in the queen's chamber."

They sat across the table from one another, Gil's deck of cards between them. Anna told the Weapon everything she remembered.

"Thank you, Rider," Sergeant Quinn said. "This gives me a better picture of what happened."

"You believe me?"

"Is there a reason why I should not?"

"I'm just a nobody, and maybe you think I meant to do something bad to the queen."

"Generally," the Weapon said, "we trust the word of Green Riders. The calling the Riders answer seems to choose honorable and honest individuals."

"But, I was not called," Anna replied. "I'm not like the others."

"Are you saying you are not honest and honorable?"

"No—I mean, I . . ." Flustered, Anna stared at the tabletop.

"We are aware of your background and how you became a Rider. Wasn't yours a calling of a sort?"

"That's what the colonel said."

Sergeant Quinn nodded. "A calling that was different from the others, but with similar intent. You *chose* the calling where the others had no choice, and that means something. Also, Colonel Mapstone is an excellent judge of character and she would not have championed your becoming a Green Rider without good reason. Not to worry, Rider, you are not under suspicion. The woman, Felice, has confessed to poisoning the queen and—"

"Poison!" Anna exclaimed. "Is the queen gonna be all right?"

"It appears so, if labor and birthing go well. That drink you saw her pour out while you were there? It was tainted. In any case, she did not receive a full dose of the poison, and the menders created an antidote to remove whatever she did ingest from her body."

Anna went limp in her chair with relief. "I hope it does not hurt the babies."

"That is what we all hope. Frankly, Rider Ash, though you may doubt yourself and your position among the Green Riders, you have proven yourself one of them. Your quick thinking saved the queen, first when you stopped Felice from using a knife on her, then when you immediately ran to get the menders. If you had not been there, we might have had a terrible tragedy on our hands."

"Why did Felice want to hurt the queen?"

"She is an agent of Second Empire," the sergeant replied. "She was determined to kill the queen and children in a single blow as a victory for her people. She was also responsible for making so many in the servants' quarter sick so she could gain access to the queen. She, and likely others, had planned this for many long months, how she would gain access and get around the Weapons, but what she didn't count on was a Green Rider wielding a flowerpot. Felice is not best pleased with you." The sergeant's serious expression broke with a smile. "That was well done, by the way. I think your colonel would be proud."

Anna's cheeks warmed from the praise, unexpected as it was from a Weapon. "What happens now?"

The sergeant stood. "We will continue to investigate whether there are other enemies who have infiltrated the castle, despite Felice's claims she acted alone. And also, we must pray that the queen and her children make it through the night alive and well. As for you, Rider Ash, I thank you for answering my questions and the service you rendered the realm today." With that, she turned on her heel and swiftly strode from the common room.

Anna did not know what to do with herself after that. Had Sergeant Brienne Quinn actually validated her status as a Green Rider? She felt both elated and exhausted. She did not think she'd be able to sleep at all that night, so she decided to wait in the common room until they received word of the queen. Many of the other Riders must have felt the same as they congregated in the common room to play cards or tell jokes. There may have been laughter and some singing, but behind it all was a nervousness about the queen's condition, the heirs, and what it meant for the future of the realm if things went badly.

As the story of Anna's victory over an agent of Second Empire got passed around, the Riders congratulated her. Gil decided to reenact the head bashing with a flowerpot, much to the hilarity of all.

Worry lent a frenetic quality to the laughter. It was a little too loud, the Riders a little too eager to horse around and find some outlet for their nerves.

Anna dreamed of bells. Bells clanging through the city enough to vibrate the table and throb in her skull. When she raised her head from the table, she realized it wasn't just a dream. The bells were ringing in actual fact, and not just the ones down in the city's chapel of the moon but from all over, including the castle.

She rubbed the crust out of her eyes and realized she'd fallen asleep at the table in the common room. Dusky morning light filtered in through the arrow slit windows. Across from her, Gil's mouth was open in a cavernous yawn.

"What is all the noise?" Merla asked in a peeved voice, her eyes squinted.

A few other Riders had also managed to keep vigil in the common room through the night, as well, and looked disoriented and spoke in hushed voices.

Why the bells? Had the queen died?

"The queen!"

Everyone woke up then and started talking all at once, wondering what it meant. Then Lieutenant Mara entered the common room. She'd dark circles beneath her eyes.

"Yes, it is the queen," she said. And then she grinned. "The queen is well, and so are her twins, a boy and a girl. Rejoice, Riders, all came through the night well."

Anna was so relieved that tears trickled down her cheeks. The queen meant so much to her beyond the fact she was the queen. She'd taken an interest in Anna, which had very much changed the course of her life for the better.

Merla and Gil did an impromptu jig to celebrate, and the others clapped and shouted.

When everyone settled down, Lieutenant Mara said, "You all know that this doesn't mean you get out of classes, training, or chores today. I expect you all to look sharp."

This was met with good-natured groans and protests, but the Riders started to disperse to get ready for what was surely going to be a long day.

As Anna began to leave, Lieutenant Mara touched her arm. "Anna, I heard all about what you did to protect the queen yesterday. Well done. I am glad the colonel chose to make you one of us."

Anna was filled with so many emotions she didn't know what to say.

The lieutenant then sighed. "With an event like this, normally we'd send Riders to all the lord-governors with the news, but they are scattered across the provinces dealing with Second Empire, and our experienced Riders are with the king and his army, and can't be spared."

"What will you do?" Anna asked.

"The lord-governors will have to wait, but there is one person who very much needs to know as soon as possible."

Anna smiled. "King Zachary."

"Exactly. And it'll be just the news he needs to lift the spirits of his troops."

"Who will take the news?"

"I'm sending Ylaine," Lieutenant Mara replied. "She is our most experienced Rider here, after Ty and Merla. Ty is not able to ride yet, and Merla needs to keep working on the castle wards."

It would be an honor to be the one to take that message to King Zachary, but Anna was relieved it wasn't her. She was not ready for a long distance errand, and she couldn't imagine trying to ride Maddie cross-country just yet. Which reminded her . . .

"I have an early riding lesson today," she told Lieutenant Mara.

She ran down the corridor to prepare for the day like all the other Green Riders even as the clamor of the bells continued unabated.

⇜ PLAYING GAMES ⇝

Karigan grunted when Tegan shook her awake. The canvas of the tent walls was infused with sunshine.

"I brought you some tea and meat rolls," Tegan said.

"What time is it?" Karigan asked, rubbing her eyes.

"Mid-afternoon."

"What?" Karigan sat up and looked about in a panic. "I was supposed to answer more questions for the king last night, and then train with the Weapons this morning."

"It's all right." Tegan passed her a steaming mug. "We reminded the king and the Weapons of how exhausted you were, but you are to go see the king when you are ready. And take your time—a few extra minutes won't hurt anything."

Karigan took her advice and savored the tea, then washed from the bucket of chill water Tegan had dragged in. She stepped outside into the brisk air and found the camp alive around her with soldiers walking or running among the tents, the babble of voices, orders being snapped out in the distance. The air smelled of woodsmoke and cooked meat. The attitude of the camp had not changed from last night, which probably meant there had been no aggression from Second Empire, and that all remained as well as could be expected under the circumstances.

She walked to Zachary's tent, determined to behave as Connly had ordered her the previous night. She would be professional and not seem to question Zachary's authority as king. She found Willis and Ellen again on duty at the entrance.

"Sorry I missed my training," she said.

Willis nodded. "Tomorrow morning will be soon enough." His countenance did not reveal approval or disapproval.

She took a deep breath and entered the tent. Zachary and a few of his officers stood over the map table, looking at what appeared to be the plans of a building, which was more than likely the Eagle's Pass Keep. The paper was yellowed and cracked.

"The problem is getting in," General Washburn was saying.

"They used magic to take our people out," said a gruff major Karigan didn't know. "We don't have the same advantage."

"It was not honorable," the third officer, General Hixon, said. He commanded the engineer companies. "Nothing about those imperials is honorable."

Zachary looked up and saw her then. "Ah, Rider G'ladheon." He excused himself from his officers who continued to examine the plans. "You received adequate rest?"

"Yes, Your Majesty."

"Have a seat." He indicated a chair at the other table, which still had an Intrigue board upon it, and sat opposite her.

"I wished to ask you more questions, get your impression on some things," he said. "I need to know more about the enemy. I have already questioned Riders Duff and Notman, and Melry, too, in this regard, but you interacted with Torq and Birch, and you've your merchant background, which has proven useful in judging people."

She relaxed. She had not known what he wanted to see her for exactly and was relieved it was purely business. She could pretend they were just king and messenger, and nothing more. She glanced at the map table and noted that the officers remained, flipping through plans and speaking in low voices among themselves. Nothing would appear untoward with her presence in Zachary's tent.

"I coaxed a fair amount out of your colonel and others who faced the Raiders in the past," he continued, "but few who encountered Torq survived to tell of it. What are your impressions of him."

"No respect for authority other than his own." It was the first thing that came to her mind. "It's his reason for existence, why he's an outlaw. He has no respect for the laws of this realm, but he also has no respect for Second Empire or Birch."

"Yes, you brought that up in Oxbridge. Would you say Torq is just using Second Empire to whatever advantage he can?"

"I think that is likely," she replied. She went into more detail than she had in Oxbridge about the interaction between Torq and Birch she'd observed after her escape from the hut. Zachary listened closely, his fingers closing around a game piece that he absently turned in his hand.

"Allies of convenience," he said when she finished. "That is a weakness. What is your impression of Birch?"

"The opposite of Torq. Very disciplined, and smart enough to not trust Torq." While she and Zachary spoke, people came and went—officers and their aides, Weapons, and servants. The servants brought tea and he poured a cup for Karigan. She was grateful for she'd grown parched with all the talking.

"Now, what of Lala?" he said. "It was her magic that allowed the keep to be taken."

"Yes, she is a strange child, but I know little about her, except that she and Grandmother stole Estral's voice, er, the Lady Fiori's voice. I had never seen her before, but she seemed to know me. I guess from when I was a captive of Nyssa's." A good deal of that night was missing from Karigan's memory, except for the whip and the agony it had brought. He, too, had been held captive in the Lone Forest, and Lala had assisted in his torture, but neither of them could do much more than speculate on her level of power, for they lacked enough information to come to any conclusions.

There was a lull in their conversation, during which Karigan was able to sip her tea uninterrupted and study Zachary. He had a faraway look in his eyes. She wondered what he thought about, where his mind wandered. He must have so much on his mind: his missing friend and advisor, strategy and counter-strategy, all that running a campaign required, and, very likely, he thought of his wife back in Sacor City pregnant with twins.

He placed the game piece he'd been fiddling with on the

Intrigue board with a decisive tap. It was a knight, its features blurred with age, the paint chipped. This was followed by more blue pieces that he formed up on his side of the star-shaped board. She recognized the set. They'd played a game on it not long after she'd arrived at the castle one spring day five years ago, bearing a message that the dying F'ryan Coblebay had begged her to deliver. At the time, she'd been aghast that Zachary hadn't wanted to hear about her journey, but found out later he couldn't speak freely because he feared spies might have heard anything she had to say.

When he looked up at her, she began to get a bad feeling, and sure enough he started setting up green pieces on her side of the board as if he intended to challenge her in another game.

Surely not.

How could he play a game at this time? Shouldn't he be standing over the map table with his generals and debating strategy? Then it occurred to her that maybe he was setting up a game for the same reason as the first time, that he had something to hide from spies, but she'd already told him everything she knew.

He set the last green piece in its spot and glanced up at her. Her expression must have clearly revealed her bemusement for he gave her a half-smile. "Shall we see if your skill at Intrigue has improved over the last few years?"

"It has not," she assured him. She did not care for the game, never had. It brought back bad memories of being stuck in the white world with Zachary's traitorous brother and his puppet master, the evil Shawdell, and his attempt to force her into a life or death game of Intrigue.

As its name implied, it was a strategy game, and she never won. Even without the bad memories, she disliked the politicking and subterfuge it required, the shades of gray. Noble children were taught to play it at a young age as a form of training for their adult lives in court. It took a subtle mind to be good at Intrigue, and she knew few would ever regard her as having such.

"Well, let us see," Zachary said. "No Triad, but as I recall, we did fine with just the two of us last time."

General Hixon appeared at the table. "Ah! His Majesty has you in his sights for a game, eh, Rider? Watch his assassins—sneaky bastards they are. I'd join you, but I need to inspect our fortifications, unless you need me, sire?"

"Go ahead," Zachary said. "We'll set you up as a Triad next time."

The general beamed as he bowed, and then he clapped Karigan on the shoulder. The game was optimally played with three people. The third person, the Triad, was the wild card who could ally with one of the other sides, or play for him- or herself. A good part of the game could be spent negotiating with the Triad. At least with that element excluded, the game would move much faster. Still, Karigan felt overwhelmed by dread.

"You look as if you've lost your best friend," Zachary told her.

Karigan attempted a smile. It faltered.

"What's wrong?" he asked her.

"It's just—May I speak bluntly?"

He leaned back in his chair, a glint in his eye. "I value honesty from my Green Riders. Proceed."

He had not been happy when she questioned him the night before, but this time she'd his permission to speak bluntly and she wouldn't hold back. Connly still wouldn't be pleased with her approach, but, well, he wasn't there.

"Why are we going to play this game when there is so much going on? The keep and Second Empire, and what about Colonel Mapstone? We could be out looking for her."

He gazed at the game board, adjusted the position of his king. "Did you know that your colonel and I play a regular game once a month?"

She shook her head. She had not.

"It's a very useful way to combine business with pleasure. Our conversations during play tend to be wide-ranging. I believe your name has come up a few times during such games." A smile flickered across his lips. "We work out many problems, and I get caught up on the business of my messengers. Your colonel is a formidable opponent."

Yes, Karigan could see that.

"You do understand, my dear Rider," he continued, "Intrigue is not just a game. For me it is a focus from which I can gain insight to strategy. It may help me solve problems with our current situation, spark fresh ideas, just as it did for your colonel. And as for your colonel . . ."

Here it comes, she thought. He was going to go cold and shut her down again.

He looked hard at her. Suddenly, all the activity in the tent, all that was happening outside, seemed very far away. "I think you know what Laren Mapstone means to me."

She did. He'd said it before, that she was like an elder sister. His gaze softened, and she saw the regret, the sorrow in his eyes.

"She is my dearest friend and I will do anything I can to get her back. And I *will* have her back. Do not doubt it."

"But we could have—"

"*No.*" There was fire in the word. "My Green Riders are excellent, but Varos . . . Varos is a very tricky situation. We must move carefully. We cannot afford a provocation, not at this time. Besides, I need my Riders here. All of them."

It seemed to Karigan that it was Varos that was being provocative. "Then how will you get the colonel back?"

Muted light gleamed on his amber hair. "First we try diplomacy."

"And if diplomacy doesn't work?"

"Like a game of Intrigue, there are many ways to approach a problem, but you need not worry about that. It is in motion."

Of course she worried—it was the colonel, the person she looked up to the most. "It?"

"The game, Rider," he said, and he rolled the dice.

✑ INTRIGUE ✑

Zachary made the first move. He pushed a scout two paces toward Karigan's side of the board. As a first move, it was not unusual. Scouts were often used to delve into enemy territory to collect intelligence and discern what an opponent was up to.

Karigan, who was, of course, given the green pieces to use, surveyed the small wooden figures, their potential for victory or defeat, sacrifice or survival. Some games of Intrigue were known to last weeks, if not months, and she'd heard of cases where games had lasted years. Those were played by dedicated enthusiasts of which she was not one. In fact, she was wondering how she might lose as quickly as possible to get it over with.

And yet, here was a rare opportunity, placed right in front of her, to spend time, perhaps hours, with a man whose attention and touch she craved. Just thinking about it made her shivery inside, and that was exactly why she had to make the game as short as possible. Being around him stoked desires that must not, and could not, be fulfilled. And it was all very painful because as much as she might wish their situation to be different, the reality was that it was not.

Zachary watched her intently. "Your move, Rider." He nudged the dice toward her.

She rolled. Not bad. Five paces. She considered her pieces once more, shrugged, and moved her merchant ship toward a region of the board known as the Sea of Passions. The merchant was usually used to collect wealth to help build a player's army.

"Hah!" Zachary said, apparently pleased she'd chosen so appropriate a piece. He set sail his own ship, a warship, on a course to intercept her merchant.

She did not defend it, but allowed him to take it. He gave her a sidelong look. She sent out an embassy to negotiate its release, but he refused it. She marched out her foot soldiers, one by one, in no particular pattern. He easily took them, or pushed them to the far regions of the board. "Either this is a most ingenious strategy on your part that I don't yet understand," he said, "or you are intentionally trying to lose."

"N-no, of course not."

He looked askance at her. "Hmm."

During play, people continued to come and go from the tent under the watchful gazes of Weapons. Some paused by the table to observe the game.

"Looks like you have an uphill battle there, Rider," Counselor Tallman told her. "His Majesty *is* a fierce competitor."

By then, Zachary's pieces vastly outnumbered her own, and she could tell he was not pleased by her poor showing. He was looking ever more annoyed.

She did not know how much time had passed, or what was happening beyond the game. She put up a half-hearted defense and made a feint at his cavalry, but it was clear it was only a matter of time before defeat.

Good, she thought.

She decided to put an enticing target into play and within his reach—her queen. If he captured or killed her queen, then the game was more or less over. She rolled the dice and picked up the queen to move it into the thick of things.

He grabbed her wrist, grabbed it before she could set the piece down. "Are you sure you want to do that?" he asked softly.

His grip wasn't hard, but it sent a shock through her so that she blushed and trembled. They were surrounded by silence, alone. Even the Weapons had stepped out.

"Are you trying to lose?" He squinted at her. "You are, aren't you."

"Well—" His intensity made her unable to put together a coherent sentence.

He held her wrist for a few moments more before he released her. When he did, she felt as though she were tumbling away, adrift in some void.

"Surely," he continued, "you are not letting me win because you felt it best not to upstage your king, or you fear for my frail ego."

"Er, no."

"Is it because you'd prefer not to be in my presence?"

She glanced around to ensure they were still alone. "Gods, no!" Though she recalled her earlier thoughts about losing quickly to get away from him.

He leaned back in his chair and appraised her, a hitch to his eyebrow. "That is good to know. Then what is wrong? I know you can do better than this."

"I do not care for the game." She decided it would be better not to broach the other reasons.

"Is that all? You could have told me that before we began."

"I did not wish to disappoint you. And you *are* the king."

His expression fell. "Karigan," he said quietly, "I thought we were beyond that."

She sat there uncomfortably staring down at the board. She didn't know what to say, her mind and emotions in turmoil. Finally, she said, "It *is* true. No matter what has happened in the past. You are my king who—who has a queen. I am just your common messenger, no matter what one or the other of us may feel."

He looked away. "I am sorry. It is hard, and I've made it harder by asking you to stay to play the game. I had thought it a way for us to see one another without any taint of impropriety, but it would appear I erred in not judging how difficult it would be for you. And for me."

Though they'd only the table between them, it might have been miles.

"The north," he continued, "the time we had together there, seems like a dream."

She gave a harsh laugh.

He looked up at her startled. "Why do you laugh?"

"Don't you mean it was like a nightmare?" They'd both been tortured, both had been near death, she from the torture, he from a poisoned wound. She had stayed by his side as he writhed in fever, thinking his every breath would be the last, and it was a different kind of torture for her thinking about what it would mean to lose not just her king, but the man she loved. Just because they couldn't be together didn't mean she stopped loving him, and the gods knew she'd tried.

"You well know what I meant," he said. "Those rare moments with none of the watchers to observe that we could be like two normal people together."

Unlike here. They were alone in the tent, yes, but just outside she heard soldiers going over a list of supplies. Somewhere nearby was the *cling-cling-cling* of a farrier at work. Footsteps hurried by, and someone laughed in the distance. She gazed at the Intrigue board, and letting her queen alone, moved a messenger forward.

"My messenger would like to meet your king," she told him.

He looked pleased. "This king," he said, "will always welcome your messenger."

She smiled in return.

A cry went up outside, followed by another, and the clamor of steel. Fastion and Donal rushed in.

"Intruders!" Fastion said. "Your breastplate, sire." And he grabbed it from a corner of the tent to help Zachary buckle it on.

"I'd better go," Karigan said, gripping the hilt of Colonel Mapstone's saber. She needed to be out there with her fellow Riders.

The uproar, sounds of fighting, a scream, moved closer.

Donal grabbed her arm. "You are staying right here."

She figured it was because she was supposed to be an honorary Weapon, but when eight more Weapons barreled inside, all ten formed a ring around her and Zachary. She looked up at Zachary uncertainly, but he gazed ahead, focused.

"What's happening out there?" he demanded.

"Warriors appeared out of nowhere," Fastion said. "In scarlet, like the brethren Sir Karigan told us about."

The Lions Reborn, she thought.

"Number?" Zachary asked.

"Nine, so far."

"The travel device," she murmured. "They must have used it to get here."

"Our Black Shields are formed up around this tent," Fastion continued, "but I'm afraid other parts of the encampment may take heavy casualties."

Karigan's stomach churned as she thought about how good these Lions were supposed to be. She prayed her fellow Riders would be well. She prayed that the greater number of Sacoridians would simply overwhelm the Lions.

"I should be out there," she said, but guiltily thought how relieved she was to be protected by Weapons.

"I am very glad you are here," Zachary said, "though I know you would wish to be with your Riders at this time. I do not like being held back, either."

He hadn't said it precisely, but she knew that he meant he was glad she was there where he, too, could protect her. And about that, why were the Weapons so intent upon—

Steel rang just outside as those Weapons engaged the intruders. Karigan tensed at the grunts and footfalls of fighters. She watched shadows dance across the tent walls. She hoped the skill of the Lions did not live up to Brother Pascal's boasts.

Shining blades stabbed through the tent walls and cut through them. Swordsmen in crimson poured in through the rent canvas. All around Karigan, the Weapons flung themselves into motion.

⤙ DEATH AHEAD AND BEHIND ⤚

"**S**tay close," Zachary told Karigan. He drew his sword.

The Weapons maintained their tight cordon around them. Blades hissed through the air as they were brought to bear against the enemy. The Weapons were like avenging gods as they clove into the Lions. Swords clashed. Blood spattered against canvas. The table holding the game of Intrigue toppled and sent game pieces flying.

The Lions proved equal in strength and grace, but they were outnumbered, and more Weapons entered the tent behind them. Black and crimson blurs of motion leaped and plunged and parried like mirrors of one another as they moved through forms too rapidly to name.

Lions fell, but so, too, did Weapons. She cried out when a curved sword gutted Willis and then was whipped around flinging off blood and was driven into Ellen up to the guard. When they fell, the other Weapons filled in their positions, keeping the cordon tight around her and Zachary. Her hand was clammy on the hilt of Captain Mapstone's saber and shook.

Steady, girl, she told herself. But she knew she was not advanced enough of a swordmaster to stand against the Lions, that her back was not strong enough, that she was out of condition. She glanced at Zachary, saw the grim intensity of his expression as he observed the action around them. Though she would die in a fight, fight she would to protect him.

The Lions pressed forward trying to reach Zachary even as more of their own fell to Weapon blades. Another black-clad warrior fell, blood gouting from his neck.

"Liam," Zachary growled. Karigan hadn't known him well.

The number of Lions dwindled and it would soon be over for them, but they fought ferociously on. One crashed into her and knocked her sword from her grasp. Before she could reach after it, the sickening miasma she'd come to know all too well descended on her. Her stomach churned as her surroundings turned fluid and spun. Torq materialized behind Zachary, ready to grab him. Before the Weapons realized what was happening and could react, she launched herself at Torq and tackled him to the ground. Shouts erupted around them. Torq lost hold of the travel device and it rolled beneath the feet of a Weapon and Lion locked in combat.

She reached after it. Torq, behind her, grabbed her and tried to push her aside, but she elbowed him in the face and crawled ahead. A boot heel kicked the orb once more out of her reach. She started to crawl after it, heard Zachary call her name. A glance over her shoulder revealed Torq right behind her and Zachary trying to break through combatants to reach her.

Torq grabbed her ankle and raised his dagger. She tried to kick free of him. His blade missed and sank into the ground beside her leg, but he held onto her with a grip like a manacle. A Lion tripped backward over him and he lost hold of her. She wormed ahead and grabbed the orb. She took a deep breath and held it with both hands.

Torq had hold of her again. Sweat poured down his tattooed face, and he pulled on her leg drawing her toward him. In desperation, Karigan rotated the two halves of the orb.

Where? it quietly asked.

An image came to mind before she could stop it, and she and Torq whirled away.

She hit the ground spinning. When she came to a stop, everything continued to rotate around her. She retched into the white earth. White earth?

Dear gods, what have I done?

She forced herself to look up despite the disorientation. She did not see Torq, but one of the Lions had crossed with her. He wobbled on his feet and gazed in shock at the strange world of the Blanding.

She thought to use the travel device just to escape, but then she realized she no longer held it. It had rolled out of her hand and beneath a bridge. There were three bridges, the same ones she had seen before when she'd come through with Duncan and the Riders. One bridge crossed back to the mountains, the second to Eletia, and the third she did not know where it went. It was under the third bridge the orb had rolled.

She rose unsteadily to her feet, and her movement caught the attention of the Lion. He bellowed and launched himself at her. She reached for her sword, but realized it was not at her hip. It was on the floor of Zachary's tent. She ran.

She ran for the middle bridge, the Lion pounding after her. As she gained the arch, the Lion was right behind her and it occurred to her that death lay both ahead and behind.

The moment the mist between worlds started to part and brighten with sunshine, the moment she felt the damp vapor of the Alluvium on her face, she dove onto the bridge's deck. Momentum carried the Lion forward and he leaped over her into full sunshine. He halted in what must have been pure astonishment and gawked at the sight before him, the rapids of the Alluvium racing their way into the valley. He looked upon what so few mortals had ever seen.

But discipline was discipline, and he turned back to Karigan, sunshine glinting on the curve of his sword as he raised it for the killing blow. At that moment, arrows thudded into his back, and the tips of their leaf-shaped heads punched through his chest. He looked down in shock. His sword clattered to the bridge and he dropped to his knees. Blood trickled from his mouth and deepened the crimson of his robe. When he crumpled over, she saw the shafts of five white arrows bristling out of his back.

She carefully crawled back through the mist into the Blanding lest the Eletians impale her with arrows, too.

She climbed to her feet and dusted white soil off her breeches. When she looked up, she saw Torq turning in circles looking bewildered. *Oh, no.* She must get the travel device before he regained his equanimity. She took a step toward the third bridge where she'd last seen the orb, but it was too late—he had noticed her.

"What is this place?" he demanded. He stared directly at her. His skull tattoo looked even more pronounced with the bleaching effect of the white world.

Karigan did not answer, but sprinted toward the far bridge. Torq was right behind her and knocked her to the ground. She kicked and flailed, broke loose, and tried to crawl away, but he grabbed her ankle just as he had back in the tent. She planted her foot in his face. He howled and let her go.

She scrambled to her feet and ran, but he was quick to recover. He grabbed her and they fell to the ground again. This time he pinned her on her back.

"You'll regret that, Greenie."

She struggled, but his weight pressed down on her. "What are the Varosians doing with my colonel?" she demanded. "Where are they taking her?"

Blood glided down Torq's jaw. "The Witch? She's to be King Farrad Vir's slave, but I'd be more worried about yourself—I promised her I would tear apart any Greenies I came across, and I aim to keep that promise."

He gripped her throat in a choke hold. She grabbed his wrist, but it was about as thick as a tree trunk and as unmovable. She struggled, wiggled, gasped, but she could not breathe, and the more she struggled, the harder it became, the world dimming around her, darkness closing in.

She heard a rustling, like wings. Was it Westrion come to take her to the heavens? Had it all been for naught, all her striving, all the battles and danger? Was this all there was?

Be at peace, Karigan, came the whispers. *Sleep in peace . . .*

Torq stood. Her vision lightened and she could breathe again, but she felt so tired and so heavy.

"What is this? What are these things?" Torq's voice sounded so far off.

She knew she should get up and try to reach the orb, but she just wanted to rest.

Yes, Karigan, rest in—

Nyssa stirred in her mind. *Get UP, you stupid Greenie!*

Karigan sat straight up, feeling in a fog, and finding herself in a fog.

Get up! Nyssa screamed at her, and kept screaming to block the whispers.

Karigan clambered unsteadily to her feet, felt the brush of a shroud against her arm. She jumped aside only to find wraiths billowing and floating around her in a graceful ballet. It was a mesmerizing dream, and they were everywhere as she turned about. Their whispers crooned in the back of her mind, a song, a calling.

Leave, you idiot, Nyssa hollered at her.

Startled, she stumbled forward and almost tripped over Torq, who lay curled on the ground beneath a blanket of mist. He slept with a tranquil expression on his face. Some of the wraiths that hovered over him turned to her. Their bloodless faces sent a jolt through her heart. One extended a clawlike hand toward her, its poison nail leaking yellow ichor.

Run! Nyssa yelled.

Run where? Karigan wondered. She was surrounded.

The bridge, idiot girl. Must I think of everything?

Karigan pushed her way through the wraiths. They reached after her. She felt a poison nail scratch along her sleeve. They called out to her, but she fought against it by reciting sword-fighting forms in her mind: *Aspen Leaf, Crayman's Circle, Raven's Sweep, Ice Slide . . .*

Then she remembered the travel device and changed course for the far bridge.

Yes, come to us, Karigan, the whisperers called.

What are you doing? Nyssa demanded, her voice incredulous.

Karigan found a cluster of wraiths beneath the arch of the bridge, tentacles extended from their torsos holding the travel device between them. The tentacles pulsed a dull red. Were they feeding off it? There was no grabbing it now.

She turned to run back to the bridge that would return her to the mountains, but crashed into a wraith. It felt much more substantial than it looked.

Rest, it told Karigan. *Sleep in restful peace.*

She tried to remember more sword forms, but could not seem to.

The world faded around her. Nyssa's voice became an irritating background noise. A pulsing tentacle whipped out and adhered its flat tip to her forehead, and the wraith's claw with its poisonous nail was poised to grab her wrist.

Sleep in restful peace, Karigan, it told her. *Sleep . . .*

⇜ FOG IN THE VALLEY ⇝

Karigan stood frozen as the mist wafted around her, but felt as though she were falling, falling, all the fight, all the living energy, being drawn from her. Consciousness faded and darkness closed in. Until . . . it did not.

Darkness lightened and she dropped to her knees, greeted by silence, and the pervasive whiteness of the Blanding. The whisper wraiths, every single one, had disappeared.

She wavered there for a time, feeling too weak to move. One of the wraiths had begun to feed off her magic. Off her. And then was simply . . . gone? A good thing, for she was not sure what would have been left of her. She gazed at her wrist. It was punctured and bleeding, but it appeared no poison had been released into her veins. She watched in dazed fascination as small drops of crimson pattered onto the white earth. There was no other sound except for the sound of her own heartbeat.

She staggered to her feet and saw that Torq slept nearby. She should move on, get away while she could. She supposed she could slay him where he lay, but there was a wrongness to it. It would be no better than Second Empire tossing sleeping Sacoridians from the heights of Eagle's Pass Keep. Nyssa made a sound of contempt, and though she said nothing, the message was clear: Karigan was squeamish.

Abandoning him to the strangeness of the white world, she thought as she stumbled toward the bridge that would take her to the mountains, was enough. He might find his way out. He had three bridges to choose from, or he might spend his days wandering the white world until he died of starvation or went mad, or was killed by whisper wraiths or any other denizens that might exist here. In any case, she was not letting him off easy by leaving him behind.

I see your point, Nyssa said. *This is crueler. You are more like me than you think, Greenie.*

"I am nothing like you," Karigan said.

Are you so sure?

She tried to close herself off from her torturer, but heard Nyssa's soft laughter.

When she reached the bridge, she had to drag herself across feeling more drained with every step. She passed over the arch and, without a backward glance, stepped through the mist into the real world, the verdant valley beneath the mountains. Late afternoon sun fell brightly on the jagged peaks. She inhaled deeply of the fresh air fragrant with green living, leafy things and rejoiced at the song and babble of birds. It made her feel much better. She stepped off the bridge and it vanished behind her. She crossed the loose masonry of the ruins of the ancient mage hall Duncan had told her about.

She knew she should return to the encampment as soon as possible to find out if Zachary and the Riders were all right after the attack, but she was bone weary. Didn't feel like she could go on. She stepped down from the ruins and found a sunny spot in a glade, and lay down to rest free of the whispers in her mind.

She woke up with a shiver. The sunny spot was long gone and the sun was lowering in the west. She shook her head and sat up only to find an oversized raptor gazing down at her.

"Oh, Ripaeria."

I began to fear you dead, the eagle said, *as you slept as still as a corpse.*

That was an interesting way of putting it.

And then, Ripaeria said, *you snored.*

"How did you find me?"

I saw your people had been attacked. It was over by the time I flew in to check on you. Your mate asked that I search for you.

"My *mate*? Ripaeria, he isn't my mate, he's my king."

That is what you *say, but you like his plumage, and he likes yours. All that is left is for you to lock talons and do the wing dance.*

"Lock talons and—?" Karigan's cheeks warmed up.

He was as worried as a true mate would be and asked that I look for you. The eagle held her head high and puffed her breast in an attitude of pride.

"The king already has a mate, and it is best you do not speak of such things to others." The idea mortified Karigan. "But," she added hastily before Ripaeria could argue further, "I am very glad you found me." She was also relieved to hear Zachary was alive. "Would you please inform the king and Captain Connly that I'm fine? And I will start walking."

Ripaeria agreed, and launched into the sky. Karigan watched after her for a moment, and rose to her feet to begin her walk. Fortunately, the sensation of being drained had been alleviated by the rest, much of her energy now restored. Still, it would be much easier if she had a horse. The encampment was not far, perhaps five miles, but she'd arrive there much sooner with a horse.

It was not long before Ripaeria circled back.

"That was quick," Karigan said.

It is not far on the wing, the eagle replied. *A Green Rider is being sent with a horse for you as four legs are better than two. Not as good as wings, but better. You wingless ones are most unfortunate creatures.*

Flying, Karigan thought, would be amazing, but she wouldn't trade her horse for wings anytime soon. She picked up her pace and questioned Ripaeria as she flew above about the aftermath of the fighting, if she knew who had lived or died.

I do not know. I smelled blood, but that is all. Besides, you mostly all look alike to me.

Karigan wasn't sure exactly how far she had walked, but dusk was setting in and she thought the Rider who had been sent with a mount to meet her should have reached her by now. She asked Ripaeria to go look, but when the eagle did not return, she grew even more concerned.

She passed the hut where she and the others had been held captive. The door stood ajar and dark. There was no sign of anyone from the Sacoridian encampment nearby, not even a sentry. She continued on into a copse of trees that grew thickly on a hill. It was the very same one she had climbed to observe the Second Empire encampment when it had occupied the area. She climbed it now, struck by the silence all around her. There were no distant sounds of a busy camp, not even that of animals in the woods. No wind disturbed leaf or bough. Her own footfalls crunching on leaf litter and cracking branches sounded abnormally loud to her.

As she crested the hill, she noticed an almost luminous ground fog snaking among the rocks and roots of the wood. A cold sweat dampened her back and sides. In her haste, she nearly tripped over a fox neatly curled with its fluffy tail covering its muzzle. She bit back a yelp. The fox did not rouse at her ungainly arrival, and at first she thought it dead, but a closer look revealed it breathing evenly. It slept. It slept too soundly.

She found the overlook where she could observe the encampment down below. Fog filled the valley and extended up into the pass. It curled and roiled among still tents where campfires burned, though some looked ready to sputter out. No life moved down there, no people, no animals. In places where the fog thinned for a moment or two, she saw the ground littered with bodies. Corpses, or sleepers like the fox? She shuddered with desperate fear it might be the former, but with the fog, she had her suspicions.

She spied movement, figures in ragged coverings seeming to float low in the fog like phantoms, drifting here and there among the bodies, confirming her suspicion. Unwittingly, when she had traveled to the white world via the orb, she had given the whisper wraiths entry to the outside world. She sensed Nyssa's amusement.

Her gaze followed the road that led across the valley and up to the pass. About halfway between the encampment and the pass was the thickest fog, a great cloud billowing on the ground. She could not tell what went on there, except there were wraiths that seemed to float amid the cloud.

What will you do now, Greenie? Nyssa asked in a mocking tone.

Karigan ignored the question. She did not have a clear idea of what to do, because if she went down there, there was a good chance she'd once more be caught under the spell of the whisper wraiths herself. Even if she deigned to ask Nyssa to help, to have her yell in her head so she did not hear the cloying whispers of the wraiths, it might not be enough.

Could she use her ability and pass among them unseen? She shook her head. They could sense magic and would be on her in a moment. It's what had drawn them to her the first time.

Nyssa's question came back to her. What was she going to do now?

Act. She had to act. Standing rooted on this hill was not going to help anything, much as she'd prefer it. The old Karigan would already be down there *doing,* not hesitating.

She growled and launched herself down the hill toward the encampment to see if she could rouse help. She couldn't do this on her own.

When she reached the edge of the encampment, she came upon soldiers sleeping soundly though their eyes were cracked open and glassy, whether gazing into dreams or visions or nothing, she did not know. She shook them, thumped on their chests, cursed them, and even kicked a couple in the shin, but they did not awaken. She looked toward the center of the encampment where the royal standard of Sacoridia hung listlessly in the mist. She wished to go there, to see how Zachary fared, but she did not think he would awaken anymore readily than the soldiers.

She was alone.

❖ INTO THE MIST ❖

Karigan drew the longsword of one of the sleeping soldiers. She'd dropped the colonel's saber in Zachary's tent when Torq attacked, and she was not going to be able to face the wraiths with only a longknife. Maybe she would scare them off as easily as she had before.

The mist stirred nearby and she looked up. A wraith drifted toward her, the ragged edges of its shroud floating in ghostly waves. She did not waste one moment, but leaped over one of the soldiers and clove the sword into the wraith. The shroud collapsed into an empty pile. She glanced around. A few others drifted among the sleepers of the encampment, but none approached or otherwise seemed to notice her. It was very odd when it was her magic that had drawn them to her before, but perhaps things worked differently for them outside the white world.

She must go to where the majority were clustered in the valley. She guessed that was where she was likely to find the travel device and the answer to removing them from her world. She adjusted the sword in her grip. It was not an elegant weapon, but serviceable. And heavy. Heavy enough that it would strain her still-weak back. There were many wraiths to battle. She took a deep breath.

And a second.

And then she dove into the mist.

I am not going to help such stupidity a second time, Nyssa informed her.

"I haven't asked you to." If Nyssa wanted to preserve

whatever remained of herself, she would help no matter what she claimed.

Karigan crouched in brush, and hid among stray trees, as she passed through the valley. She stayed off the road where she'd be in plain sight. As she went, a whispery murmur grew in her mind, like background conversation she could not quite make out. The fog deepened the closer she got, but so far the wraiths had not taken notice of her, which she thought a little odd. Being outside of the white world must have definitely affected how they perceived magic.

It will not last, Nyssa assured her.

Karigan did not have to be told. She moved on. Soon the cloud became so thick she could barely see in front of her. The murmuring in her mind grew louder, but remained unintelligible.

The fog wafted a bit and she realized why it was so thick. She was surrounded by wraiths, so many more of them than she had expected. She froze, her heart hammering in her chest. She didn't know what to do—move forward and hope they continued not to pay attention to her, or run. Everything in her told her to *run-run-run*.

Except Nyssa. *You've a sword, kill them all.*

All of them? There could be hundreds, and very likely any action would draw attention to her.

She forced herself to breathe again, tried to relax her neck and shoulder muscles. She resisted the impulse to flee and moved forward carefully evading the wraiths. It was a dance as she wove her way among them, being very careful not to touch them, going on her toes, or twirling around and side-stepping, for the wraiths were not motionless, but constantly wavering, drifting, apt to change direction with the slightest breeze or provocation.

Above the murmur in her head, she heard a familiar voice: "Do not touch me!"

It was Duncan.

"You are abominations," he said, "and you should not be here on the corporeal plane."

Karigan proceeded in the direction of his voice and

almost stumbled over a body. She paused to regain her balance and throttled down a scream when she saw it was a Green Rider—Harry, his face peaceful, the gleam of moonlight glinting on the whites of his partially opened eyes.

It took another moment to regain her calm. He was just sleeping like the soldiers of the encampment. His chest rose and fell evenly and easily. Next to him slept Hoff. As the mist shifted, she saw others—Connly, Tegan, Brandall, all lined up like a row of corpses, all dreaming away. The wraiths must have collected them from the encampment to feed off of. If the wraiths were aware of their magic, why weren't they aware of hers?

"No!" Duncan cried.

She shook herself and walked along the line of sleeping Green Riders toward his voice. She passed Trace and Sophina and . . . Ripaeria. Ripaeria slept with her beak tucked beneath her wing. And then she found a girl who was not a Rider, but Grandmother's protégé, Lala. She, too, slept. Karigan had seen the fog up in the pass. Second Empire must also be under the spell of the whisper wraiths, and the wraiths must have collected all the magic users in one place to . . . what? Make it easier to siphon the magic from them?

Karigan's grip on her sword quavered.

You can kill the girl now, Nyssa said. *Be done with her.*

Lala had stolen Estral's voice, had helped in the torture of Zachary. She had helped to kill the soldiers stationed in the keep.

Kill her!

Karigan did not know if it was Nyssa or her own dark voice urging her. She gazed at the girl, no more than eleven or twelve, with freckles on her cheeks. Adolescence had not yet set in. As she slept curled in a ball, she exuded only youthful innocence.

Kill her!

Karigan wavered. If the girl had committed such monstrous acts as a child, what might she do as an—

"Put it down!" Duncan shouted.

Karigan glanced up to observe the wraiths closing in a knot around him. One clasped his thigh bone. Then a metallic glint near his feet caught her eye.

The travel device, she thought, and thus diverted, she left Lala and carefully began to pick her way in his direction. She must get her hands on the travel device.

The wraith holding Duncan's thigh bone touched it with a tentacle. The tentacle pulsed with an icy gleam. Duncan faded out for a moment.

"You do not know what you are playing with," he declared.

More tentacles from other wraiths reached out to touch it. Duncan faded out again. Karigan hastened her steps and he finally saw her.

"No—no, dear lady. You should not have come. It's a trap."

All the wraiths faced her as one, extended their tentacles toward her. *Yes, Karigan, you have come to us and we will give you peace.*

Karigan did not know if it was her or Nyssa who roared, or both. All she knew was throwing her body forward with the sword in motion, cutting off tentacles and arms and thrusting steel into shrouds.

"Well done!" Duncan cried. "You've got them now, dear lady!"

But there were so many of them, and this time they did not scare off.

They keened. The keening hurt her head and almost caused her to drop her sword so she could cover her ears, almost rocked her to her knees. In her moment of hesitation, the tips of tentacles touched her.

Sleep, Karigan.

A weakness seeped through her body. It would be so easy to give up, to give in, to sleep, but she heaved her sword at the nearest wraith and split it in two. She ignored the sharp twinges in her back and continued to hack at tentacles, but there were always more reaching for her.

A poison nail nicked her shoulder, the whispers seeped into her mind. Sweat slipped down her face.

And then there was a pause, a moment to breathe, and a clearing between her and the wraiths. They did not keen, and the whispers ceased. The silence was far more threatening.

"There are many more of them," Duncan said. "You are valiant, but I fear you won't be able to kill them all. They waited for you, you know, instead of trying to lure you in like they had before. They wanted you to think they could not sense your presence."

She was too winded to respond, but he was right. There were too many, and her shoulder had gone cold with the venom. She needed some other way of— Just then, the toe of her boot nudged something. She took it to be a rock, but a quick look revealed the silver of an orb, the travel device.

You are ours, the wraiths whispered to her.

She looked up just in time as another tentacle reached for her. She cut it off, but cried out as crippling pain seized her back. Her sword tumbled to the ground.

The wraiths who had kept their distance, now sensing victory, formed up in a tight circle around her and Duncan.

"It was a pleasure to have known you, dear lady," Duncan said.

You are ours, the wraiths told her. *We would have given you years of gentle peace and sleep, Karigan, but you only harm us, so you will receive years of nightmares and torture instead.*

⋙ PRISONERS ⋘

Tears streamed down her cheeks at the pain in her back and she dropped to her knees. The whispers came in soporific waves, mesmerizing, and cajoling her to sleep, to give up.

She wanted to give up.

Yes, Karigan, sleep, they told her. *Give yourself to us.*

Even Duncan had quieted as if resigned to whatever end awaited him. She willed herself not to fall prey to the enticement of sleep. Even if she gave in, they'd threatened her with nightmares and torture. No, she would not have it. As they inched closer, she draped herself over Duncan's tempes stone. The travel device was an arm's length away.

"What are you doing?" he asked. "Not that I mind you on top of me, but now is hardly the time to—"

The whispers, full of promises of sleep and torment, still lulled her as they streamed through her body. Her muscles relaxed against her will. Her eyelids grew heavy. She must not—

Idiot Greenie! Nyssa cried. *Wake up.*

The torturer's voice shattered the whispers. Nyssa harangued her until she remembered herself. But she did not move. She lay there waiting. Waiting for the wraiths to close in around her.

"My lady Karigan?" Duncan asked.

Karigan tried to master her revulsion as dozens of tentacles reached out to touch her. Dozens more waited behind. The silver of the travel device glinted in the corner of her eye.

Sleep, Karigan, the wraiths commanded, *so you may provide us with sustenance. We hunger.*

"Get up! Do something!" Duncan cried. He sounded half-hysterical.

Greenie! Nyssa shouted so loud Karigan clenched her jaw.

The flat tips of the tentacles touched and adhered to her. Almost immediately she felt as if all her energy, all her life force, was draining away. She needed to act before she became totally incapacitated.

She reached and snatched the travel device. And twisted the two halves.

Where? it asked.

There was only one destination she could think of.

From darkness to darkness, she whirled. The tentacles remained anchored to her through the journey. When all stopped spinning, she remained sprawled over the tempes stone and clutched the travel device. She grew weaker as the wraiths fed, but then, over the roar of rushing water, she heard it, the whine of arrows. Their silver heads flashed and white shafts glowed in the moonlight as they descended. Wraiths fell away, one after another, until none stood.

She moved to use the travel device so she could return to the encampment, but an arrow drove through the fabric of her sleeve and pinned it to the ground. The travel device fell from her hand and rolled out of reach. Even so, she stretched her free hand after it, and another arrow descended and pierced that sleeve, also pinning it. She tried to free herself, but the wraiths had weakened her too much. She could only wait and hope the Eletians were in a merciful mood.

"They do not look pleased," Duncan said.

She did not imagine they would. Their footfalls were almost imperceptible as they approached, but their voices were sharp, even in the melodious Eltish language. Duncan responded in a placating tone. She hadn't known he could speak Eltish, but was glad, for it might very well save them.

She blinked as light blared in her face, and so could not see how many there were. She squinted and found herself at eye level with a pair of pearlescent armored boots.

"They are not happy with you, dear lady," Duncan said.

"I had no idea," she muttered.

"Yes, well, they are quite disposed to execute you on the

spot, but they know the prince did not do so when we were here last. They are seeking someone with higher authority to decide what to do with you, but any good esteem they held for you may now be null, for the crime of bringing what they call 'nothing creatures' into the Alluvium."

"It was the only way," she said.

She decided that if they were just going to leave her sprawled like this, she might as well rest. She lay her head down on her outstretched arm and tried to relax her body. The tempes stone was not particularly comfortable under her ribs, but there wasn't anything she could do about it.

She dozed without the threat of wraiths slipping into her mind and feeding off her magic, and even Nyssa had gone silent—Karigan felt nothing of her presence. She wasn't sure how much time had passed, but it felt like only a moment had passed when she was awakened by the arrival of more Eletians. An argument ensued, with Duncan interjecting.

Meanwhile, one of the newcomers knelt before her. She looked up and took in the moonlight cascading down his silvery hair and knew him. She had not seen him since the Blackveil expedition.

"Ealdaen?" she said.

"Galadheon," he replied. "You do have a way of entering a place such that all must take notice. Your arrival at this time was *not* foreseen."

"So glad I can surprise the Eletians now and then."

She thought she detected a gleam of humor in his eyes, but his tone was stern. "You have committed offences with two trespasses this night. The second is by far the more serious of the two. What were you thinking by bringing evil creatures into the sanctity of the Alluvium?"

"My lord," Duncan said, "it was the only way to—"

"Silence," Ealdaen said. Duncan immediately shut his mouth. It was the first time Karigan had ever heard anyone address Ealdaen as "lord," and she was surprised by how obsequious Duncan was.

"Your fate will be determined by Ari-matiel Jametari and the councilors of the Alluvium," he told her. "I have been directed to oversee your presence in Eletia until then."

"You could just let me go," she said, "and I promise not to trespass again."

"I could not, and such promises may be difficult to keep."

She sighed. "I guess then that I'll just lie here until your people decide what to do with me."

A slight smiled formed on Ealdaen's lips, and he pulled the arrows out of the ground, releasing her sleeves.

"I believe we can allow you more comfort than the ground. You are my guest until decisions are made."

She winced as she pushed herself to a sitting position, and gathered herself to rise to her feet. She was still weak, her shoulder was numb, and she was afraid of causing the pain to surge through her back again.

"The wraiths," Duncan said, "fed off her."

"I'm all right," she said, and forced herself to her feet. A small cry of pain escaped her lips.

"Injuries?" Ealdaen asked.

"My back hurts," she replied.

Ealdaen spoke to the Eletian archers. One retrieved the travel device, and another the tempes stone.

"Don't forget my, uh, leg bone," Duncan said. "One of the wraiths had it when we were brought here."

Karigan gazed at all the shrouds scattered about the bank of the falls, all that was left of the wraiths she had brought with her.

Duncan, following her gaze, said, "You brought dozens with us, dear lady, linked as they were by the mist they wrap themselves in."

She closed her eyes and shuddered at the memory of tentacles adhering to her, sucking the life energy out of her. "I am glad the archers got them."

"They did," Duncan said, "and those that didn't get pulled along with us here are greatly diminished. They will not be enough to keep everyone in the encampment asleep. Nor those in the pass, for that matter. Those who awaken should be able to slay them with little trouble. The strength of the wraiths lies in numbers."

His words helped ease her concern, though it was unfortunate Second Empire would also awaken. Otherwise, Zachary's forces could take advantage of the situation.

One of the archers found Duncan's thigh bone and plucked it out from beneath a shroud.

"Careful with that," Duncan told him.

Ealdaen offered Karigan his arm. "You may lean on me if it helps."

She gazed up at him, this Eletian who had tried to kill her more than once over the mere perception she might be a danger to Eletia. But then that perception had been proven wrong and he'd become one of her companions on the Blackveil expedition and their guide among the ruins of lost Argenthyne. On that long journey, deep in the interior of Argenthyne castle, he'd saved her life from a would-be assassin. She took his arm and leaned on him.

He used the light of a moonstone to guide them along a meandering path that descended gently alongside the course of the water. When her legs began to shake from weakness, Ealdaen offered her a drink from a small flask he carried.

"Take a sip of the cordial," he said. "It may help."

And so she did. It tasted of winter and clearest ice, and yet it did not chill her, but warmed her. As the warmth spread through her, it seemed to restore some of her strength, and they continued on.

"I would not expect your gift to work properly for another day and night after the feeding of the anethna wraiths," Ealdaen said.

She hoped the Eletians gave her no reason to need to use it.

They continued down the path into a wood of majestic pines. Moonlight fell through their branches and cast the trunks into great living columns of pale gray. They must be very old, she thought, to be so great of girth and so tall. Green lichen drooped like whiskers from boughs that were larger than many trees.

Ealdaen seemed pleased as he watched her take in the giants. "These are as nothing compared to the Grove."

She'd seen a grove of Argenthyne and knew he spoke truth.

They broke off the main path down a side trail illuminated by paper lanterns, and crossed a stream using stepping stones. The light of the lanterns glimmered on the purling surface of the water. The banks were carpeted in thick moss and twined with the sinuous roots of cedars. Ferns filled out the understory and quivered at the touch of a breeze.

The path bent around an enormous boulder and ended at . . .

Karigan did not know what to call it, for she could not tell if the structure was grown or built, or some combination of both. Cottage? Yes, it was a small cottage of live plantings—trees, vines, a mossy roof. From the outside, there were no hard angles, only those created by nature. Homey light flickered from windows to welcome them.

"This is the guest cottage where you will be staying," Ealdaen said. "You may wander the grounds, but do not step beyond the stream. I cannot promise you your safety if you do. Please be welcome and feel free to partake of the food and drink provided. I will send a healer to you to tend your injuries." He bowed slightly and returned up the trail, some of the guards falling in behind him. The others disappeared into the woods, no doubt to keep watch on her. The one bearing the tempes stone and leg bone headed into the cottage, and once he deposited those items, disappeared into the woods as well.

"You are being accorded a great honor," Duncan told her.

"Because they didn't kill me right away? You do know we're prisoners and not guests, right?"

"'Prisoner' might be too harsh a word," he replied.

Karigan walked to the door of the cottage and Duncan hurried after her.

"What I mean," he continued, "is that Lord Ealdaen is one of the most eminent of the ancient Argenthyne Eletians, a great warrior, too. He fought by King Santanara's side when the king took down—" and here Duncan whispered, "—Mornhavon the Black."

Karigan pushed the door open. "He never mentioned that. Nor did any of the others."

"The others?"

"On the Blackveil expedition. I traveled with Ealdaen and others across the D'Yer Wall." Six Eletians, and six Sacoridians, it had been.

Duncan's eyes went wide. "Dear lady, you truly need to catch me up."

She stepped into the cottage and found it to be, indeed, partly grown by nature, and partly built of stone and wood. Candles glimmered in glass lamps that had been blown into twisted spirals, birds, flickering flame shapes, and fish. A fire burned brightly in a fireplace made of boulders that looked as if they'd naturally tumbled into place there. Moss and lichen still grew on them.

Karigan spotted food that had been left on the table for her, and she realized she was ravenous. She'd eaten nothing since breakfast. She sampled crisp golden wine and honey cakes that tasted better than any she'd ever had. There was also a bowl of hot savory stew filled with root vegetables and mushrooms and dumplings. A half wheel of cheese and bread filled out the meal.

Yes, she and Duncan were prisoners, but their prison could have been far worse.

⤳ LIGHT AND DARK ⤲

It wasn't long before the healer arrived. Karigan had just finished the last honey cake, Duncan watching her take every bite as if he wished he could eat it, too, or maybe he just wanted to hear about the Blackveil expedition but was courteously waiting for her to nourish herself.

"I am Gweflin," the healer said. She'd waves of long blue-black hair and emerald eyes. She carried a basket over her wrist. "I am told you have an injury."

"Wrenched my back."

"I can help."

Karigan hesitated. It was not easy to reveal her back, even to those who would mend it, but when she stood and a ripple of pain made her cry out, she admitted to herself it would be best to accept Gweflin's help. Also, the wraith "sting" on her shoulder had grown itchy and it would be a relief to have it treated.

Gweflin sent Duncan away. He chose to vanish into his tempes stone. Karigan was directed to bare her back and lie on her stomach on a soft sofa-like piece of furniture before the fire. For many moments, Gweflin said nothing and did nothing aside from survey Karigan's back. Karigan could only imagine what was going through her mind. It had been the same with the others who had seen the damage wrought by Nyssa's whip, the shock, sometimes outright anger. Maybe pity. She did not expect Gweflin's reaction to be any different.

"What cruelty was this?" the healer finally asked.

"I was . . . tortured."

Silence, then simply, "I am grieved for you."

She hummed softly as she worked a lotion into Karigan's muscles that smelled of evaleoren salve.

"Hmm," Gweflin said after a time. "The first mending was well done. Your back would be in far worse condition otherwise. You might not have survived. I sense Enver, Somial's son, in the work."

"Yes." Karigan was surprised that one healer could identify another's mending, but then, these were Eletians. "I was traveling with Enver. Do you know him?"

"I know *of* him and his mending," Gweflin replied. "We have not met."

"I wonder if I could see him while I'm here," Karigan said. She then groaned in relief as Gweflin loosened a knotted muscle beneath her shoulder blade with little more than a touch. Did she use some form of true healing magic? Karigan couldn't see to confirm it.

"I do not believe Somial or his son are present in the Vane-ealdar."

That was disappointing. She would have liked to see him, try to mend what had been a difficult parting between them.

The lotion tingled and warmed the pain away, and eliminated the itchiness of the wraith sting, as she'd hoped. Gweflin's sweet voice singing and humming brought Karigan tranquility that was far more genuine than the whispers of the wraiths, and the sensation of her back muscles being turned to putty and gently remolded by Gweflin's healing hands left her limp.

When Gweflin finished, Karigan sighed. "Must it end?"

Gweflin quietly laughed. "For tonight. You would not wish me to overwork your muscles. Doing such can cause the opposite of the desired effect. You must be mindful of how you use your back. Your muscles are deeply scarred and not the same as before. They were not accustomed to your recent activity, and so were aggravated and strained."

Heaving a heavy sword to slay wraiths would do that, Karigan thought.

"You must work on stretching and strengthening your back."

"I was taught some stretches," Karigan said, and memory

of Renn and his ministrations brought her some sadness. "I just have been too busy lately to keep up with them."

Gweflin clucked her tongue. "You must make time. There is a pool behind the cottage in which you should soak. You will feel much better." She collected her basket and bade her farewell.

Karigan decided to take Gweflin up on her suggestion and found the pool just outside naturally screened by plantings. The water bubbled and steam rose up from the surface, and yet, she didn't think it was a hot spring, and there was no visible heat source to warm it. She shrugged guessing it was just more Eletian magic.

She sank into the pool with an enormous sigh, and relaxed. The heat further diminished her aches, pains, and exhaustion from all she'd been through. She stirred up the sand on the bottom and realized it had a soapy texture. She reached down and scooped up a handful and rubbed some of the grains between her fingers. It was the scouring soap she remembered Enver had carried with him on their journey north. The whole bottom of the pool was filled with it, and she gave herself a good scrubbing.

Afterward she continued her soak, gazing at stars that shone between the boughs of trees overhead. To think she'd started the day with a game of Intrigue. She tried not to worry about Zachary and her friends. She hoped Duncan was right that with their diminished numbers, the remaining wraiths had posed no challenge for the Sacoridians to defeat.

Her thoughts then moved to the child, Lala. The wraiths had been drawn to her magic, too. Would she become a force as great as Grandmother? Stuck here in Eletia, Karigan would have no answers, and it was futile to worry about something she could not help. She let go her cares to enjoy the soak.

Karigan awoke the next morning after a deep, dreamless slumber. Food, including large, ripe strawberries, was left in a basket on the doorstep. The cottage and its surroundings were peaceful in a way she had not experienced in a long time, and it was easy to forget the Eletians were debating whether or not to execute her for trespass. Nyssa continued to be absent from her mind. Birds sang and piped in the woods, and she could hear the rush of the stream when she sat by the window. The only annoyance was Duncan questioning her about the Blackveil expedition. She finally relented and told him what she remembered just to silence him.

"You shattered the looking mask the Mirare offered you to keep it out of Mornhavon the Black's hands?" he asked in incredulity.

She nodded.

"Remarkable. Is that when you got the shard in your eye?"

"Not exactly." The destruction of the looking mask had ruptured time and propelled her into Sacoridia's dark future. It was only upon her return to the present that the shard had caught up with her and lodged itself in her eye.

"Well, then," he demanded, "what happened next?"

She regarded a strawberry as she reclined on the sofa, one of several that had come in the basket, and popped it into her mouth. It was amazingly sweet and juicy.

"Well?" Duncan persisted.

"I joined the circus."

His blank expression made her laugh.

"You *what*?"

She smiled, but it hadn't been amusing at the time. Fortunately, Gweflin arrived just then to check on her back and massage it again. Duncan greeted the healer in her own language, which delighted her.

"Just how do you know Eltish?" Karigan asked. "You spoke it last night, too."

"I know a great many things," he replied. "Great mages are scholars first and foremost, and are blessed with long lives to devote to their studies, such as learning various languages. I could recite over a hundred eagle ballads by heart, if you desired."

"No, thank you."

"Not surprised," he muttered.

Gweflin once again banished him from the room to tend Karigan's back, and once more Karigan was turned into putty.

"Have you seen Ealdaen? Heard any word?" Karigan asked.

"I have not," the healer replied. "They debate in the council chamber of the Alluvium, and that is all I know. You must have patience for Eletians are accustomed to taking time in all things. You must use this interlude for rest and healing."

Gweflin's work made Karigan's back feel better, but now that she had been fed and had rested, she could think more thoroughly about her circumstances, and it set her to pacing. She found herself annoyed that Ealdaen had not returned to bring her updates on the proceedings. It was her life in the balance, after all. The Eletians seemed to like toying with her, but this time, instead of just interfering, they might actually decide to kill her.

"You are going to wear out the floor," Duncan said from where he sat in a chair of his own making, an illusion that matched the rest of the furnishings, leafy twigs, moss, and all. "Gweflin is right, you should take the time to relax and heal."

She paused. "Easy for you to say. I have no idea if they are going to execute me because I brought those wraiths into Eletia, and who knows what's happening at the mountains? I have no idea who survived when the Lions attacked, or if everyone was all right after the wraiths invaded."

"I am afraid I couldn't tell you," Duncan replied. "There was much confusion, and then everyone fell asleep and the wraiths carried my pouch away to where you found me."

Karigan paced around the room once more. How could she rest when she didn't know how her people fared? How Zachary fared? And what about the colonel? Where was she? Was she well? The peaceful spell of the cottage had dissipated and it began to feel like a cage. "I am going out for some fresh air."

"Remember what Lord Ealdaen said about not wandering far," Duncan called after her.

She let the door slam behind her. The open air soothed her, the wind stirring the trees and her hair. A squirrel scurried alongside the path blanketed by rusty pine needles. Walking along the path seemed to slough the edge on her anxiety, and the farther away she got, the better she felt.

Before she knew it, she had reached the stream. She crossed to one of the stepping stones, then the next, and the next, until she stood in the middle of the stream. On the opposite bank, an Eletian in his white armor appeared, his arrow nocked but not aimed. A warning.

She had not crossed all the way as Ealdaen had warned— she was not suicidal, after all. But she *was* stubborn and she sat down on the stepping stone, so close to the line between life and death. While the Eletian watched, she removed her boots and dangled her feet in the icy water. She shivered. It briefly reminded her of a dream. No, not a dream, but a vision she had had, she thought, while under the influence of the wraiths, but like a dream, it had faded leaving only an impression. Something to do with a stream, cold water.

When she looked up, the Eletian had returned to hiding. She pulled her feet back onto the rock to warm them after their immersion and sat gazing at the rushing water, how it whorled around rocks. The bottom was full of colorful stones. Water bugs and leaves rode along the current, their shadows trailing behind them on the bottom. It was mesmerizing, and the tension and concerns that plagued her flowed away. Her gaze became unfocused and she imagined entering a starry meadow, a starry meadow she had not seen since she traveled in the north, guided there by Enver's gentle voice. This time there was nothing to block her way, no Nyssa, nothing.

She walked through the meadow, trailing her hands along the tops of the lush grasses that shone silver-green in the starlight. She heard the pounding of hooves. In the distance, she saw two horses galloping, white and black, two horses not of the mortal realm. The white one was so white she radiated light in the dark. She was Seastaria, what Enver had called the "day horse" and her aithen. The light to Karigan's dark. But the dark was there, as well, in the form of Salvistar, the steed of the god of death and the harbinger of battle, his hide the black of the heavens, a glimpse of the infinite beyond mortal ken.

At first they took no notice of her as they galloped and frolicked. She had seen beautiful horse flesh through the course of her life, but these were more. More than perfect, more than horse flesh, they were divine beings. White and black, light and dark, life and death.

The stallion nipped the mare's rump and she bucked, then turned on her haunches, he turning with her, and they ran matching stride for stride, muscles rippling, nostrils flared. After a time, they slowed to a jog. Salvistar kept close to Seastaria, protective and possessive. But when Seastaria finally chose to take note of Karigan, she walked toward her. The stallion lingered behind, and kept watch from a distance.

Seastaria radiated love, and Karigan hugged her neck, caressed her velvety nose. Her eyes were the azure of a summer sky with the occasional passing of a fair-weather cloud. As Karigan gazed into one of those eyes, she felt absorbed, absorbed into light, absorbed by love until she was completely drawn into the mare and became one with her. She sprang into a gallop, a joyous gallop across the starry meadow, the grasses whipping at her legs, the wind caught in her mane and tail. To stretch and run was freedom itself.

The stallion ran alongside her, nipping her, taking of her scent, shouldering her. She made him work for what he wanted, made him prove his mettle, his devotion, his strength. He threw his head up and bugled his desire. He ran before her, showing her his powerful neck and flank, how fast he was. Her heart thumped rapidly and she whinnied in reply.

The running and games soon quieted and they nuzzled one another and exchanged breaths. Salvistar nibbled at the base of her tail. He curled his lip to take in her scent again. A thrill of excitement passed through her, her hide quivering. Her mind and body became consumed by instinct, and she squared up her stance and raised her tail. She wanted only one thing, she—

Karigan forcibly extracted herself from Seastaria, her heart beating hard. She trembled with arousal, watched as Salvistar mounted Seastaria and thrust into her. In a sense, she was still there with her aithen, unable to not be present and share the experience.

And then it was done. Seastaria glanced across the meadow at her. Despite having been one with Seastaria, Karigan could not say what was in that look.

Mare and stallion then stood together, Salvistar's chin resting across Seastaria's wither. They both switched their tails in contentment.

"Galadheon?"

Karigan was so startled she almost fell off her rock into the stream. Ealdaen stood on a stepping stone before her. He gazed at her with great interest.

"Uh . . ." Perspiration dripped down her face and she wiped her brow with the back of her hand.

"You seemed most distant," Ealdaen said. "I apologize for disturbing you."

She wanted to stand, but it took a moment to remember she had only two legs, not four. Ealdaen watched her curiously as she clambered to her feet.

"Were you listening to the voice of the world?" he asked.

"That is what Enver called it." She could tell he wanted to ask more, but whatever restrained him, whether it be politeness or a taboo against speaking aloud about such things, she did not know. She chose not to enlighten him. It was none of his business.

The vision left her unbalanced and she stepped with great care to the stream bank.

Ealdaen followed her. "You seem to court your own mortality," he commented. "You were very close to the forbidden side of the stream where the watchers would have slain you."

She shrugged. "I suppose it would have solved Eletia's problem."

"You are a curiosity, Galadheon," he said as he walked beside her.

"Am I allowed to leave yet?"

"No. I have come for the mage so he may speak on your behalf before the council."

"What about me? Can't I speak for myself?"

"It may be that they will ask this of you, but for now, they want to hear what the mage has to say."

"This is ridiculous," she replied. "I am sorry I brought the wraiths to Eletia, but it was the only way I knew to destroy them. I need to get back to my people. There is so much going on, and just because your people despise non-Eletians and have ridiculous laws, I am stuck here."

Ealdaen paused. "Most mortals would feel fortunate spending time in the Elt Wood." Then he shook his head. "Our laws are ancient, Galadheon, ancient beyond your grasp, and far from ridiculous. You must accept this process, for it is a trial, and it is your life at stake."

❧ WALLS OF WATER ❧

When Duncan returned that night, he declared himself exhausted, created an illusory four-poster bed that looked more appropriate for the chamber of a great emperor than a half-organic Eletian cottage, and flopped onto a very fluffy feather mattress.

"That bad?" Karigan asked.

"Worse than a pack of tired old men gumming over politics," he replied. "They have eternal lives so they can debate issues for years. Centuries if need be. All things considered, however, their questioning of me was, well, rather brief."

Centuries? She did not like to think they could hold her indefinitely while they considered her fate. Not that Eletia was an unpleasant place in which to dwell for a time, but she belonged with her own people preparing to fight Second Empire.

She pulled her feet onto the sofa and leaned back into the pillows. "What did they ask you?"

"They asked where I'd been since the Long War, which led to questions about the eagles. They did not seem amused that the eagles had kept my presence a secret all this time, but *I* am grateful they've kept their promise to me even though the Scourge was so long ago. In any case, there were many tiresome questions about my time at the eyrie, which, as I've told you, was not very interesting and so I started to recite some of the eagle ballads I know, and they relented and asked how I happened to be with you and how the thing with the wraiths came to pass. I told them everything, about your colonel being abducted, the Blanding, everything. And it's good you

391

told me the tale of the Blackveil expedition because I could remind them about that. They, of course, are quite aware of your deed in rescuing the Argenthynian Sleepers, but it didn't hurt to bring it to the front of their minds. And there is something else . . ."

"Yes?" Karigan prompted when he seemed to fall off into thought.

"Hmm? Oh, yes. Sorry. There is something else afoot here, something of great distraction and excitement occurring which may account for the questioning's apparent brevity."

"Like what?" she asked.

"I haven't the faintest. But, I can almost feel it, like an undercurrent of energy. An etheric vibration." He waved his hand in the air. "I mean, not just the natural etheric vibration that is Eletia, but something more. Something closer to its heart." He gazed at her. "It may be to your advantage they are not entirely focused on you."

Or, maybe not, she thought; if they just wanted to get her out of the way, all they had to do was declare her guilty and execute her. It would be the expedient thing for them to do.

The next morning came and there was no sign of Ealdaen. Gweflin came for her healing session, but as usual bore no news of what was happening with the council. Afterward, Karigan contemplated returning to the stream to see if she could mind-travel to the starry meadow again. She did not necessarily need the stream to do it, but it had served as such a good focus. Something of having been within Seastaria, the freedom and joy of galloping alongside her mate, called to her. However, it was not to be, for Ealdaen arrived.

"Galadheon," he said, "the council would like to see you. Please accompany me to the Alluvium."

"Good luck," Duncan called after her.

Now that it came down to it, she was nervous. As they left the cottage and walked down the trail, Karigan asked, "What should I expect?"

"You will be questioned to hear your side of events, why you did what you did." His tone was neutral, offered no clue as to how the council would rule.

"Are they going to execute me?"

He halted and looked down upon her. "I do not know, Galadheon. I do not know."

A sensation of grim foreboding settled upon her like an icy hand.

After they crossed the stream, Eletian warriors stepped out of hiding onto the trail to escort them. The sun pleasantly dappled the forest floor; birds fluttered among tree branches. Star flowers speckled the borders of the path. It was a paradise, and yet, though judgment had not yet been passed, it felt a mockery, for she couldn't help but think she walked the path of the condemned.

They followed the trail alongside the torrent that flowed down from where she'd crossed over from the white world. When they came upon a waterfall, Ealdaen turned toward it, and onto a trail she would not have seen without her guide. He led her beneath an overhang of mossy rock and behind the fall.

They emerged into an elliptical chamber in which the falling water served as a fluid, glassy wall. The rest of it was formed from natural bedrock that must have been carved out and polished long ago by the force of the cataract over the passage of many millennia.

In the center of the chamber facing the wall of water stood a throne chair that looked like it had been grown rather than crafted, a cedar, the tree of life. A twisted limb grew off the backrest toward the water wall, its flat, scaly foliage seeking sunlight. It perched upon a dais in the center of the chamber, and the throne's roots snaked and snarled around it into the natural stone floor. Beside the dais, at floor level, sat a more ordinary chair.

Statues stood at either end of the chamber, statues like she'd seen in Castle Argenthyne of winged Eletians. One was half-turned toward the fall with a glowing moonstone held aloft. A sword lay across the upraised palms of the other. It was the only real resemblance she saw between Argenthyne and Eletia.

"This is the council chamber," Ealdaen told her, and he directed her to stand before the throne, which meant her back was close to the fall. It made her uneasy. Perhaps those found guilty of executable offenses were simply pushed backward over the edge. She shivered.

"Where are the councilors and the prince?" she asked.

"They will arrive shortly," he replied.

The guards took their places along the walls of the chamber, and finally nine Eletians—five males and four females—filed in and took their places on seating located to the side, from where they could view both Karigan and the throne. Prince Jametari entered after them and sat in the chair next to the throne. He was not yet king, and so, she guessed, he would not presume to sit on the king's throne chair.

"*Au belanne oeth,* Galadheon," Ealdaen said, and he left her side to stand near the entrance. She had a feeling he'd just wished her good luck.

One of the nine stepped forward and spoke in Eletian. He paused as if he expected a response from her. She looked imploringly at Ealdaen, but it was the prince who spoke. "Use the common tongue, Councilor. The accused is Sacoridian, as you well know."

"Speak your name, Sacoridian," the Eletian said in the common tongue, a look of distaste on his otherwise beautiful face.

Karigan stood straighter. "I am Chief Rider Sir Karigan G'ladheon of His Majesty's Messenger Service, daughter of Stevic and Kariny, and sub-chief of Clan G'ladheon."

"Do you know why you are summoned here?"

"So you can decide whether to murder me for trespass."

The assembled murmured among themselves. Prince Jametari raised his hand for silence. "You are accurate in your response," he said, "but I am afraid your bald truth, the brash choice of words, disturbs my council. Yes, you are accused of trespass, not only once, but thrice: the first time when you came across the bridge and we conversed, the second time when you caused a man to cross the bridge who was subsequently slain by our archers, and the third time when you brought yourself and creatures from the anethna."

"You count only the three times?" she asked. "What of the very first?"

The councilors stirred, and again Jametari raised his hand

for silence. "I advise you to conduct yourself with decorum as the visitor to another land's court that you are, Galadheon, and restrain the impulse for outbursts of so disparaging a tone for those who judge you. Surely such behavior is not what King Zachary would expect of one of his trusted messengers."

He was right, she thought. She needed to bridle her anger and anxiety. She put her hand to her heart and bowed. "My apology to you, Your Highness, and to your councilors. You are correct. My conduct is not becoming of a king's messenger. It is just that I am anxious about what this may lead to, namely my death. I am also concerned for my people who will be facing Second Empire in battle. I wish to be there with them."

Jametari nodded. "Your hearing will be a fair one, and judgment will not be made lightly. As to the first instance to which you refer, in which you rescued Sleepers of Argenthyne from the corruption of Kanmorhane Vane, it is not part of today's proceedings, for it was of great service to the Eletian people, and at the behest of Laurelyn of Argenthyne. It is also why I granted you clemency when you crossed the bridge from the anethna the first time. Please explain to the council the circumstances of the two trespasses that followed, especially after I explicitly warned you against crossing into this realm."

Karigan took a deep breath and, in her best "messenger voice," told the councilors of Eletia everything, beginning with her captivity at the hands of the Darrow Raiders and their enmity for Green Riders, and how they sought vengeance on her colonel. She described the crossing of the white world, her struggles with the whisper wraiths, and the reasons she entered Eletia on three occasions.

"I know how good the Eletian archers are," she said. "They saved my life twice, and for that I am grateful. I had no ill intent when I entered Eletia. I simply sought help."

Debate followed among the Eletians, but it was in their own tongue. She could see that the councilors were divided, some arguing, a couple looking conciliatory, others making reasoned statements, but otherwise she could not understand what they were saying. To think her life depended on these nine, and Prince Jametari, as well.

The prince regarded her coolly, not joining in with the debate, not even seeming to listen to it. When she stared back at him, he did not avert his gaze. She felt captured by it, and the discussion of the councilors fell away until there was only the sound of roaring water and the prince's voice.

"Galadheon," he said. "I must see what you have seen."

Without either of them moving, they seemed somehow to meet in the middle. It was as though they existed aside from the world in which the councilors debated, as if they were surrounded by walls of flowing water.

He placed his hands on either side of her face and touched his forehead to hers, then pulled back. He removed her eyepatch and made a sharp intake of breath when he saw her mirror eye. Pain jabbed through it into her head. She hadn't wanted her eye revealed. She wanted to protest, to grab her eyepatch from him, but she couldn't move, couldn't speak.

"Forgive me for what I am about to do, Galadheon," he told her.

He gazed directly into her mirror eye. There was no transition of floating through the heavens and seeing the weavings of worlds and lives, but an abrupt leap to visions. Visions from her life, of fighting and defeating Jametari's son, Shawdell, who'd tried to bring down the D'Yer Wall and destroy Sacoridia by causing the overthrow of Zachary. Jametari lingered on Shawdell as if trying to memorize his features, and she felt a great well of sadness of a father for a son.

The visions followed her through many of her experiences as a Green Rider, speeding through the mundane, pausing at points of interest such as her travel back to the time of the Long War and her interaction with the First Rider upon Kendroa Mor. He paid particular attention to her journey to Blackveil and the expedition's leader, Graelalea, who, Karigan recalled, was his sister. He watched how Graelalea, mortally wounded, removed the feather of the winter owl she had worn in her hair and gave it to Karigan. *Enmorial,* Graelalea said with her dying breath. Memory. He also paid special interest to Karigan's meeting with Laurelyn, and her rescue of the Argenthyne Sleepers, of her bringing them to Eletia and meeting King Santanara.

There was the breaking of the looking mask and her journey into the future time. She saw glimpses of people and places she did not remember, but others she did—*Cade*. Jametari moved through these visions, including the intimate moments that should have remained between only her and Cade. She fought to control the visions, but could not overcome Jametari's power. It was like once again being at the mercy of the whisper wraiths, her life essence being drawn out of her.

Still he mined her memories, including her time as a captive of Second Empire, of torture by Nyssa. Over and over, she felt the whip laid upon her bare back, the helplessness of being tied to a beam, unable to protect herself as the lash fell again and again. She tried to cry out, but the spell Jametari held her under prevented it. He reviewed, in detail, the rescue of Zachary, their kiss following the Battle of the Lone Forest, her awkward parting with Enver. Relentlessly he watched her life unfold to this very moment.

And then he looked further, but she couldn't tell what he saw for it was all murky to her. Might he be looking into her future?

She is submerged in a stream. Cold currents curl around her. She need not breathe, just rest, and Enver will keep watch.

When Jametari disengaged, she gasped as if breaking the surface of water after being long deprived of air.

"You are both light and dark," he said, "as are all humans and Eletians alike, but with you it is deeper. Only time will tell how it plays out." He gently placed the patch back over her eye and bowed. "It is a very dangerous thing you've got in your eye. Should my councilors judge you favorably, I am of a mind to remove it, but it would mean taking the whole of your eye, and even I am not prepared to commit so barbaric an act. Continue to guard it as well as you can. I hope you can forgive me for my intrusion into your memories, but it has been most instructive."

She blinked rapidly. He sat upon his chair as though nothing had changed, as if he had not moved, nor had she. The councilors debated on, oblivious to anything happening between her and the prince. Had he really plundered her memories? The knowing gleam in his eye affirmed he had, and she shuddered in revulsion at the violation, that he'd made her relive the torture and the loss of Cade, that he'd seen her most private moments.

"We have come to a decision," one of the councilors declared.

Karigan's heart thudded. The chamber was silent but for the thunder of the waterfall as she awaited their judgment.

 THE HOUSE OF SANTANARA ⊰

The silence was leaden as the councilors awaited Jametari's signal to continue with the pronouncement of their judgment, but he gave no such signal and instead he stood. "We will take a recess now. I must go to the Grove. And I sense the Galadheon will need some rest and refreshment before we proceed."

He swept out of the chamber. Karigan's knees began to buckle but Ealdaen was right there and helped her to remain standing.

"Come, Galadheon," he said gently. "I am not sure what happened between you and the prince. I am not sure *anything* happened, but his departure at this moment is highly unusual. One thing I *am* certain of is that you need rest and refreshment as he suggested."

Karigan was shivering by the time Ealdaen guided her to a terrace bathed in sunshine and surrounded by a copse of white birch trees, and tall grasses dotted with purple irises. The falls and rapids of the Alluvium were out of sight, but the sound remained, if distant. Ealdaen led her to a chair to rest, and food and drink was delivered to them by attendants, including a cup of cordial that Ealdaen insisted she drink in small sips. As warmth returned to her extremities, so did her fury.

"He rummaged around my memories as if they were his to do so," she told Ealdaen. "He had no right."

"I do not understand how or why he did this, Galadheon. Ari-matiel Jametari is gifted with foresight as was his father. This must be some extension of his gift."

399

She chose not to bring up her mirror eye even though it was possible he had heard of it. "Did anything change as you watched in the council chamber? Did you see me or the prince move?"

"I am not sure what I saw," Ealdaen replied carefully. "If I had to answer, I saw you no more than shift your weight from one foot to the other, and breathe and blink, and that the prince remained seated. And yet . . . I do not know."

The one thing that was clear to her was that Jametari had known exactly what her eyepatch hid and he'd had little compunction about using her mirror eye to see what he wished. She took a final sip of the cordial and set her cup aside on a low table. There were more honey cakes and strawberries, cheeses and a dense, nutty loaf, but she was too angered by Jametari's violation to eat. It was bad enough she had to stand trial for simply trying to survive. If the Eletians were planning to execute her, how would they do it? She'd faced death before, but at least she'd been able to fight it. This made her feel so helpless. It did not bear thinking of how her father would take it, or Zachary. No, that would be catastrophic for the alliance. Would Zachary be so rash as to break off the alliance with the Eletians if they killed her?

"Ealdaen," she said, and she was surprised by the calmness of her own voice, "if they decide . . ." She swallowed hard. "If they decide I am guilty and must be executed, King Zachary must not find out. Make sure he thinks there was an accident, or the wraiths killed me, or—or I have simply disappeared, that the Eletians know nothing."

Ealdaen's eyes widened. "This you would have us do? Why?"

"For the alliance. There is reason to expect King Zachary would not react well to the execution of one of his own messengers."

"Hmm. I suspect there is more to it than that."

"Promise me you will see this done."

He stood and bowed. "I do so promise, but it is my hope that the council has not found execution necessary. I will stand by your side as a friend, and object if such judgment comes to pass. It may be that I have some influence in the Alluvium. You will not be alone."

"Thank you," she whispered. "Thank you."

"I just do not understand," he said, "why you are being made to suffer the wait with no answer. It is unheard of and cruel."

Apparently Jametari was full of cruelty, and she wondered if it was for the part she had played in the demise of his son all those years ago.

An hour must have elapsed before attendants called them back to the council chamber. It was very cool and dark there after having sat out in the sun. Prince Jametari awaited her in his chair beside the throne, his expression unreadable, and the councilors took their seats as Ealdaen escorted her to her place before the throne.

"Hope, Galadheon," he told her, and as promised, he did not leave her side.

The councilor who appeared to be the leader among the others rose and said, "We wish to proclaim our verdict." Then he waited, once more, for Jametari's word.

Jametari said nothing. There was silence but for the rush of the waterfall. Then at length, he stood and looked at the councilors. "There will be no verdict this day."

Karigan wavered on her feet. Ealdaen put his arm around her to steady her. The councilors murmured in bewilderment, their voices questioning.

"Silence," Jametari commanded. He approached Karigan, then halted before her, his gaze stern and proud. And then he went to his knee. There were gasps around the chamber.

Karigan looked to Ealdaen for an explanation, but he was just as stunned as the others.

"Chief Rider Sir Karigan Galadheon, daughter of Kariny and Stevic, and sub-chief of Clan G'ladheon," he said in a voice that resonated throughout the chamber, "I beg forgiveness for what you have been put through this day at the hands of Eletia, and most of all, by me."

An Eletian apologizing? An Eletian *prince* apologizing?

"Our people have much to thank you for in the past, and perhaps in the future to come, though the future is always in motion." He paused, then continued, "You were favored by

Laurelyn, queen of Argenthyne, and my sister, Graelalea. Laurelyn has seen more clearly than we ever have the course of events, and I honor her wisdom. You were also with my sister when she died in the ruins of Argenthyne. The feather of the winter owl she wore in her hair and gave only to you at her passing. I see you now wear a feather as part of your uniform. I cannot help but appreciate the synchronicity of it." He then spoke at length in Eltish and there was more shock around the chamber. "*Ne, Galadheon. Ne, ne.*" Then he ended with, "*Dama Cearing Asai'riel a' Santanara.*"

Ealdaen dropped to his knee beside her, and all the councilors and guards followed suit, as well.

"Uh . . ." Karigan looked about, flabbergasted. What was going on? Maybe Eletians paid obeisance to the guilty before they were thrown over the waterfall? But Jametari had said there'd be no verdict.

He finally rose, placed his hands on her shoulders, and kissed her forehead. "You are ever welcome in the Vane-ealdar, Asai'riel. You may call it home as you wish, to come and go as you are moved. Others, however, are not so welcome."

"I can leave?" She gazed around the chamber at the councilors who had also risen, but their heads remained bowed.

"As you wish."

She stared hard at him, trying to detect some guile on his part, but as always, it was difficult to say with Eletians. She glanced at Ealdaen, who still looked stunned.

"Um, then I'd like to leave," she said. "If I could have the travel device back, I will be out of your way immediately."

"That is one wish I will not fulfill," Jametari said. "Such an etheric device should not be out in the world. It has a will of its own, but we will keep it safe so it does not return to its special resting place, which, we gather, remains in the hands of the Deija."

"I do not understand."

"These types of devices have a homing imperative," he replied, "that cause them to return to their resting place after a certain amount of use or passage of time, usually a specially made coffer where their power can be replenished."

That, she thought, might explain how the colonel ended up

in the hands of the Raiders, that she hadn't actually used the device to take on a rescue mission by herself. "Yet, the Eletians might feel they can keep it for their own use?"

Jametari gave her a thin smile. "The Eletians will contain it so it is not misused as it has been by these Deija that plague your realm. I will send an escort with you through the anethna, yes? And you will soon be back where you began."

"But the travel device would—"

"No," he replied. "In this I will not waver."

She could feel the truth in that, and having just escaped execution, she chose not to push the goodwill of the Eletians. At least the Raiders would not have access to the travel device, either.

"Then I will use the Blanding to return to my king."

There was that smile on his face again, and she frowned.

"When you see King Zachary," he said, "tell him not to despair. We shall arrive when all appears most dire. I must now take my leave of you, Asai'riel, until we meet again."

"What—?" she began, but he had already strode off toward the exit, followed by his councilors. "Hells," she muttered.

Ealdaen sent attendants after Duncan and escorted her out to the terrace to sit in the sun again while they waited.

"What was all that?" she asked him, gesturing to the path that led to the council chamber. "What did the prince call me?"

He looked off into the distance, perhaps to the lake and the forest below. "To be honest, I am not sure I understand, either." He shook his head. "It is not something that has ever happened before."

"*What?* Please explain it to me."

Ealdaen gazed at her with the look of shock and wonder she had seen back in the council chamber. "He has named you a scion of the House of Santanara."

"*What?*"

"It is so, Asai'riel. It has rarely been done among Eletians, where an individual is joined into another's house, but it has never been done with a mortal."

So many questions she wanted to ask at once, but she could only squeak out, "Why?"

"I do not know." Ealdaen shook his head again. "Ari-matiel Jametari may have *seen* something when he looked into your mind, or perhaps when he ventured to the Grove. I am sorry. I do not have an answer for why. For whatever the reason, he wished to place you in the House of Santanara. It means you are Eletian nobility, a daughter to King Santanara."

"*What?*" She stood up so abruptly her chair fell over backward with a startling clatter in the peaceful setting. An attendant hastened to set it right.

These one-word outbursts must make her sound like an idiot, but really, this latest surprise from the Eletians was beyond words.

WINTERLIGHT

 So aghast was Karigan to learn she had been named a scion of the House of Santanara that she almost missed hearing what Ealdaen had to say next.

"We are no longer to call you by your surname," he said.

"What? Why not?"

"The prince finds your surname, which betokens your ancestor of Arcosia and his long-ago betrayal of Mornhavon the Black, inadequate."

Inadequate. Her ancestor, Hadriax el Fex, had committed atrocities in the effort to claim the lands of the Sacor Clans and the Eletians for Arcosia, but appalled by the monster his friend Mornhavon had become, redeemed himself by surrendering to the First Rider and the forces of King Jonaeus. After the war, he renamed himself *Galadheon,* which meant "betrayer" in the common tongue. She could not imagine what the hells the Eletians were going to call her now.

"Inadequate," she murmured in disbelief, and shook her head.

"I think you will find your new name more than adequate," Ealdaen said. "Ari-matiel Jametari has proclaimed that we call you *Cearing Asai'riel* to befit your status as a member of the House of Santanara."

"It sounds . . . nice," she ventured, but her mind was reeling.

Ealdaen laughed. "It is a very interesting name."

Interesting? Uh oh. Names did seem important to Eletians. Jametari's sister, Grae, for instance, had had her name extended to Graelalea. Karigan did not know why, or what it signified.

"*Cearing*," Ealdaen said, "suggests the long cold and darkness of winter, the sadness of the season of passing. Grief."

That, she thought, didn't sound good at all. The attendants had left them a flagon of wine and she decided to pour herself a gobletful. As overwhelming as this day had become, it appeared she was going to need it.

"*Asai* is ice, snow, frost. The Eltish language will often use several different words for a single concept such as a season, to convey not just meaning, but its complexity, with texture and other descriptive attributes."

"I imagine, then, that Eletian conversations take a while."

Ealdaen smiled. "It depends on how formal the conversation, but yes, they can. Eletians do have the time, after all. As for *riel*," he continued, "it relates to light, but not just any light. Clarity, purity, radiance, hope. Radiance that can be associated with stars, or the silver moon. It can be hot and burning, or icy cold. When paired with *cearing,* I would choose cold. Light of this nature can also be deadly, like a cutting edge, or good overcoming evil. You are familiar with our moonstones, which we call *muna'riel*, for they in fact harbor the beams of silver moons."

Darkness and light. Hot and cold. Seastaria and Salvistar. Dualities. The heat of the sun beating on the back of her neck and the background noise of the falls fell away as she tried to absorb what Ealdaen was telling her.

"So my Eletian name is 'Sad Ice Light'?" she asked.

"Very close. Cearing Asai'riel more correctly translates to 'Winterlight.' And so you are. I find it apt."

"Apt . . ." she murmured, and he raised an eyebrow as she drained the entire goblet of wine and poured herself more. "What does *your* name mean?"

"While your name is very nuanced," he replied, "mine is simple. It means 'Elder,' or 'Ancient One.'"

"Are you . . . *that* old?"

He laughed quietly. "Your folk are but the new buds of a spring tree that has not yet sprouted."

She guessed that meant he was "that old," and that what his name represented was far from *simple.*

"Ealdaen, none of this makes sense—the prince proclaiming I'm now of House Santanara, and the name. I'm not even Eletian. Your people were ready to execute me."

He shook his head as if still bewildered by it all himself. "It is indeed an unexpected development, but though you bear no Eletian blood, we are now *your* people. The prince has commanded this, and so you are Eletian and kin to King Santanara."

"Good gods," she said, and gulped more wine, not even tasting it. Then she began to wonder what the Eletians got out of this, what game they were playing, but she dared not voice it aloud.

Ealdaen stood. The sun shone on his hair as he extended his arms to the sky. "Rejoice, Asai'riel, for it is not a death sentence, but a great honor. An honor unheard of before this day."

She closed her eyes and just sat there in silence trying to absorb her new status and name, though none of it seemed to make sense. It would take time to realize the repercussions and advantages. The disadvantages. And to parse out what Jametari and the Eletians hoped to gain from it. What the hells had the prince seen in her mirror eye?

When she looked again, Ealdaen was standing on the edge of the terrace and gazing into the valley. "I am surprised Arimatiel Jametari did not request you to stay longer so you might learn more of our ways, and so we might celebrate your ascension. But he must have his reasons."

Eletians, she thought, always had reasons.

"Ah," he said, "I see the mage and his escort making their way up the trail."

Before long, Duncan stepped up onto the terrace with an armored Eletian beside him. The Eletian bore a pouch over his shoulder.

"Dear lady," Duncan said, "I am so delighted you are among the living. I hear we are to depart."

"Yes." She stood up too quickly and the wine made her head swim. Ealdaen steadied her when she swayed. "Ugh."

"Eletian wine is more potent than it may seem," he told her.

She cleared her throat, straightened her greatcoat, and said, "I can stand on my own, thank you. Duncan and I will leave now." Yes, she could stand on her own, but walking in a straight line might prove challenging.

"First things first," Duncan said. "Byrnin?"

The Eletian stepped forward and bowed, and extended the pouch to her. Karigan sighed and took it. She may have a new status among the Eletians, but to Duncan she was still his beast of burden.

"Do you like my new pouch?" he asked. "The Eletians kindly replaced the one the wraiths lost."

It was of deepest forest green, embroidered with stylized birch branches and leaves, and made of a fine woven material that was soft to the touch. "It's truly lovely," she said. "Now we can go."

"One moment," Ealdaen said.

Now what?

He removed a small drawstring purse from a pocket. He passed it to her with a bow. "A gift to you from me."

She loosened the drawstrings and found a round, faceted crystal inside, a moonstone. When she rolled it onto her palm, it lit up with purest radiance, outshining even the sun-bathed terrace. She smiled. The light seemed to clear her head of the effects of the wine, and unburden her heart. All she had learned this day might not make sense yet, but she was all right. She replaced the moonstone in the purse, and the terrace returned to its ordinary sunny self.

"Thank you," she said, "very much."

Ealdaen bowed again. "Perhaps you will not lose this one. The moonbeam within comes from a silver moon that shone over Argenthyne thousands of years ago. Laurelyn, I think, would approve."

She shivered at the thought of holding the light of so ancient a moonbeam in her hand. "I will not lose this one." She had possessed two others, one given her by a pair of eccentric sisters who lived deep in the Green Cloak. It had turned to a handful of fragments after she had used its light as a weapon during a battle with Shawdell the Gray one. The second she had found among her mother's belongings in a chest, and was lost in the future time.

"I guess we'll leave now," she said more quietly.

"*Dama,*" Byrnin said.

She looked up. The Eletian extended a small box to her.

"What is this?" she asked.

"It is from Ari-matiel Jametari," he said. "A gift on the day of your naming."

She accepted the box. It fit in her hand and was finely carved with a birch leaf design. She opened it to find a ring within. A birch leaf of emerald green, its veins rendered in fine strands of white gold, perched upon a band also of white gold. She looked up at Byrnin, then Ealdaen.

"You are kin," Ealdaen said. "The prince is making a gesture of welcome into the House of Santanara, and it will be recognized by all Eletians."

She slipped it onto her index finger, and it seemed to adjust itself to her size. The emerald glittered in the sunshine. Duncan, she noticed, looked rather thunderstruck by it all and was strangely silent, his eyes wide and mouth hanging open.

"It's . . . Well, it's beautiful," she said.

"We will tell the prince you are pleased by the gift," Ealdaen said. "And now you may leave as you wish. Byrnin and two others will guide you. It has been an interesting meeting, but I am growing accustomed to that where you are concerned, Green Rider Cearing Asai'riel. I wish you well on your journey and perhaps we will meet again soon." He bowed.

"Good-bye, Ealdaen." She would not get used to Eletians bowing to her.

"This way, Dama," Byrnin said. He led them from the terrace onto the trail that meandered upstream along the watercourse. Two more armored Eletians fell in behind them. She caught herself more than once glancing at the ring on her finger and how the emerald sparkled in the sun.

Duncan sidled over to her. "What happened today? Why are they giving you things and calling you Lady Winterlight?"

She was surprised he hadn't been told.

"Well?" he pressed.

"A very odd thing happened at the trial today," she said, and she proceeded to tell him all that had transpired, including her conversation with Ealdaen.

Duncan made a low whistle. "I have never heard the like."

She glanced at Byrnin, who walked several strides ahead
of them, and then back at the other two Eletians, who trailed
well behind. She knew no matter how quiet she made her
voice they'd hear anything they wished to; still, she asked in
an almost-whisper, "What do you make of it?"

He scratched his head. "Hard to say. The Eletians were
always cordial with us lesser folk when we were allies during
the Long War, but they still kept to themselves most of the
time. They are an enigmatic people, and I am not sure anyone
outside of Eletia or Argenthyne truly knows the culture. Of
course, I have been stuck in the eyrie for a thousand years or
so, so I've had few dealings with them."

Karigan lowered her voice to a whisper. "Any guesses
about ulterior motives?"

"I don't know, dear lady. The prince certainly has his
reasons, but as you described, even Lord Ealdaen seemed
baffled."

After steadily climbing alongside the watercourse, Byrnin halted. "We have reached the place of crossing, Dama,"
he said.

There was, of course, no way to distinguish the spot from
anywhere else along the trail, but she recognized the location,
and especially the view of the forest and lake below.

"Back into the Blanding, eh?" Duncan said.

"Prince Jametari would not give me the traveling device,"
she replied.

"Probably for the best. Such arcane devices can be more
trouble than they are worth. We'll enter the way we did the
first time."

Just as before, she used her fading ability while he spoke
an incantation in a sing-song language. The bridge shim-
mered to life.

"We need but cross," he said.

Byrnin strode past her and Duncan and waited at the arch.

"Uh . . ." Karigan said.

"Dama?" Byrnin queried.

"I thought you were just escorting us to this spot, and we
would leave you here."

"No, Dama. Ari-matiel Jametari has commanded us to deliver you directly to the Firebrand."

"But we do not need an escort."

Byrnin bowed. "I am sure that is true, Dama, but Ari-matiel Jametari has commanded it."

Duncan gazed at her with an amused expression on his face. "You are of the House of Santanara now. You probably shouldn't countermand the prince's order."

"I was hoping to avoid a spectacle upon our return."

"Three Eletians is hardly a spectacle."

It was among a folk, she thought, who had rarely seen Eletians in a thousand years, but she relented with a growl and swept onto the bridge, forcing the others to hurry after her. As she passed over the arch and through the mist, it was a jolt to go from bright sunshine and blue sky, the singing of birds and the sound of rushing water, to silence and endless white plains. She did not slacken her stride as she stepped off the first bridge, and hastened to the bridge next to it that would take her to the mountains. Having the additional protection of three Eletian warriors with her was a comfort, but even so, she didn't want to chance encountering whisper wraiths or any other dangerous denizens of the white world.

And what of Torq? A quick glance revealed no one in sight. Perhaps he had crossed one of the bridges, or maybe he had set off across the white terrain to see where it led. She had no idea, and was just as glad to see no sign of him.

She then sprinted up the arch of the other bridge and practically threw herself to the other side through the mist. Duncan followed right on her heels, breathing hard as if he had to breathe at all.

It was a relief to transition to a green and blue world again with the sun shining down on her, and to inhale the cool mountain air. She stepped off the bridge and walked across the ruins, and hopped to the ground. This was becoming a very familiar route to her, and she hoped she wouldn't have to travel it again. She set off, the Eletians ranging around her. At last she'd get to see how everyone at the encampment fared after the attack by the Lions and the incursion by the whisper wraiths.

 YOLANDHE'S ISLAND

"Go on, boy!" Beryl flung the branch up the trail and Scorch gamboled ahead to fetch it. It might have been any outing with one's dog, but Scorch was no dog, and no dog squashed swaths of brush and saplings the way he did when bounding through the woods.

He didn't quite comprehend the "fetch" part of the game and so, predictably, did not return all the way with the branch, but instead crunched it to pieces with his powerful jaws. It was an improvement, however, over his trying to breathe fire on the sticks. She and Yap played with him on the rocky shoals near camp until he learned not to burn the sticks they threw, and the forest with them.

Spending time with Scorch made up a little for her not getting to see her horse, Luna Moth. She missed the mare intensely despite the fact she was often away from her. She'd found the most trustworthy stable in Midhaven to care for Luna while she was away. But what if she was never able to leave this island? What would become of her horse? Well, Ty knew where the stable was, and if she never returned, he would see to Luna.

She walked up the path toward Scorch, hunting for a good-sized stick to throw. Her plan to make her fellow castaways regard her as unthreatening appeared to be working. Amberhill and Yolandhe cared only for one another and whatever occupied them, and Yap didn't seem to mind at all if she took Scorch exploring across the island. As for Scorch, he'd forgotten he was supposed to be her guard dog, and he'd become a grand companion as she searched the shore and island for

412

answers as to how she might drag Amberhill back to Sacor City to stand before King Zachary. Though she got to know the island on these expeditions, the answers she sought remained elusive.

She bent down to pick up a stout branch and noticed a faint trail forking off the one she and Scorch were using. She'd never noticed it before, despite having been past this spot several times. It was little used and overgrown, but definitely there.

"C'mon, Scorch," she said, and followed the path to see where it might lead. It rose upward, and she figured it must ascend the small mount. Her usual trail simply went around the base of it. She'd been to the mount's summit using a different path and had gotten a good view of the other islands of the archipelago, and the billowing sails of distant ships on the horizon. To the west she'd been barely able to make out the landmass that was the coast of Bairdly Province.

The climb started gently enough and Scorch plodded beside her, but then they came to a boulder field and she had to hop from one rock to another, hoping none rolled beneath her feet, and that Scorch would not cause a rock slide as he bounded ahead, his claws scrabbling on granite and loosening stones. A few substantial rocks clattered down the slope, but fortunately not on her head. Scorch, for his part, found a ledge above the boulder field on which to sun himself.

With a little persistence, Beryl found her way up to the ledge and sat down next to him to catch her breath. From this spot she had a decent view of the ocean through the crowns of trees that fell away with the slope of the land. Was Amberhill somewhere along the shore, interacting with dragons? She could see none of that from here. Aside from Scorch, she rarely saw the others, which, she thought, was a good thing. Not much terrified her, but *they* did when they made an appearance, even at a distance.

She enjoyed sitting in the sun. Scorch snored away emitting sparks from his jaw with his exhalations. Fortunately, there was not enough vegetation on the ledge to catch fire. The scales of his neck glimmered with iridescence in the sunshine. She climbed carefully to her feet so as not to wake him, and after a nice long stretch of her back, she turned about. Behind them the path continued between a cleft boulder, and as she approached, a current of cool air laden with the scent of damp earth and stone issued between the two halves. The path, she discovered, did not lead up the summit of the mount, but *into* it.

She stood in the opening of a large cavern. At least it felt large. She could not make out its dimensions with her sight, even as her eyes began to adjust to the dark. The sunlight flooded through the entrance past her, revealing a series of stone steps downward. There were many shapes of various sizes down in the shadows of the cavern, and the glinting of metal. She removed her specs from an inner pocket of her coat—they had miraculously survived when her dory crashed upon the shore—and put them on.

Lines and shapes became more distinct, but she still wasn't sure what it was she was seeing. There were some faint shafts of light beaming through other openings elsewhere in the cavern, but it was not enough to see details. If only she had some flint and steel. Then she remembered Scorch.

There was a pile of torches leaning against the wall of the entryway. From all appearances, they'd been there for a long time. Since they had been kept out of the weather, they might prove viable. She grabbed one and pulled the cobwebs off it, and sneezed at the dust that rose from it. She took it to Scorch and held it near his mouth as he snored. No need to even wake him up, she thought. It took some patience, but finally a finger of flame caught on the tip of the torch and flared to life.

She returned to the cavern and, with torch in hand, descended the stone stairs. The flame cast wild shadows about the walls and high ceiling, which actually made it harder to identify what she was seeing. She lit lard candles she found along the way, and only once she was on the floor of the cavern did she begin to discern the mysterious shapes she'd seen from above as barrels and chests. It was their contents that dazzled, however. Gold and silver and gems and pearls glittering in the dance of flame. Coins and jewels, and weapons with blades of shining steel and encrusted with gems like the knife Amberhill carried.

But for all the treasure, it was the ship that drew her breath away. Large and black with a dragon's head, its red eyes blinked in the flicker of the torch. She followed a path between barrels and chests and pots and ceramic jugs, but ignored the treasures they held. She steered for the ship. Its square sail hung limp in the still cavern's air. Her torch revealed it was decorated with the silhouette of a dragon, wings spread. Oars jutted from the hull, and the keel was carved with geometric interlocking symbols she did not understand. A ladder leaned against the hull.

"Come to see the remains of the great sea king Akarion?" a low voice rumbled like thunder in the cavernous chamber.

Beryl's heart leaped, but she steadied herself. "Lord Amberhill?"

"Climb aboard," he said, "but be careful. The ladder has seen better days. And leave that torch below. This ship is like kindling."

She hesitated, not sure which Amberhill she'd find today, the genial lord, or the harsh commander. She shrugged. It didn't matter which she faced, for he seemed willing to talk, and that made her curious. She placed the torch in a sconce, and taking his warning about the ladder to heart, she climbed it with caution. Once aboard the ship, she found him sitting on a chest gazing at a platform before the mast. Not just a platform, she realized, but a bier that held remains. Beneath dusty old furs lay a skeletal figure. Upon its skull was a helm engraved with symbols similar to those on the keel. It appeared the man had once possessed a prodigious head and beard of red hair.

"This is a sea king?" she said. There were those who hunted like mad for sea king treasure, and this ship burial was the mother lode.

"He is *the* sea king," Amberhill replied. "The king of kings, Akarion."

"Never heard of him." The sea kings had marauded the shores of Sacoridia so long ago, little was known of them except that they'd been bloodthirsty warriors who loved beautiful objects.

"Neither had I, but according to Yolandhe, I bear his blood and am heir to all this." He swept his arm out to take in the treasures of the cavern.

"You have come to survey your wealth?" she said. "Pity you've no place to spend it."

He laughed. It was the first time she had heard him do so. He toyed with something in his hands that glinted, and she saw with surprise it was a fine silver chain with a crescent moon pendant. It did not look like it fit with the other items that filled the cavern, and she didn't think the sea kings had worshipped Aeryc.

"I have grand fancies now and then of what to do with it," he said, "but without a boat, a seaworthy boat, it is for naught. So, it is not so much the treasure I come for, but the quiet, to sit and think."

"What sorts of things do you think about?"

"Oh, nothing important. My life back on the mainland, the family estate. My horse. My very stupid but well-bred horse. Goss is his name. I was planning he'd be the foundation stud of a breeding farm. But here I am, stuck on this island."

"Your inheritance," she said, "could buy you a fine horse farm."

"Yes, but I am not sure it is an inheritance I want."

Beryl was intrigued. This was the most she had heard him speak at one time since she landed on the island. "Why not? You could buy far more than a horse farm."

"Because it really belongs to *him*." He nodded toward the dead king. "I am not him as much as he and Yolandhe want me to be."

The ship's deck creaked beneath her feet as she shifted her weight. He was in an interesting mood without, so far, that sudden change of personality he was prone to. He remained the genial lord. At the foot of the king's bier were a shield and sword. How simple it would be to take that sword and kill him. That would resolve the problem of him becoming the future despot ruling over Sacoridia. He watched her, and she wondered if he guessed her thoughts. She did not back down, but returned his gaze.

It had not yet come to assassination, she thought. She would not abdicate her duty if it came to it, but she also would not kill him out of hand. She needed to let this conversation play out a little longer before she made any final decisions.

"What do you mean," she asked, "when you say you are not him as much as he and Yolandhe might want you to be?"

Amberhill sighed. "He was Yolandhe's great love after his ship wrecked upon the shore, and she has awaited his return for many a year."

"But he's dead," she said, pointing out the rather obvious.

"Would you believe me if I told you he isn't, exactly?"

"Now that I have seen dragons, I am rather open to believing a great many unlikely things."

He chuckled softly and said, "I suppose seeing dragons could do that."

Dragons, she thought, that he could command if she made a wrong move, or said the wrong thing.

"Akarion might be dead of body," he explained, "but he is often in my head, trying to take over. He is restless, full of need and conquest. He wishes to reclaim what was once his."

"Ah," she said, and it all came together. Karigan had described in her notes that there was more than just Mornhavon inhabiting Amberhill's mind, but she did not remember more than that. It certainly explained his swift changes of personality. "And Akarion will use the dragons to achieve what he desires."

He looked up at her. "Yes. They are his great weapon."

A chill shivered down Beryl's spine. "Great weapon" was how Karigan had described whatever it had been that caused the fall of Sacoridia in the future, although she had not learned what that great weapon was, but it confirmed Beryl's thoughts on the matter.

"Why are you able to speak freely of this to me now?" she asked. "Where is Yolandhe, and for that matter, why is Akarion, if he inhabits you, allowing you to speak of this?"

"Yolandhe walks the far shore, as she will from time to time. It is a relief, frankly. And Akarion, I do not know. He is unpredictable, comes and goes." He gazed at the crescent moon pendant now resting on his palm. "My cousin sent you to find me and to take me back."

"Yes."

"What cause has he to care if I am marooned on a distant island?"

"He has concern for your welfare." That was part of it, she was sure, but not the main part.

"He sent you all the way for that, did he?"

Beryl could try to convince him that was all of it, but he and Yolandhe had known better from the beginning. She decided she would tell the truth, and depending on his reaction, she'd feel justified to take the dead king's sword and slay him.

She sat beside him on the dusty old chest. "You know that Akarion and the dragons are dangerous, a great weapon, as you said."

He nodded.

"Well, King Zachary is aware of that danger and what it means to Sacoridia."

"I would never harm my homeland," he replied.

"Not intentionally, I'm sure," she said, "but Akarion is a different matter, and so is Mornhavon the Black."

"Mornhavon? What does he have to do with it?"

She decided not to hold back. Telling him what she knew might, in fact, help. "One of our Riders was shown . . . No, not shown. She *experienced* the future of Sacoridia. It was a bleak, terrible, and ruined place, and you were the cause." She went on to tell him what she learned from Karigan's notes.

"Mornhavon," he whispered when she finished. "It is very difficult to believe, but then I remember that I am the one carrying a dead king in my head and communing with dragons, which is beyond strange when you think about it. If not for Akarion, I would find the entire idea of myself as emperor laughable." Then he stilled before turning to gaze at her with his gray eyes. "Zachary wishes to avoid that future by having you assassinate me."

"That is not his, or my, preference."

"Dear gods, what have I gotten myself into? I don't want to die. I don't want to be an emperor. All I ever wanted was my horse farm."

"As long as we are marooned on this island," she said, "you are not a danger."

"That may be a problem," he replied. "Even if *I* don't know a way off this rock, I think Akarion does."

⇜ YOLANDHE'S ISLAND ⇝

"**O**h?" Beryl said. "Has he a ship stashed around here somewhere? One that isn't a burial ship, that is."

"I—I don't know," Amberhill replied. He absently swung the crescent moon pendant on the end of its chain. "It is only an impression I have. He does not allow me to know everything."

"That is unfortunate." She stood. If Akarion had a way off the island and was bent on conquest with those terrifying dragons at his command . . .

Amberhill gazed up at her, and his face blanched. "I know you are more than a Green Rider."

Of course he did. He'd been in the Teligmar Hills during the rescue of Lady Estora and the capture of Immerez, a captain of Mirwell's provincial militia who'd thrown his lot in with Second Empire. She'd been Immerez's interrogator, and torturer, had it come to that. Was he going to plead with her to spare him?

"Please help me," he whispered. "I don't want Akarion in my head anymore. And the dragons. . . ." He shuddered. "I keep trying to give his ring back. Watch."

He stood and Beryl spread her feet as if to take a blow, but he didn't seem to notice. He walked to the side of the bier and removed the gold ring from his finger. It was fashioned like a dragon consuming its own tail, its eye a ruby gem that shone blood red in the dim light. He pushed it onto the skeletal finger of the king. Then he stepped back.

"See?" he asked.

"See what?"

He showed her his hand. The ring was on his finger, but she had so clearly seen him place it on the skeleton's finger.

"It won't let me go," he said. "It claims me as Akarion's heir. This ring is how I—*he*—controls the dragons."

Beryl shook her head. It was looking more and more like she'd have to kill him. She hated to do so for Amberhill seemed an unwitting party to all this, a victim of his own blood. If there were a way of sparing him without endangering Sacoridia, she would, but she wasn't seeing it. He wanted her to help him, to free him from Akarion's grasp, but there was only one way she knew how to do so.

"Tell me how I can help you," she said.

"I—I don't know. You can't exactly kill Akarion. He's dead."

He wasn't helping his case. "You do not know what allows him to . . . continue?"

"This ring, but as I showed you, I can't get rid of it. I even threw it into the ocean once, but then it was on my finger again."

It sounded an awful lot like the persistence of Rider brooches. Green Riders did not lose their brooches, and they always found their way home, even after a Rider died. Arcane devices were like that, taking on lives of their own. In any case, he was not helping her to find a way to spare him. She regretted the necessity of killing him for she rather liked the Amberhill part of him, but Akarion had his hooks in him and was too much of a threat.

He turned away as if deep in thought, and she took up the dead king's sword. It was a heavy, clunky thing, more like a cudgel. The blade was rusted and pitted. She raised it for a killing blow, but he whipped around and jumped out of the way.

"So this is it, then," he said, "how you plan to *help* me."

Damn, Beryl thought. She hadn't moved quickly enough, and now it would be all the more difficult to kill him.

"It is not personal," she told him, "but a matter of protecting Sacoridia."

"I daresay it's personal to me!" He backed away.

Beryl advanced. The decking bowed beneath her feet.

Catlike, he bounded onto the bier, then leaped to the mast

and shimmied upward. "Do you care to follow?" he called down.

She did not, nor was she interested in waiting for him to tire and come down on his own. There was no telling when Akarion might make an appearance or when Yolandhe would come looking for him. She set the sword aside and swung her leg over the top rail of the ship, and descended the ladder.

"Giving up?" he called down to her.

Not hardly, she thought. The torch she had placed in a sconce still burned. It snapped and flared as she removed it. She returned to the hull.

"What are you doing down there?" Amberhill demanded, a note of alarm in his voice.

"What does it look like?" She lifted the torch to touch the hull.

"Wait!" he cried.

She paused and craned her neck to look up at him.

"You don't want to do that!"

"Seems as if it would solve all our problems."

"You would likely create an even bigger one," he said.

"Oh? And what might that be?"

"The dragons. They are awake. How will you control them when I am gone? Only *I* can, through Akarion."

"Damnation," she muttered. He could have said something earlier. She'd spent enough time around liars to know this was no lie.

"You kill me," he said, "and they go berserk. They might even go berserk on the mainland without someone to control them, and they're probably not easy to kill. I know this from having Akarion in my head."

She lowered the torch. "All right, then come down and we will discuss our options."

"You won't kill me?"

"I believe what you said about the dragons. So, no, I will not kill you."

He lowered himself down the mast, bounded over the rail, and dropped all the way to the ground, landing neatly in a crouch. He had to be half cat.

"Very impressive," she remarked.

He stood and dusted off his hands. "Had lots of practice in Sacor City."

She wondered about that, but had more pressing concerns to address, like how she was going to prevent Akarion from taking him over completely, and then getting him to Sacor City. She placed the torch back in its sconce. It was starting to sputter out.

"I wouldn't hurt my home," he said. "I need you to help me, not kill me, so we can avoid this future you spoke of."

"I don't know how," she said, "except on the end of a sword, which would eliminate the threat of both Akarion and Mornhavon. You are the one element they share in common. But, I do believe you when you say killing you could have consequences, as well."

"I would like to think I am of some importance in this matter," he replied. "Trust me when I say I don't want either of them in me. I want to be my own man again."

"Somehow you have to block Akarion," she said, "to stop his influence over you."

"What do you think I've been trying to do?"

"It will take patience and persistence, and repetition." She paced back and forth thinking about a time when someone else wished to control her mind and how she survived it. "Marching cadences."

"What?"

"Marching cadences," she said. "They helped me withstand Grandmother's attempt to break me when I was her prisoner." Grandmother had placed a spell on her that caused her pain if she so much as twitched an eyebrow. *Gold chains . . .* Only reciting the cadences in her mind had gotten her through it, but it had been a near thing.

"I don't know any marching cadences," he said.

"It doesn't have to be that. Just something that gives you focus, like a children's song, or a series of numbers. Something with a repetitive pattern. Recite it in your mind when Akarion makes himself present."

He looked thoughtful. "Hmm, all the jewels I—" He stopped abruptly and cleared his throat. "I'll come up with something."

"You need to practice it. And also see if you can find out how Akarion intends to get off the island."

"Is that all?"

There was a subtle change to his voice, a mocking tone. She stared at him. He held his body differently now, and his eyes had darkened.

"Is that all?" he repeated.

Beryl stepped back. Amberhill—or was it Akarion?—smiled.

"Let him go," she said.

"He is me," he replied. "My blood reborn. I am Akarion the great sea king, and you should bow to me."

"Lord Amberhill," she said, "fight him!"

"He can do nothing," Akarion said. "Dragons are not easy to command, but I can do it, and if I can command dragons, do you not think I can control a lordling and petty thief?"

Petty thief? she wondered. Quickly she scanned her surroundings for a weapon. There was the hilt of a longknife jutting from the top of a treasure-filled barrel. If she could get to it . . .

"I cannot allow you to threaten my plans to reclaim my lands," he said.

She edged toward the barrel. "You are mistaken if you think the people of those lands are quietly going to give them over. Even now they fight to preserve them against an ancient enemy that would claim them."

"I am not stupid," he replied. "That is what the dragons are for."

His smile was not at all like Amberhill's. It chilled her. She lunged for the barrel, but she was not quick enough. Akarion whipped his knife from his belt and threw it. At first she did not feel the pain, only the shock of impact. She looked down at the knife's hilt jutting from her mid-section and blood pouring through her fingers. Her legs lost all strength and she collapsed to the ground.

Amberhill was a shadow that hovered over her, but when she gazed up at him, she saw not Amberhill, but the king with his red beard and hair. He watched her with piercing black eyes.

As darkness overcame her vision, she thought it ironic it was all ending for her now, she who had been the one to hold the lives of others in her hands. She who held the power, whether as spy, interrogator, Rider, or assassin. It had all been turned around and perhaps in the afterlife, she'd be tormented as she had tormented others. She hoped, however, to ascend to the heavens, to be reunited with her brother.

"Riley," she whispered.

Was that Westrion's wings she heard upon the air, or the last feathery beats of her heart?

"**N**o-no-no!" Amberhill cried as he watched the light leave Beryl Spencer's eyes. "What have I done?" He dropped to his knees. "I'm sorry, I'm so sorry. Akarion made me, damn him. I'm so sorry."

"Did he?" It was Yolandhe. She had silently come up behind him.

Curse them both, he thought. "*I* would not have harmed her."

"Are you so sure? You had much to lose had she been successful in returning you to her king." She gestured at the riches that surrounded them. "Perhaps even your life, which she was prepared to take."

Yes, he had wanted to preserve his life, but not like this. "I am *not* Akarion. And yes, I am avaricious and value my own skin, but not at the expense of others. Not in this fashion." And yet, he wondered, was he blaming Akarion for his own actions? *No, no, no.*

"My love," Yolandhe said, "ambition and conquest is in your blood. It is the way of your people. You are the sea king."

"They are not my people. Those people are dead."

"They live in your blood as the ocean tides have risen and fallen for many a millennia."

There was the scratch of claws on stone, and Amberhill looked up to see the dwarf dragon that Yap called Scorch waddle by. It looked down at the body of Beryl Spencer and warbled. It then snuffled and prodded her shoulder with its beak. When Beryl did not respond, it lay down beside her and crooned. The mournful sound thrummed through the cavern.

"Dear gods," he muttered. It was like a sword through his heart. "Can't you bring her back?" he asked Yolandhe.

"She is gone. It is not my place."

"Not your place to preserve life? Then we make a good pair, for it seems my place is to take life."

"It is your instinct."

He stood and whirled on Yolandhe. "Did you know that in the future I am not just influenced by Akarion, but also by Mornhavon the Black? That a terrible future awaits the free lands?"

"I did not."

He pointed at Beryl's body. "Well, that's what she was here to prevent."

"By killing *you*, or making you her prisoner."

He wanted to shake Yolandhe out of her complacence, her unflappable disregard for the lives of those who were not her or Akarion. "She was going to help me until Akarion . . ." He shook his head. There was no use in arguing with Yolandhe. She would defend Akarion to the end of days, no matter what. He knelt once more beside Beryl, reached for her specs that had fallen askew on her face. Scorch growled and snapped at his hand. Amberhill used his ring, focused on the ruby, the heartstone, as Akarion had always done through him, and thought into it. He felt Scorch there, the dragon's simple mind and sorrow. He'd not have given credence to the beasts having emotions. He'd never felt it with the big ones, but then he'd never tried. Akarion wanted to send Scorch away with a harsh command. Amberhill pushed Akarion away and sent a calming wave into the dragon's mind, reassured it that he would not do anything untoward to Beryl, and then he broke contact. He marveled that Scorch seemed to understand Beryl was dead.

This time when he reached for her specs, Scorch made only a sad whining sound. Amberhill folded the specs and carefully tucked them into the pocket of her coat. It was then he saw the glint of a gold brooch on the lapel. He couldn't quite make out its design, but he thought it was in the shape of a winged horse, the sigil of the Green Riders. Not knowing why, he unpinned it, and stuck it in his pocket.

He lifted her into his arms and carried her from the cavern, out into the light, while Yolandhe and Scorch looked on. He descended the mount until he found a likely place facing the west. She was from Mirwell Province, and so it was appropriate that she be placed thus, facing the way of the sunset. He then built a cairn over her in the Sacoridian fashion. It took all afternoon and into the evening, even with Scorch helping to pry stones out of the earth and rolling them to him.

When he finished, he stretched his aching back and shoulders. Akarion had remained absent, much to his relief. He gazed up at the stars, thinking Beryl must be among them by now.

Yolandhe extended her hand to him. "Come, my love. Let us not dwell here among the dead, but look to our future."

"A moment. I will catch up to you."

Yolandhe nodded and left him.

When he was sure she was gone, he said to the cairn, "I am sorry, Beryl Spencer. You have my promise that I will oppose that terrible future you described. I will fight it with all I have. You have my oath on it." Then he took another moment before adding, "I should have liked to have known you better."

With that, he left behind the cairn and the sorrowful dragon curled up beside it to keep silent vigil.

⋙ THE WARRIOR KING ⋙

When Karigan and her companions came within a couple miles of the encampment, she brought them to a halt. She guessed they'd been spied by scouts keeping watch, and it wouldn't be long before they encountered sentries patrolling the perimeter. This might be the last time she got to speak to them without an audience. She gazed at each one of them: Duncan, and the three Eletian tiendan, Byrnin, Shoshan, and Kiris.

"I would appreciate it," she said, "if we kept the news about my new status in Eletia to ourselves."

"Why would you wish this, Dama?" Byrnin asked.

"It's just . . . It's just I'm still trying to get used to the idea of it myself, and trying to figure out what it means. There is already so much going on and I don't think King Zachary or anyone else needs to be bothered with it."

"I do not understand why anyone would be bothered by it," Byrnin replied. "It is an honor."

"It's well . . ." She waved her hand in the air, not sure of the answer herself.

"I confess I do not understand the ways of your people," he replied.

"It is not the sort of secret one can promise to keep," Duncan said, "but I'll do my best."

"Thanks."

She received no indication one way or the other from the Eletians for they had already moved out to take up their positions in a triangle around her. She sighed.

They encountered the first sentry before she expected. He

427

was clearly waiting for them. "We were ordered to keep an eye out for you, Rider," he said, "by the king himself, but he said nothing about Elt." He gave the tiendan a sidelong look.

"They are, er, my escorts, sent by Crown Prince Jametari."

The sentry grunted his acknowledgment and led them to the next sentry, where he handed them off so he could return to his post. When they reached the third, it wasn't just the soldier awaiting them but Tegan astride her horse, Osprey. As they approached, she dismounted and led Osprey forward, grinning.

"You're alive!" she exclaimed. "And you've brought friends."

"You're alive, too," Karigan said with a laugh, and the two hugged.

"Wish I could get a hug," Duncan said mournfully.

Karigan petted and scratched Osprey's neck, and took in the delightful musk of the sun-warmed hide of a horse. Pleased with the attention, the mare nickered for more, and Karigan, who missed her own Condor, was more than happy to oblige. "I've been worried about everyone ever since the Lions attacked and the wraiths came."

"We've been worried about you, too," Tegan said.

Karigan introduced the Eletians.

"It would appear you have quite a story to tell," Tegan said.

"You have no idea."

As they walked toward the encampment, Tegan started catching her up. "We're all well," she said. "The Riders, I mean. None of us were hurt when the Lions attacked. The Weapons took the brunt of that, and many soldiers, too."

Karigan recalled the killing of the three in Zachary's tent. She'd considered Willis and Ellen friends as much as Weapons could be such.

"The captain sent Fergal, Elgin, and Melry back to Sacor City," Tegan added, "with messages for the queen, and to get Melry out of the war zone."

Karigan could only imagine how much Mel *loved* that. She'd be champing at the bit to go in search of her mother.

"So," Tegan said, "you've actually been in Eletia all this time?"

"*All* this time? I've been gone for only a few days."

Tegan halted and stared at her. "Karigan, it's been a *month*."

"It's been *what?*"

"The Eletians probably didn't tell you," Duncan said, "as they are accustomed to it."

"Tell me what? Accustomed to what?"

"Places where the etheria is resonant, such as Eletia, seem to exist at a different pace than the rest of the world. Sometimes slower, sometimes faster. You do have a lot to learn about your new homeland."

"Your new homeland?" Tegan asked.

"Long story. I'll tell you later. And you!" Now she turned to Duncan. "It is not my homeland, and remember what I said about not talking about it?"

"I did tell you that such secrets are hard to keep."

"Well, try harder."

Duncan pursed his lips. The Eletians, who ranged at a distance, did not voice their opinion on the subject of her homeland. Tegan looked like she was dying to know more, but refrained from asking. Instead, as they continued on, she told Karigan the news of the royal infants.

"Everyone is all right?" Karigan asked.

Tegan smiled. "Yes, a healthy boy and girl, and the queen is doing fine, as well, thanks to Anna."

"Anna?"

Tegan told her about the attempted assassination and Anna's deft action with a flowerpot.

"Hearing about the babies really lifted everyone's spirits," Tegan continued, "and I daresay there's been a twinkle in King Zachary's eyes that I hadn't seen since the colonel was abducted."

It was a relief to hear about the babies and Estora on a personal level, and it was also good news for the realm, for the heirs represented stability and continuity during a time of turmoil.

"You've no news of the colonel?" Karigan asked.

Tegan shook her head. "A ship flagged with the two-headed eagle of Varos was spotted leaving Storm Harbor a little more than three weeks ago, and we assume she was on it. I am under the impression the king is doing something about it, but what, I do not know."

Storm Harbor was a town in Hillander with considerable commerce and a sizeable fishing fleet for the town's modest size. A Varosian ship would be noticed, but of interest only to the customs house. Presumably the Varosians would have kept the colonel out of sight. By now, she would be far out of reach. Once again, anger kindled in Karigan's chest that she and the Riders had not been allowed to pursue the Varosians when they had the chance.

Tegan also told her that incursions by the Raiders had become fewer and less widespread, and those that did occur were not as organized. Leaving Torq in the white world, and denying the Raiders the use of the travel device, had apparently had a positive effect. This was good news.

When they entered the encampment proper, Karigan was surprised to see how much it had expanded. On the outskirts, traveling merchants had set up wagons, carts, and booths, creating a small market selling food, trinkets, fortune-telling, and useful items a soldier could not get from the quartermaster, such as needle and thread, liniment, and personal items like hair brushes and tobacco. There was even a portable brothel in a covered wagon in which the soldiers could spend their meager earnings. The scent of sweet pies baking at one booth made Karigan's mouth water.

One vendor sold an elixir he claimed would cure any imaginable ill. Shoshan paused by his booth to sniff the contents of a bottle. The vendor, unfazed by an Eletian in her white armor stopping by his wagon, began to extol the virtues of his product.

"From foot rot to lice," he said, "from an intolerant belly to toothache, my elixir will cure all. Just for you, my lady, I will throw in a free bottle with your purchase of three."

Karigan knew all about these charlatans. He would try to sell as many bottles as quickly as possible so he could pack up and leave before his customers figured out the elixir would not cure their ills, and might possibly make them more sick. She was about to steer Shoshan away, but the Eletian wrinkled her nose and set the bottle back down on the table.

"You may keep your vile poison," she said.

"Well, now, that's not very friendly," he said. "In fact, that is downright slanderous!"

Karigan was afraid he might cause trouble, but Shoshan ignored him and walked away, and the vendor changed his tune when another customer walked up to his booth.

Shrines had been set up just beyond the merchants. They honored not only Aeryc and Aeryon, but other gods less frequently venerated in this age—Valora, goddess of war, and Faraday the Healer, among others. Soldiers lined up for the privilege of lighting a candle and leaving an offering of coins in return for a blessing from one of the presiding priests. It was appropriate, she thought, the shrines were adjacent to the market.

The encampment was noisy and smoky. Depending on wind direction, one might receive a face full of the stench of urine from the latrines, or the fumes of metal being worked by blacksmiths. Provincial units swelled Zachary's ranks, their banners posted to mark their assigned sections. They came from as far away as Wayman. Some of the units lacked the order and polish of the Sacoridian regulars, for they'd no uniforms or armor, and they'd brought whatever weapons were available to them, be it a great grandsire's notched and rusted sword, or a scythe. Their tents were pitched haphazardly, and the soldiers sat idle before their fires, smoking and drinking, and seeming to just watch the activity of the camp around them. No few made the sign of the crescent moon as the Eletians walked by.

Other units, much to her relief, looked more battle ready. Some provinces maintained standing militias, and these were better equipped, and were as disciplined as the Sacoridian regulars.

Deeper into the encampment, she glanced up toward the pass. She halted in surprise.

"What is it?" Duncan asked, and he followed her gaze. "Ah, I see. The king has been busy."

The Sacoridian front line had advanced across the valley toward the pass, though it remained well out of the range of projectiles. It did not appear as if there had been any actual combat, but the new line looked well-entrenched with earthen fortifications in place, a row of tents, supply wagons traveling to and fro, soldiers drilling, and cavalry training on open ground. It would be an impressive—and intimidating—sight to those up in the pass, especially with the main encampment of the Sacoridians massed behind the front line. None of it would make a difference, however, if a way was not found to infiltrate the keep.

It looked like Second Empire had been busy, too, barricading the pass itself. Plumes of smoke rose behind the barricades, and she imagined the troops there did not stray far from the keep. And why should they when it contained everything they needed, including fresh water and the food and armaments that had been stockpiled for the Sacoridians who had been stationed there?

It took a while to reach the center of the encampment, and when they arrived at the king's tent, they were greeted by Fastion.

"Ah, Sir Karigan, you've returned to us," he said. He assessed the Eletians with a glance. "It would appear you've an entourage."

"Er, no, not exactly." She cleared her throat. "I am here to report to the king. And Captain Connly, too."

"Then you have arrived at the right moment," he replied.

Seven horsemen rode up to the tent, six Weapons on black horses and wearing black armor. They would have been impressive enough, but at their head, like a knight of old heroic ballads resplendent in his armor, and riding upon his tall white war horse with the sun glinting on the pommel of his sword, was her king. No parade armor did he wear, but cold steel unembellished but for the etched sigil of Sacoridia on the breastplate, and marks caused by the battering of his opponents' weapons.

He lifted the visor of his helmet, and his brown eyes surveyed the encampment before him like a hawk, stern and sharp and in command.

This was her king, she thought. This was Sacoridia's warrior king.

❧ LADY WINTERLIGHT REVEALED ❧

 Zachary dismounted, and a squire helped him remove his helmet. Sweat gleamed on his brow, but he looked well, as well as he had just a few short days ago in her reckoning, a month in his. She bowed.

He did not reveal surprise at her return. "Rider G'ladheon," he said mildly, "you've decided to rejoin us at last, and you've brought company."

Karigan introduced the three Eletians. By now, others were collecting around them—Counselor Tallman and other advisors, Connly, and some officers, all looking on with interest.

"Welcome," he told the Eletians. "What brings you to our camp?"

"Our ari-matiel asked us to safely escort the Dama Cearing Asai'riel into your hands," Byrnin said.

She groaned inwardly. So much for keeping her new title quiet.

Zachary, and the others for that matter, looked confused.

"Who?" Counselor Tallman asked.

"Your Green Rider," Byrnin replied. "She is among the Eletians, the Dama Cearing Asai'riel, royal daughter of the House of Santanara."

She felt everyone's gaze land on her like hot irons. She smiled weakly and shrugged.

"She is . . . Eletian?" Zachary did not hide his incredulity.

"Yes, Firebrand," Byrnin replied.

"It is a tremendous honor," Duncan said. "The title and name translates to Lady Winterlight in the common tongue.

433

I do not think anything like this has ever happened in Eletian history. She is Eletian royalty."

"Not helping," she muttered.

Duncan grinned, and she scowled at him.

Exclamations from those observing just made her want to hide. Why didn't anyone ever listen to her and keep quiet about things like she asked? This was not how she had wanted her return to go.

Byrnin produced what appeared to be a letter. He bowed and handed it to Zachary. "From Ari-matiel Jametari. It is his word on the matter."

"But she is Sacoridian," Zachary said faintly.

Byrnin bowed again. "Yes, Firebrand. She is Sacoridian of blood, a Green Rider and knight. Now she is also Eletian, kin to our king."

"Rider G'ladheon," Les Tallman said, "I assume you've been in Eletia all this time?"

"Yes, sir."

"Did you, er, marry some Eletian nobleman there?"

Horrified, Karigan blurted, "No, sir!"

"Then what did you do to acquire this title? This Asai . . . whatever it was?"

"I, uh . . ."

The three Eletians stepped forward. It was not exactly an aggressive move, but it wasn't passive, either.

"She has been brought into the House of Santanara," Byrnin said in a calm but insistent voice, "and is recognized by all Eletians as royal kin. Her mere existence is enough to make it so. Ari-matiel Jametari would wish the respect of all as would be accorded any Eletian of noble blood. Anything else is grave insult."

"Forgive me," Les Tallman said. "No disrespect intended. I did not understand."

"It is Dama Cearing Asai'riel of whom you should ask forgiveness."

Les Tallman bowed to Karigan and her cheeks burned. This was all wrong. She was a commoner. She was—

"Rider G'ladheon," Zachary said, "might I have a private word with you?"

"Of course, Your Majesty." She passed Duncan's pouch to Shoshan, and for once the mage did not complain. She followed Zachary into his tent. This was going to be interesting.

He turned and just gazed at her before finally saying, "Dear gods, Karigan, what have you gotten yourself into now?"

"I, um . . ."

"I was worried when you disappeared for so long. I had no idea what happened to you. And then suddenly, after a whole month has passed, you return as an Eletian princess?"

"*Princess?* Oh, I don't think—"

"What else could it mean?"

"I, um . . . I'm sorry. I did not ask for this."

Zachary sighed. "*I* am sorry. I did not mean to sound angry. I know it is not your fault. It's just that it is all very surprising."

She could not disagree. "It may be hard to believe, but I was in Eletia for only a few days." She explained the discrepancy in time. "Trust me when I say I am more surprised than anyone about this Eletian kinship thing." She told him how she was put on trial for trespassing, and how that all changed when Jametari suddenly declared her kin.

He turned away and laughed. "My dear, dear Karigan. The things you do, the trouble you find. Or rather, I should call you Dama—what is it?"

She sighed. "Dama Cearing Asai'riel. And I'd rather you did not."

His expression grew more serious. "Lady Winterlight is easier to remember," he murmured. "How the hells did you end up in Eletia in the first place?"

When she explained that part of the story, he shook his head. "We wondered what had become of the wraiths. We had been overcome, helpless, but you found a way to save us."

"I had to do something."

"Where is the travel device?"

"The Eletians kept it. They would not return it."

His expression darkened. "No, they wouldn't, would they . . ."

"They believe they can keep it safe and out of the hands of those who would do ill with it, and for what it's worth, I believe them."

"Despite how useful it could have been to us at this time."

"It may have been, but I also learned it has certain negative effects, like the one that probably caused us to lose Colonel Mapstone." She told him her theory of what she thought had happened, that the device's homing spell had swept away an unsuspecting Colonel Mapstone with it when it was time to return to its coffer.

"A homing spell," Zachary murmured.

"Yes, it activates after a certain period of time has elapsed. The colonel must have been handling it when it happened."

"And it delivered her right to Torq." He shook his head. "How can the Eletians keep it if they don't have the coffer?"

"They didn't say exactly, but they *are* Eletians."

"Point taken." He then closed the space between the two of them and took her hand. "I am grateful you made it back." He gazed at her hand a moment, seeming to study the birch leaf ring on her finger, shifting it in the light to take in the emerald glimmer. "What is this?"

"A gift. From Prince Jametari," she replied.

"It is well given, and its beauty is only outshone by she who wears it."

Heat warmed her cheeks, even more so when he raised her hand to his lips to kiss it, and then also the inside of her wrist.

"Lady Winterlight," he murmured.

All sorts of interesting sensations tingled through her, and she was sorry when he released her hand. She cleared her throat and said, "I was hoping we wouldn't have to acknowledge the whole Eletian title thing. I'd prefer being called Rider, or Karigan, or even Sir Karigan."

"I am afraid it may be too late for that. It is probably halfway around the camp by now."

He was most likely correct. She frowned.

He flashed her a smile, then opened the letter from Jametari, and read. Then he glanced up at Karigan and folded it. "He does not explain much, which is not surprising, but he does say in no uncertain terms that you are Eletian and of House Santanara, hence royal kin."

She sighed.

"In light of this, I should probably remove you from active

duty and reassign you to someplace safe, if such a place exists these days."

"What? No! Er, no, *Your Majesty*. I am a Green Rider, and Prince Jametari has no say over Green Riders. Plus, Alton serves and he is the heir to D'Yer Province, and you've dozens of nobles among your officers." She wanted to bite her tongue for equating herself with nobles, but it had come to that. What ever was her father going to say about this? One problem at a time, she thought.

"But they are not you," he said very softly, "and you are dear to me."

She closed her eyes, taking *that* in. "We can't do this," she whispered.

"I know." Then he cleared his throat and said more loudly, "It is true, you are mine to command regardless of your affiliation with Eletia. Even so, it is an odd situation. I cannot offend one of our strongest allies by misusing their royal kin. Not that I would in any case, but your work is perilous."

"I think Jametari understands that," she replied. Actually, she had no idea what Jametari understood, but he had not forbidden her from doing her work.

"It is difficult to know what the prince intends," Zachary said, as if an echo of her own thoughts. "I will consider what to do with you."

She started to protest, but he shook his head curtly. She knew enough not to press him. She would save it for when he made an actual decision, whatever it might be.

"I wonder . . ." he said.

"About what?" she asked when he trailed off.

"I wonder about ulterior motives. It's not that I question your deserving to be acknowledged this way in Eletia, but I can't help but wonder about his reasoning. What exactly does Eletia gain from this?"

"I've been asking myself the same thing, and I have no answer." Was it access to her fading ability? Access to the mirror shard in her eye? She was sure they had tried to draw her into Eletia through Enver. The council of the Alluvium had ordered him to serve as her guide in locating the p'ehdrose despite knowing his unfolding was upon him. Even as he fought the urges roiling inside of him, he told her that the council must have wished "this" upon the two of them, that he lose control with her. He'd told her they would value one who could cross thresholds the way she could, and that pairing her with Enver, and any young they produced, would bind her to Eletia.

The thought of that kind of manipulation left a bitter taste on her tongue, disgusted her. She would never forget the savage, tormented expression on Enver's face as she rode away from him.

He had been strong, though. He sent her away before he could hurt her. If the council had intended to bind her to Eletia in the way Enver suggested, he'd foiled their plan. Was declaring her kin to the House of Santanara just another way of binding her? But then why go through the whole trial thing and threaten to execute her when they had her in their clutches right there in the heart of the Great Wood? She did not think she'd ever understand them. The funny part was that she was supposed to be one of them.

"What is it?" Zachary asked. "You were far away."

She shook herself back to the present. One thing was certain, she would never tell him about Enver's unfolding and what had almost happened. "My experiences with the Eletians," she said, "have been rather mixed." Now that was an understatement if ever there was one. "I never know what they are thinking. We'll only know their true motives when they are ready to reveal them."

"Agreed." He rubbed his chin. "You know, there are times I've wished . . ." He shook his head, and she wondered what he had intended to say. "Sometimes, I wonder if you are real." He lifted his hand as if to caress her cheek, but hesitated, then abruptly exited the tent.

Karigan stood there alone in the dim light. Real? He wondered if she were real? What did he mean by that? And what did he wish? She only knew she wished there were not so many barriers between them. And then, suddenly, like an unexpected wave washing over her, she realized one of the barriers had been removed. If she were now considered nobility, her status was no longer an obstacle. She stood there in shock as it sank in.

"Five hells," she murmured. So much had been happening that it hadn't even occurred to her. And now, if anything, the ache of longing would be even worse because of what had become more possible, yet remained impossible. He was married. He had children.

Tegan peered through the tent flaps. "Karigan? I mean, my lady? Everything all right?"

Karigan gazed at the tent ceiling and took a deep breath. "None of this 'my lady' business, please. It's Karigan, or even 'Chief,' if you wish to stand on formality."

Tegan grinned. "Coming outside, then? I think your Eletians would like to be released from escort duty."

"*My* Eletians?" Karigan sighed again and headed outside.

"—offer you what comfort we may," Counselor Tallman was telling the Eletians.

"Our duty here is complete," Byrnin replied. "We must return to Eletia. It is a long journey from here."

"The dama and I can open the way to the bridge for you," Duncan said.

"It has been used too much of late, and such usage does not go unnoticed."

Karigan was about to ask who, or what, would take notice of bridge crossings in the white world, but the Eletians turned to her. Shoshan passed her Duncan's tempes stone.

"May we be released from your presence, Dama?" Byrnin asked.

"Of course. I—"

The Eletians bowed to her, then to Zachary. Byrnin said something in Eletian, a farewell, perhaps, and the three turned to make their way out of the camp.

"Well," Counselor Tallman said. He turned to Karigan. "Rider—Dama? You keep life interesting."

"Please," she said, "I don't expect or want special treatment or titles. I'd prefer that this not get around."

"I am afraid you may have little choice in the matter," Zachary said, "but we will honor your request so far as it's possible. There will be times when it is not possible. Rider G'ladheon has told me some of what has transpired since we last saw her. I suggest we retire to my tent so all may hear."

When Karigan finished recounting her experiences in Eletia, she sagged in her chair. The king's officers and advisors, as expected, asked her many tiresome questions, and stewed over the prince's message to Zachary: *When you see King Zachary again*, he had said, *tell him not to despair. We shall arrive when all appears most dire.*

Connly looked particularly unhappy about everything. Unhappy, that was, with *her.* He kept frowning in her direction.

During the proceedings, Tegan's news that there had been no breakthroughs in reclaiming the Eagle's Pass Keep from Second Empire was affirmed, which would likely lead to a very long siege.

"They have all the supplies we stored in the keep for our people," General Washburn said with a mournful air. "Food in addition to what they brought for themselves, as well, and, of course, the armory."

It was dusk by the time the meeting broke up. Karigan slipped out as inconspicuously as she could. Duncan, bored by the proceedings, had vanished into his tempes stone hours ago. Many lingered to continue the discussion. Every day must be like that for Zachary, she thought, full of war talk and strategy.

Relieved to be out in the fresh air, she headed along a row of tents to find Tegan's. She stepped aside for a line of servants bearing sacks of grain to pass by. One of the smaller bearers looked familiar to her, and then she gasped in recognition.

"Lala?"

⊰ A HAZARD TO OTHERS ⊰

The child, Grandmother's flesh and blood granddaughter—not just a euphemism for an adherent—gave Karigan an enigmatic look and continued on with carrying her burden. Karigan was about to sprint after her when someone grabbed her shoulder.

She whirled in surprise, hand instinctively raised to strike.

"Karigan," Connly said, jumping back. "Relax."

She'd stopped herself just in time. "Do you know who that girl is? She's Lala, Grandmother's—"

"We know," he said.

"You don't know. She's dangerous. Grandmother trained her."

"We *do* know."

She stared at him. "Then what is she doing here just walking around our camp?"

"She is under guard, all right? We know who she is and what she can do."

"She needs to be locked away."

"She's a child."

"She's not *just* a child."

"Look," Connly said, "she is well-guarded while she helps with camp chores. It keeps her busy and she seems to like it. Apparently she was used to doing all kinds of chores in Second Empire's various camps. Those who are looking after her say that she follows directions and causes no trouble."

Karigan leaned toward Connly. "She helped torture the king."

"We know, and he has approved of the handling of her detention."

"Detention, eh? And how was she captured?"

"It was after the wraiths incident. All of us Riders woke up out in the middle of the valley, and Lala was there, too. We brought her back to camp. She didn't fight us or anything, she just came with us."

"She can't be trusted."

"She's a child," Connly insisted. "But I didn't come after you to talk about Lala. I came to talk about you."

This could not be good, Karigan thought.

"Let's go somewhere where we can speak more privately."

Karigan deposited Duncan's tempes stone with Tegan and then walked with Connly to the pickets. There was little privacy to be found in an encampment so large, but this would do. She patted the neck of a friendly mule while she waited for Connly to begin.

He absently scratched the back of his neck and shifted from one foot to the other. Finally, he said, "You did it again."

"Did what again?"

"You went on your own for a whole month. Yes, I heard your explanation about how time moves differently in Eletia. It was still a month here."

"I had no control over that."

He raised his hands as if to stave off further rebuttal. "I know, I know, but isn't it interesting how often that happens?" When she tried to protest, he cut her off. "When you *are* with us, you just seem to pull us into danger. Like the wraiths in the Blanding. They were drawn to you, which put the rest of us in danger. And when you used the travel device to take Torq there? The wraiths got hold of it, got it away from *you*, and endangered the entire encampment."

He was blaming *her* for the wraiths?

"You find danger not just for yourself," he continued, "but for the rest of us, too. Yes, thanks to you, Torq is gone and we didn't fall prey to the whisper wraiths, but we might not have encountered them in the first place but for you."

The mule snorted and stamped his hoof as if picking up on her anger. "You can't—"

"I'm not finished yet," he said. "Because you are so often putting yourself out on some individual adventure, I am stuck here without a Chief Rider. Fortunately, Tegan can step into that role pretty easily, but truthfully, having you away all the time makes our operation unpredictable and less efficient."

Unpredictability was the very nature of the messenger service, wasn't it? But *less efficient*?

"And now that you are Eletian royalty . . ." Connly said, trailing off to leave the interpretation up to her.

"Yes?" she asked as neutrally as possible.

Connly fidgeted. Scratched the back of his neck again. "I just think it will affect how the Riders relate to you. They won't see you as just their Chief anymore, but as a noblewoman."

Noblewoman, she thought, aghast. *Ugh.* Gathering all the composure she could since lashing out at him would only make matters worse, she said, "So, in other words, I have failed as your Chief Rider and you would like someone else to be Chief. Like Tegan."

Connly nodded. "She is reliable. And to be honest—and I hope you don't take offense—you were chosen without my being consulted."

"You would have chosen Tegan?"

"Yes, or Ty. Now, with the colonel gone, it is my decision as to who is on my command staff."

"What about Mara?"

"Mara stays."

"What about Beryl? Might she have something to say about this?" Beryl was a major and, so, outranked Connly. Of course, she probably had no idea she was now a major of the Green Riders, just as Karigan hadn't known she was Chief until Fergal told her.

"We never see her. I doubt she would care much who was Chief Rider, but it impacts *me* directly. If Beryl has an objection, we'll discuss it. I'm sorry, Karigan, or Lady Winterlight, or whatever you are to go by these days, but—"

Before he could finish, she unpinned the gold feather brooch and handed it to him. She walked away without his dismissal.

At first she was too stunned to feel much of anything at having what had only just recently been given to her taken away, but as she walked into camp, her fury grew. The colonel had wanted *her,* and it wasn't like the colonel was going to be permanently gone. They were going to get her back, and when they did, would she override Connly's decision?

Her anger grew even more as she stepped around a pair of soldiers tossing a ball back and forth and thought about how she had good reasons for her absences. She was doing her job on behalf of the realm. It wasn't like she'd been Chief Rider long enough to be gone so much.

And what of the Eletian title? It didn't change *her* or what she could do for the Riders. In truth, it didn't really mean a whole lot.

When she reached Tegan's tent, she dropped into a camp chair by the fire with a thump. Most hurtful of all was his assertion that she put others in danger. It was true that if she hadn't opened the way to the white world, they would not have used that route and encountered the whisper wraiths, and certainly the next time she returned to the white world, the wraiths had indeed grabbed the travel device and threatened everyone in the encampment.

However, the idea to use the white world to go after Colonel Mapstone's captors had been Duncan's, not hers, and those in charge had approved it. And was it *her* fault the wraiths were attracted to her magic? And it wasn't just hers, but Duncan's and the rest of the Riders, too. All of that concentrated magic must have been very attractive to them.

Maybe none of it was her fault, but maybe it was true that she was hazardous to be around at times. And, it was certainly true she could not be a good Chief Rider if she were not present to do her job, at least not to her captain's expectations. Still, the unfairness of it rankled. She wanted to yell and scream and kick things, but restrained herself. She laughed bitterly—if she were alone off on some "individual adventure" as Connly called it, she could kick anything she wanted. But not here. Not here in the middle of this encampment. Such behavior would be seen by all and judged unseemly.

You failed, came a voice in her mind she had hoped not to hear again.

Where have you been? she asked Nyssa.

Missed me, did you?

Couldn't get to me in Eletia, could you?

I am here now, my pet, Nyssa replied. *You thought you were so special, but you're not even good enough to be Chief among your own kind.*

Karigan didn't respond. She didn't need Nyssa to tell her to know that this was a blow to her self-worth. She gazed into the campfire. All the activity of the camp seemed far off. Her stomach grumbled, but her confrontation with Connly put her off the desire to eat. She didn't want to move for fear of running into Connly or anyone else, really. As a Chief Rider, she'd been a fraud. She hadn't deserved the promotion in the first place.

That's right, Nyssa murmured. *You are a fraud, a terrible Chief Rider.*

Karigan sighed and, as dusk set in, tossed sticks onto the fire and gazed into the flames, allowing her anger and sense of failure to simmer. After a while, she followed a spark that blew into the air and saw that she was not alone. Someone in seafaring garb occupied the camp chair across from her. Flames reflected in the lenses of the woman's specs, which she removed and folded, then wrapped in a cloth and carefully placed in an inner pocket of her coat. It took a moment for Karigan to recognize her.

"Beryl? This is a surprise."

There was a familiar intensity to Beryl Spencer, a sharp, no-nonsense demeanor even when she was not in uniform.

"I thought you'd been sent east," Karigan added. "Did the king recall you to go after the colonel?"

Beryl's eyes flickered with the dance of flames. *You must give the king a message,* she said.

"Me? Why don't you give it to him yourself?"

When Beryl's gaze met Karigan's, Karigan shivered. There was an otherworldliness to her eyes.

You must tell the king I have failed, Beryl said.

Failed, failed, failed . . . The word echoed in Karigan's mind as a reminder of her own shortcomings.

"There you are," Tegan said, suddenly appearing next to the fire.

Karigan jumped and blinked rapidly, and watched as Beryl stood, gazed meaningfully at her, then turned and disappeared into the dark. To Tegan, Karigan said, "Beryl isn't . . . here, is she?"

Tegan sat next to her. "Beryl? Here? She's supposed to be out east somewhere."

"She was just here, when you walked up. Or, that's what I thought. Maybe I dozed off and dreamed it was her, or . . ." She did not like the implication of what she left unstated.

"If you're not dreaming and she *is* here, she hasn't checked in. Or maybe she wouldn't, considering the type of work she usually does."

Karigan wasn't sure exactly what she had seen or dreamed. Was it a visitation? Usually she felt more clear about these things.

"Now that I've found you," Tegan said, "I need to tell you something."

"Yes?"

"Connly asked me to be Chief Rider."

He'd wasted no time, Karigan thought. "And?"

"He claimed you resigned. I didn't buy it, and said so. What happened?"

Karigan folded her arms and gazed once more into the fire. "I guess I did sort of resign."

"*What?*"

Karigan then related her confrontation with Connly.

"You know," Tegan said when she finished, "he just hasn't been himself since Colonel Mapstone was taken. He dithers over every decision, and is stressed and anxious. You should have kept your position. He had no right, and his reasoning stinks."

"I am thinking he may be right on some counts."

"What the hells, Karigan? You're one of the best Riders we've got."

"But clearly not one of the best *Chief* Riders. I certainly haven't been present to work in that capacity. At least, not with Connly, and as captain, it's his right to choose someone he can rely on. I think you should go back to him and tell him you've changed your mind."

"Really, Karigan, you've got to stick up more for yourself. When we were crossing the Blanding, and then looking for the colonel? You were an excellent Chief Rider."

"Honestly, Tegan, you were a better Chief Rider than I was when we were crossing the Blanding," Karigan said. "After I told everyone not to believe what they saw there, guess who fell for the first vision she saw? Me, of course. You kept me going. And, who was doing the Chief Rider job while I was in Eletia?"

"I wouldn't feel right about accepting the position."

"Don't feel bad for me," Karigan replied, though she found Tegan's support gratifying. "It would appear I have enough special titles that one less won't hurt. If you are worried about my feelings, don't be. It is beginning to feel like a relief not to have that kind of responsibility." To her surprise, it really was. She wouldn't be responsible for getting up at dawn to send Riders out on errands, ensuring they were all set with supplies and ready to go. She wouldn't have to mediate their squabbles and problems, or schedule each Rider's daily routine. It would now all fall to Tegan. So would dealing with Connly.

"Are you sure?" Tegan asked.

"I am. Now go." She made shooing motions with her hand. "Go before he finds someone less suitable."

Karigan nestled beneath the blankets of her bedroll. The day had turned into a long and unpleasant evening. It was hard to believe she had started her day in Eletia.

Tegan's blankets rustled as she turned over on her cot. After she had returned from talking with Connly, she had tried to suppress her excitement at her unexpected promotion. She'd tried not to be obvious about glancing at the gold feather brooch now pinned to her shortcoat. Karigan had smiled and congratulated her, but she wilted on the inside. Even so, she knew Tegan would prove an excellent Chief.

She sighed and was ready to sleep, but suddenly Beryl was there again, standing over her. There was a faint glow to her, a wavery-ness to her form. This was no dream.

You must tell the king I have failed, the apparition said. *Seek the flying dragon shield.*

"Shield? What shield?"

The apparition flickered, and faded out.

"Karigan?" came Tegan's sleepy voice, "are you talking in your sleep?"

"No."

"Then who are you talking to?"

"Beryl."

There was a long pause. "Um, sure you're not talking in your sleep?"

"I'm sure. Beryl is dead."

⇔ A HUNCH ⇔

No one ever wanted to awaken a king in the middle of the night, but to Karigan's relief, it appeared he'd never gone to bed. He stood alone over his map table, sleeves rolled up. A pair of moths batted against the glass chimney of a single lit lamp, their shadows a dance against the canvas wall of the tent.

"Riders?" he said after the Weapons let her and Tegan enter. Karigan had brought Tegan along for the moral support, and because now that she was Chief Rider, she possessed the authority Karigan no longer held.

They bowed, and Tegan said, "Rider G'ladheon wishes to share something we thought you should hear."

He looked from Tegan to Karigan, and Karigan thought he could not help but notice the gold feather shining on Tegan's shortcoat, and its absence on her own. He had given it to her, she was certain, as a personal gift as much as the conferring of insignia.

"Captain Connly was by earlier," he said, "to inform me Rider G'ladheon is no longer Chief Rider."

Karigan cleared her throat. "It is so, sire."

"Is that what you wish to see me about? If so, it is a rather late hour for it."

"No, sire," she replied. "This is about a different, more important matter. I have received, so to speak, a message from Beryl Spencer."

"Beryl Spencer?" he asked in surprise. The single lamp made the shadows bolder, deeper. They sculpted hollows beneath his cheekbones. "Where is she? How did she get a message to you?"

Karigan exchanged a glance with Tegan. "I believe she is dead. She came to me as an apparition."

He closed his eyes and shook his head. "Tell me."

Karigan told him how Beryl appeared to her twice, and of her message.

"That is all she told you?" he asked. There was no question or incredulity that she'd received a message from a ghost. By now it was well known to him that she interacted with spirits of the dead. Not just that, but that she was the avatar of Westrion, god of death, and she could *command* the dead. Zachary had seen her in that guise.

"Yes, sire."

"That is most regrettable. I highly valued her talent and courage. I had sent her to find my cousin, Lord Amberhill, in an effort to forestall the future you experienced, Karigan. I had hoped to prevent its possibility of ever happening. She was either to bring him back to me, or if that were not possible, to assassinate him. The last we knew, she had tracked him to an archipelago in the Eastern Sea off Bairdly. Clearly her mission failed, but whether at the hands of my cousin or by some other means, we'll probably never know. I am sorry, Riders, for the loss of your comrade. It is certainly a great loss to the realm."

Most of the Riders, at least the newer ones, would not have met Beryl, but all would nevertheless feel the loss of one of their own with great sorrow.

"Sire," Karigan said, "the second part of the message, about the flying dragon shield, Tegan and I discussed it and we think she is referring to what we've been calling the 'dragonfly device.'" It was a hint she'd brought back from the future time. Much of what she had experienced there was forgotten or sketchy, but at first, when she had returned to the present, she was able to remember more. She had written down what she could, and then Captain Mapstone had taken notes when she told all she remembered to the captain and Zachary.

One of the items she had recalled was the dragonfly device. A man she called "the professor" had taken her in when she arrived in the future, and had known much of the past's "true history." He told her of an artifact that supposedly defeated the great weapon that would be employed by the king's cousin to conquer Sacoridia and the other free lands. He'd shown her a drawing copied from a pictograph chipped into a boulder in ancient times along the shore of Coutre. It depicted the figure of a warrior who held a shield and wielded an oblong object like a sword or spear. There was the legend of Anschilde, the professor had told her, a warrior chieftain and progenitor of Clan Sealender, who had used the "dragonfly device" to defeat the sea kings. It was believed the device was located in the royal tombs, and the caretakers had been searching for it ever since her return from the future time.

"You mean," Zachary said, "we've been looking for a weapon, a device of some kind, with a dragonfly on it, when actually we should have been looking for a shield with the device of a flying dragon on it?"

"It's a hunch, sire."

"It sounds a good one," he replied. "I suppose with all the destruction you observed in the future, and the campaign by the regime to rewrite history, it is not surprising the meaning of ancient words would become so misconstrued. It is certainly worth investigating, and if true, it would narrow down the search. Word needs to get to Agemon in the tombs. Beryl Spencer may have, in her own words, failed, but if this hunch of yours is correct, she may have, in fact, saved us."

"Yes, sire."

"Is that all for this evening?"

"Actually," Karigan said, "there is one more matter I'd like to bring up." Tegan looked at her, startled.

"What about?" Zachary asked.

"Lala."

"Yes?"

"She is dangerous."

"Yes, she is. Believe me, I know."

Karigan chose her words carefully. "I was concerned when I saw her earlier moving freely about our camp."

"I appreciate your concern," he replied, "but it was the best solution for dealing with a child. If we'd a prison to lock her in, she could very likely use her power to escape it. She is watched day and night, not just by ordinary guards, but by Weapons, as well."

Karigan hadn't seen them watching, but that didn't mean they hadn't been there. Weapons were very good at fading into the background when they wished.

"Thank you," she replied. "I am reassured." She wasn't entirely comfortable with the situation, but his words helped. "Perhaps we should send for Lady Fiori so she can attempt to get her voice back from Lala?"

"I will find out from your captain if we can spare anyone to do so." He shifted, shadows half-concealing his eyes. One of the moths, Karigan noticed, lay on the table atop a map, its wings barely beating. "Perhaps Lala will, with kind treatment, be willing to return Lady Fiori's voice, and perhaps prove useful in other ways."

In other ways sent a sense of foreboding tingling through Karigan's body. He was going to try to use Lala as Birch had? She hoped he did not place much trust in her.

"I apologize for the late intrusion," she said.

"Thank you for bringing me the sad news about Beryl Spencer," he replied, "and the hope of her second message. Goodnight, Riders."

They bowed and stepped outside.

"I'm not sure I'll be able to sleep after all that," Tegan said.

As long as the ghosts stayed away, Karigan thought she—

Connly strode out of the dark toward them. He looked disheveled, as if he'd just rolled out of bed.

"Captain?" Tegan said. "What are you doing up so late?"

"Visiting the latrines. I heard your voices on my way back. Why are you disturbing the king this late at night?"

Karigan allowed Tegan to explain. His expression fell when he heard about Beryl. He raked his fingers through his hair.

"That is bad news if true."

"It is true," Karigan said. "She is gone, but her message may prove useful."

"Yes, your facility with the dead." He shook himself.

"That said, next time do not bother the king directly. Come to me first. Tegan should have known better."

Karigan noted the two Weapons who guarded Zachary's tent watching the exchange with interest. "It was im—" she began.

"Rider," Connly snapped, "I've a mind to have you assigned to latrine duty. I've had to reprimand you so many times of late. You will do as you are ordered."

Karigan had so much to say that it was a struggle to keep her mouth shut. She did not want to get on worse footing with Connly, and she certainly did not desire latrine duty. "Yes, Captain," she said.

Light flickered as the flap to Zachary's tent was pushed back.

"Would the three of you please attend me?" Zachary asked.

They exchanged glances of surprise. Once they were inside standing shoulder to shoulder, Zachary paced by them, his hands clasped behind his back.

"I have been very concerned about your missing colonel," he said. "I miss her counsel and friendship. She's been the leader of our messenger corps for a very long time. I know each of you feel her absence keenly, as well." He paused in front of Connly. "Carrying on in her absence, having to fill her boots in precarious times, is a weighty responsibility, is it not?"

"Yes, Your Majesty," Connly said, "it is."

"I do not envy you having to unexpectedly assume the helm like that, Captain. You have been doing a fine job, thus far."

"Thank you, Your Majesty. I had an excellent mentor."

"The best," Zachary agreed. "I did just overhear, however, your stern rebuke for Riders G'ladheon and Oldbrine. While normally it is wise for the Riders to follow the chain of command, I do not want any Rider to hesitate to approach me first when it comes to imparting important information. Beryl Spencer's message was for *me,* and Rider G'ladheon and Chief Rider Oldbrine chose correctly in coming directly to me."

"I understand."

Karigan chewed on her bottom lip. Did he? Really? She feared this lecture from the king would only serve to increase Connly's displeasure with her.

"Each Rider must have the ability to function independently," Zachary continued, "to solve problems and make decisions on his or her own when there is no one in authority there to do so for them. It is the nature of the job. However, a war camp like this does require group discipline and respect for the chain of command, but as we've seen this night, there are instances when breaking the chain is called for. I do not want the Riders to hesitate to come directly to me if they think the circumstances warrant it. It is the way it has always been."

"I understand, sire," Connly said.

"Yes, I think you do," Zachary said. "You have years of experience. It is not this but something else that raises your ire."

"I don't—"

Zachary placed his hand on Connly's shoulder. Connly seemed to shrink. "Yes. At this point, I believe we must address the difficulty that is Rider G'ladheon, don't you agree?"

☙ THE DIFFICULTY THAT IS RIDER G'LADHEON ❧

 The difficulty that was—*her*? Karigan had a mind to stomp right out of there. She wasn't difficult; it was Connly who was overreacting to things. She settled, however, knowing that stomping out was not a mature response, and it would only reinforce Connly's poor opinion of her. Besides, she was curious to find out in what way Zachary considered her *difficult*.

Sweat had broken out on Connly's upper lip as his king leaned toward him. But then Zachary released his shoulder and stepped back.

"The difficulty that is Rider G'ladheon is nothing new," he continued. "It is one your colonel grappled with from the start."

From the *start*? Karigan wondered.

"She resisted the call long enough," Connly said. Both men chuckled.

She could not stand it any longer. It was infuriating. "What is so funny about that? And I am *not* difficult."

They gazed at her. Zachary's eyes sparkled with amusement. Tegan coughed to hide a laugh.

"You really have no idea, do you," Connly said, and he shook his head.

"That I'm difficult?"

"Do you ever have a normal message errand, Karigan?"

"Of course. I mean, it's been a while. Actually, maybe a couple years, now that I think of it, but . . ." Her cheeks warmed. "I've been sent away on missions more recently."

"And very important and daunting missions they've been," Zachary said. "You can't guess how hard it has been for those

455

who command you to send you out on them." He returned his attention to Connly. "It does not occur to her that what she does is different from other Riders."

"But—" she began.

Zachary raised an eyebrow at her.

"But . . ."

"We know the job is dangerous for all Riders," he said, "but you tend to excel at finding danger. The question is, how does one manage someone like that?" He paused as he gazed at each one of them. "The answer is not simple, though it may sound that way, and here it is: you let them do what they're good at. You don't control them because you can't. You provide guidance and support, and then send them on their way. You trust they know what they're doing and let them accomplish what must be done in their own way. When you are a commander, it is natural to want to control someone like Rider G'ladheon, but you must resist. If it helps, remember that she is no green Greenie on her first run."

"So, do I just let her flaunt orders?" Connly asked.

"Has she been flaunting orders?"

"No, not exactly, I suppose."

Karigan reconsidered her decision not to stomp out of the tent.

"Captain," Zachary explained, "I can see you want her to be compliant like a soldier, but that kind of discipline does not work well with Green Riders. That is why the messenger corps is set aside from the regular military. Rider G'ladheon is especially not of that disposition."

"I'm disciplined," Karigan protested. "I follow orders."

Again, that sparkle in Zachary's eyes. "Indeed." To Connly he said, "There are other Riders who do not quite fit in the same as the rest. Lynx, for instance, who is often out in the northlands scouting for me, and Beryl, may she reside peacefully among the gods. She was often away on perilous assignments devised by me or my spymasters. I imagine you would not have tried reining *her* in."

"No, and I understand," Connly replied, "but Rider G'ladheon is—" He waved his arm about. "—complicated. That is why I need Tegan, who is more reliable, to be Chief Rider."

Difficult and complicated. Unreliable. Karigan stared up at the yellow stains on the tent ceiling. She struggled to restrain another outburst.

"Rider G'ladheon is reliable," Zachary replied in quiet reproof, "but clearly not in the way you need your Chief to be. I understand that. There is also the matter of her various titles, which I can see making things awkward for those who must command her. She is an honorary Weapon, a knight of the realm, a sub-chief of Clan G'ladheon, and today we have learned that the Eletians claim her royal kin and call her Lady Winterlight. All of this sets her apart. How do you handle it? What do you do with it? Of course, this is not without precedent. She is not the first of noble blood to be called to the messenger service. Currently you've Lord Alton, heir to D'Yer Province, and Lady Sophina, daughter of Lord Blackmill, filling your ranks. In the past, though it has been a couple centuries, there were even princes and princesses who were called."

Karigan hadn't known that last part.

"The Eletian aspect," Zachary continued, "does put a different slant on the situation, though she claims she is no different than she was before, and that we should treat her no differently."

She nodded vigorously at this.

"Whether she goes by Rider G'ladheon, or Sir Karigan, or Lady Winterlight, you must trust her as you would any of the Riders, and allow her to do what she does best. She will not be confined to the chain of command, and she can report to me directly as she deems necessary. Yes, she is yours to hand orders to, but she also has my confidence to decide what actions are necessary in any given situation. That is how it worked for your colonel, whether it was apparent or not."

"I—I think I understand, Your Majesty," Connly said. "I am sorry to have bothered you with this."

"I am quite fond of my Green Riders, and pleased I could advise you in the absence of Colonel Mapstone. However, please do not create a situation where I must lecture you again."

"No, sire, I will not."

"Good. You are all dismissed."

They bowed and filed out of the tent. Karigan gave Zachary a backward glance before she dropped the tent flap back into place. He was already bent over his map table once more.

Outside, Connly turned to her. "A word?"

"I'll see you back at our tent," Tegan told her.

Connly watched after her for a moment before telling Karigan, "I want to apologize for how I've handled things. Following in the colonel's footsteps has proved challenging, and I've been, shall we say, heavy-handed in my command. I plan to do better."

"Thank you for that," Karigan replied.

He nodded. "Meanwhile, Tegan will remain Chief to ensure continuity among the Riders in case you are sent off somewhere on one of the king's missions, or get caught up in some*thing*. When we get the colonel back, she may decide to reinstate you as Chief. I will explain to her why I made the decision I did, but if she is adamant, I will not object."

"Fair enough."

There was nothing else to say so they each went their own way so they could get at least some sleep before daybreak. It had not looked like Zachary planned on getting any.

Even your king thinks you are a problem, Nyssa said.

Karigan tried to ignore her as best she could, as she made her way back to the tent she shared with Tegan. Of course, as much as she and Zachary could not be together, she still wanted her king's approval, for her to give him reason to uphold his good opinion of her. He had spoken lightly of her being "difficult," but how much of a problem was she for him?

She shook her head. It was Nyssa playing with her, feeding off her insecurities. She wished she'd thought to ask the Eletians to help expel her, but Nyssa hadn't been present the whole time Karigan was in Eletia, and there'd been more immediate concerns at the time.

She ducked into the tent wondering what the next day would bring.

The next day brought eagles. Karigan was helping with the morning feeding at the pickets when a familiar voice called into her mind. She looked up and saw a pair of gray eagles circling in downward spirals into the encampment.

Ripaeria! Karigan exclaimed.

It is me, and my uncle.

"What is it?" Trace asked, as she lugged a bucket of water to a thirsty horse.

"Ripaeria and Softfeather."

"You go ahead," Trace said, "and I'll finish up here."

"Why does Karigan get to go?" Megan grumped, who was nearby shoveling manure.

Karigan did not wait to hear an answer but hurried across camp, pausing only to collect Duncan's pouch from the tent. The mage had not reemerged since vanishing the previous night.

The eagles alighted at the edge of the camp where there was open space. Zachary and his advisors had already walked out to meet them.

Where are you? Ripaeria "called" to her.

I am coming. Karigan picked up her pace, Duncan's tempes stone in its pouch bumping her hip as she went.

I was worried about you, Ripaeria said. *You were gone for a long time.*

I missed you, too, Karigan told her with a smile.

When she joined the small group standing before the eagles, she saw Connly. He seemed to note her presence, but did not send her away.

Softfeather was addressing the group, *—as you requested. Your messenger had reached her and they have been marching for ten suns.*

"I thank you for bringing word back so quickly," Zachary replied. "That is very good news. There will be no escape for Second Empire."

Who was marching? Karigan wondered. Zachary had used the eagles as messengers? Who was "her"?

There is something you may want to know about the pass, Softfeather said. *Flying over it just now, we noticed significantly less activity.*

"Our scouts haven't been able to get close enough to see what is going on there."

You could use the Eagle's Landing, Softfeather said. *You could then get a view down into the pass.*

"We checked the stairs, but whole sections have crumbled away over the centuries, and climbing the sheer cliffs is treacherous. We have been awaiting a scout with the skills to scale the cliffs, but he will not arrive for some while."

After this war is done, you must rebuild the stairs so the eagles of the Wing Song Mountains may parley with the Sacor Clans properly again.

"Agreed," Zachary said. "As for the pass, can you tell us what you observed?"

The eagle described only a small amount of livestock visible, and a scattering of people guarding the keep's gate and keeping watch on the road, especially toward the Sacoridian encampment. Others kept watch from the battlements. Otherwise, cold fire rings, few tents, and a lack of soldiers drilling and training painted a picture of a place almost abandoned.

"Most of the people could have moved into the keep," Les Tallman said. "The living spaces go deep into the mountain, and there is even room for livestock. Perhaps they have done so in advance of hostilities. It could hold hundreds, if not thousands."

Softfeather cocked his head as if considering the possibility. *Perhaps.*

Zachary was frowning.

I would scout more, were I permitted, Softfeather said, *but I have already interfered more than I should have.*

He hardly did anything, Ripaeria told Karigan. *We flew toward the coast to the lady.*

What lady?

Ripaeria paused before answering. *The sister.*

Whose—? Do you mean Lady Coutre?

That is who! Ripaeria bobbed her head. *Your queen's sister. The people were so startled to see us. It was very amusing. You humans have such funny faces when you are surprised.*

So, the "her" was Lady Coutre, and Zachary sent the eagles to Coutre Province to check on the advance of her army. Her troops could march to the pass and block it on the east side. That was how Second Empire would be trapped. It would take a while for Lady Coutre's troops to reach the pass, unless some came in from closer posts. Still, there was no telling what mischief Second Empire could get up to in the meantime.

After Softfeather spoke with the lady, Ripaeria said, *we flew back. What is so wrong with that?*

It is meddling in non-eagle affairs, Softfeather's deeper voice cut in, *which is forbidden to us.*

It is a stupid law, Ripaeria said. *I like the people. Karigan is my friend.*

You are too young to comprehend, Softfeather admonished.

When Zachary and his advisors looked confused, Karigan realized she was the only one hearing this part of the conversation.

Old eagles are so ooold, Ripaeria said in an aside. *And so grumpy. No fun at all.*

Softfeather must have heard because he clacked his beak at his niece, then said to Zachary, *It is time we returned to the eyrie.*

"I understand," Zachary replied, "and I thank you again for your assistance."

Softfeather bowed his head, then to Ripaeria, said, *Come, eaglet. It is time to ascend to the rivers of air.*

I am not *an eaglet*, Ripaeria retorted.

"Wait!" Karigan said. She ignored everyone's looks of surprise and pushed forward. "I've Duncan."

Softfeather seemed to wilt. *I see. Bring him here. I will return him to the eyrie as agreed.* He lowered his head so she could place the strap of the pouch around his neck.

I trust Duncan was not too irritating?

"Well," she replied, "I wouldn't say that, but he was helpful at times."

The eagle made a throaty sound, then said. *It is well, then. Farewell, Green Rider.*

"Good-bye, and please tell Duncan I said good-bye, as well."

He bobbed his head, and she gave him space to launch into the air.

I'm coming, I'm coming, Ripaeria said in answer to an unheard summons. *Just give me a moment.* She then gazed down at Karigan. *It makes me sad that they won't let me come here to see you anymore.*

Karigan told her it made her sad, too, and gently hugged her around the neck, trying not to crush feathers. It was a much different feeling than hugging a horse's neck—lighter, less solid. When she stepped aside, Ripaeria plucked a feather from her flank, which she gave to Karigan.

My friend forever, Ripaeria said; then she launched into the sky, circled twice, and left Karigan clutching the oversized feather to her heart.

⊰ MISFORTUNES ALONG THE ROAD ⊰

Stevic G'ladheon leaned down from his horse to show the guardsman at the castle gate his clan ring as proof of his identity. He'd been challenged by sentries even well outside the city, then at each city gate as he ascended the Winding Way.

"I am here to see Colonel Mapstone of the Green Riders," he said, his voice rough from illness.

The captain of the guard sauntered over. "I recognize him, Snylar. His girl's a Rider. Let him through."

With a nod of thanks, Stevic clucked his horse through the gate and onto castle grounds. The gelding was a sad replacement for the fine stallion he'd started with in Selium, a favorite from his own stables, but even the best of steeds did not seem to have the remarkable endurance of messenger horses and so he'd had to sell him and others in order to acquire fresh remounts for his journey. He'd made good progress until other misfortunes along the road—a thrown shoe, being robbed, and getting sick—had delayed his arrival to the city.

He rode the horse at a walk, an amble, really, with a sense of dread now that he was here. He feared Laren would blame him for Melry's abduction because he'd been the one with her at the time, supposedly looking out for her. He had included that detail in the letter he'd sent with Selium's messenger, who must have reached Sacor City well ahead of him. Apparently in the depths of a fever he had picked up along the way, he had raved about the situation to the kind wife of an innkeeper who had nursed him. He'd been unable to leave bed for a week, then was barely able to walk down the hall the next. He had rewarded the innkeeper's wife well for her care, but had not heeded her advice to stay longer. He thought that perhaps, as his body shook with another of the ravaging coughs, he should have listened. He wasn't sure the fever was quite gone.

But he was here now, on castle grounds. The eerie quiet of the place only fed his trepidation. He'd heard rumors on his journey that the king had taken his army east, and the absence of soldiers on castle grounds seemed to bear them out. Along the road, he'd also encountered provincial militia troops answering the muster of their lord-governors. The realm was in a state he had not seen since the last war with the Under Kingdoms.

He bent over the saddle with another bout of coughing, then urged the gelding ahead. He supposed sleeping on the ground had not helped his recovery.

When he reached officers' quarters, he dismounted and stood before Laren's door. As much as he was anxious about facing her, he was looking forward to seeing her. Had Melry been recovered? If not, perhaps he could provide comfort. He raised his hand to knock on the door when someone called out to him.

"Chief G'ladheon?"

He turned to find Mara Brennyn passing by. "Lieutenant!"

The Rider walked up to him. "You will not find the colonel at home, I'm afraid."

"When will she be back?"

The lieutenant looked downcast. "We don't know when, or if, she'll be back."

"What do you mean? Where is she?"

"It's a bit of a long story, and you look like you could use a cup of tea, if I say so myself."

"Please just tell me."

She licked her lips. "All right," she said softly. "She was captured by the Darrow Raiders and sold to Varosians to serve as the personal slave to the king there."

"*What?*" he roared. A coughing fit took him then, dropped him to his knees, and left him hacking up sputum and blood.

*   *   *

When he was cognizant of his surroundings again, he found himself abed in the mending wing of the castle. Mara sat in a chair nearby staring at a pile of papers on her lap, a frown of concentration etching her features.

He took a deep breath and, much to his surprise, found it came easily, not even a tickle to set him off on another infernal coughing fit. He took another, the ease of it blissful. Then he remembered what he'd been told about Laren. She'd been sold to Varosians.

No, he thought, *it must not stand.* He would not allow her to suffer in the hands of the Varosians. He would not lose her. He could not imagine the future without her, she with her red hair and sharp wit. She filled a place in his heart that had been forlorn for far too long. He would find a way to get her back.

"Lieutenant . . . Mara."

She jumped at the sound of his voice. "Chief? How are you? Can I get you something to drink?"

He asked for water, and she poured him a cup from a pitcher. "How is it my cough is cured?" he asked.

She smiled. "You know Rider Simeon? Ben?"

He nodded. "He is also a mender, as I recall."

"Well, he's very good at what he does. You may even find your lungs are almost like new."

Magic, he thought. Ben had used healing magic on him. He tested his breathing again, in and out, in and out. He still felt exhausted, but no longer feverish. It was miraculous, really, and if magic could do that, then maybe it wasn't the evil he had once supposed.

"I must thank him when I have a chance," he said.

"He is sleeping it off at the moment, in the next room, actually. His ability does that to him, and you may find yourself tired from the healing process for a while, as well."

"Is Karigan here?" he asked.

Mara looked down at her papers, hesitated. "No, we're not actually sure where she is at the moment."

"Perhaps," he said, "you would tell me everything about

the colonel and Karigan while I rest. I have been on the road a very long time, got robbed, got sick . . . It was not a good journey."

"Oh, dear," she said. "We only got an update on everything a couple weeks ago, which means our information is somewhat out of date already, but here is what we know." She gave him a rundown of events that included the Raiders, a mage, gray eagles, and wraith creatures. She gave more details, as many as she possessed, regarding Laren's capture.

He sagged in his pillows, relieved to hear that Melry had been rescued and was even now on castle grounds, but the Raiders had used her as bait to draw out Laren. The leader, Torq, had been seeking vengeance for actions that had taken place years ago. That vengeance included selling her to the king whose realm was backward, where women were not even considered people. It would be hell for a person like Laren who had lived her whole life in the comparatively enlightened society of Sacoridia with the favor of its king, and in a position of authority.

"The king ordered diplomatic envoys to proceed to Varos to insist on the colonel's return. They are on their way."

"To *insist* on her return?" Stevic scoffed. "I know the Varosians. They will not be impressed. Does Zachary intend to follow up with force?"

"I don't know for sure," Mara said carefully, "but I believe his general feeling is that he doesn't wish to escalate the situation. He does not need hostilities with Varos while he is fighting Second Empire."

"Then he won't get her back." Anger roiled up inside him, anger that there was seemingly nothing the king could or would do to get her back.

"I believe," Mara said, again very carefully, "he has another plan. The queen was hoping you would return to the city and, now that you have, is requesting your presence."

"Me?"

She nodded. "In fact we sent messengers to Corsa in an attempt to track you down."

When he started to throw his blankets aside so he could get up, she hastily added, "You can't see her right this moment. Master Vanlynn has ordered you abed and we will see how you are doing tomorrow morning. As I mentioned, the effects of a deep healing like Ben did on you can leave a patient exhausted. You will probably be wanting a good sound sleep shortly."

Nonsense, he thought. He was tired, but not immobilized. "Now, about Karigan," he said.

"She was with the king in the encampment when they were assailed by a group of Raiders, and swordsmen that called themselves Lions."

According to Mara, Karigan had simply vanished during the melee with the help of a "travel device." He was disquieted to learn she'd taken the Raider leader, Torq, and one of the swordsmen, with her. There was no sign of her after the enemy was dispatched, and the wraiths had come. That had been weeks ago, and there was no news about Karigan since.

Everything about Karigan's life as a Green Rider worried Stevic, the magic, the type of work, and her propensity for finding trouble. He tried to hide his worry from her, as it would only distract her from her job when she needed to focus on getting it done and keeping herself safe. However, she had so many close calls, and now this latest disappearance? That she had vanished with the leader of the Darrow Raiders did not bode well. Not at all. He shuddered and closed his eyes. Laren's abduction was difficult enough to bear, and now Karigan had disappeared, too.

"I know you are worried," Mara said. "Karigan is your daughter, and I am aware you have some affection for the colonel, but you should know they are two of the most resourceful and resilient people I've ever known. They'll come out of this all right, you'll see."

"I am grateful for your words and agree with your assessment." Then he paused. "You know about the colonel and me?"

Mara smiled. "We work closely together. It was hard to miss her improved moods when you were around. I came to realize all those meetings the two of you were having weren't exactly meetings."

"Well." He couldn't think of anything else to say to that.

"I had better leave you to rest," Mara said.

"I'd like to see the queen now."

"Tomorrow," Mara reminded him. "She has orders to rest, too."

And now Stevic heard the news about the twins, Prince Zachary Davriel the Second and Princess Esmere. It was tremendous news for the realm that they had arrived safely. The queen was well, but out of an excess of caution, the master mender was limiting her activity until she regained her old strength and energy.

Mara collected her papers and stood. "Send a runner for me if you need anything, and if you can't find a runner, an apprentice mender should do."

He watched after her as she left his chamber. How could he just wait here in bed, of all things? Laren was a captive of the Varosians, and Karigan had disappeared. He should be able to do something about that. He could look for Karigan and sail to Varos after Laren. If he stayed abed, he couldn't do anything. He—

He yawned as a wave of drowsiness washed over him. His eyes drooped against his will, and within moments, he was deeply asleep.

WHAT THE KING WOULD HAVE A MERCHANT DO

By the next morning, Stevic felt even better than his usual self. He was positively ebullient, joking with the apprentices who delivered his breakfast and checked him for fever. Rider-Mender Ben Simeon soon arrived for a more thorough checkup.

"How are you feeling?" he asked.

"Very well," Stevic replied, "and I understand you are the man I have to thank." He extended his hand, which Ben grasped tentatively, for a shake.

Ben checked him over and pronounced him fit.

"Good," Stevic said, "as I am to see the queen today."

"Yes, you are," Ben replied. "Rider Ash awaits. She will escort you."

Stevic dressed after Ben left him. When he stepped from his room into the corridor, he found not only a Rider waiting for him, but Melry, too. When she saw him, she threw her arms around him. It took him by surprise, but he hugged her back.

"They took my mother," she said, her voice muffled against his chest.

"I heard, but I am very glad to see you are all right. I was extremely worried when you vanished in Selium."

She stepped back and wiped her eyes dry. "I got away."

"Lieutenant Brennyn told me you were very clever and hid in a beaver lodge. It's an amazing story."

"I just want my mother back."

"We'll get her back."

"Everyone keeps saying that," Melry replied, "but no one *does* anything."

"We'll talk this over further, I promise," he said, "but right now I am due to speak with the queen. I'll see what I can find out."

She lifted her chin. "I will hold you to your promise."

He nodded, and she left, but not until after she gave Rider Ash an inscrutable look. When Melry was out of sight, the Rider visibly relaxed.

"Rider Ash, is it?" he said.

"Yessir, but call me Anna."

She was a slip of a thing, probably a little older than she looked, but still, to Stevic's eyes, so very young. There was not much that stood out about her otherwise, but a liveliness to her eyes that spoke to more going on than outward appearances might suggest. He wondered what her special ability was, but knew enough not to ask.

"Lead on, Anna," he said.

"This way, please."

She guided him from the serene halls of the mending wing into the main castle corridor, which was quieter than usual, but they did not stay there long and turned down a side corridor.

"I am sorry your colonel has been taken," he told Anna.

She glanced at him, seemed about to say something, but then thought better of it and clamped her mouth shut.

In time they came to a door which led to the gallery that framed the central courtyard gardens. To his astonishment, when they stepped outside, the beautiful, lush gardens had been transformed from naturalistic and aesthetic landscaping to extensive vegetable gardens. Workers lugged water and weeded. The rows were growing nicely. Despite the growth, it struck him as barren compared to the gardens' previous appearance. Some rose bushes, at least, and trees, remained around the edges.

"Well, this is different," he said.

"The queen thought it would be a good idea with all the shortages and war," Anna said. "They've begun to fence in the west castle grounds for livestock, too."

"The castle is becoming a proper farm."

It was clever, he thought. The Raiders had caused many folk to flee the countryside for the towns and cities. That meant that fields went untended and there was little source of food from outside. And if there were ever a siege? A regular kitchen garden, even a large one, would not be enough to sustain the denizens of the castle complex and its fighting force. He wondered if, even with the new gardens, there'd be enough food for winter. He feared it would be a hungry winter all across Sacoridia.

Anna led him onto a garden path. The paths, he noted, retained their original meandering layout, and decorative bridges still crossed the streams that flowed from King Joneaus' Spring. The paths and bridges added a whimsical aspect to the otherwise orderly gardens.

They found the queen tending a rose bush on the far side of the courtyard. She removed spent blooms with a pair of clippers. She looked content as sunshine gilded her hair. A butterfly rested on a leafy stalk beside her, and bees bobbed from one bloom to the next. It was a pretty picture marred only by the two stern guards in black standing nearby.

"Your Majesty," Anna said.

Queen Estora turned, a faded bloom cupped in her hand, and smiled. "Ah, you've brought me Chief G'ladheon."

Stevic placed his hand to his heart and bowed. "Clan G'ladheon is at your service, my lady."

"I am very pleased to see you," she replied. "We have been hopeful you would return to the city."

"I am here now. And please, call me Stevic."

"Stevic," she said with a nod.

She discarded the bloom she'd been holding. Was it his imagination, or had it looked better, more alive, while in her hand?

"Anna," she said, "thank you. You may go now."

"Yes'm." The Rider bowed and departed.

"Would you join me in the solar for tea?" the queen asked. "Of course."

She turned and walked toward open glass doors sheltered by the gallery. She moved as gracefully as he remembered.

They entered the solar, and one of the Weapons closed the door behind them. The room was sparsely furnished, but there were vases with fresh-cut roses, and a variety of other potted plants lined up in front of the window.

"I wish to congratulate you on the birth of your son and daughter," he said. "It makes my heart glad to be Sacoridian."

Her sudden smile was one of pure joy. "I must confess I am a besotted mother. I can't help but look in on them constantly, even though their nurses are with them always. Alas, I know you have come because of less happy circumstances. Our dear Colonel Mapstone has been taken by Varosians."

"Yes," he replied, wondering if she knew something about his relationship with Laren as Mara had, and if "our" included him. "I know that Karigan is most fond of her."

"Forgive me." She placed her clippers and gardening gloves on a table. "You must be so very worried about Karigan."

"Always. I cannot believe all she has done and the challenges she has faced. To hear she's missing again is very difficult."

She placed a comforting hand on his shoulder and gazed earnestly at him. "Only now, now that I have children of my own, can I even guess at how it must feel."

Humbled, he looked at his feet, unsure of what to say. At that moment, someone tapped on the inner door, and a maid carried in a tea tray. The queen directed her to set it on a table before two chairs that looked out on the gardens. She led him to one of the chairs while the maid poured tea.

"Thank you, Jayd," the queen said.

The maid curtsied and departed.

The queen took her chair. "The cooks spare me some sugar and cream on occasion if you would like some."

"Ah, the shortages," he said, helping himself to a smaller splash of cream than he might normally indulge in. He could only guess how all of this was affecting his own business.

"I pray to the gods that things will soon be back to normal," she said.

Stevic watched as a sparrow hopped from branch to branch on a small birch tree outside the window. "These times are trying for all, including the merchant class. Many will lose their businesses." He was likely losing a good deal daily. This was prime caravan and fair season. His second, Sevano, would be wary of sending out their caravans with Raiders sacking the countryside, and few folk would be willing to travel to attend the fairs with the threat.

"As for our Colonel Mapstone," she continued, "I know you are aware she was abducted and taken as a slave of the king of Varos. Zachary seems confident you may prove helpful."

"I am flattered, and I am more than willing to help if I may." She probably had no idea how much. "Though I'm not sure what the king thinks a simple merchant can do that would prove helpful."

"He knows that it is likely you've had some contact with the Varosians in trade."

"Yes. Limited, but yes." They liked fine silk.

"The colonel is his dearest friend," she said, "and mine, too, but he has known her since he was a boy. They are very close, and it is important to him to have her safely returned."

"I understand a diplomatic mission has been sent?"

"Yes, but it is doubtful it will succeed. The Varosians are peculiar in their ways, and jealous of their possessions. One with Laren's special ability is considered a great asset by King Farrad Vir."

"What is it King Zachary would have me do?"

She removed a letter from beneath the tea tray. "This will provide you with more detailed information, but his basic wish is that you go to Varos, and if the diplomats fail, *you* bring her back by any means necessary."

Stevic accepted the letter and smiled.

⊰∻ A MISSION FOR STEVIC ∻⊱

Clever was their king. The letter Queen Estora had handed Stevic anticipated his acceptance of a mission to rescue Laren. There was no indication the king knew of Stevic's relationship with Laren, but he instead appealed to Stevic's expertise in certain areas.

If the diplomats failed, Stevic was to proceed with a legitimate—that was, lawful in the eyes of the Varosians—means to persuade King Farrad Vir to return Laren. If the legitimate tactic failed, he was to employ other means using skills he had acquired before he'd become a law-abiding merchant.

Stevic's smile deepened.

He read on. So sure was the king that he would agree to rescue Laren that he'd already set preparations in motion. Three sword-hulled clipper ships, complete with crew, would await his command in Corsa Harbor. If he should choose, he could pick a dozen additional personnel whom he knew to be loyal to him and the crown. His contact in Corsa would be a man named Master Hunt. Elgin Foxsmith, Laren's orderly, had already been sent ahead to Corsa to help lay the groundwork.

The king wrote, *You will not be acting in my name at any time, nor under the commission of the realm in any form. Should you fail and find yourself subject to the laws of Varos, I will deny all knowledge of you and your endeavor, and provide no support. You will be on your own.* He added, *If successful in recovering Colonel Mapstone, you will be duly rewarded.*

There were a few other details, but when Stevic finished,

he lowered the letter to his lap and stared out the solarium's window. A gardener was watering a nearby patch of cabbage. Then he turned to Queen Estora.

"You have read this, my lady?"

"Not your letter," she said, pouring more tea for the both of them, "but one addressed to me that, among other things, describes the contents of your letter. I am to aid you as possible, but as you've seen, the king already has preparations under way. Have you an answer for him?"

"His Majesty loves the colonel very much, doesn't he?"

"My sense is," she replied, "that Laren may have been the only one, besides his terriers, who ever showed him kindness and love without condition. As a prince and possible successor to the throne, those who surrounded him thought more about how being linked to him would be in their own personal best interests. It was never about befriending the person he was, but what he could do for them as a royal prince. He'd lost his mother, of course, during his birthing, and his brother was far from kind. His grandmother came closest as a blood relative to showing him some warmth, but Queen Isen was . . ."

"A force to be reckoned with," Stevic provided.

"Just so, and too busy to spend much time with him. So, he made a family of friends with those around him—the Weapons, the horse master, the kennel master, and most of all, Laren Mapstone. She was both surrogate mother and sister to him, and his closest friend."

"I see," Stevic replied. "I thought it might be the way of it, but I did not wish to presume."

"With my own children newly born," she continued, "it is something I've thought about often. How will they be treated by those around them? I will want to protect them, but it will not always be possible. I hope their father will remember his own upbringing and do better than his father and grandmother."

It was candid of her to speak so. "Your children are lucky to have so caring a mother. Karigan's mother passed away when she was little, and I was such a wreck in my grief that I abdicated my duties as a parent for many years. I thank the gods for my sisters, that they were there to help raise her, although I must admit the result has made her very strong headed."

Estora smiled. "Your sisters did very well by Karigan. I consider her a friend even if we don't see each other often, and I hope she will become a friend to my children as Laren was to Zachary."

Stevic sobered. "If she turns up."

"I can only guess how much you worry. I know only too well the peril the Green Riders face. But I also know Karigan G'ladheon. You and your sisters raised her to be resourceful, and she has a habit of turning up when we least expect it. Fear not. I believe she is but delayed, not lost."

Stevic was humbled by his queen's compassion. He bowed his head to collect his composure. Finally, he said, "In answer to the king's request, I will bring back Colonel Mapstone. I'll do whatever it takes."

"Thank you. I know you will, and I will pray to Aeryc and Aeryon for your safety and success."

Stevic, never one to take the gods too seriously, was nonetheless moved. He stood and took his leave of his gracious queen, his mind already filled with all he needed to do.

He found Melry out by the field house using a practice sword to beat on a sand-filled dummy hanging from a post. She'd expressed her desire to become a Weapon, but this was not the image of a future swordmaster perfecting her technique, but of a young woman full of rage. Her hair was slick with sweat, her cheeks red from effort. He spied a bloody rag wrapped around the hilt of the practice sword. She'd been at this for a while. No one coached her, and in fact, all the practice rings were empty, and the area surrounding the field house quiet, except for Melry's grunts when the sword connected with the dummy.

"Melry," he said quietly.

She paused, and turned to look at him. She wiped hair out of her face with a bloody hand.

"I wanted to tell you," he continued, "that the king has tasked me to retrieve your mother from Varos."

An expression of hope crossed her face. "When?"

"I will take ship when I reach Corsa. I just wanted you to know. I *will* bring her back."

She stepped toward him. "I want to go with you."

"I don't think—"

"I'm going."

He should not have been so startled by her vehemence, but he was. He hoped that by presenting himself to the Varosians as a merchant they could come to some arrangement that would allow Laren to return home in peace, but if not, he'd have to resort to other means to free her, which meant the possibility of danger.

"My point in telling you," he said, "is to hearten you, to let you know that action was actually being taken to release your mother, not to recruit you for my crew. I fear we may encounter peril in the endeavor and I don't want to have to worry about a young—"

"I am as old as Karigan was when she ran away from school and helped save the king's throne."

The hair raised on the nape of his neck. "Citing Karigan's history is not necessarily the best way to persuade me."

"*I am going.* You won't have to worry about me. I can defend myself just fine." She raised her sword to eye level to emphasize her point.

The gods preserve him. "Don't you, er, need to get permission from someone?"

"Like my *mother?*" she asked in a cutting voice. "No, there is no one. Well, I'd write a letter to Estral to let her know I won't be back in Selium anytime soon."

He understood her desire to go, could not deny it. If anyone had a claim to join him on this voyage, it was Melry. It filled him with trepidation, however, to be responsible for her. If anything should happen to her, Laren would kill him. She'd probably kill him just for allowing Melry to come along.

"I think," he said, "you should at least inform Lieutenant Brennyn as a courtesy."

She bristled and looked as if she was going to protest, until the implication of his words set in. "You're taking me with you?"

"It would appear so. But you must promise me you will follow my every order."

"I promise!" she cried, triumph in her eyes. "I will do everything you say."

"Hmm." She was a little too ready to agree. "This will not be some lark, but important business that begins with a long and monotonous sea voyage."

She stilled herself and said very seriously, "I understand. I will do all you say. I know it's my mother's life at stake."

He nodded in satisfaction. "Then gather any belongings you have suitable for the variable weather of an ocean voyage and meet me at the castle gate by the second bell. My first order to you is to not discuss what you are doing, even with friends. It's not a secret that I'm sailing to Varos on a trading mission, but the more circumspect we are, the better. Meanwhile, I have some business to attend to at my office in town."

"I will do as you say." She sprang away with her wooden sword toward the field house, leaving Stevic to hope he would not regret this. He turned to leave only to come face-to-face with a hulking man with his arms folded across his substantial chest, which strained his tunic at his shoulders.

"Uh," Stevic said. He had not heard the man approach from behind.

"Are you G'ladheon?" the man demanded.

"Stevic G'ladheon of Clan G'ladheon, at your service." He would have given the traditional merchant bow, but his head would have thudded into the man's chest.

"I'm Drent," the man said. His face appeared to rest in a permanent scowl. "The arms master."

"It's, uh, good to meet you." He'd heard of the arms master from both Karigan and Laren. They had not exaggerated his forbidding presence.

"Your daughter does well with the sword."

"That is nice to hear." Stevic waited for more as the man stared him down. When it seemed no more was forthcoming, he began, "Well, I had better—"

"That Melry," Drent said, "you make sure to watch after her. She may one day become a Weapon, but she's not ready yet. You will make sure she trains on the voyage."

"I will? Yes, of course I will." Stevic wondered more than

ever what he was getting himself into by agreeing to take Melry with him. "You, uh, overheard us then?"

"There is little that happens on these grounds that I don't know about."

Drent bent toward him, his expression menacing. Stevic, not easily cowed by anyone, fought not to flinch or back away.

"You *will*," Drent commanded, "bring the colonel back."

"That is my aim. I will not return without her."

"Good." The arms master's posture eased. "It is not the same around here without her." Then he quickly added, "Don't tell her I said that."

Was Drent more than just Laren's friend?

"I would accompany you," Drent continued, "but I am required to stay here to help protect the queen and heirs, and to train swordmasters and Weapons who are not with the king's army." He jabbed Stevic in the shoulder with his finger. If Stevic had been a lesser man, it might have knocked him over. "You bring her back." He turned and stumped off toward the field house.

It had sounded a threat even if he'd left off the "or else."

When Stevic saw Laren again, he'd have to clarify just what was the nature of her relationship with Arms Master Drent.

⇜ HER OTHER SELF ⇝

"**I** am sorry," Karigan told Fastion, "about Ellen and Willis, and the others who died."

They stood in an open space of the encampment set aside for weapons training. The day was gloomy, the summits of the mountains cloaked in clouds.

"They died well," he replied, "doing what they devoted their lives to. They will be honored on Breaker Island. And avenged."

Death is honor, Karigan thought.

"No more talk," Fastion said. "You will show me what you are able to do." He handed her Colonel Mapstone's sword.

She licked her lips in trepidation. So here they were, her first true training session since the wounding of her back. She hadn't had time to think lately of what the consequences would be if she could not fight at the level she once had. Too much had been going on. However, on her journey from the north, she'd had more than enough time to worry about it, and now it all came flooding back. She'd lose her status as swordmaster, of course. No more black silk knotted around the blade of her sword beneath the hilt. They'd probably revoke her status as an honorary Weapon, as well. She'd worked hard to attain swordmastery, and being an honorary Weapon? She still wasn't quite sure why the Weapons had bestowed such a distinction upon her, but it had made her proud. It was a mark of respect from the realm's most skilled warriors. Nyssa's work may have stripped her of all that.

Worse, if her sword work was found to be lacking and mastery taken from her, how would she ever have confidence in herself again? What would she do? She'd be a failure.

Failure . . .

That word again. She did not know if it was Nyssa or herself who had thought it, but what was the difference?

"You can avoid this no longer," Fastion said. "We must find out the extent to which your injury limits you."

He directed her through a series of forms. She was slow and stiff, the finer points of the forms awkward. The stiffness of her back muscles eased as she warmed up, but not entirely. Her extension, and thus her reach, were poor. She could feel her efforts pulling at her damaged back, which limited her reach and threw off her footing and balance. In a fight, an opponent could easily push her away, or even knock her down.

When she finished the series, Fastion's expression remained impassive. He gave her another set, and she did her best, but experienced the same difficulties, but this time she began to tire. Not only had the muscles of her back been affected, but others in her arms, shoulders, and torso had lost conditioning from lack of use.

Afterward, she felt the taut discomfort in her back and found herself stretching this way and that to ease it. She wished for the healing hands of Gweflin in Eletia.

"We've work to do," Fastion said, "but you are doing better than I feared."

"Really?"

"You are surprised?" he asked.

"Well, yes. I—I thought I'd be stripped of my status as a swordmaster and everything."

He raised an eyebrow, which was almost all the emotion she ever saw from a Weapon.

"The lashing you received," he told her, "might have prevented you from lifting a sword ever again, physically or mentally. Probably the fact that you have had to remain active despite the pain has served you well. Yes, you have work ahead of you, and yes, we'll have to start with basics, but strength and speed can be rebuilt, and technique refined with practice."

"Are—are you sure?"

Now he raised both eyebrows. "When you lost the use of your right eye, did you find it difficult to adjust?"

She had. She'd walked into door frames, tripped down steps, and had felt generally unbalanced. "Yes, but—"

"What of your Weapons training?"

She thought back. Before she had ever lost the sight in her eye, Drent had trained his swordmaster initiates to fight with various deficits, such as having to use their nondominant hand, or having their hearing muffled. One of the toughest exercises he put them through required them to fight with one eye covered. It had changed how she perceived angles and movements and depth. With her peripheral vision obscured on one side, her sparring partner was able to sneak up on her. She'd gotten pretty bruised during the swordplay because she kept miscalculating where her opponent's sword was in relation to her own. Thank the gods they'd been using wooden practice blades at the time.

And then she had actually lost the use of her right eye and despaired of ever becoming a swordmaster, but Drent worked with her, and worked her hard, so that she could learn to compensate for her impairment. He taught her to use all her senses rather than rely solely on her vision.

"You overcame the difficulty of your sight," Fastion said. "It will be the same for your back."

She thought she'd drop to her knees in relief, and fleetingly thought of kissing him, but Fastion already had her working on stretches with forms used as the basis of many of them.

"If the pain becomes too uncomfortable," he said, "we must stop. It makes no sense to injure your back anew."

By the end of the session, there didn't seem to be a part of her body that didn't feel the strain and ache, but she was more hopeful than ever that she'd be back to her old form, or some version of it, with consistent work. She noticed Nyssa didn't have anything to say about it. If the torturer had wanted to cripple her, she was the one who had failed.

When she left Fastion, she slowly made her way through the camp. She came across a group of workers taking a rest near a massive pile of firewood they'd been stacking. Sitting by herself on the ground was Lala. She gazed intently at a black-and-yellow tiger butterfly perched on her finger, beating its wings. Her hair was tousled by the breeze and shone brilliantly in the sun. She looked like any young girl admiring something beautiful she had found, when in reality, she wasn't just any girl, but one endowed with powerful magic. Could she be swayed from the ways of Grandmother and Second Empire, or was it too late for change?

Karigan glanced at the other workers who chatted among themselves or sipped water. They seemed unconcerned by Lala's presence among them. Perhaps they were unaware of who, exactly, Lala was, or what she was capable of. Farther afield, she spotted Donal keeping a close eye on her.

When Karigan's shadow fell over her, Lala glanced up. "Do you like my butterfly?" she asked.

Karigan opened her mouth to respond, but did not know what to say. Lala's voice was a younger version of Estral's, and it was not only disconcerting, but a reminder that this girl was not normal.

"Butterflies start as ugly caterpillars," Lala said, "but then they change and grow pretty wings. You shouldn't have killed my grandmum."

"*I* did not," Karigan said, finally finding her voice, though the abrupt change of topic jarred her. "The aureas slee did. There are things *you* shouldn't have done, like steal the voice of my friend. You must give it back to her."

The girl was unmoved. "You were supposed to die."

"So you've told me."

"If you hadn't escaped, Nyssa would have finished you."

Karigan sighed. What did one do with a child like this? She thought about Connly asserting she was indeed a *child*. What Zachary intended by keeping her alive and unfettered was difficult to know. Had he some plan for her, or had her tender age caused him to hesitate?

"I am gonna make my grandmum proud," Lala said, "and Nyssa, too."

This was not, Karigan believed, a child who could be reformed. She would only grow more dangerous with time. Someone would have to make the ultimate decision of what to do with her.

The butterfly beat its wings more rapidly and lifted off Lala's fingers. It flew in the erratic way of butterflies, carried to and fro on air currents. Karigan tensed, suddenly on guard though there was nothing unusual she could see about it. She started to step out of its way as it drifted in her direction, but it blurred suddenly and drilled into her forehead, into her skull. She gasped and staggered. A spell! Her sight burst with a kaleidoscope of yellow and black wings beating, beating, and then everything and everyone fell away into blackness.

She stood in a shaft of light surrounded by dark nothingness. Where was she? Where had everyone gone? What had Lala's butterfly done to her?

Then she perceived she was not alone. Another stepped into the light, her very reflection, her twin. And yet, her twin was not entirely the same as her. She wore not green, but dark charcoal gray. No winged horse brooch was clasped to her longcoat. Her hair was long and loose as Karigan's had once been before Nyssa cut it. It was also darker. This had to be some sort of dream, a vision.

"Who are you?" Karigan asked.

"I am your other self."

"What do you mean?"

"I am the darker you. The darkness within that you fight so hard to repress."

Karigan tried to shake herself out of the dream, but could not. If it was even a dream, she could not say.

"You wanted to kill the child," her other self said. She slapped the end of a riding crop against her palm.

"Kill a child? I never—"

"You wanted to kill Lala," the other self said. "You know you did. *I* know."

"I never would."

"Not even for a greater good? To prevent her from doing anything devastating in the future?"

Karigan had considered the future and what Lala could be capable of. She could rival Grandmother in power, lead another generation of Second Empire.

And yet, she could not bring herself to kill a child.

"Then you may have doomed our people," her other self said. "All the innocents, including children. What is the greater evil, I wonder? Killing one child so all the others may live, or letting her go?"

Karigan placed her face in her hands. It was an impossible choice. She remembered the small graves at the farmstead in Boggs. The death of innocents.

"I am not like the Raiders," she said. "I don't kill children. And who is to say Lala will become like Grandmother?"

"If I am not mistaken, *you* have. She enjoyed helping with the torture of Zachary. She took Estral's voice. What are the chances she does not take after her grandmother?"

"Because there *are* chances," Karigan shouted, "she won't necessarily grow up to be evil. It's not a predetermined path."

"Is it not?"

Was it? Karigan wondered. Were they all set on a predetermined course? No, she would not believe it. She had seen too much, the workings of the very universe, the threads that intersected and diverged across the heavens, the threads of fate that snapped or endured.

Paths could be altered.

Suddenly her other self was right in front of her, grabbed her chin.

"You haven't the guts. You are too afraid. What was it you were thinking when Nyssa was lashing you and destroying your back? Let me think . . . Oh, *why me*? Why *me*? You were ready to tell Nyssa that Sacoridia's king was right under their noses if only it would make her stop."

"No!" Karigan pushed away from her other self even as a small part of her mind said, *yes*. "I don't want to think about it."

Her other self smiled. "Of course not, but true is true. You blamed Estral for your capture and torture, so why wasn't she the one to suffer?"

"She—she did suffer. I'd never—"

"Admit it!" The other pointed the riding crop at her. Light flared around it. "You blame her."

"All right. I blame her for going into the Lone Forest on her own, for getting us captured. She hadn't listened when she was told to wait. She had to run off on her own. She . . ."

Karigan stopped, her breathing was harsh. Every muscle in her body was taut. She unclenched her hands. "I forgave her. It was Nyssa who tortured me. It's Nyssa who I blame."

The other paused, half in the light, half in the dark. "But it should have been Estral chained to that beam."

"*No.*"

"In your fear and agony, that's what you wanted."

Karigan turned her back to her other self. "Go away. Leave me alone."

"Poor thing can't handle the truth."

"Go away." She didn't know how to leave this place she was trapped in.

"I can't go away," the other said. "I am part of you."

Karigan whirled. "No, you're not. You're just Nyssa trying to trick me, torture me again."

"I could tell you the names of the barn cat kittens you smuggled into your room to cuddle when you were seven and how unhappy your aunts were about the fleas. I know the boys you liked in school, then despised when they bullied you. I know your favorite chapters from *The Journeys of Gilan Wylloland*. Nyssa does not know these things. Nyssa is only a vengeful spirit and does not care. But I do because I am a part of you. *I* am *you.*"

"I don't believe you."

"The truth is, you do believe me, you just don't want to. Without me, you'd be dead."

"Oh?" She and the other had begun circling one another, in and out of the light.

"You have killed. *We* have killed. Do you remember the first?"

Garroty, Karigan thought. A mercenary who happened upon the traitorous Weapons who had taken her captive as she attempted to deliver a dead Green Rider's message to the king. Garroty had tried to— She closed her eyes and shook her head, not wishing to relive it but unable to forget his weight on her, the stench of his unclean body. The ghost of F'ryan Coblebay had urged her to action and she'd slammed her head into Garroty's face. She'd caused the bones of his nose to shatter into his brain.

"Yes," the other said, "we killed him."

"Had to, or else he'd have . . ." Karigan shuddered, unable to say more.

"Without me, he would have succeeded and killed you after. Without me, you wouldn't have killed him, or Torne the traitor, or any others who wished you ill. But why do you even fight? There is so little reward."

A third stepped into the light. Karigan stilled. It was Zachary, and she watched as the other walked around him, as if inspecting a prize stallion.

"Is it all for him?" the other asked.

"Of course not."

"He is your reward, is he not? You could take him. It *is* what you want, isn't it?" The other ran her hand down Zachary's cheek. He smiled as he gazed down at her. "Why wait? You could have him now. Who cares if he's married? A king taking a mistress is practically a requirement of the position." He took her in his arms. She rose on her toes to engage in a long and deep kiss.

Karigan turned away in disgust. Her heart pounded. Yes, she wanted him, but not like that. "Stop it," she said. "Just stop it." When she turned around, Zachary was gone, but the other stood as her dark reflection.

"Remember," the other said, "you can take your reward any time. You deserve it. I'll always be with you to help when it is time to claim it, or when it is time to kill. It's all right to take a life when we're saving our own, yes? It is all right to be angry, too, when we suffer because of the mistakes of others. Anger is good. You must not deny yourself. I am with you always, you are me."

"I—"

And suddenly she was blinking in the sunlight, standing in the very same place as she had been before the strange dream or vision. The workers who'd been taking their break gave her strange looks. She'd been talking with Lala when a butterfly . . .

"Lala?" She looked around herself. "Where's Lala?"

⋖ MIND GAMES ⋗

A hand clamped on Karigan's shoulder and she jumped. It was Donal.

"Lala!" she said.

"Yes, the child is gone," he replied.

"But I was just talking to her."

"Yes. That's the last any of us remember seeing her. She was there one moment, and then gone the next. You were left standing there like a statue staring into space."

She rubbed her forehead. There was a sore spot in the middle where the butterfly had hit. "A spell. She got me with a spell."

"We guessed as much," Donal said. "We feared causing harm if we tried to shake you out of it. What was the effect of the spell? Besides freezing you in place, that is."

She shrugged. "Not much. Apparently she wanted to introduce me to my other self." When Donal looked perplexed, she added, "I assume people are looking for her?"

"Yes, search parties have been organized and are already heading out."

They would not find her, Karigan was sure. Lala had just been biding her time at the camp.

"Probably halfway to Second Empire by now," Donal murmured.

Karigan wasn't so sure that that was where the girl was headed.

"I will escort you to the king's tent to speak with Counselor Tallman."

"What for?"

"To explain what you witnessed of the girl's disappearance."

"How long was I standing there staring at nothing?"

"A quarter hour, at a guess."

"Right."

She tried to keep up with Donal's long strides as he escorted her to the king's tent. Inside was a buzz of activity as advisors and officers came and went, argued and discussed and mused. She did not think the fuss was over Lala, but more of the usual daily business over which Zachary presided.

Eventually Les Tallman took notice of her. "Ah, Rider. You've come to speak of Lala."

"Yes, sir."

Zachary was engrossed in a conversation with General Washburn and others by the map table. She didn't think he'd noticed her entrance. Her other self would have liked to make him notice her, but she quashed the impulse.

She was attended by Counselor Tallman, Donal, a young officer she did not know, and, belatedly, Connly. She told them of encountering Lala, the butterfly spell, and the fact that when she came back to herself, Lala had already been gone for a time.

"I'm afraid there isn't much more I can tell you than that," she said.

"What of this butterfly spell?" the officer asked. "What did it do?"

"It distracted Sir Karigan for one," Donal said, "who was right there when she escaped, and caused the rest of us not to notice as well."

"There has to be more to it than that," the officer said.

"Not much," Karigan replied, and she hoped she was right. "It put me in a sort of . . . I don't know, a dream state."

"You were asleep?"

"Not exactly, no."

"What did you dream about?" Connly asked. "It could be important."

"I don't think so," she replied. "It was personal. It was me talking to myself about my life."

That seemed to make them lose interest, and she was glad. She had no desire to discuss the personal issues with which her other self had taunted her. That's what Lala had intended, she was sure, to make her question herself, to strip away her confidence much in the same way Nyssa did. Mind games.

Her questioners seemed disappointed in the lack of additional information and moved off to talk among themselves. She was about to leave, but glanced again at Zachary whose full attention was on General Washburn. She clenched her hands at her sides as her other self quietly reminded her of her "reward." She moved to stride from the tent and almost crashed into a Green Rider entering.

"Garth!" she exclaimed. She hadn't seen him in a long time.

"Hello, Karigan," he said, and then flashed her a grin before going straight to Zachary, withdrawing a sealed letter from his message satchel as he went.

Connly intercepted her. "Karigan, you are excused. If they need to question you further, they will send for you."

She was curious to know what message Garth was bearing, and to see him, of course, but she nodded and left. She hadn't any duties assigned to her until it was time to feed the horses, so she returned to her tent and, sitting in a camp chair in front of it, decided to give the colonel's saber a good polishing. Not that it wasn't already in good order, but it would keep her busy.

Camp life was one part boredom, and one part frantic duty. Those who could read and write wrote letters home for themselves or for others who lacked the skill. They gamed or carved, or visited the brothel wagon over by the market.

She worked cloth over steel, cleaning fingerprints and every speck of dust. She could do nothing about nicks and scratches, except to ensure they were clear of dirt and well oiled. The colonel had been a Rider for a long time during periods of both peace and turbulence, and her sword showed the scars.

She caught sight of her own reflection beneath the scratched surface, and for a moment, she was once again with her other self. She closed her eyes, willing away the dark thoughts that had been stirred within her. She did not like that part of herself. Her darker self wanted to see the world as black and white, where weighty decisions actually had easy answers. In her darker self's opinion, she should forget honor and conscience, and just give in to her most desired impulses. But real life just wasn't like that.

She shook herself and polished with ferocity to help erase the image and memory of her darker self.

As she finished up, some shouts of greeting drew her attention to a Rider reining her horse toward the king's tent.

"Dale?" Karigan said. She sheathed the saber and trotted after her. By the time she reached the king's tent, Dale had already been ushered inside. Tegan stood there holding the reins to Dale's mare.

"Oh, good," she said to Karigan. "Could you take Plover to the pickets?"

Karigan accepted Plover's reins while Tegan entered the tent. A twinge of disappointment prickled at her that she was no longer Chief Rider and couldn't be present to find out what had brought Dale up from the wall. But then she patted Plover's neck. Getting to take care of the horse, she thought, was the better end of the deal.

Karigan got to see her friends soon enough. They joined her at suppertime, as she sat by the fire, eating in front of her tent. One by one, other Riders came to sit with them. She introduced some of the newer Riders, including Megan, who had never met Dale. When Garth came over, he gave her a gentle hug as though she might break in his arms, a contrast to his usual crushing bear hugs. It didn't take much to gather he'd heard about her torture in the north. She responded by giving him a peck on his cheek. His blush made her smile. He then sat beside Tegan, and the two of them leaned against one another, talking quietly and laughing.

It was marvelous to see Garth and Dale again, and a happy coincidence they had arrived on the same day. There was much laughter among their group as they caught up. Their time together would not last, however, as Dale was leaving them first thing in the morning to return to the wall.

"The gryphlings are adorable," Dale was telling them, "and were just getting ready to learn to fly when I left. Poor Alton is so allergic he can't spend more than a few minutes at a time in the tower." She told them about the new gryphon they were calling "Bob" since his non-gryphon form was that of a bobcat. "He was spending most of his time out in the woods," Dale explained. "Pretty shy, but they were trying to coax him to stay close by, by offering him food." She also told them about the battle with the oversized porcupine creatures at the breach, and everyone sobered.

"That's why I'm here," she continued. "Alton hopes the king will send more troops to the wall. The forest, we think, is starting to get restless."

Karigan shuddered with the unbidden memory of black tree roots slithering across a clearing toward her beneath the eaves of the dark forest. It was only a matter of time before Mornhavon arose once more and threw the force of Blackveil at the wall in an effort to cross over into Sacoridia.

The Riders speculated for a time when and how that might happen, but then they moved on, joking and laughing again, glad to be in one another's company.

As stars gathered above their campfire, Connly made his way to their circle and joined them.

"Any word on Lala?" Karigan asked him.

"Not so far," he replied. "The searchers stopped at sundown. They'll begin again in the morning." He sounded very tired.

Brandall passed him a cup of tea and asked, "Is it wrong to say I hope no one finds her ever again?"

"I feel sorry for her," Constance said. "All her family gone and raised by that crazy old woman? It's not her fault."

"Saw her around here a few times," Brandall replied. "She made my skin crawl."

"What do *you* say, Karigan?" Constance asked. "You had more to do with her than the rest of us."

Karigan shrugged. "I'd feel better if we knew where she was." There was no telling what the girl was up to.

The Riders chewed over the subject of Lala for a while,

and when they had run out of things to say on the subject, Connly asked, "Any of you cliff climbers?"

"Not me," Sandy said, and others chimed in with a similar answer.

"The king is looking for a climber," Connly said. "Garth brought the news that the one he was expecting broke his leg and so now can't come."

From a quiet spot by the fire, Megan giggled.

"What's so funny?" Brandall demanded.

"I don't need to climb."

Connly's mouth dropped open as her words registered. Everyone else stared at her in incredulity.

"What?" Megan said. "Why are you all looking at me like that?"

Oh, Megan, Karigan thought. She had no idea what she had just gotten herself into.

THE MEGAN PLAN

"**T**his is high enough, don't you think?" Megan asked. She hovered just above their heads.

"Not nearly," Connly said.

They'd chosen a meadow area well out of sight of the encampment and pass. It would not have done to reveal Megan's floating ability to all who could see. Since Karigan had been the first to coach Megan in her ability, Connly had decided to bring her along, and Garth, too, for moral support. Zachary had directed them to test Megan's ability to its full extent to discover if she could get high enough to look into the pass.

Megan stroked her arms through the air like a swimmer, but it did little to shift her position.

"She needs wings," Garth commented.

"Try going a little higher," Connly said.

She bobbed upward a couple inches.

"Try going up a *lot* higher," he amended.

When Karigan had first tested Megan's ability, they'd been captives in the old shepherd's hut. There'd been a roof limiting how far Megan could rise. There was now no limit, but she was timid, and rose only a few more feet. They'd have to build her confidence quickly.

"You know," Garth said, with wonder on his face as he watched her, "it's like dreams I sometimes have, where I'm floating or flying. So peaceful."

"It's not peaceful!" Megan shouted. "Wind blowing in your ears, a long ways to fall. My hair's a mess."

"Higher," Connly ordered.

Megan pursed her lips and climbed some more, pausing

tentatively before pushing on. Soon they had to crane their necks to watch as she gained altitude.

Then she must have been snagged by an air current because she started to drift away. She squawked and wheeled her arms and legs, which in turn caused her to spin.

"Get me down!" she cried in a panic.

Connly and Garth exchanged glances.

"Only *you* can get you down," Karigan called up to her. "Remember to breathe—deep, slow breaths, and stop flailing."

The advice seemed to work as Megan stopped spinning, except now she hung upside down. "I really hate this," she said. "All the blood is rushing to my head."

With calm encouragement from Karigan, she righted herself, but now she drifted toward a copse of trees, and no fewer than half a dozen crows launched out of the canopy, cawing and crying and diving at Megan. She screamed.

Uh oh, Karigan thought.

Megan tried "swimming" away, but the crows mobbed her, and she screamed some more.

"Come down!" Karigan cried. "Come down, but slowly!"

"Easy for you to say!" Megan plummeted, screaming all the way, the crows flocking after her. But then she stopped about ten feet above the ground.

"Deep breaths!" Karigan cried, running toward where Megan was to land. Connly and Garth were right behind her. "Come down slow."

Somehow she managed to control her descent and land gently in the meadow grass. The crows circled overhead and called and cried until Karigan, Connly, and Garth closed in; then they flew off to their trees.

Megan lay sobbing, curled in a fetal position, covered in cuts and bird droppings.

"Kind of tarnishes the luster of the dream," Garth muttered with a grimace.

"Why why why?" she wailed.

Karigan dropped to her knees beside her, and placed her hand on her shoulder. "You did well. You're all right."

"Why did they attack me?"

"They were probably protecting their nests," Karigan

replied. "They thought you were a predator coming after their young."

"I don't want to do this ever again," Megan declared.

Unfortunately for Megan, Zachary was determined to make use of her floating ability, and so every day that week they returned to the meadow to make Megan practice, pushing her to drift higher and higher, but now with a rope looped around her ankle so she did not get carried away by the air currents.

"Like flying a kite," Garth said as he fed out more rope with her ascent. "It'd be better, though, if she could really fly."

Flying would certainly give her more control, Karigan thought, but that was not the nature of her ability. Rider magic was specialized, but weak, and only emerged at all because the gold winged horse brooches they wore augmented whatever minor gift they were born with. Maybe if Megan were a great mage she would be able to fly, and do so in a controlled and useful manner, but she was not, which meant they must work within the boundaries of her ability.

So far they had yet to discover Megan's upward limit. And all the while they made sure to stay away from the copse. As the days passed, she seemed to get an understanding of how to work with the air currents, but wind was still a problem. A strong wind could be a disaster.

They reported to Zachary one gray and drizzly day to inform him of their progress. He listened without interruption.

When they finished, he said, "Well done, Rider Notman, you have a most unique ability."

"If I may say so, Your Majesty," she replied, "I'd much rather not have this ability. I'd rather be back in my shop. I miss my ribbons and things."

"Sometimes," Zachary said, "we are called upon to endure adversity to contribute to the greater good despite our dearest personal wishes, for the benefit of our people. This is such a time for you. With your help, we will prevail against our enemies. Then one day, when the call releases you, you may return to your shop with the knowledge that you gave all to preserve your country."

Megan appeared little mollified by his words, but knew enough to keep her mouth shut.

Zachary now addressed them all. "The plan is to observe activity in the pass and the area around the keep. A perfect vantage point is the Eagle's Landing that lies beneath the peak of Snowborne." He led them to where a long map of the Wing Song range lay draped over the map table. He tapped a spot on the north ridge of the mountain that jutted out in a plateau.

"Unfortunately," he said, "a large segment of the Sky Stairs that allowed Sacoridian kings of old to climb to the landing to parley with the eagles was obliterated by a massive landslide centuries ago, and never repaired. Our scouts have verified that while the bottom of the stairs remains, about a quarter of the way up they were destroyed, buried beneath unstable talus."

He paused to gaze at Megan. "This is where you come in, Rider Notman. You will use your ability to ascend alongside Snowborne to the Eagle's Landing, and from there you will watch the activity of Second Empire in the pass."

"All the way up there?" Megan asked.

"It is high up," Zachary said, "but reasonable. You would find going all the way to the summit much less so."

"Reasonable," Megan muttered. She made the sign of the crescent moon and closed her eyes.

"She will need a day without wind," Karigan said. "It will otherwise be treacherous that high up. She could be blown clear across the range."

He nodded gravely. "I have asked Rider Oldbrine to watch the weather for us. The mission will proceed when she senses a calm, clear day ahead. It is, of course, possible the air currents in the upper elevations of the ascent will prove fickle no matter the weather. If this is the case, I have seen through my spyglass that some remnant of the stairs above the landslide survives, and they could serve as an alternate means of reaching the Landing if needed. However, Rider Notman, should you choose this route, proceed cautiously, for their viability is unknown. They have not been maintained in centuries and may prove hazardous."

"I have to do this all by myself?" Megan asked in a small voice.

It would be a daunting prospect, Karigan thought, for even the most seasoned Green Rider. She did not envy her one bit.

"Not exactly," Zachary replied. "Riders G'ladheon, Bowen, and Burns will ride with you to the base of Snowborne to provide support. Rider Burns will keep in communication with me through her link with Captain Connly. Rider Bowen will use his wayfinding ability to lead you to the right location to begin, and Rider G'ladheon, well . . ." His eyes twinkled a bit and he smiled. "She's going along for encouragement. The Sky Stairs start here." He tapped the place on the map near the base of the mountain. "A pair of old eagle statues still stand there, so it is unmistakable. It seems the natural place for Rider Notman to begin her ascent."

After that, he dismissed them. As the others filed out, Karigan lingered behind—it was a rare moment of quiet in his tent without the usual complement of aides and officers present.

"Is there something you wish to speak to me about?" he asked her, his eyes glittering with interest.

She nodded. "Why haven't you just sent me to the keep? You know I can use my ability to spy on Second Empire. Megan hasn't had long to grow accustomed to her ability."

"Did you have long to grow accustomed to your ability when the need came upon you to use it for the first time?" he asked.

She shook her head.

"I know you could infiltrate the keep and obtain the information I need," he said, "and I strongly considered it, but just as quickly discarded the idea."

"You didn't," she began hesitantly, "discard it to protect me, did you?"

A half smile played on his lips. "What would you say if I did?"

"I would say that you shouldn't. It's my job."

"Well, the truth of the matter is that I do wish to protect you." He picked up a pitcher of wine and poured himself a cup.

"I wish you wouldn't. I mean, I don't want special treatment because, well . . ." She cast her gaze down at her feet.

"The thing is," he said quietly, "if it were someone else with your ability, someone I didn't feel strongly for, I would have chosen the same course. Going into the keep, even with a fading ability, chances more immediate danger than watching from afar. You'd be right there among the enemy. It is safer for the Riders, and more likely for our spying endeavor to go undiscovered, to go with the Megan plan.

"And do not worry, Rider, lest you fear I will exclude you from future missions. I will likely be calling upon your ability very soon, whether I like it or not. Does that satisfy you?"

"Yes, Your Majesty."

"Good," he said. Then after a pause, he added, "You may not like to hear this, but I'd prefer not to put you in harm's way at all. However, the needs of the realm demand that I do. I have also learned over the years that it is not me who need worry about you." There was a glint of humor in his eyes. "It is your opponents who must need worry."

"I understand," she replied.

"Very well. Dismissed, Rider."

It was, Karigan thought as she stepped outside, the way of life for him, for better or worse, that the needs of the realm must always come first.

⤳ SNAKES AND CATAMOUNTS AND BEARS ⤳

Karigan continued arms training, sometimes with Donal, and sometimes with Fastion, along with her other camp duties while they awaited the perfect period of weather for Megan to accomplish her mission.

One morning, as Karigan and Donal took a break from sparring, the sounds of other warriors at practice—their grunts of effort, their swords clashing as their feet thudded around practice rings—were a brutal counterpoint to the fragile silver sheen of dew on the grasses of the training field.

Karigan took a sip from her waterskin, then asked, "How is the search for Lala going?"

"It has been called off," Donal replied.

"*What?*"

"Little trace has been found of her. It is almost as though she never existed. Since there has been no fresh sign of her over the last couple weeks, the decision was made for the searchers to resume their normal duties."

"She's got to be out there somewhere."

"I had no say in the decision," he replied, and that was apparently that. "Now, we will work with the staff. As you've lost yours, you may borrow this one."

Karigan's mind reeled with news of the search for Lala ending, but she suppressed her dismay and accepted the staff Donal passed her. It was made of black-lacquered bonewood just like hers had been. She missed hers and wondered if it remained along the road where the Raiders had abducted her, or if someone had picked it up. She guessed she would never know.

She shook the staff from walking cane length to full staff length. Donal did not spar with her, but coached her through a series of stretches and forms. After only a couple weeks she'd seen much improvement in her extension and precision, but it was going to take many more practice sessions to improve her strength and endurance.

When Donal made her bend at the hips to try to touch her toes and grasp her ankles, she grimaced at the pull on her back muscles. Every session she tried this, but she had not yet managed it.

"You are getting closer," Donal said.

She eased back into a standing position. Training with Donal and Fastion was almost relaxing compared to Arms Master Drent's shouting and disparagement.

Harry trotted up to the practice area. "Karigan, the captain wants to see you."

She handed Donal the staff, which he received with a nod, and trotted after Harry to where Connly was addressing Megan, Garth, Trace, and Tegan.

"Karigan, good," he said. "Tegan says tonight is the night."

Megan, she noted, did not look happy, and was winding a light blue ribbon between her fingers in a distracted way.

"It's going to be calm and clear tonight through tomorrow," Tegan said. "The winds will die down after sunset; moon will be half and on the wane. I do not expect clouds or any changes for a couple days."

"At nightfall," Connly said, "you will ride across to Snowborne. You understand the location of the old stair?"

They all nodded.

"Good. Even though Garth will find it with no trouble with the use of his ability," Connly continued, "I want you all to know its location in case you get separated for some reason. Megan goes up to the Landing before daybreak to get into position," Connly continued. He turned to her. "You will need warm clothes. The air is thinner up there, and the Landing is exposed, so it will be cold. There may even be snow in places. You will *not* build a fire. Also, the king is lending you his spyglass." He presented her with an oblong leather case with an attached strap. "Do not drop it. It's worth a king's ransom."

Megan's eyes widened as she took it into her hands. "Will I be able to see the gods with it?"

"Of course not," Connly replied, "but it will give you a good amount of detail when you look down into the pass. You understand your instructions?"

"Yes, sir," she replied. "Observe conditions down in the pass and keep, how many people and livestock can be seen, the complement of the guard on the battlements, routines, that sort of thing."

Connly nodded. "Good. The rest of you, any questions?"

When none of them spoke, he said, "Be ready to move out after sundown."

It was a gorgeous evening as they rode away from the encampment through the meadow. Crickets chirruped, and the heavens opened wide and sparkling above. Karigan rode Loon, and Megan, who was also missing her own horse, was assigned a sturdy mule. This, of course, did not please her, and she let them all know about it until Karigan silenced her with a warning that Second Empire scouts could be about.

Garth guided them through the dark, wading across streams and through marshes. Soon the terrain firmed and grew rocky as they began to ascend. Garth picked out their path over some uncertain footing. The hooves clip-clopping and clacking on rock sounded painfully loud to Karigan. She tried to keep her senses alert for Second Empire scouts, as she was sure the others were, as well.

Snowborne blotted out the moon and stars ahead of them. When Karigan looked back, the fires of the encampment were mere pinpricks of light.

She enjoyed riding in the relative silence. Camp could often feel too crowded, and there was little privacy. At night there was only a thin layer of canvas between her and the thousands with all their noise, smells, clutter, and prying eyes. It made her long for a solitary message errand where all she saw for miles was deer and squirrels and birds, and her only companion her dear Condor. She patted Loon's neck when she thought of him. Loon must miss the colonel just as much as she missed Condor.

She welcomed another silence, that which was in her mind. She had not heard from Nyssa in a while. Maybe the torturer had given up, or she'd been a fiction, Karigan's own mind warring within her. Her "other self," which had manifested with Lala's butterfly spell, had filled the void. Though it, too, was quiet at present, she didn't think it was leaving her alone. She could feel it waiting and watching.

Were Nyssa and her other self one and the same? She did not think so. Nyssa had the feel of a spirit, and her other self seemed a shadow of her own inner turmoil. Whether they were the same or not made little difference since both sought to undermine her thoughts and confidence, and she must continue to fight them both.

Up ahead, Garth halted. Not knowing why he did so, she put her hand on the hilt of her sword. Even though her sight was adjusted to the dark, it didn't mean she could make out much. She would have liked to have used her moonstone, except it would be a dead giveaway to Second Empire that the Sacoridians were up to something. Instead, she relied on Loon's senses and surefootedness to safely reach the bottom of the Sky Stair.

Garth reined his mare, Chickadee, around. "We're here," he said. "I've found the old eagle statues the king told us about."

Karigan could barely make out two huge, irregular shapes beyond him.

"We need to find a place to camp," Trace said.

"We're somewhat screened from prying eyes here," Garth said, "but I'd feel better if we used a place the scouts I talked to last night suggested. It's much more hidden, and just a short ride from here."

They turned so that the mountain was at their side, and they traveled south away from the pass. It was not long before they came upon a hillock. They rode around it to its far side. It was a fine shelter that would hide them well.

They worked as best they could in the dark to care for their mounts. There was some cursing and exclamations of pain as they stumbled about. Karigan ran into a dead branch that jabbed her arm. Trace tripped over a rock. Then, with tired sighs, they found places to sit among the rocks and trees, and eat and drink from their rations.

"I don't want to sit on a snake," Megan said. "These twisty tree roots are like snakes, but what if the root is really a snake?"

"It would bite you and then you would die," Garth said.

Megan squeaked and leaped to her feet.

Karigan, who was sitting next to Garth, kicked his leg.

"Ow! What didya do that for?"

"I didn't kick that hard. And it was for telling Megan there could be snakes. Megan, the elevation here in the mountains makes it too cold for snakes. There is nothing to worry about."

"Yeah," Garth said, "don't worry about snakes, but maybe catamounts and bears."

Megan gasped. "I wanna go home—I hate this!"

Karigan kicked Garth again, this time hard.

"That's going to bruise," he said.

"Then stop trying to scare Megan."

"But it's fun."

"Look," Karigan replied, "Megan is the important one on this mission. Don't upset her. She has a big job to do and needs to be able to rest before she does it."

"Sorry, Megan," Garth said.

"Hmph."

"I've told Connly we've arrived and he's going to tell the king," Trace said and, in an acerbic tone, added, "He also says to stop bickering."

"Who's bickering?" Garth demanded.

"You are full of it tonight, big bear man."

"We need to set up a watch," Karigan said, "with the exception of Megan, who needs as many hours of sleep as possible. I'll take second watch." It was usually the least popular because it meant breaking up one's sleep more than the others. "Who wants first and third?"

Trace and Garth argued a bit for first, but Karigan finally made them guess how many fingers she held up behind her back. Trace came closest and got the first watch. The rest crawled into their bedding on the rocky ground.

"Are you sure there are no snakes?" Megan asked in a small voice.

"Yes," Karigan replied, though she wasn't absolutely certain. She didn't want Megan to lose sleep over it when she faced a challenge in the morning far more dangerous than the snakes of Sacoridia.

✦ ASCENT AND DESCENT ✦

Second watch proved uneventful but for the distant hoot of an owl at hunt, and Garth's snoring. Karigan gazed up toward the sky and found Tegan's weather sense profoundly accurate. No clouds obscured the panorama of the heavens, and the stars punctured the velvety dark with sharp clarity. The light of the half moon did little to diminish the appearance of the River of the Gods, the hazy ribbon of celestial light the starmasters believed to be formed by gaseous vapor and concentrations of stars beyond count. How they knew this, she did not understand, except that they had access to the best scopes with which to view the heavens, and the heads for surmising such things.

The moon priests, of course, had another explanation for the formation, that in fact it was an actual river of light in the domain of the gods to which only the truest of true believers could ascend, a paradise beyond all conception. Her connection to the god of death did not convince her the starmasters were wrong, or that the priests were right. Perhaps, she thought, both were right. Or wrong. She was, in any case, content, in that moment, to simply appreciate the beauty of the night and its ambient silence before the intrusion of dawn when all that was fraught in the world would awaken abuzz and animate.

She was rewarded with the sight of a falling star whisking across the sky. She smiled and took it as a sign that it was time to awaken Garth for third watch.

Karigan didn't get much sleep on the rocky ground. She rubbed her eyes and yawned and forced herself out of her blankets. It was still dark, but the stars were setting and the moon was dipping down in the west, which meant it was time to help prepare a plainly unhappy Megan to ascend to the Eagle's Landing. Megan was dressed in layers against the cold, and carried food and water and the spyglass in a knapsack. Karigan, Trace, and Garth escorted her to the bottom of the Sky Stairs. The sky had subtly begun to lighten enough for Karigan to make out the shapes of the eagle statues looming over them, wings half-spread, beaks open in fierce challenge.

"You know I'm gonna faint when I get up there," Megan said. It was the effect the use of her ability had on her. "What if I faint before I reach the top? It's a long way to fall."

They had been over this. "If you feel it coming on," Karigan said, "find a place to land. In fact, make sure you rest along the way. You don't have to get to the top in one long ascent; do it in stages, and remember what the king said about the stairs above the landslide line."

"I remember."

"We'll be here when you come down after sunset. Ready?"

"No."

"Well, you still have to go."

"I know." Megan sounded as glum as she looked. "The ladies who used to come into the shop would never believe this."

To Karigan's surprise, Megan lifted off the ground without further prodding.

"Remember to breathe," Karigan told her.

"I know, I know."

"What is with all the breathing stuff?" Garth asked.

Karigan shrugged. "It gave her something to do when she panicked. Seems to help."

"Think she'll make it?" Trace asked.

"She is tougher than she seems," Karigan said. "I think she'll do fine."

"Dunno," Garth said. "She doesn't seem cut out for this sort of thing."

Recalling her earlier conversation with Zachary, Karigan replied, "Were any of us when we were called?"

"I sure wasn't," Trace said. "I was working in a shop, too. My grandpa's mercantile, not a fine lady's millinery shop, but still."

Garth made a noncommittal grunt.

As the dawn grayed the sky and land, the three Riders gazed up the slope of the mountain. They saw no sign of Megan.

"No body dropping from the sky," Garth said, "so that's good."

Karigan scrutinized the mountainside. She could not make out any sign of the Sky Stair, especially with this side of the range in shadow, but she could see where the rock slide had scraped the mountainside bare and left long piles of talus that skirted the slope. She stepped between the eagles and followed the overgrown path to where the steps began. The steps were huge slabs of granite, and it made her knees ache just thinking about climbing them all the way to the Eagle's Landing as the kings of centuries gone by once had.

She returned to her companions, and they kept watch for Megan. They stared above the tree line until after the sun rose, but saw no sign of her floating or climbing above. Not that they would, given the immensity of the mountain compared to one small human.

"I guess we'll find out after sunset if all went well," Garth said.

They walked back toward their campsite.

"Anybody want to take turns keeping watch while the others nap?" Trace asked.

"Oh, I like that idea," Karigan replied. "I choose napping for myself."

"Nap all you want," Garth said. "I like mornings."

"Monster," Trace said.

"I might well be a monster without my morning kauv," he replied mournfully. No fire meant no hot drinks.

He sat away from their campsite where he'd have a good vantage to observe anyone on the move near their position. Karigan and Trace retired each to her own bedroll.

"You know," Trace said, "I've been wanting to say it for a while, but there was never enough privacy to do so, so I'll say it now: Connly should never have taken away your rank as Chief."

Karigan rose up on her elbow in surprise. Trace and Connly were very close, and she would have expected Trace to support Connly's position.

"What makes you say that?" she asked.

"The way you handle Megan, for one," Trace replied. "I'm not sure anyone else could convince that girl to do what she's doing. Connly chose you to come along on this mission because he knew that of anyone, Megan would listen to you.

"Before Fergal left for Sacor City," Trace continued, "he talked about how you managed captivity with the Raiders and kept him and the others calm, active, and safe. Then, of course, there was the crossing of the Blanding and looking for the colonel. And just last night, you put Garth in his place, reminding him why he shouldn't be teasing Megan. You were a really good Chief."

"Thank you," Karigan replied, taken aback but gratified. Even if Connly hadn't appreciated her, at least others had.

"I told Connly as much," Trace said, "but he would not discuss it with me."

As well he should not, Karigan thought. It would not have been appropriate.

She fell back asleep with a feeling of pleasure, but it didn't last. Her dreams were overlain with uneasiness like the restlessness of a dark forest, of dark roots slithering through her mind, and then—

Falling. She was tumbling from the sky. The ground rushed up at her.

She sat up with a yell, sweat cooling on her forehead.

"What the hells?" Garth demanded as he sprinted into their campsite.

"She's been restless in her sleep," Trace said.

Karigan's heart pounded. She looked from Trace to Garth. "I think Megan's in trouble."

"What?" Trace said. "How do you know?"

Karigan wasn't listening. She threw off her blanket, pulled on her boots, and grabbed her swordbelt, and ran. "C'mon!" she told the others.

She led them back to the eagle statues. It was afternoon, much too early for Megan to be making her return. She looked desperately into the sky and along the slope of the mountain.

"Do you see her?" she asked the others.

"Karigan—" Garth began.

"I don't see her," Trace said, "but I see trouble." She pointed down before them where a dozen horsemen looked back at them. One had a bow and arrow, and he wasn't aiming at *them*.

Karigan looked up again, then saw her, Megan dropping from the heavens, limbs flailing.

"Breathe!" Karigan yelled. "Control!" She did not think Megan could possibly hear her, but she had to try.

An arrow sailed overhead toward Megan, but fell short.

"Control!" Karigan yelled again.

Megan seemed to get a hold of herself as she fell. She halted in midair and hovered. Karigan glanced over her shoulder and saw the archer aiming another arrow.

"Megan! Down now!"

The arrow swept by Megan, but much too closely. She yelped and started to plummet again, but this time it was much more controlled.

When she landed beside Karigan, she angrily blurted, "No one told me *they* could get up there!" And she promptly keeled over in a dead faint.

"They're coming," Garth said, drawing his sword.

"I've told Connly," Trace said.

Twelve against three. Megan, unconscious as she was, would be of no help. None of their special abilities would be of use, not even Karigan's. The sunshine was too intense and the high afternoon sun meant few shadows to aid her fading ability. She could almost hear Nyssa telling her to run, that she owed it to herself to save her own skin.

"Up the stairs," she said, "their horses can't climb up."

"What about Megan?" Trace asked.

Garth sheathed his sword and scooped up Megan and threw her over his shoulder. She hung limp like a sack of potatoes. As the horsemen rode up the final rise, Karigan led

Garth and Trace between the eagle statues and onto the Sky Stair. They needed a good place to make a stand and—

An arrow clattered along the rocks beside her.

The steps, laid by unknown hands so long ago, were too large to simply run up. They required extra effort and her thighs were already burning.

Another arrow clacked somewhere into the rocky ground behind them.

"We need cover," Trace said between ragged breaths.

"Garth!" Karigan cried. "Find cover, a good place to make our stand."

He bounded past them, Megan's body flopping on his shoulder. Karigan and Trace chased after him until he abruptly halted.

Karigan looked back and, through the scrub, could see their adversaries abandoning their horses down below and heading for the eagles. "Garth?"

"This way!" He sprang up several more steps and then off the stairs.

They scrambled up through scrub and low-growing forest, tripping over rocks and tree roots, crashing through branches. Eventually they emerged onto a ledge that was totally exposed, but Garth kept going to its far end where an outcrop forced them to a halt. They were trapped. The drop below them was breathtaking.

"All right," Garth said, "gotta be careful with this part."

"But there is nowhere to go," Trace said.

"Watch," he replied.

He pressed his body against the stone outcrop and carefully, with Megan still draped over his shoulder, inched around it, seeking purchase in the barest of finger and toe holds with only the long drop beneath him. It seemed to take forever for him to work his way around it.

When he disappeared on the other side, he said, "Easy. Just take your time."

Karigan could hear the men on the stairs searching for them. They didn't have time.

"Trace, go," she said.

"I don't know if I—"

"*Go.*"

Trace plastered herself to the rock wall, and murmuring to herself the whole time, sought the handholds Garth had used, which was difficult since he was so much bigger than her. She tried to straddle the part that jutted out to a point, but it was all taking much too long. The voices of their pursuers were getting close.

"Hurry," Karigan said.

"I—I can't," Trace replied. She was frozen.

Karigan started to look for someplace to hide. Could she survive jumping that far down? Climbing up would only expose her, and that imposing bald face offered little to hold on to. She concluded she'd have to face the twelve on her own, but then a hand reached around the rocky projection, grabbed Trace by the collar, and pulled her out of sight.

Even as the men thrashed through the scrub to the ledge, Karigan threw herself at the outcrop, not worrying about handholds. She scrabbled at the rock with hands and feet and slid.

"Garth!" she cried as she slid some more. He reached around and seized her wrist, and swung her onto a much wider ledge with an overhang above their heads. She sank to her knees panting.

"No place to go from here," Trace said, "but down."

If anything, the drop was even greater from here.

One of the enemy, clinging to the outcrop, worked his way around. Garth very simply stepped over, unsheathed his saber, and stabbed the man who fell from the cliff screaming.

"It *is* defensible," Karigan murmured.

Garth grinned, and waited for his next victim.

\prec ON THE LEDGE \prec

On the other side of the outcrop, their re-maining assailants talked quietly among themselves. Garth stood ready to skewer any who tried to work their way around.

Karigan wiped perspiration off her brow with her sleeve. "Can you make out what they're saying?" she whispered to Garth.

He shook his head.

Trace's glassy-eyed gaze was fixed on the distance. She was communicating with Connly. Megan stirred and moaned, but didn't come to.

Their foes quieted. There was the sound of shuffling as they moved about, then one said, "You're trapped, Greenies. We'll wait."

"That's too bad," Garth replied. "My sword is thirsty."

"What about the flying girl?" one of them said in a low voice.

"Shut up," the first man said.

"What flying girl?" Garth asked. "I didn't see any flying girl, did you?" he asked Karigan.

"Nope," she replied.

"If she flies again," the first man said, "we'll use her for target practice. Meanwhile, we'll just bide our time while you get hungry and thirsty."

Trace pulled Karigan aside and whispered, "Connly says they are going to help, but it'll be a while, probably under cover of darkness."

So, they would have to wait.

"Wh-what's going on?" Megan asked in a tired voice.

While Trace went to her side to check on her and explain the situation in a hushed voice, Karigan once more assessed their position. Their ledge stepped out from the bare face of the cliff. She had a good view of the valley in the distance, and the encampment beyond. It was no wonder why Connly wanted to wait until dark to cross the expanse.

The drop beneath her feet made her heart pound, and she moved back. She had no wish for her or her companions to dash themselves on the rocks below. Behind her, the exposed cliff face ascended to a great height. To scale it would first require surmounting the obstacle that was the rooflike over-hang, which meant clinging to the underside of the jutting rock at an impossible angle over the terrible drop, then clambering over it to reach the cliff face itself. There were people who could do that, find the least fissure or hollow to use as hand- and footholds, and crawl spiderlike up any wall, but she was not one of them. None of them were, and that was why Zachary had needed Megan's floating ability in the first place.

She then thought to call for Ripaeria, but if the eagle hadn't been allowed to help with spying on the pass, then she wouldn't be allowed to help them now. Karigan tried anyway, calling out with her mind. She was answered only by silence.

She shook her head, resigned to waiting, and sat beside Megan, who was beginning to look more like her old self. "What happened up on the Landing?" she whispered.

"There were men up there," Megan replied. "I didn't know they were there, and they didn't see me, either. They must be climbers unless they can float like me. Anyway, I had to pee, so when I got up to find a place, I saw them, and they saw me. They drew their swords and I panicked. I ran right off the mountain. It was like I forgot how to use my ability and I just kept falling." She shivered.

Karigan did, too, recalling the dream or vision that had awakened her. "Were you able to see into the pass? I mean, before you saw the men?"

Megan nodded. "I'll be able to tell the king something, if we ever see him again." She sounded more peeved by their situation than fearful.

She continued, telling Karigan that there was hardly

anyone to be seen in the pass. Maybe a dozen soldiers kept watch on the battlements and the gate of the keep. Civilians tended the few livestock or collected firewood outside. It certainly didn't have the look of a fully occupied garrison, she said. Her words confirmed what Softfeather and Ripaeria had reported.

It begged the questions, however, of where Second Empire's army had gone if it were no longer at the pass, and how it had left without their noticing. The possible answers were worrisome.

"I'm starving," Megan complained loud enough for all to hear.

Their enemies made much of their access to food and water.

"Come over here, Greenie," one of them said from his side of the outcrop. "I have a good meatroll here."

Megan pouted. "I'm tempted," she murmured.

Karigan was, too. She hadn't had anything to eat or drink since the previous night.

"They'd stick you with a sword before you got very far," Trace told her.

As the afternoon wore on, Karigan took a turn at guarding the outcrop. Garth and Trace sat with their backs against the mountain. Garth drowsed. Megan got up and down, up and down, and stomped around. She muttered something about being bored, looked up at the overhang, and down the cliff. She looked out into the valley.

"Hmph," she said.

Her restlessness was beginning to annoy Karigan. Apparently, it wore on Trace, too, who told her to sit down.

"No, I'm tired of sitting. I'm tired of all this."

She stepped off the ledge.

Karigan clapped her hand over her mouth so as not to shout Megan's name. Trace looked to be undergoing a similar struggle. Garth snored.

Megan floated up and past them and disappeared above the overhang. There was a chance she'd remain unseen by the enemy so long as she kept her current trajectory. Even if the enemy did see her, it was unlikely they'd get a good shot at her.

Trace got up and made her way to Karigan's side. She whispered, "What the hells is Megan doing?"

Karigan shook her head and shrugged. All she could figure was that the self-absorbed girl was put out by being stuck on the ledge and had had enough. At least her confidence in her ability had finally grown enough that she hadn't any qualms about taking matters into her own hands.

Trace then cleared her throat and pointed at the outcrop.

A hand was reaching around it. Karigan hacked at it, but the man to whom it belonged snatched it back just in time. The blade of her sword glanced off rock with a spark.

"Not quick enough," the man said with a laugh.

"Try that again and we'll see," she replied.

She scanned the sky above, then the valley below. No sign of Megan.

"Should we wake him up?" Trace asked, pointing at Garth.

"No real reason to," Karigan said. He'd kept watch for them as they had napped the morning away, then had used his special ability to find this spot. They might as well return the favor and let him rest while he could.

There was a *click-click-click* of a pebble skittering down the cliff face.

"What the—?" one of the enemy said. "Hit me on the head. Where'd it come from?"

There was more, like a handful of gravel tossed down from above. The men swore. The sound grew into more of a shower of dirt and stones as it slid down the smooth granite wall.

When the sound continued to grow into an alarming roar, Karigan wondered, *What has that girl done?* and said aloud, "We need to get back."

She and Trace tucked themselves beside the snoozing Garth beneath the shelter of the overhang. Rocks thundered down the mountainside, along with tons of soil and trees. Most did not hit their ledge, but a few bounced off the overhang. The men on the other ledge didn't seem to be faring as well if their screams were any indication.

Karigan thought they would make it, but then another boulder pounded the overhang. There was an alarming *c-r-r-r-ack!*

and a section collapsed onto their ledge. Rock shards exploded in every direction with the impact, and she buried her face in her arms to protect it.

"You all right?" she asked Trace.

"I'm shaking, but not hurt."

Karigan could hear the strain in her voice and felt much the same.

She didn't know how long the slide lasted, but it felt interminable. Finally, it ended much the way it had started, with stray pebbles rolling and plinking off the cliff. So much dust hung in the air that it was hard to see beyond their ledge.

"Good gods," Trace muttered. "You don't think Megan caused that, do you?"

Karigan rose, patted dirt off her uniform and hair, and, stepping over the rubble, tried to look around the outcrop to see what she could, but the dust was way too thick. She heard no signs of life.

When she turned back, she was startled to see Megan alight on their ledge with a very self-satisfied expression on her face.

"Well, I took care of that," she said. She dusted her hands off, and then promptly passed out into a heap.

Garth, who had slept through the whole thing, awoke with a yawn. When he saw Trace and Karigan staring incredulously at him, he asked, "What did I miss?"

They investigated as the dust settled, and discovered that the rockslide made their way back to the stair impossible. Garth, who was confident enough to edge around the outcrop, reported bodies buried beneath the rubble on the ledge, and at the bottom of the cliff. He couldn't say how many, and speculated that some of the men had gotten away. His speculation was confirmed when Trace spotted three men down in the meadow riding away.

"I got rid of them," Megan said when she came back to her senses.

"Yes, you did," Karigan replied, "and you almost got rid of us, too. Not to mention we are now stuck here."

"Oops. I didn't think about that. Too bad you can't float."

Karigan narrowed her eyes at the girl, thinking maybe she'd grown just a little too bold.

"I've told Connly we need a rope," Trace said. "Mistress Floaty here can go retrieve it for us."

As darkness fell, Megan did just that, meeting Connly and a contingent of Riders down by the eagle statues. She returned with a couple lengths of rope.

It was hazardous finding their way down in the dark, but none of them were keen on spending the night on the ledge, and Megan helped direct them from the air while Garth used his ability to find the best way.

When they reached level ground, Garth led them to the Sky Stairs, allowing them to descend the rest of the way without ropes. They met Connly and the Riders at the eagle statues.

"Well," Connly said, "so much for a stealthy scouting mission. I'm sure that rockslide was heard for miles around."

Megan could not have looked more proud.

⋙ THE SONG OF STEEL ⋘

S he was in.

　　She'd slipped in through the wicket of the keep's gate, following right behind those who had tended the livestock outside in the pass, and then through the second gate at the rear of the guardhouse. The plan was to retake the keep, and Karigan's part was essential.

She pressed her back against the inside of the curtain wall that, with its battlements and towers, sheltered the bailey and protected the keep. Her head pounded with the use of her ability and she longed to rest, but she must continue with her mission to find her way to the sally port located deep within Stormcroft Mountain. It was a door of escape from the keep, which could only be opened from the inside. A contingent of Sacoridian regulars would be waiting on the outside for her to open it.

Hinges creaked as the wicket was closed; then the drawbar clunked into place, securing the gate.

One of the guards shouted, "Gate is barred."

Chains and gears click-clacked and groaned as the portcullis was lowered. The entire process would be repeated with the secondary gate. Karigan did not have to see what was happening to identify the sounds as they were ubiquitous in fortified structures such as the castle. Soon the portcullis thudded into position and everyone, including herself, was locked inside. Her fate was sealed. There was no way out save the sally port, and to get there, she must enter the keep unseen and pass among whatever remained of Second Empire.

She took in her surroundings. Chickens pecked the

519

cobblestones near her feet. A dog followed his master into a small stable. Livestock lowed and bleated, and were so numerous that it was no wonder some had to be left outside. Somehow children found space among the milling sheep for a game of tag. Torches and lanterns provided some light, but there were enough shadows that it appeared the keep's occupants were being sparing in their use of whale oil, candles, and wood, which was not surprising in a siege situation. It was all for the better in terms of her fading ability remaining effective. Zachary would also distract the enemy by moving his army forward while she went about her business.

She gazed up at the battlements and spotted only a few guards silhouetted against the sky. Megan had been right—there was only a skeleton crew taking care of the defenses. It was always possible there were many more soldiers hiding in the keep, but she suspected this was not the case, and fervently hoped she was right.

She clung to the shadows of the curtain wall. Before entering the keep proper, she must cross the baily, and it would not do to scatter the chickens or cause the sheep to move in unexpected ways, or otherwise draw attention to herself. She set off with careful steps, wending her way through spaces between woolly bodies, cursing silently as she stepped in droppings. She stopped several times so as not to cause a stir among the milling animals, before finding another break through which she could slip. Fortunately, she didn't have to pass anywhere near the children and risk their detection. When she reached the front of the keep, she let out a long sigh and kept snug to the stone wall.

Getting inside the keep would be trickier. There was a lantern hanging by the door. She crept closer, halted when a man trotted outside and headed for the stable. After a quick glance at her surroundings, she darted through the open door. If anyone saw the blur of a person passing by the lantern, she hoped they thought it was a trick of their eyes. She had been given black to wear, lent to her by the Weapon, Erin, in hopes that she would blend in with the shadows even more. It was not the first time she'd worn Weapon black, but it felt strange not to be in her usual green uniform.

She stepped aside from the door and away from the torch-light. The entry opened right into a greathall. At the far end, a hearth crackled with a fire, and a woman tended a cauldron. Above the hearth, where some insignia of the garrison or the realm must have once hung, the dead tree of Second Empire had been painted in black. Stray drops of paint tracked down the wall from the branches in spidery runnels.

Another woman sat in a chair beside the hearth to breast-feed her baby. Others moved about among the tables and in and out the entrance to the kitchen. An air current carried the scent of baking bread to her and her mouth watered.

When Zachary and his officers had gone over the mission with her, they'd shown her the plans to the keep so she would know its layout. She had committed it all to memory. Bar-racks were on an upper level, and above that were more bat-tlements. This level was the kitchen and greathall, and other rooms that could be used as storage or expanded into more barracks. Below were more storage rooms, and the armory, cisterns, and access to the sally port. There were many more miles of corridors burrowed into the mountain that could shelter an army, but they had been closed off centuries ago, and were not of concern to her at the moment. Unless, of course, they were inhabited.

A pair of armed men approached. She held her breath un-til they'd gone well past her, then she darted into a side pas-sage that would take her to the stairs that plunged into the keep's depths.

Doors lined the passage. Some were closed, but others were open to chambers. With no windows, the chambers were lit with candles. They appeared to be occupied by families. A toddler screamed in one as his mother tried to calm him.

Karigan moved carefully, but almost stepped on the tail of a cat. The tom glared at her. Even if people couldn't see her, the cat could at least sense her.

"Sorry," she whispered, and she continued to edge along the corridor, avoiding people coming and going, and the flick-ering of the torches. It was a bit of a dance as she wove and turned and tiptoed all the way.

Finally, with a sigh of relief, she came to the end of the

corridor. A doorway led to stairs that spiraled downward. The walls were rough here, entirely carved from the rock of the mountain.

She stepped through the doorway onto the top landing of the stairs, and with no one in sight, she paused to catch her breath, and dropped her fading. The pain hammered through her skull from using her ability for so long. She stood there with her eyes closed to ease the ache. When she opened them again, a young boy with a ball in his hands stood before her. She had not heard his approach so severe was the pounding in her head. He stared at her, his mouth agape. Startled, she could only stare back at him.

"Who are you?" the boy asked.

Oh, no, she thought.

Yes, her other self said, stepping up beside the boy. *What are you going to do?* The darkness of the keep suited the other. It sculpted the planes of her face into sharp angles, shadowed the eye not covered by a patch. *You must kill him before he alerts everyone to your presence.*

Karigan's fingers twitched as she wrapped them around the hilt of her longknife. It was true, that if she did not kill him, the whole of the keep would be brought down on her and Zachary's plan foiled. They were depending on her.

Do it, her other self whispered. *A swift slash across his throat before he can scream.*

The small, fresh graves in the farmyard in Boggs.

The sound of children laughing down the corridor.

Could she take the life of a child to ensure the greater good?

Do it, her other self pressed. *They are not all innocent. Remember Lala.*

Karigan glanced at the other, the darkness that surrounded her, the eagerness in her face, and shook her head. She let go the hilt of the longknife.

I am not all dark, Karigan thought. Perhaps that was why the Eletians called her Winter*light*. They recognized the light within her, and to murder this boy who was simply in the wrong place at the wrong time would be to extinguish the light. Perhaps not all at once, but in a way that it could never be fully recovered.

She bent toward the boy and placed her finger over her lips. "Shhh," she said, and she faded.

The boy froze for a moment before tearing out of the stairwell and into the corridor. "MAAA!" he screamed at the top of his lungs.

Now you have done it, the other said.

Karigan ignored her and ran down the stairs, the boy's voice echoing behind her. With any luck, it would take some time for the adults to figure out what had upset him. Maybe they'd think it his imagination, or that he was lying.

She blew past doorways to other corridors that were sealed off as she descended and continued to the bottom landing. She paused, breathing hard. The landing opened into a rough-hewn tunnel with wooden posts and beams to brace the low ceiling. She would not have to use her moonstone for there were just enough torches to show the way.

She moved stealthily forward. Guards were more than likely stationed at the sally port. The tunnel angled downward, and she walked at great length, pausing now and then to listen for pursuit. Much to her relief, she heard none. Perhaps no one believed the boy, after all.

When the tunnel leveled out once more, she saw it, the sally port. It was a great steel-bound door, and it was indeed guarded. Two armed fellows diced before it, joking and laughing. So far, they appeared unaware of her presence.

She drew her sword and crept forward, then paused again and picked up a stone. She threw it as hard and as far as she could back in the direction from which she'd come. It clacked and clattered to the ground.

Both of the guards looked up.

"What was that?" one asked.

"Nothing, I expect," the second said, and they resumed dicing.

Exasperated, Karigan searched for a larger stone and hurled it as well. The guards looked again.

"That was something," the first said.

"Aye. I'll go check it out," the second said.

He stumped up the corridor toward Karigan and she slunk into the shadow of a post. A ring of keys clinked on his belt.

When he was past her, she hurried toward the door, then slowed as she neared the other guard. She halted to decide how to proceed. When he bent over to scoop up his dice, she knocked him over the head with the pommel of her sword. He fell face first onto the ground.

The other guard was still looking around up the passage, so she turned to the door. To her dismay, it appeared to have a complicated set of locks, and a crank-and-gear system.

"Hells," she muttered. The keys were with the other guard. She searched the unconscious fellow just in case he had his own set, but with no success.

She bounded back up the corridor with the hope of dealing with the guard the same as she had the first. She was running right up to him when he turned around.

"Whaaa—?" he began, and unsheathed his sword. "What are you?"

Hells. She was faintly visible in the light of a nearby torch. She sidestepped into darker shadow.

He swept his sword this way and that, walking in a circle. "I know you're there. Show yourself." The keys jangled on his belt.

When he turned away from her, she went after him and raised her sword to hit him over the head, but at the last minute, he turned again and saw her, and blocked her blow with his sword. This had now gone beyond knocking him out. She skittered backward and dropped her fading. Cold seeped through her veins. Could she do this? Fight without her back giving out? The doubts returned despite her good training sessions with Fastion and Donal. The fear of weakness, of failure.

What saved her was the guard seeing her in Weapon black. He froze in place and blanched. The tip of his sword dipped.

Then, in an instant, they both jumped to, swords clashing. The ring of steel was like a song to her, one she knew and loved. It took her back to a time when she was herself, back to a time before the Lone Forest and the whip of Nyssa Starling.

The guard, she thought, had believed himself overmatched when he saw her in black, and he now knew it as she made her sword sing. There was, in truth, nothing "honorary" about her ability, or the fierce joy that surged through her veins.

≈ COLD, LIKE STEEL ≈

Karigan whacked the guard's sword out of his hand. It clanged against the wall and clattered to the floor. She pressed the tip of her sword against his throat before he could draw his dagger. He swallowed hard.

"Slowly," she said, "toss your dagger aside."

When he hesitated, she pricked him with the swordtip. He obeyed.

"Now what?" he asked.

"Now we go to the door."

She forced him to lead the way, her sword now pressed against his back. Her other self was cheering her all the way. Karigan blocked the other from her mind as best she could.

When they reached the end of the tunnel, they had to step over the still-unconscious man to reach the door.

"Open it," she said.

"No."

"Do you think I would not kill you?"

"No."

"Then your choice. Death or the door. The door is opening whether you are alive or dead." She gestured at his key ring.

He hesitated. At that moment, the other guard stirred and moaned, then started to rise up on his elbows. Karigan bashed him on the head again with the pommel of her sword. She felt cold, but it was a good cold. Cold, like steel. Her other self wildly approved.

Maybe it was the harm she inflicted on his companion, or maybe it was something he saw in her expression, but the guard with the keys stepped over to the door and removed five of them from the ring and inserted them into various locks and twisted. As he worked, she discerned the sound of many feet and voices from some distance behind, and they were getting closer.

Uh oh, she thought. The little boy she'd encountered on the stairwell must have finally gotten his story across about the lady in black who could disappear.

Should have killed him, her other self said.

The guard heard the approach of his people as well, and paused his work. He looked smugly at her.

"Open it," she ordered.

When he did not comply, she jabbed the swordtip at his throat again.

"Go ahead," he said. "Kill me. I'll have the satisfaction of knowing you failed and my people got you."

He was not going to finish the job. The tunnel surely augmented the sound of footsteps and voices, and though she couldn't yet see the people, they would inevitably close in on her.

She saw a glint of brass concealed in his fist. Another key!

"Give me the key," she said.

He shook his head.

She stabbed his wrist.

"Ow!" he screamed, and dropped the key.

She grabbed it off the floor and swept by him while he tried to staunch the blood gouting from his wrist. She searched the mechanisms of the door for the sixth lock and found it near the bottom, inserted the key, and turned it. A glance over her shoulder revealed people, a whole lot of them, moving down the tunnel.

The keys had all been turned in their locks, so the door was ready to open. Now what? There was no latch or drawbar to manipulate, but there was a lever and the crank handle. She pulled on the lever and realized it was sort of like a brake on a wagon that helped secure the door in place. It was hard to shift. The people coming down the tunnel seemed to realize what was going on. They broke into a run, their footsteps turning into a thunderous charge.

At last she shifted the brake lever all the way. Then she went to work on the crank handle, turning it as fast as she could, making the gears in the door rotate in sequence. The people, a mob really, were yelling and waving weapons, and were nearly upon her like a wave about to break.

Painfully slow for all her turning, the door cracked open. Fingers and hands from the other side reached through the gap to help open the door faster, even as the hands of the enemy reached for her. The crank spun of its own volition as those outside pulled the door open. She was grabbed before she could reach for her longknife or sword. The mob pummeled and kicked and jerked her about. Someone raised a cudgel to smash her head. She struggled to break free, but there were so many hands on her, so many bodies pressed against her.

Then the door opened all the way, and the Sacoridian regulars from the Shore Unit poured inside. Suddenly she was released as the mob fled. The soldiers pounded right past her and pursued with swords drawn. A couple fell back to take custody of the door guards, binding the wrist of the one, and helping the other to his feet, before marching them outside.

Colonel Lord Pondmoor, attended by his aides, paused before her. "Good work, Rider," he said. "Are you well?"

"Well enough, sir," she replied. In truth, she was bruised and shaken, but it could have been much worse.

"You are instructed to proceed to the king's position to report."

"Yes, sir," she replied, then added, "Colonel, it is mostly civilians here—families with small children. I didn't see many true soldiers."

"All right, Rider, I hear you."

He then nodded to his aides and they set off up the corridor. She watched after him, hoping her words penetrated, that the Shore Unit would not be up against a disciplined resistance, and that a light hand would serve and minimize the number of civilians who were hurt or killed. It wouldn't be easy to stay the hand of eager soldiers who'd been waiting for this action for months. Colonel Lord Pondmoor, who was from her own province of L'Petrie, however, was a good officer, and his soldiers disciplined, and those two facts made her hopeful for a positive outcome.

She limped back down into the valley and toward the Sacoridian encampment. She discovered blood trickling from her nose and pulled a handkerchief out of her pocket to press against it. She maintained her fading all the way lest someone from either side choose to kill her first and ask questions later. The Sacoridian front line was marching its way up to the pass and she kept her distance. Zachary's command would be at the front line's previous location midway in the valley.

When she approached, she walked right past guards. She found an inconspicuous place behind command to drop the fading, then approached in a manner that would not startle anyone, as if she were merely walking up from the encampment.

When a guard finally challenged her, she said, "The king and his advisors are expecting me."

"Rider G'ladheon," the guard said. "Or is it Weapon G'ladheon?"

She gave the woman a thin smile. "Rider."

"Go ahead."

"Ah, Sir Karigan," Donal said as she stepped into the torchlight where Zachary stood with his advisors and officers. All were dressed in armor, though they were not confronting Second Empire directly.

Zachary turned, and she saw intense relief on his face. Quickly she recounted all that had happened, and he frowned when she told him how few armed soldiers there were in the keep.

"Birch figured it wouldn't take much to hold the keep," one of the officers said. "He didn't count on Rider G'ladheon. But where is his army? What is he up to?"

"There will be interrogations of the prisoners," Les Tallman said.

"You've done well tonight, Rider," Zachary said. "Go find something to eat and get some rest."

"Thank you, Your Majesty. I certainly will."

A rare smile flickered on his lips before he turned back to his advisors.

Loon was brought to her so she could ride the rest of the way to the encampment. She patted the gelding's neck and urged him into a walk. She was content to leave whatever happened next to the others.

Tegan shook her awake the next morning. Coming to was like trying to climb out of her own grave.

"That is the soundest you've slept since you got here," Tegan said, "and I'm sorry I had to wake you, but Connly wants to see you."

Karigan groaned and rubbed her eyes. "What's going on?"

"I don't know the details, but we're to get Loon ready for you."

Karigan dressed, and when she stepped outside, it was barely dawn. She found Connly outside Zachary's tent.

"Sorry to have to wake you after all you did last night," Connly said, "but you are being ordered by King Zachary, along with Trace and two Weapons, to make way for Sacor City." He handed her a message satchel. "Inside are messages from the king for the queen, castellan, and the general of the guard. Trace will be carrying a satchel with duplicate messages."

Two sets of messages, Karigan thought, in case one didn't get through. She accepted the satchel. Being accompanied by another Rider and two Weapons was unprecedented. "What is the situation?"

"After the keep was taken last night, several prisoners were interrogated. They revealed that Birch used some spell left by Grandmother to move his troops in stealth with the intention of taking Sacor City while our troops laid siege here."

Dear gods. It was exactly what she had feared, that Second Empire had somehow maneuvered past the king's army to take the largely unprotected city.

"We've had no word of enemy troops," Connly said. "Nothing to indicate an army on the move."

"Very strange," she replied.

"Yeah, it is."

She had her own ideas about how Grandmother's spell allowed Birch to achieve his disappearing act.

"It will be a race for you to reach the castle," Connly said, "to give warning. If you find the way into the city impassible, the king says you are to remember the Heroes Portal."

Ah, Karigan thought. The Weapons were going because the Heroes Portal opened only to the touch of a Weapon.

"It's one of the reasons you've been chosen for this mission," Connly continued, "along with the Weapons. It will be acceptable for you and the Weapons to pass through the tombs. You will have to do what you can to convince the caretakers to accept Trace's presence. A message for the caretakers from the king has been included in your satchel, as well, to help sway them. The king wants to be able to know what's happening in the city, and Trace is essential for that."

It was taboo for the living, aside from the caretakers themselves, royalty, and the Weapons, to enter the tombs. Trespassers were not permitted to leave and were made caretakers for the rest of their lives. The Weapons who guarded the tombs worked to prevent trespassers, but a few still got in, though infrequently. As an honorary Weapon, Karigan was allowed free passage through the tombs.

"I understand," she said. "What is the other reason?"

"What?"

"You said 'one reason' why I was being sent was because of the tombs. Was there another?"

"Oh. The other reason is that the king requested you specifically."

She wouldn't, she decided, pursue that line of questioning any further. "I assume the troops here will be preparing to move?"

"Yes. Some are already at work preparing. The rest will be ordered to do so at reveille. The Shore Unit will stay behind to mind the keep, and another, the Valley Unit, will deal with the prisoners. Harry has been sent to Lady Coutre's forces to inform them to continue to Sacor City."

Connly sent her to collect her few belongings and to have a quick bite to eat. By the time Trace and the two Weapons, Erin and Travis, were ready to go, dawn had broken and the camp was a flurry of activity, with tents collapsing in every direction, carts and wagons on the move, and irritated sergeants chivying their soldiers to step quick.

Zachary came to see them off. "You must ride hard," he told them. The Weapons each had remounts so they could keep up with the messenger horses. "There is no telling when Second Empire will reach the city, or if they're already there. Trace, you will keep me informed."

"Yes, Your Majesty."

"Very good. Off with you now."

And so they left their king behind. Karigan glanced over her shoulder, but Zachary was lost in the confusion of the dismantling encampment. They would have a hard march to the city, and it sounded as if she would see Zachary again only when battle came.

THE SELF-REGARD OF
A MAN

Birch gazed down at the body of one of his lieutenants. The man had cleaved a hatchet into his own skull.

"Throw a blanket over it," he ordered a subordinate.

The contrast of crimson blood against the white ground was shocking, and the sight of a man who had been such a stalwart officer would be, at the very least, unnerving to many others. Not that they weren't already unnerved. Grandmother had warned him about the white world when she gave him the spells. She told him lingering too long could cause madness, that there were other unknown dangers, too, but that the madness was the worst.

The lieutenant was just the latest casualty. Over a hundred of his people had gone mad with the visions the white world presented. Some of the illusions were seen by individuals and no others, and some were seen by all. No matter how much he told them that what they saw was not real, they lost their minds. And he understood why because he was not immune. One of the most disturbing visions he'd seen involved small white terriers, their whiskers dripping blood as they fed on his own corpse. Terriers that were the sigil of King Zachary's clan.

With the thousands who crossed the white world under his command, there were many illusions that appeared. Whatever the lieutenant had seen that caused him to cleave his own skull with a hatchet, however, had been for his eyes only.

"His mind was weak," Brother Pascal said.

Birch had come to appreciate the calm reserve of the commander of the Lions. The calm of all the Lions, in fact, was uncanny. Brother Pascal said daily meditation brought balance to their emotions. That, and no fear of dying. God, the brother had said, would do as God willed, and he served God.

They were a reassuring influence on many, even the horses, with their serene demeanors. The horses had been fine for some time, but then started panicking for no apparent reason, shaking in fear, shying at nothing. It was Brother Pascal who had suggested blindfolding them. With the blindfolds, they remained calm with steady hands to guide them. Birch had then considered blindfolding his troops, except for those needed to guide them, but discarded the notion as impractical.

"This is not a normal place," Birch said, "and the minds of ordinary men cannot endure."

He decided it was all Grandmother's fault. Preceding the events that led to her own demise, she had equipped him with spells to use as needed in the war with the Sacoridians, including one that allowed him to enter the white world, and a second to guide them. The guiding spell, an ever-unraveling ball of yarn, failed them. It was supposed to leave a strand of yarn behind for them to follow in order to reach their destination— in this case, a bridge to Sacor City. It worked well at first, but then just . . . died. They found the ball of yarn sitting there on the white plain, and no matter how many times Birch uttered the words of power, it would not go anywhere.

And so, he'd then pulled out a third spell Grandmother had given him, another used for wayfinding. It looked like a mass of knots to everyone else, but because it was keyed to him, he saw a salamander. A limp, pale salamander. At first, it, too, worked well, pointing its tail in the direction they needed to go, but then it also started to die. He did not discard it, for every so often, he'd get a weak reading from it. It would attempt to raise its tail, but then slump.

He suspected that with Grandmother's death, the efficacy of her spells had waned. Maybe if that dratted girl, Lala, hadn't gotten captured by the enemy, she could make these spells work properly.

So they wandered aimlessly in the strange null land for who knew how long. There was no sense of time here. When they came to bridges, he sent scouts across. A few of these ended in disaster. One pair of scouts returned gasping. Wherever the bridge had crossed over to, the air was too noxious to breathe.

At another crossing, the heads of his scouts were rolled back across the bridge. One scout made it back from a third, but he was so burned from volcanic magma that there was nothing the menders could do for him.

The situation naturally led to concern about their supplies, and if they had enough to feed and water everyone. When his officers offered their assessments, he ordered half-rations and all the slaves slaughtered. His soldiers, he decided, could be their own porters, and he permitted them one final use of the females before they were put down.

Water had become a grave concern until they came upon a fountain that spouted good, clean water. The tiered bowls the water flowed into were ornamented with etchings of horseback riders. When he examined them more closely, he couldn't help but think they resembled Green Riders. When everyone had enough to drink and every available container was filled, he ordered the fountain destroyed. His men pissed and defecated on the rubble for good measure.

He and his army trudged on. It was the only thing they could do regardless of whether they were headed in the right direction, or the opposite. He was determined they'd find their way to Sacor City, but he feared that so much time had elapsed as they stumbled around the white world that, in the outside world, King Zachary would have discovered Birch's ruse and moved his troops to the city to defend it before Second Empire even arrived.

A scream of anguish drew him from his ruminations. A display revealed itself as a mist drifted aside like a curtain. It was the slaves, as though they'd been resurrected, their grisly wounds oozing, their dead flesh even paler and more sickly with the opaque quality of the strange realm. This time it was they who did the slaying. Their executioners and tormentors watched as visions of themselves were killed in the same manner in which they had killed. A head knocked off, a knife to the gut. A throat gashed. Even worse for some was how the female slaves punished their abusers, castrating them and displaying the excised body parts before killing them.

"It's illusion!" Birch screamed at his unsettled soldiers. "It's not real."

He sent orders down the line for his soldiers to pull themselves back together, or he'd personally see to it there was a real reenactment of the killings and castrations.

Soon the tableau dissipated behind another curtain of mist, but not before a final vision of a woman who held her bloody trophy high over her head for all to see.

When they got out of this place, Birch thought, it would not be soon enough.

He called a halt so his troops could rest and the horses and beasts be tended to. There might be thousands with him, but in the vast expanse of the white world, they might have been a tiny group. The voices of his soldiers, the sounds they made, were muted. It was as if the white world were created to crush the ambitions and self-regard of a man, to render him as insignificant as a grain of sand in the desert.

Well, *he* was no grain of sand, and the white world would not defeat him. On impulse, he removed the salamander from his belt pouch and placed it on his palm. It looked languidly about for a moment before decisively rising to its feet.

Sacor City, Birch thought. *Show me Sacor City.*

The salamander flexed its tail, but then wavered, looked as if it might fall asleep.

"Sacor City," Birch growled at it.

It blinked beady eyes at him, then straightened its tail, slowly shifting it to the left and holding it steady.

"We're moving out!" Birch cried. "Hurry!" He was afraid the salamander might relapse into its torpor, so he did not wait for anyone else, but mounted his horse and charged in the direction indicated by the salamander's tail, adjusting his course as needed. He did not slow down until he came upon a bridge. The salamander pointed unwaveringly at it.

At last, he thought.

The bridge had two arches, but was made of the same

rough-cut granite as the others. He rode around it. There was a bronze medallion centered above the arches that depicted a slumbering dragon. He thought it odd, but dismissed it as his first breathless troops finally caught up with him.

Though he did not think the salamander had misled him, he sent a pair of scouts across the bridge. He could not, after all, endanger himself. He was the leader of Second Empire and, soon, to be the emperor once they broke the Sacoridians.

The scouts returned after only a few minutes, their expressions jubilant.

"The Scangly Mounds, sir," one of them declared. "The bridge leads to the Scangly Mounds."

There were cries of relief up and down the lines. The mounds were a little ways away from the city, but close enough.

"I want my officers up front," he said.

He would not make any sudden or imprudent moves. He didn't want to alert the city to their presence prematurely. Everyone needed to know their part, and exactly how they'd proceed.

"Go back out," he told his scouts. "Find out what you can about the city's complement and disposition, then report back."

"Yes, sir!" Their response was enthusiastic, and it was clear they were all too happy to leave the white world again.

He dismounted and handed his horse off to his orderly. He gazed at the salamander, and it gazed back at him with curious eyes. How intelligent was it? How alive? He did not care. He was done with it. He dropped it and mashed it into the ground with the heel of his boot. It was just knotted yarn, after all. It gave up a tiny puff of smoke and turned to ash.

Birch's mind was already on to other things, like how he'd take the city, then Zachary's bitch queen. As for the little heirs, he'd spent enough time around the Darrow Raiders to have come up with a few ideas.

✥ THE LOWER CITY ✥

The lower city overflowed with residents going about their business, and refugees from the countryside searching for work or a place to live. Anna did not think the refugees would have much luck—places to live had been taken up long ago, and there weren't nearly enough jobs to go around. She imagined a few ended up finding work with unscrupulous employers who paid a pittance for backbreaking labor and long hours. People were desperate for even these jobs. Though there had been few reports of Raider activity for a while, no one seemed eager to return home.

Maddie moved through the crowd with her ears laid back much of the time. She snapped at those who got too close, but overall, she remained remarkably steady. It helped that Lieutenant Mara rode her Firefly on Maddie's blind side. The gelding projected calm, and Maddie had warmed up to him as she had Condor. Every so often, he nickered as if to encourage her.

Anna was very glad she wasn't on this "message errand" by herself. She had not ridden Maddie into such crowds before. Lieutenant Mara considered it "training" for Anna, and a test for Maddie. Normally, Lieutenant Mara had explained, a new Rider would be taken out on extended training runs with a senior Rider before they were sent out alone. However, with most of the senior Riders away, either with King Zachary or on assignment elsewhere, the typical training routine was not possible.

"I think I have an answer," the lieutenant said, picking up on a strand of conversation they'd been having since the middle city. "I think she's jealous of you."

"Jealous!" Anna exclaimed. She corrected Maddie before the mare took a bite out of a cart horse they were sidling up along. "Why on Earth would Melry be jealous of *me*?"

"She always planned to be a Rider, assumed she'd be called, but she hasn't been. Her mother, of course, was relieved. The more the colonel didn't want her daughter to be a Rider, the more Melry wanted it. But here you are, suddenly brought into the messenger service, not because you were called—at least, not in the conventional manner—but because you were made a Green Rider by Colonel Mapstone herself. Something the colonel would not do for her own daughter."

"Oh."

Mara nodded. "You have the colonel's attention and special consideration in a way Mel has never had."

"In other words," Anna said, "she thinks I'm taking her place in her mother's heart when it's really the opposite. Her mother loves her too much to allow her to be a Rider."

"Exactly. And look, here's our turn." Mara reined Firefly down Potweld Lane.

While certain sections of the lower city might be tenements and warehouses, some tradesmen still retained their businesses there, including Arling Robinson, master saddle maker and leathersmith. All Green Rider tack and message satchels came from his shop.

"Look, I wouldn't worry too much about Mel," Lieutenant Mara said. "She's got a good heart, and in time she'll realize she's being wrong-headed."

Fortunately, Potweld Lane was quieter than the main thoroughfare of the Winding Way and they didn't have to shout to hear one another.

At least Anna now knew the crux of the matter when it came to Melry Exiter, the colonel's adopted daughter. Mel had been standoffish, even unfriendly to Anna's overtures while she'd been at the castle. Anna had been relieved when Stevic G'ladheon took her with him to go after the colonel. Her behavior had mystified Anna until now.

Master Robinson's saddle shop was a few blocks down the narrow street. The creaky, wooden buildings shouldered together like shivering old men and blocked most of the daylight from the street. Though it had not happened during Anna's lifetime, fire used to sweep through the ramshackle parts of the lower city on a regular basis. Some said they were set by the city's elite to rid themselves of lower class garbage, but the inhabitants always rebuilt. Those who could afford it used brick or stone, and Queen Isen had ordered the lord-mayor to organize fire brigades among the inhabitants to help put out fires—not just here, but throughout the city.

This section of Potweld Lane did not look as if it had burned in some time. Ugly gargoyles, covered in so many layers of paint that the details of their faces were obscured, peered down at her from the eaves.

They dismounted and tied their horses to hitching posts just outside the saddle shop. Lieutenant Mara paused before entering, and Anna followed her gaze across the street to where a pair of fellows appeared to be eyeing their horses. Their expressions were speculative.

"I wouldn't, lads," Lieutenant Mara told them.

They smirked and laughed at her.

She shrugged. "Consider yourselves warned."

She smiled and led Anna into the shop. The tinkle of a little bell over the door announced their entrance. Anna inhaled air suffused with the intoxicating scent of leather, a smell she had come to appreciate when it came to tending the tack of the messenger horses, and her fine riding boots.

An apprentice cleaned and oiled a new bridle, while another braided a set of reins. A journeyman carved intricate patterns on a side saddle. Reins, bridles, girths, and harness hung from hooks on the walls and from the rafters of the low ceiling. Saddles in various stages of creation were mounted on wooden horses. Leather scraps mixed with the wood shavings on the floor. Brasses and buckles and lengths of chain gleamed in crates and barrels.

The apprentice braiding the reins looked up. A startled expression briefly crossed her face, one Anna had seen on others encountering Lieutenant Mara for the first time. Her burn scars took them aback. People, Anna observed, had a hard time meeting the lieutenant's gaze, but then would sneak looks and stare, and even talk behind her back, when they thought she wasn't aware. Anna was pretty sure Lieutenant Mara was actually very aware, but was astonishingly good at concealing it, and managed to still treat such people with courtesy and patience.

"Can I help you, Riders?" the apprentice asked.

"Yes," Lieutenant Mara replied. "I have an order for your master."

The apprentice scampered off to a back room to fetch him. While they waited, Anna admired the craftsmanship on a saddle with fancy scrolling designs scribed into the leather. She ran her hand over it from pommel to cantle. She thought the leather so soft that it would melt beneath her fingers.

"Like it?" the journeyman asked with a smile.

"It's beautiful."

"It was commissioned by an aristocrat in the upper city, but he never came for it." He named how many gold coins she needed to buy it, and she jerked her hand away from it. He chuckled. "Truth be told, your Rider saddles may be smaller and plain, but they are just as fine and more durable, even without the exorbitant price."

An older gentleman wearing an apron then emerged from the back, his specs pushed up on top of his head. "Riders," he said with a nod of greeting. Then something caught his eye and he glanced out the window. "Those your horses? A lot of thieving around here lately, and the shortages of available horses make 'em worth something."

Anna gazed out the dusty window. The two fellows were casually crossing the street toward Maddie and Firefly. She glanced anxiously at Lieutenant Mara, who chuckled.

"Not to worry, Master Robinson," the lieutenant said. "They are *Green Rider* horses." And she handed him her list.

"Your colonel too good with her new rank to come around for a cuppa?" he asked. "Haven't seen her in a raccoon's age."

"She is," Lieutenant Mara said carefully, "away for a while."

"Hmph. Imagine that. Laren Mapstone actually gone away. She taking leave during all this upheaval? Not that she don't deserve it, but the timing's odd."

"Not exactly," the lieutenant said with a tight smile.

Master Robinson rapped his own head with his knuckles.

"Of course! She's off with the king's army. Not on leave at all. Figures. The day Laren Mapstone takes leave is the day all five hells turn to sunshine and flower gardens."

Lieutenant Mara remained conspicuously quiet.

"You tell her when she comes back to come see me and we'll have a cuppa."

"I'll do that," Lieutenant Mara replied.

"Well, then." The master propped his specs on the tip of his nose and silently read the list.

"I'll do the best I can," he said at length, "but we, like everyone else, are encountering shortages. I can barely get what I need from the tanners."

As he recounted all the materials that were hard to secure for his craft, Anna gazed out the window just in time to see one of the fellows mount Firefly. "Lieutenant?"

"Just a minute, Anna."

The gelding took it calmly and stood there even when the fellow jammed his heels into his sides.

Maddie, on the other hand, bit a chunk out of the shoulder of the other fellow as he reached to untie her reins. He screamed, and even as he started to run away, she kicked him in the buttocks and sent him sprawling across the street.

His companion persisted in ramming his heels into Firefly's sides. Firefly yawned, then lay down, and rolled on the man. The man dragged himself away, and when he stood, he had a decided limp. The two wounded men looked as if they wanted to exact some kind of revenge on the horses, but Firefly clambered back to his feet, and when the two got within range, both horses kicked. The men ran off.

"Huh," Anna said.

Suddenly, Lieutenant Mara was there peering out the window with her. She grinned.

"Shiftless transients hanging about," Master Robinson muttered, joining them at the window. "Lower city has become no better than a blighted slum, especially with these refugees mobbing the place. Customers I've had for years don't want to come down here anymore. I'd move uptown if I could, but space is scarce now. And the cost?" He shook his head. "Used to be decent here."

"I'm sorry the lower city isn't what it once was," Lieutenant Mara replied, "but those refugees are mostly just families who are scared and fleeing a war not of their making."

"I know, I know," the master said with a sigh. "Most are fine, I suppose, but there are those who take advantage of a situation."

"There are always people who will, no matter the situation, or where they are from. I'll warrant those two who tried to steal our horses were born and bred here."

"Aye, well, maybe next time you see the king or queen, you can tell them how it is down here for an honest tradesman. And don't you worry about your order. I'll get it made up as soon as I can. Don't want to lose the customers I've still got. I'll send word when all is ready."

They bade him farewell. Outside Lieutenant Mara patted both Maddie and Firefly. "Can't blame him for being concerned," she said, "but people are like to blame everything and anything on those refugees."

Anna knew. She had heard muttering around the castle blaming high prices and more crime on those seeking safety in the city. The realm had enough enemies, she thought, that people didn't need to go looking for more among those who were on the same side.

"And you two," the lieutenant told the horses, "you make a good team." Firefly nudged her pocket in search of a treat.

"You knew they'd give those thieves a hard time?" Anna asked.

"Messenger horses are pretty smart. They know enough not to be stolen. And, well, I'm familiar with Maddie's tendencies." Lieutenant Mara scrubbed beneath Maddie's forelock. The mare started to press her ears back. "Go ahead, be like that. I know you secretly like it." She gave the mare another pat and mounted Firefly. Maddie's ears went to point as if to ask where all that attention was going.

When Anna mounted up, Lieutenant Mara told her, "I'm proud of you and Maddie. You both did a very good job on the ride down. The traffic we encountered can be unnerving, but you both handled it well."

Anna was very pleased by the praise. The ride *had* been

unnerving at times, but it had helped to have Lieutenant Mara and Firefly there.

"This time," the lieutenant said, "I think Firefly and I will keep to Maddie's sighted side and see how she fares among the crowds."

"Yes'm," Anna replied, less pleased by this change, but it had to be done at some point, and it might as well happen while she had Lieutenant Mara and Firefly with her.

All was calm until they came to the end of Potweld Lane and reached the Winding Way. Anna and the lieutenant halted at the intersection, watching in astonishment people running this way and that, some dumping whatever they had been carrying, and shouting as they ran.

"This can't be good," Lieutenant Mara said.

There was too much confusion to see what the problem was.

"C'mon," the lieutenant said. "Let's go down to the gate and see what's going on."

Anna sucked in a breath and rode with her lieutenant into the fray. Maddie danced beneath her, but Firefly gave her a gentle whicker and the mare didn't go berserk. Yet.

The crowd became thicker and more chaotic the closer they got to the main city gate. There was a surge of people trying to rush into the city hauling their goods, leading livestock, and carrying children.

Anna read the lieutenant's lips more than heard her say, "What the hells?"

The horses plowed their way through the people, bumping them aside, stepping on a foot or two. Those who did not move got a chunk bitten out of them by Maddie.

When at last they neared the gate, they found the guards overwhelmed, unable to stem the tide.

"What's going on?" Lieutenant Mara yelled at the nearest guard.

"Army on the horizon," the man shouted back. "Doesn't look like Sacoridians."

A chill coursed through Anna's veins. If these were not Sacoridian or provincial troops, war had come to the city.

⇒ RESOLUTE ⇐

Lieutenant Mara did not wait. She jumped off Firefly and thrust her reins at Anna.

"Hold these," she said, and she bounded over to one of the towers that framed the gate, disappeared inside, only to reappear on top of the wall walk.

Anna could only watch as the lieutenant looked outward and talked to the guards. Meanwhile, panicked people tried to push their way through the bottleneck at the gate. Preventing the horses from being swept along in the current of the crowd occupied most of her concentration. She was not sure how long she kept this up before the lieutenant appeared beside her and reclaimed the reins to her horse.

"They're supposed to have a spyglass," she said, clearly exasperated, "but someone broke it."

"You can't tell what army it is?" Anna asked.

"Oh, we're pretty sure it's Second Empire," the lieutenant replied, and she mounted up. "If it were friendly, they would have sent messengers with standards ahead. But, I'm going to take a closer look." She clucked Firefly into the river of people.

The guards attempted to clear a path for her. "Make way," they shouted, "make way."

"Come with me," Lieutenant Mara told Anna.

The efforts of the guards proved largely ineffective, so it took a while for them to get through the gate and clear of people, and it was a relief when they did so, but it did not last long. Far afield was a mass that was the army. Anna quavered in her saddle at standing unshielded and open to the enemy, no matter that it was still far off. An urge came over her to return through the gate to the safety of the city walls, and to gallop back up to the castle and hide in the broom closet as she used to when the teasing by her fellow servants had gotten too bad. She chewed on her lower lip.

They rode out some distance, and the fear only grew on her. Tension built through her body, making her neck and head hurt. Sweat dripped down her temple. She felt naked out there with nothing between her and that army.

The lieutenant halted. "I want you to stay here," she told Anna. "I'm going to get closer and see what I can see. If I fall, or if I otherwise fail to return in, oh, a quarter of an hour or so, you ride back to the gate and on to the queen as fast as you can. Recommend to her that she send Ty to inform the king that Second Empire is marching on the city. Got it?"

Anna nodded. "Yes'm."

Lieutenant Mara flashed her a smile. "Wish me luck." Then she nudged Firefly into a canter directly toward what was very likely the enemy army.

Anna not only wished her luck, but fervently prayed to every god she could come up with. She watched as the lieutenant and Firefly grew smaller and smaller in the distance. The lieutenant rode too far away for Anna to clearly see what was happening, but she seemed to halt, then turned and rode crosswise for some time as if to gauge the extent of the army.

Anna worried her bottom lip again. Time crawled as the lieutenant scouted. Anna's concern mounted when she could no longer see her. She lost track of time. It felt like years had gone by. Should she ride to the queen?

Please come back, she thought fervently. She could not bear the thought of anything happening to the lieutenant.

Anna spotted distant movement, and there she was, the lieutenant cantering crosswise again. Anna exhaled in relief. Lieutenant Mara was, she thought, a true Green Rider, riding without a second thought right toward danger. She probably never thought about hiding in broom closets.

And then she was galloping back. When she reached Anna, her expression was troubled, and Firefly's neck and flank were lathered with sweat. He breathed hard from exertion. Anna was so relieved to have her back in one piece, tears filled her eyes.

"Let's get to the gate," Lieutenant Mara said.

They cantered back to where refugees were abandoning their tents and huts, but were trying to carry all their worldly goods into the city and safety.

Lieutenant Mara halted Firefly. "Anna, I want you to ride to the queen and inform her that the main army of Second Empire is indeed on our doorstep and marching hard. At a guess, they are three to five thousand strong. Do recommend that she send Ty to the king *immediately*. Pretty soon no one will be able to come or go. Got it?"

"What are you going to do?" Anna was afraid the lieutenant would ride off toward the enemy again.

"I'm going to try to keep these people moving through the gate, and help the guards as I can; then I'll return and report to the queen myself. Now, go. We are on borrowed time."

"Yes'm."

Anna guided Maddie into the mass of people at the gate. The guards tried to push and pull people aside so she could get through, but it was Maddie barging her way through and taking the occasional hunk of flesh here and there that opened the path for her. Once they were in the clear, she took a deep breath and asked Maddie for a gallop, a challenge any day on the Winding Way due to traffic, but Anna had been taught the quieter routes and short cuts for just such occasions.

Maddie surged beneath her, hooves clattering on cobblestones. Tenements and shops blurred by as she cut up one street, then another, and then back onto the Winding Way where she came to the city's second gate that would admit her into the middle city. She hauled Maddie to a walk, and though the gate was not jammed like the main entrance down below, she nevertheless cut the line and pushed Maddie through leaving a string of curses in her wake from others, even though it was widely known messengers had the right of way.

"What's going on, Rider?" one of the guards asked. "We're hearing rumors that Second Empire is coming."

"It's no rumor," she said. "They're here. Prepare yourselves for a possible panic."

Once she was through the gate, she didn't pause to carry on a conversation, but urged Maddie into a gallop again.

The middle city was more relaxed. Clearly the "rumors" were not yet widespread. There were shoppers on the streets, and few refugees. She passed a pair of men gossiping on the side of the road with their pipes in hand, and on a side street, a gardener trimmed a hedge. Shopkeepers cleaned their windows and arranged goods outside their doors. The tranquility would not last. She thought of Lieutenant Mara down at the main gate and hoped they'd get everyone inside before it was too late. How would the city defend itself when much of its military was off to the mountains?

She gritted her teeth as Maddie stumbled on a curve, but the mare kept to her feet and galloped as eagerly as before.

At the third gate, the guards did not ask about rumors and, being used to Green Riders riding in with important messages, waved her through. Maddie thundered across the moat bridge and up the drive to the castle entrance. A guard came forward to take Maddie, and Anna jumped out of the saddle and hit the ground running.

"Mind, she bites," she told the guard over her shoulder.

"Thanks for the warning, Rider," he called after her.

Anna missed a step. *Thanks for the warning, Rider.* It was the first time she truly felt like a Green Rider, galloping through the city to the castle, and the guard's response, his use of her title, "Rider," was like a confirmation. Despite the dire circumstances, she couldn't help but grin.

She hastened into the castle in search of the queen and found her in the nursery. She waited at the chamber's entrance with Weapon Ike and watched as the queen leaned over one crib, and then the other, before stepping outside and closing the door behind her. She nodded to Ike and he withdrew to a discreet distance.

"Hello, Anna," the queen said in a hushed voice. "The children are napping; otherwise, I would introduce you."

Anna supposed she should be flattered, but at the moment, she was not interested in babies, royal heirs or not, but passing on Lieutenant Mara's message.

"I've got an important message."

The queen looked incredulous. After all, Anna had not been sent out on any official message errands.

"Let us go to the sitting room. I don't want to wake the children."

Once there, Anna told the queen everything Lieutenant Mara had told her to say. The queen did not hesitate.

"Tell the Green Foot to summon my counselors and the general of the guard," she said. "Also, go to the lord-mayor and tell him to attend me, as well, and why. But first, tell Ty to prepare to ride."

Anna left the queen to do as she was commanded. A quick glance over her shoulder revealed the queen, a solitary figure, but standing straight and resolute. They were in good hands.

✈ YOLANDHE'S ISLAND ✈

Amberhill sat out of the drizzle in the mouth of the cave he shared with Yolandhe. Drips cascaded from the lip of the entrance and plunked into puddles at his feet. He watched Yap move about the shore looking for crabs and clawfish. The little dragon, Scorch, stuck close to his side and would not come anywhere near Amberhill. Amberhill couldn't say he was surprised as Scorch had been present at Beryl Spencer's death. Her murder. Even Yap, who had undoubtedly guessed at how she died, kept his distance, and there was fear in his eyes whenever Amberhill asked him for something.

He was not a murderer. For all the times he had climbed through windows to steal some trinket from a wealthy aristocrat, he'd never hurt anyone. It had been Akarion who had acted, but the guilt of it festered inside him. No matter how he willed the memory away, he could still feel the knife leave his grasp. He could still see Beryl Spencer's bewildered expression, and then the emptiness of her eyes.

"I am not a murderer," he whispered.

Akarion kept his silence, had been quiet since Beryl's death. Even before then. Not exactly *silent,* Amberhill amended. He sensed the dead sea king was up to something—scheming, and doing it in such a way as to shut him out.

He was doing his own scheming in turn, or at least thinking. It was easier to do with Akarion distracted. Despite his remorse over Beryl Spencer's death, it had led to the discovery that it wasn't just Akarion's will that gave him influence over the dragons. Or, at least, the smallest of them. He watched as Scorch gulped down a fish he caught in the shallows.

He decided to test his discovery, for if he could control the dragons on his own, he could challenge Akarion's hold on him. He focused on the ruby eye of his dragon ring and sought contact with Scorch's primitive mind. When he did so, it was filled with the pleasure of finding and eating fish, of bounding in the waves. *Fishes, more fishes!*

Amberhill took a deep breath and directed his will into the dragon, injected a command, then exhaled and pulled back just in time to see Scorch raise his tail and slap it on the surface of the water. Yap yelled out at the resulting drenching he received, and Amberhill laughed. He couldn't hear what the pirate said to Scorch, but he could only imagine.

"What do you find so humorous, love?" Yolandhe asked from where she knelt beside a flat rock on which she rearranged sea shells and bits of sea glass.

"Scorch just splashed Yap." Did she suspect it was more than that, that he'd succeeded in controlling a dragon without Akarion's influence? If so, she kept her peace. The real challenge would be to try something with one of the other dragons. The idea, however, gripped his insides with icy fear. Those dragons were big, big and strong, and strong-minded. Little Scorch was as nothing by comparison. There would be no innocent tail splashing. Their minds were keen and brutal. He twisted the ring around his finger. It had to be done. He had to exert control over the big ones, especially the black. He was dominant, he was the fiercest. He kept the others in line.

He would find a way to eliminate them as a threat, and then he would deal with the ring.

"Yolandhe," he said, "do you know how my ring came to be made? Who created it? Was it Akarion?"

She looked up from a piece of light blue sea glass she held cupped in her hand. "I do not know. It was not Akarion. There were many things made back in the days when the world was new, long before the Sacor Clans worshipped their star gods."

He'd not heard them referred to as "star gods" before, but it was apt. Except for Aeryc.

"Aeryc is of the moon," he reminded her.

She shrugged.

"Do you know how I might rid myself of the ring? Destroy it?"

"Why would you wish such a thing?"

"Don't you think an object this powerful is dangerous in the wrong hands?"

She gazed blankly at him. "It's in your hands. You are Akarion's heir."

"I mean, if it gets in someone else's hands."

"It is in your hands."

He wasn't going to get anywhere with that line of questioning. "Back to my original question. Is there a way to unmake it?"

She placed the sea glass in the center of her rock, then turned back to him. "The bearer must sacrifice himself in the fire of a dragon."

That certainly was not what he was hoping to hear. He loved his skin too much for immolation by dragon.

"Is that the only way?"

"I do not know."

Amberhill watched once again as Yap and Scorch combed the shoreline. Yap was dancing around and waving his hand above his head with a crab claw clamped to his finger. Scorch splashed around him like a happy, eager puppy.

Ouch, Amberhill thought, but he couldn't help but laugh.

Then the shadow of all that Beryl Spencer had told him of the future, what he'd done to her, and what he must attempt to prevent the destruction of his homeland as he knew it, fell over him. This was no game, no evening of climbing garden walls to seek some pretty trinket. No, this was the future of his home, and the preservation of his soul. He would not forget the promise he made at Beryl Spencer's graveside. He would not allow Akarion or Mornhavon to use him as a puppet for their conquests.

⇜ YOLANDHE'S ISLAND ⇝

The fog receded, revealing small islets and rock ledges down below. Amberhill perched on the cliff edge, watching waves froth and foam in shades of green and blue around them. They were not, of course, islets, and mostly not rock ledges. No, they were dragons at rest. One drowsed nearby on the island hidden in the woods, burrowed beneath leaf and loam, but the rest lazed in the ocean. There were nine all together, if one counted Scorch.

He peered around into the woods behind him as if someone might creep up on him and observe what he was up to, but Yap remained down by their camp with Scorch, and Yolandhe was walking the far shore. Akarion was quiet.

He remembered that first time he'd walked out to this cliff with Yolandhe. There had been "shadows" in his mind that he had not understood. Yolandhe had already introduced him to his "inheritance" in the cavern, but this part of it had eluded him and his dreams had become theirs, dreams of flying, of swimming, and of resting in the earth. Yolandhe had brought him here so he would understand the presences in his mind, but had recommended he not awaken them. Amberhill soon understood why, when Akarion trespassed and forced the issue.

Since then, he and Yolandhe had visited this place so he might accustom himself to entering the minds of dragons, but always with Akarion taking control, and Yolandhe there in case things got out of hand. He had managed to control Scorch on his own, but one of the big ones? Scorch was one thing, and they another. Daunted, he almost turned away to head back to his cave. Then the promise he had made to Beryl Spencer came back to him and shamed him into standing his ground.

He clenched his hands into fists. Cool damp air blew his unruly hair back. He could do this. He *would* do this. He had to, and he had to try without Akarion taking over. He unclenched his right hand and drew it up so he could gaze into the ruby eye of the heartstone, his dragon ring.

Gazing into it was not enough. He must think into it. The color red infused his senses, glistened in his mind's eye. He reached out to the somnolent minds filled with vague image-thoughts of pursuing prey, napping in the sun, skirmishing for dominance, and mating—all very much the simple ruminations of predators. As they grew aware of him in their minds, however, a more complex emotion colored their perception: hatred. Hatred for *him*.

The intensity of their regard almost caused him to quail and break off contact, but he caught himself. He could not show weakness. Showing weakness could very well prove fatal. As Akarion would have done, he forced his will into them.

Attention, he commanded them. It was more the feeling than the actual word they understood.

Heads arose from the waves to watch him with glistening eyes. They were actually too far off to see their eyes in detail, but he could well imagine the jewel facets of irises, and the slit pupils.

To his horror, the head of the big black rose up right in front of the cliff he stood on. The dragon's snout was longer than he was tall. He wanted to run, felt faint. The dragon's exhalation washed over him with visible ripples of heat. Sweat broke out on his forehead. It was no time to swoon or panic.

Go, he ordered the black, to put distance between them, and he directed him to an offshore ledge.

The black regarded him for several ominous heartbeats and seemed to consider whether or not to obey, but then he slowly slid down back into the water at the base of the cliff. He took his time swimming out to the rock ledge, almost casually.

Amberhill's legs shook and he feared they wouldn't

support him. He wiped the sweat off his brow with the back of his hand. One by one, he ordered the dragons out to the rock ledge. The others moved more quickly as their leader was already there awaiting them. When the eight were assembled, they gazed back at him, their minds poking into his even as he tried to concentrate and push his will into theirs.

He went through a series of exercises with them as Akarion would, making them swim to and fro, fly in low interlooping circles and spout fire. They grudgingly obeyed him and he was beginning to feel confident. It wasn't so hard after all. He even directed them to do tricks. He made the silver do a somersault in the air, and the red one take a deep plunge from among the clouds down into the water. He laughed and clapped his hands. This wasn't so hard at all. It was even amusing, and he threw his arms wide open to the sky, elated by the power and strength of mind he possessed to control such monsters.

A ship on the horizon happened to catch his gaze as the red did a final backflip. He shaded his eyes as he watched it make way. Three masts, as far as he could tell. It would never come to the archipelago; they never did. Many ships passed by, but the lore and oddness of the islands, and the difficult currents, caused superstitious sailors to steer well clear. Nothing he could do would draw them in for a rescue.

After watching the ship for a while, he realized his mistake. Because he had noticed the ship, so had the dragons. They launched from the water and flew in an arrow formation in its direction.

"No!" he shouted. "No!" But while his attention had strayed to the ship, they'd slipped his control.

He tried to gather his wits and stare into the ruby so he could reconnect with their minds, but he was pushed out by their excitement.

Return, he ordered, throwing his will into it.

They did not obey.

He could only watch as they shrank the farther away they went. They circled the ship. Their spouts of flame were mere sparks at this distance. It would look much different from on board the ship's deck. As the sails burned, he could only imagine the panic of the crew. Were there others on board? Passengers? Possibly families with children?

"No," he whispered.

He could not see what the dragons did to the people, and for this he was grateful. There would be no escape if the dragons decided they were tempting morsels. They hovered and lingered as the rest of the ship burned. Sometimes they dove into the water, no doubt after anyone who decided to take their chances in the ocean.

He hid his face in his hands. It had all gone so wrong. He had not meant for this to happen. The idea was to *prevent* this kind of thing.

"Oh, gods," he murmured, watching the smoke rise into the sky as the remains of the ship sank.

Amberhill now understood how the dragons were weapons of terror, weapons of destruction. Could they truly be controlled? He shuddered for what it meant for the mainland, for Sacoridia, should Akarion's monsters decide to leave the island for new hunting grounds.

⇨ UNFOLDING ⇦

No matter how hard Enver focused, no matter how he opened himself to the voice of the world, the murmur of *other* voices intruded like snakes slithering into his mind. The patch of moss in the woods he sat upon was some distance from the cottage, but he still heard his father conversing with a visitor.

Since his arrival in Eletia, the only way he could find peace for himself was to practice his meditation, to travel into the world of the aithen'a. He was watched so he would not attempt to leave to go in search of the Galadheon. He'd also been forced to make promises that he would not. It was not easy to sense her from Eletia, for the forest had its own natural energy that inhibited the outside world, and even more so, the unknown calling that was drawing Eletians home from far lands interfered with his search. Still, he was able to perceive she was alive, and he must content himself with knowing that much.

As the voices of the men continued to annoy him, he decided to give up his meditation and eavesdrop.

". . . a feeling I had about her from the beginning," his father, Somial, was saying.

"Yes, unpredictable, and the honor is unprecedented. The prince will not explain the reason, and so we must wait until it becomes apparent."

Somial's visitor was Ealdaen, Enver guessed. It was hard to miss the ancient tones in his voice, though a mortal, perhaps, would not recognize it with their less keen hearing. He wondered who they were talking about.

"So, are we to call her Cearing Asai'riel?" Somial asked.

Winterlight, Enver thought.

"That is so," Ealdaen replied. "The prince deems 'Galadheon' inappropriate given her status."

Enver stood. They were talking about *her?* He strode through the woods until he came to the cottage. His father and Ealdaen sat outside enjoying the sun beaming through the leaves upon them.

"My son," Somial said, "you have come to join us?"

"What were you saying about the Galadheon?" he demanded. "How is it we are to call her by this other name now? This Cearing Asai'riel?"

"*Dama* Cearing Asai'riel," Ealdaen said.

"Dama?"

"If you had stayed here as I had suggested," Somial said, "you would know. It seems our friend was here not so long ago."

"She was *here?*"

Ealdaen nodded. "It is quite a story, young Enver. Have a seat and I will tell you."

Enver sat upon a low-growing cedar trunk that had turned itself into something of a bench. Ealdaen proceeded to tell a tale of whisper wraiths, a trial, and a surprising announcement from Prince Jametari.

"She is of the House of Santanara?" he asked incredulously.

"So it would seem," Ealdaen replied.

"How can this be?"

"How the prince came to this decision is a great mystery."

Enver could not believe what he was hearing. The Galadheon, now Winterlight, was Eletian and a member of the highest house in the land. She'd been there, but he had arrived too late.

"When will she be back?" he asked. If she were now of the House of Santanara, she must return.

Ealdaen gazed at him with sharp eyes. "I do not know the answer, or if we should even expect her return."

"But how can we not?" Enver demanded.

"There is much that we cannot know."

A breeze stirred leaf and bough above with a restless sigh.

"Can you at least tell me how she was when she was here?"

"She seemed well enough to my eyes," Ealdaen replied, "but Gweflin would know more."

Enver knew of the healer, Gweflin, though they had never met.

"A very fine healer she is," Somial said. "The Asai'riel was in very capable hands."

Enver stood. Gweflin's cottage was half a day's walk.

"Where are you going, my son?" Somial asked.

"To visit Gweflin and introduce myself."

"Why not wait for another time?" Somial said. "There is no rush."

"I am going," Enver said defiantly, "and you will not stop me."

He put words to action and strode down the path and away. The Galadheon had been here, and he had missed her, but Gweflin could tell him what he needed to know. In his haste, he missed the significant look passed between Somial and Ealdaen, and the slight smile on his father's lips.

"This was much too easy," Somial said.

"I warned Gweflin to expect him," Ealdaen told him, "as you asked."

"May his time with her cure his obsession," Somial replied.

Enver walked relentlessly, pausing only to sip stream water from his cupped hands. He had left without his pack, without even a cloak, but this was Eletia, and if he'd had a need, he'd find it in the land or be provided what he required by the generous folk of the wood. It was unlike the outside world of the mortals where everything required payment and the people jealously hoarded their belongings, even when they could help someone in need.

Night had fallen by the time he found the pathway to Gweflin's cottage. As he approached, he found a woman kneeling in an herb garden.

"Enver, Somial's son," she said as she clipped a sprig of evaleorn. "I have been expecting you."

He stopped short. "You have?"

"Come, you are in need of a repast, for I see you have walked long and hard to reach me." She stood and, with a basket of herbs in hand, led him into the cottage.

As she set out food on the table, he asked, "How did you know to expect me?"

"Ealdaen told me."

"Ealdaen? Why would he think I would be coming here?"

She placed a loaf of fresh-baked bread on the table, as well as a crock of honey butter. "Your father wished it."

"My father? I don't understand."

"It seems he thinks you are in need of healing."

"I am not, for I suffer from no illness or injury. I have come to ask you about the time you spent with the Sacoridian woman, the Galadheon, though now she is called Asai'riel."

Gweflin sat beside him. "Yes, I expected this as well. I cared for her back while she was here. She even asked about you."

"She did?"

Gweflin nodded.

He warmed with pleasure. "How is she? How did she look?"

Gweflin patiently described her sessions with the Asai'riel and how impressed she was with the healing he had done. It had surely been a mortal wounding, she said, if he had not intervened. He barely tasted the greens and the herbed roast grouse she served.

"The Asai'riel seemed a remarkable person for a mortal," Gweflin said, "and though troubled as anyone would be after what she'd gone through, she was doing well."

Enver gazed at the bread in his hand. "Thank you. It eases my heart to hear."

"I can tell," Gweflin said, "but it is not enough, is it?"

"I am not allowed to leave Eletia to go see her," he replied.

She nodded as if it was exactly what she expected to hear him say. "Which is why your father is concerned, and why you need healing."

"I need no healing as I stated. I don't know what you are talking about."

"Deep inside," she replied, "I believe you do know. We

who heal are infamous for not treating ourselves as well as our patients. We neglect our own needs. And sometimes those needs are hidden from ourselves. You have not completed accendu'melos, and your interest in the Asai'riel has in turn become an obsession."

"She was present when it came upon me." He did not know whether to be angry, amused, or unsettled by Gweflin's insight. He decided to simply accept it. "I sent her away," he continued, "because I could not bear to harm her when the accendu'melos overtook me completely."

"It was honorable of you to do so. Mortals are not up to the rigors of accendu'melos, and it would have been even more unpleasant had it been forced upon her, a heinous act. It is remarkable you restrained yourself when every instinct, every fiber of your body and impulse in your mind, urged you to force yourself upon her." She spread honey butter on her bread. Her fingers were long and graceful. "Unfortunately, it has left your time of unfolding unfulfilled. You cannot progress without it. If you do not attend to your need, if you continue to hold it locked up inside you, the bitterness will consume and destroy you."

He knew. "But the Asai'riel—"

"She is far away, and as I understand it, she does not hear the song that is you."

To hear Gweflin say it was like shards of glass cutting him up inside.

She placed her hand on his wrist, and as soft, warm, and gentle as her touch was, it sent shockwaves through him.

"Are you suggesting—?"

"I am recommending that you allow me to heal you." Her hand moved up his arm and his pulse quickened. "You must complete accendu'melos."

"I do not know. I—"

"I am a healer. Let me heal you."

"But you do not know me," he protested.

"I know enough. You are suffering, and I can alleviate it."

His thoughts raced. He could not think clearly. His sense of her heightened, the scents of soil and herbs, the softness of her touch. Desire pulled at him as accendu'melos awakened in him, pressure building in his loins. Her song called out to him. Not in the same way as the Asai'riel, but with openness and compassion. Before he knew it, they were standing and she was in his arms.

"I should not," he said. However, he did not think he could stop himself, not this time.

"Shhh," she said. "It is time for healing." She kissed him, her lips sweet with honey.

Her kiss awoke every nerve within him to even the lightest feather touch, and he realized he could feel what she felt, as well, his lips on hers, how her hand traced the muscles of his back. He shivered.

"Yes, Enver," she murmured, "let the healing begin."

Accendu'melos took him then, and he lost all sense of himself, except for the need to satisfy the desires of his body. Over the days that followed, there was no telling where he began, and Gweflin ended, they were so entirely melded. At times, her assistants came to check on their welfare and ensure that they drank of cordial and water to sustain them. They also tended any wounds from the more intense portions of their coupling, for pain was closely allied with pleasure, but mostly, Enver was oblivious to their presence.

Still, even as he and Gweflin shared in passion, one small part of his mind remained fixed on the Asai'riel, his Karigan, and at times he imagined it was not Gweflin whom he held in his arms.

Loon's strides were unflagging as he ran through the countryside. If Karigan didn't make him slow down and walk, he'd run his heart out, run to exhaustion. It was as if he understood the urgency of the situation, and she thought he probably did. He was, after all, a messenger horse.

Even Trace's Curlew had a hard time keeping up with him. The fine-bred horses of the Weapons tended to fall behind.

"Haven't done all-out riding like this in a while," Trace said as they slowed to walk to rest the horses. A ground fog drifted from the woods into the road and twined around the legs of the horses.

"The colonel will be very pleased to hear how well Loon has performed," Karigan replied, and she slapped the gelding on the neck. "Might even give Crane a challenge the next Day of Aeryon race."

"Now that would be something to see."

They both fell silent, neither daring to broach the subject of the colonel's abduction and whether they'd actually see her again.

In time, the Weapons caught up, their black horses heaving and lathered in sweat, but neither spoke. They simply fell in behind, willing to let the Riders set the pace. Karigan and her companions were making good time, even if the Weapons were slowing them down slightly, and they'd already passed Oxbridge without stopping two days ago.

Throughout their journey, the roads had been eerily empty. Occasionally they encountered a traveler or two hastening along as if all the demons of the hells were pursuing

562

them, but mostly the absence of travelers was notable. It was like most everyone had gone home to sit out the storm, and Karigan supposed that was an appropriate way of looking at it.

At night they had made simple camps alongside the road and took turns keeping watch. There was even a Rider way-station a little way off the road where they spent one night. This evening they decided to make camp in a clearing Trace had known about. It had been used by other Riders, and she had learned about it from Connly. It was nicely screened from the road, had a firepit, and there was a stream nearby in which they could refresh their waterskins.

Karigan drew final watch and so bedded down early, looking forward to an almost full night of unbroken sleep. Her dreams did not cooperate, of course, and she launched from one nightmare featuring Nyssa to another. She was fighting, constantly fighting.

Nightmare merged into reality when someone clamped a hand over her mouth and pinned her to the ground. She kicked hard and struggled, as helpless as she had been in her dreams.

"Easy, Sir Karigan," came a whisper. "It is me, Travis."

It took a moment for his words, and understanding, to sink in, and when they did, she stopped struggling, though Travis was likely to have some nasty bruises. They had no fire, so it was difficult to make out his features as he knelt over her.

"You were crying out in your sleep," he continued, "and we have company. I am going to remove my hand from your mouth, all right?"

She nodded, and when he released her, she sucked in a deep breath, then rose to a sitting position.

"What's going on? What company?" she whispered. Then she heard it, raucous laughter in the near distance.

"A group of raiders," he replied. "Darrow Raiders."

Someone else came over. Trace, Karigan thought, because her footsteps were not as silent as Erin's would have been.

"There are eighteen of them." It was indeed Trace who spoke. "They've a couple female captives."

"What is the plan?" Karigan asked.

No one answered her at first; then Travis said, "To remain inconspicuous. Erin is keeping watch."

"That's not exactly a plan," Karigan replied.

"It would be hard for us to move without their noticing."

"Is Torq with them?"

"I didn't see anyone with that skull tattoo on their face," Trace replied.

A woman screamed from the direction of the Raider camp.

Karigan grimaced. "Don't you think we should help the captives?"

Travis paused again before responding. "It is important that your messages reach the queen, and we are outnumbered."

He was right, of course. They had to ensure they reached the castle with the king's messages. But another scream rattled her down to her marrow.

"Travis . . ."

"Sir Karigan, I don't—"

There was the sound of rustling vegetation, and a thud.

"I will go check it out," he said.

After he left, Trace whispered, "You don't think we can take on eighteen of them with just four of us, do you?"

"They *are* Weapons," Karigan said. "They'd go right through those Raiders like a scythe." Then amended, "More or less."

"You're a Weapon, too," Trace said.

"Only honorary, and my swordwork isn't what it once was."

Travis returned. "It looks like we're going to have to take some action," he said. "Erin killed one who wandered too close to take a piss. They are going to miss him soon."

"Well, then," Trace said, "that leaves only seventeen."

"My ability," Karigan said, "might come in handy."

They sketched out a plan, and indeed, Karigan's ability would prove useful, especially in the dense fog of the night. Trace's part in the plan was to sit it out, astride Curlew, and to ride with the messages in case things went bad.

Karigan stepped through the woods as quietly as possible. Water dripped from leaf and bough, and the ground was soft beneath her feet. The smoke from the Raiders' fire smelled of wet wood. They did not appear to have sentries on watch, and they probably would not have heard a herd of horses the way they were carrying on, but she was not about to take unnecessary chances.

She stepped just outside the light of their fire. They were passing around a jug drinking whatever it held, and trying to make their two captives dance by the fire. One of the women was holding her ripped chemise closed. The other was in tears.

"Dance," the Raiders shouted. "Dance and show us your flesh."

"I'll make 'em dance." A Raider rose and picked up a burning stick from the fire. He was about to light one of the women's skirts on fire.

Karigan dropped her fading and stepped into the light. "Hello. You're having a party and you didn't invite me?"

They stared agog at her. So did the captives.

One of the Raiders shouted, "It's that Greenie!"

While Karigan held their attention, Travis and Erin were cutting down some of their number who stood near the fringes of the campsite.

"Did you miss me?" she asked.

Apparently they had, for they jumped up to grab her.

"Run!" she yelled at the captives, and then she disappeared. The Raiders milled about in confusion as their captives ran off.

She moved to another location in the opposite direction the captives had gone. "Over here!" she called. Her appearance was brief before she disappeared again. The Raiders ran after the sound of her voice, and when the first one neared her, she drove Colonel Mapstone's saber through him. She thought how satisfied the colonel would be to know that her sword was being quenched in Raider blood.

She moved to a new location and called out again. The fog carried her voice in unexpected ways, seeming to make her appear closer or farther away than she was. The confused Raiders changed direction. As Karigan lured them from place to place through the woods, Erin and Travis trailed and killed them. It turned out to be almost too easy to distract and kill them. Their numbers declined rapidly. Without their leader, the Raiders were not terribly bright. Before long, the woods were still and she withdrew her sword from the gut of the last Raider. Erin and Travis had already made their way back toward the campsite, and she made to follow, fully visible but for the dark and fog. It was a mistake. One of the Raiders had been waiting in hiding for her and struck out.

She raised her saber just in time to fend off his blow. Her opponent was an amorphous shape, and in the swirl of fog, not only was sound and vision distorted, but perception as well, which made catching his blows difficult. Even worse, evergreen boughs fouled her swordwork and made defense all the harder. She slipped on a mossy rock and nearly fell. It would have been all over then if she had not saved herself.

"I remember you, Greenie," the Raider said. "Escaped, didn't you. Well, you won't this time."

Karigan followed his voice and went on the offense, but he was slippery. Her blows merely glanced off his blade. His footwork was good, steering the course of their bout, drawing her away from the campsite just as she had done with the others.

Then he stepped toward her, taking her by surprise. She jumped behind a tree just in time to avoid a blow that would have cleaved right into her neck. He seemed to have a sixth sense about what she would do next, and it made her uneasy even as they traded blows. Her new, hard-won confidence began to erode.

You were never that good to begin with, Nyssa whispered in her mind.

Hearing that voice she had not heard in so long caused her to take a misstep on a tree root that threw her balance. The Raider's sword bit into her upper arm and she cried out.

"Karigan?" Trace called out in the distance.

Karigan was so disoriented she could not tell which direction was which, and she could not answer for the Raider attacked and she barely held off his fierce buffeting. He pressed her back, and she feared she'd fall over a branch or rock, or into underbrush, and if that happened, she was finished.

She was flailing and dancing about, allowing her assailant

to command the terms of their contest. He knocked her back, and her wounded arm slammed into a tree trunk. She cried out again as pain jarred her from her fingertips to her shoulder. She almost dropped her sword. But the pain also seemed to awaken something in her, a memory of her sword training, a lesson from long ago. Arms Master Drent had hobbled her ankles to prevent the dancing and flailing, and to teach her the art of minimalism. He had taught her that she only need move when required, which conserved energy, enhanced precision, and allowed the swordfighter to exert control.

She took a deep breath and invoked stillness. Stillness inside, and stillness without.

"What's wrong, Greenie? Giving up?"

He must have smelled blood because he lunged. She did not quail. Instead she held firm and defended herself with precision. Gradually she gained control of their engagement. She made him come to her in the way she wanted, and when he did, she battered him with an array of forms he could not keep up with. Her sword slipped through his guard more than once, slicing him. She heard him gasp with effort. His footing grew unsteady and his sword work desperate.

Karigan pressed him and he fell. She discerned in the dark that he was holding his hands out to forestall the killing blow. She raised her sword in triumph to deliver it, but as had happened before, her back betrayed her. A muscle, or some other tissue, that had been damaged by the whip of Nyssa Starling gave out. She fell to her knees with a cry at the paralyzing pain, her sword tumbling out of her hand.

The Raider, seeing a reversal in fortune, dug his own sword out of the leaf litter and rose to his feet. Karigan tried to lift hers but could not. The pain was all-consuming and filled her vision with white hot agony.

The sharp edge of a blade was pressed against her neck.

"I'm gonna lop your one-eyed head off, Greenie," the Raider said, and he swung his blade back for the killing stroke.

Tears of pain pattered onto the forest floor. She wanted to call out or disappear, but the shock and pain overwhelmed her. She could do nothing but gasp for breath. This was it, she thought, and though she'd some regrets in life, at least the pain would be done. All the striving and darkness would be done. She called Zachary to her mind as the last image she'd see, his brown eyes gone soft as they sometimes did when he looked at her, a slight smile to his lips, a lock of amber hair hanging over his forehead.

Then, when it seemed to take a long time for the death blow to come, she looked up and saw the body of the Raider fall. Erin removed her sword from his back, and knelt before Karigan.

"Sir Karigan, can you stand?"

"I—I don't know. My back . . ."

Trace came through the woods. "Karigan?"

"Let us get her to the campfire," Erin said.

They helped her stand and she cried out, but it was a little better once she was upright and walking.

"Your arm is bleeding," Trace said.

The pain of her back had overwhelmed all else.

"Let's get you back to the campsite so we can bind it up," Erin said.

Each step jarred her back, and she bit her lip to prevent herself from screaming.

"The women we rescued are a mender and her apprentice," Erin said. "Perhaps they can help."

When they reached the campsite of the Raiders, the bodies had already been dragged to the side. Travis was conversing with the two women.

"Menders," Erin said, "we require your assistance. It's her back, and a wound to her arm."

Before Karigan knew what was happening, they'd removed her coat and were helping her lie down on her stomach on a blanket. It was a position with which she was all too familiar.

"Arm will need stitches," one of the women said.

"Fetch our satchels, Aldena, and set about suturing the wound," the other said. To Karigan she added, "You are in good hands, Rider. We'll do what we can for you."

 DRAGONS FLY

"Unfortunately, such injuries do not simply go away because we wish it, or because we'd find it convenient," the mender, who was named Bertine, said, her face aglow in the light of Karigan's moonstone. Igniting it had lessened the hurt a little and made it much easier for the menders to tend her. Bertine, who struck Karigan as quite pragmatic, had not been impressed by the fact it was an Eletian moonstone but by how useful the light was for her work. She and her apprentice, Aldena, had been walking home from a birthing when they were overtaken by the Raiders. They hadn't been badly hurt, but were roughly handled and frightened.

Karigan, lying prone by the fire, said little in the haze of pain. The wound to her arm had been sewn up by Aldena while Bertine gently examined her back. Trace stood nearby watching, and Erin and Travis appeared to be rummaging through the Raiders' belongings and disposing of their bodies. They must have determined that Karigan wasn't going to move or be moved from her spot by the fire this night.

Bertine was calm and professional as she examined Karigan. "Your superiors returned you to active duty too soon," the mender continued in her brusque manner. "These wounds to your back were traumatic, and the gods know who the evil person was who did it, or what this has done to your mind."

"My mind is fine," Karigan said.

"Hmm," Bertine said, not sounding at all convinced. After a pause, she said, "Just because a wound feels better doesn't mean it has finished healing."

Karigan did not know if she was referring to the wound to her back, or to that of her mind, or to both.

"You said this original *injury* occurred at the end of winter?" Bertine asked.

"Yes."

Bertine muttered under her breath. "Well, it weakened much of your musculature, and so where one muscle is weak, others accommodate by taking on extra work. My dear, I think we are seeing muscle strain, though I can't be certain how much tissue damage is involved, or its extent, but you are in considerable pain, yes?"

"I can hardly move."

"You need a few days of rest before attempting anything physical."

"But—"

"You will only make matters worse if you force yourself to ride and carry on. Aldena? Is the tea ready?"

"Yes, Bertine. I will bring a cup over."

"We have brewed you a medicinal tea. It will relax your muscles and help with the inflammation."

Karigan glanced up at Trace, who looked stricken. She did not know if it was Trace's view of her back, or the play of light that cast her features thus.

Bertine and Aldena shifted Karigan onto her side, and had her tuck her knees into a fetal position.

"This will ease the pressure and pain some," Bertine said.

Erin came over with an armload of gear. "Sir Karigan's bedroll."

"Sir?" Bertine asked. "You're the realm's one knight?"

"Don't look it, do I," Karigan murmured.

"It's not that. I had heard the king had made a knight a few years ago. First one in a century or two. Didn't expect it to be a messenger."

"Two centuries," Erin said, "and she is an honorary Weapon, as well."

"Well, well," Bertine said, "that is impressive. But I'd be more impressed if you did as I advise and rested for a few days before attempting to get back in the saddle."

"Here's the tea," Aldena said.

Bertine helped Karigan sip from the mug. It was bitter, but anxious to subdue the pain, Karigan drank it without complaint. The menders then shifted her to her bedroll, positioning her on her side once more. Aldena placed a warm waterskin against her back before covering her with a blanket. The waterskin was very soothing, and she sighed.

"I am leaving the herbs and tea with your companions," Bertine said, "as well as a liniment. It must be applied three times a day, and you are to take the tea and herbs two times a day."

"Two times a day," Karigan said dully. Her eyelids felt heavy, and her tongue had grown thick. They had dosed her with a soporific.

"Perhaps we can offer you this in payment," Travis told Bertine. He held a very full purse in his hand. Coins jingled when he passed it to the mender.

"What is this?"

"We collected it from among the Raiders and their belongings. You may take their horses, as well, if you wish."

Karigan's vision had grown blurry, so she could not see Bertine's expression. There was a long silence.

"This will be most useful," the mender said at last. "It will go toward helping our village and the families the Raiders harmed. There are orphans."

Their voices faded away, and Karigan knew not who said what, for the warmth and comfort detached her from the world, and she drifted away into a deep sleep.

Discomfort woke her. It was still dark and she had no notion of the time, but the others were up and about.

"—if she can't ride," Trace was saying. "You urge me to continue on, but neither of you will accompany me?"

"Our duty is to protect Lady Winterlight," Travis said.

Karigan blinked rapidly, fighting off grogginess. Did he really just say their duty, his and Erin's, was to protect her? Had he really just invoked her Eletian name?

Trace must have been equally stunned for there was a long

silence before she said, "The king sent you to protect Karigan? I know there is something between them, but she's a Green Rider. She can't do her job with bodyguards."

Karigan agreed. But maybe it was Bertine's medicine that made her slow to react.

"The reasons do not concern you," Travis responded. "The messages must reach Sacor City as soon as possible. You are fit to ride, and Lady Winterlight is not. We stay with Lady Winterlight."

"It's just *Karigan*," Karigan said in a raspy voice. "No Winterlight."

They looked down at her in surprise.

"Forgive us," Erin said. "We did not know you were awake."

"Hmm. Well, perhaps one of you can explain about your duty being to protect Lady Winterlight."

Erin and Travis remained silent.

"Figured as much." Weapons and their secrets. They had many, perhaps even more than anyone, including Zachary, knew. Why were they particularly interested in protecting Lady Winterlight? Or had Zachary indeed ordered them to do so? She pushed herself into a sitting position and grimaced at the flash of pain and stiffness in her back. It was not, to her surprise, as bad as she thought it would be. "We all ride to Sacor City together."

"Your injuries," Trace said.

"I'll live. Aren't you the one who once rode all the way from Westford with a broken ankle? We all ride with injuries from time to time."

"Sir Karigan—" Travis began.

"Oh, so it's *Sir Karigan* again, is it?"

"Sir Karigan," he said, as if she hadn't interrupted him, "the mender was clear about your need to rest your back. It is possible you'll slow us down. If we send Rider Burns ahead—"

"*Together*," Karigan said. "I may need some help saddling Loon, maybe other things, but I can ride as fast as anyone."

She climbed to her feet and caught a breath at the twinge in her back. Dawn was lightening the world, and she could see the resigned expressions on the faces of her companions.

"If you like," Trace said, "I can rub some of that liniment of Bertine's on your back for you."

Karigan consented. Anything to help. The liniment had a pleasant scent that reminded her very much of what Renn Harlowe had used when they'd been prisoners of the Raiders. That seemed ages ago, but thinking of him and his death brought on a wave of melancholy.

As Trace worked, she told Karigan that the menders had opted not to spend the night at the campsite with them but to continue on back to their village as they had other patients in need.

"So late at night?" Karigan asked.

"Menders work all hours depending on how many patients they have and what their needs are," Trace replied, "but I suspect the fact that the Raiders held them captive here in this spot was the greater reason."

Karigan nodded in understanding. She did not think, were she in their shoes, that she'd want to spend the night here, either.

The Weapons readied the horses, and Karigan "allowed" a leg up from Travis, but in truth she didn't think she would have made it into the saddle on her own. Each stride Loon took sent a jolt of agony through her back, but she had expected worse, possibly because she had known much worse.

The rising sun warmed her back and shoulders as they rode, and this helped. Loon seemed to make his gaits extra smooth for her. During breaks, she walked around and stretched, and Trace spread more liniment on her back. She also drank a partial dose of Bertine's tea concoction. Even the lesser dose made her drowsy in the saddle, but Loon didn't let her fall if she dozed off, and Trace kept an eye on her to make sure she was all right.

The days passed in a fog and sometimes she heard Nyssa whispering in her mind, and sometimes she heard her other self. Often the two merged and she did not know who was who.

Can't be a Green Rider with a bad back, they told her. *Zachary will be so disappointed in you. You are useless.*

"Shut up," she told them.

"What?" Trace asked.

They were trotting through a narrow road with a tunnel-like feel with trees hanging over it. The shade made Karigan shiver.

"Nothing," she said.

Some while later—she did not know how much time had passed—she saw someone standing on the side of the road. She reminded Karigan of Beryl Spencer. As she neared the woman, Karigan was sure it was Beryl. She was attired in the seafaring garb Karigan had seen her in, in her last vision. She pulled Loon up in front of her.

"Beryl?"

Beryl's gaze was distant. Her eyes glinted with an otherworldly sheen. Her form was fluid, wavery.

Dragons fly, Beryl said. *They breathe fire. You must find the device.*

Karigan shook her muddled head, and Beryl was no longer there. Instead, Trace was there, talking to her.

"Are you awake?" Trace demanded. "Why did you stop?"

"Beryl," Karigan said. "It was Beryl."

"Beryl?"

At that moment, the Weapons caught up with them.

"Is there a problem?" Travis asked.

"I think maybe we should cut back some more on that tea Karigan's been taking for her pain," Trace replied.

Karigan thought this was probably a good idea, but she also knew that seeing Beryl was not an effect of the tea. Or, maybe the soporific helped open her mind to seeing Beryl. In any case, she knew she must try to remember Beryl's words: *Dragons fly. They breathe fire. You must find the device.*

Hoofbeats began to pound in her head, growing louder by the moment.

"It's a Green Rider," Trace said. "Looks like Crane, so that means Ty."

Karigan looked up, surprised to find that the hoofbeats weren't in her head but real. She definitely had to cut back on the tea. She blinked hard to clear her eyes, and when the Rider pulled up before them, she saw that Trace was correct.

"Is the king's host still at the mountain encampment?" Ty asked without greeting.

"No," Trace replied. "We retook the keep and learned Second Empire is on the move to take Sacor City. We're on our way to inform Queen Estora."

"She already knows." His expression was grim. "Second Empire has set up for a siege, and the gates to the city are closed."

⇝ HEROES ⇜

K arigan was submerged in pain and misery
as the horses pounded at a mad gallop.
Arrows and crossbow bolts zipped past them.
Since the city was closed with the main body of
Second Empire's army before the gate, as Ty had said it would
be, Karigan and her companions had sought the Heroes Portal, but they were spotted by Second Empire's scouts, who set
off after them. She did not know how many pursued them.
She cared only about keeping far enough ahead of them to
reach the portal and safety.

An arrow passed right over her head and thudded into the
ground in Loon's path. He trampled the shaft as he surged
forward. In the haze of pain, Karigan had a vision of arrows
arcing through the sky, a vision that seemed familiar. Arrows
raining from the sky toward her, but she never saw where they
landed.

She shook her head. She must stay focused. She wasn't
even on a half dose of Mender Bertine's concoction and she
was still having visions. Or maybe visions of visions?

Travis brutally whipped and spurred his horse forward.
He and Erin had released their remounts when Second Empire came after them. The poor horse was managing to keep
up with Loon, but it wouldn't last. Travis reined the stallion
sharply into the trees, and Loon and Curlew sprang after
him, with Erin on her horse trailing. They did not slacken
their pace through the woods. Loon flew over a blowdown,
the dead branches scraping his belly, and pushed on without
missing a stride and bounded after Travis and his horse. They
whipped by a pale obelisk, and the nonexistent path turned

into the remains of an ancient road bordered by a grove of tall hemlocks. Somber and dark they were, fitting sentinels to an entrance of the tombs.

They passed a granite slab that was a coffin rest set beside the road. After that, the portal came up quickly, and they plowed to a halt before a ledge that loomed above them. Into its face, the round iron door of the Heroes Portal was embedded. Travis flung himself at the door and pressed the glyph of Westrion in its center. A handle popped out and he hauled the portal open. Cool air flowed from the depths of the tombs.

"Go in," he ordered.

"We're not leaving our horses," Trace said.

An arrow hit the ledge above the door and stuck in a thick mat of moss.

"Take them!"

Karigan hissed in pain as she dismounted. It made her lightheaded. Darkness stained the edges of her mind. Travis grabbed her arm and dragged her through the doorway. Loon trotted in behind her. Trace and Curlew were up ahead. Travis then disappeared behind and waited for Erin and her horse to enter, and then pulled the door shut behind them. It closed off the world, and only the harsh breathing of Karigan's companions and the huffing of the horses filled the tube-like corridor of stone they stood in.

The sound of running feet echoed up the corridor. A pair of Weapons appeared, and Travis hastened to greet them. They had a short discussion; then he waved them to come on. They followed him to a chamber that was a nexus to other corridors, one that was, fortunately, large enough to accommodate several people and four horses though the ceiling was a little low.

Karigan had been here twice before, though she truly only remembered the first time. A coffin rest dominated the center of the chamber, and on the walls, murals of battles came to life in the flickering lamps: swords raised to take down the enemy, horses bearing knights at full charge, the enemy trampled beneath hooves.

"Sir Karigan, Rider Burns," Travis said, "these are Weapons Gord and Harris."

The two tomb Weapons nodded solemnly.

"Your unexpected entrance will—" Harris began, but suddenly there was the sound of someone falling, a thud on the hard stone floor. Karigan looked behind and saw that Erin had collapsed. A broken arrow shaft protruded from her back. The Weapons rushed to her side.

"She's alive," Travis said.

"I'll get help," Gord replied, and he hastened off into one of the corridors.

Travis dug through his saddlebags, withdrawing bandages to staunch the wound, and a cloak with which to pillow her head.

"Will she be all right?" Trace asked.

"Weapons are strong," he said simply as he worked.

The motto of the Black Shields, *Death is honor,* rang through Karigan's mind. In her own misery, she couldn't shake a certain darkness.

"Gord will bring a death surgeon," Travis told Erin.

If she replied, Karigan could not hear it. Erin had been their rear guard, and had paid for it.

"I guess we didn't all make it unscathed," Trace whispered to Karigan. "I've told Connly we've made it, and the king is apparently very relieved. They are marching hard to reach the city."

Karigan nodded, distracted by her own pain, and wishing there was something she could do to help Erin.

"Won't Second Empire try to get in?" Trace asked Harris.

"They can try," he replied. "The structure of the door is sound and strong, and is enhanced with spells. The area is also warded, so they'll become disoriented and perhaps lost."

"But we didn't."

"You were guided by a Weapon."

Soon a man in long dark robes strode into the chamber, followed by four caretakers in drab white and gray bearing a litter. The caretakers gawked at the newcomers, especially the horses. The death surgeon went right to Erin's side, knelt down, and examined her wound. Death surgeons not only prepared the dead for interment in the tombs, but served the caretaker community as menders. To Karigan, the tombs always seemed a place of contradictions—death surgeons who preserved the dead and healed the living, caretakers who lived among the dead.

Erin was gently lifted into the litter so that she lay on her side as the broken arrow remained in her back. She groaned, and Karigan was glad to hear some sign of life from her. The litter bearers swept her from the chamber with the death surgeon leading the way.

"Aren't you going with her?" Trace asked Travis.

"My duty is to stay with Sir Karigan. And you."

Karigan narrowed her eyes. She'd heard that pause after "Sir Karigan" before he included Trace in his statement of duty. She would have to have a conversation with him the moment she could pull him aside.

"What now?" Trace asked. "Shouldn't we get moving?"

"We await Agemon," Harris said. "This is his domain, and, well, with an outsider and horses here, our approach requires delicacy, and his blessing for your passage."

"But we've urgent messages for the queen, and a letter from the king allowing us to pass."

"Even so," he said. "Agemon is the chief caretaker, and his word is law here. He will not be long."

Karigan hoped not. The cold was adding to the ache in her back. It wasn't freezing cold in the underground environs of the tombs, but it was persistently cool enough that the Weapons wore extra layers even in the midst of summer. She leaned against Loon, taking in his warmth and sweaty horsey scent. He turned his head to nuzzle her shoulder. She'd grown immensely fond of him, but could not wait to see her own Condor. That reunion, however, would have to await the chief caretaker and her duty to the queen.

Trace fidgeted. "Outsider," she muttered. "I am a servant of the king as much as this Agemon is, and these tombs are Sacoridian."

"There are reasons why entry is limited," Karigan said, thinking not only of the priceless treasures that were hidden within, but the fact that they also held artifacts of a more arcane nature that must be kept hidden from those who would misuse them. She did not know how many there were, or what they were, just that caretaker culture had evolved to consider the intrusion of outsiders, the living, as offensive to the dead, and that intruders must never see the outside world again.

"Easy for you to say," Trace replied, "since as an honorary Weapon they let you in."

Grudgingly, Karigan thought.

Fortunately, Agemon did not dawdle, and he entered the chamber with Gord striding beside him. The chief caretaker was in his elder years with long gray hair, but his face, like that of other caretakers, was curiously pale and unlined from a lifetime of inhabiting the tombs. He wore robes that were of muted and dusty tones, shroudlike. He adjusted his specs on the end of his nose.

"Not horses," he muttered. "Not horses."

"I am afraid so," Harris told him. "This is the only way into the city right now, and these Riders carry important messages for the queen from King Zachary."

"This green!" Agemon pointed a shaking finger at Trace. "It must never depart the tombs to see the living light of day again."

"We've a letter from the king for you about that," Karigan said. Not that such ever carried much weight with Agemon.

"*You!*" he cried. "You and your green, you and your horses, and your infernal dragonfly device."

"Yes, me," Karigan said, fighting to keep her tone even and patient so as not to escalate the chief caretaker's agitation. "And yes, we do need to discuss the dragonfly device."

He gave her a sour look. "Indeed."

"But first, more urgent business," she said, and she handed him the king's letter.

While he read, Trace whispered, "Is he slightly . . . mad?"

"The caretakers don't deal with outsiders, with only a few exceptions. It makes them nervous." She recalled her first visit to the tombs. She, Zachary, and others were sneaking into the castle via Heroes Avenue during Prince Amilton's coup attempt. Upon their first meeting, she'd thought Agemon quite mad, as well. He did tend toward expressing his dismay and querulousness, but he knew his tombs and his people, and was not mad.

When he finished reading Zachary's letter, he passed it back to Karigan and she stowed it in her satchel.

He sighed. "Might as well invite the world in, build a road through the tombs."

"It's just one outsider," Harris reminded him.

"And four horses. Oh, the mess. Always the mess in my tombs."

"Agemon, these Riders need to see the queen. Immediately."

"Yes, yes, always some emergency with these greens." Agemon tugged on his hair, then turned, muttering to himself, to lead them into the one lit corridor.

To Karigan's mind, the sooner they were out, the better. Though the tombs were well-lit, dry, and kept spotless by the caretakers, they made her skin crawl. She did not like being surrounded by so many corpses no matter how long ago it was that they had died. She never felt that way in graveyards, but then she wasn't underground with the dead in those. There was an intensity about Heroes Avenue and the royal tombs, the number of sarcophagi and chambers and artifacts, that overwhelmed. It was as if the dead and death pressed in against the living.

She grimaced in pain as they set off after Agemon and Harris, the clopping of horse hooves on stone reverberating down the corridors. Travis and Gord brought up the rear, leading the Weapon horses. She had stood too long in one place, and even with Loon acting as a live hot water bottle, her back had grown stiff. What she really wanted was a hot bath and her own bed, so long as Second Empire wasn't overrunning the walls. Maybe even if they were. In any case, it was unlikely they'd make any major moves for a while. It took time to arrange one's siege.

The first few chambers they passed through lacked corpses, but there were symmetrical rows of granite slabs awaiting dead heroes of the realm. This was, after all, the part of the tombs reserved for Sacoridia's heroes. When finally they entered a chamber where the slabs were occupied by remains, she heard Trace's sharp intake of breath.

Some of the dead reclined in full armor. Others were

covered by shrouds or wrapped in linens. Others, still, were encased in sarcophagi with lifelike effigies on the lids. Karigan kept her gaze straight ahead, but when they came to one room in particular, she kept an eye out for a specific slab of granite. When she saw it, she pointed it out to Trace.

"The First Rider."

Lil Ambrioth's remains were just lumpy shapes beneath a shroud. Blue-green plaid was draped from her feet to her hips, and her swords—a two-handed greatsword and a saber, along with a battle ax—were mounted on the wall behind her. Lil's portrait was painted on the ceiling above her slab. She rode astride a warhorse and wore the plaid about her shoulders. She bore her saber, and a shield with the device of the gold winged horse on it.

Karigan felt a brief flush of warmth from her brooch, a recognition that she was in the presence of the great Lil Ambrioth, the hero who had founded the Green Riders, and it was an acknowledgment that Karigan was her descendent— not by blood but by the brooch both had worn.

Karigan had traveled to the past and met the living Lil Ambrioth, a person far more vibrant and interesting than the ceiling portrait made her out to be. She was indeed heroic, but also flawed, and so very alive. Karigan found she could not look at her remains. Trace, conversely, halted and stared.

"Come, come," Agemon entreated. "You must leave my tombs as soon as may be. Yes, yes."

Karigan understood Trace's awe. It was something to confront the person who had created the life you now lived, a person of legendary proportions who all Riders revered. And the horses. If Karigan had been looking in a different direction, she would have missed it, the bob of Loon's and Curlew's heads toward the slab.

"*Come,*" Agemon insisted.

Trace nodded and, with reluctance, fell in step. "That's really the First Rider?"

"Only her remains," Karigan replied, glad she'd gotten to meet the living woman and not just see her mortal husk.

"It's a little disappointing in a way," Trace said.

"What is?"

"To see that all these heroes are so very human. That they turn to dust just like the rest of us. It makes them kind of ordinary."

Karigan thought she understood. Heroes were bigger than life, seemingly infallible, and to learn they were just like anyone else? Yes, she could see being disappointed. But to her, their mortality, their ordinariness, made them human, and their feats all the more astonishing. The legends made great deeds seem unattainable, but seeing the humanity behind the legends brought them within grasp. She bet few of these heroes set out to be such. They were just trying to defend their homeland or do the right thing. They might have chosen to stay home in safety, but the true heroic deed was that they did not, even knowing the danger they faced.

And had they truly turned to dust? Karigan glanced over her shoulder, but the remains of the First Rider had already vanished from sight. The physical form might disintegrate with time, but even after so many centuries, Lil Ambrioth's name and deeds lived on, as did her progeny, the Green Riders.

❧ ADJUSTMENTS ❧

Karigan concentrated on putting one foot in front of the other and ignored the hundreds of sarcophagi and granite slabs encumbered with the dead that they passed. Loon might as well have been leading himself. He stuck right beside her, nostrils flaring. She wondered what he must think of it all, how he perceived the world of the tombs in that horsey noggin of his. Along the way, the horses did what horses were prone to naturally do, and out of the corner of her eye, she espied caretakers seeming to appear out of nowhere to clean up droppings. Agemon was visibly distraught, muttering to himself and tugging on his hair.

After some time passed, he apparently needed to vent at someone, and so he dropped back to talk to her. "I do not know what the king is thinking by allowing so many who are not permitted to enter the haven of the dead. And horses. *Horses!*"

"He is the king," she said, "and much is going on in the world beyond the tombs." She wished Brienne Quinn were here to provide a buffer. She seemed to have a talent and the patience required for managing the chief caretaker.

"And *you*," he said. "You told us to look for a dragonfly device. We searched every corner of the tombs, our archives and storage and workshops for anything with a dragonfly on it, or that was in the shape of a dragonfly. Do you know how much time and effort this cost? Hmm? And then I get a note from the king: *Agemon, Sir Karigan does not think it is a dragonfly, this thing, but a flying dragon.*"

"I am sorry you had to go to so much trouble," she replied, "but I gave you all I had to go on at the time."

"Now we must tear apart this domain," he continued as if he hadn't heard her, "this sepulcher of serenity, the final resting place of the great and royal ones, to find this flying dragon device on a shield. Do you know how many there are? Hmm? *Hmm?*"

Karigan had no idea, of course, and then she recalled her vision of Beryl. "Look for one that is a device of not only a flying dragon, but one that breathes fire, too."

"Yes, yes, breathes fire." Agemon sounded anything but mollified.

Karigan hoped that that one detail of a fire-breathing dragon would help narrow the search somewhat. "Remember," she told him, "it could nullify the effects of Mornhavon the Black's great weapon and avert destruction and disaster."

"What of the destruction of my tombs to find it, hmm?"

Having had his say, Agemon wandered off among the funerary slabs to straighten a shroud. Karigan sighed. Did he not understand that the tombs would likely also suffer if they were not able to overcome Mornhavon's great weapon, whatever it was? She shook her head and focused on walking again. It was easier than riding, but she looked forward to getting off her feet. Trace continued to be sunk in her own thoughts, or perhaps she was conversing with Connly.

"Ah," Harris said, "here we are."

They arrived in a rotunda from which other corridors spoked, very like the chamber in which they had started, but much more ornate. Solemn statues of kings and queens watched them, and down the corridors lay the sarcophagi of the royal dead. Harris guided them to a set of doors that Karigan knew led to another chamber. It was a warming room for the Weapons and a transitional space between the outer world and the tombs, the receiving room for the newly dead who were to be interred either along Heroes Avenue or the sections reserved for royalty.

They entered through a pair of doors into the receiving room with its somber decor of heavy hangings, velvet and brass, and the blazing fireplace. Karigan finally felt like she could breathe easier, that she was no longer hemmed in by the dead. Even more so, when they were all inside and the doors to the tombs were closed. She was further pleased to find a pair of familiar faces there waiting for them—Weapons Brienne and Lennir.

"Welcome back, Sir Karigan, Rider Burns, and Weapon Travis," Brienne said. "I am sorry I was not able to meet you myself down by the portal. I hope there were no issues?"

She meant Agemon and the passage of Trace and the horses.

Trace smiled. "Well, your chief caretaker didn't make me stay for the rest of my life, though he clearly wasn't happy."

"To be honest," Brienne said, "he is never truly happy unless there is someone of prominence to inter." She paused before adding, "You may also be interested to hear the death surgeons are giving Weapon Erin their best care and are cautiously optimistic about her chances for full recovery, but this first night will be critical."

Travis nodded, but gave no other indication that he cared beyond that. Karigan assumed he did, but all Weapons wore stony countenances.

"Shall we?" Brienne said.

There were two sets of doors that led out. One pair led to the castle's royal chapel of the moon, and the other to the commoners' chapel. Lennir opened the door to the commoners' chapel. It was quite plain with a coffin rest that also served as an altar, and wooden benches for congregants to sit on. Two Riders awaited them there—Anna and Gil.

Happy greetings were exchanged among the Riders.

"I've missed you," Anna told Karigan, a little shyly.

"And me, you," Karigan replied. "I've heard very good things about how well you've been doing."

Anna smiled and blushed. She and Gil took command of the horses, and after saying farewell to Harris and Gord, Karigan, Trace, and Travis followed Brienne and Lennir from the chapel. The queen awaited them in the throne room, Brienne said. It meant more walking, starting with a flight of stairs. Karigan glanced back at Anna, Gil, and the horses, and wondered how well the horses would manage the stairs.

The pain in her back was expanding. She was overdue for liniment and Bertine's tea concoction, but it had to wait. She strode on doggedly, and it seemed to take forever to reach the throne room. Brienne, meanwhile, described the current situation with Second Empire as they walked.

"They have arrayed themselves in a siege pattern," she told them. "They appear to be constructing siege engines, and in the meantime, they have made some feints to test our defenses and the strength of the city gates."

"All of those soldiers against so few of us and civilians," Trace murmured.

"The guard has been, at the queen's behest, recruiting the able-bodied among the refugees to help in the city's defense, whether that means training with the guard, making and repairing weapons, joining the fire brigade, or assisting the menders. Many have been eager to help."

Well, that was something, Karigan thought, but would it be enough to hold off Second Empire until the king arrived?

Finally they reached the throne room. The walls fell away, and the chamber's tall windows and the lofty ceiling gave it an airy feeling.

Estora stood within at a table with what appeared to be maps unrolled atop it, very much like Karigan had seen of Zachary at the encampment. She was dressed in a gown the cobalt of her clan. It was a stern color, but elegant on her. Her advisors surrounded her, including Castellan Javien and General Meadows of the guard. Mara was there, too, and her face lit up when she saw them.

Karigan and her companions bowed before Estora. Karigan grimaced at the sharp pull in her back.

"Welcome home, Riders, Weapon," Estora said. "What news do you bring?"

When Trace and Travis appeared to wait for Karigan to respond, she cleared her throat. "Your Majesty, we bear messages for you and your advisors from the king." She dug through her satchel and passed the messages to the appropriate recipients. Then she waited with the others as the messages were read. At one point, Estora raised her eyebrows and looked at Karigan in surprise before continuing on with her reading.

When Castellan Javien finished his message, he said, "It is clear the king did not know Second Empire was so close when he wrote this message."

"No, sir," Karigan said, "but we encountered Rider Newland on the road and he told us, and Rider Burns passed the news on."

"Are you in communication with the king now?" Mara asked Trace.

"Yes, Lieutenant, and he has questions, but first he sends his heartfelt regards to the queen and, of course, greetings to everyone else. The army is now two days west of Oxbridge."

There was some murmuring among the advisors, and then a conversation ensued between Zachary and Estora, relayed through Trace's connection with Connly. Soon advisors at both ends interjected with opinions and questions. Someone thought to have a goblet of wine brought to Trace to moisten her throat, and a chair as her ability began to tire her. It was probably much the same for Connly on the other end. At length they needed to take a break. The ache of Karigan's back was giving life to a stiff neck and pounding head, and she longed to lie down. Perhaps they wouldn't notice if she stretched out in one of the alcoves beneath a window.

"Your Majesty," Travis said.

"Yes, Travis?"

"Sir Karigan has recently reinjured her back. She needs to see a mender. Perhaps you would wish to excuse her?"

Karigan could have hugged him at that moment, and was grateful for the ability of Weapons to read the language of bodies.

"I did not know," Estora said. "His Majesty requested that I ensure she visits the menders for examination, but I did not realize it was more urgent."

"She strained her back when we confronted the Raiders," Travis said.

"You encountered Raiders?"

He explained.

"Then she must go see the menders," Estora said.

"I will ensure she reaches the mending wing."

Karigan sighed. They knew her too well. She just wanted to go to her own chamber and collapse, maybe see the menders at some other time.

"One more thing before you go," Estora said softly to Karigan. "I am made aware of your new station, my lady. Adjustments will have to be made."

"Adjustments?"

"New quarters, for one," Estora said. "We cannot have the high nobility of another nation living in common quarters."

"Please, don't move me," Karigan said. "I like my quarters. I don't want any fuss."

"We shall discuss it later when you are feeling better. Now you must go to the menders. In the meantime, I am very pleased to have you back, Lady Winterlight."

Those nearby who overheard looked her way in surprise. Karigan twisted the birch leaf ring around her finger, then hastily half-bowed and turned to leave.

When Mara started to join her, the queen said, "Lieutenant, I will need you here."

"Of course, Your Majesty." To Karigan, Mara added, "I will check on you when I can, and maybe you can explain your new . . . station."

Karigan gave her a brief nod before following Travis out of the throne room. That was not how she'd wanted her friend to hear about her Eletian status, but it was done, and there wasn't anything more she could do about it at the moment.

When they reached the central castle corridor, she paused. It wasn't as crowded as usual, but those who used it strode purposely on business of their own. She was sorely tempted to disobey orders and head to the Rider wing to her own chamber. She could cuddle with Ghost Kitty, and there was Condor to visit, too.

Travis placed his hand gently but firmly on her shoulder. "This way, Sir Karigan." And he steered her in the direction of the mending wing. After a couple steps, she halted and planted her feet. Here was her opportunity, after all, to address the protection that the Weapons seemed to be offering Lady Winterlight.

"I'm going no farther until you explain why you are acting like my bodyguard," she told Travis. "Did the king order you to? Trace was right—I can't do my job with a bodyguard hanging around."

He regarded her with classic Weaponish impassivity. "No, Sir Karigan, the king did not order me to be your bodyguard."

"He didn't?" she said in surprise.

"Aside from helping to ensure his messages reached the queen."

She rubbed her knuckles into her aching back. She'd been so sure it had been Zachary being overprotective of her.

"Then why," she asked, "have you been so particular to protect Lady Winter—*ow!*" Sharp pain jagged through her back. "Ow ow ow . . ."

"It is time we got you to the menders," he told her. "Lean on me."

She hated to admit she needed his help, but she took his arm. She was too immersed in pain to pursue her questioning of his motives, or to even think about it. Weapon mysteries would have to be solved at another time when it did not feel like her back was being torn apart.

❧ HEALING ❧

"This process is going to take a while," Ben said.

"Define 'a while,'" Karigan said. She lay on her stomach on an exam table with her back exposed.

"A few days, with periodic checkups thereafter."

"A few days?"

"Calmly, Rider," Master Vanlynn said. "A few days is not long for the damage we see. You are lucky it is not worse, and this after you did not heed Mender Bertine's advice. Ben will work on it for only short periods of time, which is better for the both of you. The process, we have learned, can exhaust both mender and patient, and we cannot afford to have Ben totally incapacitated for any length of time. You will be able to leave the mending wing between treatments so long as you obey our orders."

"What orders?"

"To rest. You are forbidden to ride or lift things, or exert yourself in any manner that will stress your back."

In other words, she would be next to useless until this was all done, even as Second Empire tried to overcome the city's walls.

"Do you understand, Rider?" Master Vanlynn asked.

"Yes." Only a few days, she thought, only a few days, and in between sessions she'd get to see Condor, Ghost Kitty, and her Rider friends.

"Your arm wound is healing just fine without magical intervention," Master Vanlynn said, "and so we will not interfere with it except to provide salve and fresh bandages. But it is looking very good."

Karigan thought it looked rather ugly, herself. The scabbed, puckered flesh. Erin had removed Aldena's sutures a couple days earlier.

"A warning," Master Vanlynn continued. "I mentioned that the process of healing can be exhausting. I am not exaggerating. You may find the treatments make you very sleepy afterward, so I would not plan to accomplish much until all is done. It is asking much of one's body to heal so quickly."

Which brought Karigan back to the thought of how useless she'd be. She listened to the slow footsteps and tap-tap of the master mender's cane as she departed, and finally the opening and closing of the chamber's door.

"Go ahead," Karigan told Ben, "make me a new back."

"Karigan . . ." he said.

"What?" She didn't like the tone of warning she heard in his voice.

"I can't make it like new."

"But—What about Sperren's hip?" The former castellan had fallen and broken his hip, but Ben, new to his special ability, had made him a new one.

"I worked on it right after he injured himself," Ben replied. "It was fresh. These days Vanlynn wouldn't allow me to be so, um, thorough. And in truth, it was not a new hip, just a lot of repairwork. In any case, I can't undo what has already healed and scarred, just the more recent damage, and maybe some of the older that hasn't quite mended all the way."

Her hopes had risen when she learned that Ben would be allowed to use his true healing ability on her. She could be her old self, she thought, maybe even better, the violence committed on her would be wiped away. Now she must lower her expectations. She'd retain the skin of a monster. But, if he could at least eliminate the pain . . .

"You will have to continue rebuilding your back muscles," Ben continued. "I can't create new muscle for you, but you can strengthen what you have. On the positive side, someone, or it sounds like a few someones, have done excellent mending work on you, which makes it easier for both of us. Are you ready?"

When she gave him her consent, she was aware of him placing his hands above her back. A warming sensation that alternated with cooling flowed across her skin and deep into the tissue. It was quite pleasant.

"It may begin to feel a bit odd," he murmured after some time had passed.

It was an understatement. It felt like worms wriggled through her muscles. She wanted to shift and stretch.

"Hold still," Ben warned.

The wormy feeling continued and she fought not to squirm. Even worse, it was followed by a tingling and itchy sensation as he continued to work. What she did not feel was pain, but she assumed he was numbing it. Soon he stepped back from the table.

"That will do for today, except for some liniment."

He warmed it before applying it to her back. When she turned her head to look at him, she saw that his features were drawn, his complexion wan.

"What was done to you was inhuman," he said, shaking his head. "There are scars on the surface, but I can see how deep they go and the damage that was done. You had good care at the outset, and that saved your life and prevented a crippling deformity."

Enver, she thought. The melancholy she felt whenever she thought of him and their parting came back to her. Enver had saved her. Would she see him again?

"I want you to rest for a while before you go anywhere," Ben said.

"But—"

"Mender's orders." He smiled and poured her a cup of water from a pitcher. "Drink this. Your body needs fluids after such a healing." He left the cup for her on a table. "You'll feel achy and sore, probably, but the liniment I put on should help. Remember what Master Vanlynn said about no lifting, riding, or exertion."

"I remember."

He gave her a doubtful look, then smiled. "It's good to have you back, Karigan." Then he departed.

Left on her own, she moved hesitantly, not wanting to ruin

his work. She pulled on her shirt and obediently sipped the cup of water. Then she paced about, experimentally stretching and bending. There was still pain, but the intensity was gone.

A tap came on the door, and Mara poked her head in. "Hello."

"Mara!" The two hugged—Mara doing so gently—and started talking at once, then laughed.

"Welcome back," Mara said. "It feels like ages since I last saw you."

"It has been."

"Ben says you're free to go if you feel up to it, but to rest. Join me for supper?"

Karigan followed her friend to the mostly empty dining hall. Servings were smaller than she remembered, though there was a quantity of fresh greens available thanks, she was told, to Estora's foresight in planting more gardens. Their stew was thin on meat but full of root vegetables.

As they ate, Mara caught her up on all that had been happening at the castle. She was pleased to hear that Anna was doing very well as a Green Rider and getting on with a one-eyed mare with the unlikely name of Angry-Mad, or Maddie. There was no word on the colonel, but then Mara told her who had been sent to Varos to reclaim her.

"*My father?*" Karigan's exclamation was loud enough that the few in the dining hall looked her way.

"I don't know all the details," Mara replied, "but he has gone in his capacity as a merchant to bargain for her release. He took Melry with him."

Melry, Karigan thought, certainly had a vested interest, and so did her father. It was canny of Zachary to send him— he had traded in Varos before, was persuasive, and if the effort failed, he possessed other skills. As for his vested interest? He loved Laren Mapstone and he wouldn't leave Varos without her. She was sure Zachary had known all this. However, it left her in the unusual position of being the one doing the worrying instead of her father.

Mara leaned in. "I heard Connly demoted you."

Karigan yawned, feeling suddenly very tired. It wasn't just

the exertion of the day, she was sure, but the healing session catching up with her. "It's for the best."

"Best for who?" Mara demanded. "Tegan is fine Chief Rider material, but you are better. Frankly, I could strangle Connly—the colonel and I chose *you*. When the colonel gets back, she'll set it right."

Karigan was not sure she wanted it set right. Being Chief was a lot of responsibility. She yawned again.

"Looks like it's time for you to be abed," Mara said. "Ben told me the healing session would make you sleepy. Here, I'll walk you to your room, and then I have to return to the throne room. They'll make poor Trace use her ability until she collapses unless I intervene. They barely allowed her a supper break."

As they walked through corridors toward the Rider wing, Karigan could not stop yawning, and she staggered like a drunkard.

"One thing I have to know," Mara said as they went along, "is what the queen meant when she referred to your new station and called you 'my lady.'"

That was certainly something Karigan did not feel up to broaching that moment when she was nearly falling asleep on her feet.

"It's a long story," she said through another yawn. "Can't it wait until morning?"

"It will kill me by then."

Karigan paused unsteadily. "All right. I am now an heir to the House of Santanara." She thrust the ring under Mara's nose.

"*What?*"

Karigan chuckled. Gods, she felt drunk. "The Eletians made me one of them."

"How on Earth is that possible? Why? When did you see them?"

"Like I said, long story." And she toddled down the Rider wing.

"I guess I will have to wait," Mara said. "I'm not sure you're making much sense just now, anyhow."

Karigan was never so happy to reach her bed chamber. A lamp had been left at low glow for her. Her gear had been deposited by her bed.

"We aired it out and put fresh linens on the bed," Mara said. "And when I say *we,* I mean Anna and Merla."

"It's so wonderful." Tears unexpectedly streamed down Karigan's cheeks. To be home and among her friends again. "Kitty!"

Ghost Kitty was curled on her pillow, but considering the feline look of disdain he cast her, her presence clearly disturbed him. When she sat on the bed, he leaped off and ran out the door.

"He's so happy to see me," she murmured.

Mara helped pull off her boots. "Do you need help with anything else?"

Karigan lay on her stomach, her limbs sprawled out. "Nope." Her eyes were already closed.

"All right. We'll talk more in the morning."

Karigan was barely aware of Mara shutting the door, and started to sink into blissful—

Shaking. Someone was shaking her.

"Mmmff?"

"C'mon, Karigan, wake up!"

"Wha—?" She woke just enough to see Fergal hovering over her. "Fergal?"

"You awake?"

"I am now," she said, unable to withhold the crankiness from her voice. She glanced at the lamp that was still aglow and noticed it was the same as when Mara had left her. "What time is it?"

"Just after seven hour."

"In the morning?"

"No. Mara just left."

Karigan pushed herself into a sitting position. "The better question is why you woke me up."

"We have to talk."

"Can it wait till morning?"

"No. I've been holding this secret too long. I was going to tell you back at the encampment, but then you disappeared, and I was sent back here with Melry before you showed up again."

"A secret?" She tried to focus her attention on him, but sleep was clawing at her, pulling her back into oblivion. She shook her head. "What secret?"

"It's about King Zachary, and you're the only one I dare to tell."

He had her attention now. "What are you talking about?"

He glanced around as if there might be spies hiding in the shadowy recesses of her room. In a low voice, he said, "The king is bespelled."

⋙ THE KNOTTED HEART ⋘

*T*he *king is bespelled.*
  "You saw his aura?" Karigan asked.
  Fergal nodded. "Like black, barbed knots tied around his heart."

It was an image she could envision clearly, the barbs piercing into Zachary's beating heart. Grandmother had cast spells on him when he was her captive in the Lone Forest. The knot spoke of her particular work.

And very good work it was. Nyssa stood beyond Fergal, shadowy, the tendrils of her whip, as always, trailing blood.

"Karigan?" Fergal patted her cheek. "You with me?"

"Knots," she blurted, blinking rapidly to sharpen her focus. When she could see normally again, Nyssa was gone. It was like she was only half aware, the other half of her asleep and trying to drag the rest of her down with it.

"How many?" she asked.

"Er, how many what?"

"Spells. How many spells did you see?"

"I can't say for sure. It may be one complex spell, or—?" He shrugged.

"Who else knows?"

"I haven't told anyone else."

"*What?*"

"You just don't go around saying things like that about the *king*," he said in a low voice. "That can get you in a heap of trouble. I didn't feel like I could tell anyone but you. Or, maybe the colonel if she were here."

"Oh, Fergal." She lowered her face into her hands. It felt

good to close her eyes. It shut off the world and its problems. It was followed by a pleasant drifting sensation.

Shaking. He was shaking her again. "Karigan, what's wrong with you?"

She came up for air, fought to keep her eyes open. "After effect of the true healing. You should have told Connly the moment you saw the spell."

"The one who demoted you?" Fergal snorted.

"He's a Green Rider and your captain."

"I dunno, Karigan," Fergal replied. "I just wasn't sure he would handle it right."

She had to admit that Connly wouldn't be the first person she'd want to tell. "Mara. You could have told Mara."

"I guess, but I don't know her like you do. You're the one I know and trust."

Karigan sighed. He had been her trainee, and she'd taken him on a long distance run. Their simple message errand had grown more complicated when they found themselves having to rescue Lady Estora from kidnappers.

"You never told anyone how I ended up in the river," Fergal explained.

He hadn't known how to swim and jumped off a ferry to force his special ability to surface. Special abilities often emerged when Riders were in life-threatening situations. His hadn't, and he had almost drowned for his trouble. However, his statement about her not telling anyone wasn't true. She had told one person all the details, her best friend, Estral. But Estral was discreet and very good at keeping secrets. Apparently Fergal was, too.

"I appreciate your confidence in me," she said, "but Connly and Mara know the nature of your ability, and they'd have handled it so there were no repercussions to you."

"What are you gonna do?"

Karigan scrubbed her face. "Know any secret stashes of kauv?"

"I might," he said cautiously.

She raised an eyebrow. "Well, then, if you do, I am going to need a few cups to stay awake. I want you to get me some."

He nodded. "Then what?"

"We tell Mara. And then after that, she'll probably want you to go to the queen with her."

"The *queen?*"

"Fergal, she is the same person you traveled cross-country with after we rescued her."

"No, she's not. She's the queen. She'll lop my head off."

"Oh, dear gods. Get me that kauv. Mara will handle it so no one's head gets lopped off." He did have a point though, she thought, that being queen, with the position's incumbent power, could not help but change Estora. If she ever learned about the closeness Karigan and Zachary had shared up north, she might decide to lop off Karigan's head. She shuddered. She'd have to make sure Estora never found out. As for the situation at hand, she thought Estora would handle it sensibly.

She didn't remember Fergal leaving, or that she'd closed her eyes, or dropped off to sleep. There was only the insistent shaking.

"Nooo," she moaned, and flung her hand out. It bounced off a fleshy surface.

"Ow!" Fergal cried. "If I have a black eye, it's your fault."

"Ha! Consider us even then." She turned over to go back to sleep.

He shook her awake again and pulled her to a sitting position.

"I brought you a whole pot of kauv," Fergal said. Karigan sniffed the pleasant and bracing aroma that filled her room. "Also," he continued, "as much sugar as I could. And Mara is here."

"Would anyone care to explain to me what this is all about?" Mara demanded. "Karigan is supposed to be resting as ordered by Master Vanlynn, and I'd like to learn how Fergal got his hands on so much kauv and sugar."

He shoveled sugar into cups of the steaming liquid for each of them. "Er, best not to ask about the kauv and sugar, and Karigan can explain the rest."

"No, Fergal, I cannot." Karigan took one of the cups and blinked against the overwhelming drowsiness. "This is your lot to explain."

"Fergal?" Mara asked. She was looking irritated. "What is this about?"

He set the pot aside on Karigan's desk, looked at the floor, and cleared his throat. "Here it is." In a halting voice, he told her what he'd told Karigan.

Karigan, meanwhile, only half-listened, her mind wandering to thoughts of her pillow. She loved her pillow, and it loved her back. It was so soft with its downy filling, so comfortable.

"Oh, no you don't," Mara said, shaking her awake. Fergal, who must have extracted her cup from her hand, returned it, once again filled to the brim.

"I am sorry to ask this of you," Mara said to Karigan, "but I want you to go to Queen Estora with us."

"You don't need me."

"We do. You had the most experience with Grandmother, and you were there in the Lone Forest when King Zachary was held captive."

A memory came back to her of Zachary tied down to a table. He'd been covered in Grandmother's knotted yarn.

"It'll be best," Mara added, "that she hear about it from a friend."

"Isn't it too late? She'll be abed."

"It's just after eight hour," Mara replied, "and I doubt the queen will get much sleep tonight anyway with Second Empire on our doorstep."

Fergal glanced at Karigan, then asked Mara, "D'ya think she can manage?"

Karigan realized she was tipping over sideways. Mara and Fergal pulled her upright again.

"More kauv," Mara ordered.

They made her drink two more cups. Her sloshing bladder, she thought, would keep her more awake than the kauv.

The three of them made their way to the royal apartments, Mara having to usher along a reluctant Fergal, who kept dragging behind, and a yawning Karigan, who kept stopping to sit on a bench or chair along the way to rest for just a minute. It was jarring to be constantly awakened by Mara in a different place each time. The wakeful properties of the kauv, clearly, were having little effect. Karigan found the pull to sleep as strong as the Rider call, and at one point, Mara took her left arm, and Fergal the right, so she would not lie down on the floor in the middle of the corridor.

It was slow going, but at last they found their queen in her public sitting room of the royal wing, conferring with her advisors. The last thing Karigan remembered saying before once more being shaken awake was, "Your Majesty, we request a private audience. It is urgent."

The next Karigan knew, the room was empty of all but the queen and a pair of Weapons by the door, and three Riders.

"What is this about?" Estora asked. There were furrows etched across her forehead that Karigan had never seen before.

Karigan's attention wandered and began to fade. There were an awful lot of plants around. Estora liked plants. Plants were nice. They smelled good and softened the harsh stone walls. She began to smile. Yes, plants were nice.

Mara patted her cheek. "Stay with us, Rider, and tell the queen what we came here to tell her."

Karigan shook her head in an attempt to stay awake. "I beg your pardon, my lady. The healing has made me unbearably sleepy."

"So I understand. What is this urgent news?"

Estora's curt tone, rare as it was, was enough to snap Karigan awake more than all the shaking and cheek patting ever would.

"You are acquainted with Rider Duff's special ability?" Karigan asked.

"Of course. He can see magic in others."

"Yes. He can see magical auras and is able to tell something about the magic through colors and the occasional vision. When Rider Duff saw King Zachary at the encampment in the mountains, he was able to see that a spell had been placed on him. Fergal described it as a black knot around the king's heart."

Estora's expression fell. "Grandmother."

Karigan nodded. "When we had rescued the king in the north, he had been covered in Grandmother's knotted yarn that she used for spell-making. She and her granddaughter had worked the spells during his captivity."

"Yes," Estora replied. "He had been fearful that the witch had succeeded in planting a spell, or many spells, upon him. He lost much sleep not knowing what exactly she had done, what it would do to him, or make him do. Rider Duff's ability only confirms that there is a spell attached to our king."

"That is correct, my lady."

Estora leveled her gaze at Fergal, who seemed to shrink beside Mara. "Why was this not brought to my attention sooner?" Estora demanded.

"Out of discretion," Karigan replied. "An *excess* of discretion. Rider Duff was understandably reluctant to speak of anything that might cast even the slightest hint of a bad light on the king, and he feared the consequences of doing so."

"Why now?" Estora asked.

Fergal stepped forward. He gazed at his feet. "I could trust Karigan. Er, Rider G'ladheon, and I've only just gotten to see her."

"Rider Duff," Estora said, "I am disappointed."

"I am sorry, Your Majesty." He knelt before her. "I will take my punishment, even if I must lose my head."

Estora's eyebrows rose in surprise. "Lose your head? You misunderstand. After our travels together, I would have thought you'd feel comfortable enough to come directly to me."

"Begging your pardon, my lady, but you weren't queen back then. You were Rider Esther."

She'd been disguised as a Rider for her safety as she and Fergal traveled cross-country together.

She nodded. "And now, as queen, I have the power to take off heads."

"Yes, Your Majesty."

"Fergal, believe me when I say I understand the Riders have special abilities and they are meant to be helpful. We do not remove the heads of Riders just because of what their abilities tell us. Next time something of this nature arises, you must tell your officers right away, and they can inform the appropriate authority."

"Yes, Your Majesty."

"It is something I will impress upon all the Riders as a reminder," Mara said.

"Do so," Estora replied, "with royal backing. We cannot afford for this sort of information to be withheld out of unfounded fear."

"Not unfounded," Karigan murmured. "Messengers are often subject to the ire of the powerful who receive messages not to their liking."

"Perhaps that is true in other realms," Estora replied, "but there are laws in this one to protect the Green Riders."

Laws were not everything, Karigan thought. Those who held enough power would not give a second thought to breaking them, even in Sacoridia. She knew enough, however, not to speak her dissenting view aloud.

"Go get rest while you may," Estora told them. "It will not be long before I must make use of the Green Riders at their fullest capacity."

⇜ SLEEP AND AWAKENING ⇝

They stepped outside the queen's apartment. "You see?" Mara told Fergal. "No one lopped off your head."

"Not yet," he said in an undertone.

Karigan yawned, merely happy now that she could return to her chamber and sleep without interruption. But someone was standing in her way. Someone in black. She looked up.

"Travis?"

"Master Mender Vanlynn is displeased."

"About what?"

"You are not following her orders."

She then noticed a journeyman mender beside him. She'd seen the young woman around the mending wing and thought her name was Aisla.

"I was needed," Karigan said, "to, um . . ." Mara and Fergal were welcome to jump in with their support at any time.

Mara said, "Rider G'ladheon was needed to go before the queen on delicate business."

"Nevertheless," Aisla said, "Master Vanlynn was explicit in her orders, and when she witnessed Rider G'ladheon disregarding those orders, she sent me to return Rider G'ladheon to the mending wing for the duration of her healing." She turned to Karigan. "Forcing yourself to wakefulness like this will only undo what has been accomplished thus far, which is terribly selfish and disrespectful of the work Rider Mender Simeon has done, and regrettable for you."

"I'm sorry," Karigan replied, startled by the rebuke. "I certainly did not intend—"

"Please accompany me to the mending wing," Aisla said.

"If you wish to be healed, now is the time, before we must turn our attention to those wounded when the fighting begins in earnest."

Karigan didn't know what to say.

"I'll check in on you," Mara told her and then, with a significant look at Aisla, added, "and I'll have a word with Master Vanlynn."

Karigan watched after Mara and Fergal as they made their way down the corridor.

"Will you come willingly," Aisla asked, "or must Weapon Travis assist?"

Karigan glanced at Travis with his dispassionate expression. Being lugged through the castle over his shoulder was not the sort of lasting impression she wished to leave on anyone who witnessed it.

"Er, no. I mean, I will go willingly. I am all for getting some sleep." Her words won her no approval from the stern mender, who, on second look, appeared to be, perhaps, a year or two her junior.

"Come on, then," Aisla said.

Karigan dragged herself after Aisla, too tired to engage in conversation, and doubtful the mender would even respond. It was, in any case, easier to remain silent. Aisla, on her part, appeared content with silence. When they arrived at the mending wing, it was abuzz with apprentices and journeymen rushing about and moving beds, winding bandages, and carrying piles of fresh linens.

Aisla brought her to a room and indicated she should enter. Inside, three beds had been stuffed into the small chamber making it feel rather crowded.

"You will change and sleep there." Aisla pointed at a bed against the far wall.

Karigan recognized one of her own nightgowns folded on it. Anna, or another of the Riders, must have fetched it. She waited for Aisla to leave, but the mender did not.

"Change," Aisla ordered. "I haven't all night, and I am not leaving until I see you abed."

She was as bad as Drent, Karigan decided. One might expect an arms master to order his trainees about in a harsh manner, but one would expect a mender to offer a little more compassion and understanding.

She went to the bed and, her back to Aisla, started disrobing. She laid her folded clothing on a nearby chair and slipped on her nightgown. When she once more faced Aisla, the mender's countenance was unchanged even though she could not have missed seeing the misshapen wounded flesh of Karigan's back.

"Now to bed," Aisla told her.

Karigan climbed into the narrow bed without argument and lay on her belly. She was out almost before her cheek touched the pillow. When she awoke some indiscernible time later, two figures hovered over one of the other beds.

"The swelling should be better by morning," said a familiar voice.

"Ben?" she asked.

Both figures turned. Ben's companion was not a mender, but a Green Rider whom she did not know.

"How are you feeling?" Ben asked.

"All right, I guess."

"Well, you shouldn't be awake so soon."

"But I am, so I can leave, right?"

He sighed. "Not yet."

"But—"

"You'd best listen to him," came Merla's voice from the other bed, "or he'll fill you with vile potions."

"Merla? What are you doing here?"

"She overworked her ability," Ben replied. "Again."

"I am all puffed up," Merla said. "I could hardly breathe when they found me."

"Oh, dear," Karigan replied.

"You need to rest more," Ben said. "Both of you."

"But I feel all right," Karigan said. Truth be told, she was still drowsy, but she was determined that now that she was awake, she should return to her own chamber. She sat up and swung her legs over the side of the bed. Ben turned to his companion and said, "Green Riders are almost as bad as menders when it comes to being a patient. Do you want to give it a try?"

His companion nodded.

"Karigan," Ben said, "meet Mason. He's our newest Rider."

"Hello," she said.

Mason extended his hand, and she, thinking he meant to shake hers, reached out, but he bypassed her and touched her forehead just above the bridge of her nose. A cool sensation tingled through her head, and she remembered no more.

"I think it's working."

"—never done this before."

Ripped out. She was being ripped out, out of the silence, out of the dark serenity. Gluey threads of it clung to her, but the force in the light kept pulling, pulling, pulling . . .

"She's coming to," one of the voices said.

She tried to dive back into the serenity, like a fish into its pond, but the light, the noise, the irritation pursued her and tore her out.

She awoke yelling and batted at the nearest face that hovered near her. Hands grabbed her wrists.

"It's all right," someone told her in a soothing voice. She thought it was the new Rider, Mason.

"It is not!" she shouted.

Ben came into her vision. He dabbed a handkerchief to his bloody nose.

It took a few moments for her to place herself. She was in a chamber in the mending wing. She'd been made to sleep there. She remembered Mason touching her forehead and— and then nothing. Pure, sweet nothingness.

"Let me go," she growled at him.

"You won't hit me if I do, will you?" he asked.

"No promises," she grumbled.

"Let her go," Ben said, his voice muffled by the handkerchief.

Mason released her and hastily stepped back.

She rubbed her wrists. "If you ever touch my forehead again," she told Mason, "I will break your finger." She felt odd, like some part of her lingered in the nothingness of sleep, as if she were not fully there. "I thought the idea was for me to sleep," she told Ben.

"I'm sorry, Karigan, but the queen insisted we wake you. I've never done that before—brought someone out of healing sleep. Didn't even know if it could be done."

Gray morning light poured through the chamber's small window. She rubbed her eyes. "Why won't anyone just let me be?"

"Sorry, Karigan," Ben mumbled. "You best ready yourself to meet with the queen."

When they left her alone in the chamber, she closed her eyes and took some deep breaths. The dark place called to her, sang of sleep as strongly as any whisper wraith of the Blanding. However, the waking world and duty loomed. She dressed, and though not feeling wholly herself, she stepped out into the corridor where she found none other than Travis waiting for her.

"Come," he said.

She followed after him. If she were more herself, she would have asked after Erin. Asked him what Estora wanted. Instead, she brooded behind him, feeling unmoored, and paid little attention to her surroundings until she realized they were not going to the throne room or the queen's apartment as she expected. Travis led her to a lower level in the west wing that lacked the ornamentation of the corridor where the royal household was located above—no plush carpets or polished woodwork, no paintings or fancy chandeliers. This area was raw stone, the corridors narrow with a low ceiling, and more fortress-like as the castle had once been.

Travis turned beneath an arched doorway, and Karigan found herself in an arming chamber. A narrow window channeled in dull daylight that gleamed on an array of armor and arms.

"The royal arming chamber," Travis said.

An armored figure stood in the center of the chamber, shining in silver and filigreed gold, with stylized rose blossoms in enameled reds, the leaves and thorny stems in green. It was such a stunning suit of armor that it took Karigan a moment to realize it was Estora wearing it, her golden hair tucked beneath netting.

"Your Majesty," Karigan murmured, and bowed. She had

to look again to ensure she was not mistaken, for she'd seen Estora in gowns, and only the once dressed as a Green Rider. Estora in armor was unexpected.

"Excellent," the queen said. "Mender Simeon was not sure he'd be able to reverse the healing sleep that had been placed upon you. Are you awake enough to ride?"

"I believe so."

"Good. I am to parley with General Birch, and you will be riding out with me."

"*Me?* Surely there are better—"

"We will not be alone. There will be others. But you must never forget that you are more than a mere messenger, but a knight of the realm. Your place is to accompany me to the parley."

"Um, of course, Your Majesty."

"And I must admit," Estora added, "your status with the Eletians does add an interesting dimension to your position." She smiled, but it was a tired smile. "The most important reason I wish you to accompany me is that it will be good to have a friend along."

The matter of their friendship, Karigan thought, even without Zachary added into the equation, was complicated. She believed that Estora sometimes forgot what her powerful status as queen meant, that what she thought of as friendship was actually an unequal relationship between a servant and sovereign. The servants were all too well aware they must obey the queen and serve at her whim, friend or no. Once Estora had ascended the throne, the friendship she and Karigan had once known could not endure when she was able to command Karigan as she saw fit.

"Master Vasper?" Estora called.

A brawny man with a thick mustache entered from an adjoining chamber. He wore a leather apron with pockets that held an array of tools. Karigan surmised he was the royal armorer.

"Madam?"

"This is Rider Sir Karigan. Do you think it will fit?"

It? What was Estora up to?

Vasper squinted at her with steely eyes, gazing her up and down with such thoroughness that it unsettled her.

"I do believe it just might," he said at last. "I will need to measure to make sure."

"Very good," Estora replied.

Vasper pulled out a length of knotted string and started by measuring the length of Karigan's legs.

"Uh, what am I being measured for?" Karigan asked.

"To see if you will fit in Princess Florence's armor," Estora replied. "I had it brought up from the tombs just for you."

THE ARMOR OF PRINCESS FLORENCE

"**P**rincess who?" Karigan asked.

"Florence," Estora replied. "While Elgin Foxsmith was researching historical documents related to Green Riders in wartime, he came across a reference to her, a snippet of verse from five centuries ago. It went something like this:

> *Fair warrior maiden of the Sacor Clans, was she,*
> *Sealender's scion,*
> *Daughter of kings*
> *For whom the storm glass sings,*
> *Champion of Alendriel Field*
> *and fell enemy of the Urzek Horde,*
> *Rider of swift Swallowtail,*
> *Princess Florence Aventine.*

"It turns out," Estora continued, "the verse was her epitaph, and that the caretakers in the tombs were aware of her, for there is a memorial dedicated to her in the Sealender wing of the tombs."

Vasper moved behind Karigan to measure her shoulders.

"Why would you want me to wear *her* armor? A princess from five centuries ago?" It then dawned on Karigan that Elgin had been researching *Rider* history, and Swallowtail was the name of a winged creature, a butterfly. "Of course. She was a Green Rider."

Estora nodded. "When she died upon Alendriel Field, far out on the Wanda Plains, it was a great loss to the realm. She sacrificed herself so her brother, King Darien the Second, could win the day."

Karigan thought back on her history lessons at Selium. About five hundred years ago, King Darien and his forces drove the mysterious Urzek people out of Sacoridia, and there had been a decisive battle on the Wanda Plains. She recalled no mention of this Princess Florence, or of any Green Riders whatsoever. Of course, she hadn't been the most attentive student at the time, so she might have missed it, or, as was typical when it came to anything having to do with the Green Riders, the historians had, unwittingly or not, failed to preserve the contributions of Princess Florence.

"Her remains were interred beneath a cairn where she fell," Estora said, "but her armor was brought back, or perhaps this was a second suit she owned. In any case, it has been well taken care of down in the tombs."

"The armor will fit," Master Vasper announced. "Not exactly perfect, but as well as we can expect when it is not tailored specifically to Sir Karigan."

"Well enough for a parley," Estora said. "Please arm Sir Karigan."

"Yes, madam." Vasper left them for the adjoining chamber.

"Who called the parley?" Karigan asked.

"Birch," Estora replied. "No doubt to set the terms of our surrender."

Karigan was not surprised.

As Estora stepped out to attend to other preparations, Vasper returned with the armor to begin the arming process. First she had to remove her shortcoat, then draw on a padded doublet. Afterward he presented her with Rider Princess Florence's armor. It did not look five hundred years old, and shone at high polish. The plate was etched with feathers in gilt. It was not ostentatious, and it reminded Karigan of the gold embroidery on Colonel Mapstone's coat. For all that it was in amazing condition for its age, it was not pristine parade armor, for there were scratches, dints, and dents that were the evidence of battle.

Vasper cradled a greave in his arms like a baby. "Beautiful armor, is it not? Made by a master of his craft of the period."

"It is," she agreed.

He clad her, starting with her feet and working upward. While Karigan had worn cuirasses before, she'd never worn full plate, at least not of the Earthly kind. The star steel armor she had worn as the avatar of Westrion did not, she thought, count.

The armor was not heavy, though not insubstantial like star steel, of course, and the hinges of the articulated plates made movement easy, almost flexible. A warrior could fight unhindered in this armor, which was most desirable.

Vasper buckled a sword around her waist. "It didn't belong to Princess Florence but comes from our stores. Weapon Travis has knotted a swordmaster's silk around it."

She half-drew the sword and observed the black silk tied beneath the guard. Each of the knots was symbolic of a Weapon attribute. She remembered Fastion going through them for her the night she'd passed her swordmaster's test. *The first is for loyalty*, he had said. *The second is for honor. The third is for protection, and the fourth is for death.* The purpose of swords, after all, he had reminded her, was to reap death.

She slid the sword home and sighed. *Weapons.*

Then she thought of the verse Estora had recited, the epitaph of Rider Princess Florence. "Master Vasper," she said, "do you know what the 'storm glass' was that was mentioned in the epitaph?"

"I do not," he replied. "I was wondering about it myself, if it were some sort of weapon."

She guessed it would have to remain a mystery for the time being.

Vasper finished the arming with the brevor and helmet. This part she did not care for because it limited her vision and muffled her hearing. She immediately pushed back the visor. It helped, but not greatly.

The arming had not taken long, but a weariness settled on her, probably from having been awakened too soon. And there was still the unsettling sensation that a part of her was absent, perhaps still dreaming far away from the waking world.

She stepped up to a full-length mirror to get a look at herself. She could not believe how she looked, like a knight of legend. Had Princess Florence once gazed into a mirror to observe herself in this very armor? Karigan turned one way, and then the other, to view herself at different angles, how light flowed over the steel. She was pleased, very pleased, and so was Estora when she returned.

"Why did you wish me to wear Princess Florence's armor in particular?" Karigan asked. "I realize she was a Green Rider, but I am sure there is other, less important plate I could wear."

"The fact that she was a Green Rider is the obvious reason," Estora said, "but also that she was a great hero of her time. She was beloved by her people. The caretakers found many scrolls of ballads, poems, and laments that were written in the years following her death. Everything we do for this parley is symbolic and about appearances. Though Birch may know nothing of Florence, *we* do, which is an important reminder of past triumphs by our people. He will sense our pride as we approach him." She gave Karigan a half-smile. "It is good to remember that not all battles are waged on the cutting edge of a sword."

Their party consisted of six Weapons in black armor, one who bore a plain black banner to represent them, a guardsman bearing the banner of the firebrand and crescent moon, a city guard who unfurled a pennant representing the walls and castle of Sacor City, and Karigan, who, it turned out, was to carry the banner of the Green Riders. It was not the one King Santanara had given Lil Ambrioth in ancient days, but a perfectly fine specimen embroidered with a gold winged horse on a field of green. Another Weapon joined them belatedly and raised the queen's royal standard, a field halved by the Hillander terrier and the cormorant of Coutre.

The Winding Way emptied for the queen and her company. At first, the bystanders watched in silence as they passed, but then a roar of approval began to rise along their route to deafening levels. Estora did not wave or acknowledge the crowds as she normally would but rode ahead with an unwavering gaze and an air of determination.

"The Rose Queen!" someone shouted, for her armor

gleamed even in the dim, cloudy light of the day and outshone the armor of those who rode in her party, including that of Princess Florence. Others took up the cry until thousands shouted in unison, "The Rose Queen! The Rose Queen!"

Karigan patted the strong neck of the handsome, heavily-muscled warhorse she'd been given to ride. She did not know why she hadn't been given Condor, except for what Estora had said about the importance of appearances, and this big dappled gray was certainly impressive. She did not know to whom he belonged, but he had an unaffected, genial nature even when the crowds and noise could have so easily made him nervous. His gait was easy, but he was so wide it was rather like riding an extra large barrel. With no name attached to him, she decided to call him Pumpkin.

Riding in Princess Florence's armor was not difficult, but with her legs sheathed in steel, she did lose some contact with Pumpkin's sides. She was also conscious of the subtle impact on her center of balance, tipping this way or that with the additional, unaccustomed weight, but she soon grew used to it.

When they reached the lower city, the civilians were kept away from the gate and wall, out of the way of the city's defenders. The guard, and those who more recently had taken up arms in defense of the city, stood on the wall's walkway or tended the gate.

Karigan, and the rest of Estora's entourage, halted before the gate. The cheers and shouts died down until there was almost silence. In the distance, back in the middle city, the bell of the chapel of the moon started tolling. Estora nodded and the guard began the process of opening the gate.

Karigan waited on Pumpkin with some curiosity and dread, but also feeling disconnected, separated from the world by plate armor and the odd sensation that part of her remained asleep. She shook herself to stay focused. While it was likely Birch would obey the customs of parley, there was no guarantee, so she must keep her wits about her.

It took several guards to crank and lift the gate open. It was extremely thick, constructed from ancient oaks from the deeps of the Green Cloak, and bound with iron. Once the gate was open, wind blew into the city as though to herald a coming storm. Banners snapped and fluttered, and the party rode out.

They passed the remnants of refugee huts and campsites. There was the unwelcome stench of death emanating from corpses impaled by arrows. Brienne, Karigan recalled, had mentioned that Second Empire had made feints at the wall and gate. The wind lifted cloaks of the dead lending them unnatural life.

In the distance, across far-flung fields, the enemy massed like a bruise upon the land, the clouds brooding overhead. Estora led the party into a canter. Karigan clucked Pumpkin on and at last felt the power of his gait as he surged forward. It was rather pleasant, like sitting on a rocking horse.

The banner of the Green Riders rippled on the staff she bore. Her place was a flank position with no one to her right, and yet, she sensed someone there riding along with them. At first, when she looked, she could see no one, but a second glance revealed a ghostly horse and rider charging alongside her and Pumpkin. The ghost rider wore armor, but no helm. Instead, a circlet shone upon her brow, her long hair flowing behind her. Her horse ran silently beneath her, her gaze fixed on some unknown point beyond Karigan's ken.

And then the ghost gazed in Karigan's direction, and Karigan knew it could only be the spirit of Rider Princess Florence Aventine, daughter of kings and the champion of Alendriel Field, astride swift Swallowtail.

⤳ A PARLEY OF GHOSTS ⤳

Karigan did not know if the ghost of Rider Princess Florence looked at her, or through her, or even if she saw her at all. Perhaps she looked into another time, upon another scene very like this one. The ghost made no indication one way or the other and simply faded away like a mist evaporating with a breeze above the tips of the fallow field's tall grasses.

Karigan released a breath and turned her attention to the business at hand. It was not the first time she'd seen a ghost, and she doubted it would be the last.

When the party reached the agreed-upon spot for the parley, they all came to a halt, and Estora rode ahead with the Weapon who bore the royal standard. She met Birch and one of his officers midway. Tension rose throughout Karigan's body. If there was a time that anything would go awry, this was it with their queen face-to-face with the enemy. She tried to reassure herself that if Birch did not abide by the peaceful conventions of the parley, half a dozen Weapons would be on him in an instant.

Estora and Birch, astride their respective mounts, began their dialog. Karigan could hear their voices rising and falling with the wind, but not what they were saying, though she caught a few words now and then: *the empire, your aggression, sovereign land, surrender or . . .* She imagined Birch was making all sorts of threats should the queen of Sacoridia not comply with his demands for surrender.

Pumpkin stomped his massive hoof. Bees droned on the white and yellow flowers of late summer that dotted the field. The tall grasses waved and bent in the wind. She made sure

she kept the banner of the Green Riders straight and proud
so it did not droop or become tangled around its pole, the
emblem of the gold winged horse unmistakable. Birch's party,
she saw, carried among them only one banner, that of the
dead tree. The soldiers didn't wear any regular uniforms or
armor, but whatever they could make or scrape together. One
might mistake them for some ragtag collection of cutthroats,
but that would be a fatal mistake when Birch was their commander.

"My children?" Estora cried incredulously. "You are insane."

Birch laughed, and her Weapon leaned toward her as
though to whisper counsel.

A mist rose up among them, and at first Karigan thought
it was some trickery of Birch's, but he and Estora continued
as before as though oblivious to it. The vapor twisted into
insubstantial forms. The figure of Florence astride Swallowtail arose beside Estora's Weapon, and a crowned figure who
must be her brother, King Darien, enveloped Estora. Facing
them were two unrecognizable figures. They wore head-
dresses incorporating antlers, but they were too blurred and
shifting for Karigan to see clearly. It was as though she were
looking at a mirroring between past and present.

Far off in the distance, a ghostly army waited, and near
her, a group of figures sat mounted behind their king bearing
banners and pennants just as she and her companions did.
Their features and shapes shifted and swirled and remained
undefined. No one else appeared to be aware of the presence
of spirits, or even of a mist upon the field.

Then a wave of vertigo assailed her. She jerked in her saddle at the sensation of falling. While the mist rose and fell
around her, everything else slowed almost to stillness, her
companions, Estora and Birch, even the wind. It was like, she
thought, the wild ride, in which she had traveled quickly in
time with the aid of ghosts. All that was in the present had
slowed to a standstill even while she surged ahead, allowing
her to outrun her enemies, and even arrows. The figures of
the ghosts around her grew more sharply defined. Florence
remained the most clear of all, almost solid.

There was a reason the ghost of the princess appeared to Karigan. It wasn't just that Karigan was wearing her armor, though it was likely a conduit that connected them. She could only wait and see what it was Florence intended.

King Darien gestured as he spoke, his voice distant, whispery and unintelligible. An unnaturally slow breeze rolled along the tips of the grasses. Swallowtail pranced and tossed his head. Misty figures rose from out of the grass where they'd lain hidden. It was an ambush. Florence dug her heels into Swallowtail's sides and reined him around to shield her brother from spears the enemy threw. One, and then a second, bounced off her armor. Karigan felt buffeted as though it was she the spears hit. The impacts almost dislodged her from her saddle.

Florence grabbed the reins of her brother's horse and spurred Swallowtail on, hauling the king along with her and leading him to safety toward the castle as his other retainers moved to engage the spearmen.

And then it started all over again. The ghost parley, with Florence beside her brother, the spearmen rising from the grass, Florence moving just in time to rescue her brother. It repeated a third time.

The fourth time, Florence glanced back at Karigan as if to ensure she was watching. When she completed the rescue of her brother, the mist whirled away and vertigo washed over Karigan once more. She grabbed onto Pumpkin's mane to steady herself. The sounds of insects among the flowers, the snorting and hoof stamping of horses, the raised voices of Estora and Birch, assailed her ears. All was in motion once more. She did not hesitate.

"Ambush!" she cried, and she spurred Pumpkin's sides. He leaped—leaped unexpectedly into the air in an aerial maneuver which the finest warhorses were trained to execute. She almost tumbled off his back, but by some miracle stayed her seat.

When Pumpkin landed, Estora and Birch were watching her in surprise. Pumpkin dug into the ground and charged toward Estora.

Karigan did not see if Birch had given some signal, but

now men arose from where they had buried themselves in the earth beneath the grasses. They shed layers of turf and strung arrows to bowstrings.

Pumpkin thundered beneath her. The Weapon who'd stayed beside Estora acted uncharacteristically confused. The others were in motion right behind Karigan, but she reached Estora first. Just like Florence, she placed herself between her queen and the enemy as a shield. Arrows exploded against the armor. The force of impact rocked her in the saddle. The din of steel arrowheads battering steel plate deafened her, but she followed Florence's example and grabbed the reins to Estora's horse and spurred Pumpkin into a gallop.

"What—?" Estora cried.

Karigan did not answer. She did not look back, but she was still aware of the Weapons closing in behind her and Estora. Another arrow smashed into her backplate and shoved her forward. The fine craftsmanship of Florence's armor that Vasper had so admired continued to deflect arrows. When Estora collected herself and urged her horse on herself, Karigan let go and dropped back to shield her from behind, but Pumpkin must have been hit because one moment they were charging full ahead, and the next she was launched into the air. The last she recalled was a blur of sky and field and horse, and slamming into the ground in a great clatter of steel.

"Ung . . ." Karigan moaned. Her head was throbbing. Drops of water plopped onto her face, and there was much movement and shouting around her. A figure in black loomed over her. She blinked to clear her eyes. More drops, a light rain, splashed on her face, thunked on armor. Armor. She was wearing armor . . .

"Karigan?" said the figure in black.

That was odd, a Weapon with Trace's voice. She touched her hand to her head. Her helmet had been removed, but her hand was still in its gauntlet. "What the hells happened? Estora! The queen, is she—?"

"Queen Estora is shaken, but fine, thanks to you," Trace

replied. "For your part, you had a pretty spectacular fall when your horse went down. Everyone was quite impressed."

Karigan had to think for a moment to remember what had happened, and with what horse. "Pumpkin?"

Trace looked puzzled by her question.

"My horse. Is he—?"

"His name is Pumpkin? Doesn't sound like the sort of name the king would give his warhorse."

"The king?" This was all so confusing. She blinked rain out of her eye.

"You didn't know? He's one of King Zachary's. The king suggested you ride him for the parley. He'd come up lame before the king took the army to the mountains, so he got left behind to heal up. I guess he was fine until today. He'll be lame for a while again."

When Karigan remembered that Trace was connected to the king through Connly, her knowledge of the horse's origins made sense, and so did the fact that Trace had been armored as a Weapon to ride beside Estora at the parley. It meant Zachary was right there, in a manner of speaking, and Birch would have never known the difference.

"Will Pumpkin be all right?" she asked.

"They think so," Trace replied. She didn't say who "they" were, but explained that Pumpkin had stepped in a hole and flew haunches-over-nose. It was a miracle he hadn't broken a leg or squashed Karigan. Even Princess Florence's armor would not have saved her from *that*.

Karigan was pleased that Pumpkin would be all right. He'd been such a nice horse. She would have felt terrible if worse had befallen him.

Trace further explained that the Weapons had dragged her through the gate.

"Did everyone make it back?"

Trace shook her head. "Two didn't, but if you hadn't given warning . . . How did you know?"

A filmy figure formed behind Trace and gazed over her shoulder at Karigan with an inscrutable expression.

"I had help."

Trace seemed about to ask her to explain, but then looked

up. "Here comes Travis with a cart to take you up to the castle."

"A cart? Don't think I'm hurt." Karigan flexed her limbs. Yes, she'd feel battered later even with the armor, and her head throbbed, but there seemed to be no serious injury.

"You don't want to walk all the way to the castle, do you?"

"Oh. Guess not."

Trace helped her to rise to her feet as Travis drove up with a donkey cart. It would not be as impressive a return to the castle as riding Pumpkin would have been, but Trace was right, she didn't want to walk all the way.

She saw that she'd been placed on a corner of an intersection beside a closed shop. City defenders were running about or keeping watch on the wall. Members of the guard rode up and down the Winding Way.

Before she climbed into the back of the cart, she mouthed a "thank you" to the ghost of Rider Princess Florence Aventine. There was a quirk of the ghost's eyebrows and the slightest of smiles before she vanished.

Karigan picked up her helmet from the ground with a groan, then crawled up into the cart. Trace deposited the banner of the Green Riders beside her, then mounted up on her black Weapon's horse and rode ahead, leading Travis' steed behind her.

On the bouncing, slow ride up the Winding Way, Karigan patted her breastplate. There were new dents and scratches to the steel from the impact of arrows, not to mention from her fall from Pumpkin. Agemon would not be pleased by the damage, but she didn't care. The armor had saved her life, which in turn allowed her to lead Sacoridia's queen to safety. It had also provided a connection with Florence's spirit. Without her help, Karigan, Estora, and the rest of the party would now likely lie dead in the field outside the city wall.

✥ REUNION ✥

Vasper was unbuckling Karigan's backplate from the breastplate when Estora appeared in the doorway of the arming room. He paused and bowed. "Your Majesty." He moved as though to abandon Karigan to attend to Estora's armor.

"Finish with Sir Karigan first," Estora told him.

Karigan was relieved. Her head hurt and made her feel a little unwell, and all she wanted was her bed, although her superiors might have other plans for her.

"Karigan," Estora began, as Vasper resumed the removal of Florence's armor, "I thank you for what you did today. Those men were so well concealed. How did you know there was an ambush about to be sprung?"

"I didn't, exactly," Karigan replied. She hesitated as Vasper removed the back- and breastplates at last. She observed more fully the new and numerous scratches and dents the armor had received from Second Empire's arrows and her fall off Pumpkin.

Estora, picking up on her hesitation, said, "Vasper, please leave us for a few minutes."

"Yes, my lady."

After the armorer disappeared into the adjoining room, Karigan said, "It was Florence." At Estora's blank expression, she explained.

"The spirit of Princess Florence." Estora murmured when Karigan finished. She shook her head. "Thank the gods you were out there with us to see her warning. I guess we should have assumed Birch would cause a breach of custom with so underhanded an act."

624

"You were prepared for the possibility," Karigan said, thinking of all the Weapons who had accompanied their queen onto the field. They just hadn't been expecting that level of stealth. "It would have turned out worse if you hadn't."

"Still, I am glad you were there," Estora said quietly, "and Zachary, too, through Connly and Trace. Birch is a vile man. He demanded I turn myself and my children over to him."

Karigan rubbed her temple. "Did he figure out the king was advising you through Trace?"

"I do not believe so. I hope he does not figure it out, or other things, either." Estora did not elaborate, but called out into the corridor for tea to be brought.

When she had turned in the doorway, Karigan observed a new dent or two in Estora's armor, as well.

"Tea should help settle my nerves," Estora said. "Fortunately, we do not seem to be short of it. You look like you could use a cup, yourself."

Servants soon brought a tray of tea and biscuits, and Estora enjoyed a cup while Vasper finished disarming Karigan. Though the plate had not been terribly heavy or restrictive, its removal was a relief. Karigan sipped tea while Vasper, in turn, disarmed Estora. While it did not cure her headache, it warmed and heartened her.

"Queens do not seem to have squires to help with their armor," she said as Vasper pulled off one gauntlet, and then the other. "Jayd, who dresses me, wouldn't have the faintest idea of how to deal with this." She chuckled.

"Most queens," Vasper said, "would not ride out to parley."

"It had to be done."

When Estora's armor was removed, it revealed her plain shirt and breeches beneath. Vasper brought her cloak to wrap around her shoulders. He then carried her armor off to the adjoining room to be polished, and he did not return.

Estora sat beside Karigan, sighed, and closed her eyes. "This is all very difficult. I do not wish to step out the door where I must face the reality of what we are up against. My advisors and officers, and very likely the lord-mayor, await me."

Karigan did not doubt it was difficult to have the defense

of a city on one's shoulders, and not just any city but the royal seat of Sacoridia. Should Second Empire overcome their defenses, it would be a huge blow to the realm and would allow Birch to attack from a place of strength. It was certainly not a burden Karigan would care to carry. Estora looked small and fragile beneath her cloak in that moment.

She poured more tea into Estora's cup and handed it to her. "I think you have time for another cup and a biscuit before you have to go out that door."

"Thank you, my friend. You save me yet again. And I am remiss. I haven't inquired as to how you are after that fall you took off Storm."

His name was Storm? She supposed it was a more appropriate name for a warhorse than "Pumpkin."

"I'll live," she said.

"See that you do," Estora replied. "You've proven yourself too valuable to this realm. I would miss you a great deal, besides."

Karigan smiled, sipped her tea, then sobered. "What happens now?"

Estora tugged her cloak closely about her as if to stave off a chill. "As I understand these things, Second Empire will array themselves outside our walls just out of arrow range. They have already tested our defenses, so they have an idea of our capabilities, which I fear are not great in the advent of a sustained attack. But we've strong walls and good people."

"And the king is on his way," Karigan added.

"Yes, yes he is, but his army is being harried by Second Empire. His soldiers are being picked off—the enemy does not stand and fight in the usual way but attacks in small numbers from concealment. It takes time to bring them down, and the chaos they sow slows the army even more. But they will come, and Birch will be caught between the city walls and the might of Sacoridia."

"What about our allies?" Karigan asked.

"I sent messengers to Mirwell and Adolind for additional help, and also to Rhovanny, but I fear Rhovanny is now entrenched in battles with Second Empire themselves, and they will not be able to come. We have not heard anything from our emissaries to the p'ehdrose, and, of course, nothing from Eletia. I fear those two peoples do not consider Second Empire to be worth their effort. They await the awakening of Blackveil. Unless you know more?"

Karigan shook her head and thought Estora was probably right about the Eletians and p'ehdrose.

Estora sighed and set her teacup aside. "I have tarried overlong and must now face what is to come."

When she rose and stepped through the doorway to the outer world, Karigan peered after her. A crowd of advisors, officers, and nobles descended on her, all talking at once. She watched them all move down the corridor with their queen at their center. No, in this she did not envy Estora one bit.

Karigan wrapped her arms around Condor's neck, his hide silky warm against her cheek. He blew gently through his nostrils.

Finally, she was reunited with her friend, her partner, her beloved companion. She petted him, scratched him in his favorite places, snuck him a handful of oats, and told him how much she had missed him. He, in turn, lipped at her hair and nickered to encourage more scratching. The world might be falling apart around them, but they were finally together again, and together they could face anything that came their way.

After she left the arming chamber, she'd made her way to Rider stables carefully so that she would avoid anyone with the authority to order her elsewhere. It was wrong of her to do so, but she didn't care. She supposed, as she stroked Condor's velvety nose, that she should report to the mending wing as she'd been instructed, but it would have to wait.

She gazed into Condor's shining brown eye. "I think we've got some hard times ahead," she murmured. He flickered his ears. "I'm afraid."

Those two words surprised her, spoken aloud. *I'm afraid.* Speaking it to her gentle friend unlocked something inside, freed her to not hide what frightened her. She'd been hiding it, not just from others but from herself. With her admission, a sense of peace settled over her, enhanced by the quiet whickers and shuffling of content horses in their stalls.

She was afraid of what was to come for the realm and those she loved, and she was afraid for herself, too. Accepting her fear would not stop the nightmares or the all-too-vivid memories, or the hesitations, but maybe now the true healing could begin.

Healing, her other self said contemptuously. *You can't show your fear. They'll take advantage and use your fear against you.*

Karigan pressed her face against Condor to block the image of her other self leaning against the neighboring stall, her dark attire merging into shadow as she tugged black gloves on. There was truth in her words, that it was important to show strength, to not let them, whoever "they" were, take advantage. But didn't it make sense to acknowledge one's fear so one knew what to prepare for?

Thankfully, her other self did not offer an opinion, but Condor made a deep rumbling sigh of contentment that she could feel through her contact with him, and everything was once more all right.

⇜ BRACING FOR
A STORM ⇝

Alton stood outside Tower of the Heavens and stared at the granite ashlars. He steeled himself for entry. He didn't really want to go in, but currently, with Dale not yet returned from her errand to King Zachary, he was the only one able to. The towers were particular about who they allowed in. At one time, there had been D'Yerian keepers who watched over the wall, and they may have had some level of magic, or some other affinity, that allowed them access, but long ago, the clan had stopped maintaining the wall. So, there were no keepers. The towers permitted Green Riders, Eletians, and one particular and special minstrel inside. Alas that Estral was not here and that her voice had been stolen.

You can do this, he told himself.

It wasn't that he was worried the tower might reject him as it had in the past, no. It was what he'd find inside. He took a deep breath. He had to get in there to commune with the wall. After another deep breath, he made himself step through solid stone. The sensation was much like passing through water—slight resistance, a certain fluidity, and a moment of breath holding.

When he emerged on the other side into the tower chamber, his worst fears were realized when the little monsters pounced on him—all five of them at once, wings aflutter, tiny claws piercing through his clothes into his skin.

"Ow! *Achoo!*"

His sneeze sent the gryphlings wheeling through the air with many a squeak and meep. He glared at Mister Whiskers in his orange tabby cat form who lay sprawled on the long table licking his paw. There was no sign of Midnight. She could be up in her nest—it was too far up and shadowed to tell at the moment, or she could be out hunting. He did not blame her if she had decided to take a break from the little darlings.

The place was a disaster. It smelled of cats and dead things, and there were bones and patches of animal hide strewn everywhere. Maybe having gryphons reside in the towers as a defense against an invasion of powerful and deadly dark Sleepers wasn't the best idea, after all, but Merdigen had thought the gryphons could take them on. Alton had fought a dark Sleeper once and almost perished, so he'd been eager to gain any edge he could against the enemy.

The dark Sleepers were Eletians who had not escaped Argenthyne after Mornhavon the Black conquered it. They had been peacefully sleeping the great sleep in the massive boles of trees, as Eletians who were tired of their eternal lives were wont to do, and were left behind as their folk fought and fled the forces of Arcosia. They slept on oblivious to the woes of the outside world, but, in time, absorbed the corruption Mornhavon wrought in the land and became tainted themselves. Their hearts turned black. All that was beautiful and light in Argenthyne succumbed to his rot, and the realm became known as Blackveil Forest.

The towers of the D'Yer Wall were fussy about who and what they admitted. Among those allowed to enter were Eletians. Unfortunately, Alton had learned, nearly at the expense of his life, the towers did not distinguish between ordinary Eletians and dark Sleepers. It was how, he believed, Blackveil would invade Sacoridia, by sending those creatures through the towers. With a heavy sigh, he supposed he could put up with the messes the gryphons made if they proved as useful against the dark Sleepers as he hoped.

Since there was no time like the present to do a serious house cleaning, he set to, telling Whiskers, "You need to teach your offspring to go *outside*. And no more eating in the tower."

Whiskers rolled onto his back and purred.

"Big help," Alton grumbled.

The youngsters zoomed around him as if to see who could

fly closest without crashing into him while he worked. They skimmed his head and careened beneath his arms. Yelling at them only seemed to encourage them.

"Zag!" he cried, almost tripping over the gryphling. Zag was one of the four who took after his mother. He was completely black and, in his gryphon form, had the body of a panther cub and the visage of a raven.

His partner in mischief was Zig, also black, but the tips of her toes were white. The other two black gryphlings were Soot and Shadow. The fifth looked like his father with a tawny catamount cub's hide and raptor visage in gryphon form, and was a roly-poly orange tabby as a kitten. He was named Whiskers the Junior, but was just called Junior for short.

Alton gagged over a recent pungent pile of regurgitated fur, bone, and . . . whatever that was. At least Bob, the bobcat gryphon, did his business outside. Of course, he did not dare enter the domain of two adult gryphons who were very protective of their young.

Alton continued to sweep and clean, and after dumping the debris outside, he found Merdigen moving about the tower chamber.

"Ah, boy, there you are," the great mage said. "What are you up to?"

"Cleaning," Alton replied.

Merdigen gazed about. "Doesn't look so bad."

"That's because I've been *cleaning*, and you don't have a sense of smell."

"Sadly, that is true."

"Not so sad in this instance," Alton replied. He was still feeling a little green after his encounter with the gryphling puke.

Merdigen, a great mage of a millennium past, and long dead, described himself as a "projection of the great mage, Merdigen." Some essence of his being, his consciousness, perhaps, resided in the large egg-shaped specimen of tourmaline that sat on a pedestal in the center of the chamber. The tourmaline Soot and Shadow were currently trying to bat off the pedestal.

Merdigen shrieked and ran across the room. "Shoo!

Shoo!" he yelled at the gryphlings. "Bad kitties!" He created an illusion of a moth to distract them. They bounded after it in kitten form, mewing and meeping.

"You have got to have a talk with Whiskers and Midnight about taking the gryphlings out more and getting them to behave," Alton told Merdigen.

"Yes, I see that now. They've clawed up some of my books."

Alton glanced at the stacks on the table. He had already discarded two that had been shredded beyond repair. He shook his head and entered beneath the eastward arch of the chamber that led to a short corridor. The corridor intersected with the wall. It was time to do what he had originally intended when he'd entered the tower: commune with the wall.

He pressed his hands against granite. Runes flickered on stone, and he closed his eyes. His mind traveled among the crystalline structures that pulsed with power. He heard the steady song of the wall guardians—the souls of magic users who had been slain during the Scourge to strengthen the wall. Forever trapped in stone, their song kept the wall strong. Alton lent his voice, and it helped, but he wasn't Estral Andovian.

Everything seemed well with the eastern section of the wall, though there was, he thought, an underlying tension. He was not surprised, not with the restlessness of Blackveil. There had not been any incursions through the breach of late, but the sense of waiting for the inevitable was there.

He disengaged and returned to the main chamber only to find Merdigen and the gryphons were not alone. Dale sat at the table with all five kittens curled up on her and sleeping contentedly. She was having a cup of tea with Merdigen, though Merdigen's was illusory, of course.

"You're back!" Alton exclaimed.

She smiled and raised her cup to him. "I am. Did you know it smells kind of catty in here?"

"You picked up on that, did you?"

They exchanged greetings, and she said, "The king's message for you is in my satchel." She nodded to where it lay on the table so as not to disturb the kittens. "Lots of news when you're done reading, and not a lot of it is good."

He took the satchel and pulled the king's message out,

addressed to Rider Lord Alton D'Yer. He broke the seal and read the contents with growing dissatisfaction. King Zachary wrote: *The quills you sent me impress upon me the urgency for more troops to be stationed at the wall. I have not forgotten you, but unfortunately, until such time as hostilities with Second Empire cease, I just cannot spare them.*

Alton tossed the message onto the table in disgust.

"Bad news?" Merdigen asked.

"He can't give us any troops because of the war."

"I was under the impression that was the case," Dale replied, "though I wasn't told directly. They were still waiting out Second Empire, holed up in the Eagle's Pass Keep when I was there, and there are detachments north and west fighting factions, not to mention the Darrow Raiders."

News of the Darrow Raiders had reached the wall. They had hit some farms in D'Yer Province, and people had fled the countryside for the relative safety of Woodhaven.

"What else?" he asked.

"You should know that the colonel has been abducted."

"What?"

Dale then launched into an incredible tale of the Raiders, a magical travel device, whisper wraiths, great gray eagles, and the secretive realm of Varos.

"Well, well," Merdigen said, "so my pupil, Duncan, somehow survived all these years."

Alton just sat there stunned.

Dale shifted a kitten and poured him a cup of tea. "I know. It's a lot to take in."

"Is the king just going to leave her there, a captive of the Varosians?"

"Karigan seemed to think he had some plan in mind, but he had not revealed it to her."

Whiskers rose to sniff at Alton's teacup. When he raised his paw to dip it in the cup, Alton shooed him away and sneezed. His eyes were watering and he just wanted to claw them out.

"I've heard of such travel devices," Merdigen said. "There were one or two present during the Long War. Surely the king could use it to rescue your colonel."

"Well," Dale said, "that brings us to the next part of the tale."

"There's more?" Alton asked.

Dale nodded and moved Junior as he climbed up her coat. The next part of the tale was as remarkable as the first, and involved an attack by elite Arcosian warriors who called themselves Lions, more whisper wraiths, and Karigan ending up in Eletia and being put on trial.

"I assume she was exonerated," Alton said.

Dale laughed. "More than that; they named her the heir of King Santanara."

"What?" Alton almost spewed his tea. His outburst elicited an annoyed meep from Whiskers.

"They call her Lady Winterlight," Dale said, "though she just wants to be known as Rider G'ladheon."

"That is unheard of with a non-Eletian," Merdigen said. "It's extraordinary. I do not understand what could have prompted the Eletians to bestow this upon her."

"Karigan doesn't understand either," Dale said. "Apparently, the Eletians looked ready to convict her, and then something made Prince Jametari drop the accusations and basically name her his sister. The other Eletians, she said, were astounded, too."

"Karigan," he murmured, and he shook his head.

"I know what you mean."

Dale then told him how Connly had demoted Karigan and made Tegan the new Chief Rider.

"He finds Tegan more reliable," she said.

Alton thought he could see Connly's reasoning, considering all the madness Karigan got herself into. Eletian royal status? That would certainly change her life going forward. If the two of them were still together, it would have made her a more suitable match for him as the heir of Clan D'Yer. Though their relationship had never panned out, a part of him always felt some regret. She'd been much different from the noble girls and women who had thrown themselves at him, and he found that maybe he still loved her a little.

"How is she?" he asked.

Dale stroked Zig, who kneaded her chest with little mews,

her gaze thoughtful before she answered. "I'm not sure. She is much as I remember her, yet not the same. She's thinner, harder, and yet more fragile. Tegan says she has lots of nightmares."

Alton nodded. He knew something of Karigan's nightmares.

"There is another thing," Dale said.

"More?"

She nodded. "Sad news. It's believed that Beryl is dead."

"Dear gods." He had hardly known Beryl, but it was always a punch to the gut when one of their own died. "How?"

"We don't know, and only know of her death because Karigan saw her ghost."

When they finished catching up and Dale left the tower to visit Captain Wallace, Alton decided he needed to commune with the western part of the wall. Of course, he could only check the section between the tower and the breach. He'd have to physically travel to the breach or one of the towers on the other side of it to access the rest.

The impression he got from the wall guardians this side of the breach was a great deal of worry. They were always nervous near the breach, but this time it seemed a little more intense. He hoped he wasn't leaking his own emotions into the wall after all the things Dale had told him. He tried to calm them with song, carefully tapping the cadence like the beat of hammers cutting stone that had been used to form the granite blocks of the wall. Slow and steady.

His efforts helped, but when he parted from his connection, he had a strong sense that the guardians were bracing themselves for a storm. What kind of storm, he did not know, except that it would come from Blackveil.

⊰⊱ A BAD DAY ⊰⊱

A nna hardly recognized the lower city. Civilians ordered to stay clear of the wall area were relegated to neighborhoods several blocks away. If Second Empire broke through the gate, the civilians would evacuate to the middle city. An air of desolation hung over the area with so many shops and taverns boarded up and closed, except for those taken over by the military as field offices or the menders to use as houses of mending. The people she saw were mostly uniformed—the black and silver of the wall and gate guard, and the gray of city guard.

It was noisy. Sergeants yelled for archers to keep sharp on the wall. Carpenters hammered extra bracing onto the gates. Hooves clattered on the cobbled streets as soldiers galloped past her.

She reined Maddie out of the way of menders bearing an injured man on a stretcher. There was rubble in the street where the enemy's war machines had succeeded in catapulting projectiles over the wall. A contingent of soldiers jogged by in orderly formation despite what appeared to be chaos everywhere.

"Git outta the way!" a drover yelled as he whipped a team of four horses straight at her at full gallop. She gave Maddie a kick and the mare practically jumped across the street. Anna was too surprised to see what was in the wagon, but it must have been something important.

More than a little shaken, she steeled herself and urged Maddie toward the gate in search of Captain Nolder.

"Move, Greenie!" a carpenter yelled at her as he and his helpers lugged more timbers to the gate.

This time she didn't make Maddie jump, but she reined the mare away from the vicinity of the gate. She knew everyone was at a heightened level of intensity and anxiety, but it still stung to get yelled at. All her life as a servant she'd been harangued and yelled at no matter how well she did her job, and it had made her sensitive to raised voices and slamming doors and the like.

She dismounted and tied Maddie to a post in front of a closed inn, and slung her message satchel over her shoulder. "You be good while I look for the captain."

Maddie just rubbed her neck against the post with a grunt.

"Good enough," Anna muttered.

The mare had actually done very well on the ride to the lower city, this time with no one accompanying her. Anna might wish for Lieutenant Mara to be with her, but she was much too busy attending the queen, and had said it was time for Anna to spread her wings anyway. It was time for all of the newest Riders to spread their wings. Riding lessons and weapons training continued with new fervor, but all other classes were canceled, and the green Greenies were now busy conveying messages around the city.

She strode past the gate on Compass Way, the street that ran the perimeter of the city along the inside of the wall, until she found a soldier who had just climbed down a ladder.

"I'm looking for Captain Nolder," she said.

"Tower three," he replied, and he pointed her in the right direction before heading off on his way.

She continued on. There was a good deal of activity on the ground beside the wall, but she deemed it easier to make her way on the street rather than climbing up onto the narrow wall walk.

Tower three appeared ahead, and she ran to the entrance. Once inside, she sprinted up the spiral stairs, plastering herself against the wall when soldiers in a rush thundered down the steps.

When she reached the middle landing that opened onto

the wall, she asked the archers stationed there, who kept
watch through arrow loops, where she'd find Captain Nolder.
She'd expected them to point to the stairs going to the top
level of the tower, but instead they pointed along the wall
walk.

"Be careful," one of the archers admonished her as she
stepped outside.

More archers stood lined up gazing outward between merlons and through arrow loops. She spotted Captain Nolder
ahead. He hung out over the wall between a pair of merlons,
peering through a spyglass. Wondering what held the captain's attention, Anna glanced over the shoulder of an archer,
then stopped in her tracks. She had not looked out upon the
enemy since that day she and Lieutenant Mara had ridden
together into the lower city to visit Master Robinson's saddle
shop. Back then, Second Empire had been well off in the distance, but now they had advanced, and had apparently done
so since the parley three days ago. They were nearly in arrow
range, close enough to make out individual figures of soldiers,
and there were thousands of them. Towering overhead were
three siege engines.

"Hah! It *is* broken," she heard the captain say. "They're
pushing it back to work on it."

There was chuckling among the archers.

"What's broke?" Anna asked.

The archer she stood behind turned and grinned. "Their
catapult. They'll probably have it fixed pretty quick, but it'll
give us a short reprieve."

She supposed such things commonly happened in war.
Things broke and needed to be fixed. Seeing the captain ease
back from his precarious perch, she approached and pulled
out a message from her satchel.

"Captain Nolder," she said, "I've a message for you from
General Meadows."

He handed his spyglass to one of his aides and took the
message and opened it. He read through it quickly, then
asked, "You have paper and pen with you?"

"Yessir." She passed him the supplies and the small writing board she carried in her satchel. While he wrote, she

looked outward to see what Second Empire was up to. It appeared there was a reorganization of the front line happening.

"Sir," a lieutenant said, "they're bringing up the archers again."

The captain looked up, then thrust his letter at her, the ink still wet. She frantically waved it in the air before folding it and placing it in her satchel.

"Let them waste their arrows," the captain told his archers. "Don't shoot unless you are sure of a target."

Anna thought she'd better move on and get out of the way. She was only three steps along when arrows hissed through the air. Some hit the merlons and wall, but others arced overhead and rained into the street below. People scrambled, but it appeared, miraculously, that no one had gotten hit. She hurried now.

"Another volley," someone shouted.

She was about halfway to the tower and sheltered behind a merlon with the friendly archer who had told her about the catapult. The arrows whizzed overhead again.

"They're just trying to soften us up," the archer explained, "before they attempt a major assault. They're not real accurate at this range."

That was reassuring, she supposed.

He moved to peer between two merlons, and before Anna could register what was happening, there was a *thunk!* and he spun around, an arrow impaled in his throat, and he fell from the wall walk to the street below. It had happened so fast that Anna's scream came belatedly.

Someone barked orders, and another archer came to take the spot of the fallen man.

"Best get on," the new man told her in a kindly voice. "And keep your head down."

Anna ducked and moved, but she was numb all over. After she ran down the tower steps and reached the street, she dashed to where she had left Maddie, fearing stray arrows.

Still in a state of shock, she rode up the Winding Way, oblivious to her surroundings. All she could see was the scene replaying in her mind, of the archer spinning around with the arrow stuck in his throat, and the expression of surprise on his face as he fell.

After Anna delivered Captain Nolder's message to General Meadows in the throne room where all the war planning was taking place, she returned to Rider stables to brush down Maddie and make sure she was ready for another run if called for. Anna hoped she wouldn't have to do another, shaken as she was.

Grooming Maddie on the crossties calmed her. The mare wasn't in her usual snappish mood, which helped, and the quiet of the stables seemed far removed from the activity in the lower city. She was aware of Sir Karigan in the other section of stables helping Riders get off on runs.

When Maddie was groomed to Anna's satisfaction, she returned the mare to her stall. She was checking her water bucket to ensure it was full and clean when there was a *bang!* and explosive, "Fekking goat balls!"

Anna rushed out of the stall to see what was the matter and found Sir Karigan hopping on one foot.

"What is it?" she cried.

Fury rolled off Sir Karigan. Anna took a step back. She'd never seen Sir Karigan so angry before. She'd noticed she'd been a bit short of late, and haggard looking, and assumed it was because of the stress they were all under. Even though Sir Karigan was no longer Chief Rider, Lieutenant Mara had her working in that capacity.

"Anna," Sir Karigan said, "is this yours?" She pointed at the floor.

Her grooming kit. The very sturdy wooden carrier was tipped over onto its side and the brushes and combs strewn across the floor.

"Yes'm," she replied in a small voice.

"I have very nearly broken my neck, and my toe, too. Do *not* leave your things in the middle of the aisle." The last came as a shout.

"I'm—I'm sorry." It was like being stabbed in the heart to have Sir Karigan raise her voice at her. She got on her knees and started picking up the brushes. "It won't happen again."

"It wouldn't have happened in the first place if you hadn't been so careless."

Sir Karigan stalked off, and Anna rubbed tears from her eyes. It wasn't just being yelled at by the person she admired most, but having that man killed right in front of her, and the other people shouting at her, and everything in an uproar. She missed the colonel, wherever she was, who rarely showed anger and looked out for her. Anna once again began to doubt her decision to become a Green Rider. She just wasn't tough enough.

When she put her gear and grooming kit away in the tack room, assiduously avoiding Sir Karigan who was preparing Carson's horse for an errand, she bolted from Rider stables and made her way to the central courtyard gardens where she might have some peace. It would take them longer to find her if they needed another Rider to make a run, and it was not right of her to hide, but she needed time to collect herself, maybe have a good cry.

The gardens were yielding well, it appeared, with tall poles burdened with bean stalks, and plump squashes and pumpkins growing on vines along the ground, neat rows of cabbages and greens, among other types of produce. Gardeners weeded and harvested and watered. Amid the orderly sections of vegetables stood an oasis that was King Jonaeus' Spring.

She crossed the stepping stones of the trout pond. A frog plopped into the water and shattered the mirrorlike surface. She continued along the path into an area of dense shrubbery and boulders that had not been removed when the ornamental gardens were converted to vegetables. She hoped no one else was there, but when she stepped into the secluded nook sheltered by the boulders, she found that a young woman sat on the rustic bench. After a moment, she realized the young woman was sobbing and that she hadn't heard it over the burbling of the spring.

Guess I'm not the only one having a hard day.

She started to retreat thinking she'd have to find some other hiding place when it dawned on her who the young woman was. She halted and turned around. "Nell Lotts, is that you?"

"Go away, Mousie," the servant said, her voice muffled through her handkerchief.

"Now what are you getting on about?" Anna, who had certainly never gotten along with Nell, thought she should just leave and feel some sort of satisfaction that her nemesis was having a worse day than she, but for whatever reason, she did not.

"Go away," Nell told her again.

Anna ignored her and sat beside her on the bench. "What's wrong?"

"What do you care? You hate me."

"I'll leave if you want, but I'm not having the best day, either. Maybe if you tell me what's wrong you'll feel better."

Nell blew her nose and settled, and gazed at the spring. Anna didn't think she was going to reveal what was troubling her, but then a short time later, she said, "I'm pregnant."

Oh, no, Anna thought. "What of the father?"

Nell sobbed again, which answered Anna's question. The father was either dead, or was disavowing the child, which meant Nell was on her own.

"Master Scrum," Nell whispered. Master Scrum, who oversaw the general castle servants, would not go easy on her. In fact, he'd be downright harsh and he might even dismiss her outright, which meant Nell would be unable to provide for her child and would be at the mercy of others.

"Was he nasty to you?" Anna asked.

"He . . . He's the father, and he will not accept it."

Aeryc and Aeryon, Anna thought.

"I just want to die," Nell wailed.

The image of the poor archer with the arrow in his throat passed before Anna's eyes. "No, you do not, Nell Lotts," she declared. "Not if I have anything to say about it."

~ MISTRESS EVANS ~

Anna searched the west wing for Mistress Evans, who oversaw the royal household and its servants, and though she did not directly supervise the general castle servants, she had the highest status among them and reported directly to the queen. Anna found her folding sheets in a chamber devoted to the royal linens. She stepped into the palatial room that boasted its own shiny brass and crystal chandelier, marble statuary of maidens and knights, and grand paintings of landscapes. It was filled with shelves and racks and tables for folding and storing the linens of generations of royalty, some exquisitely stitched by the nimble hands of queens and princesses. The pleasant scent of cedar suffused the entire room, for the walls were lined with it to repel moths.

"Anna, what a surprise," the older woman said. She claimed she'd no royal blood, but her bearing was regal and Anna had to fight an impulse to curtsy.

"I am sorry to disturb you," Anna said, "but I was wondering if I might have a word."

"You may, but your hands need not be idle while we talk."

Anna smiled and took the corners of one end of a sheet featuring the embroidery of Hillander terriers frolicking among flowers, and inhaled deeply. It smelled of a spring day. She spoke of Nell Lotts' situation while she helped fold.

"Does she know who the father is?" the housekeeper asked as she placed the folded sheet onto a shelf.

Anna nodded, then hesitated.

"Well, child?" Mistress Evans pressed.

"Master Scrum," she said at last. "He refuses to accept

643

responsibility and will dismiss Nell if she makes an issue of it."

"Do you believe the girl?"

"Yes'm, I do. You don't go around telling tales about Master Scrum. He has ways of finding out, and when he does, he makes sure you pay."

"Which means the girl must be removed from servants quarters immediately." Mistress Evans sighed. "Between you and me, Anna, I have never cared much for Master Scrum's manner and have been suspicious of certain of his records for some time. Nothing I could ever prove, of course, and it is not my place to interfere with the management of his domain, just as it is not his to interfere in mine. It is Castellan Javien who oversees him, but this crosses a line."

"What will you do?"

"I daresay, it would be best to bring this Nell Lotts into the royal household for the time being. Escort her over, if you would, Anna, and put her into the care of Sharri. Sharri will see her settled."

"Yes'm." Anna was relieved that Mistress Evans had come to the decision to take in Nell herself.

"I will broach the matter with the queen and castellan," Mistress Evans continued, "as much as I dislike the thought of disturbing them from more pressing problems." She shook her head, then drew another sheet out of a basket to begin folding. Anna once more caught the other end to help. "It sounds as if the unwed individuals in servants quarters need to be reminded of the measures they can take to avoid finding themselves in such a predicament. No doubt it is time to instill a dose of proper discipline there, too, which I'll also recommend to the castellan."

To Anna's mind, such a reckoning was well past due. Master Scrum was a terrible person, and she thought Mistress Evans' suspicions about him, whatever they were, were undoubtedly true.

She continued to help with the folding and found herself missing working for the even-handed head housekeeper. She never raised her voice, not even in rebuke. Her stately and composed manner was enough to put a situation to rights. In fact, might it not be good to work in the royal household again? Surely, with Queen Estora so busy with the war and twin babies, she'd need all the help she could get. And it would be safer than riding down to the lower city.

"Anna?" Mistress Evans said. "There is more on your mind, yes? What is it?"

To Anna's dismay, tears started to roll down her cheeks. Mistress Evans offered her a neatly folded handkerchief off of one of the shelves. Anna blew her nose and proceeded to tell her about the archer impaled with an arrow in his throat, and ended with, "Then Sir Karigan yelled at me because I left my grooming kit in the middle of the floor."

"Oh, my dear." Mistress Evans folded her into her arms. "You are a gentle child, and seeing a man killed right in front of you like that was not easy." She held Anna and patted her back until the sobs abated.

When they parted, Anna said, "Can I have my old job back, please? I'll clean hearths, scrub floors, anything."

Mistress Evans stood very erect and appraised her with an unswerving gaze. "That is the last thing I expected to hear from you." When Anna tried to interject, Mistress Evans hushed her with a curt shake of her head. "You've worked very hard to become a Green Rider, and if I'm not mistaken, you were well aware of the dangers. But yes, I know what you saw today is different than just hearing about such things."

Anna shuddered. "Yes'm, it is."

"I am afraid, before all is said and done," Mistress Evans continued, "we'll all see frightening and tragic things as people commit violent acts upon one another. In war, it is never just the warriors who are affected. Do you think you could stand being cooped up in the royal wing while your friends ride to battle, never knowing what is happening at any given moment?"

Anna smoothed a pillowcase she had just folded. She would worry a lot about her friends. It would be hard, she had to admit, not being right there to make sure they were all right.

"Could you stand wondering if the enemy will make their way through the city's defenses and assault us in even our most fortified place?" Mistress Evans asked. "If that should happen, none of us will be safe. In a way, I envy our warriors because they do not have to wait. They can actively work to stop the aggression of the enemy."

Keeping busy, Anna thought, and involved, was often useful, and she could see how being stuck in her old duties would cut her off from what was going on, from what was important. Still, the arrow in the man's throat . . .

"I do believe Colonel Mapstone and Queen Estora put a good deal of faith in you by, shall we say, breaking convention to allow you into the ranks of the Green Riders. The colonel, in particular, stood up for you, and I suspect she, were she here, would be most disappointed to learn that you wished to leave the messenger service so soon."

Anna stared at the floor worn by the footsteps of generations of servants who had come into the linens chamber over the centuries. Nothing could have made Anna feel more guilty than the invocation of Colonel Mapstone's name. Mistress Evans was certainly correct that the colonel had taken a chance by supporting her entry into the Green Riders. Anna's leaving would reflect poorly not just on herself, but the colonel, as well.

"As for Sir Karigan," Mistress Evans continued, "if she is not commonly given to shouting at you, you must question yourself as to why she did so today. The answer may prove illuminating. Ultimately, it is likely to have less to do with you than you may imagine."

"I know she has been short of sleep," Anna replied, "but even so, it's unusual."

"That should tell you something right there." Mistress Evans then collected a pile of folded linens into her arms. "I've my duties to return to. The needs of the royal household do not abate for anything, not even war. If it is truly your wish to return to work in the queen's household, I would gladly have you back. You were a good and earnest worker. However, think carefully about it before making a final decision. Think about how you would feel if you turned your back on the messenger service, and if you could live with the decision."

Anna bowed her head. The neat handkerchief she'd been lent was now all crumpled. "Thank you, Mistress Evans."

"I am glad I could help. You take care of yourself, Anna, and do bring Nell Lotts to Sharri."

"Yes'm."

Mistress Evans' skirts swished as she walked from the chamber bearing her burden. Anna stood where she was in the quiet among the linens. The war felt very remote from here. Even the activity of the castle seemed far off. She thought about all the head housekeeper had told her. If she had expected an easy answer, she had not been given one.

Anna carried a sack of Nell's scant belongings down the corridor away from servants quarters.

"What do you think Mistress Evans plans to say to Master Scrum?" Nell asked anxiously as she strode beside her.

"I haven't the faintest," Anna replied. She wasn't even sure if Mistress Evans would confront him directly.

They continued on in silence for a while. Nell shifted her basket in her arms. It contained a few more belongings—sewing supplies, a rag doll, a comb, and some ribbons. "Why are you doing this for me? I've never been, well, very nice to you."

"It isn't just for you," Anna replied. "You've got that baby coming, and while it's nice and quiet up here at the castle, it's not so good in the city with Second Empire trying to break through our walls." It was, she thought, no time to get kicked out onto the street. "People gave me a chance to get out from under Master Scrum's thumb, so maybe it's my turn to help someone."

Nell's gaze was downcast. "He threatened to throw me out if I didn't allow him between my legs anytime he wanted," she said.

Anna grimaced. If she had stayed among the general castle servants, would she have found herself in a similar situation?

"I didn't care for it," Nell continued, "but he did favors for me in return, like giving me little gifts and treats, and he let me get away with cutting out of work, so long as I kept my mouth shut. If I refused him when he wanted a poke, he slapped me around. You can imagine how he was when I told him I was missing my monthly and started getting morning sick."

Anna nodded. "No one will hit you or ask for a poke in the royal household," she said softly. "Mistress Evans keeps her lot in good order."

Nell released a long breath.

"She will not be lenient if you cut work," Anna added. "She's strict, but fair so long as you do a good job."

"I don't know how to thank you."

"Just do good."

"I will. I promise."

Anna left Nell with Sharri in the west wing, and then headed for the Rider wing, thinking that at least one thing had gone well this day, but the cloud of indecision once more hung over her head. She had questioned her ability to be a Green Rider often enough, but it was easy to say she'd been fine about it when her daily life had revolved around classes and training, and not actual experience, and then there was today. How did the others handle it? She guessed the Rider call gave them no choice in the matter and they faced whatever they had to face. Even after all that Lieutenant Mara and Sir Karigan had been through, they kept going because they had to. It only made her feel more ashamed.

When she arrived in the Rider wing, Lieutenant Mara stepped out of her chamber. "Ah, Anna, there you are. Do you have a minute?"

"Yes'm." She felt another tinge of guilt for avoiding the Riders and her duty.

Lieutenant Mara ushered her into her chamber. It was a comfortable place with colorful art on the walls and a patchwork quilt on the bed, upon which Ghost Kitty napped. Her desk, however, was worse than even Colonel Mapstone's ever was, with an old apple core, a pair of socks in need of darning, and what appeared to be a stack of a week's worth of dirty dishes on it.

Anna expected to be berated for her absence, but instead,

Lieutenant Mara asked, "As Karigan's friend, I was wondering if you had noticed her being a little surly of late?"

"Yes'm." Anna explained the incident with her grooming kit.

"Hmm. She snapped at me this morning, too. It's out of character, but the gods only know what's normal for her these days."

It was a validation to hear that Lieutenant Mara did not think Sir Karigan was herself either. "She seemed fine when she arrived, but the past few days, not so much."

"I agree," the lieutenant replied. "I've tried to get her to visit the menders, but there is never time, and Ben is occupied down by the wall. I was on the verge of ordering her to report directly to Vanlynn, but she slipped out to take a message herself to the east wall because no one else was available to take it."

Anna gazed at her boots, ready to confess her digression and unworthiness, to pour out all that had happened this day and that she was thinking of leaving the Green Riders.

The lieutenant, however, sighed and said, "I guess that's all, Anna. Thank you. You are dismissed."

Anna hesitated before leaving, again wishing to unburden her heart, but Lieutenant Mara was already digging into a pile of paperwork, a frown of concentration on her face. Maybe later, she thought, when the lieutenant wasn't so busy, though she had no idea when that would be. She returned to her chamber, feeling all sorts of turmoil, and not just for what she hadn't told the lieutenant. If anything happened to Sir Karigan, it would be all her fault because she should have been the one to take that message, and as she had learned today, dangerous things were bound to happen when you went near the battle zone. She did not deserve to be a Green Rider.

⋘ FIGHTING NYSSA ⋙

 Karigan berated herself for yelling at Anna, but the smallest irritations set her off. She had not slept for three days. She was exhausted, yes, but mind and body would not cooperate. She drank chamomile tea, and when that didn't work, she sipped of the whiskey her Aunt Tory had left her on her last visit. That didn't work, either.

She wearily tightened Condor's girth, and buckled on her cuirass. There was a message that needed to be delivered to the east wall, and no one else to take it. Anna should have been available, but she'd disappeared. Karigan didn't blame her really, not after being yelled at for such a minor transgression.

You are not a good friend, Nyssa said.

"Shut up," Karigan told her.

Making matters worse, Nyssa had stepped up her presence nearly tenfold, whispering disparaging words constantly and appearing around every corner. Currently, the torturer made herself at home in Rider stables by sitting on a bale of hay. She worked the bloody whip through her fingers.

When Karigan finished tacking Condor, she led him out of the stables, and there was Nyssa sitting on the fence rail. Karigan wanted to squeeze Nyssa's neck or batter her head against a rock. She fantasized about driving her saber through Nyssa's torso and burning the whip. The problem was that Nyssa was already dead.

It was the same all the way through the city as Karigan rode. Nyssa standing on a street corner or staring into a store window. She joined a group of people meeting in front of a

650

tavern. She was everywhere, on wagons, leaning out an upper story window, flicking her whip with a spray of blood as she crossed the street.

I am so tired, so tired of this, Karigan thought. *Why must she haunt me?*

Because I like it, Nyssa replied. *Because I enjoy breaking you, and I will, over and over.*

Sweat dribbled down Karigan's face, and she rubbed it away with the back of her hand. This had to end. It had to end one way or another.

Nyssa flashed her a smile before bending to examine vegetables at the market.

In order to reach the east wall, Karigan needed to pass through the gate between the middle city and the lower city. Nyssa was, of course, there, attired as a guard checking pedestrians through. Karigan rubbed her eye and saw that she was mistaken. It wasn't Nyssa at all but an actual guard. On the other side of the gate, there were Nyssas everywhere. She might not have nightmares because she could not sleep, but she had horrible waking dreams.

"No," she whispered. Her hands shook. Nyssa laughed.

After passing through the gate, Karigan turned, unseeing, off the Winding Way onto Skeller Lag Street, a distilling and brewing district in the city. Like so much else, the distilleries and brewers had gone quiet because of the shortages, in this case, of hops and grain.

She urged Condor into a fast trot, hoping to leave Nyssa behind, and it seemed to work. Everything remained heavy and dull to her from the lack of sleep, as though she moved through a thick fog. She wanted to speak to Ben about it, as she largely suspected he had done something when he forced her out of the healing sleep. He had, however, been inaccessible working near the city's main gate to assist with the wounded, and she'd been much too busy to seek him out. Maybe after she delivered the message, she'd go looking for him. She could not continue like this for much longer, and she was needed, which meant she had to be awake and well. The city had too few defenders.

As she rode down the final stretch of Skeller Lag, the east

wall came into view. She was told she'd find Major M'Gyre near the intersection with the Compass Way. There were no towers at this location. The closest was about three blocks down. Few guards and archers stood on the wall walk, as the defense of the city was focused near the main gate where Second Empire's army was massed, the gate being the weakest link in the wall system.

She found Major M'Gyre outside an abandoned brewer's house that faced the wall.

"Major," Karigan said, "a message from the general." She handed it down to her.

"Thank you, Rider." The major was a thickset woman in her middling years, and from what Karigan could tell in their few interactions so far, she was quite sensible and calm. Karigan liked her, and it helped that the major made much of Condor and patted his neck. "How are things up at the castle?"

"To tell the truth, I've been in the stables most of the time," Karigan replied. She did not add that when she was off duty and couldn't sleep, she roamed the mostly empty corridors of the castle because she could not stand lying in bed and staring at the ceiling of her chamber. "The throne room is pretty busy, I guess."

"I do not doubt it," the major replied.

A shout went up nearby.

"What is it, Corp—" the major began, but just then, arrows sang over the wall. Several of her people were struck and fell. "Damnation," she muttered. Without hesitation, she ran for the wall even though arrows rained around her. "Rider," she called, "we could use your help."

"Do you want me to go get—"

"On the wall! Now!"

Karigan licked her lips and shuddered.

Afraid? Nyssa asked with a tone of amusement. She leaned in a nearby doorway.

The archers were scrambling on the wall, the major climbing a ladder to reach the walk. More arrows landed near Condor's hooves. There was no time. She dismounted and slapped Condor on the rear so he would run down Skeller Lag Street to safety.

Then, with a deep breath, she headed for the ladder. Someone up top was blowing a horn, which would summon help faster than she could on horseback.

She had to step over bodies to reach the ladder, and tried not to think about it. She tried not to think about anything except what she must do right at the moment, and at that moment, she must climb the ladder.

It's not too late to run away, Nyssa told her. *They're too busy to notice.*

Karigan placed her foot on the bottom rung and climbed.

You will probably die, Nyssa said.

Karigan looked up and saw the torturer standing there on the wall staring back down at her. An arrow passed through Nyssa, but she did not even flicker. Karigan turned her gaze to the next rung and climbed.

There was an uproar on the wall, and the horn rang out again in desperate notes. Then she heard the unmistakable clang of swords above.

Oh, no, she thought.

Someone fell past her and crashed to the ground below. She closed her eyes for a moment.

That could be you, Nyssa whispered. Her laugh was like a snake that slithered through Karigan's mind.

Karigan fought with herself, tried to block out Nyssa's disparagements, then gathering any shred of courage she had left, forced herself to climb.

When she stepped onto the wall walk, she found Sacoridians engaged in melees with the enemy, who had climbed ladders from the other side of the wall. How had they done so without having been spotted? She then remembered that back at the mountains, Second Empire had hidden its army with some kind of magical shield.

There was no time to think about it for there was the enemy to engage and archers, who were generally better at shooting arrows than swordfighting, needed help, though Major M'Gyre was doing a good job of thrashing the enemy soldiers left and right.

Karigan unsheathed Colonel Mapstone's saber—she'd not yet acquired a new one of her own after the Darrow Raiders had taken hers—and quickly found herself an adversary. They engaged in a quick exchange of blows, the sun glancing off the steel of their blades, but Karigan reached and delivered a slash across her opponent's neck and ended the bout almost before it had begun.

From the corner of her eye, she saw the major and some of her people attempting to heave Second Empire's ladders over to stem the flow.

She took out another soldier who had nearly gotten the better of a young archer. When the next turned to fight her, it was Nyssa, Nyssa with a sword instead of the whip. If Karigan hadn't been wearing the cuirass, she would have been skewered in her moment of surprise. Nyssa used her hesitation to get past her guard with a thrust.

"I hate you!" Karigan cried.

Nyssa laughed.

Karigan's exhaustion fused into rage. She aggressively lunged after Nyssa. It turned out that Nyssa was not so good a swordswoman and she was felled by Karigan's saber, but Karigan's triumph was short-lived, for another Nyssa came after her. Karigan screamed her fury and exchanged blows with her. Her swordmaster training held her in good stead for fighting on the narrow wall walk. She held a strong, steady stance while her opponent danced and jumped around flailing her sword. All that movement made for poor, insecure footing and led to tiring oneself out, and an opening for Karigan. She thrust, and this Nyssa fell from the wall.

When the next Nyssa challenged Karigan, Karigan screamed in enraged frustration. She could not seem to free herself of the torturer. A fever came upon her, and she was determined to destroy them all until there were no more. She did not worry about her back, she was not concerned about getting hurt, she only saw another Nyssa to cut down, and she did so, one Nyssa after another.

She did not know how many she killed. She had begun to slip in the blood left by those she had defeated. At some point, and she did not know how much time had passed, the action on the wall settled down. No new Nyssas presented themselves to her. She paused, her lungs raw from effort, sweat burning her eyes. A figure ahead turned around. Nyssa! This one did not raise her sword, but Karigan did, and she leaped forward to take her head.

"No, Rider!" someone shouted.

Ben Simeon stumbled out the door of the tavern-turned-mending house into the side yard where three apprentice menders rested on a weedy patch of grass. He threw his bed-roll down beside them and, still stained in the blood of a wounded guard he'd worked on, sank onto his blankets with a groan.

Master Savell had ordered him to get some actual rest after days of tending the wounded using his nonmagical mending skills. Oh, there was the occasional touch of healing he provided a patient if he or she were showing signs of infection, or if it relieved someone's excruciating pain, but he had to do it when no one was looking, for he was under strict orders from Master Vanlynn to use his healing ability in dire circumstances only. She told him his learned skills were more precious than his magical gift because he could treat more people in the ordinary way. When he used his special ability to any extent, he was useless for hours, if not days, and right now they needed all the menders they could find. However, he'd been working long shifts for days, and when he did get a chance to bed down, his sleep was awful, rendering him almost as useless as if he'd been overusing his ability.

He wrapped his blanket around him and sighed. Despite his exhaustion, sleep eluded him. There was the heavy snoring of two of the apprentices, full daylight bleeding through his closed eyes, and the noise of traffic on the street, but it wasn't so much those irritations that kept him awake as the knowledge that if he did fall asleep, he'd be assailed by nightmares. They'd started maybe two or three days ago and were bad enough to wake him several times a night and leave him drenched in sweat. It got so bad that he was almost afraid to close his eyes.

An amorphous shadow lashing a whip that splattered

blood stalking him. The one he loved being ripped from him as cataclysm caused the world to collapse around him. A black forest full of monstrous creatures that lunged out of a thick vapor at him. And more. The shadow, however, was always present, always there to rend his flesh with its barb-tipped whip.

When he admitted he was suffering from bad dreams to Master Vanlynn, she had tried to give him a soporific, but *sleep* was not the problem. It was the dreams.

After a while he started to drowse despite himself, the ambient sounds around him falling away, even the snoring of the apprentices, until the distant, urgent notes of a horn rang out, drawing him back to wakefulness.

"What's that?" Claris, one of the apprentices, asked in a sleepy voice.

"Trouble," Ben replied, but he did not get up. The trouble, he thought, or more likely its result, would find its way to the menders soon enough. "Guards somewhere on the wall calling for help," he elaborated.

"Shouldn't we be doing something?" Claris asked, sounding more awake now.

"They'll get us if they need anything. Best that you rest while you have the chance." He closed his eyes. He could hear shouting down by the gate, and the clatter of hooves, no doubt the guard responding to the call for help. If Second Empire overran the wall, Master Savell would most certainly come out and wake them so they could evacuate the wounded. Until then, he would rest, and at last he drifted off, too exhausted to worry about enemy incursions, or even nightmares.

"Umf . . ." Ben muttered. He was being shaken awake from a better sleep than he'd had in some while.

"C'mon, Ben, you got to get up," someone said urgently.

He sat up. "Wounded coming?" But it was not Master Savell, or any mender, kneeling beside him, but a Green Rider.

"No," Anna Ash replied. "Lieutenant Mara wants you up at the castle. It's Sir Karigan."

⋙ DESCENT ⋘

"**S**he went berserk," the corporal said.

Mara gazed at Karigan behind the bars of the block house. They'd manacled her wrists and attached them with a chain to the back wall of her cell. That was how crazed she'd been, they told Mara. Currently, Karigan seemed to be involved in a conversation with herself. The name "Nyssa" kept coming up, and the words "I will kill them all," as well. There were dark rings beneath her eyes. Mara had already sent Anna for Ben.

"She killed, I dunno how many, a bunch of the enemy," the corporal continued, "and it made the difference. They'd have overrun us, otherwise."

A contingent of Second Empire's soldiers had somehow approached the east wall unseen. She strongly suspected magic. The east, west, and north walls were sparsely guarded, with much of the city's forces concentrated near the gate at the south district where they faced the bulk of Second Empire's army. Mara did not know what the queen and her advisors would decide to do in light of this new tactic, but they were spread too thin. She prayed that King Zachary and his army would arrive soon.

"We were lucky to have a swordmaster there," the corporal said. "She cut 'em down like hay at harvest. But then when there were no more, she turned on us. She nearly got Major M'Gyre, but we tackled her and brought her here. Wasn't easy."

No, it didn't look like it had been. The corporal and his companions, two privates, were bruised and cut, had bloody

657

noses. All of that could have been a result of their melee with Second Empire, but she kind of didn't think so.

"Thank you, Corporal," she said, "you may be excused."

He nodded, and as he and the privates exited the block house, they all glanced one last time at Karigan with wide-eyed expressions of awe.

Mara sighed. Karigan had clearly snapped. When one thought about it, it wasn't really surprising, given everything she'd been through over the last year or two—travel through the evil that was Blackveil Forest, the loss of a man she had loved in the future time, then the torture up north, and captivity by the Darrow Raiders. Frankly, Mara was surprised she'd held it together for as long as she had.

She approached the cell. Karigan seemed not to notice her. "Karigan?"

Karigan did not acknowledge her, did not even look her way.

"Karigan, can you hear me?" she asked more loudly.

This time, Karigan seemed to hear. She raised her head. "Go away," she growled. "Get out of my mind."

"I am not in your mind. I am right here outside your cell."

Now Karigan looked. Mara's hair stood on the nape of her neck for she hardly recognized her friend. Her expression was feral. Then she collected herself and leaped at the bars with a snarl. Her chains, which didn't extend that far, snapped her back. Still, Mara was spooked enough that she jumped.

"A real animal, that one," said the block house guard. He sat with his feet up on his desk, and picked at his teeth with the tip of his knife.

"Karigan—" Mara began.

"I will end you," Karigan said, "all the Nyssas until there are no more." She looked a wounded, crazed animal.

"Oh, Karigan," Mara said. She hoped Ben would be able to help.

It felt like it was taking forever for Anna to return with him, and she had to endure seeing her friend in this state while she waited, and listen to her muttering madly to herself. When finally they did arrive, she saw how haggard Ben looked as he dragged himself in. Blood splatters and splotches stained his mender's smock. Mara gave him a rundown, and as she did, he moved closer to the bars to watch Karigan. She had turned to face the wall and had quieted.

"She's not talking strange anymore," Anna observed.

"You say she hasn't been sleeping well?" Ben asked.

"No," Mara replied. "Maybe not at all."

"She isn't the only one," he mumbled. "I am afraid that after we woke her for the parley, we didn't follow through with getting her back into the mending wing for more rest and healing. It's been . . . busy."

A vast understatement, Mara thought. "Can you help her?"

"I don't know. This sounds more like a sickness of her mind. As you said, what she's been through is more than enough to break anyone."

"Lieutenant," Anna said quietly. She pointed at the cell.

At first Mara didn't get what Anna was seeing, but she noticed Karigan standing more erect, her head held high. She still faced the wall so they couldn't see her expression, but the attitude of her body had changed, and there was something else, a change in the air or the light, almost like the downsweep of great wings about her.

"You will *DESCEND*," came a voice that was Karigan's, but somehow not. It was not loud, yet it reverberated through the entirety of Mara's body and raised gooseflesh on her arms. It came from nowhere and everywhere, and was so full of command that she felt compelled to obey, though she knew not how.

"I will end you," Karigan told the Nyssa on the other side of the bars. "All the Nyssas until there are no more."

It is too late, Nyssa said, a tone of glee in her voice. *You are broken, and you are mine.*

Karigan clenched her hands and faced the back wall of the cell. *I don't know who I am or what is real anymore.*

Nyssa laughed.

I can't take this anymore, Karigan thought. *I want to die.* There were no tears. She couldn't seem to make them. There was only the exhaustion she felt bone deep. She wanted to die, but would there be relief even in the grave?

I will always be with you, Nyssa told her.

Karigan had not felt this hopeless since the north in the days following her torture. There was a time when she had been strong, strong enough to command the dead, at least as Westrion's avatar, but though she had tried, she could not rid herself of Nyssa. The command had failed her. Westrion had abandoned her.

You need me, Nyssa said. *You want me because I remind you of how weak you are, of how much of a victim you are, which you can use as an excuse for your fear and evoke the pity of your friends, and especially your king.*

It was not true.

Is it not? You revel in the attention they give you. The attention he *gives you.*

A part of Karigan knew this was not true. She didn't want pity. And yet, another part doubted. Was it all a ploy she used to draw Zachary closer? She just wanted to bash her head against the stone wall to rid herself of the sound of Nyssa's voice, but doing so meant Nyssa won. Giving in to the grave was a victory for her. Giving up meant the torturer won all.

"I have had enough," Karigan whispered. "I own my fear."

Nyssa laughed again. *It's so adorable when you try to defy me.*

"I own my fear," Karigan repeated, "and I will be free."

The Nyssa standing in the cell with her seemed to yawn. *I wonder how you will manage that, especially when you want me with you. You want me to stay.*

Karigan paused and gazed at the unwavering figure of the ghost in her cell. *You want me to stay,* Nyssa had said. Her words suggested she could leave, or maybe even be gotten rid of.

You're wrong, Nyssa said hastily. *You can't be rid of me. I will always be with you.*

Cold washed through Karigan's veins, the cold of the heavens. Maybe this time . . . Maybe this time she could compel Nyssa to leave her alone, to cast her away. "I own my fear," she whispered. "I have no need of you."

You do. You NEED me.

Darkness flooded the edges of Karigan's vision, where the stars of the heavens pierced the vast tapestry of the infinite. Though not clad in the star steel armor of the avatar, the power of that office filled her.

The spirit of Nyssa Starling fluctuated in an otherworldly breeze. With a twitch of Karigan's finger, the torturer's whip dissolved into a wisp of supernatural smoke.

No! Nyssa cried. *Don't do this—you need me!*

Karigan smiled. She thought to draw the moment out, to make Nyssa beg, but she tired of her existence. "You will *DESCEND.*"

No!

Karigan pointed at the floor. It began to absorb Nyssa's feet. She screamed.

You can't do this! You need me!

"I do not," Karigan replied. *"DESCEND."*

Nyssa screamed and raged as she melted into the floor to her knees, then to her hips and shoulders. Another flick of Karigan's finger took away her voice so that the torture of descent was silent, animated only by her contorted expression and voiceless scream. She would seep into the hells, drawn from one to another until she reached the worst, where she would suffer worse torments than those she had inflicted on her victims.

When Nyssa was finally gone, the otherworldliness, the cold presence of the heavens seeped out of Karigan's being. She felt as if she would simply float up from the floor. The silence in her mind, but for her own thoughts, was amazing. There would always be some echo of Nyssa, and reminders of her, always the reminders, that the descent of the torturer would not erase, but Karigan was now free without that voice constantly undermining her and trying to break her.

She turned and saw Mara, Anna, and Ben watching her with bewildered expressions on their faces. She smiled, then laughed. "I'm free," she told them. "I'm finally free."

"**I**'m free," Karigan said, "I'm finally free."

Mara studied her friend's face. Joy had replaced the wildness in her eye. Tears slipped down her cheeks. She laughed. Was she better, or had she sunk deeper into madness?

"What are you free of, Karigan?" Ben asked.

"Nyssa. She has haunted me since the north. I—I couldn't get her to shut up in my head. I couldn't get rid of her until now."

Ben looked at Mara with questioning eyes.

"Her torturer," Mara reminded him, then whispered, "and you know her ability with spirits."

He nodded, then turned back to Karigan. "How are you feeling now?"

"Relieved," she replied. "So much lighter. You have no idea. Exhausted, though. So terribly exhausted." She brought her hands to her face to scrub it, the chains clinking.

Mara pulled Ben aside, and Anna went to the bars of the cell to speak quietly with Karigan.

"What do you think?" Mara asked.

"It is clear she needs rest. I think we should get her released, and return her to her quarters. Lack of sleep, and whatever duress she's been under with this—this ghost, will have taken a toll."

"We could really use her help with things," Mara said. "All hands are needed."

"I know, but she will be of little help to you or the realm without some healing rest. Think of her as having an injury you can see, say, something as debilitating as a broken leg.

She is at least that bad and needs some time. She will probably never recover fully from the trauma of torture—none of us would, but if she can heal in some ways, she should have the strength to cope with it, something I think you understand."

Mara did. The burn scars on her face and other parts of her body were only on the surface of what had been injured. She was the first person on whom Ben had ever used his true healing ability. "Are you up for it? The healing? You look like you've not been sleeping either."

"Bad dreams. Nightmares. Couldn't tell you exactly what they're about, but they've been waking me up in a cold sweat. Not pleasant."

She didn't expect so, and thought they were likely an extension of the horrors he saw when treating the wounded. She turned back toward the cell.

"—and I bedded him down real good," Anna was telling Karigan, "and made him a nice bran mash."

"Thank you," Karigan told her, "for looking after him. I am sorry I yelled at you earlier. I wasn't myself."

Anna gazed at her feet. "I know that now, but it was still wrong to leave my kit in the middle of the floor."

"I was too harsh," Karigan replied.

There was, Mara thought, a serenity about Karigan that she hadn't seen in far too long. Not since before Karigan had left for Blackveil. There was still fragility, but also strength. Karigan had always been strong, but having overcome all she'd experienced had only made her more so.

"I can't fix her mind," Ben said quietly, "but I can help by facilitating the physical healing, and that includes the rest she needs."

Mara nodded and stepped up to the bars beside Anna. "Karigan, we are getting you out of here."

Saying it, it turned out, was much easier than doing it. The block house guard was stolid in his insistence that Karigan was *not* to be released.

"You didn't see her when she came in," he said. "It took four of us to handle her."

"She needs mending," Mara told him.

"You can do it here."

"No," she said. "Private, I am ordering you."

He gave her a long look. "I don't take orders from Greenies."

"You do from a superior officer."

"Not a Greenie one."

Mara leaned over his desk. "Your captain might have something to say about that. Don't think I won't have a word with him about you."

"Go ahead." He folded his arms across his chest and tilted back in his chair.

Mara decided she needed to try another tack, as Guard Captain Grayhouse was probably too busy down at the gate for her to bother. "I suppose, then, I'll have to invite Arms Master Drent to come over here."

"Arms Master Drent? Why?"

"She is one of his swordmasters, you idiot, and an honorary Weapon. Didn't you see the insignia on her sleeve?"

That got his attention.

"Not to mention she's a knight of the realm. The *only* knight of the realm."

"Oh, she's *that* Greenie?" He sat up but still looked undecided.

"Anna," Mara said, "please go fetch Arms Master Drent." She had no idea if he would come, but she hoped the mere threat of the intimidating arms master coming to the block house would be adequate.

"Yes'm!" Anna crossed toward the door. Her hand was on the handle when the guard finally pushed himself back from the desk.

"No need," he said. "You'll just have to sign the papers and take responsibility for her."

Mara did, and the guard took his key ring to the cell and, with an expression of misgiving, unlocked it. Then he handed another key to Mara. "For the fetters. You'll have to unlock them yourself."

"Oh, for gods' sakes," she muttered.

When she took the key, the guard hastily backed away.

Just how much damage had Karigan inflicted when she'd been brought in? She shook her head and entered the cell.

After she unlocked the manacles, Karigan rubbed her wrists and said, "Thank you."

"Let's get you to your quarters," Mara replied.

They gathered her gear, her weapons and cuirass, and started to leave, but Karigan halted before the guard. He looked about ready to bolt. She put her hand out, palm up. He just stared at it.

"My ring," she said, "and the crystal."

"What ring? A crystal?"

"You know very well. You took them away from me when I was brought in and hid them in your desk."

"I did no such thing," he said. "One of the other guards must have taken them."

"It was you." She got into his face. "Hand them over. *Now.*"

He scrambled behind his desk and pulled a drawer open, then he handed her the items, the beautiful ring with the emerald leaves, and the shiny crystal that Mara knew was a moonstone.

When everyone else had stepped outside, Mara paused in the block house and told the guard, "I am still going to talk to Captain Grayhouse about this. He happens to be a friend of mine. Also, you might reconsider stealing from prisoners. Not only is Rider G'ladheon a knight and honorary Weapon, but kin to the king of Eletia. I do not think Queen Estora or King Zachary would take kindly to your poor treatment of a royal personage representing the realm of an important ally."

She left the dumbfounded guard standing there and, with a sense of triumph, headed out the door.

Back in the Rider wing, Mara excused Anna so she could attend to her other duties, leaving just her and Ben with Karigan in Karigan's chamber.

"Aching," Karigan was telling Ben. "I think whatever I did down at the wall is catching up with me."

"Do you remember any of it?"

"Not a lot. Flashes of fighting, and Nyssa being everywhere."

"I'll do what I can for you," Ben said. "Just don't tell Vanlynn I did it in one go."

"Ben," Mara said in a warning voice, "Master Vanlynn isn't the only one who has say over the use of your ability."

"Oops," he said, looking chagrined.

Karigan laughed, and it was good to hear.

"Don't overdo," Mara told him.

"I understand," he replied. To Karigan, he said, "I am going to put you into a healing sleep and work on your back to finish what was started."

Mara and Ben stepped out into the corridor while Karigan changed into her nightgown.

"Think she'll be all right?" Mara asked.

He ran his fingers through his hair. "She seems much better mentally. Whatever she did to that ghost, whatever happened back in the block house, it has helped dramatically. Only time will tell if it sticks. Physically? I'll know more when I do the healing, but she seems to be doing pretty well for someone who went berserk on Second Empire, then struggled with guards all the way to the block house. She's bruises, maybe some cuts, and achiness, but no major injuries. She's the most interesting patient I've ever had."

Mara chuckled. "That's our Karigan."

A short time later, Karigan further challenged Ben when he tried to use his ability to put her into a healing sleep as she lay beneath the covers of her bed. He had touched the bridge of her nose, but nothing happened. He tried several times, and still nothing.

"I can feel the energy of your ability," Karigan said, "but that's it. Ever since you woke me for the parley, I've felt like a piece of me has been missing, or maybe it's asleep without the rest of me."

Ben scratched his head.

"Does this mean I'm going to be awake for the rest of my life?" she asked.

"I hope not," he replied. "It would not be a good thing. Let me try again."

It did not work.

"I am going to get you a regular soporific," he said, and he left, but returned only a moment later with Mason right behind him, the two discussing the situation. "Mason was passing by, so I grabbed him," he explained, and he encouraged him to try putting Karigan into the healing sleep.

"She said she'd break my finger," Mason protested.

"If she does, I'll heal it," Ben replied. He, of the infinite patience, sounded exasperated.

"Do it," Mara ordered.

"Yes, Lieutenant," Mason said.

"I won't break your finger," Karigan told him. "I promise."

He started to reach for the bridge of her nose.

"I might bite it, though," she said.

"Ha ha," Mason said. He did not look amused, but he did not hesitate.

Ultimately, he failed to put Karigan to sleep just as Ben had.

"Looks like it's time for the soporific," Mara said.

"I am thinking," Ben replied, "that won't do much good for the underlying problem." He paced back and forth. "Karigan says part of her is still asleep. We need to find that piece and reconnect it with the rest of her. Somehow, when I took her out of the healing sleep, I didn't bring all of her out. She's disconnected from it. I messed up."

"I don't know if that's the right way of looking at it," Mason said, and the two launched into a full-on debate that erupted into an argument. Karigan threw her blanket over her head.

Mara sat on the side of her bed. "You all right?"

"I am wonderful because Nyssa is gone," Karigan said, "but I am terrible because I'm so tired and can't sleep."

"Certainly not with these two arguing. I'm sure they'll figure out something."

"Hope so." Karigan did not sound hopeful.

Another mender appeared in the doorway and, looking at Ben, said, "There you are."

"Is that Cranky Aisla?" Karigan whispered from beneath her blanket.

Mara laughed. The severe expression on the journeyman mender's face made the appellation apt. "Yes," she replied.

Karigan groaned.

Ben and Mason told Aisla about the problem they were trying to solve.

"Well," she said, "did you try giving back the sleep you took away?"

"We tried to put her to—" Mason began.

"That's not what I asked. I asked, *Did you try giving back the sleep you took?*"

"Give back," Ben murmured. He paced back and forth a couple times. "When I took her out of her healing sleep, I actually took her sleep? I wonder if that would explain the dreams and nightmares I've been having."

It sounded rather obvious to Mara.

Karigan peeked out from beneath her blanket. "Give me my sleep back. You can keep the nightmares."

 ALONG THE MIND PATH ⫷

"**I**'m going to try what Aisla suggests," Ben said. "I don't know if it's actually possible to *give* you your sleep back, but we'll see, and Mason can back me up if needed."

"Please, let's just do it," Karigan said.

"We'll check on you regularly if this works," he added.

"I will, too," Mara said. She had moved away from the bed to give Ben space and stood with her arms folded. Karigan wasn't the only one feeling impatient.

"Just relax, Karigan," Ben told her.

She withheld a tart reply and tried to do as he asked, and closed her eyes. As before, he touched the bridge of her nose and she felt tingling in her head. She did not fall asleep. Instead of withdrawing, however, he kept at it, and the tingling turned into waves, gentle waves that rose and fell, rose and fell. It was pleasant and soothing, but it wasn't putting her to sleep. She . . .

It hadn't worked.

She opened her eyes astonished to find her room empty but for herself and Ghost Kitty who had curled up beside her. She hadn't slept, had she? But then she realized she felt rested and *good*. And her bladder was extremely full. She got up and took care of that business, and now realizing just *how* well she felt, she laughed and danced around her chamber, pausing only to take in the sunshine glowing in the window. Then she twirled around with a feeling of such lightness that it was almost as if her feet did not touch the floor.

Free of Nyssa, fully rested, moving without pain—it was like being reborn, like the blossoming of the first spring in a new world and baby birds chirping in their nests, and speckled fawns frolicking around their mamas for the sheer delight of having legs. She almost broke out in song, but stopped abruptly, deciding that her tone deafness would ruin the perfection of the moment.

She glanced at Ghost Kitty still curled on her bed, watching her with an expression of disgust. He then shifted so that his back was to her.

"Fine," she said, "be that way."

She grabbed her robe and stepped out into the corridor. The Rider wing appeared quiet. No one moved about, and the common room was empty. She then checked the bathing room and found she could have it all to herself. She'd take a nice hot bath and then report to Mara.

She entered and closed the door behind her, plugged the tub, and released the valve on the tank that always held heated water, warmed over coals in a sort of hearth, and filled the tub.

She did not know how long she soaked, but it was long enough for her to prune up. It was a blissful interlude before she must confront the world, or at least her part of it. Since the water was still warm, she lingered as it was unlikely she'd have much of a chance to rest once she returned to duty.

She closed her eyes and decided to try something she hadn't attempted since Eletia. With Nyssa now banished to the hells, the way was likely open to her. Since she hadn't a burbling Eletian stream to serve as a focus for entering the starry meadow this time, she used the imagery Enver had once given her. She followed along the lapping shore of a lake, through an emerald forest on a path lined with ferns. Without Nyssa to block her, she traveled with ease along the mind path. Before she knew it, she stood in the meadow where the dew on tall grasses glistened like stars. And there, waiting for her, was the most beautiful and perfect white mare.

"Seastaria," Karigan murmured.

Her aithen, her spirit animal. This time, the great black

stallion, Salvistar, was not present. It was a relief. But as the mare approached, it was clear that something of him remained.

"You're pregnant," Karigan said, observing Seastaria's bulging sides.

When the mare reached her, she blew through her nostrils. Karigan stroked her neck.

"Is it even possible for you to be pregnant?"

Seastaria did not answer, but shifted her position beneath Karigan's hands as if to give her permission to stroke the side of her belly. Karigan felt the contours of the foal. It quivered beneath her touch, and a sensation like a jolt of energy crackled through her veins. She stepped back, startled. Seastaria flickered her ears and gazed curiously at her. She touched the mare's side again, but the sensation did not recur.

"Your foal is well along," Karigan said, which was curious since the mating she'd observed had been only two months ago, but, she reminded herself, this was not the ordinary world but the aithen'a, and Seastaria and Salvistar were not ordinary horses.

She supposed anything was possible here. It wasn't clear to her where or what the aithen'a was, or if it was simply a vision in her mind, which would mean Seastaria could simply be a figment of her imagination, but she felt so real, so warm, her coat silky. And when Karigan had been inside Seastaria running with the stallion? That had transcended anything she understood of the world.

Seastaria seemed to enjoy the attention, but after a while, she nudged Karigan with her nose.

"What? I, er, don't have any treats with me if that's what you're wanting."

When she tried to pet the mare again, Seastaria shoved her toward the path she'd used to enter the starry meadow.

"You want me to leave?"

Seastaria stamped her hoof and swished her tail.

A little hurt, Karigan asked, "Did I do something wrong?"

Seastaria nuzzled her arm as if in reassurance, then nudged her again.

"All right, you need me to leave."

In that moment, she glimpsed a storm in the mare's eyes that usually reflected the azure sky and fair weather clouds. The storm that raged, Karigan knew, represented battle.

"You are right," she said, "I need to return."

She kissed Seastaria's nose and hurried down the path. When she was back in the world, she found the bath water uncomfortably tepid. She got out and dried herself off and, wrapped in her robe, stepped out into the corridor. She paused and listened, but the Rider wing was still eerily quiet.

Back in her chamber, she dressed quickly and tied her damp hair back. The last thing she did was buckle on Colonel Mapstone's sword.

The corridor remained empty. Even Ghost Kitty had disappeared. She knocked on Mara's door, but no one answered. The common room was abandoned, motes of dust floating in the air where the sun came through the window. She tried knocking on other doors, but no one was around. Her earlier mood of joy turned to one of consternation. She told herself that with the siege, all the Riders would be busy, but usually there'd be at least someone around.

I guess I'm the someone.

She headed for the main castle corridor. It, too, seemed abandoned. Karigan's heart started pounding. Had everyone been magicked away while she slept?

When a servant armed with buckets and a mop appeared from behind a door, she exclaimed and ran to him. He took a step back with a startled expression on his face.

"Where is everyone?" she demanded.

"I, uh, dunno where *everyone* is, Rider. Bunches of folk are guarding the walls, I 'spect. Others here and there."

"Riders? Have you seen any Riders?"

He gave her a pointed look, then shrugged. "I don't keep track of 'em. Gotta get back to work." He hurried off, dirty water sloshing in one of his buckets.

Her stomach roiled with hunger so she decided the dining hall was as good a place as any to search for Mara. That was what she told herself, anyway. And it wouldn't do anyone any good if she fainted.

When she reached the dining hall, she found its

atmosphere subdued, with a few servants and some exhausted-looking guards grabbing a bite to eat. To her relief, she saw a figure in green hunched over a bowl of soup. She grabbed a bowl for herself and a meat roll, though the meat looked scant. She sat across from the Rider.

Fergal slowly gazed up at her. He was unshaven and his hair tousled. He looked as if he'd been rolling around in the dirt. It took a moment for recognition to register in his tired eyes.

"You're up," he said.

"Yes, and feeling good."

"Took you long enough. Been what, three days?"

Karigan nearly dropped her spoon. "I've been abed three days?"

"Aye. Mara and Anna kept an eye on you when they could. Ben, too. Wish I could have three days."

"You've looked better," she said. "What have I missed?"

He told her that Second Empire had stepped up their attacks. King Zachary and his army were still on the march, and General Birch seemed to know that he had to seize the city as soon as possible. Having King Zachary on his flank would place him between a hammer and an anvil.

"The south lower city is a mess," he explained. "Their catapults are knocking down buildings. So far, the walls seem to be holding, but it's only a matter of time for the gate. They've got a battering ram and have been making use of it."

"Our Riders?" she asked.

"Most are all right. Carson and Trace are in the mending wing. Carson got blasted with rock shards when the catapult sent boulders over the wall. He'll be all right, Ben said."

"And Trace?"

"Overuse of her ability. Yesterday she collapsed and hasn't woken up. Mara says the queen has been using her to talk to the king almost constantly."

That was not good to be cut off from Zachary. Their connection to him was one of their advantages against the enemy.

Fergal continued to tell her the Riders were, of course, carrying out their duty to convey messages about the city, but also pitching in where needed, whether keeping watch on one of the walls, patrolling the city, or assisting the menders.

He could not tell her how Estora was faring, though she'd ridden down to the gate at least once in that rose armor of hers to rally the troops and hearten her people.

"I don't know how much longer we can hold the outer wall," Fergal said. "We've lost a lot of people, and it's hard to cover the whole thing. Second Empire has tried to climb over the sections with fewer guards, like that day when you went berserk on the east wall."

Ignoring his reference to her loss of control that day, she asked, "How much longer, do you think?"

"Dunno," he replied, "but I don't think the king will arrive in time."

A HERO AND
A MADWOMAN

As soon as Karigan located Mara at Rider stables, she was put to work much as before, readying horses and Riders to go out on errands throughout the city.

"Glad to have you back," Mara told her.

Mara hadn't time for conversation, however, and left the stables with haste to attend the queen. She looked tired and careworn, a look Karigan would become accustomed to seeing on the faces of all those she encountered before long.

As she saw Gil off on a run, Mason strode into the stables and slipped into the stall that held Carson's horse, Puffin. Karigan peered over the stall door and saw him squatting down to peer at Puffin's legs.

"What are you doing?" she asked.

He looked up in surprise and stood. "Good to see you up and about. I'm just checking Puff's knee. He got hit by debris when Carson did."

She didn't see much evidence of injury, and she thought it odd he'd be checking on Puffin. "Thought you'd be helping out the menders."

"I have been," he replied, "but people are not my area of expertise."

"What? I thought . . ."

"I'm an *animal* mender," he said, grinning at her confusion. "The healing I did on Puff looks good. He'll be more than ready to go when Carson is fit to ride again. If I hadn't been here, he might not have made another run. Ever."

"Dear gods," she breathed. It was good news they had a

true healer of animals. She stepped aside as he opened the stall door to exit.

"I need to go check on the horses of the guard," he said. "They've been used hard, and there are lots of injuries."

"I see."

"Don't break anyone's fingers," he told her with a wink as he strode away.

She smiled. "I'll try not to." Smiling seemed to come a lot easier now, and she once again felt that sense of euphoria whenever she thought about being free of Nyssa.

A Green Foot runner trotted down the stable aisle and passed Mason on his way out. With so few Riders available, the runners had begun to bring messages in need of delivery directly to Karigan. The problem at this moment was that, once again, she didn't have any Riders available except for herself.

"The general has another message to go to Captain Nolder," the runner told her, and he handed her the missive.

Since the captain was overseeing the defenses at the gate and vicinity, she supposed it only made sense there would be frequent communication between him and the general.

She quickly tacked Condor and buckled on her cuirass, and rode out. She found the demeanor of the city's populace more tense than it had been the last time she rode into the city. The people hurried around the streets with their heads down. The walls were keeping them safe thus far, but it was not a sure thing, and the reality of being surrounded by the enemy had undoubtedly set in, especially as shortages became worse. She'd heard there was a thriving black market and that legitimate merchants were selling their goods at exorbitant prices. What must be the hardest of all for them to bear, however, was that many of their loved ones who were defending the city were getting wounded and killed.

The tension was even more apparent as she passed into the lower city with the refugees they'd allowed in huddling together around fires on street corners and begging for coins, even the smallest among them. She dug around in her pocket and handed all her coins, a couple coppers and half silver, to a boy who looked no more than four. He ran to his parents in triumph with the coins clasped in his fist. His father lifted him into the air and laughed.

The closer she got to the gate, the more destruction she saw from the pummeling of the catapults—roofs smashed in, rock debris in the streets.

She left Condor tied to a rail at a stable where the guard picketed their horses. It was a safe distance from the wall, and she was glad of her decision when, as she jogged toward the gate, arrows whistled overhead and the steel heads sparked on the paving stones around her. The gate, she saw, had been bolstered by piles of debris. It was difficult to assess its condition on this side, but Fergal had told her that Second Empire had been using a ram on it.

She hurried toward the gate, hoping to evade another volley of arrows. At the bottom of one of the towers, she asked after Captain Nolder.

"Up top," she was told.

She climbed to the very top of the tower, open to the sky and crowned by merlons. She gasped when she looked upon the land that spread out before the city's entrance. Second Empire had withdrawn just out of arrow range. The ground was churned up and littered with bodies from their attempts to force their way into the city. In the distance, the rest of Birch's army swarmed like ants. Beyond, lay their encampment. Whole thickets of trees had disappeared to apparently feed the numerous fires that produced columns of smoke darkening the sky.

"They're readying one of the catapults," a soldier said, "and forming up their archers again."

"Getting ready for another run at the gate," Captain Nolder said.

Karigan took in the three siege engines. Foremost was a catapult with several soldiers clustered around it. Greasy black smoke rose from a fire beside it. A dozen or so men stood closer with a ram between them, the trunk of some massive tree. Shieldmen stood beside them and would protect them when it came time to ram the gate. Archers had formed up in two long lines to help cover them.

"You have something for me, Rider?" the captain asked when he noticed her.

"Yes, sir, from the general." She handed the message over and waited while he read.

He nodded and said, "Tell the general I understand."

"Is that all, sir?"

"Yes." He squinted at her shoulder, and she realized he was gazing at her Black Shield insignia. He grinned. "Ah, the famous Rider G'ladheon, hero of the east wall."

"Uh . . ."

"Best get out of here before they spring that catapult," the captain told her.

"Yes, sir."

As she left, she heard one of the captain's aides say, "They're lighting it afire."

When she reached the bottom of the tower, she sprinted, anxious to be away before Second Empire bombarded them with more projectiles.

She'd just reached Condor when she heard shouts back from where she'd just come, followed by the blaring of horns. She gazed upward at balls of fire that sailed overhead into the next block.

Oh, no. That was where the menders were working out of an old tavern. She made a decision right then not to go straight back to the castle with Captain Nolder's response, for there was more immediate danger at hand, and she could help. She mounted up and clucked Condor into a quick trot, and cut through alleys and yards to reach the street where the fireballs had landed. Plumes of smoke were already rising from buildings a few blocks down.

"Fire!" she cried to any who could hear as she urged Condor on. People looked out their windows or stepped outside to see what was going on.

She halted in front of the tavern, dismounted, and ran inside. Startled menders looked up at her from setting bones and suturing wounds. Her nostrils flared at the iron scent of blood and the stench of corruption that herbs could not cloak.

"There a problem, Rider?" a master mender asked.

"Second Empire is sending flaming projectiles over the wall, and they've hit down the street."

"I thought we were out of range," the mender said.

"You should get ready to evacuate," she told him, then left without waiting for a response. The closeness of the buildings, their age, and wooden construction were sure to increase the chance of the fire spreading quickly, and devastatingly.

She ran to Condor and mounted up once again and trotted him down the street shouting, "Fire!" in an attempt to rouse anyone she could. She could feel the heat radiating from the flames as she approached. Fortunately, a bucket line had already formed to combat them.

"Rider," a man on the line called to her, "could you send the brigade on Spring Street to us? We could use the help."

She nodded and reined Condor around. As she rode, more fireballs streaked overhead. Flames roiled across rooftops. Whatever Second Empire was using, the flames burned with unnatural ferocity. If left unattended for long, the fire would rage out of control.

As she once more passed the mending house, she saw the master mender standing outside with his hands on his hips, observing the smoke down the street.

"Sir, I wouldn't wait," Karigan told him. "I'd evacuate *now*. This is no ordinary fire."

"I hear you, Rider," he replied, and he rushed inside the tavern shouting orders as he went.

As Karigan rode to Spring Street, she saw plumes of smoke rising from the eastern side of the city.

"Oh no."

The fire brigade was gone from its post, undoubtedly fighting one of the other conflagrations that had arisen elsewhere. She cantered the length of the street but found no sign of them.

More fireballs hissed against the darkening sky. Horns blared in various parts of the city.

A woman stepped outside of her small house. "What is going on, Rider?"

"The lower city is burning," Karigan said, and the woman

gasped. "Collect anyone who lives with you, and your neighbors, and head for the middle city."

She decided the most useful thing she could do was to ride through as many neighborhoods as she could to alert the residents to the danger and instruct them to make their way to the middle city. As the fire spread from building to building, she discovered people were all too aware of their peril and were fleeing to the Winding Way carrying children, pets, and precious belongings.

"Leave that," Karigan told one man who was lugging a behemoth of a chair that could have rivaled the king's in the throne room.

"My papa made it," he replied, "and I'm not leaving it." He doggedly hauled it along.

She shook her head. On one street, where a whole cluster of buildings had caught, a mother with a bunch of children passed an infant to her.

"Please, Rider, take him and Little Penny to safety. I can't carry them all."

Karigan took the baby and held him awkwardly. She hadn't a lot of experience around children and certainly not babies. He seemed content at first, looking about and waving his tiny fists, but then his gaze locked onto her face and his placid expression crumpled like a precursor to a storm, and when the storm broke, he bawled and screamed and squirmed. Little Penny was lifted onto the saddle in front of her. Using her legs to guide Condor, since she must use her hands to hold both the children, she rode for the Winding Way.

The Winding Way was already flowing with people evacuating. Those who had brought along too many possessions were slowing down everyone else. Worse still, the fire was starting to spread toward the Winding Way from various directions. Smoke filled the air.

She rode at a canter, passing the man with his chair, wagons full of wounded, and menders hauling stretchers, and many frightened people making their way the best they could. Some ran in a panic. One tried to grab Condor's reins, but Karigan booted him away.

When she neared the middle gate, the area was clogged

with people. It appeared no one was gaining entry to the middle city. There was angry shouting. She pushed Condor through the crowd and some of the anger was directed at her.

When she reached the gate, she discovered it was closed.

"Open up immediately!" she yelled to the guards up in the towers.

"Sorry, Rider," one of the guards responded, "but we haven't had any orders to let people through."

"*I'm* ordering you!"

"You don't rank us."

"If you don't open this gate," she yelled over the crying baby, "I'll come up there and make you."

The people around her yelled in agreement. When the noise quieted for a moment, she thought she heard one of the guards say something about the "crazy berserker Greenie from the east wall."

She'd acquired a reputation, it appeared. A hero to some, and a madwoman to others. If they didn't open that gate, they'd be seeing a crazy berserker Greenie in short order.

SILVER SMOKE

The guards were no longer paying attention to Karigan or anyone else on her side of the gate. They looked the other way into the middle city. Smoky haze descended on the evacuees, and the baby's scream tore at Karigan from the inside out. Who knew such small beings possessed such large lungs? She tried bouncing him in her arms, but then Little Penny, who had remained quiet till now, whimpered and started to cry, too.

Dear gods. To the guards, she shouted, "We've got wounded and children down here! Open the gate!" An inhalation of smoke made her gag.

To her amazement, the gate started to open. Desperate people surged past her to cram themselves through the opening. Condor took it stoically. She did not.

"Wounded first!" she yelled at the people, but they were beyond listening.

Finally the gate was fully open and the press moved forward in a relentless wave. She urged Condor to move with it. When she got through to the other side, she saw a young moon priest watching the inflow of people. She worked her way over to him. When she reached him, he looked questioningly at her.

"Could you take these children, Father? Their family will be along shortly."

"Yes, of course," he replied.

She handed the baby down, and once in the priest's arms, he immediately stopped wailing and actually cooed and smiled.

"Huh," she said in consternation.

She then lowered Little Penny to the ground and the girl clung to the priest's robes and jammed her thumb in her mouth. Relieved to be free of the children, Karigan reined Condor around, and wondered what had prompted the guards to finally open the gate. There were no military officers around, but at the base of the tower, she saw a figure in luminous white. It was the luin prime. The chapel of the moon was but a block from here and Prime Brynston must have come down to see what was happening in the lower city. It must have been he who ordered the gate open. The guards had listened to *him,* but not her. Well, she wouldn't let it bother her. She was just grateful the gate had been opened.

She turned against the tide and maneuvered Condor back through the gate and into the lower city. There would be more people needing help. Connly, she thought, would disapprove of her deciding this on her own. He would have wanted her to return to the castle to make her report, but, she thought, this was an emergency. Lives were at stake and seconds counted.

She clucked Condor into a canter. She needed to see what was happening down by the outer wall so she could provide the latest details to Estora. Smoke burned her eyes and nostrils, and she doubled over coughing. She hated to force Condor into the smoke, but he did not balk.

More evacuees made their way to the street, covering their noses and mouths with handkerchiefs. The farther along she got, the thicker the smoke. Fire raged in various places and the brigades would never be able to contain it all.

When she reached the main city gate, she saw soldiers formed up before it with weapons and shields at the ready.

BAM! The gate shuddered.

The ram, she thought. She spotted Captain Nolder speaking to some of his people on the ground. She reined Condor in his direction.

BAM!

The soldiers shifted uneasily where they stood. The captain, in contrast, was very calm when he looked up at her approach.

"What are you doing back down here, Rider?" he asked.

"I wanted to check on you one more time before I report to the queen."

"You should have evacuated," he told her, "but since you are here, you can tell the queen that the gate will not hold for much longer. We will make a stand and defend the lower city for as long as we can." His tone was matter-of-fact.

BAM!

Fire flared on a nearby building with a blast of heat that showered sparks on them. Karigan patted them out as they landed on her sleeves. Condor merely shook them off his hide. The captain had not flinched, even as the orange tint of the flames lit the contours of his face.

"I will tell her," Karigan said quietly.

"Very well." He turned to give orders to some aides.

She thought the captain a man of quiet courage, and one resigned to his fate. He and those who guarded the gate and outer wall might very well perish before the night was over, and from the looks on their faces, they were well aware of it, but still they held their positions.

She turned Condor back up the Winding Way.

BAM!

The sound of Second Empire battering the gate might not seem to perturb Captain Nolder, but it rattled her nerves.

The smoke had grown even more dense in the short time she'd been with the captain. She coughed and tears rolled down her cheeks. Condor snorted and tossed his head. The sun had gone down, and the descent of darkness, combined with the thick smoke, made it hard to see and know exactly where she was.

"I'm confused," a man said in a high-pitched voice. "We should be there by now."

Someone else sobbed.

"Over here!" Karigan called, and then she coughed and hacked.

"Who's there?" the man asked.

"Green Rider. I'm on the Winding Way."

She continued to call to them until an older couple, or maybe it was just the ash in their hair that made them look older, emerged from a side street holding on to one another.

"Thank the gods," the woman said. "A building collapsed in our path and we had to find another way out. I thought we would die."

They still might, Karigan thought, and herself, too, if they didn't get out of the smoke. She thought to tell them to hold on to her stirrups so they would stay together, but then had a better idea. She pulled the moonstone Ealdaen had given her out of her pocket. Its brilliance cut through the smoke and ash, and she could see the road ahead. The light heartened her, seemed to calm the harshness in her chest.

"Let's go," she said. The moonstone revealed the stunned expressions on the couple's faces.

It was slow-going with the couple on foot, but the moonstone led the way, and they emerged into an area where the air was easier to breathe. She glanced over her shoulder and was surprised to find others trailing behind. More people came down another street and ran to her, the relief on their faces plain to be seen.

A little farther along, a weary fire brigade joined her group.

"We were ordered to retreat," their captain explained, "and told that we'd be needed to look after the middle city just in case."

Karigan frowned. That meant the lower city was going to be left to burn.

"Saw your light," he added. "We were a little lost until we saw it."

The fire brigade helped their wounded along. One man overcome by smoke was supported between two of his fellows. They had brought civilians with them whom they'd found lost in the haze. By the time she reached the gate to the middle city, she was astonished to find so many people, maybe a hundred or two hundred souls, perhaps even more, had followed her.

She watched as they filed through the gate, then extinguished the light of her moonstone. There was an audible sigh of disappointment from all who watched.

"Rider," one of the gate guards, a sergeant, said, "you shouldn't do that."

"Do what?"

"Douse the light."

"Why? I need to go report to the queen."

"One of us can take any message you have," the sergeant replied, "but you're needed here to shine that light so folk can find their way."

It wasn't proper, and she could only imagine what Connly would say about it, but he wasn't here and there were more people who could be helped. She couldn't ride into every neighborhood to find every single person, but she could light the moonstone and hope that people would see it and be drawn to it.

The sergeant chose one of his men, a private named Seften, whom she recognized, to go to Estora in her stead, and she told him Captain Nolder's words and described the scene down at the main gate. She made Seften repeat it all back to her and, when she was satisfied he had it just right, allowed the sergeant to send him on.

Karigan rode Condor back into the lower city a couple of blocks. She stood in her stirrups and raised the moonstone over her head. Blades of light streaked between her fingers and turned the swirling smoky haze silver. Brilliance luminesced around her and Condor in glimmering waves, and shone nearly as bright as day.

It was not long before people started to appear by ones and twos and, in some cases, large families and groups. Sometimes there was a constant flow and, at other times, pauses where she wondered if anyone else would come, but then they would in large numbers. Some were injured, others confused or sickened by the smoke, but the light drew them, and she directed them up the street to the gate where they could receive aid. In the distance, horns blared and she thought she heard fighting, which meant the main gate to Sacor City had fallen and the lower city was lost not only to fire but to the enemy. Still, she kept her vigil despite the waves of smoke that left her gasping, for once the gate to the middle city was closed, residents of the lower city would not be able to enter, and would be at the mercy of the flames and Second Empire.

Eventually, the guard sergeant made his way down the street where she had positioned herself.

"Rider," he said, "we've got to close the gate. The horns are telling us that Second Empire has entered the city and are heading this way."

"But there could be more people," she said. She wanted nothing more than to leave, but—

"Undoubtedly," he replied, "but you've helped many, and we have to close the gate before the enemy arrives."

She nodded and lowered the moonstone but did not extinguish it. The sergeant walked beside her as she slowly rode Condor back to the middle city.

She glanced one more time over her shoulder into the lower city, but no one else appeared, and the gate was closing. The light of the moonstone faded, and she reined Condor up the street.

Sacor City burned, or at least the lower city did. Zachary stood on the highest hilltop of the Scangly Mounds, watching the flickering orange glow rise and fall in the distance. Now and then an enormous surge of twisted flame erupted as the fire found new fuel.

General Washburn, Captain Connly, Fastion, and Lord Penburn stood with him, and they were ringed by Weapons with their shields and swords at the ready and facing outward. Some distance away, his warriors fought the enemy that had been harrying his weary troops the whole long way from the mountains. It had taken a toll, not just in terms of casualties but in mood. The spirits of his warriors had risen the closer they got to Sacor City, until they had seen the fire.

"Still not able to reach Rider Burns?" he asked Connly.

"I cannot, sire." He had been distressed when he lost contact with Trace Burns. The two Riders had been used hard and Connly had almost collapsed from overuse. They guessed that his counterpart had succumbed. Connly clearly worried about her though he tried to hide it. It was left unsaid that something worse might have befallen her and that she had perished. Zachary could only imagine what it was like to suddenly lose contact with one with whom you were almost always in communion. Even when the two were not conversing back and forth, or otherwise in active contact, Laren had once explained that there was always some thread of connection between them. But now, Connly said there was nothing, nothing at all where he usually felt Trace, and he confessed he hadn't felt so lost since his first counterpart, Joy Overway, had been killed some years previous. Zachary wondered if such a connection with a loved one was more a curse than a solace, though he couldn't help but envy it.

Lord Penburn pointed. "Look, there it is again."

A silver light grew above the orange flames and surged up above the smoke, blazing into the sky in a majestic beam that seemed to unite with the crescent moon. A thrill coursed through Zachary. It was *her,* his Karigan. He knew it.

"Some magic afoot, I'll warrant," General Washburn muttered.

"It is Sir Karigan and her moonstone," Fastion said. Silver light glistened in his eyes.

Zachary started in surprise and took a second look at his Weapon. Were those tears gliding down his cheeks? How odd, he thought, until he realized his own eyes brimmed with tears, moved, as he was, by the sheer magical beauty of the light, how it transcended all that was common and elevated all that was good in the world.

"Truly?" Lord Penburn asked. "The lady who rode to Darden with, er, no clothing on?"

Zachary smiled. "That is her, but she was attired."

"Barely," General Washburn said, "as I hear it."

The cool silver light supplanted the angry orange of destruction. Zachary had no way of knowing *why* Karigan called upon it. Perhaps it was meant as a warning or a signal, but he rather thought she was using it as a kind of beacon to aid those trying to escape the fire. It had certainly seemed so when they had seen the light before cutting through the smoke as it moved about the city. Now it was stationary, a bold column of crystalline silver lighting the path to the gods.

He passed his hand through his hair and shivered. His heart expanded knowing who called it forth, and that she did so most likely to help others. She was more than an Earthly messenger, his Karigan, even more than the avatar of Westrion. She was truly Lady Winterlight.

"The moonstone is well bestowed." He hadn't known he'd spoken aloud until Fastion replied in a hushed voice, "Yes, it was."

Zachary gauged Connly's expression. It was hard to read, but he thought he saw . . . resignation?

They gazed in wonder at the silver moonbeam for a time until the strident notes of horns sounded in the distance.

"That's ours," General Washburn said. "Second Empire has breached the city gate."

It had only been a matter of time. The din of fighting still came to him from the near woods, delaying their approach to the city. Despite their best efforts they had not made it in time.

Lord Penburn asked, "What is our next step?"

"Captain," Zachary said.

"Yes, sire?"

"Would you please bring Rider Notman? I've a task for her."

As Connly jogged off the mount, Zachary returned his attention to the silver light and wiped a tear from his cheek as it faded to dark.

❧ SPIRIT OF SILVER LIGHT ❧

The news was not good, Estora reflected. Fire raged through the lower city, and the main gate was likely to fall this night. Trace Burns remained unconscious in the mending wing, and without her connection to Captain Connly, they no longer received the benefit of Zachary's advice or knew exactly the location of his army. He could not arrive soon enough. Now she and her small contingent of advisors must make decisions on their own and pray for the army's swift arrival.

She ran her fingers through the fragrant leaves of sweet fern. She'd had several of her potted plants brought to the throne room where they thrived in the light that fell through the tall windows. Her apartments had turned into something of a jungle, and bringing some of the plants down cleared out her living space to a degree, and had the added benefit of providing calming greenery to a chamber that was anything but with all the battle talk.

Currently her advisors were discussing what they'd be up against if Second Empire took the lower city, and any additional measures they could take to contain the fire.

The throne room doors opened and a figure covered in ash was admitted. A Green Rider. The eyepatch helped her quickly identify that it was Karigan. Karigan came before her and bowed. Soot was smeared across her face, and there were pinprick burn holes in her green coat. She smelled strongly of smoke.

"Rider?" Estora said. Had Karigan been ordered to ride

into the fire? The look of consternation on Lieutenant Brennyn's face suggested she had not.

"My lady," Karigan replied, "Second Empire has entered the lower city."

Estora closed her eyes as the voices of her advisors rose. Zachary would arrive soon, but would it be soon enough? When she opened her eyes, Karigan was doubled over in a coughing fit, and Lieutenant Brennyn had her hand on her shoulder. Estora summoned Castellan Javien to her side.

"Send for Mender Simeon, and have a servant bring some water for Rider G'ladheon."

"Yes, my lady."

Karigan tried to explain between coughing fits all she had seen in the lower city. Water helped her some, but it wasn't until Mender Simeon came and placed his hand on her back that the coughing subsided. She had looked at him in surprise, and Estora suspected he'd done a true healing on her. He also gave her a cup of herbal tea.

"The honey," he told Karigan, "will help your throat." Apparently satisfied that she was doing better, he left.

Estora watched as Karigan took a deep breath without coughing. An expression of relief crossed her face.

"You have heard much of what I had to report from Private Seften," she finally continued. "Captain Nolder said that he and his warriors would try to hold the lower city for as long as they could."

"Yes," General Meadows replied. "They'll harass the enemy all the way up the Winding Way. The fire might actually prove an advantage to us, and a hindrance to Second Empire."

"Anything else, Rider G'ladheon?" Estora asked.

"Not concerning the enemy," she replied. "I tried to help people evacuate the lower city as I could, but I'm afraid there are many who are still trapped there."

Estora was not surprised that Karigan had done this.

"We tried to prepare the people," the general said. "Warned them to be ready, but it's inevitable that not all listened or could be helped."

"Well done, Rider," Estora said. "You may be excused."

Karigan bowed and strode from the throne room.

Strategizing continued with messages coming in from the city, though little of it clarified what was actually happening. The Winding Way stymied General Birch's army, as intended. The street did not travel in a direct line to the castle, but rather looped around the city. If an invading army attempted to use side streets, their narrowness would cause a bottleneck. Choosing either route for its advance, Second Empire would find itself an easy target for the city's defenders. Unfortunately, the defenders were few.

Something else came out from those reporting in, tales of a silver light that had helped guide civilians out of the smoke and mayhem, of a Green Rider leading families, the wounded, and many others out of harm's way. Some spoke in awed voices of how she was like a miracle of the gods and described her as a "spirit of silver light."

Karigan, Estora thought. They were talking about Karigan and her moonstone.

"Hundreds," the sergeant said. He'd been stationed at the gate between the lower and middle cities. "She helped hundreds find their way to safety with that magic light of hers," he said, "and then went back into the smoke for more. That light was a beacon—it shot clear to the heavens. I swear it!"

"How many hundreds?" Castellan Javien asked. Estora liked to think of him as the court skeptic.

"At least five hundred," the sergeant replied. "Maybe more. She would have stayed longer, but we had to close the gate and I made her come back."

Estora shook her head. Karigan, who was the Winterlight of the Eletians, had become a guiding light for the residents of Sacor City. There were tales of heroic deeds being made by many all around the city this night, and there were undoubtedly more to come as battle with the enemy continued, but with Karigan, there was always that extra *something*, whether it was traveling through time to the future, and returning to warn of the realm's imminent peril, or the light of a moonstone she used to show people their way to safety.

The evening continued with Estora and her advisors poring over plans and a map of the city, a map that would be much altered as soon as the damage from the fire was assessed, and she received ongoing reports from exhausted and smoky soldiers and Green Riders. The Sacoridians were slowing down the advance of Second Empire but, of course, not stopping it. The fire continued to burn, but the remaining fire brigades had halted its advance west and to the north. Second Empire did not send anymore flaming projectiles. Perhaps, Estora thought uneasily, they were saving those for the middle and upper city.

When the sergeant from the middle gate returned, his expression was grim.

"The enemy has not reached the gate in force," he reported, "but they've pulled one of their catapults some distance into the city and cast the heads of Captain Nolder and some of his warriors over the wall."

Estora stifled a cry and forced herself to retain her composure. The heinous nature of the act made her want to rush to the nursery to seek the comfort of holding her children in her arms, but she must not. In Zachary's absence, she must remain strong for her people, if not for herself.

"Thank you, Sergeant."

He bowed and left to resume his watch at the gate.

"Captain Nolder was a capable and good man," General Meadows said.

The throne room grew quiet as those present remembered a friend and colleague, and mourned the loss of so many good Sacoridians.

Anna Ash then entered the throne room and made a beeline to Lieutenant Brennyn. She whispered into the lieutenant's ear. Lieutenant Brennyn's posture straightened, and surprise registered on her face.

"Is something wrong?" Estora asked.

"I do not believe so, Your Majesty, but may I be excused for a few minutes to attend to some Rider business?"

"Anything we should know about?" Javien inquired.

"That's what I'd like to verify," she replied.

"You are excused then," Estora told her, her curiosity piqued.

"Thank you. I will not be gone long."

The lieutenant was true to her word and soon returned accompanied by another Green Rider, one Estora had not met before. The Rider was small and plump, with pink ribbons in her curly hair. Lieutenant Brennyn brought her before the throne. The girl's eyes were big and round as she took in everything in the throne room, including Estora herself.

"Your Majesty," Lieutenant Brennyn said, "this is Rider Notman. She bears word from King Zachary."

There was an uproar among the officers and counselors. Estora once again fought to maintain her composure. This time it was a surge of hope that filled her.

"Rider Notman," she said, "how is it you bring word from our king?"

The Rider actually curtsied. It was gracefully done, odd as it looked that she had done it in her uniform. Had the circumstances been different, Estora might have been amused.

"It is such an honor to meet you, Your Majesty," Rider Notman said. "I can't tell you how much I admire you."

"Megan," the lieutenant said in a tone of warning.

"Well, *it is*." Rider Notman then cleared her throat and leaned in, and whispered, "I floated here. And let me tell you, it was really smoky. I don't know if I'll ever get the stench out of my clothes and hair."

A smile twitched on Estora's lips despite herself. She now recalled that this was one of the Riders who had been abducted by the Darrow Raiders. Trace had spoken of how Rider Notman's ability had been used to spy on the enemy in the Eagle's Pass.

"The king, girl!" Javien demanded. "Has he arrived?"

"Nearly, my lord. He holds the Scangly Mounds. I certainly couldn't have floated all the way from the mountains, could I?"

"*Megan*," an exasperated Lieutenant Brennyn exclaimed.

The Rider's impertinence did not seem to register with the others, not even the castellan, but the news that Zachary had finally reached them did.

⊰ MESSENGER OF
THE GODS ⊱

Smoke hung in the air even up on castle grounds. There was no getting away from it, but Karigan had heard that the fires were dying down on their own, which sounded suspiciously as if there were some magic behind it.

She trotted Condor along the Winding Way through the hazy dark. Ben had done something when he touched her in the throne room to make her lungs well, but now she wore a scarf over her nose and mouth to protect them. She worried the smoke would make her sick as it had after having inhaled so much at a lumber camp in the north when ghosts had used it as a means of communicating with her, but thanks to Ben, she felt all right. A little tired, maybe, but not suffering from the all-encompassing need for sleep as her previous true healing.

Mason had likewise attended to Condor, and she once more thanked the gods that the Riders now had an animal mender among them. Condor snorted as he trotted on with his usual vigor, his hooves rapping out a sharp report on the street.

Though the hour was nearly midnight, there were many folk out and about. A good number of them were soldiers and guardsmen, and her fellow messengers, but also other folk who had been displaced by the fire, and those wishing to help them. They rushed along like ghosts in the haze. She did not need a moonstone to show her the way. Unlike the lower city, streetlamps had been lit, and they cast a misty, golden glow.

She was bound to stand watch on the middle wall. She smiled thinking the notion not so grim as she'd have thought it just a while ago, for Mara had given her the news that Zachary and his forces had reached the Scangly Mounds. She wasn't happy just because he was bringing his army, but because it presented the mere prospect of seeing him again.

Before she reported to the gate captain, however, she had a message to deliver. She reined Condor by the fountain that stood on the plaza in front of the city's chapel of the moon, an edifice of granite and marble that stood above most buildings in the vicinity. Evacuees sat on the rim of the fountain's basin or on the chapel's vast steps. Children ran across the plaza. Others had spread out blankets on the hard paving so young children and elders alike could rest.

Moon priests and acolytes moved among the weary and frightened people, offering sustenance and prayer where they could. One, however, in his stark white robes, stood on the top step before the great doors of the chapel. The luin prime. Torches to either side of the door created a halo about him as he gazed out upon all the activity below.

She halted Condor when she saw familiar faces—Little Penny, the baby, and their siblings and parents.

"You all made it," Karigan said.

They looked up at her in surprise, and she pulled her scarf down so they could see who spoke to them.

"Oh, Rider!" the mother, Elise, cried. "We made it thanks to you."

Karigan dismounted. "I was happy to carry Little Penny and the baby out of the lower city."

"You didn't help just the littles," Elise said. "I mean, you helped *all* of us." She cradled the baby in her arms. The tiny mite cracked his eyes open at Karigan and immediately howled. "We saw your light and followed it. You led us out of danger."

Karigan smiled, despite the baby's reaction to seeing her again. "Glad I could be of some help."

"Hey, everyone!" Elise yelled loud enough to drown out even the baby, and now Karigan knew from whom he got his lungs. "This is the Rider with the silver light!"

The shout and announcement startled Karigan and roused many of the people in the plaza. They started to come forward, the young and old, by ones and twos, and in groups, and they all gathered around her and Condor. A small girl reached out to lightly touch her sleeve and look up at her with earnest eyes.

"Thank you, Rider," she said.

A gentle murmur of thank yous came from the assembled, and someone said, "You gave us hope." There was a chorus of assent.

"Messenger of the gods," others said.

"Oh, no," she responded with a smile. "I am an ordinary messenger of the king."

But they all seemed to want to touch her and Condor as if by doing so some blessing of the heavens would rub off on them. There was gratitude in their eyes, awe, as well, and even tears.

Oh, dear, she thought.

"The Spirit of Light," they said. "Messenger of the gods."

"I'm glad I could help, but I'm just a Green Rider," she told them over and over, her feeling of discomfort growing.

"You led us out of destruction," a grizzled old man said.

"She carries Aeryc's light in her hands," one woman told another, and others repeated it and agreed.

She didn't know how many surrounded her—a hundred? Two hundred? All wanting to touch her arm or shoulder.

"I'm a regular messenger," she insisted, "a Green Rider." She turned round and round looking for a route of escape.

"Blessed by Aeryc."

"Spirit of Light."

"Messenger of the gods."

She had to end this now. "You're welcome," she told them. "But I need to see the luin prime. Please let me through."

They parted, creating a solemn silent path for her and Condor. Condor blew through his nostrils and swished his tail as she led him away. Best as she could tell, he had enjoyed the attention. She glanced over her shoulder and all the people were watching her. The baby had stopped howling.

She left Condor at the base of the stairs and climbed. The luin prime watched her approach, his expression one of displeasure.

Uh oh, she thought. She'd heard from Anna and others that he did not like Green Riders very much. His demeanor said as much.

When she reached the top step, she bowed. "Luin Prime Brynston, a message for you from Her Majesty the queen." She removed the message from her satchel and handed it to him. He took it without a word. His expression lightened as he read it, but his fair features darkened once more when he gazed at her.

"Have you a response you'd like conveyed to the queen?" she asked.

"No."

She'd been told not to expect one. She shifted uncomfortably waiting for him to excuse her.

"Is there something else, Your Eminence?"

"Yes, there is." He leaned toward her. He wasn't just unhappy; he was incensed. She took a step back. "You Riders with your evil abilities are bad enough. Your ancestors should have been eradicated long ago."

She couldn't help but gape at the waves of hate that seemed to roll off him like heat. Apparently he knew about Green Rider abilities.

"You messengers exert undue and corrupt influence over our king and queen, over their decisions and court life, and their *personal* lives."

Karigan's toes curled in her boots. Was he implying he knew something about her and Zachary? Or, maybe he was referring to just her friendship with Estora.

"You are unclean," he continued. "The lot of you, with your cursed magical filth, and yet I tolerate you because *they* do." He leaned even closer. "But this display out here, courting the people to exalt and look worshipfully on you as though you were sent by the gods, fashioning yourself as one among the heavens when you are the spawn of the hells. *That*, I cannot abide."

"It's all a misunderstanding," Karigan began, suddenly afraid he would clout her there on the steps.

"*Silence.* Know that I am not without power and influence

in court. More so than you might imagine, and as head of all moon priests, I will, by the gods, see you branded for heresy."

Karigan backed away without being excused, shivering at how ugly and twisted his beautiful face had become. She turned and ran down the steps to Condor as the luin prime hurled imprecations after her, everyone on the plaza aghast as they watched the scene.

"Deceiver! False idol!"

She swiftly mounted and trotted back onto the Winding Way.

He hadn't liked how the people had responded to her. It had made her uncomfortable, but it had definitely riled the luin prime. She could sort of see why, but he was overreacting. And did Estora, who so often counted on his companionship and counsel, realize how much he hated magic and Green Riders?

Would he really brand her a heretic? It would require a trial and everything. It wasn't so long ago that those deemed guilty were burned at the stake. How would he react if he knew she actually did have a link to the gods, that she had served as an avatar to Westrion?

As she neared the gate, she tried to push thoughts of Prime Brynston to the back of her mind. There were more important matters to worry about at present. Perhaps over time, the luin prime would forget about her.

Karigan rubbed her bleary eyes as she stared into the graying of dawn. She'd been assigned a spot a ways from the action. Apparently Major M'Gyre had requested her, despite the fact Karigan had tried to kill her in the midst of her berserker rage, to stand watch on the east wall of the middle city.

Even in the predawn light, there wasn't much to see. Smoke hung over various neighborhoods in the city below, though the one that skirted the wall had not been touched by fire. She still wore her scarf over her nose and mouth even though most of the fires had died out or smoldered. Unless a good wind came through, the smoke would just linger.

The archer beside her yawned. His name was Rol and he

was only thirteen years old. He'd been a refugee with his family from D'Ivary when the Darrow Raiders were terrorizing the countryside. Hunting had made him a superior archer, so he'd been assigned to the wall, though on a quiet section, in deference to his age.

"They'll be coming around with tea and bread soon," he told her with the air of a veteran.

"Good," she replied, "I'm starving."

"I'm always starving," he said.

Karigan smiled. Considering his age, she wasn't surprised. He kept her entertained and awake through the night with tales of his sisters and brothers in what sounded like a large and boisterous family. She wondered what it would have been like had her mother not succumbed to fever, to have had a sister or brother, maybe even a half dozen or more siblings. Then she recalled the images of an alternate life she'd experienced while under the power of the whisper wraiths, and frowned.

"Hey," Rol said, "didya see that?"

"See what?"

He pointed down below, but she didn't see anything.

"The smoke and shadows may be playing tricks," said an older archer, named Graves, who stood nearby. "I know I'm about seeing double at this point."

Karigan could relate, but she scanned the area before the wall carefully. It was silent, too silent, and nothing moved. Then someone down the wall shouted, and suddenly arrows filled the air.

⊰ A FRESHENING WIND ⊱

Defenders on the wall cried out as they were impaled. Karigan ducked behind a merlon, and saw that Rol had done so, too.

Major M'Gyre ran behind them. "Archers! Loose at will!"

Karigan grabbed her bow. It wasn't a great longbow like Rol and many of the others bore, for she hadn't the strength in her back and shoulders yet to draw it, nor the expertise. She'd been given, instead, a shorter, easier-to-shoot bow. It lacked in range and power but, if used well, could be just as deadly. She nocked an arrow to the string, aimed, and drew. The ground down below swarmed with Second Empire. Where had they come from? She loosed her arrow. It sailed sideways and tumbled into a tangled garden.

"Damn." Her archery skills were, she thought, nearly as "good" as her knife-throwing. She could always blame it on being one-eyed and how that altered her vision, but it would not excuse the knife-throwing since she'd had the use of both eyes back when Drent had tried to train her in that particular skill.

Rol laughed at her, then set his arrow loose. She didn't watch its flight, but was sure it hit the desired target.

Second Empire sent another volley over the wall. It became almost rhythmic—duck, nock, shoot, repeat, but she also knew there was a danger in falling into repetitive actions. It made one predictable to one's enemy.

After she finally took out an enemy soldier, Rol congratulated her.

"Thanks." She hadn't the heart to admit she'd been aiming for someone else. The shot had been a lucky one for her, though, but not so lucky for the fellow she'd inadvertently hit.

Down below, enemy soldiers charged out of the smoke with ladders, while their archers provided them with cover. Arrows hissed over and past Karigan. The challenge for the defenders was to hit the soldiers before they could lean their ladders against the wall and start climbing, and to do so without getting impaled, but there were just too many of them.

It was the east side of the outer wall all over again, and cold fear streaked through her veins, but it was normal fear. Nyssa Starling did not whisper in her ear to augment it.

Soon she set aside her bow to help push a ladder down. She and her comrades grunted and sweated with the effort, and they only succeeded when Major M'Gyre added her strength to theirs. Meanwhile, bouts broke out along the wall walk where they had not succeeded in pushing down ladders.

She turned to Rol. "You should go."

"Go? Where?"

"Head for the upper city, safety." He was too young for this, she thought. He did not have a steel cuirass like she did, only a hard leather vest.

He did not answer, but aimed his arrow and loosed it.

She unsheathed her saber when more of Second Empire's soldiers spilled over the wall. The first one she faced was out of breath and hadn't even had a chance to grasp the hilt of his sword before she sank hers between his ribs.

It was like the last time, taking on enemy soldiers who were not equal to a swordmaster's level of skill, but she did not go berserk this time. There was no Nyssa tormenting her. Still, the soldiers were strong and determined, and though her back was healed, she hadn't regained full strength and remained largely out of practice and condition.

She found she could only concern herself with what was right in front of her, not the many skirmishes happening along the wall, or the enemy soldiers who got past the defenders into the middle city. Those with stronger backs kept trying to push the ladders down, but the enemy simply raised them back up. Horns rang out in urgent blasts on various sections of the wall—it wasn't just their section that was getting hit. This must be Birch's big push to take the city.

She hacked off the arm of a soldier reaching from his ladder to pull himself between a pair of merlons. He screamed and lost his balance, gouting blood as he fell. She was ready for the next, and the one after that. Sweat streamed down her face, and the periodic waft of smoke made her eyes burn. She blinked away tears even as she clashed with the enemy, the screams of the dying and shouts of combatants all background noise.

There was a cry nearby, and she saw Rol knocked down by one of the enemy, who raised his sword to plunge into the young archer's chest. She stabbed him in the back and kicked him off the wall. She didn't wait to see how Rol was—there was no time—and turned to block a thrust from another soldier.

This one was more skilled than the others, a little quicker, better at handling a sword, and while he kept her occupied, more and more of Second Empire's soldiers climbed onto the wall walk and fought their way to another ladder or tower that would allow them to descend into the middle city.

She was tiring; her hand wrapped around the hilt of her saber had gone numb. Her back and shoulders ached as she fought with the soldier. He pounded on her blade like he wielded an ax instead of a sword. Sweat stung her eyes, but then she became peripherally aware of a freshening breeze cooling the perspiration on her skin.

Her opponent pushed her into the opening between merlons, their swords locked as he pressed in closer. She hadn't the strength to push back. If she moved the wrong way, he could slice off her head, or he could toss her over the wall. They were practically nose to nose, he grinning, but then a look of surprise crossed his face, and he lurched away, an arrow in his back.

Rol stood there with another in his hand and jammed it hard into the man's throat. The man gurgled blood, fell to his knees, and Karigan finished him with a thrust to his gut.

"Thanks," she told Rol.

He nodded, then went back to work, shooting arrows at Second Empire's troops.

A lull followed as defenders pushed over the closest ladder, and she needed it to catch her breath. The day was lightening, and the breeze was starting to blow the smoke away.

The respite was brief. All too soon, more of the enemy made their way to her position, and she found she'd lost any finesse she'd had and just did the best she could to stay alive. Her cuirass saved her more than once.

A horn ringing out in the distance caused her current opponent to pause, and she used the moment to slide her blade into his neck.

"Look!" Rol shouted, and he pointed where the soldiers of Second Empire had been based to make their assault on the wall. They were abandoning their posts and running away. Even the soldiers who'd been on the ladders jumped to the ground and ran. The horn had been a signal of retreat.

"Keep shooting those arrows!" Major M'Gyre bellowed. An ugly gash on her cheek bled freely. "Keep fighting."

Melees continued on the wall, and in the middle city, but Karigan's section was free. She grabbed her bow, but it had been broken at some point, maybe by someone stepping on it. She glanced out across the city. Much of the smoke had been carried away by the wind, and the sun had fully risen beyond the horizon, leaving a blush of orange in the sky. In the distance, she could see the mass of Second Empire contracting as it pulled its troops together.

To their east was another army. The sun glanced off metal like ripples on a lake. King Zachary had arrived! As the news passed among the defenders, a *hurrah* rumbled along the wall like building thunder.

When Major M'Gyre's defenders cleared their section of the wall of Second Empire, Karigan found the major peering through her spyglass toward the two armies. It was too difficult to make out what was happening with the naked eye, just that the two armies had sort of merged.

"What do you see, Major?" Karigan asked.

"Hard to say exactly, even with my glass," Major M'Gyre replied, "but it would appear King Zachary is hitting the enemy with his heavy cavalry before Birch can organize his defense."

Karigan felt fierce pride for her king, and much hope. Birch must have put all his plans into the capture of the city. He could try to retreat to the lower city and find some defense there, but then he'd be sandwiched between the city defenders and Zachary, with nowhere to escape.

"Birch is too good an officer to not pull his people together," the major said, "but at the moment, the battle is in our favor. Have you paper and pen? I'd have you take a message to General Meadows."

"Yes, Major." A messenger always had her satchel with her. Almost always, at any rate.

As she rode off with the major's message, she found the way fraught. Soldiers of Second Empire who had gotten over the wall and had no hope of joining the retreat were at large, and she came across fights in the street and city defenders on the hunt. She rode with her saber bared.

She made it to the castle without incident, and when she reached the throne room, she found the mood there one of intense relief. News of the king's arrival had already reached her superiors.

"We don't have enough personnel left to hold the outer wall," General Meadows was telling the assembled officers and advisors. Estora was nowhere to be seen.

"Maybe just the gate?" Castellan Javien suggested.

General Meadows frowned. "Perhaps. We need an assessment of its condition. Send some of my people, a carpenter, and an engineer." He looked up at Karigan's approach. "Rider? You've a message?"

"Yes, sir, from Major M'Gyre."

She slipped it out of her satchel and handed it over.

"Mostly good news," he muttered when he finished reading. "The king has engaged Second Empire."

"Do you wish to send a reply, sir?" she asked.

"Not yet. Go get some rest, Rider, something to eat, but don't go far. We may need you before long."

 JUST THE MESSENGER

Karigan carried her mug of tea into the common room of the Rider wing. Gil was sprawled in the large, cushioned chair in front of the cold hearth, softly breathing in sleep. Anna sat at the table with her head nestled on her arms. Both were stained with soot and smelled strongly of smoke. Karigan had been able to wash some of it off herself, but was sure all of them would smell of it for some time to come.

She sat across from Anna. There was a long-forgotten game of cards spread out on the tabletop. She peeked at the hand closest to her. Three knights. Not bad.

After cleaning up, she had eaten and rested as General Meadows had told her to, but had not yet received new orders, nor had she heard further news of how Zachary and his forces fared on the field of battle. She'd sent up a prayer for his safety and success.

Anna stirred and rubbed her eyes.

"You all right?" Karigan asked.

Anna looked up in surprise. Her nose was tipped with soot. "I guess I'm alive," she replied. "Been running errands everywhere for everyone." She wiped some ash off her sleeve. "If I wanted this much smoke and fire, I'd have stayed an ash girl. Maybe would've been better."

"And miss out on the excitement?" Karigan had asked it lightly, but Anna gave her such a jaundiced look that she was sorry she had said it.

"Maybe you're used to seeing people get hacked to pieces all the time, but I'm not. There's a reason I didn't hear the call

706

like the rest of you. It's because I'm not cut out for this." She stood and walked out.

Karigan was so flabbergasted that Anna, mild, good-hearted, down-to-Earth, Anna, replied with so much heat, that her mouth dropped open. Only belatedly she tried calling her.

"Don't bother," Gil said without moving in his chair.

"I thought you were asleep."

"Kind of drowsing."

"What's going on with Anna?" she asked.

"Oh, it's been since that archer got killed in front of her, and of course since then she's seen some pretty horrific stuff out on errands. We all have. Dying soldiers crying for their mommas as they hold their guts in with their hands. That sort of thing."

"That's not easy for any of us," Karigan replied.

"I know. I keep trying to tell her that, but she's been thinking about joining the royal household as a servant again."

"Oh, no." The idea of it was very disappointing to Karigan because she liked Anna so much and thought her a capable person with a lot of common sense. Maybe it was that common sense that was leading her to think about becoming a castle servant once again, but Karigan thought she had come so far along with her training and everything that it would be a shame for her to turn her back on it all now.

"She has the one thing the rest of us lack," Gil said, "whether she knows it or not."

"What's that?"

"A choice in the matter. *We* can't leave the messenger service until our brooches abandon us, unless we die first, of course."

Anna, Karigan thought, hadn't had to go through the same process as those who were traditionally called. She had *chosen* this life. The rest were forced to deal with whatever fate dealt them. Gil stood and stretched, and turning to her, he said, "And we can't all be like you."

"What do you mean?"

His expression and tone were aggrieved. "How many of us

have special titles and magical crystals, huh? How many of us get to travel to the future? There is only one, and that's hard for us lesser folk to live up to. I think even the First Rider would have a hard time living up to Sir Karigan G'ladheon. If it's hard for those of us who have been magically called, think of how it is for Anna."

She could only sit there dumbfounded. Gil walked from the common room, yawning. Her tea got cold as his words churned in her mind. Did the rest of the Riders really feel less because of her? It wasn't as if she set out to receive a moonstone or titles. Would they really want to experience the trauma of time travel or the things that had resulted in her attaining those titles? Any of them could ask to train toward swordmastery, though they probably wouldn't achieve the status of "honorary Weapon." She still didn't understand herself why she had received that one.

Gil, however, hadn't seemed to take into consideration the loss of one of her most recent titles, that of Chief Rider. She'd been demoted, and though she accepted it and understood why, it still stung. As for being proclaimed a scion of the House of Santanara, it could not mean anything good, and all of it was a weight she carried. She would not wish it on anyone, and simply wanted to go back to being just an ordinary Green Rider.

As for Anna, she'd track her down later and see if she could help. In the meantime, she'd let her have some space.

At suppertime, she found Mara in the dining hall listlessly stirring her bowl of soup. Karigan sat down at her table with a bowl of her own.

"You all right?" she asked Mara.

Mara looked up in surprise. "Oh, hello." She shook her head and straightened. "I'm fine. You?"

"Fine."

They sat silently for a time, each sipping spoonfuls of chicken soup. The chicken was largely missing from it, but the broth was flavorful with the addition of vegetable chunks and barley.

"Anything new on the war front?" Karigan asked.

Mara paused. "We got some reports from those watching from the walls but not much detail. Our troops and Second Empire's have met head on, but it's, so far, impossible to see who has the advantage. I really wish Trace would wake up."

"What does Ben say?"

"He doesn't know when she will regain consciousness, but he thinks she'll be fine when she does."

"Well, that's somewhat positive," Karigan replied. She broke off a chunk of bread from a loaf she shared with Mara and sopped it in her soup. "What about Megan? Can't she bring news?"

Mara rolled her eyes. "That girl! She's gotten cocky." They both laughed. "She returned to the king before daylight. Don't know if she'll be able to come back. It's quite a distance for her to use her ability, and if the wind picks up anymore, forget it."

They discussed how the Riders were doing. Carson was ready for some light duty, and Mara was taking up some of those that Karigan had been doing. When Karigan told her about Anna and Gil, Mara looked unperturbed.

"I wouldn't take it too hard," she told Karigan. "Everyone is under stress, and as new Riders, they're being thrown right into the middle of this mess. It can be pretty overwhelming. You and I didn't become Riders in the middle of a war. Plus, you've got to admit, you do have rather a lot of titles, and a lot of Riders tend to be envious of that moonstone of yours. Most of them know, however, what you've been through to be a knight and other things, and if they just thought about it for a moment, they'd understand the price you've paid."

"It's not like I asked for any of this."

"Well, you know me," Mara said, "I like staying close to home and out of trouble. You can have your fancy titles. A moonstone would be nice, but probably not worth it."

Karigan smiled. "I take it you don't want to trade places, then."

Mara laughed hard in answer.

They spoke quietly together of their worries and hopes as they slowly ate, until a Green Foot runner approached their table.

"Riders," the runner said, "the queen asks that you attend her in the throne room."

"Both of us?" Karigan asked.

"Yes, ma'am."

She exchanged a glance with Mara. Apparently General Meadows had decided what to do with her.

When they reached the throne room, they found Estora and her advisors leaning over a map with wooden markers that represented the placement of the armies. The map looked recently drafted and rough.

"Ah, Riders," General Meadows said. "Very good. You got some rest, Rider G'ladheon?"

"Yes, sir."

"Good, good." He cleared his throat. He had a prodigious mustache and a habit of combing it with his fingers. "This map represents what Rider Notman was able to tell us of the king's position last night, and we were able to get scouts out of the city to survey the situation, though they could not make it through to the king. Four of them were killed, and one made it back to give us some information, but with three arrows in him."

Karigan glanced at Mara, who seemed to guess her thoughts and shook her head to indicate none were Green Riders.

"We don't know if Rider Notman will be able to reach us again," the general continued, "and our surviving scout discovered a weakness in Second Empire's position that the king might want to exploit, which is why, Rider G'ladheon, we're sending you out."

"You, Karigan," Estora said, "are the one Green Rider who we think can get through to the king."

Because of my ability, Karigan thought. "I understand."

The general proceeded to detail for her how Second Empire was situated, where their sentries were located, and where she'd find the king.

"I will not be giving you a written message," the general said, "in case you are captured."

Karigan had not expected he would. He gave her the information about the supposed weakness in Second Empire's position, and a plan to take advantage of it. It sounded dubious to her, but that wasn't for her to decide. She was just the messenger.

"If Rider Notman does not appear by midnight, you will then depart," the general said. "Moon is almost new, which should help. Any questions?"

"No, sir."

"Then good luck, Rider."

"Thank you."

"I'll make sure Condor is ready to go when the time comes," Mara said.

Karigan nodded and started to leave when Estora stepped forward. "Karigan, a moment, if you please."

"Of course, Your Majesty."

"I have something I would like you to take to my husband." She produced a gold case small enough to fit on the palm of her hand. She unclasped it, and it opened on hinges to lay flat like a book. On the inside of each lid was a tiny painting of an infant.

"I had miniatures painted of the children," she explained, "so their father could see them. Would you please take it to him?"

"Of course."

Estora closed the case with a snick and passed it to her. Karigan felt a little awkward at the moment, taking the portraits of Estora's children to be delivered to her husband, the man Karigan happened to love. She closed her fingers around the case and bowed. Regardless of how she might feel, however, she really was just a messenger.

"I'll see that he gets it."

"One more thing," Estora said in a quiet voice. "You know what Rider Duff saw in Zachary."

"Grandmother's knots," Karigan replied, just as quietly.

"Yes. You know him well."

Karigan did not know how to take that statement.

"If you see him not being, well, himself," Estora continued, "you must tell Counselor Tallman or one of his Weapons. They are aware of the spell within him."

"I'm sure they'd pick up on it if anything were amiss."

Estora tilted her head to the side. "Perhaps. If Colonel

Mapstone were here, I'd be confident she'd pick up on any changes immediately. As she is not, I am positive *you* will be attuned to the nuances of his mood and well-being, even more so than his Weapons who serve him day and night."

"I—I don't know about that," Karigan stammered. "But I will keep watch as you ask."

"Very well."

Karigan hastened from the room feeling flustered. Estora thought she'd know the "nuances" of Zachary's mood and well-being? Unless Karigan was reading too much into it, it was almost as if Estora knew she and Zachary had been close. She did not think she was reading too much into it.

☙ GREENIE HEART ❧

Anna thought to find solace in the central courtyard gardens, and it *was* quiet there. A lone gardener picked up his tools and carried them away. The air was better here, less smoky, it seemed, and seeing the greenery of plants, even if they were simple beanpoles or low-lying rows of herbs, and not the beautiful ornamental plantings of before, soothed her. The muscles of her neck and shoulders eased. Battle and devastation and fire felt miles away. Maybe this was why the queen surrounded herself with so many plants, for their restorative powers.

Anna was sorry she'd been so short with Sir Karigan. She'd been in a dark place, still was, and did not understand how the other Riders coped with witnessing such violence and death, terrible wounding and anguish. Such scenes kept playing through her mind. She would never understand how people could bring such harm upon one another.

Birds chittered and flew among the remaining trees and bushes, going about their ordinary bird business. They didn't care that two factions of humans were trying to destroy each other. It would affect them not at all, and quite suddenly she wished she had been born a bird. She could just fly away from trouble. She'd be an ordinary brown house sparrow, she thought, and no one would pay her any heed.

Her contemplation of life as a bird was interrupted by a cry coming from the direction of King Joneaus' Spring. Startled, she stood rooted in place.

"No!" a woman cried. "Leave me be!"

A man responded, but not loud enough for Anna to make

out his words. She looked desperately for someone to help the woman, but she was the only one around.

You're a Green Rider, Anna, she told herself. *Like it or not, you're the one who's got to help.*

She sent a small prayer to the gods, then sprinted down the path to the spring, her hand on the hilt of her saber. She'd never used the sword for anything but training and, even then, only against straw dummies.

When the woman started to plead and cry, Anna hurried. She crossed the stepping stones of the stream to where the boulders and shrubbery sheltered the bench by the spring. She was taken aback to discover Master Scrum and Nell Lotts struggling. Master Scrum's meaty hand was wrapped around Nell's throat, and he pressed her up against one of the boulders. In his other hand, he held a knife against her heart.

"Anna!" Nell gasped.

Master Scrum looked her way. "Well, well, the little Mousie. I'll kill you, too, for what you've done."

"Let her go!" Anna cried.

"Don't you sound all brave and everything in that green uniform," he mocked. "Worthless little bitches, the both of you. After you two, I'll go cut the throat of that Mistress Evans. You cost me my job and good name, the lot of you."

Anna unsheathed her sword. Master Scrum laughed.

"Let her go," Anna said.

"Gonna prick me, eh, Mousie? You don't have it in you."

"No more warnings," Anna said.

He laughed again, then drew back his knife as if to plunge it into Nell's chest. Anna did not think; she reacted as she'd been trained, and thrust.

Master Scrum howled and dropped his knife. He clasped his bloody bicep. Nell edged away.

"Run and get help," Anna told her, and Nell grabbed her skirts and obeyed.

Master Scrum turned on Anna. His face was red and contorted with rage. "That was a big mistake, Mousie."

"The name's *Rider Ash,*" Anna said.

This only seemed to make him more angry. "You are

nothing. Just a little ash girl no one cares about trying to wear britches too big for her."

"You're wrong," she replied, but there was a quaver in her voice.

He backed away, but bent and swiped his knife off the ground.

"Toss it aside," she told him.

"You squeaking at me, Mousie?" He lunged.

Her training came into play again. She stepped aside as he made his move, his side unguarded, and she plunged her sword into him. She felt the momentary resistance of muscle, the blade scraping on bone. What she would never forget, however, was the look of utter surprise on his face that she had actually done it, that she had actually put her sword through him.

Anna stood over the dead man who had once held so much power over her and watched the blood pool beneath him. She watched even as Lieutenant Mara, Sir Karigan, and members of the castle guard arrived. Lieutenant Mara pried the blood-stained saber out of her hand.

"Anna?"

She swallowed hard. She felt like there was a knot in her throat. "He came at me with his knife."

People talked around her and gazed at the body.

"Nell said you saved her," Sir Karigan said gently.

"Is she—is she all right?"

"Some bruises. Scrum was not gentle with her. Mistress Evans is looking after her."

"He was gonna kill her—Mistress Evans, too—after he killed me and Nell."

"It is good you arrived here when you did," Karigan said, "and that he underestimated you."

"She can answer questions later," Lieutenant Mara was telling someone. "Karigan, can you look after Anna for now? I've got to return to the throne room."

"Yep."

Sir Karigan put her arm around Anna's shoulders and turned her around, and guided her away from the spring.

"It will never be the same," Anna said.

"What won't?" Sir Karigan asked.

"The spring, the gardens."

Sir Karigan squeezed her shoulder. "We're going to get some tea, all right?"

Karigan ensured Anna was comfortable in the cushioned armchair in the Rider common room, and lit a fire in the hearth and made a pot of tea. Anna stared into the flames with her hands wrapped around her mug.

"You need anything else?" Karigan asked, relieved to have something helpful to do other than worry about what Estora did or did not know about her and Zachary.

"I didn't mean to kill him," Anna said.

"This won't make it any easier," Karigan replied, "but you were defending yourself. He would have definitely hurt you, if not killed you, had you not. As a Green Rider, you knew one day you would be faced with such life and death decisions." She had killed her first man defending herself, too. "I wish no Rider had to go through this, but the uniform seems to attract all sorts of trouble."

"But I wasn't on an errand or anything. I went to the gardens for fresh air."

"You still did your duty as a Green Rider. You saved Nell and yourself, and, potentially, Mistress Evans, from a man intent on murder. We are well rid of him, frankly. How would you have handled it had you come upon the scene of Scrum hurting Nell and you were still a servant with no Rider training?"

"I—I don't know," Anna replied. "Run for help, I suppose."

"And while you were going for help, what might have happened to Nell and the child she's carrying?"

Anna's silence was as much an answer as if she had spoken.

Karigan sipped her tea, then said, "Your training as a Green Rider saved four lives today. I know you've been thinking about leaving the messenger service, but I hope you stay with us. You've got a good head on your shoulders, and you've shown a lot of courage. Not just today, but when you helped us fight the ice creatures of the aureas slee last winter. Remember that? And when you protected the queen from that assassin as she went into labor. I know our work is dangerous, but as you saw today, being a servant, like Nell, can be dangerous, too."

Anna heaved a long sigh, then gazed at Karigan. "I don't think I could go back to servants quarters now that I'm a killer."

Karigan sat in the rocking chair next to her. "You are not a killer."

"Then what am I?"

"You are Anna Ash, a bright young woman who cares about others. Look at what you've done for Nell, and I'm not just talking about you defending her today, but the other things you did to give her safety and security during her pregnancy, and you did so even though she had not been kind to you. And, you are a Green Rider. A very special Green Rider."

Anna looked at her in surprise. "What do you mean?"

"You came to the Green Riders on your own. You chose it. The rest of us were coerced by the call. None of us came because we wanted to, but you did. You are unique, and have a true Greenie heart through and through. You have been trained and equipped, and your training proved true today. I know Arms Master Gresia will be proud when she hears how you handled yourself. *I'm* certainly proud of you. But, for all your training, it is really your Greenie heart that shines through and makes you who you are."

Karigan rocked for a bit, then continued, "I know it seems like things like war and violence don't affect some of us, but believe me, they do. It's just that we can't hesitate when it comes to doing our job, whether it's out on the battlefield, or defending a servant from a man like Scrum. And, we certainly can't hesitate when it's a matter of us or them. We see some horrible things in the course of our work, but that's so others don't have to. Sadly, we can't protect everyone." She shook her head. They hadn't even been able to protect their own colonel.

"Thank you, Sir Karigan," Anna said in a quiet voice.

"Anytime, Anna, but one more thing. It's just Karigan, all right? I am no more special than any other Rider." Anna gave her such a look that she hastily added, "It's true. I am flesh and blood like everyone else. I make mistakes, lots of them, and I don't always like my job. And believe me, having a title is not the perk you might think it is."

At that moment, the captain of the castle guard and a sergeant entered the common room. Both Anna and Karigan stood.

"We need to ask Rider Ash questions about what happened," the captain said.

"Anna, are you ready for this?" Karigan asked.

She nodded.

"If you don't mind, Captain," Karigan said, "I'd like to be present for the questioning."

"It's no problem," he replied. "It's really just a formality. The man, Scrum, shouldn't have even been on castle grounds today. The queen had ordered him expelled, but somehow he got past us, so it's *our* failing the incident took place. Fortunately, Rider Ash prevented any tragedies from being on us, as well." He gave Anna a respectful nod. "We've statements from Nell Lotts and Mistress Evans, and they and the queen speak highly of Rider Ash and her character."

Karigan smiled. Anna may not comprehend it just this moment, but many people cared for and respected her, and some of them in high places. That was something with which no title could compare.

The wind picked up after sundown. Megan never appeared, so Karigan set out at midnight on her errand to reach Zachary. The ride through the middle city was uneventful. Units of the guard patrolled, seeking remnant invaders. If there were any left, they were keeping a low profile.

Portions of the lower city, however, had become another world with the unfamiliar shapes of burned buildings lending a forbidding atmosphere. Ash and smoke swirled like banshees in the light of streetlamps. Odd knocking and scratching sounds, and wind whistling amid the ruins, made her hair stand on end. The dim streetlamps only seemed to make the darkness beyond their glow more mysterious, denser, otherworldly. Though tempted to use her moonstone, she did not because she didn't want to alert Second Empire that something was afoot. If the moonstone flared as it had during the fire, it would certainly draw unwanted attention.

It was with relief when she finally approached the main city gate with lanterns and torches set around it, and blacksmiths and carpenters at work to repair it. Guards stood up on the towers and wall, keeping watch. They would not be able to stop a forceful incursion by Second Empire, but they could certainly defend against smaller-scale attempts or, at least, slow them down.

Rubble still filled the street, which would provide readymade projectiles for the catapult Second Empire had left behind, which now stood facing outward, ready to fling havoc upon the enemy that had made it.

The gate did not look too bad. She guessed it was the

mechanical parts that had taken the most damage under the assault of the ram. Sparks flurried from the blacksmith's anvil as he hammered on a molten piece of metal.

She halted Condor as a guard approached her. "Heading out, Rider?" he asked.

"Yes. How are things out there?"

"Not much moonlight to see by," he replied, "but we haven't seen anything unusual, maybe some Second Empire patrols in the near distance. I reckon there are enough of those about that you'll want to be real careful, but the king seems to be holding the main army's attention."

She nodded. "Thanks for the warning."

"Think your horse can fit through the pedestrian gate? It'll draw less notice than if we start cranking open the main gate. Right now it's real hard to operate and takes longer. Makes a lot of noise, too."

"No need to announce that someone's on their way out," she said.

To her relief, Condor was narrow enough to fit through, and he just had to bow his head a little to clear the lintel.

When she reached the other side, the guard said, "May the gods be with you, Rider."

He closed the pedestrian gate, and suddenly she was alone on the midnight plain that lay before the city. The enemy no doubt had her in view, or was otherwise aware of her. She mounted up quickly and squeezed Condor forward. Once she was away from the light by the gate, she called on her ability.

She felt as though she floated disembodied until her vision adjusted to the dark. Off in the distance, hundreds of fires belonging to both armies twinkled like stars on a black tapestry. Closer by were the rotting corpses no one had dared to collect from either side. She pulled up her scarf to help alleviate the reek of putrefaction.

She halted Condor and sat stock still at the sound of scurrying, fearing a scout of Second Empire had found her, but then she thought she saw an animal scavenging a meal off the corpses. She recoiled in disgust when she realized it was a feral-looking man going through pockets and belt pouches of the dead. He placed his treasures in a sack before moving to the next corpse, from which he removed the boots.

She shuddered and urged Condor on. Once away from the city, the wind blew away the stench of the dead.

They traveled slowly, Condor seeming to pick up on her need for quiet. Voices and camp noises came to her from across the dewy grasses, even as she gave Second Empire a wide berth. Crickets chorused in waves, and occasionally bats weaved about her. As tempted as she was to drop her fading, she was all too aware the enemy could be nearby keeping as quiet as she. She'd have to endure the headache and fatigue of using her ability until she reached Zachary.

It paid off. She heard a horse nicker close by. Probably it sensed Condor, but Condor, being the intelligent horse he was, did not respond in kind. She halted him and sat while whoever the horseman was swept the area. Only when she thought him well away did she resume her journey.

It felt like it took forever to reach the Sacoridian camp. She dropped her fading before she encountered the outlying sentries and sagged in relief. She was ushered into the encampment and found her way to Zachary's tent. Either someone had awakened him ahead of her arrival, or he had never gone to sleep. In any case, he was waiting for her.

When they came face-to-face, at first they just gazed at one another, and feeling a little shy, she glanced down and bowed.

"Your Majesty, I bear a message from General Meadows."

He smiled and it lit his eyes. He looked good and strong. No injuries she could see, and his demeanor did not suggest he was under the influence of any spell. She was relieved.

"I am very glad to see you," he said quietly, and he took a step toward her. "More than—"

At that moment, Counselor Tallman entered. "Your Majesty," he said, "the others are on their way." Then he nodded to Karigan. "Good to see you again, Rider."

"Sir," she replied, disappointed her moment with Zachary had been so brief. "If you haven't summoned General Hixon, you will want to." The general oversaw the engineers.

"It happens that I have," Counselor Tallman replied.

They waited for all of Zachary's advisors to file in.

Lord Penburn paused before Karigan. "Ah, the lady of the light has found her way to us." He bowed deeply.

Karigan's cheeks warmed.

Connly nodded to her as he entered the tent. He looked shrunken to her, his forehead creased with worry.

"We'll speak afterward," he told her.

"Yes, Captain."

Finally, when all were assembled and watching her expectantly, she turned to Zachary again and said, "Your Majesty, General Meadows wishes me to convey to you that one of his scouts discovered a possible weakness in Second Empire's position."

She described that the land they stood on was low lying between the mount upon which Sacor City was situated and the Sleeping Waelds, a hilly upland to the south of the city. That meant that often in spring, between snow melt and rains, the ground could get boggy. If summer brought a lot of rain, it could remain boggy into the fall. It was one reason why the area had not been farmed.

"Second Empire has placed itself in something of a bowl near streams that run off the hills," she said.

"Easy access to drinking water," Counselor Tallman said. It was imperative for any army to have such access.

"This is all true, Rider," General Washburn said, "but it is not spring, nor have we had a lot of heavy rains."

"That is correct, sir," she said, "but the scout grew up hunting in the Waelds and has climbed them all. He says there is a murky lake dammed up back there—"

"A lake?" General Washburn demanded. "What lake?"

"I wonder . . ." Zachary said, looking off into the distance.

When his words faded, they all waited for him to finish his thought.

Finally, he said, "I think that may be the fish pond my great-great-grandfather King Geoffrey had made. He was, it is said, quite fond of casting a line." He cleared his throat. "Which is neither here nor there. Please continue, Rider."

"Yes, sire. The scout said that the dam is old and neglected and sure to give out in a handful of years. When it happens, all the water will flow downward into the streams between the hills and directly where Second Empire has set up camp, and fill it, like, well, a bowl. It is enough water that it would swamp the ground."

"You are suggesting," General Hixon said, "that our engineers make the dam fail sooner."

"General Meadows is suggesting it, sir," Karigan replied, "but with caution. Second Empire's scouts and some units have worked themselves into the hills. Also, he says the water may choose some other course to flow than the one desired."

"If the land does flood as he suggests," General Washburn said, "it would mire the enemy's movements and make life very difficult for them."

"The dam would have to be broken at night so it happens before they are aware," Counselor Tallman said.

As the king and his advisors discussed the possibilities, Connly sidled over to Karigan. "Well done," he told her. "How is everyone in the city holding up?"

"Weary, and working hard, but very happy the king has arrived at last."

"Megan gave us a rundown when she returned last night, of all that was happening in the city. But . . . do you have any news of Trace?"

Karigan was not surprised this was foremost in his mind. "From what I hear, she's still unconscious, but Ben is confident she will soon awaken and be her old self."

Connly visibly relaxed. "Thank you. It has been difficult." He swallowed hard and still looked lost, but the creases on his brow eased, and his demeanor brightened. "I've sent for Tegan so she can show you someplace to rest while they—" he pointed at the king and his advisors "—debate what to do."

"I do have one more thing for the king," Karigan said, "but of a personal nature from the queen."

"You'd best present it now. You may not have a chance later."

He got Zachary's attention, though she wasn't sure his attention had really ever left her. She'd been aware of his gaze returning to her even as he spoke with his advisors.

She withdrew the case from an inner pocket of her coat. "Your Majesty, for you from Her Majesty the queen." She passed it to him with a bow.

He received it with a look of curiosity. He studied the case, then found the clasp and opened it. He was a master at concealing his thoughts, but now all facade fell away revealing surprise and amazement. Emotion rippled across his features.

He glanced up at Karigan. "These are them? My children?"

"Yes, Your Majesty."

He found a chair and dropped into it, staring at the pictures. "Zachary Davriel the Second," he murmured, "and Esmere." Then he looked to his advisors and showed them. "My son and daughter."

They patted his shoulder and congratulated him.

"The young prince looks ready to take on a pack of groundmites," General Washburn said.

"It would appear they take after the queen," Lord Penburn said, "which is fortunate for them."

There was good-natured laughter, and Zachary glanced once more at her. "Have you—have you seen them?"

"No, sire," she replied. "Circumstances have not permitted."

"Of course. Thank you. Thank you for these."

"I only carried the case," she said. "The queen had the foresight to have the miniatures made."

He smiled. "Thank you, Karigan." And he returned his attention to the pictures.

"I think you can leave now," Connly told her. "This was just the boost to his morale he needed."

Tegan awaited her outside, looking as if she'd been awakened from a deep sleep. She hugged Karigan and led her back to her tent.

"Dawn is in a couple hours," she said, "but you might as well relax while they decide whether or not to send you back. Brandall is taking care of Condor, and I've brought your gear back to my tent."

"If they don't decide what to do soon," Karigan replied, "I won't be able to go back until tomorrow night."

In Tegan's tent, instead of sleeping, the two sat in the dark and caught up. Karigan described the ruin of the lower city, and Tegan spoke of the chaos of battle.

"We haven't participated directly yet," Tegan said of the Green Riders, "but have provided support in various ways." The Riders, she said, had helped mind the horses of the heavy and light cavalries, and carried messages between the various unit commanders. "And, the king calls upon those of us who might have a useful ability, of course. I get to give daily weather updates."

As though mentioning her ability were a summons, Connly spoke to them from outside the tent. "Glad I'm not waking you," he said.

"Are they ready to send me back to the city?" Karigan asked.

"No," he replied. "They want to know the forthcoming weather."

"Huh," Tegan said. "A little earlier than usual. Tell them clouds building in throughout the morning. Drizzle and light rain becoming heavier in the afternoon and through the night. Not the best for battle."

If the king and his advisors were going to use the lake of King Geoffrey to their advantage, Karigan thought, the weather conditions Tegan foretold would be perfect.

 IN THE TENT OF THE MENDERS ⤜

The encampment was roused ahead of day-break, and before long, voices, the sounds of equipment being readied, and the whinnying of horses filled the air. Karigan was alone in the tent when she woke up. Tegan had already been up and about as a good Chief Rider ought.

She rubbed her eyes and stepped outside into the dull morning light. She was greeted by Riders she had not seen since her departure from the mountains—Brandall, Garth, and Daro, among others. They gave her cheery greetings and a mug of tea.

"Good to see you all," she told them. "We were getting a little anxious in the city."

"Got here as fast as we could," Garth told her. "Second Empire was on us the whole journey."

"And what was left of the Raiders," Brandall said. "Nasty."

"I'm glad you're all in one piece," she told them.

Constance brought over bowls of gruel, and they caught up while they ate. Sandy appeared, and when he saw Karigan, he retreated to his tent.

"Something I said?" she asked.

The others laughed.

"I think he has something for you," Daro said.

When he reappeared, he came bearing a swordbelt equipped with saber and longknife.

"Missing something?" he asked her.

"Wait . . . Is that mine?"

He grinned. "Not sure who else it could belong to. It's a Rider sword with black silk wrapped beneath the guard. We found it tossed into some brush near that old hut where the Raiders kept you prisoner."

"What Sandy means to say," Daro told her, "is that *he* spotted it. There was no *we* involved."

Karigan took her words to mean that he had seen it with his special ability.

"Cleaned it up a bit," he told her as he handed it over.

"I don't know what to say," she replied. She'd been given it after she'd lost her first saber in Blackveil. "I've been using the colonel's all this time."

"'Thank you' works well enough," he said.

She smiled. "Thank you. Now I won't have to beg a new one from the quartermaster." Thus avoiding any stern rebukes.

She unbuckled Colonel Mapstone's swordbelt and left it in Tegan's tent. She then buckled on hers, the leather smooth and pliant. If it had been sitting out in the weather for so long, it was clear that Sandy had cleaned it up more than "a bit." She drew the sword and was taken aback at how much longer and heavier it was than the colonel's. She might, she thought, want to keep using the colonel's until she was back to her old strength.

Just then, Tegan joined them.

"Good news," she told all the nearby Riders. "Trace is awake and back in contact with our captain."

There were murmurs of relief. Karigan hoped they didn't overextend Trace again, especially during her recovery.

Tegan turned to Karigan and said, "Now that we've contact with the castle again, you are not to return. You are ordered to stay with the army and perform duties as required."

"And what duties are required of me?"

"Helping me get those Riders mounted up. The army is preparing to meet the enemy on the field of battle again, and our Riders will be essential for running messages and errands for the king."

Karigan did just that, rushing with her fellow Riders to the pickets to help them ready their horses and mount up. Tegan, meanwhile, handed out orders.

"Constance, you're liaison to Horse Marshal Martel.

Sandy, you're going to be General Washburn's second pair of eyes."

And on it went until each Rider was off on his or her assignment. It was only then that Karigan realized that much of the encampment was emptied but for support personnel. She could not see the action from where she stood at the pickets.

"We should saddle our horses, too," Tegan said, "in case we're needed to ride."

Karigan checked Condor over as she groomed him, and found him in good condition and spirits. He seemed to want to join his fellows in battle. He arched his neck and dug at the mud.

"You'll get your chance, boy," she told him. "Don't get yourself all splattered." She left his girth loose and secured a blanket on him to help keep off the rain.

"Now what?" she asked Tegan.

"The hardest part. We wait."

They were posted outside the king's tent where Zachary and his officers coordinated their strategy. Several Weapons stood in the rain with them, on guard. Fastion gave her an assessing look and what appeared to be a nod of approval.

"Welcome back, Sir Karigan," he said.

She returned the nod with a smile.

Riders came and went with messages for Zachary. Mostly Karigan played the part of groom, holding the reins of horses, and walking those that were sweating and breathing hard from exertion. Fortunately, with the cloud cover and light drizzle, it wasn't overly warm, the condition of the horses a testament to how hard they were working.

She gained little sense of how the battle was going. The Riders couldn't waste time informing her, and she couldn't really hear what was being discussed in the tent. Of the battle itself, she heard distant horns and drums signaling troops to do one thing or another. There was the occasional roar of the soldiers, a sound that sent chills through her body, but none of it indicated how it was going.

Tegan was in and out of the tent, passing messages to the Riders, the feather brooch on her shortcoat gleaming. Had things been different, Karigan would be the one wearing that feather and directing the Riders. It was just as well she was not, she thought, because Tegan was doing a very good job.

She pulled up her hood when the rain fell more persistently, glad of her greatcoat. Harry, on Bumble Bee, trotted right up to the king's tent. He staggered when he dismounted.

"Harry?" she said.

"Got nicked is all," he mumbled. He held a wet, bloody rag against his thigh and limped into the king's tent. It didn't look like just a nick.

They would not send an injured Rider back out, so Karigan led Bee to the pickets, where she untacked him and tried to slick the rain off him as best she could before blanketing him.

She slapped his neck and said, "Harry'll be just fine."

Bee grunted and swished his tail.

She hurried back to the king's tent where Tegan was emerging with Harry.

"Karigan," Tegan said, "could you see that Harry gets to the menders' tent?"

"Don't need help," he said.

"Orders," Karigan said.

He insisted on limping along without assistance, however.

"How is it out there?" she asked him.

"Second Empire is using the catapults," he replied. "Throwing our lines into chaos, lots of hurt people." Then he snorted. "Moving those things, though, has gotten hard in the mud, so they can't be easily aimed."

That was good, at least, and boded well if Zachary decided to go forward with breaking the dam that held back the lake. However, the rain created problems for their own side, as well, forcing the army to slog through the mud, and drenching soldiers. It would be exhausting and unpleasant work. She thought back to a long-ago sword training session she'd had with Master Drent. He had made her train in a downpour. When she grumbled about it, he'd demanded, *Do you think the battle stops for a little rain? It slows troops down, it rusts steel, it makes soldiers miserable, but battle does not stop for rain.*

And so it did not, which was more than apparent as she

and Harry approached the large tent of the menders. Other wounded were being carried in on stretchers or over shoulders. Some limped along, like Harry.

The interior of the tent was a scene of chaos with wounded everywhere and menders shouting and hastening from one patient to the next. The tang of blood and bile was thick on her tongue, and she tried not to look too closely at what went on in there. An apprentice in charge of checking in the wounded, her expression unfazed, glanced at Harry.

"Yes?" she asked.

He peeled the rag from his leg. She looked at it briefly and said, "A few sutures most likely, but you'll have to wait while we treat the more critically injured." She directed him to sit on a bench with other of the less wounded.

"Will you be all right here?" Karigan asked him.

"Not liking it very much," he replied, "but, yeah, I'll be all right."

She turned to leave, but a mender caught her arm. "Rider, I need you to help hold this man down."

The man in question was stretched out on a table. He wore the colors of her own province, L'Petrie. His leg was a mangled mess and she grimaced.

"I must return to my post," she said. And she was no mender.

"I need to take care of this man's leg now, and there are no extra hands to help. Hold him down *now*. Orsin?"

"Yes, Master Clemmet?"

"Tourniquet."

That didn't sound good, Karigan thought. She placed her hands on the man's shoulders. He was moaning insensibly, which was probably a mercy, because the master mender suddenly produced a saw. Orsin, a journeyman by the knot on his shoulder, tightened the tourniquet above the wound. He passed Karigan a thick strip of leather with bite marks in it.

"Put this in his mouth so he doesn't bite his tongue off," the journeyman told her.

Karigan obeyed, trying to speak in soothing tones to the soldier while she worked his jaw open, her hands trembling.

When the saw cut into his limb, she had to use all her strength to hold him down.

Upon her return to Zachary's tent, Tegan asked, "Is Harry all right?"

"Probably."

"Probably?" Tegan then gave her a long look. "You're kind of pale."

Truthfully, Karigan wasn't sure how she'd managed to keep her gorge down. She'd seen a lot of things since becoming a Green Rider. She'd even severed limbs off enemies. But to actually be present as a man's leg was being sawed off? The sound of the toothy blade scraping bone, the soldier's screams of agony . . . It felt like it had taken forever. She closed her eyes and took a deep breath, then told Tegan about the experience, how the soldier's leg had been smashed by a large rock hurled by one of Second Empire's catapults and was too damaged to be repaired, how she tried to soothe him as he screamed and thrashed, and how Master Mender Clemmet, when he'd finished with the sawing, simply tossed the dismembered leg aside.

"Thank the gods *you* went with Harry and not me," Tegan said. "I'd have passed out."

Karigan had been close. She would never make it as a mender, but those who chose it as their vocation seemed to thrive on it.

As she resumed her post in front of Zachary's tent, she could not shake the image of the poor soldier from her mind. The method of mending used on him had seemed cruel, but she did not doubt its necessity. She knew only too well that he had a long road ahead of him to overcome the trauma, if "overcoming" were even possible. She fisted her shaking hands and thrust them into her pockets.

ᵂ REGRETS ᵂ

As the day waned, Karigan watched the king's advisors leave his tent, some singly, some with aides in tow, and head off into the rain. She stood discreetly to the side and overheard snatches of conversation. Most were grumbles about the weather, some were about the plan.

Of most interest was hearing Horse Marshal Martel mutter to his aide, "With their colonel gone, they should be under my command. They are essentially light horse, after all."

He was, she was certain, talking about the Green Riders. The Green Riders were only nominally military, and served the king directly as an independent corps. To rein them under the authority of the light cavalry would be to terminate their independent status, and to suggest doing so in Colonel Mapstone's absence was unfair. She did not think Zachary would allow such a thing to happen. After all, the Green Riders were *his* voice, but it was disturbing to think about all the same.

The last to exit the tent were Connly and Tegan.

"We're done until after supper," Connly told her. "Fighting has broken off for the day, too, so you may be excused."

Donal stepped out of the tent. "If I could have a word with Sir Karigan, please?"

"I'll see to Condor," Tegan told her, "and catch up with you later."

The Weapon waited until they were out of sight and hearing before speaking. "It is actually the king who wishes to have a word with you."

It wasn't the most discreet way for Zachary to ask to see her, but what else could you do in a war camp?

Donal escorted her into the tent. Rain drummed on the roof.

"Thank you, Donal," Zachary said.

Donal, and the other Weapons present, filed out of the tent. Zachary approached her with an assessing gaze.

"You're soaking," he said.

"Tegan was right about the rain."

"The better for us," he murmured.

Which indicated, she thought, they were going ahead with breaking the dam. Her cheeks warmed when he helped her remove her greatcoat. He placed it over the back of a chair to dry by a brazier. He then poured her a cup of tea and ordered her to sit near the warmth.

"It was hard knowing you were just outside all day, so close, and yet so far," he said, "and standing in the rain."

"It was my duty," she replied.

"I know. And it was better than worrying about you out on the field."

She set her tea aside on the table. "Your Majesty, you must not worry about me."

He gave her a sharp look. "You are now telling your king what to do, Rider?"

"No, Your Majesty. It is simply that I do not wish your concern for me to interfere with the needs of the realm."

"Karigan," he said in a quiet voice, "there are no others here. It is you and me. Please dispense with the formal address."

"I am not here as one of your Riders?"

He sat beside her, took her hand, and held it between both of his. "No. I simply wanted to see you before tomorrow when we make our big push to finish Second Empire. I am confident we will prevail, and I will be leading the troops into battle myself. There is always the chance we will fail, of course, and that Sacoridia's king will fall. I wanted to see you on this eve of battle, and going forward, I would be reassured to know that you were safely out of the fray."

She reclaimed her hand. "I have been *in* the fray for some time helping defend the city. You need every Rider you've got doing what they were trained for."

"And it is important," he said, "to have someone based here supporting them."

"I will not be that person." Even as she said it, she felt that old desire to actually be that person, to be out of the immediate danger. Fortunately, Nyssa was no longer there to reinforce her fear, and she knew the best way to overcome it was to face it.

"That is not up to you," Zachary replied.

"If someone needs to be left behind for support purposes, it should be Tegan. She was marvelous today coordinating the Riders."

"Karigan . . ."

"And another thing," she said with quiet determination, "you *will not* fail, and Sacoridia's king will *not* fall. Not if I have anything to do with it."

"Your faith humbles me and I love you for it. However, regarding your involvement in the battle, there is another point I must consider. You are not just Rider G'ladheon anymore, but Lady Winterlight."

"Will Lord Penburn be fighting? Lord L'Petrie? For that matter, what about you?"

"Yes, but—"

"What, then, makes me so special?"

He smiled. "Many things, of course, and you should know that I do not dream of kissing Lord L'Petrie."

Her cheeks heated. Damn the blushing. "I am being serious."

"And so am I. You have been made the scion of the royal house of a foreign land that also happens to be our ally. I am not certain what their wishes would be in this matter, and I am responsible for your well-being."

"So, if Prince Jametari were to ask to join the battle, you would deny him? I am a Sacoridian and a Green Rider first. If the Eletians didn't wish for me to be involved in Sacoridia's fights, they should have kept me in Eletia, but they did not. Clearly they are not worried about me going into battle."

He sat back with an exasperated sigh. Then he laughed.

She demanded, "What's so funny?"

"You are still her," he replied, "the girl who came into my

throne room five years ago and told me how I needed to take better care of the realm's roads to promote commerce. You are still *that* Karigan G'ladheon."

She thought back to that day, their first game of Intrigue, he sitting on the step of his dais, and the portraits of his ancestors on the ceiling gazing down at them. "I believe I also brought up taxes and safety on the border. You laughed then, too. It's a wonder you didn't throw me in a cell for my insolence."

"I was intrigued by this runaway schoolgirl who had taken on a dangerous mission passed to her by a dying Green Rider, who was then pursued cross-country by those who would do her great harm, and despite the dangers and trials she faced, she persisted and survived. Insolent or not, you were a breath of fresh air when you swept into my throne room, and you . . . you awakened something in me I had never felt. Karigan, I know I sound overprotective, and no doubt I am, but I could not live with myself if something happened to you. You have already endured so much, and you are my heart."

A wave of warmth passed through her. He was her heart, too, but she must not be diverted. "Today I held down a soldier in the tent of the menders while his wounded leg was sawed off. Have I endured more than others? I don't believe so. You've many who serve you who are suffering great trauma and giving their lives to fend off the enemy, and they do so willingly knowing their deeds will likely go unsung."

He bowed his head and seemed not to have a response.

"I know what can happen in battle," she continued. "I've experienced a few myself, and yet I would go willingly like those others. It would feel like a betrayal if I didn't ride with my fellow messengers. You'd have to lock me up to keep me away."

He gave her a sheepish smile. "The thought had occurred to me."

"And I would not forgive you," she told him bluntly. She stood and grabbed her coat. "It is probably best I leave now."

He caught her hand. "Please don't go," he said.

She saw the desire in his eyes, how much he wished to be with her, all that remained unspoken.

"I will not come between you and your family," she told him, gazing toward the case with the miniatures he had propped open on the table. She tried to conceal her own regret. "Besides, on this eve of battle, you will be wanting to go out among your troops and visit them. They will be putting their lives at risk not just for Sacoridia, but for you."

He bowed his head again, but did not release her. "I was wrong."

"About what?"

"About you being the same girl you were five years ago. You've become a woman of great wisdom and character. I am foolish and ashamed, and I beg your pardon." He bowed. "We will go into battle together. You will attend me as an honorary Weapon."

She raised an eyebrow, but did not protest for it was more a concession than she had expected. "As you wish," she said softly.

"There is much that I wish." The yearning was still in his eyes, but he let go her hand and stepped back, freeing her.

She rushed outside, her tears blending with the rain drops streaming down her face.

When she reached Tegan's tent, she found her friend sitting beneath the tarp at the entrance, darning a sock in fading daylight. She looked up at Karigan's approach.

"Didn't want to go into battle with a hole in my sock," Tegan said.

Karigan nodded and stood beneath the tarp.

"What did Donal want?"

Karigan cleared her throat and hoped her voice remained steady. "I am to ride with the Weapons tomorrow." Best, she thought, not to reveal it was Zachary who had decided this.

"Really? I know you're an honorary Weapon and all, but you were a Green Rider first."

Karigan shrugged, not trusting herself to respond without spilling everything. Tegan was a good friend and could be trusted, but you didn't just talk about the love you did or did not share with your king. Even good friends had lapses, and that was how rumors got started. Several Riders seemed to know or suspect something, which meant things had already gone too far, and she was not going to throw more fuel onto the fire.

"When I get done with this," Tegan said, indicating her sock, "do you want to get some supper?"

Karigan nodded and sat in a camp chair next to her.

"You're a talkative one," Tegan said.

"Sorry."

"It's all right. People all act different on the eve of battle. Let's hope the king's plan works out tonight."

She'd let Tegan believe that was the reason for her quiet. "So they are going ahead with it?" she asked.

"Yes, and the Forest Unit is positioning itself in the Waelds should Second Empire try to seek higher ground."

Karigan surmised Tegan spoke of it to her only because she'd brought the original message from General Meadows. "Any sign of the troops coming from Coutre?"

"The king sent Ty to find them days ago. We've had no word, and it doesn't look like they'll arrive in time. We made some inroads today, but Second Empire pushed back with those accursed catapults of theirs, so I hope breaking that dam works; otherwise, I don't know how it's going to go tomorrow. Ow!" Tegan sucked on her finger. "Impaled myself. It's getting too dark for darning." Then she looked up. "Oh, the king is walking among the troops."

Karigan could see him the next row of tents over, pausing by a campfire to speak with some soldiers. He accepted a mug from one of them and laughed at something that was said. Weapons ranged about him, but not so closely that they intruded on the one-on-one exchanges he was having with those who would fight for him the next day.

"Want to get supper?" Tegan asked. "Or, do you want to see if the king heads this way?"

"Let's get supper. I'm starving."

Karigan wasn't actually hungry, but it was the best way to avoid another encounter with Zachary. She feared being in his presence just now would lead her to giving in to her own weakness, which then could only lead to regrets on both their parts.

≪ HARBINGER ≫

"**L**ooks like gruel again," Tegan told Karigan, craning her neck to watch as those ahead of them in line received ladlesful of the stuff. "Big surprise."

Keeping an army supplied and fed was an enormous challenge, so indeed, Karigan thought, no surprise. The line shuffled forward, everyone with their bowls in hand. Her thoughts kept going back to the scene in Zachary's tent and the look in his eyes before she'd left. She shook her head, trying not to think of it. It was not easy, but then a conversation going on behind her between an old-timer and a couple of young recruits caught her attention.

"It was third watch last night," the old-timer was saying, "black as pitch with the rain, and I demanded they show themselves, but no one answered. There were the hoofbeats of just one horse. I strained my eyes, I did, and then saw him out on the field where we'd battled only two hours earlier. Blacker than night, he was, and no rain touched him. A breeze flowed around him. He weren't any horse of ours, and not any of theirs." Then he whispered, "He weren't of our world."

The young soldiers gasped.

"Aye," the old-timer said, nodding, "the harbinger of strife and battle himself. But then, who else would it be?"

Some other soldiers scoffed at his story, but Karigan did not.

When they reached the big kettles, her attention turned to receiving her portion of gruel and a wedge of pan bread. She heard no more of the old-timer's story. Even if he'd not seen

Salvistar and was just putting one over on the youngsters, she knew the story to be more than plausible. She'd had, after all, personal experience with the death god's steed, and this was a battlefield.

Later, after she'd turned in for the night, she burrowed under her blankets, feeling restless on the eve of battle. Even as she twisted and turned, a compulsion came on her to rise, and before she knew it, she was outside the tent, the ground soft and wet beneath her bare feet. The rain had stopped, but a mist hung in the air. The camp was silent, but for her own breaths that curled off her lips in a wisp of steam.

She wrapped her arms around herself against the chill and passed among the still tents as though in a dream. Perhaps it was a dream. She wasn't sure. As she walked, not a soul stirred, and even the land lay quiescent. Crickets and night creatures kept silent, and no breeze whispered among the boughs of trees. Sentries did not appear to challenge her; no one kept watch.

She passed between stakes driven into the ground with sharpened ends pointed outward as a defense against enemy cavalry. On the field of battle, not all the dead had been recovered by their respective sides. Some lay slumped where they fell, their flesh pale in the dark, others stretched out as though they only slept. She stepped around helms that still contained severed heads securely strapped in.

Luminous, transparent figures moved about the battlefield. A ghostly sergeant silently yelled at his dead soldiers. A warrior attempted to lift his sword from the ground over and over, but the sword was of the living world and he was not.

Some of the spirits began to move with purpose in the same direction. She followed, and they were joined by more. A young drummer boy strode by her, an eager expression on his face.

From the silence came the pounding of hoofbeats and she knew it to be Salvistar. He galloped across the battlefield, the wind that rolled off him collecting spirits. Fluid and powerful, he surged through the night.

He was not alone.

On a knoll a short distance away stood a monumental

figure, man-shaped, his raptor's visage and wings limned by ghostlight. Westrion, god of death, staff in hand, surveyed the harvest of souls. Those spirits not swept in the wind of Salvistar's passing were subtly directed by Westrion, whether by a nod of his head or a gesture, and either drifted upward toward the heavens, or sank into the ground. Karigan, as avatar, had wielded such power, but she did not join in the dispersal of souls now.

After a time, Westrion seemed to note her presence with a glimmer of light in his eye. Then he extended his great wings and, with a few powerful strokes, ascended into the air and flew away.

Salvistar trotted up to her with a snort and toss of his head. His hide absorbed the night, and his mane and tail flowed in no Earthly breeze. He presented his side to her, an invitation. Curious, she accepted and vaulted onto his bare back. His flesh was neither warm nor cold, and it was as though she sat upon the air, but then she realized, when she looked at her hands, that she, like the souls Westrion had collected, was translucent, not present corporeally. Nor was she clad in the armor of the avatar as she had been the other times she'd ridden Salvistar. She did not feel Westrion's presence within her.

Salvistar picked his way into the middle of the battlefield among the corpses of people and horses. Equipment—bits of armor and weapons, and the small items carried with them, such as spoons, tokens of luck, waterskins—were scattered on the ground. Arrows impaled the earth and bodies in uneven thickets.

A celestial light gleamed on a figure who strode across the battlefield. She wore bronze scaled armor and a helm of ancient design, and carried spear and shield. A short, double-edged infantry sword was girded on her right hip. She was, Karigan knew, without knowing how she knew, Valora, goddess of war. Her hounds, Soro, Heth, and Bella, ranged around her. Often she was depicted riding in a war chariot across the field of battle, exulting in the carnage, or among the stars, the home of the gods.

She was not alone. Lodan appeared in their long robes.

Neither male nor female, Lodan united both as one and symbolized balance in their role as the goddai of justice. Lodan represented the rights and wrongs of the universe, the laws as handed down to humanity. They bore a scroll tucked beneath their arm in which the laws were inscribed.

Karigan understood why Westrion and Valora would visit a battlefield, but not why it had drawn Lodan who presided over the court of the heavens.

Valora strode toward Lodan and joined them in the middle of the field. Westrion descended from the heavens and alighted on the ground beside them, and folded his wings back.

"Has your harvest been acceptable, brother?" Valora asked.

"Yes," he replied.

They spoke a language that had lived beyond time and was no longer known in the world of mortals, not even to the moon priests, and yet Karigan understood. Some thread of her avatar nature must be active for her to comprehend their speech.

"It will be even better on the morrow," Valora said.

"The two sides are nearly evenly distributed," Lodan said with approval.

"In which case," Valora replied, "it will come down to strategy and whose is best."

They did not seem to perceive Karigan's presence as she sat upon Salvistar eavesdropping. Except for Westrion, she thought. He was why she was there, and it was he who must be shielding her from the others.

Two more gods arrived, and Karigan felt a thrill, for they were Aeryc and Aeryon, the twins. Aeryon blazed with such light that she was difficult to look upon. A corona of flame seemed to flare, twist, and arc around her. Aeryc, the moonman lover of Queen Laurelyn in song and legend, remained in shadow but for the side of him that faced his sister. They were sun and moon come to Earth.

They spoke of the impending battle, debated who had the advantage, the better strategy, the better fighters, and she wondered again why Aeryc and Aeryon, and Lodan, too, cared enough about this battle to descend from the celestial realm to concern themselves with warring mortals.

"*Our* mortals must claim victory," Aeryon said, "lest we lose dominance to the one god."

And that was when Karigan understood. This battle didn't have life and death consequences just in the mortal realm, but also for that of the gods. If Sacoridia lost, the god of the Arcosian conquerors would take precedence. Second Empire would not stand for the defeated Sacoridians to continue to pay homage to their gods. Clergy would be persecuted, chapels of the moon destroyed or converted to houses of worship for the one god. Those caught worshipping the old gods would be severely punished. Without supplicants to provide the old gods with sustenance in the form of belief, prayers, offerings, and rituals, they would diminish and fade from the world.

The flame that was Aeryon flared, and Karigan felt the heat of her regard across the space that separated them.

"Salvistar," the goddess said, "do come forward and show us who has been spying upon us."

Her voice carried the power and weight of an order, and Salvistar swished his tail and carried Karigan before the gods. She looked wildly about for a way to escape, but she could not move, no matter how much she willed it.

"It is a mortal," Lodan exclaimed in surprise.

"A warrior," Valora added, an unfriendly smile on her face. Karigan could not meet her gaze, for her eyes were filled with turmoil, violence, hate, and the maggots of the dead.

"How has this spy come among us?" Aeryc asked. He did not burn bright like his sister, and was visible only where her light illuminated him.

"Mortals who look upon us must have their eyes burned out," Aeryon told her, "and be made mute so it cannot be spoken of."

"The mortal is my servant," Westrion said in his rumbling, deep voice. It was then that Karigan realized his raptor's visage was more a headdress and mask than a bird's head, as she saw through to more human, chiseled features beneath.

"Even the servant of Westrion is not permitted, unless in the guise of avatar," Lodan said.

"This one shall remain unharmed," Westrion said. He gazed at Aeryc. "Do you not see the light of Laurelyn on her?"

There was a ripple of emotion on Aeryc's face, the part that did not fall into shadow. "I do," he said.

"You, sister," Westrion said to Valora, "see the warrior she is. Much would have been lost to us had she not been one. How much will be lost if she is blinded and made mute?"

"Verily," she replied, "this one must continue to fight. She brings courage to battle, and death to her foes."

He turned next to Aeryon. "My servant has driven back the hordes of the damned on two occasions and repaired the seals through which they transgressed. The first includes the one located in the cavern where we were first envisioned and described by mortals. Had she not, this world would be overcome by the dark, the mortals feasted upon, and no one left to worship us."

Through her link as avatar, Karigan understood him to mean the caverns beneath the royal tombs. It was a memory that Westrion had originally suppressed in her but later restored. Demonkind had nearly escaped their hell and would have brought that hell to the living Earth, but in her role as the avatar that first time, she had prevented the end of the world.

Aeryon did not speak for a while. The corona of flame expanded and receded and, at times, roared with turbulent radiance.

"What are you called, mortal?" she asked Karigan.

"Karigan G'ladheon. I am a Green Rider."

Again, the long consideration. Then, "I see you can speak with the dead, and you've the ability to cross thresholds. This is why my brother favors you. I also see you have been marked by the Mirari, who are powerful tricksters. The Eletians favor you, as well. You are a very unusual mortal creature. Lodan, what say you?"

"The weight of justice carries in favor of this human." The goddai unrolled their scroll and examined it. "Yes. The qualities extolled preserve this one from immediate maiming. But it must not speak of this meeting."

"On my honor," Karigan said, "I will not."

"So mote shall it be," Aeryon declared. "Be warned, however, mortal, I now know your name and your soul, and none go unpunished who have seen our aspect. You will continue with your life for now and serve my brother, Westrion, as he sees fit. Your punishment is what I see in your future, and it is that you will know true suffering."

 THE BAYING
OF HOUNDS

Karigan awoke with a gasp and sat straight up in her bedding. It was still dark, but horns blared through the encampment, summoning all to awaken. She scrubbed her face. Had it been a dream? Meeting the gods?

Tegan yawned on her side of the tent. "Morning." It sounded more a groan.

"Morning," Karigan replied.

"It's like I just put my head down to sleep," Tegan said.

"I know the feeling."

There was no time to contemplate dreams and gods, for the camp scrambled to prepare for another day of battle.

As Karigan finished a quick bowl of gruel for breakfast, Connly approached her out of the thick fog that had settled over the land. The horn of the First Rider, she noticed, was slung over his shoulder, as was proper.

"You are to report to Donal at the king's tent as soon as you're ready," he told her.

"I need to get Condor ready, too," she said.

"You will not be riding," he replied, "but going on foot."

"What?" She was a Green *Rider*.

"The ground is too soft," he said. "Even the heavy cavalry is going in on foot."

"What about you and the other Riders?"

He gave her a thin smile. "We still ride."

"But—"

"Good luck, Karigan."

"You, too," she said as he walked away.

She put on her cuirass and helm, and chose to gird herself

with Colonel Mapstone's sword. Lighter in weight than her own, it would not tire her out so quickly in a fight. As she strode to Zachary's tent, she realized she hadn't had a chance to give Tegan a hug or wish any of her fellow Riders, except Connly, good luck. Now it was too late.

At Zachary's tent, the Weapons were assembling, and donning light armor. She found Donal, who looked gravely upon her and nodded. "You are to stay by the king's side."

That meant she'd be ringed by Weapons and well-protected, just as Zachary wished. The Riders would not have that kind of protection, and guilt weighed on her that she would not be riding with them.

Donal reached behind himself and presented her with a plain black shield. "When one of us yells *shield,* you will position this above you like so." He demonstrated, holding it like a small roof over his head. "All our shields will overlap so arrows do not penetrate. Do you understand?"

"Yes."

"Good. Glad to have you with us protecting our king."

She almost laughed at that, and wondered how much he and the other Weapons actually resented the fact they were having to guard her in addition to Zachary. They certainly didn't show it, but then, they wouldn't.

Getting all the units and divisions and companies into position and ready to move appeared chaotic, but was underlain with good order. She was placed in the center of a square of fifty-nine Weapons, who formed up three to four deep on each side, and she thought she would not want to be the enemy confronting them. Zachary was nowhere in sight.

They marched to the front of the army. As she looked upon the assembled, the long lines of fighting men and women, the archers, men-at-arms, infantry, she saw only a small portion of the combined armies of Sacoridian regulars and provincial militias as the ranks extended into the fog. The colors of banners and uniforms were drab in the dim morning light. No wind rustled the banners so they hung limp and lifeless.

She wondered how the poor visibility would complicate the battle. Archers might accidentally loose their arrows on their own people, and troops could lose track of one another, or head in the wrong direction. It threatened to throw off the coordination of precisely planned troop movements. She, of course, had not been made privy to much of the actual strategy; only the officers had been, so she did not know how it was all expected to work.

Zachary arrived mounted on one of his warhorses, accompanied by Fastion on his black steed. They cantered along the line, and soldiers banged swords on shields as he passed. He rode toward the other end, disappearing into the vapor. The sound of shield banging followed him, and it was the only way to tell where he was. Finally, he reappeared at a hazy distance and halted before his troops.

"Today we march to rid our land of the aggressors," he said, projecting his voice so all could hear. "We do it for Sacoridia, for our sovereignty, for the gods, and most of all, for ourselves and our way of life.

"Last night, I walked among you, heard stories about your families, of your children who have made you proud, of the wives and husbands you miss; of your work when not fighting a war. Some of you are carpenters and wheelwrights, farmers and fishermen, foresters and stonemasons. You told me how you'd like to live peaceably in pursuit of prosperity for you and yours. These are all things Second Empire threatens. They would subjugate us, take what is ours, and force us to worship at the altar of their one god."

This was followed by hissing and booing from many quarters.

"Fight for Sacoridia," Zachary boomed. "Fight for our people and our families. Fight for a future in which we may all live in peace and prosperity."

Karigan joined in with shouts of affirmation and the beating of shields. It was not a side of Zachary she had often seen, this role of him as warrior king leading his troops in battle. He was not one for making loud speeches, but rather quiet gestures. However, he stepped into this role masterfully, and it made her heart sing with pride to see him up on that horse rallying his people.

"I am proud of every one of you," Zachary continued. "You have brought Sacoridia much honor, and today you will bring her victory. Today, we are all Sacoridia."

The army took up a great chant: "Sacoridia! Sacoridia! Sacoridia!"

He drew his sword and held it above his head, and galloped along the lines to the chant and pounding of shields. No doubt Second Empire could hear it over in their encampment, but they, too, would be receiving a rousing speech from their commander, General Birch.

Over the sounds of the cheering and chanting, she thought she could hear the baying of hounds.

"Do you hear the hounds?" she asked Joshua, the Weapon who stood to her right.

"What hounds? Just all this yelling and noise."

She frowned.

Zachary returned and dismounted, and handed his horse off to an attendant while another brought him his shield and helm. He then gave instructions to the field marshal, who raised his baton. Horns rang out up and down the line with the signal to march. Drummers beat out the pace.

Zachary walked in front, accompanied by Fastion and a standard bearer.

"I thought the king would be with us," she said to Joshua as they took their first steps forward.

"He will, but it does the troops good to see him leading."

Not that many could see him through the fog.

Her legs shook. She'd been in battles before, but never one so orchestrated with thousands of troops on either side. She wondered how the newer, younger Riders like Megan and Hoff were faring. They'd have even less experience in this level of warfare than she.

The fog deepened her fear. They could not see what lay ahead, and what could not be seen, the imagination built into something far worse. She thought she heard the baying of the hounds again but did not mention it to Joshua this time. Hooves pounded and a chariot drawn by a pair of horses shot ahead into the fog, three hounds running alongside the spinning wheels. Karigan had an impression of jubilation on the charioteer's face.

"I don't suppose you saw a chariot driven by Valora just now, did you?" she asked Joshua.

"A chariot? The goddess of war? Are you feeling ill, Sir Karigan?"

That answered that. "I'm fine," she murmured, though she wasn't sure. It seemed her meeting with the gods had actually been more than a simple dream, though there was always the chance she was hallucinating, but she knew better. Her life had gone down too many strange paths not to accept the reality of the surreal. In Joshua's case, it was probably a good thing he did not see Valora, for the gods would burn out his eyes if he had.

The cadence of the drummers quickened, and Zachary, Fastion, and the standard bearer dropped back and were absorbed into the square of Weapons.

"Good morning, Rider," Zachary said as he fell in beside her.

"Your Majesty," she said. "I think today I am more of a walker than a Rider."

"I am told," he replied, "that walking is beneficial for the heart and lungs."

She had never seen him quite so ebullient. His cheeks were flushed, his eyes sparkling, and his manner eager.

"I am told the enemy woke to a rather soggy morning," he said, and grinned.

"The plan worked?"

"The dam was broken, yes. Whether it helps our cause, however, remains to be seen."

She glanced over her shoulder to take in the Weapons who were their rear guard, and at the standard bearer directly behind Zachary. He was large and broad, and . . . familiar.

"Flogger?"

Her old sparring partner from swordmaster training nodded to her. "It is Weapon Clarence now."

He must have excelled at Black Shield training on Breaker Island to be wearing Weapon black so soon. She had wondered if he'd the right temperament to make it as a Weapon. Apparently those who decided such things had deemed him fit.

The square of Weapons fell back so as to allow other troops to advance before them, providing a greater buffer for Zachary. She was sure he wished to be at the head of the army the entire way, but, no doubt, his advisors had argued against his participation at all, and this was a compromise.

Soon they bypassed the pointed stakes that were defense against enemy cavalry, and they began to encounter the dead and debris from the previous day's fighting.

Archers, strategically positioned, blindly sent rafts of arrows sailing into the fog with the intent of thinning out Second Empire's forward ranks, but there was no telling if they hit any of the enemy.

It was not long before the enemy answered. They hurled rocks and metal shards out of the vapor and over the heads of the Sacoridians, and hit into the troops somewhere behind them. Soldiers screamed.

"Damn those catapults," Zachary muttered.

Karigan's hands shook, but she kept walking even though she wanted no more than to run from the danger. Zachary would probably even excuse her if she asked, and be glad of it, but she gritted her teeth, remained silent, and continued on.

The archers, homing in on the general direction of the catapult, filled the air with more arrows. This time cries could be heard through the fog. The archers did not relent, and soon projectiles from the catapult stopped coming.

Enemy arrows, however, screamed out of the fog in answer.

"*Shields!*" Donal cried.

Karigan threw hers over her head as she'd been instructed. They were almost too late in creating a shelter over themselves. The arrows hit like hail on a roof, but none penetrated their formation. Soldiers in other units were not so fortunate, and their cries of shock and pain were wrenching.

The tempo of drums increased and they picked up their pace to a jog. When more arrows rained upon them, they shielded themselves again, but did not pause or slow down. Ahead, the fog thinned enough to reveal armed figures running out of the gray gloom to meet them.

Thousands of booted feet thundered on the earth as the front lines of the two armies charged toward one another. Over the battle cries and screams of determination that propelled the combatants forth, over the clamor of horns, drums, and steel, and the pounding of her own heart, Karigan was sure she heard the baying of hounds.

⋙ A PALE IMITATION ⋘

Time ceased.
   Weapons leaped ahead in slow, extended motion. The shouts of soldiers droned, and the march of the armies lagged to a standstill. Arrows hovered in the air. Karigan's pulse throbbed in her ears in ponderous measure, her breaths harsh and drawn out. She saw the eagerness in Zachary's face, the joy in his eyes, the glint of light on his sword. The wet air carried to her the tang of first blood.

Time resumed.

The lines of Sacoridians and Second Empire collided. The earth seemed to quake with the crash of steel and thud of bodies. The hiss of arrows in flight; the screams of the mortally wounded.

The Weapons kept a cohesive formation around her and Zachary, which meant she had yet to engage the enemy. She could tell Zachary very much wanted to charge between his guards and fight. He was known to go berserk, and the need to attack must call to him. The king, of course, was a target, so he would no doubt get a chance to ply his skill as a warrior soon, though not many could stand before the deadly expertise of the Weapons.

They pushed forward, and at times were pushed back by the enemy. It was impossible to know how the battle was proceeding elsewhere because of the poor visibility. She wondered about her fellow Riders and where they were located, and what their part in the battle was to be.

They pushed forward again, stepping over fresh corpses of both their own soldiers and Second Empire's, and onto new, wetter ground churned to mud. It sucked at her boots. It would compromise their footing, make everything harder. It was all like a dream with the billow and wisp of fog around and between them, soldiers appearing and disappearing in it. It closed around them like a suffocating blanket. She lost all sense of time, felt like they'd been at this for hours, but it had probably been only minutes.

A line of enemy crossbowmen stepped out of the mist directly in front of them, and Donal barely shouted, "Shields!" before crossbow bolts hurtled at them. One thunked with such force into Karigan's shield that she was knocked back a step and the wood was split in half. Several Weapons fell, including Joshua next to her. Zachary sprinted through a sudden opening between his defenders in front of him.

Hells! Karigan thought.

She threw her broken shield aside and rushed after him with the Weapons. He bore into the crossbowmen even as they attempted to reload with fresh bolts. Many, in the face of the onrush of so many angry, black-clad Weapons and their berserker king, dropped their crossbows and ran. Any who remained or tried to fight were quickly cut down.

What had been a solid fighting formation among the Weapons had turned into a mad dash to keep up with Zachary as he slashed his way through the next wave of enemies, one after another. She had not been present when he'd gone berserk during the Battle of the Lone Forest, but now it was something amazing and terrible to behold as he left a trail of bodies in his wake. She slipped and slid in the mud as she tried to keep up with him.

Flogger—*Clarence!* she reminded herself—huffed and puffed behind him with the standard. She raced to his aid when several of the enemy took him on at once. Capturing the royal standard would be a great prize. She splashed through the mud and ran one of his assailants through, and when another turned to her, a quick exchange of blows ended his life with a good solid thrust through his gambeson. Flogger used the butt of the standard to knock a third down, and the Weapons took care of the rest.

"Thanks," he said as he rushed on after Zachary.

Karigan gave him a nod. So often they had been opponents in swordmaster training that he'd become something of a nemesis, but not today.

She scrambled on the mucky ground in an effort to reach Zachary. By now, the fighting had turned into a messy all-out brawl.

"For Arcosia!" a soldier howled, and he swung at her.

She intercepted his blow and pushed back. He slipped in the sludge. Before he could recover, she slashed his throat.

As the fighting wore on, the ground became a mire of blood and entrails mixed with the mud. Karigan no longer had time to think, just to thrust and parry and survive, until, suddenly, no other attackers came at them. They breathed hard in the relative silence. The cloying stench of ruptured bowels and churned, wet earth was thick in the air. Somehow they'd been cut off from the rest of the army, enclosed by the wafting mist. Even Zachary had stilled to catch his breath. The battle fever was still in his eyes, but he seemed to retain some control of himself.

Around them were the sounds of clashes, the fog too dense for them to see. Horns rang out in the distance.

"Regroup," Donal ordered.

Fastion grabbed Karigan's arm and led her to Zachary's side, and the Weapons once more closed around them. She tried to wipe mud off her face, but only smeared it around. It was like she had rolled in the stuff. Somehow Zachary and the Weapons appeared only mildly splattered.

"How many have we lost?" Zachary asked.

"Eight, in the volley with the crossbowmen," Donal replied.

"Injuries?" Zachary asked.

The Weapon reported only minor cuts and bruises.

"Sir Karigan?" Zachary asked.

"No injuries," she replied.

"Good."

"Your Majesty?" she asked.

"Yes?"

"Injuries?"

There was a quick flash of amusement on his face. "None,

but surely you can tell as I am not caked in mud. Any injury would be apparent. With you, it is decidedly difficult to tell." He then grew serious again. "From the sounds of it, our troops to the north and south have pushed on. The fact Second Empire hasn't tried to send any horse units against us leads me to believe that breaking the dam worked, and the ground is too wet for them to be effective. In fact, I've found their resistance to be on the light side."

"A trap, sire?" one of the Weapons queried.

"I am guessing there is more resistance where our forces are more concentrated, but it wouldn't be unlike Birch to have a surprise in store for us. Let us move ahead with caution, and keep close together, shields ready. Where is yours?" he asked Karigan.

"Broken."

Flogger removed the one he had worn slung over his back and handed it to her.

"My hands are full with my sword and the standard," he said, "so you might as well have mine."

"Thank you."

They moved forward, keeping together as Zachary told them to. A tall object loomed out of the mist.

"One of the catapults," Fastion said.

Bodies of Second Empire's soldiers lay about it, bristling with Sacoridian arrows, with no one left alive to operate it. It stood with two of its wheels buried to the hubs in mud. One of the rear wheels had broken. It was useless.

"Hah!" Zachary said. "No wonder they stopped lobbing debris at us."

As they continued slogging across the churned ground, about a hundred members of the Penburn provincial militia found them and advanced with them.

"We lost our bearings in this fog," their sergeant said. He explained that Lord Penburn was with another unit.

They overpowered groups of enemy soldiers as they marched forth, but otherwise continued to meet with little resistance.

Zachary paused, and they all halted. The odors of horses and woodsmoke drifted in the air, indicating Second

Empire's camp was near. Also not far off, the sounds of rushing water could be heard.

"It would appear we are close to Second Empire's camp," Zachary said, "but it is impossible to know the situation down there."

Karigan summoned her nerve. Mostly, she was proud of how well she was doing. She had not broken down and run off, but kept focused on the job at hand. Still, despite the absence of Nyssa the torturer, the long-lasting effects of her presence remained nibbling at Karigan's confidence. It would take a long time for her to get over it, if she ever could.

"I can go take a look," she said.

"No." Zachary's answer was a little too quick.

"But you know how good I am at this sort of scouting." She had no wish to reveal to the soldiers of Penburn just what kind of scouting she meant.

"That is not in dispute, Rider," he replied, "but we stick together."

"Sticking together won't help if we walk into a trap," she replied.

The Weapons watched their exchange stoically, which was the way of Weapons, but the Penburnians who were close enough to hear appeared agog that a mere common messenger would contradict the king to his face, and so soundly. She took note and bowed.

"Your Majesty," she said, "forgive me. I simply wished to offer an alternative."

"Sire, if I may," Donal said, "it is a sound idea."

As they debated, the curtain of fog thinned ever so slightly.

"Sire," Fastion said softly.

Zachary looked up, and Karigan followed his gaze. Hazy figures surrounded them, curved swords at the ready.

"Lions," she whispered.

"Birch's surprise," Zachary muttered.

"Form up!" Donal ordered, and the Weapons tightened up around Karigan and Zachary.

One of the Lions stepped forward, and Karigan recognized him as their leader, Brother Pascal.

"The last king of Sacoridia, I presume," he said. "On behalf of General Birch, I offer you the opportunity to surrender. Your death will be swift and dignified, and as painless as possible, and we will allow the ordinary folk in your army to walk free and return to their farms, shops, and families. I am afraid that all officers and these Black Shields, however, must also be executed."

Karigan guessed there were seventy-five or so Lions. It was hard to get an accurate count with the ever-shifting mists. They clearly outnumbered the Weapons, and she suspected they would not find the Penburn contingent much of a threat. Still, the Penburnians combined with the Weapons outnumbered the Lions, and it might be enough to even up the odds a little.

"Why should I surrender?" Zachary asked. "My forces are winning."

"Are you so sure?" Brother Pascal replied. "You can see so much through this fog? The field is littered with dead Sacoridians."

"There are casualties on both sides."

"But where is this grand army of yours?" Brother Pascal demanded. "Certainly not victoriously marching into our camp."

Zachary laughed. "Your camp is by now a flooded mud pit. I daresay many of you woke up this morning with sopping-wet blankets."

"I make the offer one more time," Brother Pascal said, "and one more time only. If you surrender, we will spare those of your soldiers who are otherwise ordinary citizens. Before you answer, you should know that we, the Lions of Arcosia, have been training since childhood for this moment. We outnumber your Black Shields, and are more skilled."

Fastion issued an uncharacteristic and derisive snort.

"Well," Zachary said, "my Black Shields will simply take that as a challenge. As for myself, I like to recall how my ancestors valiantly held off, and eventually defeated, the aggressors from Arcosia who encroached on this land and its sovereignty. The Sacor Clans had not the mechanicals or concussive weapons that the Arcosians possessed, but they had spirit, and the passion to defend their homeland. Second Empire, and its so-called Lions, are but a pale imitation of that adversary my ancestors faced and *defeated* a thousand years ago."

Brother Pascal scowled particularly at the words "pale imitation." "You will regret your inso—"

"Attack!" Zachary shouted before the Lion could complete his sentence.

The Weapons exploded into action, dragging Karigan along with them.

⤳ DANCE OF DEATH ⤳

The Weapons swept Karigan along with them as they took on the Lions as a cohesive unit. It was the outer rows of the square that battled the enemy, and if one Weapon fell, another was right there to take his or her place. Steel clanged and blows thudded on shields. She and Zachary were in the center of the square and so could do little more than wait.

In contrast, the Penburn militia was fully involved in clashes. The unit's hornsman managed to sound off an urgent call before he was slain. She feared they would be massacred, but it seemed the Lions were concentrating the force of their attack on the Weapons as if the Penburnians were but an afterthought. That was to the advantage of the Penburnians, and they were able to double and even triple up on a single Lion.

Because all she could do at the moment was observe, she took in how fluid and graceful the Lions' style of swordplay was. It was quite different from that of the Weapons, who were restrained in their movements. The Lions were not. They bounded, leaped, and twirled like dancers, and they were quick. At times they seemed almost to fly. That said, their actual swordfighting forms resembled those she knew.

"Theatrics," Donal grumbled, as though he had read her mind.

Zachary leaned his shoulder against hers. "Are you doing all right?"

"Yes." She was boxed in by protective layers of Weapons. What else could she say?

"I should have sent you back to the castle."

"I would not have gone," she replied.

"I know, but I—"

One of the Lions must have tired of banging on the shields of the Weapons and the failure of his brothers to break the square, for he took a running leap and lithely somersaulted over the heads of the astonished Weapons and landed in their midst. He was quickly slain, but it jostled the center of the square, which sent ripples outward and created cracks in their outer wall.

The Lions apparently perceived the somersault move a good strategy for another attempted it. He fell behind Zachary and Flogger—Karigan just couldn't think of him as "Clarence." Zachary quickly impaled the Lion with his longsword.

The damage had been done, however; the cracks in the outer line of Weapons ultimately weakened the integrity of the square. A knot of Weapons still securely surrounded her and Zachary, but the rest were embroiled in melees. Had the circumstances been different, she might have been more appreciative of witnessing this display of swordsmanship at its pinnacle, the quick gleaming blades, catlike grace, and pure artfulness of the practitioners, but people were dying, Lions and Weapons both. And, she could no longer tell what was going on with the Penburnians.

Another Lion leaped into their knot, sword ready to thrust into Zachary, but Donal knocked him away with his shield and killed him. A madness then seized the brethren. They leaped one after the other onto the knot in an attempt to reach Zachary. One knocked Karigan to the ground. Zachary stabbed him, then turned to a new assailant, leaving her stuck beneath the body of the Lion. Warriors stepped on her, and she turned her head in time to avoid being kicked in the face. So many feet moved around her in a deadly dance of swordplay.

After some effort, she managed to squirm out from beneath the Lion, grab her sword, which had slipped her grasp when she fell, and clamber to her feet. Everyone was involved now, blades cutting through the air in a spectacle of deadly efficiency.

As she attempted to regain her bearings, Brother Pascal,

apparently disregarding her as a threat, moved to strike Zachary from behind. Zachary was involved with another opponent and unaware of the threat from the Lion. She blocked Brother Pascal's blow and he gave her a reassessing look. His blade moved like a flicker of lightning. Her reaction was comparatively sluggish, but she managed to sweep aside a killing blow.

He watched and gauged her with calculating blue eyes, then launched into another series of forms that she could barely keep up with. She stumbled back into other combatants, and he stalked her like the predator his order was named for.

She felt like a child barely able to hold a sword against him, and he toyed with her, presenting an opening she fell for. He was quick with his parry, and she stepped back just in time to save her life, but she received a cut down her left arm. She hissed with the sudden stinging pain.

This, she was sure, was how it was going to end. In this muddy field, at the end of a sword wielded by Brother Pascal, and it was mud that was almost her undoing. She slipped and fell, and lost her grip on her sword.

Brother Pascal wrapped both his hands around the hilt of his sword to plunge it into her. With her sword now out of reach, it was as though some other force guided her hand into her pocket. She whipped out her moonstone. The light flared bright and pure right into Brother Pascal's eyes and gave her the moment she needed to grab her sword and rise to her feet, but it was not she who ended his life. Zachary pivoted just in time and thrust his longsword through the Lion's back. The tip emerged from his chest, and when Zachary withdrew his sword, Brother Pascal dropped to his knees and toppled to his side.

"Thanks," Karigan said.

Zachary flashed her a smile and went back to work.

After the demise of Brother Pascal, the spirit of the Lions faded. Karigan and Zachary fought back-to-back, moving in accord as though linked mind and body. Each guarded the other, their swords darting and flashing as they faced the enemy. Karigan focused on her swordplay, but was always aware of Zachary like a pleasant warmth against her back, and his nearness lifted her with renewed energy and determination.

When a Lion pressed her to reach Zachary, even as tired and hurting as she was, her desire to protect Zachary made her fierce. She met the Lion form for form, and when in frustration he made a final drive to break through her guard, she ducked beneath his blow and, in one fluid movement, drew her longknife and thrust it between his ribs.

Eventually, the Weapons were able to pull together to create another knot of protection around them. It was a relief for her wounded arm hurt too much to use, and she had, in fact, let go the shield she'd been using. Blood ran down her sleeve and trickled off the ends of her fingers.

The Lions made a final push to reach Zachary. Flogger went down and the standard started to topple. She caught it before it could fall, and Zachary dispatched the assailant.

"I'll take that," Fastion said, reaching for the standard.

She handed it over and knelt in the mud next to Flogger. The Lion had stabbed him through the arm hole of his cuirass, and into his chest.

"Flogger?" she said.

"Weapon Clarence," he whispered. "It's Weapon Clarence."

"Yes," she replied. "Yes, it is."

"The standard—I dropped it."

"No, you didn't. It still stands tall and proud."

"Good, good." His voice faded and he closed his eyes.

"Hey," she said with a gentle shake of his arm. "Stay with me now, Clarence, we're going to get you help." Where she was going to get it from, she wasn't sure.

"Too late." He coughed and blood spattered his lips. "Tell—tell my ma . . ."

Whatever message he had for his mother died on his lips. She checked for breathing, but he was gone. She closed his eyes and bowed her head. She'd never gotten a chance to really know him and she was sorry.

She stood unsteadily and gazed about her. The fighting

was done. Bodies of Weapons, some she had known, and many she had not, lay entwined with those of Lions as though they'd been engaged in some dance. It had been a dance of death.

No Lions stood, and perhaps thirty or forty Weapons remained, some helping their injured fellows. Only a handful of the Penburnians had survived.

"It was our armor more than anything that saved us," Donal was telling the king with a shake of his head. "They wore only thin jacks under their robes. If they'd been wearing something more substantial, I don't know that we'd have won."

"Anything heavier would not have accommodated their acrobatics," Zachary said.

They looked up at her approach. Donal appeared to be favoring his right leg, and blood smeared his face, though it was unclear if it was his or an opponent's.

"You're bleeding," Zachary told her.

She glanced at the blood mixing with mud on her sleeve, then back at him. "You are, too." A cut on his cheek flowed freely into his beard.

"Just a scratch." He was much less muddy than she, and he produced a white cloth from a belt pouch and tied it snugly around the deepest part of her wound to help staunch the flow of blood. "You need to have that looked at by menders."

She sighed so heavily that he chuckled.

"My lord!" cried the Penburnian sergeant. "Look!" He pointed down the slope.

The fog was lifting, and they could see the Sacoridian forces pushing Second Empire back toward their camp. Three once-tame streams now roared down from the nearby Waelds and flooded the camp. A horn rang out signaling a retreat, but it was not a Sacoridian horn. Second Empire's soldiers stopped fighting and ran away from the Sacoridians who gave pursuit.

"They'll escape to the west," the sergeant said.

"I'm not so sure," Zachary murmured.

The fog lifted like a curtain revealing an army standing on higher ground in the way of Second Empire's escape. It was too far off to tell for sure, but Karigan thought she could see the cormorant banner of Coutre, the crossed sword banner of the light cavalry, and the gold winged horse banner of the Green Riders.

"Coutre's army caught up with us after all," she said.

"Not exactly," Zachary replied. "They are still two days out."

"What?" But when she realized what she was seeing, she laughed. "Hoff!"

"I don't understand," the sergeant said.

"Collect any of your able-bodied warriors," Zachary told him. "We go to receive Second Empire's surrender and round up more prisoners."

"Aye, sire."

"Rider G'ladheon," Zachary said, "I understand you've a fresh horse?"

She nodded.

"Then please take word to the queen that we've contained Second Empire."

"Won't Connly—"

"Yes, but you will be a direct witness. Get that arm looked at, too. And beware stray enemy soldiers along the way that may have gotten separated, or otherwise separated themselves, from their units."

"Yes, sire."

She watched as the Weapons closed around him and they all strode down the slope accompanied by the Penburnians who were able to walk.

A couple Weapons remained behind to care for their wounded. She looked down upon all the corpses, at Flogger peacefully laid out in the center, Brother Pascal sprawled beneath the body of another Lion. She thought she perceived wingbeats just overhead, the wingbeats of Westrion, god of death, but she could not see him. He was there, though, she knew, for this was his harvest.

She shook her head and began her trek through the carnage on her mission to bring her eyewitness account of victory to the queen.

❧ THE GIFT OF LODAN ❧

She walked carefully among the scattered corpses on her way to the Sacoridian encampment. Enemies lay side by side in death. Those who had fought for Second Empire had been Sacoridian citizens, but had chosen to reject that affiliation and commit war on those who'd been their neighbors for centuries, rather than continue to live in peace. They refused to acknowledge that their blood was, in fact, more Sacoridian than Arcosian. Instead, they embraced the idea of an empire of the ancient past that no longer existed, rather than coexist in the land that had, for centuries, accepted them.

She glanced over her shoulder as she walked. The Sacoridians were closing in around Second Empire's camp. Fighting had ceased. Hoff's illusion of an army remained, but she didn't think he'd be able to hold it for much longer, which didn't appear, at this point, to be a problem. How would General Birch react when he realized he'd surrendered to an illusion? She wished she could see his face.

Mostly, however, she was just terribly tired now that the fighting was done and her blood no longer surged through her veins with excitement. Fighting was hard work, and muddy conditions had made it much more toilsome. She could almost drop right there on the ground, among the dead and wounded, and sleep. But she did not. She continued to trudge on, the wound of her arm throbbing. The sooner she reached the castle, the sooner she could fall into bed and rest.

She was walking past a clutch of dead soldiers when the hand of a corpse darted out and grabbed her ankle and

765

yanked her foot out from beneath her. She screamed as she thudded to the ground. The dead man then rose over her.

He was, of course, no corpse, even with the skeletal countenance of his face.

"Torq," she whispered.

"Well, well. What luck it is that it would be you," he said. "I'd have been happy to have grabbed any Greenie, but it's you, *you* who stole my travel device, and then left me to die in that strange white place."

She started to climb to her feet, but he kicked her legs out from beneath her.

"Going somewhere, Greenie?" he asked.

She attempted to push herself up again, and this time he kicked her wounded arm and she fell with a cry of pain.

"Looks like you are going nowhere," he said with a harsh laugh. "And I will have the pleasure of killing you. Slowly."

"Where have you been?" Karigan asked, trying to buy herself time.

"I bet you think I was lost wandering around that white place, eh? Well, no, as luck would have it, I crossed one of those bridges and found myself back at the mountains."

Too bad, she thought, he hadn't crossed over the Eletian bridge.

"Bided my time to see which way the wind would blow with this little war," he continued. "Watched the lower city burn. Watched the two armies position themselves. Thought that with the king and his people here, I could fulfill my promise to the Red Witch and grab a few Greenies to tear apart."

"Seems like there are better uses for your time," she muttered. "Maybe take up embroidery or something."

He laughed. "A Greenie with humor, how amusing. It's vengeance that eats at me. It is a sickness, I know. I will destroy any Greenie I can find."

She had started to crawl away, but he kicked her arm again. The pain caused her to nearly faint, her vision blur. When she could see normally again, she saw he held not a sword, but a warhammer.

"Picked up this beauty on the battlefield," he told her.

Her other self, whom she had not seen in some time, stood beside him. She was dressed as before, in sleek dark grays and blacks. With Nyssa banished to the deepest of the hells, it was now abundantly clear that the other was indeed an independent manifestation arising from Karigan's own mind, which would make her difficult to eradicate.

You cannot do that, the other said. *I am you. But we will both be "eradicated" if you continue to sit there waiting to be killed.*

No, she was not waiting to be killed, but she was exhausted and hurting.

You've been worse off.

She knew it was true, but it didn't change how she felt at this moment.

Trust me, her other self told her, *he will make sure getting killed hurts.*

Torq admired his warhammer. "Imagine what I can do with it."

Karigan could.

And yet here you still lie, the other said in exasperation.

"I'm not just lying here," Karigan protested, "and you're not being very helpful."

Torq gave her an odd look and she realized she'd spoken aloud. He followed her gaze to where her other stood, but of course he could not see her.

She sank her hand into the muddy, churned earth. It was strangely warm and had a smooth, clay-like consistency. When Torq turned his attention back to her to say something, she flung a ball of mud at him. It hit his chest and splattered his face.

Mud? That's your defense? the other demanded.

"Mud?" Torq echoed. "You are going to fight me with *mud*?"

It was not a defense but a distraction, and it worked. It gave her the moment she needed to rise to her feet and draw her sword.

"Are you perhaps a little mad?" Torq asked as he wiped the splatter off his face with the back of his sleeve.

"Not just a little," she said.

"I am still going to kill you, slaughter you like a butcher." He swung the warhammer about as if to warm up his muscles.

The warhammer could punch through her cuirass, or her skull. He could hook the sword out of her hand with it. She must be careful.

"You do realize I'm a swordmaster, don't you?"

"Swordmasters are made of flesh and die just like anyone else."

He lunged, but she had anticipated it and stepped out of the way. A man like Torq would always try to seize the offensive position with aggression rather than skill. That was something she could use against him.

They circled one another, each assessing the other. She knocked away another blow with her sword. Her left arm hung uselessly, but the pain was a distant thing as she focused all her attention on her opponent.

She maneuvered so she was on a slight downslope position from him. She could see the calculation in his eyes, and his pleasure at what he perceived to be her disadvantage.

Once again, she anticipated his next move. He was like a cat preparing to pounce on a mouse, tensing his muscles and holding his body just so. He was not subtle, but those who were accustomed to using brute force generally were not.

When he lunged, she sidestepped and tripped him at the last minute. Momentum sent him sprawling onto the ground. He'd lost hold of his warhammer, and she kicked it out of reach even as she pressed the tip of her sword into his back. But it wasn't *her* sword, was it . . .

"What are you waiting for, Greenie?" he demanded.

When he started to crawl away, she let the swordtip trail along his back, cutting into his flesh.

"I'm waiting," she said, "only to tell you that this sword that I am about to kill you with belongs to Colonel Laren Mapstone of the Green Riders, who you know as the Red Witch."

He stopped. "What? No!"

She plunged it into his back.

He slumped and sobbed, "No . . . Not the Red Witch. No . . ."

"This is for Colonel Laren Mapstone and all the Green Riders you ever hurt," she told him, so that the last words he ever heard, the last thoughts he had in his mind, were of his old enemy.

She withdrew the sword and heaved it into him again, and twisted the blade. He did not speak or move this time.

"We got him, Colonel," she murmured. "We got him."

Karigan was not, she knew, the only one who suffered nightmares. The colonel must have had many about the Darrow Raiders over the years, and yet, she had never let on to her Riders how she must have been haunted by the atrocities she had witnessed.

The only thing that would have made killing Torq more satisfying was if it had been the colonel who had done it, but she was not here. Telling her about it would not provide very much closure. Karigan knelt beside his body.

You know what to do, her other self said.

"It's not the sort of thing *I* do," Karigan replied.

You are not doing it for you.

She closed her eyes and heaved a deep breath, then hacked into his neck with her sword. She had to saw a bit to cut all the way through flesh and sinew, and the bones. As she did so, she murmured over and over, "This is not me, this is not me, this is not me . . ."

It hadn't been a clean job; messy, really, but when she was done, she turned his head over to look at his face. His eyes and mouth were open in an expression of astonishment and denial. The skull tattoo lent a macabre embellishment to his head.

"Dear gods," she muttered. "What am I doing? This is not me."

No? her other self asked. *Zachary said it. You are no longer that schoolgirl running away from Selium. You are a warrior. You have killed many. Even Valora recognized you as such. Remember, you are not doing this for you.*

Karigan wiped her swordblade on Torq's sleeve, then stood and sheathed it. With great reluctance, she grasped Torq's convenient topknot and lifted his head.

As she made her way across the battlefield, soldiers and

menders who had begun to search for wounded gaped at her with her burden. She did not blame them.

A loud shout went up from Second Empire's camp. She paused, but couldn't make out what was happening. She located a spyglass on an enemy captain's corpse. It couldn't have helped him much in the fog.

She set Torq's head aside, and removed the glass from its case and gazed through it. The remaining troops of Second Empire were ranked up and surrounded by the Sacoridians, though Hoff's illusions were long gone. Their weapons had been removed and heaped in a great pile. The ground of the camp looked like a bog.

A man with his hands tied behind his back was shoved into an open space where all could see. His neat, close-cropped white hair and fighting leathers identified him as General Birch. The muddy water splashed when he was forced to his knees.

Zachary then approached him and appeared to address the assembled troops. He paused, looked down at Birch, then drew his sword. Before she could glance away, he swept his sword through the air and decapitated the enemy general. Birch's head slopped into the mud face-first.

"Dear gods," she murmured, jerking the glass from her eye. She might have just cut Torq's head off his body, but it didn't mean she wanted to view another decapitation.

Zachary is a warrior, as well, her other self said, *and you must never forget that he, too, has blood on his hands. The lives he has taken, however, were for the benefit of the realm he rules. He is a warrior king whose duty is to mete out justice. This is the gift of Lodan.*

Karigan knew this. It was not the first time she had witnessed him carrying out an execution, but it was at times difficult to reconcile the gentle, scholarly, and caring man she knew him to be, with the warrior king.

≼ THE GIFT ≽

Covered in blood and drying mud, Karigan stepped into the castle's central corridor. Her ride to the city from the battlefield had gone without incident, just the uncomfortable sensation of Torq's head in its burlap sack bumping against her leg with each of Condor's strides.

She had enjoyed passing on the news of victory to the gate guards as she entered the city. It was a fine thing to make people happy. People in the castle, however, already seemed to know, most likely because of Connly's connection with Trace, and good news would have traveled fast. It was a pleasure to see faces that had once been so drawn with worry for so long, now smiling and laughing.

She ran into Fergal just as she was about to turn down the Rider wing.

"You're back!" he exclaimed. "But maybe a little worse for wear."

"It's been a long day," she said.

"How are our Riders?"

"I actually don't know, except Hoff created a very nice illusion at the end of the battle that stopped Second Empire from escaping."

Fergal *whooped*. A few courtiers looked his way, but such was the mood of the day, they smiled at his high spirits.

"Would you mind putting my things in my room?" she asked him.

"Nope."

She handed him her saddlebags and gear, and the burlap sack with its stain of blood.

"What's this?" he asked, with a frown.

"A gift," she replied.

"You shouldn't have."

She laughed and patted his shoulder. "Not to worry. It's for the colonel when we get her back."

He looked at her questioningly, but she offered no further explanation and hurried down the corridor in the direction of the throne room. Normally, if her business were less important, she would clean up before going in front of her queen, but the victory in battle was too momentous to waste time, and when messages were of such import, the condition of the messenger did not matter.

Like the other parts of the castle, the mood in the throne room was lighter, more relaxed. Courtiers had once more been permitted inside and the map table pushed to the side. People gazed sidelong at her as she strode down the length of the chamber to the throne. She assumed she was the first to arrive from the battlefield, and she couldn't begin to guess how she looked.

Estora was not seated in her throne chair, but stood before the dais, conversing with some nobles and sipping wine. Karigan halted and waited for Estora to notice her.

"Karigan?" Estora asked.

"Yes, Your Majesty," she replied with a bow. "His Majesty asked me to bring word of our victory as an eyewitness."

She described what she knew of the overall battle, and made sure to highlight Zachary's prowess. She ended with: "General Birch of Second Empire is no more."

There was clapping and cheering at that pronouncement. Afterward, Estora took her aside.

"I thank you, Karigan. You are certain Zachary is well?"

"When last I saw him, he was very well."

"No signs of the spell Grandmother placed on him?"

"I saw nothing like that," Karigan replied. "It may be that the spell went dormant with Grandmother's death, or has since dissipated."

"That is good to hear," Estora replied with evident relief. "He was quite concerned he would inadvertently do harm."

"You would have been proud to see him today."

"As were you?"

Karigan studied Estora's face for a moment, trying to discern if she sought some sign that Karigan was in an illicit relationship with Zachary.

"As were we all," Karigan replied. "He led us well."

Estora nodded. "And you gave him the miniatures?"

"Oh, yes. He was overcome, really, so very proud and happy to see images of his heirs. He was showing them off to his advisors."

"I do hope he will come see them soon, for they are growing and changing fast. I am afraid they will not resemble their portraits much by the time he returns. In any case, I thank you again. Perhaps you will take tea with me tomorrow?"

"As you wish, my lady."

"Good. Now, you must go look after yourself. You've a wound that needs tending, and you are undoubtedly exhausted and could use some rest."

Karigan bowed. She *was* exhausted and, as she left the throne room, wondered if she could get away with a nice hot bath *before* visiting the menders.

Common sense had prevailed and she had gone to the mending wing first. Most of the menders were down by the battlefield by now and it was quiet. To Karigan's dismay, Aisla had been the only one available to clean and stitch her arm wound.

"You are going to be one giant scar," the mender had told her.

Karigan had not been amused then by the comment, and still was not. Now she headed for the Rider wing, her left arm bandaged and in a sling so it could rest, and with instructions to drink willowbark tea and keep an eye on the wound. If it showed signs of festering, she was to report back to the mending wing immediately. There'd been mud and fine gravel packed into the cut.

The Rider wing was quiet, too, the Riders most likely out on runs or down on the battlefield, which meant she could have the bathing room to herself, and Aisla said she could bathe so long as she kept her wound out of the water.

She entered her chamber with a sigh of relief. Fergal had

left her gear at the foot of her bed, including the sack. She'd have to deal with it, but not until after she—

It moved.

The sack rustled and wobbled. She jumped back with a cry, then a furry gray tail flicked out of the sack's opening.

"Ghost Kitty! No!"

She reached in and pulled him out by the scruff. He licked his chops. Repulsed, she dropped him out in the corridor, but he scampered back in before she could close the door, straight for the sack. She grabbed it and held it out of his reach.

"MEEEOOOWWW."

"No."

She needed to do something with the head sooner rather than later, and she wasn't going to stow it in her wardrobe just to keep it safe from the cat. With a noise of irritation, she put off her bath and strode out into the corridor.

Karigan accessed the royal tombs from the commoner chapel. Brienne Quinn accompanied her, it seemed, more out of curiosity than Karigan's need of an escort.

They entered the caretaker administrative area of the tombs and went straight to Agemon's office. When they stepped inside, the chief caretaker stared at them.

"You do not have an appointment," he told Karigan in a querulous voice.

"Nevertheless," Karigan said, and she set the sack on his desk with a *thump.*

Agemon pushed his specs up on his nose. "What *is* this?"

"Sir Karigan requests a favor," Brienne told him.

"A favor, hmmph. I'm the one who should be asking favors, yes, yes, for all this green has put me through." He gave Karigan a myopic look. "Muddy green," he amended. "She had better not be dripping mud in my tombs."

Karigan pointed at the sack. "Take a look."

When he hesitated, Brienne said, "Look, as Sir Karigan asks."

He muttered to himself and reached into the sack and pulled the head out. He was not at all taken aback or repulsed by it. After all, he lived among the dead and it was his job to care for their remains. Karigan, on the other hand, did not care to look at it again, even though she was the one who had cut it off. Instead, she gazed directly at Agemon.

"Can you preserve it?" she asked.

"Yes, yes," Agemon replied, as if it were the easiest thing in the world. "But who is this? A great hero of the recent battle?"

News of the victory had apparently already reached the tombs, too.

"A very evil man," Brienne told him. "The leader of the Darrow Raiders."

Agemon almost dropped the head. "What? You brought the remains of a villain into my tombs? My sacred tombs of royalty and heroes? You must remove it at once and dispose of it. I will not have it here." He held it out to Karigan.

"I need it preserved," Karigan told him. She explained Torq's connection to Colonel Mapstone.

Agemon looked a little more interested and set the head down on top of the sack. "Yes, yes, we have a special place for the heroic colonel."

She assumed he meant a funerary slab on Heroes Avenue for when the colonel passed away. She wondered if the colonel knew about it. She had a feeling she did not.

"Sir Karigan killed this monster," Brienne said. "The colonel didn't get a chance to do it herself, but seeing his remains might . . . help her."

"The head would remain here only temporarily, until the colonel decides what to do with it," Karigan added.

"But she is missing, is she not?" Agemon asked.

"There is a mission under way to rescue her."

"Very well, very well. I will do this thing." Agemon gazed at the head. "It looks like an animal has nibbled on the meat of the neck where it was cut."

Karigan was *not* going to let Ghost Kitty sleep with her tonight. "Please be sure the lines of the tattoo remain well defined so there is no mistaking who he is."

"This is not a problem," Agemon said. "I will preserve the head, and I will preserve the tattoo. You will take the head away when the colonel returns."

"Thank you," Karigan replied, anxious for her bath. "We'll get out of your way now."

"Not so fast," he snapped. "Since you are here, there is something I must show you."

Karigan wondered what in the hells the caretaker would have to show her in the tombs.

BANISHER OF
DRAGONS

"**T**his way, this way." Agemon's robes flapped against his legs as he strode down the corridor.

He led them past offices and workshops, and Karigan wondered what he wanted her to see. When she'd looked Brienne's way, the Weapon had just shrugged.

He stopped abruptly at a big, carved door and took a lamp from an alcove.

"This is the storeroom," he said.

"For what?" Karigan asked.

He did not answer, but pushed the door open. They followed him inside and found the room stacked from floor to ceiling with shields.

"Oh, my," Brienne said.

"Look for the dragonfly device, the king told us," Agemon said. "So we looked for all the objects with dragonflies on them. Then, oh no, Sir Karigan says it is not a dragonfly, but a flying dragon." He yanked on a tendril of his gray hair. "The hours, the sacrifice of finding all the dragonfly things! But we obeyed and looked for all the flying dragon things. Then Sir Karigan says, a flying *fire-breathing* dragon on a shield. The work! The hours!"

Karigan gazed at the towering stacks with dismay. Brienne pulled out a shield. It was rectangular and featured a field of red with a stylized dragon, wings extended, spouting flame. A tag dangled from it.

"That one doesn't look old enough," Karigan said. "Anschilde lived during the time of the sea kings, so it would be kind of ancient."

Agemon groaned.

"Well," Brienne replied, "that may narrow it down some." She gazed at the tag. "Says 'Prince Halden,' followed by a lot of numbers."

"Those are catalog numbers so we know its history and where it is supposed to be by looking in our records," Agemon explained.

Even if the ancient age of Anschilde's shield would help eliminate some of those that were piled in this room as Brienne suggested, Karigan was no less daunted.

"How many are in here?" she asked Agemon.

"The caretakers I assigned to the task stopped counting after one thousand," he replied. "You will begin looking through them soon, yes?"

Not today, she thought. She wanted that bath and nap. "Soon," she replied. "I don't . . ." She trailed off as a ghostly shape took form near one of the stacks. Its features resolved so that Karigan recognized Beryl Spencer. She stood there, or maybe *floated* slightly above the floor, and stared at the stacks of shields. She did not speak.

"You don't know what?" Brienne asked.

Beryl turned to Karigan, expressionless and silent. Then she left the room. Karigan rushed after her out into the corridor.

"Sir Karigan?" Brienne called. She and Agemon followed.

"Where does she think she is going?" Agemon demanded.

"I don't know," Brienne replied.

Karigan ignored them and concentrated on following Beryl. Sometimes the ghost faded out, only to reappear again some ways down the corridor. She led them past more workshops until she came to a door. She paused and gazed at Karigan expectantly, then passed right through the door. Karigan opened it and found Beryl waiting on the other side.

"This leads to the Sealender crypts," Agemon said. "I do not understand. What does she want here?"

"I don't know," Brienne said, "but she seems to be onto something."

The iconography of the domed crypt integrated the Sealender gull with familiar symbols of the gods carved into the walls. The winged figure of Westrion was present, of course, and Salvistar, and the crescent moon of Aeryc. Karigan shivered to think she had seen these gods and spoken with them.

An obelisk bearing the names of Sealender royalty stood in the center of the chamber. Their remains rested on shelves inset into the walls. She spotted the remains of King Darien the Second, brother of Princess Florence, whose armor she had worn, and other names with which she was familiar. Some of the shelves lacked linen-wrapped dead as though the Sealenders had not expected the line to end abruptly with King Agates some two hundred years ago.

"Where is King Agates?" Karigan asked.

Agemon pointed to a lowermost shelf. She bent and peered into shadow at the lumpy form. A gold, jewel-encrusted crown rested atop what must have been his chest. She shivered again. Two hundred years in the past, she had seen the corpse of Agates being carried on a bier by Weapons just after he had died, that same crown resting on his chest. Pulled by time, she'd been, to witness the roots of the Clan Wars. That Agates had been placed in a low, shadowy shelf was testament to the turmoil his dying without an heir had caused, which some believed had been an intentional act to sow chaos. And yet, without the turmoil, the Hillanders, and thus Zachary, would have never come into power.

"Was there something you needed to see here?" Brienne asked her.

Beryl waited beneath an archway, her luminescence fluctuating as she pointed beyond.

"Um, no," Karigan said.

She hurried to the archway and followed the ghost into another chamber devoted to the Sealenders. Murals of ocean scenes featuring seagulls aloft, and fishermen in sailing dories plying their trade, brightened the walls. There were sarcophagi in this chamber of royal clan members, and, prominently, a lifelike marble statue of a heroic figure clad in armor with a cloak draped over her shoulder. In her hand she held a saber. Karigan did not have to read the inscription on the pedestal to know it was Rider Princess Florence Aventine. Florence gazed into eternity from across centuries, and as cold as marble might be, and as distant as they were in time, Karigan could not help but feel kinship with her.

"Sir Karigan?" Brienne asked.

Her voice brought Karigan back to the present, and a swirl of ghostly translucence drew her attention to Beryl, who stood before a wall with a mural that depicted men and women repairing fishing nets. As Karigan watched, Beryl walked through the wall. Karigan stepped up to it and stared at the mural.

"What is it?" Brienne asked.

"I'm not sure."

"Come, come," Agemon said, "I have not all day for a green who wishes to admire artwork. I have much work to do. Yes, very much work."

On a hunch, Karigan felt around the stonework until she came across one block that protruded more than the others. It featured a gull perched on pilings painted on it.

"Of course," she said, and pushed the block.

The sound of mechanisms that had not moved in a very long time suddenly came to life with much creaking and grinding from somewhere within the wall. It made even Brienne jump.

"What? What?" Agemon cried. "What is this?"

The wall slowly opened, and fetid, dusty air flowed out of a chamber beyond. They could see little inside, so Brienne grabbed a wall lamp.

When they entered, they found a crude chamber with natural rock as the rear wall. Agemon seemed offended by the existence of a chamber he had not known about, and that had cobwebs and dust everywhere.

"This should not be here," he said. "It does not exist. If it did, we would know of it, and it would be clean, perfectly clean."

"It may not be in your records," Brienne told him, "but it surely exists." She sneezed.

"It can and it does," Karigan said. "And so does the shield."

The lamplight fell on a boulder upon which sat a crude wooden box. The shield leaned against the boulder. It was an oval of wood, and beneath the many layers of dust was painted a flying dragon spouting flame.

"Thank you," Karigan murmured to Beryl.

The ghost nodded in return, and her form dissolved to nothing, perhaps never to be seen again, leaving Karigan with a sense of melancholy.

"What does it say on the lid?" Brienne was gazing at the wood box.

Karigan looked. Old Sacoridian glyphs were carved into it, along with the depiction of a flying gull.

Muttering to himself about dust, Agemon joined them and gazed at the inscription. He adjusted his specs and said, *"Here lies Anschilde, who banished the sea kings and their dragons.* Hmmph! His bones have been here all along and we did not know." He lifted the lid, and sure enough there was a pile of human bones inside, upon which sat a skull. "This is a disgrace; yes, yes, we have disgraced the dead." He walked in a circle tugging on his hair. "We must clean this place immediately. We must honor Anschilde, progenitor of the Sealenders!" He exited the chamber, still pulling on his hair and muttering to himself.

"Poor Agemon," Brienne said. "This is really sending him over the edge. He prides himself on knowing everything there is to know about the tombs, and he doesn't handle surprises well."

Evidently, Karigan thought.

"How did you know the shield was here?" Brienne asked.

"I didn't. I had guidance."

A knowing look came into Brienne's eyes and she nodded. "What of the shield? What will you do with it?"

"I suppose we leave it here for now," Karigan replied, "and let the king know it's been found. After that, it's up to him."

The two exited the chamber, and Brienne said, "So Anschilde was a banisher of dragons. Do you suppose that means they really existed?"

Karigan shrugged. She'd seen so much that was strange over the last five years that she would not have been surprised if they had.

*   *   *

Back in the Rider wing, Mara asked Trace to pass word of Torq's death and the discovery of the shield to Connly, who could then relay it to Zachary. That left Karigan to her own devices so she could finally bathe and rest. Ghost Kitty was banished from her chamber for a time. She might have been the one to cut off Torq's head, but she hadn't tried to eat it, and the thought of the cat licking the tip of her nose like he sometimes did was not to be borne.

The next day, she arose sore but rested and unmuddy. Someone must have let Ghost Kitty into her chamber because she found him curled at her feet. She smiled and petted his head, and forgave him his natural carnivorous inclinations, so long as he didn't acquire a taste for human flesh on a regular basis.

She went about her day, arm in sling as instructed, checking on Condor, Loon, and Bluebird, and trying to unknot the Rider accounts for Mara. Both she and Daro had been away too long, leaving Mara to do the best she could with everything else going on, which meant the ledgers were a disaster. She heard also that Zachary was likely to return to the castle later in the day.

At the second bell in the afternoon, she had an appointment to visit with Estora. It would be a relief to step away from the books for a while. They were giving her a headache.

Truthfully, it was all nicely normal, and knowing that she would not have to raise a sword against anyone this day was freeing and made her feel immensely light and happy.

She left the Rider wing, looking forward to visiting with Estora, her friend, as opposed to Estora, her queen. Maybe she'd even get to meet the royal heirs.

MEETING THE ROYAL HEIRS

"The army from Coutre will arrive by nightfall," Estora said, "and they will help with the detainment and interrogation of prisoners. Many—the ordinary folk, the farmers, shopkeepers, and the like—may be able to go back to their old lives so long as they take an oath not to bear arms against king and country again."

Karigan sipped her tea. Estora's sitting room was an oasis of calm, especially with all the plants, largely ferns in this case, softening the stone surroundings. The castle had become very busy with soldiers and courtiers coming and going, but the sitting room exuded peace. Her visit with Estora had begun with the usual niceties of how the other was faring, but conversation naturally turned to the battle.

"It sounds like a positive way to proceed," Karigan carefully replied, "but there will still be factions that remain active."

"So it is with zealots," Estora agreed, "and not just in Sacoridia. King Thergood in Rhovanny has apparently been putting down outbreaks of insurgency, too. We did warn him."

Karigan nibbled on a piece of pound cake and closed her eyes in ecstasy. The buttery, moist, sweet-but-not-too-sweet cake was the best thing she had tasted in ages. It was all she could do to stop herself from greedily stuffing it whole into her mouth.

Estora set her teacup aside and fell into silence for a few moments as if deep in thought. Then she said, "Karigan, there is something I wish to address with you."

Uh oh, she thought. It could only be about her and Zachary.

Instead, Estora said, "The luin prime came to me with some very disturbing comments."

Karigan swallowed a mouthful of cake. She was almost relieved. "He does not like me for some reason."

"It is not just you," Estora said, "but all Green Riders and their historic association with magic. But he was very clearly displeased with how the people whom you had led out of the fire in the lower city responded to you as though you were god-sent and divine."

"He was a bit harsher with me," Karigan replied. She wondered what he'd think if he learned she'd spoken with the actual gods. "I believe he wishes to try me for heresy."

"Yes, he did say that. I have dissuaded him for now, and told him not to mistake the gratefulness of the people who had suffered a horrific night, with some desire on their part to worship a Green Rider."

Despite the seriousness of the subject, Karigan was amused by the thought of people worshipping Green Riders. "Thank you. It is a relief that you spoke to him."

"I must tell you," Estora continued, "he will likely remain suspicious and antagonistic. Even more so now that he knows of your affiliation with the Eletians. I think *he* thinks I have been blinded by Green Rider magic."

"I can't imagine any Rider having that kind of power," Karigan replied. She would have to ensure she steered clear of the luin prime, and to warn Connly that the others should, as well.

"Me, either," Estora replied. "But Prime Brynston is of the school of thought that all magic is evil, anathema, and not to be tolerated."

It was an old bias, Karigan thought, and unfortunately, the head of all moon priests, with all his influence, was likely preaching against magic to the faithful.

Travis entered the sitting room.

"Yes, Travis?" Estora asked.

"My lady, we have received word that the king has entered the castle and is on his way up."

"Thank you."

He bowed to both of them. Karigan raised her brow as she

watched after him. He'd called her "Lady Winterlight" upon her appearance at Estora's door.

She set her cup on the small table that held the tea service and cake.

"I will go now," she said, "before the king arrives."

"No, wait," Estora replied. "I wanted you to meet the babies when they woke from their nap, but now you can both see them."

Karigan settled back into her chair a little apprehensively. She was not sure she wanted to be there when Estora and Zachary had their reunion. Estora's eyes glistened with excitement, and she smoothed her skirts nervously. She tinkled a small bell.

Her maid appeared within moments.

"Jayd," she said, "please ask the nurses to prepare the children to meet their father."

"Yes, my lady."

"Do I look presentable?" Estora asked Karigan.

Karigan almost laughed. "You are as stunning as usual, my lady." Estora looked startled by her words, but it was no lie. Motherhood had only deepened her beauty. For Karigan's own part, she was just pleased she wasn't covered in mud.

When Zachary arrived, his presence dominated the room. He'd removed his armor, but he was clearly fresh from the battlefield with mud on his boots and cloak. The cut on his cheek was nicely cleaned up and looked to be healing well.

He bowed over Estora's hand and kissed it. "My lady. It pleases me to see you looking so well. Your leadership while I was away has been hailed as exceptional by your advisors, particularly General Meadows and Castellan Javien."

"That is gratifying to hear from those two crusty gentlemen," she replied with a laugh. "I am very pleased to see you, Your Majesty, well and victorious from the field of battle."

He then turned to Karigan and she bowed.

"Lady Winterlight," he said with a nod. "A surprise to see you here."

"We were having tea," Estora replied, "and I asked her to linger so she could meet Dav and Ez."

"My son and daughter," he murmured with barely

concealed excitement. "I can't tell you how much the gift of the little portraits meant to me. I've kept them here, even during the battle." He tapped a pocket over his heart. "I couldn't wait to see them."

Estora smiled. "Then the wait is over." She rang the bell, and when the maid reappeared, she said, "Now, Jayd."

Two nurses appeared, each bearing a swaddled infant.

"This is Prince Zachary Davriel," Estora said pointing to one. "And this is Princess Esmere," she added, pointing to the other.

They kind of looked the same to Karigan. In fact, they kind of looked like any other baby she had ever seen with their chubby cheeks and fuzzy tufts of hair, but she had to admit they were much cuter in person than how they were portrayed in the miniatures.

She was much more interested in Zachary's reaction as he saw his heirs for the first time, than the heirs themselves. A smile of profound happiness formed on his lips as he leaned forward to get a good look. His eyes were bright, his expression unmasked and . . . vulnerable. Estora practically glowed.

Then something changed. His features hardened and the corners of his mouth sagged. But it was his eyes that alarmed Karigan. They clouded, turned black as night.

"Get them out of here!" she yelled at the nurses. They stared at her as though she were mad. Estora looked confused.

Zachary's hand went to the hilt of his sword.

"Run!" Karigan cried. "Get out!"

Estora glanced at Zachary's face and gasped. She turned and pushed the nurses away.

"TRAVIS!" Karigan screamed, and she threw herself at Zachary so he wouldn't charge after Estora and the nurses.

He flung her back and she crashed into the tea table. The teapot, cups, and treats crashed to the floor. Instead of pursuing Estora and the twins, he drew his sword and turned to Karigan. She lobbed the first thing that came to hand at him. It turned out to be the pound cake, which was unfortunate on two counts, the first being that it merely bounced off his chest and did nothing to slow him down. The second was that she had sacrificed the pound cake, the very ambrosia of the gods, with no good results.

Zachary's blade swept down and she rolled out of the way just in time. She climbed to her feet. She dared not draw her sword against him. To do so, to draw on one's sovereign, was tantamount to treason, even in self-defense. A king had absolute power to kill one of his subjects if he so chose.

His expression was cold, like iron, the blackness of his eyes like smoldering coals. She darted away from a thrust.

"Zachary," she said, "it's me, Karigan!"

If he heard, it did not register on his face.

Travis ran in at last.

"Travis!" she cried. "He's bespelled!"

The Weapon seemed to comprehend what she meant, that there was some reason Zachary was trying to kill her other than she deserved it.

"Your Majesty," Travis said, approaching carefully from behind.

Zachary paused. Then, with Travis just within arm's reach, he whirled and smashed the pommel of the sword into the Weapon's face. Travis crumpled to the floor.

No! Karigan thought.

Zachary came after her again. She leaped over the sofa, but he was unnaturally quick and grabbed her arm. He threw her at the wall. She crashed into potted plants and the back of her head hit the stone wall. She blacked out for a moment as she slid to the floor. Her eyes fluttered open to discover the tip of his sword pressed against her chest.

"Zachary," she whispered. "It's me, Karigan."

"Must kill you," he said. "Must kill what I love most."

"No," she said. "That's Grandmother's spell. You are stronger than that."

He applied pressure to the sword, but not enough to stab her. "Must kill what I love most."

She closed her eyes expecting to be impaled at any moment. "I love you, too," she whispered.

The stabbing did not come, though she still felt the pressure of the swordtip. When she looked, there was a flicker in his eyes, a wavering in his stance.

"Zachary," she said, "this isn't you. It's Grandmother's spell. Come back, please. You are stronger than her."

"I . . . I don't know," he replied. "I must kill what I love."

"That is not you, Zachary, it's Grandmother. Do you remember? She tortured you, placed a spell on you. You can defeat her in this."

"I think . . . I think I remember." He wavered again, and there was the slightest slackening of pressure against her chest.

"That's right," Karigan said. "Don't let Grandmother win."

The black in his eyes diminished. "Karigan," he whispered.

"Yes," she said. "It's me."

"I love you," he said.

"And I love you."

He threw the sword aside and it *thunked* on the carpet.

"Dear gods," he said, and suddenly he was himself, all the black gone from his eyes, and the iron from his features. He dropped to his knees beside her and took her in his arms. "I am so sorry. I'm so sorry. I would never—"

"I know, I know," she said, and she wrapped her good arm around him. The change in him was so profound she had no doubts he'd overcome the spell, that the knots tied around his heart had come unraveled. She could *feel* it in her connection to him. "I know."

"How could I have even . . . ?" He sobbed.

"It's all right," she whispered. "You didn't, and you defeated Grandmother."

The sounds of fighting quieted, and Estora made to open the door of her bed chamber to see what was happening. She'd bade the nurses lock themselves and the heirs in the nursery. They'd be safe there.

"My lady," Jayd said, "you mustn't."

"I need to see what is happening."

She stepped outside and made her way toward the sitting room. She heard no yelling, no more fighting, just the low murmur of voices. She peered into the sitting room. Travis sat on the floor bent over, blood dripping from his nose. Zachary knelt on the floor with Karigan in his arms, cheek to cheek in the attitude of lovers. He rocked her, and was sobbing.

"I would never mean to hurt you," he told Karigan. "I love you."

"I know," she whispered.

Estora was not shocked.

He kissed Karigan's forehead, then suddenly released her and stood. He backed away.

"What—?" Karigan asked.

"I'm—I'm a danger."

Fastion and Lennir ran into the room.

"My lord?" Fastion said.

"Travis and Sir Karigan need the attention of menders," Zachary said, "and I am going to the Chamber of Proving, where I will not be a danger to my children or . . ." He looked up at Estora. "Anyone." He swept from the room with Fastion tailing him. Lennir knelt to help Travis.

Estora stepped into the sitting room and surveyed the damage. Karigan, who still sat on the floor, looked dazed. Blood stained the sleeve of the arm that had been in the sling.

"What came over him?" Estora asked, but she already knew.

"Grandmother's spell," Karigan replied. "Seeing his heirs seemed to trigger it."

"What is this Chamber of Proving, and why is he going there?"

"It's a place, a room in the castle that nullifies magic. I think he must fear a resurgence of the spell and that he is a danger to you and the little ones."

No, Karigan, Estora thought, *he thinks he is a danger to* you.

THE CHAMBER OF PROVING

The figures in the ledger swam in Karigan's vision. She pushed the book away and rested her aching head on the cool wooden surface of her desk. She'd an egg-sized bump on the back of her head from being flung into the wall by Zachary the previous day. After Lennir had ordered her to the mending wing yet again, Master Vanlynn had asked if they should set up a permanent room for her.

The mending wing had been crowded with wounded from the battle, the busiest Karigan had ever seen it, and the menders very busy. Master Vanlynn herself checked her, and resutured her arm wound, which had reopened in the tussle with Zachary.

When asked how it had happened, Karigan had been ordered to respond with a falsehood. "It was a training accident," she had told the master mender. Vanlynn had given her a strange look, then told her to return to her quarters and rest.

Rest had proven challenging because she incessantly reviewed the previous day's events and worried about Zachary, which was why she had attempted to work on the Rider accounts, but clearly that was not going well. Ghost Kitty jumped onto the desk and rubbed his cheek against her elbow with loud purrs. She sat up and scratched him behind the ears.

She had received no word of Zachary and could only assume he was still down in the Chamber of Proving, racked with guilt and believing he was a danger to her. She didn't think he was still under the influence of the spell—she'd seen his eyes, his expression after the attack, his remorse. She was sure that she had somehow *felt* his change deep within.

In addition to having to lie about how she had received the bump on her head, she'd been ordered not to speak about anything that had happened in Estora's sitting room, nor was she to reveal Zachary's location. She did not know how long he would be able to remain in his self-imposed exile without questions being asked.

A knock came on the door and Ghost Kitty jumped to the floor.

"Come in," she called.

A Green Foot runner stepped inside. "Rider," she said, "the queen requests your presence."

Estora's hands were folded before her as she stood in the sitting room at Karigan's arrival. The debris from the previous day had been removed.

"Karigan," Estora said.

Karigan bowed. "Your Majesty." She shifted her sling on her shoulder and waited, curious as to the reason for the summons.

"You are doing well after yesterday?" Estora asked.

"Bruised, a bump on the head, but I'll live."

Estora nodded. "I have asked you here because the king refuses to leave the Chamber of Proving, and he will not allow me near, even though the chamber supposedly suppresses the spell upon him. Is it true you believe the spell is gone from him?"

"I can't be absolutely certain," Karigan answered carefully, "but he stopped the attack of his own volition, and his whole manner changed. He no longer seemed . . . maddened."

"We need him to return to his duties," Estora replied. "His generals and lord-governors are asking to see him, and I can't keep this fiction of his being abed with a sudden sickness for much longer. Counselor Tallman is holding them off for now, but they are already suspicious."

It was paramount to keep the incident secret, Karigan knew, because if word got out that the king of Sacoridia had been under the influence of an evil spell and gone mad, he'd lose the trust of his vassals, which could stir up an enormous amount of trouble.

"And frankly," Estora said, "I need my husband back."

Karigan flashed back to the incident. Her memory was dim on certain details thanks to banging her head on the wall, but Zachary holding her and telling her he loved her was quite sharp in her mind.

She cleared her throat. "How may I help?"

"I would like you to coax him out of that chamber," Estora replied.

"I don't think it should be too hard," Karigan replied after a moment of thought. "Just need to convince him he is no longer a threat."

"How will you do that?"

"The same way we learned about the spell in the first place," Karigan replied.

"Of course," Estora said faintly. "Rider Duff."

Karigan nodded. Then, because she needed to know, she gathered her courage and said, "May I ask why you have chosen me for this?"

Estora stood very still, her expression unchanging until she lifted her chin and replied, "I think we both know why." Then she turned and strode from the room.

Karigan wavered where she stood, feeling rather unbalanced, whether from her concussion or Estora's answer, she did not know.

"Sir Karigan?"

She whirled to find the Weapon Erin had entered the sitting room. The last time she'd seen Erin she was being taken into the care of the death surgeons down in the tombs.

"How are you?" Karigan asked.

"Doing well," she replied. "I am only on light duty for now. I have been instructed to escort you to the Chamber of Proving."

"We need to find Rider Duff first."

It turned out Fergal had just returned from a run to the battlefield. He gawked in surprise to find Karigan and a Weapon standing outside his door. Mostly he gawked at the Weapon.

"Fergal, this is Erin," Karigan said. "She is going to guide us to a secret place in the castle. We have need of your ability."

He brightened. "A secret place? That sounds interesting."

"You will be blindfolded," Erin told him.

"*Blindfolded?* Why?"

"Because it is a *secret* place," Karigan replied.

"Then how can I use my ability? I need to see."

"We will remove the blindfold when we get there," Erin told him.

He grunted. "Guess I'll find out soon enough. Are you going to be blindfolded, too?" he asked Karigan.

"No," she replied. "I'm an honorary Black Shield." She had been blindfolded on her first and only time to the Chamber of Proving for her swordmaster test. It had not been a pleasant experience.

They took him to a lower level of the castle where the records room was located. Dusty, unused passages in this ancient part of the castle yawned off the corridor they stood in.

Erin blindfolded Fergal and turned him round and round, then picked up a lantern she had brought along, and they set off into one of the abandoned passages. Karigan led Fergal, helping him negotiate stairs and preventing missteps. Erin backtracked and took so many side passages to confuse his sense of direction that even without a blindfold, Karigan didn't think she'd be able to find her way on her own.

As they went, Fergal cheerfully filled them in on what was happening down at the battlefield, his voice echoing hollowly down the empty stone corridors.

"They're calling it the Battle of the Sleeping Waelds," he said, "even if most of the battle didn't take place in the Waelds themselves."

He told them that many of the prisoners had been put to work digging graves under the watchful eyes of the Coutreans, and that the ultimate fate of the prisoners was being debated among the generals and nobles, and that they were troubled not to have the king's input.

"On the brighter side," he said, "some refugees are leaving the city for home to see what they can salvage of crops and such." He told them that residents of the lower city were already tearing down badly burned structures and rebuilding.

His news helped keep Karigan's mind off Estora and what

she appeared to know. *I think we both know why,* Estora had said as to her decision for choosing Karigan to be the one to convince Zachary to leave the Chamber of Proving. It confirmed her fear that Estora knew there was something between her and Zachary, unconsummated though it may be.

Soon, a glow of light appeared in the near distance—some lanterns at the entryway to the Chamber of Proving. Two Weapons stood guard at the door. One was Rory, and the other Travis, with a swollen, broken nose and black eyes from his encounter with the pommel of Zachary's sword the previous day. Karigan grimaced, and was frankly surprised he was on his feet. She wondered if he had to tell people it was a "training accident," as well.

"Are we there yet?" Fergal asked.

"Yes," Karigan replied. At Erin's nod of approval, she pulled off the blindfold.

Fergal blinked rapidly as his eyes adjusted. "What is this place?"

"The secret place," Karigan replied.

"He is within," Travis told her in a muffled voice.

She glanced through the entryway into the Chamber of Proving. It was an impossibly immense space. Lantern glow was too feeble to illuminate it. Far in the center of the room, Zachary sat hunched over a table lit by candles and a lamp. He appeared to be looking over papers.

"Was he told I was coming?" Karigan asked.

"No," Travis replied.

"Right." She adjusted her shortcoat and stepped into the Chamber of Proving.

⊰ ISLANDS OF LIGHT ⊱

Stepping into the Chamber of Proving was like falling into an abyss blacker than night. It might have been her concussion, but vertigo assailed her and she had to close her eyes until the sensation passed.

When she opened them again, it wasn't much better. Some light filtered in from behind, and there was Zachary straight ahead working at his table. It was as though he were a castaway on an island of light. The expanse of darkness between them was vast enough that she might as well cross the heavens in order to reach him.

She clasped her hand around the moonstone in her pocket. The Chamber of Proving suppressed magic, and in fact she could feel the effect on hers as a discomfort, like having one's sense of taste or touch taken away. A dulling and weight, an absence. What might the Chamber of Proving do to a magic user over a long period of time? She did not think she wanted to find out.

She decided to see if her moonstone would work. She drew it out and light exploded from her hand. It reached into the barrel vault ceiling and pushed back the curtain of dark around her like a stroke of lightning. It revealed the stony countenances of statues along the walls and the surprise on Zachary's face. Even so, it could not reach the far edges of the chamber, and the light quickly faded to a soft glow around her, another island in the vastness of the dark, and left the chamber largely a mystery.

"Karigan?" Zachary said. He stood.

"Your Majesty." She walked forward, and the moonstone

weakened with every step until it was no better than the meager glow of a firefly.

When her light finally merged with Zachary's, she placed the moonstone back in her pocket.

"Lady Winterlight, in truth," he breathed.

Fastion, she saw, stood just outside the light. With his black uniform, he was barely visible.

"Rider G'ladheon," she countered.

There was the hint of a smile on Zachary's face. "I see my Weapons chose to ignore a direct order by allowing you in here."

"We received a conflicting order from the queen," Fastion said.

"Did you now? You know mine was for the safety of Rider G'ladheon, yes?"

"Of course, sire, but she is not in danger."

"That is my determination to make," Zachary said, "not yours." He actually looked and sounded angry.

"Yes, sire." Fastion appeared unperturbed by the rebuke.

"Rider G'ladheon, since you are here, what brings you?"

"Her Majesty the queen asked that I come. She requested I encourage you to leave this place and resume your duties."

"I am attending to my duties from here. I cannot leave. You saw me yesterday." He brushed his hand through his hair. "I—I lost control and almost . . . I might have killed my children. And *you.*"

"We believe the spell is broken," Karigan said, "and can ensure that it is."

"Oh?"

"Yes. The same way we knew the spell was definitely there in the first place. I have brought along Rider Duff and he waits outside."

"I forgot about Rider Duff with all that has been going on. I suppose a war will do that. Now hope *wars* with dread at what he may see."

"Perhaps the sooner we step outside, the sooner we can reassure you all is well."

"How are you so certain? You saw me yesterday. It was . . . It was like someone or something took me over and there was nothing I could do about it. I could only watch myself try to—I can't even say it. It was a nightmare. Karigan, I hurt you and I cannot bear it."

"The spell hurt me," Karigan said, "but *you* saved me before it could kill me."

He gazed at her in wonder. "Is that how you really see it?"

She nodded. "If you recall, I, too, have had dealings with Grandmother. She was powerful, powerful enough to ensnare the avatar of Westrion. You fought the spell, and by fighting it, you saved me. I am thinking that took a lot of strength to overcome the compulsion she placed on you."

He bowed his head. "You reached me. With your words. I do not know if I could have stopped but for that."

She wanted to reassure him with her touch, but she kept her distance. She had to. "Shall we go see what Fergal has to say?"

He nodded, and together they walked to the chamber's entrance with Fastion following. Zachary halted just before the door.

"Fastion," he said, "you and the others must stop me if I am overtaken by the spell again, and return me to the chamber."

"Yes, sire."

He took a decisive step across the threshold to the outer corridor. Karigan felt a tingle over her skin as she left the chamber, and once more felt whole, as if there were color in the world again, the "sense" that had been suppressed now restored.

"Rider Duff," Zachary said. "You are to tell me if you still see the spell within me."

Fergal bowed. "As you command, Your Majesty." He studied Zachary hard for a time. It felt like hours, but probably wasn't even a minute, and it meant that Fergal was being thorough. "I see nothing," he said at last. "No sign of any magic at all."

Thank the gods. Karigan had been sure the spell was broken, but she always could have been wrong, too.

Zachary's response was restrained. "You are sure, Rider?"

"Yes, Your Majesty. I'd have puked on the floor if I saw that knot on your heart again, or anything like it."

Zachary gave him a half-smile. "I am glad we are spared, then. My thanks to you. Erin, would you and Rider G'ladheon please escort Rider Duff back?" To Karigan he said, "You may tell the queen I will see her just as soon as I can." And he reentered the Chamber of Proving.

He wouldn't stay. She was sure of it. He just needed to gather his belongings.

Erin blindfolded Fergal again and repeated the process of spinning him around before they set off once more, with Karigan as his guide.

"Well, that was interesting," he said.

"You are to say nothing of this place or what occurred here," Erin warned him. "The Weapons will hear of it if you do."

"Riders know how to keep secrets," Karigan said, annoyed by Erin's tone.

"It's all right, Karigan," Fergal said. "She's being careful. I understand what's at stake." As they continued along, he asked, "What was it like in that room?"

"An abyss," Karigan replied with a shudder. "Very uncomfortable. It took away my ability, and it was kind of like a part of me died."

"Why would there be a room like that?" he asked.

"It was created following the Long War during the Scourge," Erin replied, "as a place to detain magic users and put them on trial."

"Oh."

His "oh" was laden with the knowledge of how magic users were systematically purged during that time by those who blamed the crimes of Mornhavon the Black on *all* magic users, whether they fought on the Arcosian side or that of the Sacor Clans.

Karigan helped him up a set of stairs, then at the top said, "Erin, when I tried to use my moonstone, I saw statues. Who were they?"

Erin did not answer immediately. She gazed down the corridor, carrying the lantern with one hand, the other resting on the hilt of her sword. It was some time later when she finally said, "Black Shields. The founders of our order."

Of course, Karigan thought.

"Black Shields?" Fergal asked. "Why would their statues be hidden down there?"

"Back then they were not hidden," Erin replied.

"Aye, but a place where magic users were imprisoned and judged? Why there?"

"Think about it," Karigan said. "And step to your left unless you want to walk into a wall."

Fergal seemed to think for a while as she suggested, the echoing of their footsteps the only sound as they walked in silence.

"The Black Shields had something to do with the Scourge," he said at length.

Erin turned a corner ahead, and Karigan hastened so she and Fergal would not be left behind. The lamps that lit the corridor outside the records room glimmered in the distance.

Erin blew out the candle in her lantern, leaving them in dusky darkness. Karigan removed the blindfold from Fergal's eyes.

"The Black Shields," Erin said, "were the Scourge."

≪ AWAKENING ≫

Enver traveled often between his father's home and Gweflin's, deepening his knowledge of healing from both. His father was an excellent master, but because he possessed an innate etherical ability, there were techniques he could not pass on to his son. Gweflin filled in the gaps and he learned much.

She also continued her healing of him though the urgency of accendu'melos had long subsided. Sometimes they'd be working in the garden and the desire would overcome one or the other, and they'd make love where they were, the scent of crushed herbs wafting in the air around them. Or, she would find him in a forest glade where he liked to listen to the voice of the world. The soft moss was sensuous against his bare skin as they coupled.

He did not love Gweflin, though he appreciated her as his healer and teacher, and considered her a friend. Her healing helped quell his obsession, but he never forgot the Asai'riel. Gweflin asked him about her, about his feelings for her, and he sensed she considered this part of his healing, as well.

She did not love him either, he knew, but she clearly found their time together pleasant. She never sent him away, nor did she ever express annoyance at his needs. She, as often as he, initiated their intimacy. Though to the eyes of a mortal she looked young, Enver knew she was one of the ancient ones, and her patience was great.

A constant in the background was the calling. It vibrated through every living thing in Eletia. One late summer day, Enver and Gweflin were sitting by the garden, taking tea and enjoying the fall of sunlight on leaf and stem when the calling changed, grew more urgent.

Gweflin stood.

"What is it?" Enver asked.

"I must attend the Grove," she replied.

"Which one?"

"The great Grove."

The great Grove was the sanctuary of the eldest of Eletians, including those of Argenthyne.

"I am coming with you," he said.

She did not protest, and they departed immediately, their tea left to grow cold on the table by the garden.

Others called out to them as they walked, asking what the change indicated. Gweflin said she was not sure, but she felt she needed to go to the Grove. Many followed, and they encountered others along the way who were also drawn. By the time they reached the Grove, hundreds of Eletians had already arrived, and the call thrummed in Enver's chest, pulsed through the whole of his being.

The Grove arose in the valley beneath the Alluvium, with the lake between. Ordinarily it was a place of serenity, a peaceful glade where the massive boles of the Eletian conifers grew, reaching above all others. Higher than a castle's turret they grew, and as wide around. Paths into the Grove wended around, over, and under immense roots that could have been large trees themselves.

Gweflin did not pause to see what was to happen, but hurried inward into the heart of the Grove. There, they found a dozen attendants in white robes, standing beside one of the largest trees. They nodded to her, and she glanced at the tree. Then she turned to Enver.

"We will need some water."

"What do—"

But she hastened by him to a stream. He followed. A silver bowl sat upon the mossy bank. The stream was called Ilyonbourne, and it was known to have healing properties. While the trees of the Grove might receive enough of a watering from nature, the attendants were known to periodically water the roots of the great trees from the Ilyonbourne. It promoted healing, not only for the trees themselves but for those who slept within.

Enver stepped down the steep bank into the icy water that sang and jingled and laughed down its course. Its current was strong and crisp, the clarity of the water that of glass. He dipped the bowl into the water, filled it, and handed it up to Gweflin. He climbed up the bank, feeling lighter, more buoyant, even though he had only stood in the stream.

Back in the Grove, Gweflin bore the bowl to the attendants, and they indicated she should wait with them.

More Eletians came and stood around and throughout the Grove. The calling became palpable. No one moved; no one spoke. They waited.

Time was largely irrelevant to Eletians, but Enver was only half Eletian and he grew impatient. Hours might have passed as they stood in silence. Many of the people appeared to be in deep meditative states as they absorbed the energy humming through the Grove.

Before evening fell, Prince Jametari arrived. He approached the attendants and gazed at the great tree they stood by. His presence changed the tenor of the event to a frisson of excitement. Those who meditated opened their eyes to the present. There was some murmuring from others.

When Enver returned his attention to the tree, he realized he had almost missed the event itself, the emergence of a Sleeper. He had not been there one moment, but was the next.

The attendants washed the golden fluid that was the tree's life blood from the Sleeper with the water from Gweflin's bowl. Then they clothed him in white robes.

He had a deformed hand. It was clawlike and blackened, and when he submerged it in Gweflin's bowl, steam rose up. Finally, it dawned on Enver who he was.

"Behold!" Prince Jametari called out. His voice resonated through the Grove. "Our great king stands with us once more. Born beneath the stars of Avrath was King Santanara; here, among the leaves and limbs of Eletia, he stands." The prince then went to his knee before his father. Everyone in the Grove did likewise.

". . . will remove it," the king was telling Gweflin quietly.

Enver only heard it because of his close proximity. "It does me no good. I can hold nothing with it, and it brings only great suffering."

His voice carried the strains of the ancient times, before the mountains, before Eletia, before the world, and yet he looked a man in his prime, broad-shouldered, his long flaxen hair shining in the dusk.

"I see my son," he said, "and I have been glad of his visits to the Grove. I heard his voice even as I slept. But where is my daughter?"

Those who heard his question were openly stricken and cried out. Some wept.

"Graelalea is passed," one of the attendants told him.

"I know of my Grae, my Graelalea," he replied. "To Avrath on the wings of the winter owl she has returned, no longer present in this life. I grieve for her, and I will avenge her death. But I speak of my other daughter, the Cearing Asai'riel."

It thrilled Enver to hear her spoken of by the king.

"She fights in a war among her other folk, my father," Prince Jametari said.

"Ah," the king said, indicating neither approval nor disapproval.

He gazed out upon his people and stepped forward. He became a commanding presence.

"Rise, my people," he said. "It is time to rise for there is much to do. I have come back among you because of the unease I felt in the roots of the earth. Our great enemy, he who visited such atrocities upon fair Argenthyne and our people, stirs once more. Our allies cannot face him alone and hope to win. It was our—*my*—responsibility to destroy him, but, in that, I failed. He was defeated for a time, and the Sacor Clans coped the best they could to prevent his return with a wall, but he is too great a force.

"He rises again, and this time I *will not* fail. We will destroy him utterly."

Inspired by the great king's words, Enver strode across the glade and knelt before him. "I will gladly follow you, my lord, even if it means entering the black heart of the dark wood itself. I pledge to you my sword."

Santanara gazed down at him. "I see in you more a healer than a soldier, young one."

"I have fought and will fight," Enver replied, "and I will do so for my king and all Eletians."

There was a sparkling in Santanara's eyes as he considered Enver, like the glint of a long-past silver moon. Enver felt as though years passed as he knelt beneath the king's gaze.

"A warrior and a healer then," Santanara said at length. "So be it."

He flexed his clawed hand. Flesh had rotted on it, leaving the fingers skeletal, the result of his handling the Black Star, a powerful magical device crafted by Mornhavon. Santanara had stabbed it into its creator at the end of the Long War. It had brought about victory for the allies who fought against the Arcosians for over a hundred years.

Enver stood, bowed his head, and stepped aside so others might approach the king and declare their intent.

Gweflin came to him and gazed quizzically at him. "Why have you done this?" she asked.

"Our king has returned to us to defeat an old enemy," he replied. "Is it so strange that I vow to join in that struggle?"

"Perhaps not, but I am thinking you are not as healed as I had thought."

She walked away before he could ask her what she had meant by that. But in truth, he knew. He had done it for the Asai'riel. He would earn favor with her father, the king, and perhaps, in war he would win her approval.

⊰⊱ YOLANDHE'S ISLAND ⊰⊱

Yap gazed at the charcoal remnant of the fish on the end of his stick. Smoke wafted up from it.

"No, no, Scorch," he told the little dragon. "Ya did too much all at once."

Scorch cocked his wedge-shaped head questioningly.

The experiments using dragon fire to cook their food were a failure. Scorch couldn't seem to control the intensity of his blast. Yap tossed the stick onto a pile of overly crisp fish they'd already burned this morning. He would have to continue to cook the old way, but at least Scorch was good at starting cook fires.

The dragon made a whimpering sound and bowed his head as if he understood he'd failed.

Yap patted the rough scales of his head. "It's all right, lad. No harm, just wanted to see if we could do it."

Scorch then jerked his head up. Lord Amberhill was approaching down the beach, stones clacking and clattering beneath his feet. Scorch scuttled behind Yap and peered around him to watch.

Ever since the death of Beryl Spencer, Scorch had been this way, nervous around Lord Amberhill, scared even. It only reinforced Yap's conviction that Lord Amberhill had been responsible for her death. No, not Lord Amberhill but King Akarion. He watched on a daily basis how the two personalities struggled for dominance. He wondered which one he was about to face now.

The waves lapped against the shore with a sigh while he waited, the tang of charred fish lingering in the air. Lord

Amberhill halted a couple yards from him. The sea breeze tousled his hair, which had grown long since their landing on the island.

"Come with me," Lord Amberhill said, then he turned and started to walk inland without waiting for a reaction from Yap.

Akarion, Yap thought with misgiving. Scorch was not the only one who feared the sea king. He dared not disobey an order.

Scorch shambled after him as he followed Akarion into the woods. The birds of summer were moving on, so the woods were quiet with foreboding. It would be another long winter on the island.

They kept going, clambering over boulders, and through thick underbrush, and across streams until they reached the far side of the island. They then followed the shoreline until Akarion paused to take in the view of a headland.

"What do you see?" he asked Yap.

Yap scratched his head. "Rocky cliffs, sir. Scrub trees. A cove tucked down below."

Akarion nodded, but did not comment. He simply continued on for a few yards, then stepped off the high edge of land they were on and started to descend. Yap was surprised to find there were stone steps that allowed them to climb down with ease. At the bottom, they came to a broad, protected sand beach. Yap thought it was the only sandy one on the island.

"What do you see?" Akarion asked again.

Yap examined the fissured rocky cliff face of the headland that bordered the beach. "The same, sir."

A strange smile crossed Akarion's face that did not at all resemble Lord Amberhill, and he led the way across the beach to the far side where it met the headland. He did not pause, but waded into the water and skirted the edge of the headland until he turned toward the rocky face and seemed to vanish through stone.

Yap halted in his tracks. "What?" Then he splashed forward and found that a jutting column of rock concealed a fissure, but not just a fissure, he realized, but an entire cavern.

He waded inside and gradually stepped up onto dry sand where he was met with the amazing sight of a ship on log supports within.

Akarion gazed at it with his hands on his hips. "It is *Roko-ranak*," he said.

It looked very much like the funeral ship deep in the island that held Akarion's remains, with its dragon head bowsprit, multiple oar ports, and runes carved on the keel. Yap walked right up to it and ran his hands along the lapped wood of the hull.

"It's a very fine-looking ship, sir," Yap said.

"And beyond ancient. It is in good condition considering all the years it has awaited my return, but it requires repair."

Yap could see that. Some of the lapping gapped and looked weakened by moisture. It was impossible to judge its condition from below. He'd have to climb up to get a better view from topside.

"You have carpentry experience aboard ship, do you not?" Akarion asked.

"I was a simple hand, sir, the low dog. That's why I'm called Yap." And they'd kicked him around like he were some miserable stray. "But I helped the ship's carpenter sometimes."

"Good enough."

Yap watched as Scorch snuffled one of the support beams. "I am not skilled enough to fix this ship, sir."

"We will work on *Rokoranak* together," Akarion replied, "so that it will be ready to sail come spring."

Yap thought that an ambitious plan. And with only two of them to sail it? Or, would Yolandhe be coming with them?

"Where will we be sailing to, sir?" he asked.

"I intend to make for Corsa Harbor in Sacoridia," Akarion replied, "and thence overland to Sacor City so that I might present myself to the king."

Yap gazed at him askance. "Weren't ya afraid he planned to arrest you?"

Akarion laughed, laughed so hard that it echoed through the cavern and startled cave swallows from their roosts. "He can try, but my dragons will ensure he regrets the attempt."

So, Yap thought, Akarion planned not just to present

himself to the king, but to begin his reconquest of the lands the sea kings had once ruled.

"No one will be able to stand against me," Akarion murmured, "least of all a king bearing the weakling blood of the hill people."

THE PURR OF GRYPHONS

A lton ran out of his cabin at the sounds of shouting and gryphons roaring. He buckled on his saber as he went.

"What in damnation is going on?" he demanded of a young archer running by.

"In the sky, sir!"

Alton squinted into the morning light, fearing that more creatures of Blackveil were attacking, this after a night of dreams in which inescapable darkness descended on him and the encampment. Whiskers and Bob flew overhead like arrows toward another winged creature that circled high above. At first he thought it was another gryphon, but as he continued to watch, he saw it was larger than Whiskers and Bob, and it was all bird, a gray eagle.

His relief was immense. It was not a nightmare creature of Blackveil at all, though a thread of anxiety remained. Not about the eagle. It was the nervousness of the wall guardians bleeding off on him, which was probably the source of his dreams, as well.

A human appeared to be riding the eagle, a peculiarity, but then he recalled Dale filling him in about a great mage named Duncan who stayed with the eagles in their eyrie, and rode around on them now and then.

"Don't shoot," he told the archers who were lining up.

The eagle rolled away on a wingtip from the gryphons hurtling toward it. The flight must be quite dizzying for the passenger, or maybe as the projection of a great mage, Duncan didn't get those stomach-churning sensations one would expect.

Alton needed to call off the gryphons before there was an unfortunate incident. "WHISKERS!" he shouted.

"What the hells is going on?" Captain Wallace demanded as he ran up to Alton.

"We need to keep the gryphons from attacking the eagle."

The eagle plummeted in a dive. Bob swiped at its tail feathers but missed.

Several of them took up the cry to call off the gryphons, but it was only when Leese joined them that they listened.

"Well, now we know who they like best," Alton said as Whiskers and Bob landed.

"Meep," Whiskers said, as if in confirmation.

"Who's riding the eagle?" Leese asked.

"A great mage named Duncan, I believe. The eagle could be the one named Softfeather."

The eagle back-winged as it landed. It bore a pouch around its neck in addition to the passenger on its back.

The gryphons hissed and growled from their crouched positions. The eagle kept its wings spread and hopped toward them.

"Back off, lads," Leese told Whiskers and Bob.

The eagle's rider was saying the same to his mount. Alton was afraid there was going to be a full scale talon, claw, and feather fight on their hands, but the gryphons backed off with Leese's encouragement, and the eagle seemed to decide to ignore them.

Duncan, the great mage, slipped from his perch on the eagle and strode forward. He gave them an ostentatious bow.

"Greetings," he said. "I am Duncan, and my companion is Ripaeria of Snowcloud Eyrie."

So, not the eagle called Softfeather, after all. "Welcome," Alton said, and he introduced himself, the captain, and Leese.

Duncan appeared very interested in Leese. He seemed the sort who commonly pursued flirtations with females, the way he wore his shirt open to reveal his chest and held himself, his hair brushed back just so. He was quite a contrast to Merdigen and the other great mages Alton knew.

He then gazed at Leese with new eyes. She was a brilliant mender, and that was how he saw her, but now he also saw a young woman who, if not extraordinarily attractive, wasn't unpleasant to look at.

As for Leese herself, well, she had eyes only for Ripaeria.

"Your eagle is beautiful," she told Duncan.

I am not anyone's eagle, Ripaeria replied tartly, startling them all by speaking into their minds.

"My apologies," Leese said, with a half bow to Ripaeria. "I meant no offense."

Accepted, and no offense taken.

"What brings you to our encampment?" Alton was curious. Dale had told him the mage was sort of a renegade who had run away and hidden during the Scourge, rather than face the judgment of King Joneaus.

"After being among your people by the mountains," he replied, "I found the eyrie dreary and boring beyond belief, and so I talked Ripaeria into bringing me here."

I am in very big trouble, the eagle said. She sounded very pleased with herself.

Duncan smiled indulgently at her. "I also found myself wanting to see my old teacher."

"Merdigen?" Alton asked.

"Yes."

"I'd be happy to take you to him."

"Excellent."

Alton started to lead the way to the tower, but Duncan cleared his throat.

Alton paused. "What is it?"

"My pouch. If you wouldn't mind carrying it for me?"

Alton glanced at the eagle. The pouch would have his tempes stone in it. "Right."

He approached the eagle, and she was much more imposing close up than even the gryphons. Her beak could eviscerate him in seconds.

She made a chuckling noise in her throat. *I would not eviscerate you. I am a Green Flyer, which means we are friends.*

She had heard his thoughts? He tried to clear his mind, but *Green Flyer?*

She chuckled and dipped her head so the pouch strap slid off her neck. He grabbed it before it hit the ground.

"Thank you," he murmured.

You are most welcome.

He slung the pouch over his shoulder. The tempes stone was heavy enough, but there was something else in the pouch that jabbed at his side as he walked. A stick, maybe. As they headed for the tower, Leese strode toward the eagle, no doubt full of questions.

"How is my old master?" Duncan asked Alton.

"Often grumpy, and always eccentric."

"Ah, then he has not changed much."

Alton felt that something was off the moment he passed into the tower. The wall guardians felt "itchy." He didn't know how else to describe it. Their angst vibrated against him, an irritation. The gryphlings were even more naughty than usual, knocking objects off shelves and performing impressive acrobatic stunts in the air, and diving at him, trying to catch his hair in their talons.

When he paused to blow his nose, Merdigen appeared and demanded pillows to be placed around the pedestal that held his tempes stone lest the gryphlings succeed in knocking it off. Alton didn't have pillows, but he pulled a couple blankets from a cabinet. One contained the half-gnawed rotting leg of some creature, and he groaned.

Meanwhile, the meeting between Merdigen and Duncan did not seem to be going well, and he kept one ear open to their conversation.

"Decided to show yourself here after all these years, eh boy?" Merdigen demanded. "To visit us in our prisons?"

"I guess the answer to that would be yes, but you don't seem to understand I was in a prison of my own living with the eagles."

"Hah! A prison of your own making."

Shadow swooped down and grabbed the rotting leg out of Alton's grasp and flew back upward into the nest. Alton gazed up and saw only a pair of intense green eyes staring back at him. Midnight. He sneezed.

"Your *bones*?" Merdigen shouted in incredulity. "You

have *your bones*? Clearly none of our teachings and laws got through that thick skull of yours."

"How was I supposed to burn me?" Duncan demanded. "I was dead and the eagles can't light fires. My bones are safe in the eyrie."

If Alton thought about it, it was a rather weird conversation to overhear.

Merdigen shook his finger at Duncan. "No mage bones are safe. That is the first thing we pound into the heads of our students."

"Like I said, nothing I could do about it. Extreme circumstances."

Merdigen paced in a circle and muttered to himself.

Alton placed the blankets around the base of the pedestal. The two mages sounded as if they had been apart only hours, not a thousand years.

From his current location in the very center of the tower by the tempes stone, he saw not the tower's interior, but vast plains going off into every direction. It was one of the strange properties of the tower. Once he stepped between the columns that circled the space around the tempes stone, the plains disappeared and he was in the tower again. And, just now as he did so, three gryphlings pounced on him. His explosive sneeze scattered them.

"By the gods," he muttered.

"Because I didn't want to be sacrificed!" Duncan shouted. "All of you just gave yourselves up."

"No, no," Merdigen said, waggling his finger again. "We did our duty to our people because we were pacifists and would not fight in the war. This way we could serve the realm without killing."

Duncan crossed his arms. "A worthless sacrifice. From what I hear, they just left you here and forgot about you."

"Worthless sacrifice? You are not my son." Merdigen turned his back on Duncan.

Son? Alton wondered.

"Can you believe him?" Duncan asked Alton, pointing at Merdigen.

"Um, I think I'm going to go check on the wall," Alton replied.

He almost tripped over Junior in his haste to enter beneath the west arch.

"Achoo!" Even his allergies were stirred up more than usual.

He paused, listening to the angry voices rising and falling in the main chamber.

"Whew," he said. There were definitely some unresolved grievances between father and son there, and they had simmered for centuries.

He found no peace in communing with the wall. As he pressed his palms against granite, it was like holding handfuls of buzzing bees. He sent his mind into the wall, but pulled out immediately. The guardians were hysterical. Runes lit up on the wall as if to scream, *Danger, danger, danger . . .*

Alton rushed out into the main chamber. It had quieted, but for the low growl of Midnight and the higher pitched growls of the gryphlings.

"There is something very wrong," Alton told Merdigen and Duncan.

"Indeed there is," Merdigen said.

It was then he noticed the two mages and the gryphons were staring at the chamber's rear wall, the one that was on the Blackveil side of the tower.

With a prickling on the back of his neck, he slowly turned just in time to see a Sleeper step through the wall. It lacked the natural light of an untainted Eletian, but emanated the dark through the black pits that were its eyes. Hair hung about its face in cobweb strands, its body thin with spidery limbs, and flesh taut like parchment. It exuded a roiling hunger.

Dear gods. Alton unsheathed his saber. This had been his deepest nightmare, that the dark Sleepers, the tainted ones, would enter Sacoridia through the towers.

Another stepped through the wall behind the first, and another, and then another . . .

"We need help," Alton said.

"We can do nothing," Merdigen replied.

"You have my pouch," Duncan added. "Send me out."

Alton ran for the Sacoridian side of the tower. "Warn them," he said, and he tossed Duncan's pouch through the wall. The mage vanished.

They were his last words before the Sleepers, ten of them, at least, rushed him. He met them with his sword slashing. Midnight dove into them, snarling and tearing. Her gryphlings also joined in with ferocious high-pitched cries.

The Sleepers expressed their hunger in unnatural wails, and fought with blackened fingernails and serrated blades that were not of any Eletian make. Alton parried a thrust and decapitated the first Sleeper. Another knocked him to the floor. Soot flew into its face and clawed at its eyes.

A flurry of feather and fur streaked into the tower— Whiskers and Bob, growling and snarling, claws and talons extended. Alton climbed to his feet and stabbed another Sleeper, but it didn't slow down. He scythed his sword at its neck. Only decapitation seemed to kill them.

Whiskers threw one at the wall and bones audibly snapped. The creature did not expire, but it could not rise because of its broken body.

Alton parried the thrust of one of the Sleepers, and its serrated blade almost jerked his sword out of his hand. He tried to recover to block the next blow, but he just wasn't fast enough. He screamed as the blade tore into his midsection.

Silence. Darkness. Then confusion. Concerned faces hovered over him. *Pain.* He cried out.

"Stay with us, my lord," Leese said. Then she was talking to blurry others around her.

They were outside, he thought. Somehow he'd been brought outside. He could smell the soil of the Earth beneath him, the clean open air. Whiskers peered at him down his bloody beak and crooned.

"Warn king," Alton gasped. "Tainted Sleepers."

"We're working on it, my lord," Leese said. "Do not worry."

Alton closed his eyes. "Tainted Sleepers invading."

This was, he thought, his ending. It was not unpleasant. A gentle vibration filled him, and he realized, as the darkness took him, that it was the purr of gryphons.

❧ STAR STEEL ❧

As the weeks passed following the Battle of the Sleeping Waelds, it felt to Karigan that a sense of normalcy had begun to prevail over the castle and city. Summer waned and brought shorter days and cooler nights. Food supplies were still low, but neighboring Rhovanny and the Under Kingdoms were only too happy to sell their excess for a good profit.

The sounds of rebuilding in the lower city were like music, the cadence of hammers and the rough song of saws. Neighbors helped raise walls and shingle roofs. Master Robinson, whose saddlery shop had been spared, lent his apprentices and himself to help rebuild. Prisoners were also put to work under the watchful gazes of the city guard.

After the fall of General Birch and the defeat of Second Empire's main army, several factions laid down their arms. The king and his generals were busy processing and judging prisoners. Those who committed atrocities and played leading roles in Second Empire's insurgency were executed. Those who were not deemed to be dangerous were put to work.

Several factions did not surrender, and were pursued by the Sacoridian regular military and provincial militias. Others disappeared into the countryside, perhaps biding their time until they could exact revenge, though it was hoped that many would just meld back into ordinary Sacoridian life.

There was no sign of Lala, no sightings, no rumor of a magic user causing mayhem, nothing despite the fact that scouts, soldiers, and messengers kept watch for her. Captives under interrogation knew nothing of her fate. It left Karigan with an uneasy feeling that they did not know Lala's whereabouts, or even if she still lived. Karigan believed, however, that the girl was alive and would make her presence known when they least expected it.

Likewise, they received no word of Colonel Mapstone either, but it was not expected. Varos was quite a distance away, and Green Riders did not go there. Karigan could only hope that her father had reached that country by now and had found the colonel alive and well. Loon and Bluebird moped, but did not appear to be highly distressed.

As for Karigan herself, life took on a fairly normal routine as she untangled the Rider accounts and assisted Tegan with Chief Rider duties. She was assigned to short distance errands about the city and to the Coutre encampment out by the battlefield, but was not sent on longer errands. Connly said it was because they wanted to ensure she was up to full fighting strength. To that end, she was attending training sessions with Master Drent, who was working with her to strengthen her scarred and damaged back muscles. The consistency of the sessions helped tremendously though they often left her exhausted and aching.

"We stop with these baby steps next time," the arms master announced.

Baby steps? Sweat dripped down her face. She was so tired she just wanted to throw herself on the ground.

"No more practice swords," he said. "Steel."

She glanced at the wooden sword in her blistered hand. He'd attached progressively heavier weights on it with each session to increase her strength.

"Come with me."

She stumbled after him from the outdoor practice field into the arming room of the field house. It always reeked of old sweat, leather, and oil. It was, in its own way, not an unpleasant combination of scents. She placed the practice sword on its hook.

"Wait here," Drent said, and he headed into his office.

She fidgeted, wondering what he was up to. He wasn't the same Drent she'd started swordmaster training with, though he was still gruff. He reserved most of the yelling for the beginners. He'd been careful with her workouts, for overdoing it would only impair her further. She was given to understand he'd spoken with Vanlynn and Ben to find out the best way to go forward with her training.

He returned shortly with a longsword in a plain black scabbard. "Here. This arrived today."

"What?" Karigan said in surprise.

"A swordmaster requires a longsword, and you'll be needing it for training. As I recall, you lost your other one up north, did you not?"

She hadn't *lost* it. She'd lent the previous sword she'd received upon passing her swordmaster test to Zachary as he went into battle in the Lone Forest. He'd never returned it, and she'd felt odd about asking for its return, so she hadn't.

"Thank you," she said, accepting it.

"Don't thank *me*," he replied. "I'm just the messenger."

Was that an actual joke? She glanced at him but couldn't tell.

The hilt and pommel of the sword looked much like her previous one, unornamented and serviceable. Drawing it from the scabbard revealed the black silk knotted beneath the guard to denote her swordmaster status, but that was where all resemblance ended. The blade was like none she'd seen before. It rippled with wavy blue-black, purple, and gray iridescence.

This most definitely was *not* her old sword.

"Nice, huh?" Drent asked.

"Very," she replied.

She turned the blade this way and that to see how it shone and changed in the dusty light that filtered through the window. What steel was this? How had it been made?

"Glad you like it," Drent said. "It's the envy of the Weapons. We're done for the day, so you can go."

Karigan hurried back to her room in the castle to look over her new sword more thoroughly. She swept it through the air.

Ghost Kitty, who had been napping on her bed, was singularly unimpressed. He gave her a toothy yawn and rolled over.

She did not know how long she had been gazing at the sword when someone knocked on her door.

"Come," she said absently.

Garth stepped into her room. "Tegan and I wondered if—" he began, but when he saw what she held, his eyes rounded. "Whoa!" He was across the room in a moment and stared unwavering at the blade.

"That's star steel," he whispered.

"What did you say?" she demanded.

"Star steel. Well, not the actual star steel of the gods, but it sort of is. The steel comes from falling stars—meteorites. My brother showed me a knife blade like it down at his shop last week and told me about a sword one of his master's rivals was forging. I bet this is it."

His brother was a blacksmith for one of the premier royal armorers in the city, and now she understood. She had heard of such blades forged from the ore of meteorites before, but had never seen one. As the avatar of the god of death, she'd been clad in armor and wielded weapons of actual star steel, the kind the gods forged.

"May I?" Garth asked, holding out his hands.

She passed him the sword, and he admired it anew as he gazed up and down the blade and checked its balance. "Here's the maker's mark, and yep, it's Master Wolff's. He's the one my brother was telling me about."

He showed her the flat of the blade where a wolf's head was etched just below the silk.

"They use different kinds of steel, and in this case, including the ore from the meteorite, and forge 'em in layers to create the iridescence. It's an intense process, but if you're gonna forge from a meteorite, you might as well make it special. Meteorites are rare, and a master craftsman who possesses one might go a lifetime waiting for the right project to come along before using it."

Karigan swallowed hard. No wonder it was the envy of the Weapons. It was by the foremost armorer who had used rare materials.

"This is your swordmaster sword?" he asked.

She nodded, a little numb.

"I know your clan has got some wealth, but this is princely."

"It's not from my clan. I received a sword with my mastery

that, uh, ended up with someone else last winter. This is a replacement."

"Nice replacement. You must have a prominent patron."

"Er, no. Swordmasters receive swords upon mastery." Even as she said it, however, she realized it didn't sound quite right. Even a swordmaster wouldn't simply be issued such a fine and unusual blade. As she thought about it, even the previous sword had been much too fine.

Garth looked askance at her. "I don't know what you heard, but Fastion says swordmasters buy their own or have a patron."

Karigan made a single, but likely, guess as to who her patron was. "You've been talking to Fastion?"

"Interesting fellow," Garth replied. "Knows a lot about history and such. So, you've got a secret patron, eh? Well, let's see." Before she could respond, he pushed the knotted silk up toward the guard. He raised his eyebrows when he saw the mark. Karigan already knew what he'd found.

"Clan Hillander." He showed her the mark of the Hillander terrier. "An important patron."

The name of the patron stood between them. Karigan almost laughed at herself for having thought all swordmasters received the same sword, when really she'd been given a gift. Zachary and his Weapons had kept that bit of information from her. But now, she knew.

"Garth," she said before he could speculate too much about what it meant that their king was her patron, "what did you want?"

"Oh, I was just going to ask if you wanted to go to midday meal with Tegan and me."

"I'll meet you there. I've got to clean up first."

She closed her door after Garth and gazed at the sword and the mark of Hillander. It was a beautiful object, beautiful and deadly, and weighted just right. The symbolism of the "star steel" was not lost on her, either. Zachary had seen her as the avatar and was referencing it with this special gift.

"Oh, Zachary," she murmured. She could not imagine he gave out swords to every new swordmaster. It was too great a gift for a common messenger. Gifts, acknowledgments of this kind, just made it harder to push away from him as she must. As he must push away from her, too.

She should decline it, return it to him, but she would not. If he could pretend to have nothing to do with it, she could pretend not to know who it was from. She sighed and sheathed the beautiful thing and set it on her bed. Ghost Kitty rubbed his cheek against the pommel and purred.

"You like it now, do you?" she said.

It would be much easier to distance herself from Zachary and move on if forces didn't always seem to be pushing them together. In some cases, the force was Zachary himself, as in the gift of the sword. She reminded herself she wasn't supposed to know it was from him, and yet, she knew.

She groaned and went to her wash basin and poured water in it. They hadn't crossed paths in a while, and maybe that trend would continue.

"Who am I fooling?" she muttered. She *wanted* to see him as much as she knew distance was the safer option.

She splashed cold water on her face and shivered as it dripped down her neck. It felt like the cold finger of fate, reminding her how little control she had over her life at times. What would be, would be, and she'd have to weather the future best as she could.

Karigan smiled as she gazed at the group sitting two tables away in the dining hall. Anna, Gil, Megan, and Brandall sat with Nell Lotts and two other young women wearing the livery of the royal household. They chatted and laughed, and it was good to see the smiles and hear the laughter. She was also pleased to see Riders making friends outside their own cadre, and it was largely thanks to Anna.

"Everything looks well in that quarter," said Tegan, who had followed Karigan's gaze.

"I haven't heard a single word from Anna about wanting to leave the Green Riders since the incident with Scrum," Mara said as she broke a hunk of bread off a loaf.

"Good," Karigan replied, and she meant it whole-heartedly.

"She's been a good addition," Garth said. "The colonel was right to bring her on."

At the mention of the colonel, they quieted for a moment, each with his or her own worries and hopes for her return.

"Whether or not Anna realizes it," Mara said, "her horse has grown to adore her."

"She doesn't adore *me,*" Garth told her. "That Angry-Mad about bit off my hand."

"Because you didn't read the sign on her stall door," Tegan said.

"I'm tall. The sign was low."

"Her name is Maddie," Mara reminded him, but his mind was already onto other matters as he reached for Karigan's apple tart.

"Hey!" She threatened to impale his hand with her fork.

"I forget," he said, leaning back, "that you are a mighty forkmaster."

"Don't forget next time."

Her companions laughed. She was about to take a bite of the tart when a Green Foot runner stepped up to their table. He could be there for any one of them, Mara being a particularly good candidate as lieutenant, but it was not to be.

"Rider G'ladheon," the boy said, "the queen wishes you to attend her in the solar."

"Any reason given?" she asked.

"No, ma'am, just that you attend her."

She watched after the boy as he ran off, and sighed.

"Now can I have your tart?" Garth asked.

"Greedy lad," Tegan chided with a poke to his arm. "You've already had five or so, including mine."

"I know, and the cooks won't let me have any more." His expression was so morose that Karigan could only shake her head.

"Go ahead," she said, "you can have my tart, but you owe me."

"You know I'm good for it," he replied.

"You're going to share this one," Tegan told him.

Karigan was sorry to leave her friends. Everyone's mood was much lighter after the defeat of Second Empire, and it was pleasant to spend time together without the worry of the world on their shoulders. It had also been a long time since the cooks had dug into their stores to make special treats, and she was sad she wasn't going to be able to enjoy hers. And, she had to admit, she had a good deal of trepidation about visiting Estora. What would she want? Especially since it seemed clear she knew about the feelings between her and Zachary.

Fastion admitted her into the solar. It was fragrant with greenery growing in many pots great and small. She found Estora *and Zachary* gazing through the big windows out into the gardens as birds flitted about in the near shrubbery.

Zachary, as if sensing her, turned first. "Karigan?"

What was he doing here? Was the summons a mistake?

Estora, elegant as always, today in silks of pale green, turned as well. "Thank you for joining us, Karigan."

Karigan bowed. "Your Majesties." What was this about?

"What is this about?" Zachary inquired, echoing her thoughts.

"There is something I wish to discuss with you both," Estora replied.

Uh oh, Karigan thought. Her fear about Estora confronting them seemed to be confirmed, as well as imminent. She saw the concern in Zachary's eyes, and she attempted to brace herself against any accusations Estora might level at the two of them.

"Please approach," Estora said.

Karigan nervously stepped forward between rows of potted roses.

"I have thought these weeks long and hard about just what I would say at this moment," Estora said, "and how I would go about saying it, and I am still not sure how to do it, but the time has come, and so here it is. This past year has not been easy for any of us. For my part, my husband was abducted by the aureas slee and I was relegated to overseeing the realm while in my long confinement. There was also, of course, the war. Fortunately, these things have come to positive conclusions, but there is an ongoing issue that I must address."

Karigan chewed on her bottom lip, waiting for the accusations to fly. She could not tell what Zachary was thinking. He stood there calmly, waiting.

"You know that I understand what it is to lose one's true love, one's true heart," Estora continued. "That is who F'ryan Coblebay was to me, though our love was forbidden. The Riders kept our secret, for if my family had learned of it, I'd have been cast out. And do you know I was prepared to forego all that I had ever been, everything I knew, so I could always be with him?"

Karigan hadn't known that part. It would have been a considerable adjustment for her to have forsaken her title and status to marry a commoner.

"But of course," Estora said, "I lost *him*, my heart. After that, nothing mattered." She then took Zachary's hand in hers. "My husband, and my liege, the father of my children, I do love you, but I am not blind. I have known for some while that your heart lay elsewhere." He tried to protest, but she shook her head. "Please do not try to placate me with false sentiments. As I said, I have known for some while. I have known it is Karigan who holds your heart."

Dear gods, Karigan thought. There it was, right out in the open. Was this really happening? To her surprise, Estora also took *her* hand. Her touch was soft and warm.

"I know," Estora continued, "Karigan feels the same for you, my husband, and that for years now, you've both been fighting your feelings and natural attraction for one another so as to preserve the honor of the throne, and for me. I want you both to know I understand. Because of how it was for me with F'ryan, I understand how you feel."

Karigan gaped. Did she just say that she understood her husband loved someone else, and that that someone was her friend?

"Respectfully—" Zachary began.

"I am not finished," Estora said. "You and I were contracted to marry for a very important reason—to solidify Coutre Province's allegiance to the crown and, thus, that of all the eastern provinces. I had hoped for more, but the basis of the marriage was not for love, but was the product of a legal document between great lords. It was a good decision. You are king, and you must keep Sacoridia strong.

"But I also recognize it when two people I care about are in pain, and their love denied. I know pain and do not wish them to suffer needlessly."

Karigan almost cried out in startlement when Estora placed her hand in Zachary's and held them together. Zachary searched Estora's face as if to understand.

"I will not have the two of you tearing yourselves apart because you are trying to spare my honor. If it is my permission you need to be together, you have it with no ill will, no jealousy. Well, perhaps some envy for what you share and what I've been denied since F'ryan's death. All I ask is that you remain discreet. Not just for me, not just to silence the court gossips, but for the children." She squeezed their hands. "You've my blessing."

She gave them a faint smile. "I will leave you now. You both look rather overcome and perhaps need a little time to consider my words."

She left them then, and Karigan overheard her tell the Weapons outside not to let anyone disturb them.

Karigan felt a little lightheaded. Neither of them said anything at first. She gazed at Zachary's hand still clasped around hers.

He cleared his throat. "That was most unexpected."

"Not what I was expecting, either," she whispered. She found she could not meet his gaze. There was so much to think about. She could be with Zachary without guilt. But could she really? It could not be out in the open. He was still Estora's husband.

"It seems like I should feel free," he said, "but now I am burdened with regret for any disappointment I have caused her."

"I feel as if I have betrayed my friend." She looked up at him. "Despite her consent, I just . . . I just . . ."

He folded her into his arms. It felt good, it felt right.

"I know, dearheart," he said. His voice rumbled nicely against her. "There is something I need to tell you," he said, "about the spell. Something that requires more explanation."

They parted.

"Grandmother's spell?" Karigan asked.

"Yes. When I lost control. I have had a while to think about it, to remember what happened. The spell was meant to force me to kill those who I loved most. Seeing the children triggered it, as I believe Grandmother intended, and at first I meant to kill them. Thank the gods you were there and got them out of the way. But then I saw you, and I was consumed with the need to kill *you*. You were what I love most. I had no impulse, none whatsoever, to attack Estora. Not even a little bit."

That was Grandmother, Karigan thought, trying to hurt her enemies in personal ways, and not necessarily practical ways, which must have been a considerable annoyance to a man like Birch. What if she had placed a more useful spell on Zachary that had caused him to surrender to Second Empire? And yet, she revealed the depth of her evil by creating a spell to cause a man to try to kill his own children.

"Your love stopped me," he continued. "Your love blocked the spell. You brought me out of it. For that, and so much more, you are my light, and not just winter's light, but my light of every moment of every day." He dug into an inner pocket of his longcoat and produced a velvet pouch. He placed it in her hand.

"I can't accept any—" she started to say.

He gently placed his forefinger over her lips. "Take a look."

She loosened the pouch strings and withdrew the horse-hair bracelet he had made for her in the north. Her subsequent travels had damaged it, and so she'd stashed it in her message satchel to protect it. She'd thought it lost.

"When Condor arrived without you," he said, "Laren removed it from your satchel, guessing its personal nature. She gave it to me, and I repaired it."

There were white horse tail hairs entwined with Condor's red.

"The white?" she asked.

"From my stallion, Storm," he replied. "I believe you called him 'Pumpkin'?"

She laughed and allowed him to tie it around her wrist. After, she stood on her toes and kissed his cheek. She then rested her head against his chest, and he held her close.

"What are we going to do?" she asked. She knew what she wanted to do, but it was not the same as what she *should* do.

"I believe Estora was earnest in—"

Someone banged on the door and they abruptly pulled apart.

Fastion entered the solar.

"You were told not to disturb us," Zachary said.

"My apologies, sire, but it is really urgent."

Zachary gave her a look of *what now*? "What is it?"

"The castle guard reports a giant eagle has landed on the roof and is asking for you."

*　　*　　*

They emerged onto the castle rooftop.

Karigan!

Karigan smiled to hear the voice of her friend, Ripaeria, in her mind. She had not known if she would ever hear it again when they had parted in the mountains. She'd placed the feather Ripaeria had given her in a drawer of her desk with other special mementos.

Hello, my friend, she answered.

The castle roof was a complex of walkways, drainage systems, towers, and crenellations, and it took a bit to walk to where Ripaeria had landed. She and Duncan were surrounded by soldiers with their hands on the hilts of their swords.

"It's all right," Zachary told the watch sergeant. "These are friends."

The sergeant ordered his soldiers to stand down and return to their posts, leaving Zachary, Karigan, and the Weapons standing before Ripaeria and Duncan.

"This is a surprise," Zachary said.

Duncan bowed. "Greetings, Your Majesty, and so it is, but we were sent with grave tidings."

"From the mountains?"

"No. We have come from the Deyer Wall, or D'Yer as it is now called. I was, er, visiting my old teacher, Merdigen."

We snuck out of the eyrie, Ripaeria confided to Karigan. *Duncan was so upset to find himself back there, and I was bored, so we conspired to go on an adventure. The elders will be furious with me.*

Ripaeria's tone sounded so very delighted at the prospect of her elders being furious that Karigan had to chuckle.

"What are these grave tidings?" Zachary demanded.

"Sleepers, from Blackveil, attacked the Tower of the Heavens, and also scaled the breach and attacked the main encampment."

"How many? Casualties?"

A sick feeling grew in Karigan's belly. She'd confronted dark Sleepers and knew how strong and hard to kill they were. Alton and Dale were down there.

"We hadn't exact numbers by the time we left," Duncan

explained. "There were only a handful of Sleepers at each site, and the gryphons and Ripaeria hunted them down. We believe we got them all."

I shredded them into tiny pieces, Ripaeria said. She made a gnashing sound with her beak.

"Even so," Duncan continued, "there were numerous casualties, especially by the breach. Your Captain Wallace perished, and Lord Alton may not see morning."

Karigan gasped. Zachary clasped his strong hand on her shoulder, steadying her.

"Fastion," he said, "send for General Washburn and Counselor Tallman."

"Yes, sire."

It was only Zachary's touch and proximity that kept Karigan balanced on her feet. *Alton . . .* she thought in anguish. Zachary and Duncan kept talking, but she didn't hear them. Tears brimmed in her eyes. Ripaeria cocked her head this way and that as she gazed at her.

You are very sad in the human way, Ripaeria observed.

Alton and I are friends. Close.

You liked his plumage and he liked yours? Were you mated?

No. It never went that far. How was he hurt?

Stabbed, I believe, Ripaeria replied.

Karigan closed her eyes, tried to master her emotions.

"I will write up the message immediately," Zachary was saying.

"We will await your word then," Duncan replied.

The next thing Karigan knew, Zachary was guiding her through the doorway that led off the roof into the castle. The door slammed behind them. Zachary ordered the Weapons to go on ahead and out of sight, so there were only the two of them on the stairway.

He took her into his arms. "It does not sound good for Alton. I'm sorry. I know he is important to you. He may yet pull through, though, and we must pray that he does."

He offered comfort and strength, and Karigan swallowed back tears. She would indeed pray, and try to remain strong for Alton's sake. "What will you do?"

"I will do as Alton has asked me many times—send troops. Now that the worst is over with Second Empire, and the threat at the wall has increased, I can spare them. I doubt this incursion from Blackveil will be the last. I fear that any time you won for us when you wounded Mornhavon in Castle Argenthyne has been lost."

She thought he was probably right on both counts. She shuddered even as she found comfort in his arms. That it had been dark Sleepers who had found their way to the Sacoridian side of the wall meant only one thing: Mornhavon the Black was stirring once again in Blackveil Forest.

⋙ A FINAL MESSAGE ⋘

Leese Callan, master mender and chief of the menders at the wall, was up to her elbows in Lord Alton D'Yer's blood as she worked to staunch his wound. She was damned if she was going to let him die.

They had swiftly moved him from outside to the large mending cabin so she could be within reach of her supplies, but every second had cost them. He had gone in and out of consciousness, mumbling about Sleepers and warning the king. She and her assistant, Nera, tried to reassure him the best they could, but she doubted he heard them.

The injury was bad. The serrated edge of the blade had done significant damage. She tried to repair as much of it as she could and stop the bleeding, but she did not know if she'd gotten it all, or if it was in time to save him.

The door burst open and a figure in green rushed in. She, too, was covered in blood—not her own for the most part, but that of Captain Wallace. Her face was a torment of grief. Dale Littlepage looked down at Alton where he lay on the table more dead than alive.

"Dale," Leese warned. As sorry as she was for the Rider's loss, for all their losses, she did not need this distraction.

"Is he—?" Dale began.

"Please leave, Rider," Leese replied. "We are doing the best we can."

"Master Callan," Nera said, "he's stopped breathing."

Leese checked his pulse and listened for breaths. *Nothing.* "Damn it."

Before she could do anything about it, Dale grabbed

Alton's shoulders and started shaking him. "Alton! Don't you dare die on me, too! Do you hear? Don't you die!"

"Get her out of here!" Leese ordered other menders who were working on less critically wounded patients nearby.

Even as they grabbed the struggling Rider and dragged her out of the cabin, Leese and Nera worked to revive Alton. Nera breathed for him while Leese pounded on his chest to get his heart pumping blood again. The third time she hit him, she felt his sternum break beneath her fist. It would be the least of his problems if he survived. *If.*

The night was so clear that the stars seemed close by. Alton gazed at the heavens in wonder. A falling star whisked through the deepest midnight blue, trailing a tail of light.

He stood upon a hill that looked like the one he used to play upon when he was a child. It was just far enough from Woodhaven to feel like an adventure to his younger self, but close enough to be safe. In winter, he and his friends went sledding down it.

However, where he should have seen the lights of Woodhaven, there was nothing. Though the semblance was strong, this was not the hill of his childhood. He walked a different path now.

The circumstances that had brought him here were dim. He remembered little except flashes of pain, confusion, violence. His life had held many dangers, but he'd hoped he'd overcome them and live on for many years with Estral at his side. He regretted not being able to see her one last time.

He continued to follow the path that had brought him up the hill until he came to a bench of wrought iron with a swirling leaf and branch design that one might find in an estate garden. It was not unoccupied. Beryl Spencer sat upon it, gazing into the distance. She wore her Green Rider uniform. Had he actually ever seen her wear it? He'd only seen her attired otherwise for whatever mission the king had in mind for her. How odd, he thought, that it was she whom he encountered on his way to the heavens. Shouldn't it be those he'd been close to? His grandparents, maybe? Even his bitter cousin, Pendric?

The stars reflected in her eyes. Her expression was distant. He sat beside her.

After a time, she spoke. "I must follow the path to its end."

"What is at the end?" he asked.

"Eternity? Peace?" She shrugged. "I do not know."

"Looks like I'm headed that way," he said. "I could keep you company."

"No."

"No?"

"We do not travel the same path."

"But—"

She gazed at him at last, her eyes all stars, infinite. "You must turn back."

"What? I thought—"

"This is not your path to walk yet. Turn back."

"I don't understand."

She stood and pointed back down the trail. "Go."

"Why? Aren't I dead?"

She still pointed. "Go."

"All right, all right," he said, and he stood. "I will go, but what will happen?"

She did not answer, but started striding away from him until she vanished into the dark.

He turned to walk in the opposite direction as Beryl had ordered him, back the way he'd come. He did not know what would happen. He glanced over his shoulder, but saw no sign of Beryl.

He continued on and on. The night gradually turned gray and the stars faded from view, but not because of a sunrise. As the world brightened around him, Beryl's voice came to him: *There is a final message you must take with you.*

"Master," Nera said, grabbing Leese's fist before it could fall once more on Alton's chest. "It's been too long. He's gone, he's gone. You've done everything you can. This won't help."

Leese staggered back, gasping for breath. Alton lay lifeless on the table, flesh pale, the ghastly wound exposed. The heir of Clan D'Yer, her friend, and she had failed him. No, this couldn't be happening.

Nera moved to pull a blanket over him. A shroud. As if to conceal the evidence of their failure, or to somehow diminish the pain of his loss. *Why do we hide the dead?* she wondered. He had been a whole person, full of life, animate, and now they were just going to cover him up and forget about him?

"Master?" Nera said.

Leese had lost many patients there at the wall. It was never easy, but this one hit hard. He'd been her friend.

"Master?"

She shook herself, saw that Nera had paused, had not finished covering Alton's body. "What is it?"

"I think he's breathing."

"What?" Leese jumped to the side of the table, leaned over him, and listened for breaths again. Nothing. Despair set in again after the brief surge of hope, but then, just as she was giving up, she felt the slightest exhale of breath against her cheek. With a shaking hand, she checked for his pulse. It was weak, but it was there. His heart had begun to function again.

"Thank the gods," she said, despair now turning to elation. She needed to be careful, though. They could lose him again.

His eyes fluttered open.

"Lord Alton," she said, "can you hear me?"

His gaze was dull. His lips moved, but he made no sound.

"Welcome back," she told him. "You have been through a great deal, but we are here to help you. Even so, you must fight with us."

"Message," he whispered. "Must . . ."

"Don't worry about messages," she told him. Green Riders made the worst patients after menders. They were obsessive about their work. "We'll take good care of you."

". . . come," he said.

"What now?" She leaned close to hear his soft whisper.

When he finished, she stood up and watched as his eyes closed and he fell unconscious again.

"We will need to keep a close watch on him," she told Nera. "His condition is precarious."

"What did he say?"

Badly injured patients sometimes got out of their heads and spoke nonsense. She supposed that was what this had been.

"He said he had a message from Beryl, who I think is another Green Rider."

"What was it?" Nera asked.

"It sounds mad, but he said, 'Dragons will come.' That's it. He said, 'Dragons will come.'"

ACKNOWLEDGMENTS

Many, many thanks to my "sister from another mister," Melinda Rice-Schoon, who listened to this book chapter by chapter and across nine or so states, and provided essential feedback and support.

My gratitude, as always, to my book mom and editor, Betsy Wollheim, the amazing crew at DAW Books, copyeditor Annaliese Jakimides, and my agents, Russ Galen, Danny Baror, and Heather Baror-Shapiro.

Bravo to Donato Giancola for the truly epic cover art.

A book is nothing without its readers, and I am humbled by the community that has arisen around the Green Rider Series. From this community, the *Green Rider* book soundtrack album, composed by Kristina A. Bishoff, and its companion art book, crafted by Madeline Shayne (each with permission) were crowdfunded via a Kickstarter campaign in 2018. The resulting album, recorded with a live orchestra, can be listened to and downloaded in the usual places. It's amazing what beauty we can bring into the world when we work together.

Thank you to Jay Bishoff, Pascal Doisteau Frerot, and Megan Notman, who heard the Rider call and pledged contributions to a special tier of the Kickstarter that entitled them to "Tuckerizations" of their names in this book. *Heh heh heh . . .*

Thank you to Laura Richardson for being an amazing liaison to the fan community and, among other things, coordinating, along with Megan Notman, Melinda Rice-Schoon, the Jesup Memorial Library, and Sherman's Books, and marshaling the aid of Jamie Pandy, Laura Schroeder, Amanda Tillman, and Steve and Barbara Moody, the launch party we held for my novella, *The Dream Gatherer* ("murder blanket" and all). She also took the lead as cat herder-in-chief in organizing online events we held for the Green Rider community during the Covid-19 pandemic.

I am deeply grateful to my Patreon patrons who helped make life less stressful. *Thank you, thank you, thank you* to

Sherise Mitchell, Matt Weber, Anjali Jindal, Hildie Johnson, Jessica Madnick, Kyle Schwerdt, Heather Robinson Lindsey, Natasha Mueller, Steve Moody, Malena Jax, Carna Steimel, Bethany Sheffer, Rebecca Elo, Amber Jessup, Stephanie Hinden, Lisa Wells, Tracy Frost, Catherine Kidd, Michelle Carter, Eve, Ted Hart, Wilmelyn Santos, Tirzah Conway, Kelly Trahan, Theo Da Kaffei, Rosie Brown, Laura Laubach-Richardson, Risa Kay, Jeremy Violette, Rosalie Boel, Jerri Stepp, Bethany McGee, Shakota Petrie, Margeet Kikstra, Joshua Kahn, Michelle Carter, Erin Cochran.

Finally, I am so pleased to get this book into your hands (or ears, in the case of audio editions). It takes time, and I always marvel about all the things that have happened in the course of writing a book, whether in my personal life or on the national/international stage. Each book is like a snapshot of history, and this one has had more than its share of history. I hope there is a little less as I continue work on book 8. Please, all of you take care of yourselves and be well.

~Kristen B.

Kristen Britain is the author of the bestselling Green Rider Series. She lives in a woodland cottage on an island in Maine.

www.kristenbritain.com